O9-AIE-222

m.   LEONOR DEL VAL

O CARO   JUAN LUIS

Servants and Their Masters
A NOVEL

BOOKS BY FERGUS REID BUCKLEY

Servants and Their Masters
Eye of the Hurricane

SERVANTS AND THEIR MASTERS

A Novel

FERGUS REID BUCKLEY

Doubleday & Company, Inc., Garden City, New York
1973

ISBN: 0-385-04160-8
LIBRARY OF CONGRESS CATALOG CARD NUMBER 72–76128
COPYRIGHT © 1973 BY FERGUS REID BUCKLEY
ALL RIGHTS RESERVED
PRINTED IN THE UNITED STATES OF AMERICA
FIRST EDITION

CONTENTS

BOOK FOUR

The Countess of a Thousand Tears

PART TWO

THE PILGRIMS

BOOK ONE

The Commencement of a Wake

BOOK TWO

Hidalgos

BOOK THREE

Civil War

BOOK FOUR

The Exposure of Insurrection

Servants and Their Masters
A NOVEL

PART ONE

The Marchioness of the Pilgrim

Book One

THE MARQUESA

Fifty or so years ago, Madrid was a town of plazas, parks, fountains, and trees. It was the gracious, languorous capital of a lost empire, where dreams are more precious than one's daily bowl of garbanzos, and old stories, and old quarrels, and the most defunct glories, were revived in garrulous tertulias at which Spaniards of every class gathered to expound what they no longer possessed the might or energy to impose.

Solana, the mordant painter, whose eye was a good deal less cheerful than Goya's, would have us believe (*Escenas y Costumbres*) that Madrid was also a town of debased and mutilated humanity, swarming with thieves, pimps, whoring wenches, and diseased mendicants batting their empty eye sockets or flapping in one's face gangrenous stumps, all wallowing in physical and spiritual degradation, and hungering to prey on each other. Well, prosperity has today cleaned up the populace. Common whores now prowl about in taxis, with tourists their prey. Thieves are discreet, having discovered finance. Pimps swill scotch-and-sodas in the lounge of the Castellana Hilton, and beggars have largely disappeared. It is the city that has been mutilated.

Anyhow, chopped away, leaving stumps as terrible as the blown legs of a penniless veteran. Avenues once laced with locust trees, fragrant in the spring, leafy and cool in the torrid summers, have been bulldozed down before the inexorable logic of the motorcar. Ah, the juggernauts! Plaza after plaza is shrinking, parks have been asphalted over, and formerly broad sidewalks laid for a race of people that still cherishes its postprandial paseo are being gouged at steadily, so that sidewalk cafés— the heart of Spanish life—are reduced to a thin red file of painted tin chairs.

There are still quarters—known as barrios—where a more traditional spirit obtains. These are the quarters of the very poor, or the sometimes very rich. Both incline to a way of life sovereign in its tradition. For centuries, poor and aristocrat were interdependent, because the peasant was needed to work the land off which the noble lived, and the noble was needed to provide and protect the land off which he permitted the peasant to support him. The sweat of both classes has soaked into Spanish earth, and even their blood has intermingled, in ways that were once as common as today they are rare.

I write of the great scandal that took place in 1967, coinciding with the Six-Day War between Israel and the Arab states. The scandal rocked Madrid. It helped shatter the Spain of Solana, the Spain of the Generation of '98, and the derivative Spain of the Franco Era. I had many of the antecedents to this complicated affair from the mouths of protagonists; victims, actually. Others I researched. States of mind and heart I have occasionally inferred. I am overwhelmed—intimidated—by my incompetence as chronicler. Francis Bacon gained courage from an ancient Spanish proverb: *Di mentira, y sacarás verdad.* I fear the contrary.

Calle Don Pedro dwindles down off the oldest barrio of Madrid. It trickles out of Plaza Julio Romero de Torres, and it would spill into the muddy Manzanares River were it not blocked by the massive ego of the Royal Palace. On summer evenings, the Barrio de Latina (to which Don Pedro belongs) fattens the air with effluvial smells. Human and animal sewage, straw, hot horse hide, the nectar of putrifying fruit, tomatoes, garlic, rancid olive oil and sardines spitting in it, the black fulminations of carburetors and the toxic fumes of diesel engines, all enjoy layers in the surheated atmosphere. At night, when it cools, these layers condense, and are only disturbed by feet wading through them. At night, gas lamps dimly draw moths down the crooked length of Calle Don Pedro, and nighthawks dive and bank across the narrow corridor of darkness between the buildings.

Two and a half stories high, and neoclassically proportioned, each house adjoins its neighbor in an unbroken rampart. Escutcheons pilaster the façades, because Calle Don Pedro is chockablock solid with mansions erected by nobles the most prognathic of Spain, whose Castilian lisp came as naturally as sucking their gruel through straws; which, indeed, many were compelled to do. The buildings are masoned out of fieldstone. Scabs of protective stucco chip off now and then, but this propensity has had its uses. Back in 1808, when Murat occupied Madrid, platoons of puffed-up hussars rode through the streets to bugle above the roll of kettledrums a sundown curfew in a city that recognizes no bedtime at all. Calle Don Pedro retaliated with an avalanche of rubble that stampeded the horses into a rout now known locally as Don Pedro's Patada—or, loosely, Don Pedro's Kick-in-the-Behind. Behind each building today pushes the weight of two or more centuries. One, Number 14, an exquisite architectural achievement, was the gift of Philip II, who assigned Herrera to the project.

Its tall, inhospitable windows are grilled and girded. Double doors, joined by bolts of iron as thick and as long as crowbars, oppose eight feet of nail-studded oak to the knuckles of a visitor.

Alas, doors such as these have withstood the siege of everything but time. Within, the woodwork is wormy. Ancient brocades and velvets peel off walls. Plaster falls from the high, molded ceilings, and rats leave prints on the warping surfaces of furniture. There is generally a fading marchioness, a widowed woman, hanging on in the shadowy interior. I am thinking of one. Her bedroom is lit brightly by electric lamps. The bed is narrow and short, as far as sleeping accommodations go, but it dominates the room. Designed by a master of the seventeenth century, it belonged to her father, and to his great-grandfather, and to that great-grandfather's grandfather. The wood is mahogany, and garnet-red. There are four posts. Each is worked with the High Baroque exuberance of the Churrigueras. They are immense posts, thirteen feet tall and a foot and a half thick, their every twisted boll crawling with vines out of which bulge grapes in orgastic clusters. The bed is canopied. From the outside, it can suggest a congregation of four brooding vultures, frozen in the last glow of the sun.

The bed is set against the center of the north wall, because the kitchen flue comes up through the wall, and it gives warmth. Our particular Marquesa requires more warmth every day, no matter the summer heat. Her headboard, shaped like a giant conch shell, is upholstered. Brocaded into it in gold and silver thread are heraldic symbols, surmounted by a crown. Out of the center of the crown, and rising in place of the conch's finial, is a crucifix. The Renaissance Christ is carved out of yellowing ivory. It is a tortured Christ, with gaping, sanguinary wounds, and gaping, upturned eyes. It is also a mutilated Christ, because one arm is missing from shoulder to wrist. The separated hand, clutching at the rusty head of the nail transfixing it, has a life of its own.

The rest of the Marquesa's room, which is small, is devoted to a pouf, a chaise longue, an immense armoire, and a delicate marble fireplace. There is a dressing table, with vials, bottles, and a silver-backed set of brushes belonging to her late husband. Pasted to the mirror are devotional polychromes glorifying the Sacred Heart of Jesus and Santa Teresa of Avila. The walls of the room are covered in saffron silk, and grouped on them are icons, military and ambassadorial decorations, and portrait miniatures of antecedents, each of whose names, rank, position, and titles, the Marquesa remembers to the very last barony. All these mementos jiggle on their pegs as the bass drum of an orchestra next door pounds out a "big beat" rhythm.

The Marquesa, lying like an overstuffed doll in her grand bed, does not approve of the Santo Dominican gangster to whom her dear friend, the Condesa de Magascal, has rented her adjoining palace; she does not approve of the nightclub, nor of the throngs of scantily skirted young women and their hirudinoid escorts who every evening battle their way into the club and then, some hours later, stagger their scandalous way out. But she does rather *like* the music, and she does rather *enjoy* the beat, and she has to confess that her evenings are less lonely with the noise thudding through her bedroom wall, and sleep more easily courted. Still, it was un*pardonable* of Marisa Magascal to have rented the west wing of her house. It was simply dismal of Nacho Pelau, Conde de las Dos Tripas, to have acquiesced in the conversion of his palace into a restaurant. And it was absolutely un*thinkable* of Carlos Lapique, *Duke* of Centollos, to have surrendered the major floors of his magnificent mansion to that pair of simpering Scandinavian decorators, who, despite their Viking physiques, spoke with elbows glued together.

Our Marquesa sighs. She reclines on her back, propped up at the shoulders by three swansdown pillows, her covers and the eiderdown comforter drawn up to her wobbly chin. The sheets she lies between are of Irish linen, with borders into which good nuns of yore embroidered the family arms. The sheets have been torn in places and carefully stitched. Under the heel of her left foot, the Marquesa can feel the horny scar of a long tear. She had always to remember to clip short her toenails, because once the big toe of her right foot opened a terrific split in her last sound top sheet; and when she heard that rip, and realized what she had done, the Marquesa wept.

Now she lies securely in her ancestral cocoon, composing herself. Her plump, diminutive hands peek out of the covers on either side of her face, palms up. One of them grasps a rosary; she is fingering the third decade in the Sorrows of the Blessed Virgin, and managing, even while she concentrates devoutly on that particular Sorrow, to drift away with the thumps that pound rhythmically through the wall behind her head; and think of Marisa Magascal, Nacho Pelau, and Carlos Lapique (who nowadays peered like a beleaguered tortoise out the hoods of his dormer windows), and conjure up briefly the image of her late husband, and two of her five dead children, and one of her three living children, and frown as she considers whether she ought not pare her midday meal to a single course, perhaps fish, which she loathes, and frown in an irritated fashion as she recalls her maid's tiresomely lugubrious rehearsal of household catastrophies; and then slump a little, her forehead smoothing insofar as the defeats of a long campaign permitted, that vestigially active seat of her brain pondering whether she might imbibe just another ounce or two from the rock crystal decanter on the onyx table top at arm's length from her bed; and finally sink until her jowls sag, and her cupid lips wilt apart like petals, and her eyelids shut, and her plump fingers cease palpating the beads; and she has fallen asleep, a thunderous and rhythmical snore escaping her open mouth, the electric lights burning, burning, burning through the night, and her dreams taking her to Bethlehem.

Nati, the Marquesa's sergeant at arms, discovered her thus in the morning as she kicked through the door of the bedroom, bearing a breakfast tray. The maid's slipper-shod feet came together in a noiseless clap of disapproval. She sucked a disapproving sucking sound through her colorless (but still handsomely cabriole) lips, and smacked a disapproving smacking sound with her sharpened (but still as pink as salmon) tongue. "The old sow has drunk herself to sleep again," she thought. Onward, she strode. With a bang and a clink and a clash and a rattle, Nati slapped the tray on the dressing table. Striding back to the bedside table, she pulled up the cord and thumbed off the lamp's light. She went to the tall, single window next, pushing aside the draperies and hauling on the strap of the persian blind. Five vigorous wrenches, and the blind rumbled up on its roll. Sunlight, in five gulps, swallowed the room. Nati returned to the dressing table, picked up the tray, kicked the pouf out of her route, stood there, looked down on the grinning, snoring, indecently comatose Marquesa, her mistress of fifty-six years, sucked again through her lips, smacked her tongue against the roof of her mouth, cleared her throat, and shouted: "Wake up! It's ten o'clock! You'll never make the eleven o'clock Mass!"

The Marquesa's eyelids batted wide, batted shut, and then capitulated. "Oh!" she let out, her legs jerking. "Oh!" she sighed. "Morning already?"

"Bright and hot. It's ten o'clock. You'll never make the eleven o'clock Mass. You won't make the twelve o'clock. I doubt you'll make the one o'clock." And then, with grim pleasure: *"And there is no evening Mass today!"*

Nati dumped the tray by the Marquesa's right side. She drew back a step, brought her feet together again, placed her hands behind her back, and resolutely looked over the Marquesa's head and across to the next wall, where, as she had suspected, the new stain from the thrice-repaired new water pipe was again spreading.

The Marquesa was struggling to life. With the heel of her palms, she pushed herself out of the covers, until the two fatty balloons of her bosom bubbled over the turned-back sheet. Nati, with stiff prods of one iron arm, helped her adjust the pillows, until the Marquesa was propped up cross-legged.

Who, taking the tray and placing it in her lap, said, "Do fetch me my peignoir, Nati."

"Where'd you drop it? On the floor again?"

"Somewhere by the foot of the bed."

"Hah! Are you sure?"

"Claro!"

The maid picked up the tumbler that was resting on the bedside table. She sniffed into it, bringing the rim of the glass so close that, to the Marquesa's dismay, the frequently moist septum of Nati's nostrils nearly touched the rim.

"Fetch me my peignoir!" she said sternly.

Nati put the glass down, went to the foot of the bed, searched, did not find it, looked about her, spotted the flimsy pink garment lying on the floor, stooped quickly, picked it up, looked back at where it had lain, looked over at the Marquesa, sucked her lips, smacked her tongue, took the peignoir to her mistress, whom she helped into it, saying, "I haven't brought you last night's mail. Stuffed with Día de la Caridad appeals. I stuffed them into the wastebasket. You had a card from one of those creatures squatting in the Señor Duque's palace. Engraved. Coroneted, if you can believe it—*Graf auf* something-or-other, who can be expected to pronounce all the barbarous names thrown at one nowadays?"

"What did he want?"

"Your money. Anyhow, the prestige. An opening. One can well imagine the sort of people who will go, all the new-rich of Madrid. Americans, theater people, riffraff."

"But I like openings!"

"This one's not for you. An exhibition of old chairs and tables. I tore up the card, as if we could do with more."

"Is that all?" the Marquesa asked, sighing a little interior sigh.

"You're invited Wednesday next to Puerta de Hierro, for lunch, by the Argentine ambassador. It's for the polo team, I telephoned María, she tells me your daughter will be there, but you can't do it."

"Why!" The Marquesa nearly jumped in bed. "I'd *like* to go!"

"Ballroom day."

"Let's change it!"

"A schedule is a schedule. Make any sort of change, and it all goes. And then where are we? I haven't brought you the *ABC* either. Needed it to light the stove. Don't complain, you never read anything but the society page anyhow. There wasn't much in it today. Everybody's in Athens, those who could afford the trip. Why that handsome young fellow wanted to marry an infanta as skinny as the Greek princess is beyond me. What fun is he going to get out of a crown in bed? He'll be punctured, like as not. Hah! Your 'friend' the Countess of Estepona telephoned. *She's* up early. Her voice was sweeter than a bombón helado. She's been sick—she says—but she wanted to find out whether you had gone to Athens. I told her not since the old King sent his yacht to Barcelona just to pick you up. That stopped her mouth. As for the other news, the war in Vietnam, wherever that is, goes badly; a woman in Calle Mayor stabbed her husband to death, probably for good reason; the Pope has called for peace, simple enough to do; and those granujas, the British, say they'll fly over our airspace whether we like it or not—they would. I hope all the apes in Gibraltar get rabies and bite them; and that's about it, unless you want to know who else died."

Having delivered the morning's news, Nati drew back a full pace, brought her feet together, placed her hands behind her back, and resolutely looked over the Marquesa's head and across to the next wall, where, as she had known it would, the new stain from the thrice-repaired new water pipe was about to consume the old stain from the thrice-times-repaired old water pipe.

"*Who!*"

"No one since Pidal. He was pushed, by the way."

"Nonsense."

The Marquesa had gulped down her orange juice. She had poured her coffee and sipped at it. She had buttered her starchy croissant, spread fig and peach jam on it, and munched half of it; and she was feeling more awake, although heavy-eyed and heavy-headed (Eugenio Pidal had not been pushed), and she could not remember what happened after the Virgin and St. Joseph and she had gone off on a picnic with the Infant Jesus—couldn't remember whether it was then that Alfonso XIII, the late King of Spain, appeared in her dream, or afterward, and was vexing her memory trying to decide—when Nati again spoke.

"They've come from the mantequería this morning."

"Oh, what a bore!"

"They want to be paid."

"I'll pay them."

"They want it today."

"Oh, what a bore!"

"It's nine thousand pesetas."

"But that's rubbish!"

"It's nine thousand three hundred and fifty-two pesetas," the maid answered eximiously. "They haven't been paid since February. That's three months, now. If I didn't steal soap from the Condesa de Magascal's pantry, it would be double that amount."

The Marquesa's breakfast was ruined. Of late, few breakfasts had been eaten in peace.

"Nati, you're enjoying this. What else?"

"We owe three thousand five hundred pesetas to the bodega, and we're out of whisky, not to mention good table wine. By the way, if you want to souse yourself, why not do it on wine, it's cheaper and healthier?"

"Mind your own business."

"Do you think I want to be left alone in this rotting old hulk of a house?"

"You're the one who insists we have to save it. How much did you say we owed the bodega?"

"Three thousand five hundred."

That was 284 new francs, the Marquesa calculated. It was 26-and-something pounds sterling, and 58-something dollars.

"Well, it's not such a fortune. They can wait. *They*'re rich."

"They were banging at the back door at eight-thirty sharp. Even I wasn't up. The farmacia telephoned at nine o'clock—two thousand five hundred pesetas. The supermercado sent a boy at nine-fifteen—seven thousand three hundred pesetas. The electricista arrived at nine-thirty, late, as usual, he said he'd be here by ten past nine to look at the fan in the laundry room—twelve hundred pesetas. And the fontanero had the cara dura to show up at nine-forty, while I was fixing your breakfast, but I told him he was a robber, and that's the God's truth, that trap in the kitchen sink leaks still, you might have noticed the leak in the wall, there, before it ruined the material . . ."

"All right! How much do we owe him?"

"*He* says five thousand pesetas. *I* say not a duro, not a single penny, until he really fixes the pipe."

The Marquesa now took a gluttonous gulp out of her coffee, which was tepid. "I suppose you've added it all up."

Out from beneath her apron Nati yanked a scrap of ruled notepaper.

On it, she had itemized the Marquesa's bankruptcy. "I've included the peluquería," she announced: ". . . and, of course, your clothing bills."

The Marquesa ran dull eyes down to the total. "Coño," she muttered, deriving her sole satisfaction out of the morning at Nati's empurpling reaction. "Well," she demanded, "don't you people shout it into the skies whenever one of you cuts his finger? Me—why, I'm bleeding to *death!*" she declared with a fine, histrionic gesture, slapping her bosom with an open palm and then flinging the palm back at Nati. "One hundred and twenty-two *thousand* pesetas!" she wailed. "A fortune! Im*possible!*"

Like all improvident people, the Marquesa was first shocked by the huge and unexpected total and then within seconds indignant at the knavish merchants who had permitted her *without a single warning* to run up such staggering indebtedness. She ranted. She quite lost her temper, upsetting the coffee cup. Well over $2,000! "They're thieves, every last one of them," she finally gasped.

"True," said Nati, who had kept stolid vigil to the performance, "but you're extravagant."

"I live like a church mouse!"

"You had no business buying the two Balenciaga suits. At your age, you don't need them."

"At my age, I need whatever can be done for me. *What* will I do!"

"What you've been doing for the past five years—beg."

She hates me, thought the Marquesa, regarding the implacable face of her maid. Nati really hates me . . .

Dully, she said, "Fetch me the telephone."

Nati took the tray and left.

The Marquesa slumped back against her pillows, closed her eyes, clasped her hands over an oblate belly, and wished she were dead; an access of loneliness welling up in submerging waves. There was no remedy, no hope. Only two months before, she had humbled herself again at the desk of Ignacio. She had *flown* to Sofía afterward, and sobbed in Sofía's dear arms, Ignacio's roll of fresh bank bills fattening her chic pocketbook, which had been handcrafted at *Loewe's*. After all the years of dreary toil, it was too much, she could not continue, she was getting old, old, and she did not have the strength.

How had Odette Caro Pérez de Barradas, XVIIth Marchioness of the Pilgrim (Marquesa del Peregrino), widow of the gallant Count of Obregón, Ramón Prades, come to such a sorry pass? Her husband had been everything a woman could have desired, himself a grandee, grandson of a marquis (by grace of Fernando VII, hélas, not that it mattered), a hero from the Riff wars who had fallen defending True Spain (actually, he had died in a motorcar accident on his way to the Battle of Brunete, but that was splitting hairs)—a gentle, kind, and luminously handsome paladin of a man who had indulged in only one minor indiscretion during the twenty-three years of their married life. But: however: desgraciadamente: he had had not an iota of business acumen. Ramón had only to drill for water for it to come up salt. He had merely to glance at a reclaimed iron mine for the principal shafts to cave in. Rumor had it the King was straitened? Ramón mortgaged his plantation in Alicante. The Nationalist cause was in urgent need? Ramón smuggled into France one mediocre Velázquez and two superlative Zurbaráns, sold them and delivered their value in gold to the Movimiento, scorning a receipt. And so he left his widow with the farm in Segovia, her own, that in 1940 produced an ample income of 900,000 pesetas, but that the past year had yielded an exiguous 375,000 pesetas. All other property, saving the house, which was also hers by inheritance, was placed in trust to their children. It wasn't much. Ramón had had faith—poor, decent, impractical, honorable man —in so many evanescent hopes! The King had never recovered his throne. The Marquesa was glad her husband did not live to know it, nor learn how little Old Spain would rake out of the ashes. Her course, her duty, was clear. Hostilities concluded, she entrained at once for Madrid (closing down the family refuge in Biarritz), bringing with her a freight car filled with baggage and household effects, nine servants, and the three children: Consuelo, then twenty, Ignacio, then sixteen, and Sofía, a soft and dimpled three-year-old. With Nati supervising the other domestics, the Marquesa cleaned up and repaired the gutted Número Catorce; and from that date began the long but hopeless squirming between the jaws of a vise.

Nati, one mandible of it, now entered with the telephone, trailing a long cord. She plugged the cord into a low socket near the door, stooping with a creak to do so. Straightening, she dumped the machine on the bedside table, handed the receiver to the Marquesa, muttered "Good luck," and left.

The Marquesa dialed the seven digits that attached her to Consuelo.

"Está la Señora Condesa? Su madre, la Marquesa de . . . oh, hello, María, I didn't recognize you, there must be a million bees hiving in the wires. You are well? Good . . . oh, not good? That swollen ankle again? *Pay no attention to the doctors, do what I told you to do!* Yes, bathe it nightly in *hot* water and Epsom salts, then wrap it tightly, *but not so tightly that you cut off circulation*, and . . . You've tried it. The swelling is still there. It's worse. Ah. Oh. Are you sure the water was *hot?* It scalded your wrist, yes, well, that certainly ought to have been hot enough. I suppose you had might as well try the diet, I don't believe in them myself, doctors are forever starving infirmities into submission, but don't tell *me* they don't as often kill their patients, yes, well, is my daughter up? Thank you."

She waited several moments. Her eyes began bulging, as though they would press through the impersonal black cup in an effort to capture the reality on the other end of the wire.

"Hello, darling. So early? Why the day's half done. I've been up and around and busy . . . He *did?* Now I wouldn't worry, dear, all men go quite off their rockers at least once in their lives, revives their spirits, fifty is a disconcerting age for men and women both . . . Oh! She *didn't!* She *is* a ramera, isn't she? Next time you see her, cut the little chit, that's the thing to do; but Consuelo, do it like a lady, mind, show your breeding, it wouldn't hurt to remind people she has none, I mean her grandfather was a mayorista in Valencia, yes, bought up oranges by the cartload and peddled them in Madrid, a fruit vendor, really, everybody knows it and everybody's forgot it, they're so very rich, but I wouldn't get upset, dear, these things pass like the rains of San Isidro . . . Jaimecito! But how *is* the poor love? Doctors again! I'm old despite them. Give him a purge, all boys his age need them occasionally, they always stuff themselves . . . Appendicitis? What nonsense, he had it out, didn't he? Oh, that was Angelica. But of course it was, makes no difference, I'd *still* give him a good purge, it won't hurt, don't you go listening to every . . . Yes, María told me. I can't stop her from reciting . . . Yes, it is a bore, they're all alike, a swelling here, a bump there, and they're sure they're about to die . . . Oh my dear I know, those long faces, yes, it's a lot to endure, as a matter of fact, that's what I'm telephoning you about, Nati . . . I said that's what . . . Do you hear me? Drat the bees, there, it's clear now, I said that Nati came in about cobra . . . cobra*dores,* yes, everybody coming to collect, insolent folk, gets worse every year, it's not as if it's so *much* after all and that I don't *pay* my bills, they know I do, it's just that everything comes higher and dearer . . . Yes, darling, oh, that's very nice, I'm so happy for Amparo, such a sweet, sweet girl. I have no favorites among my grandchildren, but perhaps I love her just a teeny bit *more* than the others, you understand, but about these bills, I . . . Who? C. O. Jones? Asked poor Julio where the money went? How boorish of him! But, querida, what can you expect? Mixing with Americans and bullfighters and Flamenco artists is all right *up to a point,* but you know

what they are, and where they come from, and you can't expect them . . .
Now darling, I'm suggesting nothing. All I'm saying is that you young
people—you *are* still young to me—expect too much out of that sort, and
you're too easy, too easy by far, a certain distance, a certain reserve . . .
Well, I suppose I am an old woman, I'm past seventy . . . No, no, I'm
not insulted, I know that times are . . . Yes, I'm fine . . . Well, it *is*
that I've telephoned you about, I haven't been extravagant, it's just that
. . . Read them out? Whatever for? Yes, I have a list . . . Well, there's
nine, no, actually" —begging the good Lord forgiveness for the fib— "I
mean there's just a *little* over three thousand pesetas I owe the mantequería, yes, and let me see, yes, the plumber, now he *says* it's five thousand pesetas, but that's rubbish, we're not going to pay him a third of it
. . . My dress bills? Well, they are a little higher than . . . But darling,
of course I'm not going about naked . . . How much is the total? Oh,
well, the total . . . yes, I have it, don't rush me, let's see . . . yes, really
an unimportant sum, I mean a bit over fifty thousand . . ."

Now was the crucial moment. The Marquesa clutched the receiver
as though it were a stump rooted in the face of a precipice, and she dangled from it. She held on through the shrill crackling of her daughter's
voice, eyeballs swollen, mouth parted, tongue gliding out dryly and
licking at crusts on her lips. Then her expression softened, and relaxed,
and a sort of serenity warmed her blood, rushing to her brain, so that she
felt giddy.

"My *dearest* Consuelo, I will try. Oh, yes, I *will*. And you'll send me
. . . Twenty-five thousand pesetas?" The shock was cruel. Red veins on
the whites of her eyes bubbled and burst. "No," she said, "I'm very grateful, of course it's difficult for you, and with Jaime carrying on now as he
is . . . No, no, no, I meant to imply nothing, Consuelo darling. I just
meant that if you could spare a *little* more . . . Oh, you *are* an angel! An
angel! And I *won't* forget about that brooch you've always wanted, you
know I've reserved it for you, my darling, and why don't you send the
children over . . . You must run? I thought you were in bed? Oh, yes,
your bath. Yes, well, I have to run too. Call whenever you want anything,
dear, yes, do, and so many thanks . . ."

She was sweating when she replaced the receiver on its cradle. Her
temples were soaking, and soaking her jet black hair, so that she feared
for the dye. Nati sprang up at the doorway, broom in hand.

"How much?" she rasped.

"Thirty thousand."

"That's nothing. You need at least a hundred thousand more, there are always odds and ends. Who did you speak to?"

"Consuelo."

"That golosa!"

The Marquesa threw herself forward from the pillows. Ferociously, she said, "Don't dare ever again allude to my daughter in such fashion!"

The two women stared at each other—old friends, old adversaries. Nati did not blink. The Marquesa let herself fall back on the pillows.

The maid said, "Call Don Ignacio. He never lets you down. But hurry. No Mass, and no lunch. Not now. There's the rose room today."

With that, she shut the door.

The Marquesa, left alone, gazed out vacantly across the foot of her bed and into the blinding roar of light. It cascaded through the window with eager, kinetic leaps, all the dust motes writhing in their beams like maggots desperate for carrion. It was hot already in the bedroom; outside, it would be a kiln, consuming even thirst.

She had been a fool—to spend 35,000 pesetas at Balenciaga, not to mention her bills at Rodriguez and Vargas Ochagavía, six months in arrears (at least). She *had* spent too much at the bodega on whisky, but that was such an insignificant amount, a few thousand pesetas, and such an insignificant indulgence. There was no excuse whatever for the cocktail party she had given, she supposed . . . but then what use was there in keeping up such a house, if she couldn't show it off from time to time? All her other bills were plain necessities.

Not that she blamed Consuelo. Not a bit. Nati, if she weren't indispensable, would have been summarily dismissed for her remark. (Consuelo gluttoned out of unhappiness, her mother knew.) Daily was the maid more disrespectful, daily more of a Tartar, as if the sun rose and set . . . No: the Marquesa was grateful to Consuelo, forgiving her that she had become dull and complaining in her middle age, and close with her money. Consuelo had, after all, seven children to think of. Jaime, her husband, did not earn such a very great deal with that construction company, it had been rather a setback when the lintel over the doorway of the newest project fell at the mayor's feet as he was about to cut the ribbon, *some* things did not change so very much . . .

No! The Marquesa battled against the necessity of telephoning her other daughter, Sofía, who had had the ill fortune of marrying a nice young Englishman of perfectly acceptable antecedence, but who undoubtedly had been dropped on his head as an infant. Sofía, the darling, would send at once as much money as she could afford, and probably more, because she knew that she was loved by her old mother more deeply than any of the other children . . .

No, no and no! She would *not* call Sofía. She would nerve herself into telephoning her son.

He never lets you down. Yes, the implied reverse of that coin. Who had: who would call for the accounts of breeding against the grand-daughter of a fruit vendor but who had sanctioned the social miscegenation of her surviving son with the daughter of the infamous Baltazar Blás, smuggler, pirate, and (as was rumored) murderer. Ignacio, Conde de Obregón, and someday (probably, hopefully, soon) to inherit his mother's unique title along with Número Catorce; Ignacio, in whose interest the Marquesa and Nati slaved . . .

The Marquesa began to hum. She went *hum-tum-tum,* a tuneless fit of distracted humming that beset her whenever she worried about her relationship with her son, which was less and less frequently as the years passed. *Hummm.* She neither advanced in her vague explanation for it, nor probed back further than safety recommended. *Tum-tum.* Her shock had been complete, and merciful. She had respected her husband for his confession, yes she had, *tum-tummm,* and for the manful resoluteness with which he had recited it. She had never been able quite to forgive him, nor reanimate her stunned love; nor feel for the infant then huge in her womb more than duty. Oh, it was dreadful, dreadful, to grow up finally after so many years, and then to have to spend so many long years more growing old, and carrying all the time a whole attic full of encumbering wardrobe trunks from another era that ought to have been cleaned out ages before! But she had forgot—forgot truly—what her husband had confirmed one glowing afternoon early in the June of 1924, that preposterous operatic score she had intuited eight months before, handled with charity, and erased: erased out of her mind, out of reality, a phantom swept out of the house. He had brought it back in. *Hum.* With every word, he had packed *hum-t'tum-tummm* flesh on the shadow, and thrust it at her. It was more than she could endure, yes, she was young, young, and not so strong, and she had let out a wail, falling to her knees, and fainting; and Ignacio was born in a hemorrhage.

The Marquesa now shivered in her bed, ceased humming, and began bobbing her attention in an aimless figurative arpeggio along the miniatures pegged to the walls. Oh, how lovely! She absorbed herself in the regal train of her great-grandmother's gown. She would not give in. She refused to recall that she had nearly died—that when she had awakened, it was only because during her coma she had fought interiorly a mortal and valorous battle. She had stripped the phantom of flesh; she had hurled it back into the world of bad dreams. Well, who hadn't? Was there a woman anywhere who had endured seven decades without having put her dreams to rout?

She snapped back to the present. There was nothing else to do. The Marquesa picked up the receiver, dialed her son's private number at the bank, and spoke to him for fifteen minutes.

Of which he appropriated twelve. In that dry, distant, tutorial voice; as *if* she were an irresponsible child, pushing toward that final transgression for which her wrist would have to be slapped!—he had told her, now emphatically, that she ought to sell Number 14. Sell it! His bank, he reminded her, last year offered 14,000,000 pesetas. This year money was very tight in Spain, but the bank might consider 17,000,000, five cash, the remaining 12,000,000 in two notes payable over twenty-four months. He called to her attention that a flat amply "responding to" (he was subject to that sort of phraseology) her "forseeable" needs (the cold of the grave blew into her ear) ought not cost more than 3,000,000 pesetas, leaving her with a fortune of 2,000,000 to carry her until the first 6,000,000-peseta note matured. Moreover (yes, she was still listening, what he had to say was something to consider, most interesting): moreover—he had begun again—several institutions might be willing to discount the bank's notes at not an excessive dilution, yielding her (did she tarry that long in this world) an estimated total of 1,150,000 pesetas per annum, or over 95,000 pesetas every month; which, he reminded her (now severely, although it was an avuncular severity), was a munificent sum, permitting her (the tone implied) every sort of luxury that a woman her age really had no business asking of life.

Hanging up after many expressions of gratitude, the Marquesa wondered how in the world Nacho had attracted the wealthiest and most beautiful heiress in Spain. She felt weak and ill, and colder than ever, although the sheets near her body were drenched. But by hearing him out, she had exacted a promise of a 50,000-peseta advance. She had now raised 80,000; she needed another 50,000. Where they would come from, she did not know.

Nacho, of course, was perfectly right. He had been right five years before, when he first suggested she sell the place. And her reply (it sounded to him ever more unreasonable) remained no. What had Ramón, Ignacio's father, IVth Count of Obregón and IIIrd of the Caribs, died for? For what had her beloved first two sons spilled their young blood? Except to save Número Catorce. Except to preserve tradition. Except to throw a gauntlet into the works of that frightening juggernaut of time, and declare to it, stop here—at least in Spain—because here, beyond these doors, you will not advance, and never enter. She, the widowed wife and bereaved mother, was not going to betray the fallen.

As the Marquesa yanked her covers down, pivoted on her firm bottom, and dropped her short legs over the side of the bed, she said no again. While she wrestled with her brief matinal ablutions, she said no. As she kneeled beside her bed, and gazed up at the crucifix given to her by Emilio, count, warrior, royalist, pederast, priest, republican, and finally saint, her lover, she said no. And as she dressed, she said no once more . . . but each no sounding more hollow to her, and more obstinate—old-lady-obstinate. She could have wept.

The Marquesa had donned basic underwear (it always included the most rigid girdle she could find) and an old blue bathrobe. On her feet were slippers. Because this was her working costume. She sighed when she thought of the task confronting her. She went to the cord that dripped over the headboard of her bed, ending in a fat, plastic bellbutton; but before depressing it, she paused. She sighed once more. She waged a weak, interior battle, like a badly mauled army that turns unconvincingly for a final growl at the foe. She was not vanquished, she said to herself. She was being wise, playing for time, letting the enemy exhaust itself on her desert plains and forbidding sierras. All she needed was time, she insisted to herself, turning, pacing the room, absently tucking her coal-black hair into the sort of turban she had contrived to cover it. Then, decisively, she went back to bed, plumped down on its edge and dialed a number.

Nati entered just as she was replacing the receiver.

"Well," the maid said, "I see we're finally on our feet. If you think I've been idle, you're very much mistaken. I've beaten the corridor rugs already."

The Marquesa regarded the maid with annoyance. Nati was in her usual, bombazine black; her yellowish-white hair was protected by a turban similar to the one worn by her mistress. Turban and uniform were furred with lint and dust. She looked as though she had been crawling through an attic.

"There's no need to belabor the rugs. Why did I buy a vacuum cleaner?"

"You can use it," answered the maid, stripping the Marquesa's bed with a yank of her long, stringy arms. "Did you get the money?"

"Eighty thousand." The Marquesa was tidying up her dressing table.

"Is that all? What are you going to do?"

"This afternoon, I'm visiting the Condesa de Magascal."

"How's that going to help?"

"You'll see."

Nati straightened up, sheets folded over her arms. She regarded her mistress suspiciously.

"You're not going outside the family!"

"I've raised thirty thousand from my wealthy daughter, and fifty from my wealthier son."

"Why didn't you ask Don Ignacio for more?"

"I did," the Marquesa lied, enjoying for an instant the incredulity and doubt in her maid's eyes, "but he wouldn't give it to me. Admit it, Nati! Nacho couldn't care less about the place."

Nati did appear momentarily stunned. Then her faith surged back, she who had wet-nursed the infant while her mistress had been insensible. Her passionate dark eyes snapped.

"You didn't dare ask him for the full amount! You didn't dare confess your clothing bills. It's you, your extravagance, that'll drop the roof on our heads!"

"Think what you like, but finish up here while I start downstairs."

There were twenty-two major rooms in the palace, not counting a closed suite in the back courtyard. Each day of every week in the year, excepting Sundays and feast days, one of those rooms was thoroughly overhauled by the Marquesa and Nati. It was whacked, buffeted, bullied and tamed. Not a niche was overlooked. Not a panel of any piece of furniture was left unoiled. The paintings were taken down, their backs inspected for dirt. Porcelains were washed, bronzes rubbed, silver polished, and loose slats of veneer glued back into place; and if the slightest incipient tear was discerned in the smallest cushion, it was at once stitched together. This was their great secret, the labor of love that bound the two women. Not for the world would the Marquesa have had it known that like any scullery maid she dropped her knees on protective gray rags and waxed the parquet floors. Not for the world would Nati have wanted anyone to know this, because it was demeaning to the house, and demeaning to her, and not in that order of things they both sought to perpetuate.

She, the principal ally in this struggle, joined the Marquesa in time to help her with the removal of an awkwardly long Zuloaga portrait. The two women, looking much alike except that the Marquesa was short, plump, and soft, and her maid tall, scrawny, and strong, worked with scarcely the exchange of a word. It was not merely a matter of economy, that they should vent no valuable breath, but a sensible appreciation that whatever they had had to say to each other had been said long ago, or belonged to private chests whose lids would be forever shut. Nati, who despite her iron constitution (itself partly a matter of will, which was adamantine) looked ten years older than her mistress, was actually two years the younger. She had been reared on the estate in Segovia, but of her life before 1911, when she had been assigned to the Marquesa, she now remembered very little. She had been thirteen, third daughter of the head gamekeeper, ordinarily destined to become the wife of a peasant and the mother of more, with a life circumscribed by the boundaries of the fields her husband worked. But she was a remarkably pretty child, slim and fair-haired, with eyes like black olives set above blooming cheeks. The old Marquis picked Nati out himself. She was gay. She was saucy. The little Marquesa, at fifteen, was already becoming a young lady, but she was still sufficiently unself-conscious to enjoy escapades with Nati. They limed a deep pool at the bottom of a ravine, into which a creek fed sluggishly, watching with horror and fascination as first fish floated up to show their pale bellies, and then eels wriggled desperately to the surface, and finally a snake or two lashed the poisoned waters. They sneaked through the rafters of the stable in order to watch a stallion cover an ass. They raided the coops for fresh eggs, which Nati punctured with a sharpened twig, letting out the white. The two girls then filled the shells with sugar and milk, and after shaking the eggs vigorously, sucked on them. This was bad for the Marquesa, who was developing even then voluptuous proportions. But Nati made up for it by taking her friend and mistress on long jaunts across the wheat fields, and up through the sage-scented hillsides, where partridges erupted out of the heather. They climbed to the top of a meseta, exploring the ruins of a Moorish watchtower, following a spiral of stone steps to the windswept top. There jackdaws wheeled on black wings dizzily about them, gabbling with consternation. They could see for miles and miles over plains rippling with grain, and over numberless bleached steppes, pastured to their clay roots and eroded to their gypsum foundations. They felt like the queens of creation, which in the case of the young Marquesa was understandable. Her father owned, and she as the only child would inherit, most of the land visible from horizon to horizon.

In Madrid, their intimacy flourished. The Marquesa had found a sister, to whom the wonders of the city were delicious to show. It was by no means all pleasure for Nati. She was initiated into her duties by the Marquesa's infirm mother, who was strict with the girl, and often impatient. Nati learned deference. She learned, although it went hard with her animal vivacity, how to be demure, silent, and long-suffering: and somehow fascinated by a hypothetical lure in space somewhat to the right of the old lady's left ankle, which was the correct, modest attitude of the properly trained servant.

She had a champion in the old Marquis. He was a stout and jolly gentleman, who treated everyone with the benevolence of his well-being. He had taken a liking to his daughter's saucy little maid. Her eyes were assuredly Celtic, and her complexion Asturian. He had no doubts whatever that there was a strong bourdon of the Visigoth in her blood. Perhaps one of his forebears had swung a seigneural leg over one of her maternal ancestors, he had no idea, it was customary in jollier days, but as an innocent epicure in the matter of female flesh, he gave high marks to the graceful bend (but never bent) neck of the girl, and he was indulgent with her lapses into childish impertinence; as when he playfully pinched her taut little bottom and she wheeled like a cat, pinching the rufous bulb of his nose until he bleated. Besides, his daughter's soft, imploring arms winding round his neck were irresistible. At Odette's behest, and with his amiable concurrence overriding the sharpest objections of her mother, he agreed that a bed be placed in the young Marquesa's dressing room, which Nati occupied. Many long hours of a thousand dark nights did the girls spend whispering confidences to each other through the open door.

By the time the Marquesa was eighteen, she was a beauty; yet of the alarming kind, with a bosom already warning about its own weight. The Marquesa's ankles were dainty; her calves were finely articulated; and her thighs were sensually molded; but her legs, from knee to hip, were too short, and they met hips that though pert, and plumply appealing in youth, augured heaviness in maturity. At sixteen, Nati was still a long and slender stalk, bowing modestly (but never quite humbly) under the flower of her face.

It was she who first fell in love.

A shooting weekend was being held at the finca. Oh, the preparations for this one! The Monarchist party had just triumphed at the polls; so overwhelmingly, in fact, that it hardly mattered that the elections were rigged. The wines, the viands, the company! Gathered were the resounding dukedoms from Spain's one hundred golden years of might. King

Alfonso, slim and courtly, and as shy as a fawn behind the bushy black grill of his new mustache, was the guest of honor. King and Queen swept into the courtyard escorted by the two royal equerries, twenty-four-year-old Cavalry Captain Emilio Guzmán y Stuart, Conde de Cortijos, and twenty-four-year-old Cavalry Captain Ramón Prades, Conde de Obregón. These were the nation's Achilles and Patroclus, whose exploits in the dismal Riff war had earned them both the Military Medal. They were a pair, those two, *noblemen:* loyal of heart, pure of mien, and long of limb. But if Ramón Prades towered over his sovereign, Emilio Guzmán towered over his intimate friend Prades. And if Ramón was deemed handsome, Emilio put Phoebus to the candle. Nati watched these cavaliers clatter over the cobbles behind the King's coach, capes swirling as they kneed their stallions into the shock of a flat, four-legged halt. She was struck dumb. The Conde de Cortijos was too godlike for her powers of assimilation; she was blinded, could not raise even vicarious sights that high. It was the lesser of the two, the Conde de Obregón, who bound fast her gaze until King, Queen, and their barons disappeared into the house.

To Nati, Ramón Prades was of course as unthinkable as he was unreachable, and his marriage a year later, in 1915, to her mistress ful-filled her every seventeen-year-old ambition.

She had been very young, had Nati. She had not known what dark serpents coiled in her loins. The Marquesa, as was the custom of the time, bore one-two-three-four-five children in the gasp of less than a dec-ade. That voluptuous bosom billowed with maternal fullness; the pert hips thickened. She was in mourning much of the time, losing her mother and father in quick succession, miscarrying once, and then watching two of her infants languish and die. She herself succumbed to a fever con-tracted in the fetid marshes of Seville, where the couple had spent feria in King Alfonso's retinue. It was only through the solicitude of maid and husband—as the Marquesa firmly believed—that she survived. Maid and master took turns bathing her dry, hot forehead; day and night, they alternated at her bedside. Her convalescence was complicated by another pregnancy. Many feared she might take after her invalid mother: she was frequently bedridden, and subject to malarial attacks that tempo-rarily yellowed her fine Castilian complexion without melting any of her excess poundage. Nati, meanwhile, had burst from the chrysalis. Her legs were long. Her hips were narrow. Her bosom was compact, high and firm; and when, in her duties, she stooped and stretched for an article, the tightening of the uniform over her breasts pronounced their virginal beauty. Her skin was an especial wonder. The pores were tiny and tight, so that it felt as it looked: like satin hung out at dawn.

Nati's worship of her master deepened with the years. In his presence, she was as tremulous as a dove, which annoyed the Marquesa. Nati defended him fiercely in the occasional spats between master and mistress, which further irritated the Marquesa, although Nati was unshakably loyal to them both. After a tiff, she did her earthy best to reconcile the couple, encouraging her mistress to drink another *Chinchón* dulce before bedtime, placing fresh clean sheets on the matrimonial bed and festooning the room with flowers. Mornings, when she changed the sheets, noticing the evidence of her success, her cheeks flamed with happiness.

After a year or so, that happiness was poisoned by thoughts she tried at first to banish—wicked, envious, and hateful thoughts, scandalously carnal thoughts, ones she did not dare confess, and which led to a gradual falling away from the Sacraments. The master had his valet, of course, a poor boob called Percival, but Nati was so intelligently responsive to his needs that he took to calling upon her for many small services. The Marquesa began to frown. "Nobody asked you to polish the Señor Marqués's chaps," she might say, "but my shoes, Nati, *they* look as though they've been dragged behind an automobile!" Nati was filled with remorse. She was wicked indeed, and growing wickeder. It was simply not possible to refuse the master when he bid her fetch him his polo boots (*not* the hunting pair, Percival, ignorant lout, would never learn the difference); and she would not, had she been able to, deny herself the reward: lifting her eyes to his when he thanked her, and for one, brief moment abandoning herself to the spell of their grave and veiled regard.

It was a matter of time only, and the occasion. On 14 September 1923, the King was virtually deposed by General Primo de Rivera. That night, the Marquis remained alone in his library, drinking. His beloved sovereign was preparing for exile. The peerless and once no less beloved Guzmán had turned traitor. Odette was away, up north, visiting Sacedón. Hours Ramón Prades paced the library, the floorboards of his anguish quaking in Nati's heart. Lying in her bedroom, listening to church clock towers clang out each its version of midnight, and then one o'clock, and then two, she could not bear it. Rising, she went to him; and drained from his astonished lips nine long years of suppressed adoration.

Three of the four walls were now done. Together the two old women huffed and puffed dragging an immense sixteenth-century vargueño—a cabinet desk with a fall front—away from the fourth wall. The effort was almost beyond the Marquesa's strength: it was midday, and a throbbing sun—an unseasonable, July sort of sun—beat hammer-blows on the shuddering belly of Spain. Nati, bone and leather, and bitter, unforgiving, herself weary to the rim of exhaustion, growled, "Push harder on your side . . . Work some of that fat off!" The Marquesa was too blown to reply. Her turban had come askew; sweat collected on her plucked brows, and trickled stinging into her eyes. Whenever she wiped at them, sweat and grime from the back of her hand smeared the sweat and grime on her face, so that her eyes were now constantly smarting. Finally the vargueño was moved.

After resting a few moments, the Marquesa went to the vacuum cleaner and began swiping at the faded rose velvet on the wall. Nati watched at a scornful distance, arms crossed over her skinny bosom and hands nested in her armpits. Her aversion to anything mechanical, and anything new, was absurd, but it exasperated the Marquesa nonetheless. Nati would have beaten the velvet with a cloth, giving whacks capable of flaying the hide off an alligator. It was her way, of course, the peasant way. Yank, wrench, push and if that doesn't avail, kick. Naturally—an intelligent response to rural experience. If one met a stump in a field, one pulled it out. If a shed door stuck, one hauled back on it until it sprang open, or the latch came off in one's hands, as generally happened. Nati, for all her training and pretensions, was no different. She was a demolisher of porcelain. It was a serious drawback in a maid, but one so generic to her class that the Marquesa, along with hundreds of thousands of other Spanish women, lived with it as she (and they) lived with perpetually running toilets, bursting water mains, and mystifying draughts. For the Marquesa, however, there were compensations in the shattering of some priceless platter or figurine. Nati was abashed. "Even paragons, Nati!" her mistress would exclaim—and for hours afterward this paragon of a maidservant walked about the palace with a welcome humility.

Both women now went to work on floor and furniture, dusting and oiling and waxing: and then, when that was done, they transferred their labors to the pantry, first polishing lamps, their bases and even their bulbs, and replacing them on the furniture (which had been put back in place), and after that returning to the pantry, and piece by piece taking the objets d'art, silver, bronze and brass (Nati), ivory or porcelain (the Marquesa), and giving each piece the attention it required. By four o'clock that afternoon, whatever was able to shine shone, or gleam gleamed, and the great rose room was finished.

They were both done to the ground, but the Marquesa tottered with her weariness. It seemed as if ten years of wretched toil had been heaped on her today. She was stiff and sore. She felt as though termites had burrowed into the marrow of her bones—so frangible that if she collided with some hard object, she would herself porcelain-like shatter. Maid and mistress went to the kitchen. Neither had the energy, nor was there the time, to confect the standard Spanish lunch. Nati viewed the concept of the sandwich with gimlet distrust, but when they ran late, she accepted it. Certain formalities were observed. Although the Marquesa sat by the kitchen table, she merely sat. Nati did all the work, slicing the bread fine and paring off the crusts. Her filling was a salad tossed out of lettuce, tomato, watercress, and partridge vinaigrette. Standing by the sink, Nati nibbled at one sandwich. The Marquesa consumed six of them. Nati sipped water from the tap. The Marquesa drank an inexpensive claret, three glasses of it. She now felt wearier than ever, but with a wonderful lassitudinousness, and a little light-headed as well, as much from physical exertion as the wine. She relished the prospect of one of her few luxuries: she would go upstairs, presently, and wallow in a hot, scented bath; and then roll into bed for a full hour's nap.

Meanwhile, she tarried in the kitchen, watching Nati cascade the dishes into the sink, scrape and wash them. Nati was no longer the tower of strength she imagined herself, and the Marquesa pitied her. She seemed not to have perspired at all, which was unnatural. And she had become so skinny of late that when she leaned over the vertebrae of her spinal column nearly punctured the bombazine.

"Nati," the Marquesa said, "we can't keep this up much longer."

She was accorded no answer; Nati began putting dishes and silver away, treading in and out of the pantry.

"We're getting too old," pressed the Marquesa, "and Don Ignacio doesn't want the place anyhow."

"Who says he doesn't!" demanded Nati, whipping coffee cup and saucer out from under the Marquesa's elbow. These she washed.

"He says so. He's been after me to sell it to his bank."

"So that he can have it. So that he can move into it, as he should."

"He's not yet Marquis of the Pilgrim, Nati!" Then, sorrowfully, "Don Ignacio doesn't *own* the bank. He's just one of the directors. Sooner or later, before or after we die, they'll take over Número Catorce. They'll tear it down . . ."

"Never!"

"They will, they'll tear it down and build some sort of office building on the premises, or perhaps an apartment house."

"Don Ignacio would never permit that." She was now rubbing oily drops of dishwater out of the cup's bowl, using a soggy towel.

"Well, Nati, whatever happens, I'm wearing out. Every month, I feel older."

"You're staying up too late, reading books and drinking."

The Marquesa shook her head. "It's age, Nati, nothing else. And I'm still fifty thousand pesetas short. Where will I get it? And if I get it this time, how about the next time?"

"You can stop spending so much money on yourself."

Again the Marquesa shook her head, slowly. "Can't do that, Nati. Can't not dress. Can't not have a few people in now and again. What else makes this worthwhile?"

"It's your extravagances," said Nati, walking into the pantry, "your self-indulgence," she called back over a shoulder, "that mean the end of Número Catorce."

"No, Nati," the Marquesa mumbled, "it's time . . . But you wouldn't understand that." She raised her voice. "Nati, what if I found a way out, a way around, not what either of us might choose, but a way to keep the place, at least until we die?"

Nati strode back into the kitchen. She had a spoon in her hand. Bobbing it above the Marquesa's nose, she said, "Don't you try to change anything. It's mine, every bit as much as yours. It's the Marquis's! There's nothing else. There's nothing left. Don't you do anything but what we're doing now."

The Marquesa looked up at Nati in some surprise. The maid's lips were clenched. The skin was warped away from the bones, in an ugly manner. It was as if Nati were announcing some kind of threat. Rebellion leaped up inside the Marquesa at the thought. Her stout little back stiffened. Her own face grew stern. Many things she would tolerate from Nati, but this sort of nonsense never.

And then weariness, and the narcotic complacence of food and drink, took their toll on the old woman. The muscles of her face relaxed. "Well, Nati," she said, rising, "I'll do what has to be done, and you'll see eventually that it is the right thing."

Bathed, already somnolent, the Marquesa clambered into bed. Nati had prepared it while her mistress was in the tub. The maid now let down the roll of slats outside the window, until only infinitesimal cracks of sunlight showed through. Drawing the draperies, these cracks were shut out, and the room was plunged into darkness. "Que se descanse" —may you rest—she muttered ritualistically, finding her way out of the bedroom and shutting the door behind her.

The Marquesa squirreled under the covers, sighing contentedly. She permitted herself the rotund satisfaction of a belch. Aaaah, she went. "Mine . . . as much as yours," she murmured, asking, "*Because* it's" —she yawned— "whose?"

Made no sense at all.

But: what a queer, crazy look had come into Nati's eyes—standing over her, agitating that spoon in front of her face! The Marquesa's right foot reached out uneasily to satisfy the horny callus of its heel on the hornier scar of the rent. *Was* the woman going mad? It happened—in the best houses. Marisa Magascal's waitress of over twenty years announced dinner one night stark naked. She was an angel, she explained. There was that dreadful story from Biarritz. Reportedly, the ancient maid of old Princess Hofendorf borrowed a ball of twine from the concierge of the Hotel Palais, spun her mistress into a cocoon, and then plucked her to death with a pair of tweezers. The Marquesa did not entirely credit this story. In her experience, nobody had ever succeeded in borrowing so much as a postage stamp from a French concierge. Still, maids did seem to relieve the tedium of their existence in Grand Guignol fashion.

The Marquesa yawned again, scratching herself uneasily under the right breast. She frowned, feeling and poking her breast all over. No, it was all right, no lumps, just an itch. One had to be candid. Maids did not lead exciting lives. Their tasks were repetitive and menial. They were on call from eight or eight-thirty in the morning until (often) well past midnight. They were granted one afternoon off every week, as well as an afternoon every other Sunday, and a month's vacation during the year.

Dreary. From the moment they entered service, they were as good as doomed to spinsterhood. During their hours of liberty, the young walked out with their beaus, but these were liaisons that dragged for years and years, and that rarely advanced beyond a scuffle of bodies in secluded doorways. They flocked to the movies with their familiars, or gossiped about their employers. What other topics they explored, the Marquesa could not imagine, but it all had to be very dull, they read nothing of interest, they were children, really, and dim-witted ones at that . . .

But Nati, what did she do all day? Nati rarely consorted with other servants, unless it was with that second fixture and marvel, poor Juan Luis's Herminia. Most of Nati's contemporaries had died; her contempt for the younger ones she scarcely concealed. She no longer went to the movies. She stayed home. And Nati hadn't availed herself of her vacation time in ten or more years. What *did* she do?

All day. During her free hours. Now, while her mistress was napping and chores had been attended.

Nati sat in her room, that's what Nati did. No fancy sewing. She read not at all. She turned the radio on loud, but never listened to it. She sat.

She *brooded,* that's what Nati did.

What about?

Twice, the Marquesa had come across Nati, wandering through the gloom of the shuttered palace, shoulders hunched, hands sheathed in her armpits, making those dreadful sucking sounds. There seemed to be no purpose to her wanderings; she stared at a chair; she gazed into the penumbral perspective of a corridor. Once, the Marquesa asked Nati whether she had lost something. The woman scorned to answer, walking on with those hissing *ethsss-ethsss-ethsss* sounds sluicing into her mouth.

What did Nati think about?

The Marquesa's forehead knotted. It was perplexing—an aggravating puzzle. If she churned her brains any more about it, she would get no sleep at all.

The Marquesa put Nati out of her mind, resolutely. Nati did what thousands of other maids did with themselves, that was what. Nati thought what thousands of other maids thought about, that was what. Nati brooded—*if* she brooded—about the injustice and hopelessness and progressive disillusionment of life, and who did not?

Forget Nati. Sleep.

The Marquesa was loosening her limbs into oblivion when she sat up with a start. What a bad Christian she was! She'd nearly forgot— after missing Mass for the third consecutive day! Out of her sheets she pushed herself. Turning about, so that she faced the crucifix above her head, the Marquesa knelt on her pillows and recited an Our Father, a Hail Mary, and a Glory Be. One never knew, when closing one's eyes, whether one would wake up in this world or the next. She dropped her fanny on her heels, still looking up at the cross, whose cruciform, especially the dismembered claw clutching at its agony, glowed palely in the dark. "Please," she implored, "please give me strength—and luck."

Sighing then, she turned around, slipped her short, fat legs between the covers, snuggled deep into them, and slept.

Don Emilio Guzmán—paladin, apostate, and priest, saint and pederast, the traitor—times his call at this hour, four-forty. From her initial whimpers, he judges it must have awakened her. Then his tone of voice tolled through.

"You've heard the second knock!" she blurted into the receiver, frightened.

"No," he said to her, "not yet. But I beg you to implore God, that it need not be so."

Don Emilio will not talk about it. He is held to be quite demented, now. It transpires nevertheless that he had had one of his visions, or seizures. He speaks of hearing the Marquesa's "labored breathing." (Her heart?) I say she guessed he was in one of his revelatory states. Plainly, Don Emilio did not want to divulge about what—make her frantic. I annoyed him with my persistence. He rejects imputations of prophecy with an irritation that scratches on choler. "If I sensed a threat—a humdrum phenomenon of the human psyche, and in my case the more explainable because of my intimacy with the family—from what quarter and aimed at what target?"

"You warned Sofía. Accurately."

"I was ambiguous!"

I wait. He subsides. I discount official opinion. He did not rise from the pyre deranged. His intensity, his desperation, steam rather from the grill on which his soul continues to broil.

Gently, "What did you tell her?"

"Odette?"

"She must have asked you about what to implore God?"

"For the souls of the thousands about to meet Him. The Jews, remember, prepared to attack."

I remind him, "This was on the afternoon of the thirtieth of May, a week before the Israeli strike."

At which, another frown of irritation revenges itself on the serene nobility of his features, with whose beauty he feels he was cursed, because they deceive the world, whereas he, despite the injunction of his bishop, wants the truth to be believed: his monstrous sinfulness. "A matter of military deduction," he says patiently, "no supernatural divina-

tion." He pauses. "I was, after all, and God forgive me, once a soldier"—
a note of bitterness there, the information hardly necessary for anyone
beholding that warrior's physiognomy, depleted as his frame may now
be by age and starvation. "I could think of nothing else to say," he
concludes.

"What do you imagine to have been Odette's reaction?"

He smiles. "I'd imagine Odette reached for the rosary on her bedside
table, began a decade while wandering in her mind to other matters—
perhaps that luncheon at the club for the Argentine polo team she wanted
so badly to attend—for which she probably chastised herself, resolutely
recommencing the rosary only to fall asleep with it wound about her
wrist."

"You loved her deeply."

"I will love her to the grave."

Nati, downstairs, stood in the library. Long moments she stared at
the leather armchair and footstool. Nothing had been changed. The room
was preserved as if the Marqués might at any moment walk back into
it, sit at the desk, and ring for the day's mail. He would return, in the
form of his son.

What ensued that night forty-four years gone by was never repeated.
Two people raised in a code of service that commanded their lives,
each according to rank, had for less than half an hour surrendered: to
the moment, and at least in the case of Nati, to passion. Each had
betrayed honor, and a woman esteemed by both.

They were not cynical people, Nati and Ramón Prades. They
shunned each other thereafter. When unavoidably in the Marqués's presence, summoned by her mistress, Nati kept her eyes downcast. Both knew
she would have to leave the house that had become her home. When
five weeks had gone by, Nati's departure became imperative.

The Marquesa reacted with consternation at Nati's announcement:
she had become affianced, Nati said, to one of the lesser gamekeepers
on the Segovia estate, and would thus have to quit Número Catorce
within a matter of days. The Marquesa's consternation dissolved almost
at once. She pardoned Nati the inconvenience her abrupt departure
would cause, suggesting that Nati enjoy a vacation before the wedding,
beginning that very day, and saying that she was happy for her and
would provide her with a suitable dowry. She then of her own volition
went to Nati and kissed her on both cheeks, patting the maid's shoulders.
Nati was weeping. Fourteen years, they had shared, the first heady wine

of youth, to which nothing, ever again, can be compared. "None of that!" had snapped the Marquesa. Her throat seemed tight, her diaphragm convulsive. "None . . . of that," she had repeated, turning then, turning away from Nati, going to her writing desk and fiddling with a paperweight. "We will miss you, Nati, both of us. But the Señor Marqués and I wish you every joy . . . It is better this way, Nati."

And Nati, of course, then realized: not that the Marquesa had knowledge of what had happened five weeks back in the library (perhaps she had: Nati would never learn), but that it had not been a sudden thing, it had been imminent for longer than Nati herself would have guessed, and it had not been one-sided, but an unacknowledged growth in the Marqués as well, of which her frivolous, shrewd mistress had been aware.

Nati returned to the farm of her childhood and married lovelessly. Her husband, a consumptive individual, was poor even by peasant standards. Their house was a three-room hut, an agglomeration of stones and rubble, held together by a lid of pink tiles. There were a pen for goats, and a pen for pigs, and an attached, lean-to shed occupied by a few sheep and a malevolent donkey. The front yard held a well, with an arched iron hoop from which dangled a bucket. Two fig trees flanked the well. They were sickly. Everything was scorched by the sun in summer, and then flayed by a cold wind off the Guardarrama mountains in winter. Here, seven months after her wedding, Nati's boy child was born. As she had promised, Nati dispatched her husband donkey-back on a thirty-kilometer ride to the nearest telegraph office, advising the Marqués and Marquesa. Two days later, the Marqués arrived at the ranch.

In a cart, he drove the ten kilometers from the main house to Nati's hut. Gladly did her husband give his consent. He was overcome by the honor of the visit, and by the importance of the mission. The Marquesa was ill—not one of her usual illnesses at childbirth, but gravely ill. She could not nurse. And the child, also a boy, was very weak. He needed healthy milk in abundance. It was a great thing, that the Marqués trusted wife and child to no one more.

Wrapping her infant in a shawl, Nati drove off with her master. She returned to the finca two weeks later, alone. The Marquesa was recovered; her son was in robust health. But Nati was dressed in deepest mourning. On the evening after her arrival at Número Catorce, her child had died.

Spain's curse is the sun, pitiless, insatiable, the ruminant horde that munches the land down to its roots, the goats that tear the cropped follicles out of the baked earth, and the ravens that pick over bleaching bones. Loneliness, and the demise of hope, combine in human entrails into a radium solar lump. Nati had now lost everything. Never again would she return to Número Catorce. Forever gone, and even dimming in her memory, were the voyages to Naples, Rome, and Paris, and the picnics in the Bois de Boulogne with the Marquesa and her brood, where he, at Auteuil, ran his steeplechase horses. Nor again would she promenade behind master and mistress along the boardwalks of San Sebastian in the brilliant summer season; nor accompany them on royal yachts, and help dress her for royal balls. Nati had lost all that, lost her, who could never again be a friend, and him, him forever, the sight and the incarnated memory. And Nati withered with the injustice, consumed by the interior fire, so that her heart was charred to ashes, and the meat shrank from her bones, and she became the peasant woman she was born to be, hauling on the bucket for well water, voiding herself between planks set over a stinking hole, hoeing the lumpy, brittle clay in her melon patch, and cursing the rain when it poured, the wind when it blew, and the sun when it shone. The desolation of her marriage was not, she knew, her husband's fault. Long had he courted her; he had been able to accept her sudden submission to his desires, and her undissimulable lack of love. On their first conjugal union, he had learned that she was not a virgin. In his humility, he had been able to accept the "premature" birth of their son. But that son's death had struck his soul also a mortal blow.

Nati nursed him dutifully. Affection, she could not give him. Her bosom had dried away; her loins were leather. But she fought for her husband's life, requesting that he be retired from his duties, and that one of the whitewashed cottages near the main house be made available to them. Within two years, the patient was bedridden. In the fourth year, with all expenses paid by the Marqués, he was removed to one of the sanatoriums on the southerly flank of the sierra, where Nati visited once a fortnight. For the rest of the time, she kept busy in the main house, cleaning and dusting, and it was she who supervised preparations for the infrequent visits of master or mistress.

One autumn, four years after Nati's husband had died, and four years before the Civil War, a grand shoot was planned. It was to last three days. A houseparty of twelve guns and their wives was expected. Nati spent a week scouring the house down to its last floor tile. The Marquesa surprised her, arriving twenty-four hours earlier than planned.

Nati was in the master bedroom, piling wood in the fireplace. She did not hear the motorcar drive into the courtyard; she was only vaguely aware of the bustle downstairs. Then the Marquesa walked into the room, startling Nati, who straightened up and pivoted. The two women gazed at each other.

The gaze held a moment. Then Nati's eyes darted from the face of her mistress to the corridor. There, in his priest's soutane, loomed the heroic figure of Emilio Guzmán y Stuart, renegade, yet once equerry of the King, once Conde de Cortijos, and once the bosom comrade of Ramón Prades. Nati's eyes darted back to her mistress, incipient horror seeded in them. But the Marquesa, as though moved by some inchoate emotion, took five quick steps toward Nati, placing a gloved hand on the younger woman's left cheek. Tears glistened in the Marquesa's eyes, and she said, "Oh, Nati, my poor Nati!"

Nati was bewildered. She could not look her best, certainly. She had been fetching and carrying all morning. She was in her black, ragged workaday clothes, not in the neat, carefully preserved uniform she donned for the visits of the Señores. Probably her graying hair had slipped out of the severe bun she now wore it in, and her face was flushed, and her armpits (undoubtedly) stank. Withal, the Marquesa's impulsive demonstrativeness alarmed Nati. Her mistress turned at once to other matters, slipping off her gloves, inquiring about two dozen details, assigning Guzmán (in a careless, almost shrill aside) to the suite next door, where he now headed on his own. His shadow removed, the Marquesa turned to Nati, saying as though the notion had occurred to her at the moment, "My personal maid—the seventh since you abandoned me, by the way—is a disaster. They all are, chits with no upbringing and no sense of responsibility. Why don't you come back with us to Madrid?"

And with those words, Nati realized what had happened, what had sprung the tears to the Marquesa's emerald eyes, and prompted the Marquesa's plump, perfumed hand to touch her cheeks.

She turned slowly. The door into the bathroom was open, which is the natural state of doors anywhere in Spanish houses. Nati looked into the bathroom and at the mirror over the washbasin. She stared at herself. There was nothing any longer to tempt the Marqués. Burned out of Nati was even the desire.

Guzmán left at dawn. At noon, the Marquesa was at the courtyard to greet her husband and their children. She was merry all the long weekend with her guests. Monday evening, Nati rode back with master and mistress to Número Catorce, Ignacio sleeping in her gaunt lap. She served faithfully through the outbreak of war, through the flight to Biarritz, and through the sad, victorious return. She would remain with the Marquesa until one of them died. But she would never forgive her mistress.

Standing in the shadows of the library, Nati's hand descended to the telephone, clutching the receiver a moment before she raised it, without looking down, to her ear and mouth.

"Herminia? This is Nati." She allowed the woman no opening, going right on. "What we talked about last week, how long does it take?"

There was a hesitation during which, apparently, her fellow conspirator's mind raced back to the relevant conversation and then weighed the risk.

She replied, "To be certain, fifteen minutes."

"Does . . . it hurt very greatly?"

"What should that be to you?"

Nati dialed a second time—the number of the Condesa de Magascal. She waited long rings. Finally one of the Magascal slatterns answered the call. Nati asked for the butler. In a tone so low she scarcely heard herself speaking, Nati arranged for a breach in faith that only a greater betrayal could excuse.

Nati called the Marquesa at five-fifteen. At five twenty-five, the maid again came to the bedroom door, rapping one of the stained lozenges with knuckles swollen by work. "Get up!" At five thirty-five, a no-nonsense Nati banged through the door, stomped to the window, and yanked brusquely on the cord of the blind. A sizzling afternoon sun bored into the bedroom, excavating the darkness with a blowtorch.

"How cruel of you," murmured the Marquesa.

"Up you get," said Nati, turning her back to the window and surveying the bed. If treachery was to be done, better now than later. "Your friend, the Condesa de Magascal, serves her merienda at six-thirty sharp, and if you want to beat her to the cakes, you'd better be there on time."

The Marquesa yawned, rolled over on her back, and stared stupidly at the open furnace of her window. "I'd just . . . got to sleep," she pleaded. Her mind rambled. It had to be 40 degrees Centigrade outside, miserable for May. Marisa might serve something cool, perhaps gazpacho, no, not that, although it would taste good, white gazpacho, the nutty kind made out of garlic and oil and the milk of crushed almonds. What did she have to say to Marisa? Ah, yes. Courage.

She shuddered suddenly: from cold; from a crypt-deep ice block of cold lodged in her entrails. Fuliginous terror possessed her, reaching to embrace her from out of the nightmare. She had been a girl again, watching eels and snakes rise to the surface of a whitened pool. They began writhing toward her. She was rooted to the bank. Nati had run away. Nati was calling to her, get up, get up, but she was unable to move, and the snakes and eels began winding around her bare legs. And then, when the Marquesa had thought she had awakened, it was to stare into a tall, dark cell, whose ceiling was supported by four columns. Round each column twisted a huge serpent, slithering down, coils choking the wood so tightly that it bulged between them. Thank heavens Nati had roused her when she had, because the loathsome heads of the four serpents had reached the floor and were gliding toward her.

The Marquesa shuddered again. She had not slept well at all. Her eyeballs ached. But there was important business to do: and with a determined gathering of her faculties, the old woman pushed herself off the bed.

It might be that she was only going next door. No matter. The Marquesa dressed with care. She had reason to feel a certain pride when she gave her appearance a final appraisal in the full-length mirror attached to the inside of her closet door. She saw a short, somewhat stout, but distinguished lady, who surely looked at least a decade younger than her seventy-one years. Glossy black hair curled tightly behind her petite (and prettily formed) ears, pressing close against her cheeks and temples, setting off nicely the powdered whiteness of her complexion. Her skin was still quite good, with hardly a seam. Because she did not subscribe to the contemporary shibboleth of female starvation, and was therefore plump; because she led a vigorous existence, and thrice daily patted her chin a hundred and fifty times with the backs of two fingers, and twice daily slapped her face with water as cold as the pipes flowed it; and if her chin had imperfectly fissioned, well, neither it nor its half-born image jiggled. Her eyes were still marvelous—gray-green gems behind a grid of black lashes.

She might owe Vargas 16,000 pesetas, but the results were worth it. Her dress, burgundy-red, pleased her. She was old-fashioned enough to order a garment for the material's sake, and this color was a feast. The silk was purest Shantung, the feel of it on her shoulders heaven. Jesús Vargas had cut it for her just at the pretty cap of her knee, so that she could walk with a courageous nod to the current mode. All in all, quizzing her appearance in the mirror quite lifted the Marquesa's spirits.

She rang for Nati. Years earlier, she had learned to do without a maid when dressing herself, which she would have thought impossible when she was a young woman. But for the final touches, she still required Nati's attendance, anyhow her approval, and she waited impatiently for the maid to come in.

Nati entered looking haggard, with the bright sun falling on her sallow, wrinkled, long face, and exposing the yellow scalp beneath her sparse gray hairs. At something, she must have been working very hard indeed, because tiny beads of sweat frosted her upper lip. Looking at her, the Marquesa again felt a surge of pity. No one could have imagined that Nati had been beautiful.

"I wish you'd use that deodorant I gave you," the Marquesa said.

"Ah, you're ready—and it's just six-fifteen."

"Well, do you like my dress?"

"I suppose it cost five thousand pesetas, or something equally immoral."

"Much more! When I indulge myself, Nati, I want it known. Fetch me the lizard-skin bag."

"Black, or brown?"

"Black, of course. Have you learned nothing in half a century?"

"A few things," Nati muttered, rummaging in a drawer. "That butchers cheat on weights. That you should never let a grocer add the bill up for you . . ." She handed the bag to her mistress. "You'd better take something for your shoulders. It will be chill when you come out."

The Marquesa finally rejected the idea of a shawl or stole. Her furs were too shabby to expose to harsh sunlight. Shawls made her feel old. She would risk the chill of evening.

Emerging from the great doors of Número Catorce into the open furnace of the afternoon, the Marquesa was almost able to put out of her mind that her mission was sad and distasteful. Because this was her reward for the hard work she did every day: to be bathed, rested, and beautifully, expensively, faultlessly dressed, and to be going somewhere, even if only next door, and to be seen, even if only by a woman she had known since childhood. What matter? What matter that she was a pauper, in debt to half Madrid? She remained Odette Prades y Caro Pérez de Barradas, in her own right XVIIth Marquesa del Peregrino— the "Imperial Marquisate," as it was known, drooled over by the highest lords in the realm. She remained the widow of the gallant Ramón, Laureado de San Fernando, and the mother of two gallant sons who had also earned entrance into that world's most exclusive hall of valor. And she remained, at least for a little longer, doyenne of Número

Catorce, whose very stones embodied True Spain. At Marisa's there was always the chance of other company, perhaps Nacho Pelau or Carlos Lapique, gentlemen of her generation. They would talk as if times had not changed. After the merienda, they might drink a cool whisky, and the gentle shadows of evening would make the men (even Nacho Dos Tripas) look courtly and herself at least reminiscently handsome, and it would then be easier for her to return alone to her palace, to which she and Nati had become drudges. Nati, poor thing, had no such compensations. But the Marquesa might prevail on Marisa and her other guests to step next door for a nightcap, and she would then usher them into the rose room, and Nati would witness in their faces that one reward shared by maid and mistress: the disbelief. What magic was it, the guests would ask themselves, that maintained the palace as if a legion of domestics danced to its needs? "Oh, we manage, do Nati and I, don't we?" — handing the maid her gloves. Nati would give her stiff bob of a curtsy while Marisa trumpeted, "She's a *sorceress!* There isn't a house in Madrid kept the way Número Catorce is kept up! Why, it's the envy of us all, really it is, and you, dear" —speaking to the Marquesa— "you're the envy of all Madrid, having Nati." This would fill Nati with pleasure, which she would try to suffocate behind a rigid mask, but which seeped through anyhow in a faint return to her cheeks of the roses she once owned. And she would hurry off, and return with startling speed, bearing glasses, ice, and liquor on a silver tray. Carlos Lapique, Duke of Centollos, who was the soul of gentility, would thank her in his wheezing, emphysematous croak, and she *might* truly blush then, and she would disappear once more . . . but to return! Oh yes, Nati would be back with one of her surprises. As if blessed with telepathy, or some other nearly mystical sense, Nati always somehow knew when the Marquesa would bring in company, and Nati somehow was always prepared. Before Carlos had finished pouring the drinks, she was back in the room, bearing one of the massive George III trays, a beautiful piece, really, a museum piece, and on it would be ice cold Beluga caviar patties, and pâté de foie gras on thin, circular cuts of toast—something in the order, something delicious and expensive, as this was Nati's reward, Nati's indulgence, Nati's sublimation, which she respected by never even nipping at the delicacies.

All these things the Marquesa envisioned as she clickety-clacked the twenty meters to the entrance portal of her friend, the Condesa de Magascal. But, pulling on the bell cord, she dismissed the dreams. She had important business, a mission to complete, and for this she must be left alone with Marisa. She did not want others to share her first experience with shame and defeat.

The heavy doors swung back almost at once, revealing a black, rectangular shield that stopped the light dead at the jamb. Into this space, obtruding his bulk, blocking the Marquesa's passage into the interior, stepped a creature so ruffianly that she nearly jumped.

He stood tall as a statue in some grim Gothic basilica. Hair hung raggedly over a thick metopic plate, screening eyes that were sunken into cones of flesh and gristle. Paleolithic arms dangled by his sides, well below the buttocks, protruding from the gray sleeves of his livery four inches at least of thick, red wrists, from which in turn pendulated the weights of an enormous pair of hands.

"What . . . do you want?" he asked, as though speaking with a tongue swollen by thirst.

"I," said the Marquesa—with suitable hauteur, recovering her composure and jutting her chin-and-a-half forward— "have come to visit la Señora Condesa! Who are *you?*"

He stared at her. From deep within the cones glinted suspicion. "Tomás," he finally extruded out of his throat. "You the Marquesa?"

"Yes!"

He did not budge. "The famous one, from next door?"

"Idiota, soy la Marquesa del Peregrino! Déjeme pasar!"

He contemplated her, that swollen, strongest muscle in the human anatomy thickening under the agony of its burden, to deliver: "Come in, then" —and he lurched back into the shadows of the interior.

Odette must have been of two minds, but she stepped after the voice into the cool, sepulchral dark. The creature shot the bolts home behind her. She could see nothing, and she stood there helplessly blinking. Regrettably, the man was not what she had at first supposed, a bouncer attached to the nightclub. Tomás, he had said. Nati had expressed herself in round terms about Marisa's newest curiosity. Now that the Marquesa had met him, she did not for a moment doubt Nati's opinion—that the man would cut anybody's throat for twenty duros, and for an extra five pesetas bring back an ear or a nose as proof of his deed.

The entranceway in which the Marquesa stood was really a portico, a passageway into the courtyard through which carriages used to rumble. There were cobblestones beneath her small feet. Shod as she was in high heels, she felt insecure. When the blow came—on her left side—she nearly fell.

She staggered, flinging her arms out. A paw landed on her right shoulder, closing on it and jerking her upright.

Her heart thudded. Her mouth was twisted in a frozen scream.

"You . . . all right?"

Blundering by her, the man had nearly knocked her down. He did not wait for her reply, pushing ahead. Indignant, but still flustered by her fright, and breathless, the Marquesa tottered after him.

He went lurching into the east wing of the house, with no deference to her age, position, or state of near blindness—rapidly, without a backward glance. Trailing him in a stretto of emitted puffs within which nearly squealed her outrage, she mounted a broad, carpeted stairway. It rose along the right wall to a landing, from which it doubled back on itself, ascending along the left wall. On this first landing, Tomás turned, staring down at her impatiently. Really! The Marquesa was beside herself with indignation. She could not *wait* to deliver a broadside at Marisa! It was bad enough that she had never known how to train servants once she had picked them, but her penchant for the Goyaesque had been indulged too far this time, the dwarf was acceptable, but in this . . . *grotesque* Marisa had clearly overreached.

The grotesque, however, intimidated the Marquesa, infuriating her the more as she puffed hurrying up the stairs, risking perspiration. No sooner had he satisfied himself that she was following than he went lumbering across the landing and up the next flight, leaving her to the dim light and her own devices. What a wretch, what a boor, what a monster! How she longed to lash him with her tongue! But she held it. She composed herself. She would *not* hurry on her short, fat legs, *not* disarray her careful toilette. At the landing, she rested, panting. Then she engaged the last flight of stairs.

She gained a small hexagonal parlor. It was empty. Tomás had vanished. At once, on the first chair, the Marquesa flopped down, breathing heavily, patting her chest above the heaving bosom. After a few moments, tranquillity repossessed her. The parlor was, of course, all lit electrically, because the persianas had been let down against the heat, and the draperies drawn tight. The Marquesa's eyes now began a comprehensive study of her surroundings. Nothing had changed. There was nothing new. She felt comforted.

It was not the stability that reassured her. It was the condition of decay that everything showed. The draperies displayed rents she had memorized. Slats of veneer had fallen off the Second Empire rolltop desk, and the knee of its right foreleg was still missing its ormolu. Nothing had been mended or replaced, and only the most cursory cleaning had been attempted. So that it was plain that Marisa, for all her boasting over the nightclub, for all her defiance of tradition, was as helpless a housekeeper as ever. And this proved something to the Marquesa that she had ever believed, that Ignacio, her son, did not seem to understand, and that was: *money did not change a thing.*

The Marquesa was therefore armed when Marisa, with a flourish of joy, came billowing through a small door that had been flung open for her by the churl.

"Odette, corazón de mi alma!"

"Querida Marisa!"

The friends embraced, left cheek to left cheek, right cheek to right cheek. Ladies of fashion, they held each other as if they were petals on a Meissen bouquet, scrupulous to crush nothing in the other's habile. Did they ponder on the tangle of their loves and lovers? One doubts it. The web of the past, however, held them both. The Countess of Magascal, rejected by Emilio Guzmán, straightarmed her friend away, studying her as though she had been famished for the sight, her own hippic features flaring with every manifestation of pleasure. She is a tall, roached, angular woman, with a long Spanish nose out whose thorough-bred nostrils she habitually hoots her greetings. "Come, dear one," she now bugled at her dumpy, elegant friend. "You look smarter than ever, and younger! Can it be a week? Ten days? An age by the measurement of the old!" She half hustled the Marquesa through the inconspicuous door by which she had entered, which opened unexpectedly on an immense reception room, crammed with the singular, oppressive, ornate, and sumptuous vulgarity of nearly all Spanish palaces, superfetated with satins and silks, velvets and velours, all clashing in a profusion of incompatible patterns and shades, a fussy parquet floor geometrically vertiginous under the Persian rug whose intricate trellises themselves warred with the massive whorls of tapestries, many bad oil portraits so heavily varnished that nothing more than the melancholy ghosts of faces could be deciphered, one jewel in the seraphic Flemish school, a David certified by the Prado Museum, a dour, dubious Ribera that should have been on a church wall, a humdrum Goya landscape showing bodies being carted off for burial under a rose and turquoise sky, and massed everywhere hunks of mahogany of the most opulent Napoleonic period, Dominican fiddleback, Cuban plum pudding, each a galleon freighted with fruit woods, brass, bronze, and Perugian marble, every last one fussed about by half a dozen little barges—overstuffed, carved walnut chairs—

through which maze navigated Marisa Magascal, guest in tow, flapping along in her beige, three-quarter-length tea gown, the error of a usually infallible house of haute couture, so that she seemed to have been cut adrift from some English promenade deck out of the early 1930s, and to have been blown by freakish gales over Spain's Cantabrian coast, and thence picked up and dropped in Madrid. She did have English blood, on her mother's side, and English directness, of which she was resoundingly proud; but in that characteristic she was hardly a match for her friend.

Who, no sooner had they sat down, declared, "That verdugo, Marisa, that Frankenstein's monster you've hired—*dismiss him at once!* At . . . *once!* Or you'll find him in your bedroom one night with a carving knife in his hands!"

The Countess blew two gales of laughter out of her nostrils, which caused the Marquesa to clutch instinctively at her curls.

"Isn't he ab*surd?*" she trumpeted. "Isn't he wonderfully, frightfully, horribly, impossibly *just* the perfect butler?"

"He's nothing of the sort!" said the Marquesa severely. "Wherever did you . . . ?"

"Muñoz González, querida, from whom else!"

"That gangster!? The owner of the nightclub?" The Marquesa was horrified.

"Yes, and gangster or no, I couldn't care less—a charming, handsome man, pays the rent on the dot, sends me two dozen roses a week, found Tomás in Extremadura for me . . . I can't begin to describe his thoughtful little attentions, Odette, I feel *courted* once again, *protected!*"

The Marquesa was not impressed. Marisa's enthusiasms were as passionate as they were brief, and without fail mistaken. "You had better take my advice. Now, tell me who has died . . . No, tell me first what you have to eat."

The Countess obliged. The Marquesa approved. "Very good," she murmured, "very good indeed. Is anybody else expected?"

"No one! We're quite alone, and we can gossip as much as we like!"

"Excellent. Start by telling me more about Eugenio. Nati insists he was pushed."

It had been unjust of Nati to say that the Marquesa read only the society page in the *ABC*. Actually, it was the necrological section that received her special attention. Eugenio had *not* been pushed, said Marisa, but although the Countess related every tidbit with appropriate gusto, she had nothing really new to add to the simplicity of poor Pidal's accident, who had stepped from his ninth floor apartment into the elevator only to discover too late that it was not there. Presently, as the Countess elaborated on the difficulties encountered by firemen in extricating Eugenio's mortal remains from the machinery at the bottom of the shaft, the Marquesa's stomach began to gurgle.

"I'm sorry," she apologized, "but it is almost seven o'clock, and I'm hungry."

Marisa Magascal was at that moment being growled at unintelligibly by Tomás, who had come up from behind the two ladies and stood hulking over them. The Countess smiled at him, nodded, smiled at the Marquesa, and rose. "The dining room is too gloomy," she announced, sweeping her friend into a small adjoining parlor, where food and tea had been set on a sideboard near a card table. They entered discussing the servant problem in Madrid, which was daily more acute; and then they fell to.

The Marquesa attacked the food with open, ferret-like greed, her chubby little hands darting out to snatch a sandwich or a tart, her fastidiously penciled lips not an instant still as she chatted and masticated with simultaneous dexterity. It was a joy to stuff herself out of Nati's tyrannical eyeshot, four cream puffs and five eclairs (chocolate, mocha and vanilla), and it pleased her friend, the Countess, who herself devoured sweets as though she had a pet tapeworm to pamper. They prattled first about people both had known since childhood, reviving old tales and laughing at them until tears sprang to their eyes, and the Countess had to blow her nose twice into a dainty square of lace that seemed hardly adequate for its mission. Mention of Emilio Guzmán they avoided out of common tact; but would Odette attend Luis Sacedón's memorial Mass on the morrow? If God willed. They spoke then about their children, most of whom were either dead or just as effectively gone, leading lives so separate and different that the generations seemed unconnected. The children of their friends engaged them perhaps more: Juan Luis, who had so tragically inherited his father's dukedom, and was it so his gypsy mistress had conceived by him?; Julio Caro, who had so tragically inherited his marksman father's bankruptcy, and was it so that he had been humiliated by C. O. Jones, the uncouth American magnate? Next they reviewed the latest infidelities, one of which (they agreed with an access of charity) had *not* been proved; and this particular case wound them naturally into the scandal of the bank that had failed, and how the president, son of another dear friend, also dead, had had to escape to Peru from the hands of the law, where it was said he supported himself by selling lottery tickets. After which, their spirits refreshed, their tongues deliciously exercised, and their distended abdomens warmed by a last cup of hot tea, they relaxed back in their chairs, sweating discreetly, and spoke about money, their favorite topic, Spain's favorite topic, everybody's favorite topic; and one of absorbing interest to aristocrats of their generation, who had once had such a lot of the stuff, and who now had so relatively little.

"It's simply phenomenal!" trumpeted the Countess, shuffling a pack of cards. "Oh, do press the bell right next to you, dear, will you? Ring twice. I want you to see Tomás struggle with a tray, watch him, he's almost sure to drop it."

The Marquesa, who was shuffling a second pack, obliged. She was not pleased by the interruption. Tomás lumbered in through a service door that was hidden behind a tall, chinoiserie screen. He cleared the table, dumping everything haphazardly on the tray and squashing a few eclairs in the process. But though he swayed under the unequal balance he had created, and very nearly collided with the screen, he dropped nothing, much to the disappointment of the Countess, who declared that if Tomás wasn't going to amuse her, she had might as well let him go.

"It is extraordinary," remarked the Marquesa, dealing out a hand of gin. She referred back to the subject of money, which was what she had come to explore. "Practically any building lot anywhere in Madrid fetches a fortune."

"Yes," said the Countess, picking up her hand and swiftly placing three queens by two kings, and an ace beside a four-card run. "It's spades," she cautioned, although it was unnecessary, because the Marquesa was a vigilant player who never permitted herself to become distracted. "I don't want it," the Countess went on, refusing the marker. "But it's not helping us, is it?" she mused, accepting a jack off the top of the pile and snuggling it between her three queens and two kings. She discarded the ace, which was foolish. The Marquesa pounced on it, saying, "That's true. Nacho tells me Blás got forty-five million for that corner lot on Velázquez and Lista—as if the man needs it! Have you noticed, only the very rich and the very stupid are benefiting from all the speculation? The very rich never needed to sell; the stupid didn't sell when they should have, ten years ago. Do you want it or don't you?"

"I can't make up my mind," snuffled the Countess, who had been agonizing over a ten discarded by the Marquesa, which she really had no use for at all; but she had made a great mess of her hand, changing her mind too often, and it was now (she suspected) irreparable. She took the ten, discarding an eight out of her run, which the Marquesa snatched up almost before it had touched the table top. "Yes," agreed the Countess, irritated by her stupidity—it should have been evident the Marquesa had a run from ace to jack— "those of us who need it don't seem . . ."

"Gin," stated the Marquesa, fanning her hand out. "Well, poor as I am, I still wouldn't dream of renting my place—and I must say I haven't got over my surprise at you."

The Countess forked her eyebrows as she marked the score. "Now, why?" she asked. "Both Centollos and Dos Tripas have followed suit. Damn! What's seventeen and twenty-five?"

"Forty-two—and don't forget the marker, spades, it's all doubled. Which is all the more shocking. We're giving way, Marisa, and we shouldn't do that. This was just about the last street in Madrid where the old life went on."

"Driving us all into bankruptcy," said the Countess, accepting and sorting her ten new cards. She almost whinnied. The marker was spades again. She lacked but an ace for gin. "The new has to be built on the old, querida," she asserted with a smug, herbivorous grin, "and we either take a hand in it, and help control or influence it, or we are out completely, and nothing is preserved."

"Well," said the Marquesa, "has it helped much? I mean, has it been worth it to you, the inconvenience, strange people traipsing into your courtyard, the noise at night?"

"Oh, I don't mind it," muttered the Countess, frowning, wondering why the Marquesa had taken the two of hearts.

"I think it would drive me to distraction."

"Oh," said the Countess (a two of hearts, why that—and should she have taken it herself?), "does the music reach you? Does it disturb you? I hope not."

"I go down with two," said the Marquesa, shocking her friend, who was caught with a pair of aces in her hand, sixty points less four. "Frankly, it does," she confessed then, taking the other pack and dealing it as the Countess painfully annotated the score. "The music is barbarian. The drums pound through my bedroom wall, shaking everything that hangs, my crucifix, pictures . . . Really, Marisa, some nights I don't sleep a wink."

Now the Countess was concerned. Had the Marquesa come to warn that she was about to lodge a complaint with municipal authorities?

She said, not reaching for her cards, "You know, querida, I do need the money."

"We all do," retorted the Marquesa.

"But some of us aren't as magical as you and Nati," the Countess said worriedly. Yet another spade. "*I* can't live without a cook. I need a maid. I simply *have* to have a man around the house to do the heavy work . . ." She examined her hand, which was a horror. "Frish?"

"I'm afraid not."

Not throw in her hand, nor reveal it . . . "Super," the Marquesa announced on the fourth card, shattering her friend. The score was whopping. She had carried off the first two columns blitz, and she had 140 points in the third. Marisa was not concentrating. The Marquesa did not wish to be cruel, and keep the Countess in suspense, but she must ascertain how much precisely a rental brought in.

"Well," she said, after Marisa had credited her with 36 points, worth 180 pesetas, "I can't believe renting the west wing pays for everything. I'm sure you could get along as you were before."

"But I couldn't!" cried the Countess, highly upset. "You remember, Odette, how bad things were. I didn't have a spare céntimo to my name, no flowers, plain biscuits with my breakfast . . ."

She broke off, staring hard at her friend. And then she laughed—laughed until the chair quivered beneath her.

The Marquesa smiled sheepishly. "You've guessed!" she said.

"You had me fooled," gasped the Countess, "me, Marisa Magascal, who has known you since we first fought over beaus—fooled!"

The Marquesa began to laugh. It was such a relief, for Marisa to have divined what she was after! Tears went streaming down her cheeks. They were started by the laughter. Then the laughter died away, and the tears kept streaming down.

Marisa stretched a bony hand across the table, taking one of the Marquesa's marzipanish little hands, and squeezing it.

"Is it that bad, querida?"

The Marquesa nodded. She could not speak. She was weeping. And that in itself was a relief, because she had not wept, really wept, for years and years and years.

"Your children?"

"I . . . can't ask . . . any more."

"But how much do you need?"

"Fifty . . . thousand."

"I can't let you have that much."

"I know . . . you can't! I haven't come to ask it. I can't . . . go on this way, Marisa, the children . . ."

"That dreadful Ignacio!" snorted the Countess of Magascal, wrathful. The card game was forgot. Her friend wept uncontrollably, chin trembling, mouth gone suddenly batrachoid. She was stammering, on the verge of revealing something, something she had buried in her heart more than forty-four years. The Countess encouraged her, pressing her hand, saying, "Go on, Odette, tell me. You know you can tell me." It was time! Ignacio, the slug, bore his father's title. But he had no more right to Número Catorce than the garbage man.

She waited. Nothing forthcame. The Marquesa was choking on it, unable to get it out.

"Very well," said the Countess decisively, withdrawing her hand. "I'm going to tell you a story, Odette—one I should have told you a long time ago. Will you listen to me?"

The Marquesa nodded.

"In 1830, my grandmother's first cousin, John Peel, emigrated to the United States. That was the Darnley connection, you recall, the link between the Smith-Burtons and my mother's family."

The Marquesa nodded again; the Countess was certain of her grounds, the intricacies of lineage, at least, were indelible in her kindred mind.

"He bought a plantation near New Orleans, where he grew cotton or indigo, I don't recall. He prospered, and he married a Creole girl of good family. This didn't prevent him from contracting a liaison with an octoroon, as they were known, beautiful creatures with a touch of Negro blood, bred and trained to be courtesans. She became pregnant at just about the time that his wife conceived her first child. But his wife, toward the end of her time, caught the yellow fever. She very nearly died. She was in delirium. And her child was stillborn.

"Are you listening to me, Odette!"

"Yes." The Marquesa had ceased crying.

"Well," the Countess said doggedly, "the octoroon gave birth to a healthy boy child a day or two after the legitimate child was born dead. John Peel was not conscienceless. He felt an obligation to the love-child; and he was distraught about his wife. She did not know that her baby was dead. She was still raving, and although the fever had broken, he feared the effects of shock on her system when she learned the truth. And so he took a coach, Odette, and drove all night to New Orleans, changed horses there and drove straight back to the plantation. Bundled in his cloak he held his illegitimate boy, and it was this boy that he laid beside his wife."

She paused. The Marquesa was regarding her with a curious, blank, unsettling expression.

"I . . . I think your story is very romantic," she finally offered—in a tone that implied she felt called upon to say something, although she did not know why or what.

"Yes, isn't it?" replied the Countess. "I told it to Ramón not long after you were married."

"Strange he never repeated it to me," said the Marquesa. She did not so much as blink.

The Countess was now herself utterly perplexed. She regretted having mentioned the tale, asking, "What is it you want from me, Odette?"

"Ah," said the Marquesa, smiling, as if pleased to get back to the matter at hand. "I want to know how much you get for the rent. Yes, Marisa. And I want your help in renting my place." But she warned, "I want nothing changed, Marisa. I mean, surely that Muñoz González has had to redecorate your west wing. I couldn't permit that with my house."

"So that it will keep for Ignacio?"

"Of course."

She was such a fool, the Countess thought. She had not before realized this about her friend—that she was a courageous but hopelessly romantic fool. "You're making it harder," she said, "but we'll try."

They discussed the possibilities then. Both women became excited. For the Countess, it was an adventure. And now that the Marquesa had accepted the idea, gulping down her pride, she wondered at her long obstinacy. One hundred and twenty thousand pesetas was Marisa getting, a fortune! It promised rest after a decade of struggle. It meant a comfortable, chatty sociable last few years, which she felt she had earned. She nevertheless requested Marisa to maintain the highest secrecy until a rental contract was signed. For one thing, she would have to prepare Nati.

They finished the game. The Marquesa was so grateful to Marisa Magascal that she forgave her that ridiculous story, and even permitted her to recoup part of her losses by throwing away the third column. They kissed good-bye. Shown out of the house by Tomás, the Marquesa reached impulsively into her lizard-skin handbag, pulled out a five-duro piece—one fourth of her winnings—and pressed it into one of the man's damp, ungracious palms. The great doors slammed behind her.

It was nine o'clock, and still light. Lavender motes flaked silently off a cooling sky, but the stones of Calle Don Pedro were still hot. Nothing stirred. The Marquesa was entirely alone on the street, which surprised her, because at this time of evening there was usually some activity, guests arriving at the Scandinavians for a soiree of chamber music, or early diners—tourists—debouching from cabs at the restaurant. But now no one at all moved through the narrow lane, not even the lamplighter. Doors were shut tight. The persian blinds of countless grilled windows were still let down, and outside shutters on third-story dormers were drawn and bolted. All the odors belonging to Don Pedro mingled with sluggish muscularity, coiling into sleep. The Marquesa's bosom rose and fell, in rhythm with her light steps. She felt a great peace.

Her own keys let her into Número Catorce. She did not bother to bar the doors behind her. The carriage entrance was as cool as a cave. There was a vast silence. Nati must have fallen asleep, in her bedroom or the kitchen, because not a light greeted the Marquesa. She felt her way up stone steps that stopped at another door. Again she used her keys, this time shoving the iron latch on the interior through its brackets. She was now at the bottom of a staircase well. A single electric bulb burned above her, from the second floor hall. She climbed the familiar stairs. On the carpeting, her feet were soundless. Down the hall she walked, pushing through a portiere that trapped behind it a vestibule. A narrow, arched doorway to the left of it opened into a corridor, which would lead her around the courtyard and into the kitchen and servants' quarters. She entertained taking that route, and rousing Nati. But another doorway beckoned, an imposing, double door framed in a neoclassical wicket. She went through it, entering a large receiving parlor in which two lamps alone dropped their pools of light. She passed along this room, separating the sliding doors of the library. Here it was entirely dark, except for the dim relief behind her. The glass panes of the bookcases shone like moonstones, opaquely. Only by straining her eyes was the Marquesa able to catch the glints of ivory and mother-of-pearl worked into the arabesques of the Mudejar ceiling, whose blunt, pentagonal cubes of sandalwood, pine, cedar, and olive were fragrant in the still air. From the library, she moved into the yellow parlor, where Eugenie de Montijo visited with her mother on their way to France, whose last Empress she would become. In the rose parlor, which was brightly lit—as if Nati had expected guests—the Marquesa's fingers trickled over a spread fan of finest Cordovan workmanship, pierced ivory inlaid with gold, abandoned there one afternoon by Queen María Luisa, whose adenoidal face had shriveled year after year with lust and jealousy over a Goya cloaked in his unabatable wrath. The Marquesa heard a footfall behind her. She turned, half expecting to glimpse the wraiths of queen and lover, but she saw nothing.

Next she wandered into the grandiloquent ballroom, where, as a child, she had peered through the jalousied minstrels' gallery to watch her mother and father waltz; where her engagement party had been held; where kings and queens, princes of the realm, statesmen, poets, and financiers (not to mention many notorious rascals), had for more than ten generations congregated under the round, frescoed, eighteenth-century dome, eating and drinking and dancing. It was dark also in the ballroom, but the round marble dance floor, the marble Corinthian columns, and the white-and-gilt pilasters and decorative molding, all gleamed with a light of their own under the silver stars embedded in the dome, so that she could distinguish the busts of the twelve Caesars in their niches under the arcade, and the soapstone-smooth back of a beautiful, libidinous Leda enveloped by the wings of her swan. Near her, shining dully, standing on its serpentine pedestal, was one of four lavish Meissen cachepots that had been given by Carlos III, the best of the Bourbons, to her great-great-grandfather, Mauricio Caro, IIIrd Marqués de la Romana, whose grandson (her grandfather) had become XVth Marqués del Peregrino. Now the seventeenth in that succession ran a hand over the cold plinth of the cachepot, the royal reward for having protracted negotiations with John Jay, the American ambassador, whose infant child had died in Aranjuez and was then sepulchred here, in the chapel of Número Catorce, out of pity. The Marquesa began humming to herself the bars of *Wien;* and presently she was waltzing with an invisible partner, swooping around the circumference of the floor, gliding from pedestal to pedestal as from corner to corner, grinding the marble under her feet into grains as bright as diamonds. People began to fill the chamber. The men wore military tunics, with gold or silver epaulets. Off their chests dangled silver and gold decorations, suspended by bright ribbons. The women entered in white flounces, and every shade of pastel. They were young and beautiful. Tiaras sparkled in nests of dark hair. Colombian emeralds, or rubies from Burma, pulsed between their excited bosoms. They swirled to the violins, whose bows now stabbed frantically at the air. Then a baton, like a scimitar, flashed downward. The music stopped. All stood still. There was a flourish, the imperial anthem was struck, and in entered . . .

Nati, approaching from across the ballroom. She was dressed in her inquisitional black, her eyes no more than vacant shadows on a grim and ghostly visage. But of course! Nati had every reason to disapprove. She

ROSENDALE LIBRARY
ROSENDALE, N.Y.

would begin sucking her lips soon, and smacking her tongue against the roof of her mouth. Because they *had* begun dancing before the entrance of the King; they *had* commenced the ball before he had taken out the first belle.

But Odette Caro Pérez de Barradas was undisturbed. She rested a hand on one of the pedestals, breathing rapidly, a smile fluttering on her lips. The King would excuse her; Nati would excuse her; because it was she who would be selected for the honor of the first dance, she among all the beauties of the land, among all the noble ladies, who would be singled out . . .

Nati halted some five paces in front of her. She stood absolutely still. One pale hand gleamed in the dusk.

"Lo hiciste!" she hissed.

"I've done what, Nati?"

"You plotted with the Condesa—to turn this place into a hotel, to betray me, el Señor Marqués . . . and Don Ignacio!"

The young beauty laughed. It was silver laughter, that tinkled through the chamber.

"What a shameless witch you are, Nati! You paid that miserable Tomás to spy on us, to eavesdrop! *Aren't* you ashamed?"

"Miserable, vain, weak-willed creature," the maid said, moving closer.

"Enough!" snapped the Marchioness of the Pilgrim, letting go of the pedestal and drawing herself up. She was out of patience. "There'll be no hotel. We will rent Número Catorce to an ambassador, for a chancellery, which will keep it just as it is. And then we're free, Nati—don't you see that?" She stepped toward the maid now. "We'll make an apartment for ourselves, with a new kitchen, a living room, a bedroom and a bathroom for me, and a bedroom and bathroom for you—out of that suite in the north wing of the courtyard that we never use anyhow. We'll have our private entrance, the back stairway, a little paint, that's all, and sconces. We'll have everything we need, Nati, and plenty of money, and no worries, and no more horrible, terrible, ghastly, every-single-day . . ."

"Ramera!"

The Marquesa recoiled. *Whore,* the epithet had exploded out of Nati's mouth. The woman was trembling, shaking with rage.

She hissed now with the full sibilance of her Spanish tongue. "Serpiente! Hija de Satanás!"

The Marquesa did what not once in her life had she permitted herself, no matter the provocation. She drew back an arm, swung it wide, and slapped Nati, her maid, across the mouth, slapped her a stinging, flat-out slap, a slap so resoundingly sharp that all the skin on the palm of the Marquesa's hand tingled with pain.

The force of the blow flung Nati's head back. In no other way did she react. She stood as though immovable, staring at the Marquesa. Her mouth opened. Shadows gushed out of it, like blood. "You should have done that forty-four years ago," she said, "or never." And then she went after her mistress.

She sprang for her, elbows wide, forearms raised from the elbows and hands raking the air. She missed on that first spring. The Marquesa— rearing back from the base of her spine, almost tripping as her fat diminutive feet back-pedaled—ducked around the pedestal. Nati followed. The Marquesa back-pedaled again, trying to keep the pedestal and its cachepot between them. Nati pursued, stiffly, briskly, in a series of pounces.

"Nati!" the Marquesa cried. "Nati, stop!"

Again the maid sprang; once more she missed. She kept coming. Hoarsely, she let out, "I won't . . . let . . . you do this to . . . our son!" —with those final two words, now and forever, prying the lid off: forty-four years of deceit and resentment and suppressed fury, everything in Nati that was feminine and that had been dashed against the mirror in Segovia. And with their utterance, in a single flash, the Marquesa perceived everything, and could not hum it away, and realized her danger was mortal; yet, and nevertheless, and within the panic of her retreat, cried pluckily, "*My* son!" —hurling the lie at Nati. She was dizzy from scuttling backward round and round the pedestal, with Nati relentless, Nati now stalking her, Nati waiting for her to drop. The Marquesa cried again, "My ungrateful, miserly, insensitive pedant of a son, who doesn't care about this, believe me, Nati, who does not care—but *my* son!"

She stopped then. She would retreat no more—nor could she. Nati rounded the pedestal, halting in front of her. Both women breathed with a shuddering of their lungs, even Nati; but the maid, so much the stronger, manacled her aging body to her will.

She said, "The . . . son I would have had, if the trip hadn't killed it. The . . . son who caught a chill, and died, whom . . . I nursed, and gave up to you, my one legacy, the . . . one thing he left me, the . . . one thing that made . . . everything else, all right."

And that pale hand flicked out, catching the Marquesa by the throat, and squeezing it with a terrible strength.

The Marquesa gasped once. Her eyes bulged almost instantly. The grip was a vise, and death was coming with the swiftness of rushing water.

She fell back against the pedestal, dragging Nati with her. The weight of the bodies of both women toppled the stone column, and the cachepot fell, smashing on the floor into thirty dozen pieces.

The grip was loosened at once. Oh, thank God, thank God, swirled through the Marquesa's brain. She and Nati had also tumbled to the floor. They were sprinkled with porcelain dust. Nati breathed like a bellows. The Marquesa gasped and gasped and gasped.

Gasping out, "Now see what you've done! A broom . . . a dustpan . . . quickly!"

Nati rose in two stiff and separated lunges, sucking the heel of one palm, which was cut. She walked away. The Marquesa remained on the floor, panting still for breath, thanking God again and again, and wondering how she would remove her demented maid to an asylum.

Nati seemed quite normal upon her return, carrying equipment, switching on all the ballroom lights, one by one. She laid a flannel cloth on the floor, after having first carefully brushed the area underneath it. Then she stood on the cloth.

"Here," she said to her mistress, handing her a whiskbroom. "Brush me, and then I'll brush you."

That done, both women spent an hour on their knees, gathering up every last fragment.

"I think that's it," said the Marquesa at last.

"What about under your legs?"

"I've looked, they hurt, it's worse than a church floor. And my stockings are ruined."

"Never mind about your stockings. Look again."

"I tell you I have! You're the one wearing long skirts."

"I've been careful."

"Don't think I haven't! And how do you know? There are splinters everywhere."

"Well, then, search me."

The Marquesa discovered a sliver, tiny, sticking to the back of Nati's hem. "Hah!" she said triumphantly, holding it up to the woman's face.

Nati looked away. "All right," she mumbled, extending the dustpan. "Drop it in."

Having done so, the Marquesa pushed herself to her feet. She was bone weary. Her throat hurt. It would be badly bruised. She would have to cover it with something if she went out.

She said, "You can take everything tomorrow to the Commission of Fine Arts." Adding, "You should know everybody there, by now."

Nati grunted, using an arm to help her up. She walked stiffly to the flannel, emptying the last crumbs of porcelain from the dustpan into it, then laying the dustpan down. She turned. The Marquesa was gazing across the ballroom, toward the statue of Leda. Nati was glad of that. Because she was a true romantic, and stepping up behind her mistress, she now finished choking her to death.

Book Two

HEIRS TO TRUE SPAIN

Juan Luis Seguismundo del Val

Standing uncertainly (uncertain, that is, of his feet, knees, stomach, past, present, and future), brain blocked, belly blown, scrotum sore, sacs empty, a slim, silver ignition key dripping out of his right fist like the collapse of the male ego (addendum oh most limp!), he arrived at (without having progressed to) certain Truths. To be alive is an exercise of will, an achievement, as stunning an event as the conquest of night by day. In Madrid, to be alive, and awake, during the dawn hours (and, moreover, during a clear, hot month of May) is delectable. Or (thought he) should be. How vast the African sky, and how translucent its pearls and clear washes of aquamarine—a sweeping, romantic sky, an optic treat and an alveolar joy! For, at six o'clock in the morning, the cool brisk air of Madrid is (used always to be) an elixir, a pleasure to suck into one's lungs. Into tired lungs. Into lungs sodden with the tar of sixty tasteless cigarettes, and funky with the fumes of whisky. It purifies. It bubbles into deepest recesses. Down sluice cleansing crystals of dew, each bearing the fragrance of locust blossoms, like lilac in their perfume. Oh, it is a rare privilege, to greet the dawns of May in Madrid!

Exercised, he made note, by few people. Far along the rails of perspective, where parallels nearly meet, he spotted three midget firemen who, in their black rubber boots and brown baggy uniforms, had been hosing down the area since midnight. Nearby, night watchmen were giving the pavement of the sidewalks final *tap-tip-top-tip-taps* with their long billybats, scuttling off one by one to disappear into undiscoverable dens like those mysterious crabs in rock grottos at night that have vanished by dawn. Around a corner lumbered traperos, garbage collectors, driving their mules and donkeys, sitting high on the bridges of carts heaped with refuse, their dark nomadic visages mobile with the glitter of soft dentine, their eyes chatoyant, liquidly moonstone-white, and flashing as they tongued out their dulcet Andalusian diphthongs.

Such as these, the humble, the very poor, drank in the regal dawns of Madrid; and such as he, peccable scion of impeccable antecedence, ample of means, of girth, of bottom, in rank and fortune suitably steatopygous, and therefore solidly embutted member of the superior

order of señoritos who, having caroused all night, prepared now to return
to their mothers, wives, or (the luckier ones) bachelor apartments. His
name was—is—Juan Luis Seguismundo del Val, XIVth Duke of Sacedón,
a winsome, worthy, worried individual (oh son of Adam! oh issue of
Eve!) positioned equidistantly between his twentieth and thirtieth year,
between the natural vigor of his early manhood and the sag (under the
eyes, under the chin, and under the belt) of round-the-clock self-
indulgence, tall for a Spaniard (nearly six feet), with curling, sable hair
worn long at the nape of the neck and behind the ears, and brushed forward to conceal the curse of the bon vivant, that fate curled into the
glossy black ringlets of Mediterranean scalps: the tendency to thin. His
small feet are shod in basketweave suede shoes, of Italian make, with
paper-thin soles and gigolo toes, long, tan, pipe-stem trousers hugging
calves innocent of muscle, and short, plump thighs ignorant of exercise,
over the upper third of which hang the flaps of a neo-Edwardian double-
breasted blue blazer, flaring in double vents from the navel. His waist,
once supple, helping from adolescence to imply a boyish character, still
does so, although its roll of jiggling fat (not wholly winked away by the
cut of his jacket) now implies the character of a boy who has been stuffing too much on sweets. His hands are small, pale, and beautiful, with
trained guitarist's fingers, all muscle and bone. His arms are short, with
flabby biceps, ironwood forearms, and delicate, steely wrists. His
shoulders are a tailor's nightmare, narrower than the expanding waist
and bottom, sloping forward from the weight of indolence and dropping
pronouncedly on the left.

Look at him, power, potentate—poor child of privilege! Seguismundo.
Sigismundo. Aye, his world. See him squeeze the sight of himself out of
his eyes, and rock from his defeat. Sir! Sir! How do you be a Duke?
Madam, did you spot a stray noble running down the street? Catch him!
—the harried, well-fed insouciance of the expression, peachdownpuppy-
dog, muzzlemoist, wag-eager, the chin a soft, fleshy, manipulable lollop
to a jaw somewhat undershot (or overcooked, or underchromosomed),
the mouth small, moue-ing and petulant between the puffiness of its
hinges, the nose pudgy above the septum and thick at the upper bridge,
from which meaty flanges of skin shining like scar tissue fork downward
and out, suggesting impacted sinuses and a rather high, nasal voice. His
eyes (open now) pop a bit from murky whites. His temples are narrow,
and his forehead narrow and high.

Physically unprepossessing he may be, but nova most luminous in
his social constellation: primarily bachelors, either rich and titled already,

or waiting for their noble sires to pass on. His Grace had had it, by the neck—a year ago to the hour or so. Despair, Juan Luis had commented, is a virgin with a girdle on. Why? Whencefrom? Every right to ask. He is, after all, unchallengeably Duke of Sacedón, among the most important peers in the realm. Yet is he given to doleful seizures in company that defies the melancholic spirit; in his orbit something of an enigma, unsettling, the unique and unexpected silence at a ribald jest, the hands that went for the throat of Julio Caro over nothing at all, one of Julio's crop of sexual fantasies, but that had required the intervention of three comrades to pry loose. It was rumored Juan Luis read.

Once upon a time, when he disposed of it, before driving his deal, wrenching his independence from the weeds of his widowed dam, to tug now vainly at the dry dugs of existence . . .

Ah, humanity! Bartleby and Leopold Bloom; Quixote, Niggle—in so many respects representative of his class and time, the one dying, the other wasting away, each tine on the comb currying out its tribute of scales. Newly the Duke, Juan Luis had ground out his grief in a trip round the world, discovering (as all men must) that the center of the universe is that place everyone seeks to escape but to which everyone is obliged to come back. Months ago, he defied the girdle in Mozambique, thirty-two days of safari, gunning down everything stalkable and learning that bullets in the gut of dik-dik or pachyderm are weight enough to topple the sun from the sky; but he did not have the courage. Last week, educated in resignation, he flew to Greece, to assist at the spiking of a royal hymen; and just yesterday afternoon, he duly adorned the ceremonious christening of yet another infanta, dressed again in full ducal regalia, plumed helmet, shining breastplate, and tight Napoleonic trousers and tunic, resembling (as he in fact felt in the unseasonable heat) a goggle-eyed prawn being grilled in its armor. After the reception, he showered and changed as rapidly as possible, checked his telephone messages, tried to forget them, and then visited a brace of cocktail parties, the one stuffy, given by a stupendously rich American oil tycoon who invited always the same, indigent, dry-bosomed, withered old dowager duchesses, and the same indigent, hopelessly-out-of-the-direct-line Princes of the Blood; the other not so de rigueur, but much more lively, a bash held by a Romanian ex-mogul movie producer in a seedy penthouse near the Avenida de las Americas, this one attended by the gayer studs of Spain's pedigreed and financial aristocracy, assorted pederasts (the Scandinavians; Magascal), and a gaggle of Spanish, English, Italian, and French whorelets, who, by the time he arrived, were sufficiently primed to oblige almost anybody, which opportunity Juan Luis did not eschew, selecting a lusciously mammiferous young thing from St. Tropez, whose muddy complexion under the impasto of her make-up he did not notice until after he had relieved his tumescence with her in a back bedroom, where a reproduction of Murillo's "Madonna and Child" gazed serenely over the proceedings. He lingered on through another couple of vodkas, luctual, shaking the girl; proceeding thence through a snarl of bad-tempered traffic to *Jockey*—that incorruptible rock in the rapids of change—where he joined his intimates and their dates in a private dining room upstairs. The meal lasted two hours, langostinos in a rich champagne sauce, pheasant roasted in grapes and chitlin gravy, garnished with red cabbage, chestnut purée, and souffléd potatoes; ending at one o'clock. Gay, bibulous—not a few of them gastroenteric—they roared off into the night, rocking the now still back streets of Madrid with the rodomontade of their four-cylinder sport coupes, fetching up first at the new discothèque in Marisa Magascal's west wing, a club of somewhat louche reputation and perhaps for this reason favored by the younger haute monde. There Juan Luis sweated to the Beatles and The Stones and Los Brincos, as uncomfortable with rock as the other ninety-nine out of one hundred male Spaniards, grateful for "Strangers in the Night" and the Cuban interlude following Sinatra. He was able then to enjoy the revolution in female Spanish morals, one that had occurred during the two or three years past. In the pelvic clutch of a mambo, Inmaculada Urquijo, nineteen-year-old Countess of Cáceres, expertly erected him and wrung from his member the first lubricative drops. He in turn, under the cover of a stroboscopic storm, fitted knee and thigh up under the broad scalding crotch of Asunción Mendoza, while fondling her left breast until the nipple blossomed. When the bombardment was turned off, she smiled daintily at him and drifted away, Juan Luis at that moment turning to see Muñoz González, the gangster, observing him behind parted, grape-purple lips and a blinding flash of white teeth, their brilliance accentuated by the ultraviolet beam of a projector.

A bow, somehow mocking, from the waist. "Está todo a gusto, Señor Duque?"

"Gracias."

"Siempre al servicio de Vd."

His tenant: fading away now with the cushioned, nearly feline gait of perfect muscular fitness—a South American chulo if ever one had been bred.

The man impaired that part of the evening for Juan Luis. It was two-thirty in the morning. Julio Caro suggested they push on. Suisa, Beltrán, and Amontefardo seconded. In the street, Juan Luis glanced once at Número Catorce—shuttered, barred, and bolted. Boozy tears stabbed their stingers into his eyes; he plucked them out, forbade his memories. Ten minutes later he and his fellow revelers had fetched Las Brujas, a surly Flamenco cave, a dingy, dungeony tunnel vaulted with brick arches, where they pushed their way through tourists to a prepared table in an alcove near the front, and drank and drank and drank, enduring the heat steaming from bodies pressed buttock to buttock and thigh to thigh, enduring the thick, eye-smarting fog of tobacco smoke, and the eardrum-shattering, skull-detonating torrents of clacketing palms from on stage, where megacephalic male singers with gynandromorphic bottoms bulbose beneath their short jackets tore out their larynxes hurling twangy atonal love lyrics at bored beauties who stomped through ritualized versions of once passionate folk dances, cracking their spines bending back on them, jutting at the stucco ceiling the chitinous cones of their bosoms, snatching up the ruffles of their gypsy costumes to flaunt satin-sheathed pudenda and smooth, brown, muscular thighs, between several esculent pairs of which Juan Luis had whinnied out his lust.

The lights went on. It was three-thirty. Waiters were hailed, bills were paid, revelers crowded out into the dim alley. Juan Luis bade his companions good night, barooming out beyond the city limits to a Flamenco roadhouse uninhibited by the metropolitan curfew, where he collected Flora (she had been waiting for him, dancing in one of the cells), taking her to the flat he had provided near Calle Dr. Fleming; and there made strenuous, stertorous love to her, both falling asleep even as sweat trickled between their as yet spreeted pelvises, the male and female oils of progeneration trickling uselessly down their thighs.

He had set the alarm. Less than half an hour later, he staggered up from the bed. The morrow was upon him, the maternal tug. He staggered into the bathroom, turning on the shower, which dripped hot water inadequately, so that with effort he scrubbed off Florita's greasepaint, her carmine, sticky lip rouge, and her sweet and sickening tuberose perfume, pungent with genital musk. Dressed in his now rumpled clothes (he was fastidious; he demanded fresh, fluffy linen, and trousers creased to a cutting edge), he tiptoed out (he was not unthoughtful, not unkind), shut the door noiselessly behind him, risked the cacophonic elevator downstairs, rapped his ducal ring on the glass pane of the entrance door, vaporized with blank unseeing eyes the sereno who toddled up to let him out, stuffed into the creature's hand ten pesetas, walked to his Lancia, looked up at the inspiriting vault of the dawn sky, and gulped in air.

Gulped down all the air his lungs would ingest, to the distended limit of their capacity; gulped it in and wheezed it out; and gulped it in again; and felt dizzy; and recoiled from the bile rushing acidly up his throat, up his nasal passages and into his mouth; and gulped that down; and gulped in more air; and then, casting a last glance at his surroundings, unlocked the driver's door, slid onto the cool, damp, black leather seat, twisted the key in its ignition socket, listened to the Lancia hoick coughing like a leopard in the early chill, and swung away from the curb, purring his way out of the cul-de-sac of newly laid streets and into the broad, beautiful, nearly empty Avenida del Generalísimo. Ten minutes later he had reached Calle Almagro, where, at Number__, a romantic new building, he parked the car.

He sighed. It was good to be home. The condominium had been designed by Jaime Orbaneja. No one in Spain was more imaginative, nor so discussed. The portico through which he now navigated dripped with marble stalactites, one of which had dripped off two months before, impaling Señora Pareda's Alsation. Those things happened, philosophized Juan Luis, weaving with hunched shoulders and a watchful eye until he had cleared the portico. It opened into a charming patio whose fountain, when it worked, spurted into a Gaudiesque pool. This morning it was flooding with all the ebullience of the sinks and bathtubs in the building, whose drains channeled into a pipe that for some mysterious reason seemed to possess no outlet—none, at least, discoverable by the crews of plumbers and masons who periodically tore holes out of walls and then went away muttering. Juan Luis, wading through two inches of water, peered into the copper-green shallows of the pool, to ascertain whether his favorite carp—a scarred, fan-tailed old patriarch with a carapace of brassy scales—had escaped one more night the claws of Countess von Leddhin's cat. It had. Pleased, Juan Luis reared all the way back to gaze at the heavenly parallelogram, that patch of blue and gold stamped out of the sky by the tall cube of the courtyard.

It was a mistake. Two jolts of pain shivered into his occiput. His memory went blank. He tottered. The sky would become a bronze bell, and its sun the clapper. The sky would clang with heat, and then the bell would descend, to snuff out Madrid. And he could not remember.

He was now—and just now—drunk. His feet stuttered up the four steps of a portal. His right hand fumbled in a pocket for the key. He poked. He jabbed. Slid it in. Turned it. Pushed with his left shoulder.

Pulled the key out. Reeled inside. Fell back with his back against the door, shutting it. Reeled to the elevator. Yanked at the art nouveau grill. Stumbled in. Clanged the grill shut. Pushed button six. Waited. Pushed button five. Not a tremor. Seven-four-three. Three-two-five. Six. Six. Dead!

He banged on the instrument panel. Pidal had not been pushed; one makes one's own destiny, excavating it out of a solid block of indifference. Out of the elevator he yanked-stumbled-pushed-clanged-reeled—to the stairs. Up a flight. Sweat. A top spinning in his skull. Oh God his stomach. The landing queasy under his soles. Up another flight, hauling on the bannister rail. Holy Mother his stomach. Drenched with sweat. Steps above him.

Jaunty steps, firm steps, prosperous steps, well-satisfied steps, down-from-the-top-of-the-building steps. Up another flight. Air like rigging in his hands. Up, m'bully. Oh. Oh. Oh! Three more yardarms above him, mast pendulating while below heaved the bosom of the sea . . .

Flat-footed steps, glottal steps; steps gay with the clicketing of steel-tipped heels. Nearer, ever nearer.

Pull himself together!

You, Juan Luis Seguismundo del Val! You, Duke of Sacedón, twelve times a count, seven a marquis, and six times over a grandee of Spain.

The wall. Support: cool and clammy. Better!

Steps on the landing above. Bulk turning importantly down the flight. Pate balder than an egg. Belly the boll of a tree trunk. Duck-footed. Ruhr-rooted. Perforated, brown-and-white shoes. Dacron lightweight gabardine suit. White silk tie, monogrammed in pale blue. And a trencherman's smile, a smacking, porcine roll of the lips—a veritable canyon across the face of the moon.

Manners, Juan Luis!

"Buenos—pop—días."

"Wie geht's?"

Pop. Pop.

"Est ist so schön heut' früh . . . leider ist es geschlossen!"

Pop.

At least smile!

Weakly. Broad-brimming back, gleaming, machined dentures, polished on carborundum, steady, appropriative steps down, jerking an amiable, hip-out bow—in passing—like a hockey check.

The Duke of Sacedón shivered. He had glimpsed the past, present, and future. Down, down, down went the steps, to the final landing, and out the door, for the visitor seemed to possess his own key—to the world. And as for Juan Luis Seguismundo del Val: up. Ohhh, up! Three tilting, warping, buckling flights. I will not take off my tie. I will not bow to your Republic, to your tyranny, to your monstrous, mechanical State. I will not deny God—and for that, do with me what thou wilt. Up.

Into his apartment. Into his bedroom. Stripped. Naked between sheets. Eyelids clamped against the dread of the day to be anticipated. He had promised . . . He had promised . . . Eugenio had said . . . His mother . . . Jaime would not let him . . .

Herminia. Herminia would wake him. Herminia would take care of everything. Now . . . sleep.

T W O
Jacobo Rivas, Mantequero

Nine o'clock the same morning—a splendid morning, the last few days of the month making up for a cold and rainy spell that had dispirited the San Isidro bullfights, which, traditionally, expect some inclemency, but not quite so much as the season of 1967 brought. Jacobo Rivas (striding through the old Puerta de Moros, now fancified by City Hall with the name of Plaza Julio Romero de Torres, who ever heard of him? a painter, they said, but what did he paint? nobody knew, naturally not, one more silly notion by cretins who could never leave well enough alone, changing street signs every ten minutes, blocking squares, mystifying traffic, routing a body one way here, one way there, day-after-next all changed about again) snorted. He was in high good humor. Basque by birth and God's grace, bullocky ex-portero (goalkeeper) for the once renowned Atlético de Bilbao professional soccer team, and now perforce and by God's mysterious will a mantequero, this glorious thirty-first of May signaled the beginning for him of a whole new future. He was sure of that. Sharp at seven-thirty in the morning, his eyelids had popped open. Just like that! Like a child, popping out of sleep and ready to pop hopping out of bed. But he had not budged. No indeed! He had lain, lingered, in wonderment. Breathless. Awed. Because, to his immense delight (and to tell the truth his astonishment), he had awakened to discover an immensity between his legs.

It was a true immensity. Not in nearly a decade had such a thing happened. Needless to say, he was all macho—but fifty-three years old, after all, and well beyond the time for priapian thaumaturgy. But there it was, undeniable, thicker than the stem of a young oak!

Nearly bursting with pride, he had rolled out of bed. He had stripped off his pyjama bottoms, admiring himself in the sheet of hammered tin tacked to one wall. What a spectacular sight it was! Thudding around to the other side of the bed, he shook his wife awake.

"Marisol," he shouted at her, "look!"

One subfuscous eye, at once menacing and at the mark, opened. "What," she had growled, "do you think you are doing?"

"But look, woman, just look! In the morning! Is it not beautiful? Is it not grand?" He sucked in the hummock of his belly, throwing out the hummock of his chest.

"It is disgusting. Put it away. Go to the bathroom. I want to sleep."

"Woman, prepare yourself!"

When it came to exercising his conjugal rights, Jacobo, Spaniard to the hilt, brooked no nonsense. He yanked Marisol over on her backside, eliciting from her a yelp of outrage and dismay. He ignored it, ripping the covers down, springing her thighs apart, and thrusting himself into the thickety fen. Oink-oink-oink, and done! Just like that! Oh, it was magnificent, a regular rape. Even Marisol was impressed. "Jacobo! Corazón! *Amo!*"

At breakfast, he had pounded on the kitchen table. The coffee was not hot enough. It lacked chicory. The rosquillas were too doughy—leaden! And a glass of aguardiente he would have. Marisol was all humility. Marisol served him instead of hurling at him his food. Of course, it might not last. She was volcanic, and well able to swing over her head a hundred-liter pail of milk: a fine, fearsome figure of a woman, Jacobo's match, and he would have asked for no other. But he delighted in her rare deferences; he basked in the admiring smiles of his children—button-black eyes, merry, blooming Cantabrian cheeks. Probably the older ones had overheard the great event of the morning, packed together as they were in the spare room separated from their parents' sleeping quarters by a thin partition. He beamed at them, most of all at Soledad, whom he adored: his darling, his rose, the fifteen-year-old daughter who virtually ran the downstairs store for him, who was quick with the customer, quick at taking inventory (which he hated), and even quicker to intuit the occasional glooms that weighed his heart; who, sadly, was old enough now to earn her way in the world, and who had recently applied for

several positions, none of which he hoped she would obtain. He loved
her and loved them all, even the postscripts born in Madrid, Amadeo,
Teresa, Asunción, and Calamidad, who were somewhat of a blur to him,
as yet undifferentiated bundles of protoplasm. They screamed, they
fought, they laughed, they wept, they had appetites, they needed clothes,
they crawled over him, they shredded his cigarettes, they overturned his
bottles of hard cider and tore his team photographs; but they all smelled
of himself and Marisol, of the butter and cheese sold out of the shop. He
was very much the idol of his children. "Oh, Papá!" Soledad exclaimed
for no reason at all, her sweet young bosom heaving as she spoke. He
pulled in his stomach. He puffed out his chest. Yes, her father was a
macho indeed. Let Madrid, let all the world, know it!

"Marisol," he demanded, "what have you done about the Marquesa's
bill?"

"I sent over Amadeo just yesterday."

"And?"

"Promises."

"Well," he announced, "today I am going to Número Catorce myself. I will exact payment!"

"Jacobo!"

"Yes," he stated. "I, Jacobo Rivas, will go. Not you. Not Amadeo.
Not Soledad. But I!"

"Jacobo! Children, listen to your father—*look* at him! *There* you have
a man indeed!"

They devoured him with round, worshiping eyes, even Primitivo
and Serenidad, the two eldest, who between them brought in 20 per cent
of the family budget, and were thus on the threshold of skepticism. Everyone knew how their father loathed pressing debtors. They all knew how
he hated the shop; how he longed for the hills of Sacedón and the sea
he had once conquered.

"How much does the old lady owe us?" Jacobo inquired, thoroughly
pleased by the sensation he was causing.

"Soledad," said his wife, "how much does the Marquesa owe?"

"Nine thousand, three hundred and fifty-two pesetas, Papá!"

"*How* much?!"

"Nine thousand, three hundred and . . ."

"Disgraceful!" roared Jacobo, even as he paled inwardly at the
thought of trying to collect such a sum. Cowardice prompted real indignation. "How could you permit such a scandal?" he hurled at his wife.

"Con cuidado," she murmured, kindling.

But he was too angry to care. "Who is to caution whom! Is it proper that I, a Rivas de Sacedón, chief of the clan, should have to act as my own cobrador? Is it dignified? You forget your place! Who sweated in the mines? I! Who saddled me with nine hungry mouths? You! Cuidado, you say! Is it not enough that you thwarted my career, the greatness I might have achieved, making a shopkeeper out of me in a city filled with Arabs and Jews and not a true Christian anywhere . . ."

"Take care!" repeated Marisol.

"Take care! Take care!" His excitement was producing the most extraordinary physiological response. "Who is to take care from now on? You *dare* so address the person who should be to you as the Lord Christ (may He forgive me) to the Church? Shame on you, woman! Am I, a Rivas! an hidalgo! to tolerate impertinence on top of everything else?"

"Enough!" The bulk of Marisol was suddenly looming across the table. She had risen.

"Ha!" snorted Jacobo, staring up at her. On any other day, he might have quailed before that mushrooming cumulus cloud, from which thunder was the least to be expected. Or backed prudently beyond the reach of her palms, which had more than once clapped an entire electrical storm inside his head. Not this morning. He spread his own pachidermic palms, grasping the corners of the table, quite obliterating the faces of several small children flanking him. "Niños," he commanded, keeping his eyes fixed on the flashing vortices under Marisol's thick, black brows, "be off. Be off about your business. Soledad, Amadeo, open the store. You, Marisol, will go to your room."

Now were the heavens sundered. "I'll do no such thing, you lazy lump of pork fat!"

"Woman!" he bellowed. "*Do . . . as . . . I . . . say!*"

It was magical. The children scattered. The thunderhead seemed to inspissate before his eyes. No pious resignation, even. No stiff-lipped, contemptuous acquiescence. Marisol was shocked. Marisol was overwhelmed. Could he be suggesting . . . after just forty-five minutes ago?

A rubious flush rose from the woman's neck, suffusing her cheeks: that virginal alarm he had known when those cheeks were not so heavy, when they were merely plump and juicy, when thirty-odd years before, he had begun his long courtship of her among the slopes and orchards of their homeland.

"Sí, Jacobo." And she turned into the bedroom.

He waited a few moments. The magic held. He got to his feet. It was true. He was not boasting. He was able.

He yawed after his wife, hippopotamic hips swinging left and right, backhanding the flimsy door of their bedroom behind him; and found her (magic indeed) in bed already, shrugging the covers up close under her chin, shoulders naked, eyes meek, submissive, peering at him as if fearful, with the fear and wonder of their wedding night. And this time he contained the plenishment of his lust. He could not say whence came the inspiration, but he made it an objective that Marisol should derive from this encounter as much gratification as he was able to provoke. And it was with ardor that she responded. He knew it; she tried to dissemble it; neither would ever confess it to the other. But within moments she was pent, moaning and groaning. He held steady, unconquerable the rod on which her gender seized. She sobbed. Her fists pounded on his chest— cursing him, calling him a goat, a donkey, a foul beast. Because it was shameful, a terrible sin, the overthrowal of the middle-class female Spanish empire for her to have betrayed more than passive endurance. He grinned down at Marisol: sphingine, august. He was a beast indeed, goat and donkey—and a bull and a lion too! Not in her thousand-and-one previous conjugal unions had ecstacy been vouchsafed. Never had she imagined the delirium that a man had it in his power to induce. Again! he thought. Let Marisol's mammoth buttocks and thighs thrash beneath him in the mounting calamity of climax. Now! He rammed her into a second, shrieking convulsion, soaking her womb with his prepotent seed; saying, "And if I want to have a drink or two with my friends, you, woman, will not open your mouth."

Ah! For weeks, perhaps months to come, Marisol would gaze on him with tremulous awe. Merited. She had rushed off to seek her confessor, as well she might. He and she had made a most amazing discovery. Women, respectable women, enjoyed it! Oh, had he known that this was the case—long ago! From now on, Marisol would shush the children if he wanted to nap, and say nothing if he emptied a bottle or two of cider, and let him sleep through Sunday Mass if he felt like it. Her soul, after all, was in by far the greater peril.

Ah! Ah! Ah! It was *good* to be a man, a Basque, man among men and Spaniard amongst Spaniards! Proudly Jacobo strode through the Plaza Julio Romero de Torres, heading west, past San Andrés and down into the broad mouth of Calle Los Mancebos. His destination was the back door of Número Catorce—which would open to him, as all doors must from now on. He had the bill in a pocket, with all the vouchers. It was as clear as day. Five, six months had gone by without payment. Incredible! He should punish Marisol. (She might enjoy it, now.) He should upbraid Soledad. (Gently.) To let this go on! He feared nothing, not the Marquesa, not even that witch of a housekeeper, that Nati, with her imperious airs and necromantic eye. Coño! As if he, Jacobo Rivas, Basque, hidalgo de Sacedón, had anything to fear from anybody!

THREE

Juan Luis Seguismundo del Val,
Duque de Sacedón

A battery-powered alarm whined him awake.

Out went his left hand, slapping at the plunger. Erratic and occluding eyeballs tried to focus on the luminous dial.

He refused to believe it. Nine o'clock. Stygian, his room. Yet instinct told him it was morning, not night.

He groaned. Herminia was responsible. But why this dreadful hour? What duties loomed all along the day?

He would avoid them. (He shut his eyes.) He would devour Time in sleep until the time came for it to devour him.

Long moments he felt nothing—neither pain, nor joy, nor regret. Then the craving of the addict seized him.

He stirred. His left hand went groping about the bedside table. The lamp base. The agate hollow of an ash tray. His wallet. The telephone . . .

Not there!

With his right hand, he began batting at shadows above him. The shadows were cobwebby. *Where* was the bellbutton? *Who* had deprived him of it: umbilicus, sole connection with life; and at the moment sole slender chance of survival?

He stretched higher, toward the center of the headboard. A cord slipped between index and third fingers. Ah!

Murmuring little moans of thanksgiving, he ran its cool length along the fleshy junction of the fingers until he had the plastic egg lodged between them. Whereupon, using his thumb, he depressed the nipple twice; hanging on and falling asleep.

Eons later, the opening of his bedroom door awoke him. A scrap of gray light penetrated.

"Señor?"

"Huh?"

"You rang, señor."

Ah yes. "Tráeme los pitillos."

The maid walked in and searched through his jacket, which was flung over a chair, coming to his bedside in the scarcely relieved darkness and placing in his outstretched left hand a pack of Kents and a throwaway propane lighter.

"El desayuno, señor?"

"Sí!"

She departed. He lay still. Then, slowly, he lit a cigarette. Aaah. Aaaaaaaah! The indescribable joy of the day's first! Nicotine ballooned his lungs and filtered into the bloodstream. Each drag helped revive him. His head cleared. Where had he ended up? Oh yes: with Florita.

What a cheat life was! Now, upon first waking up, did the serpent in his loins hiss most importunately. He swelled. More and more often, reminiscences roused in him keener response than acts so frequently performed when half besotted. He would have liked his mistress in bed with him this moment, Herminia permitting, which she never would. Which was idiotic. Which one of these days he would change. Were Florita within reach, *what* he would do! *How* he would astonish her!

Compressing the few muscles remaining in his belly, he snorted smoke down from his nostrils. In his imagination, he fleshed out the dancer. The face he was unable to visualize very well, except for the stunning Semitic scythe of her nose. The shape and texture of her buttocks were nearly palpable. He disagreed absolutely with Julio Caro, who, although a hog at the swill, professed that the bodies of women become unmemorable after the first dozen or so. Faces, maybe: bodies never! Since his violent renunciation of chastity—eight years, it was now—he, Juan Luis, had bedded perhaps a gross of women. Yet he would never forget the sensation of furring his lips on Lady Hume's nape, which was downy; nor how amusing and incongruous were the tiny pink teats on La Húngara, famous for the size of her breasts. Françoise Lacouste's armpits possessed a special French fragrance: scullery maid's sweat steamed in cabbage and sprinkled with Jolie Madame—irresistible! And La Chata, who could ever forget her? The silken tassle of her dome alone distinguished her from all other women . . .

He was immersed in such reveries when the maid returned with a tray. As she set it on the bed beside him, he noticed her figure. It was neat, compact, well-turned. What was her name? he wondered. Pilar? Paca? Herminia, the perfectionist, changed them about so often nowadays that he was forever confused. This one, whatever she was called, went to the window and began hauling on the strap of the persian blind. Daggers of light stabbed between the crack of the curtains and into his eyeballs. Oh-oh! Deep in the cerebellum he felt the first, premonitory throb of what was going to be an epic hangover. "Don't," he begged, "—for the love of God don't draw the curtain!" He chanced a sip of coffee. Acid and bitter, it nauseated him. He snuffed out his cigarette, lighting another. It tasted less good. But he watched the girl, who was shaking his clothes out of the chair. She was meek-seeming; and, he guessed, not yet eighteen. The very thought pierced him. How poignant! What a plum! She collected first his underpants. He wondered what she felt about handling them. She evinced no squeamishness, although after the stand-up bang with the Marseilles tart they were sure to be stained. Did she know about that? She must, daughter of some peasant from the provinces. Lewd little images prospered in his mind. "Few delights," Jaime Orbaneja had noted, "charm the voluptuary more than voyeuristic fancies." "Ascribing to innocence," Billy Smith-Burton had added, "secret perversions." Juan Luis ruminated. When tucked into her cozy bed, had this particular innocent ever felt her sweet young nipples stiffen and her slumbering genitals curl; and had her fingers crept to the pitch of her womanhood, there to squander her treasures alone? What if one night he sneaked in, and caught her writhing and moaning and . . .

She was examining his jacket, delving a small, swift hand into each pocket, fetching out his car keys, change, and a money clip, all of which she placed on the marble surface of an armoire. She stooped then for his trousers, which he had kicked off into a corner. Despite the gloom—more intriguingly in the gloom—he could see up the backs of her sturdy peasant thighs, as smooth and cool to the sight as alabaster.

He puffed rapidly on his cigarette. His being palpitated with an abdominal thunder. How naked and rank he felt under the light covers! She wore a loose, belted blue uniform. He was acutely aware that little more than a bra and rippable cotton panties protected her. She would be delicious.

Should he take her now, while she was absorbed, while her back was to him? He could be out of bed cat-quick. Before she jerked upright, he would have jammed his lust hard against her bottom, and—arms enveloping and imprisoning her arms—palmed and gripped her plump young breasts with the tenacity of a barnacle. She would go, "O! O! Dios mío, Señor!"

She would struggle, calling upon the saints. All that would heighten his pleasure. Limp she would finally become, the risk of her profession, the fear of her parents, the tradition of centuries . . .

But she had straightened up, turning briskly. He had lost his opportunity. What he really wanted to do was pass water.

"I'm getting out of bed," he announced in an irritated tone. Now he began to feel the hangover in earnest. And he remembered at the same time what he had in store for him. There was the Utilidades Españolas board meeting to preside over. There was more. Eugenio, his administrator, had telephoned late yesterday afternoon about something worrisome he wanted to discuss after the junta, and about which he would reveal nothing to Herminia. This made Juan Luis angry again: the Catalan's eternal caution! And he became angrier yet when he recalled that the meeting wasn't until eleven o'clock, and he could have slept a whole hour more.

"Take the clothes out," he yipped at the maid. "Bring me the light gray suit, a white shirt, black socks, and the new, laceless black shoes. And the studbox. And leave them on the bed, I'll be in the bathroom. And tell Herminia I want to see her!"

"Sí, señor," came the toneless reply. She bunched up his clothes, carrying the bundle out and shutting the door behind her.

Juan Luis was on his feet before the door had shut. He swayed. Pincers were closing on his optic nerves. His tripe gurgled, and gall simultaneously geysered up his esophagus. He staggered into the bathroom.

He sat on, rather than stood at, the toilet. This was surrender, but he could not help it. It was painful to urinate; he had confused nature with conflicting demands. He was like an old man, waiting with anguish for the first stream, short, spastic spurts that did not begin to empty his bladder. He had to contract the urethra in order to squeeze out last dribbles, and then, as he was rising, he was compelled to sit back down for a senile flow that all at once came of its own.

He gazed at himself in the mirror. How loathsome! Weak-chinned, sullen—spoiled-brat-who-didn't-get-what-he-wanted. His tongue felt like a a coating of phlegm. He stuck it out. The sight of it nearly caused him to gag. A strong shower was what he needed.

He stepped into the tub, yanking at the shower curtain so that he was half enclosed by it. He whirled the upper pair of chromed faucets wide open, standing to one side until the hot water began to run. He was now ashamed of himself. Once, seven or eight months ago, he had pounced on just such a bon-bon. He had been surprised by her instant accommodation and, as he discovered quickly, the professional case of crabs she bequeathed to him. Herminia had found out. She fired the maid at once. With him, she was livid, telling him she did not care what he did so long as he did it on the other side of town; but that she would not tolerate his molesting a single girl in the household. "As if you don't blow enough bellows!" she snorted, her kind old face wrinkled with scorn.

Juan Luis blushed at the memory. Rarely had he seen Herminia in such a tantrum. He had felt like the swine he was. Sometimes he thanked God that circumstances had prevented even courting the woman he loved.

He stepped into the rushing cone of water, yelping from time to time as either the cold or hot flow was interrupted and he was by turns scalded or chilled. The series of shocks helped; but when he got out of the tub, his knees felt wobbly. He gasped. A heavy iron helmet was being hammered to his skull. This was going to be a morning of purgatory.

"I deserve it," he thought. He marched himself to the mirror again. He forced himself to look at himself. "Eres una miseria," he said aloud. He prayed, "Merciful God, punish me with all Your Might!"

The Lord needed little encouragement. Twice he had to drop the razor for two loose and explosive sessions on the toilet. Moment by moment, he was feeling worse. Other people—Julio, for instance—were able to throw up with ease. He could not. He preferred death by the garrote to vomiting. The poisons therefore bubbled away in his gut, knotting his intestines, doubling him with spasms. God was merciful. God had listened to his prayer. God was castigating him now, on earth, instead of waiting to catch him in Hell. He wished he felt more heroic: able, without massive hypocrisy, to plead with the Lord to redouble the torments. But he was and ever had been a moral and physical coward. He whimpered.

He was dousing cold water on his face when Herminia pushed the bathroom door open, catching him stark.

"What are you *dooo*ing!" Juan Luis squealed, grabbing for a towel and whipping it about his waist.

"Hijo, a una viejecita como yo, qué importa?"

"But you shouldn't just walk in like that!" he insisted petulantly, knotting the towel at his waist. "I am no longer a child!"

"You are nothing else," said the woman with sorrowful affection. And she wagged her old head.

It was impossible for Juan Luis to be angry with her. She had come to the family in 1942, a middle-aged woman whose infant daughter had just died and whose husband, a bull herder on the ranch near Jerez, had been gored months earlier through the brainpan. If she had had other children, she never mentioned them. Juan Luis had become her life. Whereas conceding with objective candor that he was the least likely child to amount to a hill of beans, she had been his stout protectress from babyhood through adolescence. She reproved him. She could be strict. But it was she, after that cataclysmic afternoon twelve years ago, who nursed him back to sanity. She was his confidante, more to him than mother or father, the only person privy to his hopeless love. That had commenced also in 1955, although not until five years later, when he was seventeen, did he acknowledge it for what it was. In the beginning, he had identified Sofía Prades, daughter of Cousin Odette, with the Virgin; and when he prayed, the polychromed image of Mary in Sacedón's new church—all blue and gold, with raven hair and the cherry tint of a maiden on her cheeks—merged innocently with the flesh-and-blood image of the living woman. Then, as he advanced in puberty, an awful perturbation entered, a shattering ambivalence. He noticed the swell of Sofía's bosom. Shockingly, he noticed at the next Mass that there was a similar swell on the statue of the Mother of God. His confusion increased with the rapid growth of his sensuality. Infamous dreams attacked him at night. They terrified him. He was appalled by them. He could no longer pray to the Virgin. That was sacrilege. He could no longer trust himself to dwell on Sofía, and soon he was reduced to a rack of blushes when in the presence of any young woman. That quandary of emotions followed him back to Madrid, worsening during the fall and winter. It was Herminia who had perceived in him the conflict of body and soul; and who intuited how it had become unbearable and in what way he tried to abolish it.

To his unforgettable mortification, she had trapped him one afternoon, waiting by his bedroom door, opening it, and catching him in the act of his release.

"Hijo," she said sadly, "how often does this happen?"

He found it impossible to reply.

"Once a week?" she persisted gently.

"Yes . . . more." He had begun to cry.

"Would you like Doña Sofía to know about this?"

"Oh, God, Herminia!"

"This is bad for you; you must not let yourself. Come, now, put your trousers back on and follow me."

He thought he was surely going to suffocate with shame, but he obeyed her. They slipped out of the back door of the palace on the Castellana. Herminia hailed a cab. She stopped it halfway down the Gran Vía, paying the fare and then leading him to a shabby building on a sordid little lane behind the avenue. They walked up several flights of dark, rickety, dusty wooden stairs, stopping in front of a door. He remembered the brass placque of the Sacred Heart. He remembered the impulse to flight. It was Herminia who pressed the buzzer, who spoke to the lady, who slipped a bill out of her purse, and who then pushed him inside. Half an hour later, he had come out, more miserable and depressed than he believed possible, certain that he was condemned to hellfire. Herminia smiled in understanding. Old, wise, and tolerant, she told him that young men always felt like that the first few times, but that he would grow used to it, and no matter what those eunuchs in black said, God would not condemn him for something so natural; adding that when he grew older and married, the experience would enable him to instruct his wife and establish his authority over her.

Juan Luis's problem being that his goddess, six years older, was already the mother of another man's children. Several times more he visited the house behind the Gran Vía. Herminia indulged him. When he was out of funds, she lent him the twenty duros it cost. Then one day she refused. He was too young, she said, for excesses. That happened to coincide with a searing attack of conscience. Was he not sublimating his love in the foulest and most ignoble ways? Didn't he owe her, who had not once blamed him for what had happened, a worthier sacrifice? He made his resolve. Total renunciation was the answer—a dramatic conversion. He went to confession. He became a daily communicant, poring over the New Testament and even tackling Aquinas. His mother was euphoric, his father less so. Herminia viewed the newly pious Juan Luis with good humored skepticism, which irritated him. But he was happier during those twelve months than at any period of his remembrance; until that late summer afternoon when his father forbade him this (the only!) escape out of his dilemma.

He was eighteen then, ready to embark on his university career. Juan Luis had indicated no preference. Luis—père was growing impatient. "It can't be put off any longer," he declared to his duchess. "Leave that boy to himself" (he spoke always as though Juan Luis were out of earshot) "and he'd drift from here to Brazil and back!" A conference was scheduled for after lunch.

This culminating clash with the man who was known as the Duke

of Steel took place in the grim sixteenth-century ruins of the castle at
Sacedón, the Cantabrian hamlet from which all the barons of the line had
sprung; on the townfolk first, and later on the enemies of Spain. With
his father's blow, the world came crashing down. Juan Luis, sobbing in
his room, spoke to Herminia about running away. "Now don't be so foolish," she chided him. "Your father knows you through and through, and
he is right." Juan Luis protested. He went to church, kneeling on the
cold stone flags and trying to pray. Dust. His long and on several occasions (he felt) heroic battle against the flesh had come to nothing. God
had failed to succor him.

It was once more Herminia at the breach, locating the big-breasted
peasant's daughter who, for the balance of the summer, was at least willing to suckle him.

She was not quite five feet tall. Although she was his housekeeper,
and entitled to dress more suitable to her position, she went about still in
the starched white uniform and apron of an ama. The garb became her.
She had clear, creamy Andalusian skin. Her cheeks were smooth and
round, her lips were usually curled as though tasting fond memories, and
she walked habitually with arms hugged under her bosom and supporting
it. She was a little old woman with immense moral authority—the only
one to have persuaded Juan Luis's mother that he would be safe (under
her surveillance) in an apartment of his own. She managed everything,
hiring and firing and training the staff of two maids and a cook, keeping
his personal accounts, and inventorying pantry or linen supplies to the
last item.

Still, he fretted at her. "The board meeting isn't until eleven. Why
did you rouse me so early?"

She wagged her head again. "You have the Requiem Mass."

"Oh my God!"

"Hijo," she said reproachfully, "you *must* remember these things."

"I'm sorry. I did remember. Then I forgot." He turned from her,
spraying Monsieur Givenchy over his cheeks and chin. The sting of it,
and the fresh scent, made him feel better. He began brushing his hair.
"I'm not going," he blurted at the mirror.

"What a silly thing to say! The Señora Duquesa . . ."

"I am not going to go!"

Herminia was silent. He sneaked a look at her out of the corner of
his left eye. Her sharp, concerned old eyes were studying him.

"You have been out every night this week," she said severely.

"What of it?"

"How often with that gypsy?"

"Only twice."

"That's twice too often. You had better get rid of her."

"I'm thinking about it . . . Why?"

"What if she becomes embarrassed?"

By which Herminia meant, in the quaint Spanish usage, pregnant.

"Oh," Juan Luis said, combing his long sideburns, "she isn't likely to do that."

"Don't be so sure." Herminia stepped closer to him. "Hijo, you let everyone take advantage of you. If I weren't here, Heaven only knows what would happen. Listen, you are getting tired of her. She surely senses that. In a matter of seconds, she can put chains around you for the rest of your life."

This was something to ponder. He took a plastic squeeze bottle of talcum powder and began dusting his body, dropping the towel as he did so. It made no difference, after all: Herminia knew him inside and out.

"What should I do?" he asked.

"Pay her off. Throw her out."

"It . . . it may not be so simple."

"Must I take care of it?"

"Would you?"

She sighed. She looked him up and down. He felt (in the English sense) embarrassed again, squatting to retrieve the towel and once more wrap it around his waist. His belly bulged.

"Just look at you!" Herminia exclaimed. "It's a shame. You were never a wonder, I must say, but now you're like calabash left out in the fields too long. You're eating too much, and drinking much too much . . . It has to stop, hijo mío, before you look so terrible no young lady will want you. If I let your mother know half how you spend your time she would be very upset indeed. Why not spend this one evening at home?"

"I may," he mumbled unconvincingly, tottering toward the door.

Herminia stepped aside for him to pass. Arms still crossed under her bosom, she followed him into the bedroom. He saw his clothes laid out on a chair, and he began dressing.

"It may cost quite a little sum," she remarked, picking his wallet off the bedside table and peering inside.

"What?"

"Ridding you of that puta." She fished two 1,000-peseta notes out from under her apron and folded them into the wallet.

He sat on the bed, struggling with his socks. Leaning over the rolls of his own belly was painful. "I gave you one hundred and fifty thousand pesetas last month."

"And you borrowed back eighty-five thousand of it for what I don't know."

"Well, how much do we have left?" He was bilious, now, and stifling hiccoughs that wanted to ground themselves in retches.

"Ten thousand in cash," she said, gazing on him sorrowfully, "and less than fifty thousand in your checking account. But that gypsy will demand one hundred thousand at the very least. More! You had better go to the Mass, hijo, really you had. You may have to borrow again from the Señora Duquesa. Of course, tomorrow we collect the rent, which will help."

Juan Luis looked up. "I've been meaning to ask you about that. Who actually lives next door?"

"What do you mean?"

"Well, Muñoz González rents the place, but I've never seen him. Here, that is."

"*I* have!" snorted Herminia. "Twice, at an indecent hour, with cabaret girls. El Riscal types. I gave him such a look! But he has a cara dura, that one. You ought to speak to him."

"Me?" Juan Luis was genuinely startled.

"Yes, hijo, you. Your old nurse isn't the one to do it. Permitting the apartment to be used for that sort of thing is *not* good. Don Eugenio, of course, thinks of nothing but money. You must mind your reputation."

"He pays awfully well."

"Sixty thousand? I should say! That's twenty more than anyone else would give . . ."

"But for what?" He was standing before a small, gilt-framed mirror now, fingers fumbling with the necktie knot. Herminia went to him, and with neat little tugs charmed a perfect dimple into the silk. "I mean," he continued as she straightened the back of his shirt collar, "there are cheaper places to take girls to. Last night—this morning—I met a German on the stairs. I'm sure he was coming down from the apartment. A few months ago, there were those two NKVD types, I think I told you about them, meaty, Slavic faces, shapeless suits . . . They stared at me as though I were a spy in the Kremlin! Oh. Ohhh!"

A long, long gurgle drained his insides. He clapped both hands over his stomach, tottering backward and sitting once more on the edge of the bed. His gut felt like a can of earthworms.

"There is still time to make the Mass, hijo," said Herminia, bearing on her face a half-reproving, half-commiserating smile.

"I . . . am *not* going! I—I am not up to it."

"Anyone can see that." She held out a large, nickel-plated pocket watch, which was attached to her waist by a steel chain. The dial showed nine forty-five.

Juan Luis said, "Take the breakfast tray! Bring me the *ABC!*"

The tone was ducal. It's more than likely Juan Luis doesn't recognize this when it emerges. The servant in Herminia did. She pressed him no more, doing as she was told. Lying back on his rumpled bed, he skimmed through the guest list at the christening ceremony yesterday. There was little other news of interest; none, anyhow, that he was prepared that morning to take interest in. King Hussein had delivered his troops to Egyptian command, poor ducks. No more on Barcelona in these discreet pages, where maidens and young matrons of good family had been seduced by professionals, lured into prepared hideaways, photographed in their transports, and then, the glossy prints held against them, forced into the service of visiting textile merchants, who paid the ringleaders premium fees. Juan Luis pondered his fascination by the scandal. Would he have himself paid for one of those wretched girls? Possibly. Would knowing them to be victims add a special sadistic zest to his lust: the humiliation of the helpless, the normally untouchable? Probably. What a disgusting creature he was. How normal. How normally disgusting is the male animal. About love, Thomas Aquinas had written that it was "in all the soul's powers, but also in all parts of the body . . ." If he shut his eyes, and did not move at all, his head stopped aching and his stomach subsided. He needed peace, and hours more sleep, and perhaps this one night to stay home as Herminia suggested, and eat a light supper, and not drink at all, and read as he had not had the time for in months and months, and go to bed early: and think. And that, of course, was the trouble. He would think. He would not be able to bear it, and he would be tempted to telephone Sofía, just to hear her voice. If by luck she invited him to drop by, he would throw away the hours in talk with Billy, her husband, talk that increasingly terrified him; and then, upon leaving the couple, he would not be able to stand it, and he would go to Florita or hunt out some other girl; and while rutting say to himself, "Would you want to defile her like this? Even were it possible, can you bear imagining her beauty and goodness subjected to your unspeakable lust?" And that would tap fresh despair, provoking either a brusque and bitter orgasm or the humiliating toil of impotence.

He thought of Augustine, and the paradox the saint spoke about when he was in Carthage. "To love then, and to be loved, was sweet to me; but more, when I obtained to enjoy the person I loved, I defiled, therefore, the spring of friendship with the filth of concupiscence, and I beclouded its brightness with the Hell of lustfulness . . ." This described Juan Luis Seguismundo del Val, Duke of Sacedón, who, if granted the opportunity, would befoul, and thus betray, even the love he honored and whose purity was just about the only thing in his life that honored him. And the paradox he lived was that only when having fornicated himself into a state of physical insensibility was he able to meet Sofía's eyes without shame.

He dozed.

Herminia closed her master's door; and then with brisk, determined, rolling little steps followed the corridor into the kitchen and thence into a back room where the maid (whose name was neither Paca nor Pilar, but Petra) was laundering the Duke's shirt.

She stopped in the doorway, watching the girl a moment. Petra rubbed the linen over the slanted enameled washboard with a sluggish, rocking rhythm of her arms, shoulders, and upper back. It was a good, strong rhythm and a good, strong back. A pity, thought Herminia, because the girl was docile and had been well received; and with everyone making money right and left, it was getting harder and harder to find replacements.

"Is Magdalena still asleep?" she inquired in her gentle, authoritative voice; referring to the other maid.

Petra sprang up and back from the washboard, wheeling. "Sí, señora," she replied, bobbing a curtsy.

"You look tired, my dear."

"Oh, I am!"

"The work is becoming too much for you."

"Oh no, señora. It's close to my time of the month, that's all."

"Well, suppose you come to my room when I ring. We can have a chat, you and I."

Herminia retraced her bowlegged little steps into the corridor, passing the Duke's bedroom and a guest room, and then entering her modest but neat and cheerful quarters, where she had a desk, a telephone, an upholstered armchair, and a little work table for her sewing materials. The desk was rolltop, its writing surface stacked with receipts in flimsy pink and yellow and white, beside which lay a long blue checkbook between whose stubs had been stuffed a bank statement. Herminia sighed when she looked at it. Her poor old brain was taxed hard by the heavy mental labor of balancing accounts; but she was dogged, and she prided herself on having erred by but two pesetas in the past year. It was likely that this month she would be obliged once again to dip into her personal savings in order to tide her little boy over; but she had become accustomed to that sort of thing these past ten or fifteen years, and right now there were more immediately pressing matters to deal with.

She sat at the desk, reaching for the telephone.

First she rang the executive offices of Utilidades Españolas.

"Deputy Inspector Stepanópoulis Grau," she heard reply.

"Who?" Herminia was startled.

"Deputy Inspector Stepanópoulis Grau, at your service. I hope, anyhow."

"I am ringing Utilidades Españolas."

"Well, you got me. The lines must be crossed, they generally are. Can I help you?"

"I don't see how."

"Seems to be my lot. If I can be of service in the future, do remember me, Deputy Inspector Stepanópoulis Grau, anything from stolen pocketbooks to homicide."

"I'll remember, Inspector."

She hung up, disturbed, dialing anew. This time she connected with the firm, giving her name and asking for Don Eugenio. He was at once switched on.

"Don't tell me he's not coming!" the administrator yelled.

"You needn't worry."

"Are you sure! You had better have him out of the house by ten forty-five at the latest!"

"He is dressed."

"Well, thank God for that."

"Is it big trouble?" she asked.

"It is very big trouble." And the man hung up.

Herminia smiled. Catalans rarely exaggerate, Don Eugenio least of all.

Now she dialed another number. She asked for Doña Isabel.

Minutes passed. A hoarse, full-blown female voice came on the line, growling, "Yes!"

"This is la Señora de Lima speaking," said Herminia with some sharpness, appropriating to herself the "de" ordinarily reserved for gentlefolk.

"Ahhh," came from the woman, tone mellowing instantly. "Doña Herminia! You have something for me?"

"Her name is Petra. She comes from Guadalajara. She is strong, clean, reasonably obedient, no more stupid than most, and will do."

"I'm not sure I can use a new girl now. Is she good?"

"Yes."

"She pleases?"

"Very much."

"How old is she?"

"Seventeen."

"They're all seventeen!"

"This one was exactly seventeen two weeks ago. I gave her a locket."

"Does she need training?"

"I've done my best. She can be lax, but she is well-intentioned."

"How much?"

"Fifteen thousand."

"That's too much."

"Everything has gone up."

There was a ruminative pause over the line. "All right, send her over, I'll look at her. She had better be clean."

"I can assure you of that," said Herminia, hanging up.

Herminia mused a moment. Then, delving a hand into the depths of one of the pigeonholes in her desk, and feeling with her fingers into the secret compartment at the rear of and beneath the pigeonhole, she fetched a purse-sized address booklet bound in leatherette. Reading from it, she dialed once more, replacing the booklet as she waited for an answer.

"Café Paraíso?"

"Sí!"

The man was busy; she could hear the hiss of espresso coffee levers, the clatter of saucers, the shouted orders.

"Kindly inform Señora Rivas of *Mantequería Jacobo Rivas* that Señora de Lima will be paying a call later this morning."

"We don't run a message service!"

"You will nevertheless deliver this message. For which I thank you."

She had no doubt whatever that her request would be honored. Herminia now depressed a bellbutton twice. While waiting for Petra, she picked a white, crested envelope from another pigeonhole, winking from under her apron at the same time a roll of 1,000-peseta notes. Six of these she stripped from the roll, folding them in half and slipping them into the envelope, whose flap she licked and pressed down firmly.

There was a knock on the door. "Come in," she called.

Herminia did not turn around when Petra entered; she was busy writing a name and address on a slip of scrap paper.

Finished, she swiveled about.

"Come all the way in, dear, and shut the door behind you."

The maid did so. "These are for you," said Herminia, smiling, handing envelope and paper to the maid. "I've selected a nice home for you."

Petra stared at her hands, and then gazed questioningly at her mistress.

Herminia said, "It was Magdalena's turn to sleep, and yours, querida, to keep watch."

"But I'm sorry, Doña Herminia," the girl quavered. "It won't happen again, I promise you! I was just so tired my eyes shut for an instant and before I knew it . . ."

The old woman wagged her head. "You young girls! You have no resistance. Why, at your age, I could work all day, dance all night, and be back in the fields by dawn! I'm afraid there's no excuse, Petra. I can't keep you on."

The girl fell to her knees. "Please," she said. "I've been happy here!"

"I'm sorry," said Herminia, kindly but firmly, placing a wrinkled hand on that glossy dark head and caressing it. "I warned you when you came that orders are orders. Now don't cry, dear. I can vouch that you will be well contented in your new position. There's a little gift from me in the envelope. But be good at Doña Isabel's; no more than I will she put up with frivolousness. Now, now, don't carry on so! The work there is actually easier. You'll have more company, and nothing at all to do in the mornings, and you will be able to send to your parents as much or more every week."

They were always tearful at parting, and Herminia felt for them. One had to be stonehearted not to become attached to these babies, despite their deficiencies. She did her best to comfort the girl, who, sniveling, finally accepted her fate.

As soon as the door had closed, Herminia reached a final time for the telephone.

She connected with a manservant, who put her on to his master.

"Good morning," she said primly.

"And a very good morning to you!" came the languid, purring baritone.

"Qué sinvergüenza!" thought Herminia. She said, "We are to expect you, aren't we?"

"At eleven o'clock. No Moors on the coast by then, right?"

"As far as we are concerned, although Countess von Leddhin walks her cat at that hour."

"I have her animal rubbing its spine against my legs."

"I don't doubt it. But *he* is getting suspicious."

"That puppy? Why?"

"Your German friend left late this morning; he was just coming in, and they met."

"Why should he care?"

"My position is difficult."

"I'm sure you can handle it."

"How much more time do you need?"

"A few days, perhaps another week. Have you loaded the cameras?"

"All three."

"In English I would call you a 'living doll,' Herminia."

"What is that?"

"Something very nice."

"Compliments from men have never interested me."

She listened to him chuckle. He said, "I thought you were an idealist!"

He was teasing her. She smiled despite herself. "I am also a practical old woman."

He laughed. She liked that rich, tropical sound. All women, she supposed, did, and even at her age she was not proof against it.

He told her, "I'll keep my promise, you know that."

And with great distinctness she told him, "I have a letter with my notario in case you forget."

She hung up on another burst of laughter. Her eyes wandered to the wall above her cot. Three framed photographs had been pegged there. The one on the left showed her with the three-year-old Juan Luis in her arms. His pudgy little face was swollen from a squall that had taken place minutes before the picture was snapped, because he had had removed from him a jar of English hard candies. She held him tight, looking straight at the shutter. She was still handsome then, with hair just beginning to gray. How time flew!—for those with the patience to wait.

The photograph on the right showed Juan Luis's father, the late Duke of Sacedón, dressed in the boots, baggy khaki jodhpurs, and belted military jacket of an artillery officer. He was in his prime, a colonel. Short, scrawny, and stiff-backed, he exuded military elegance, sword and sash as natural to him as the field glasses he was pincering with his left hand. He looked sternly ahead, perhaps at the very shell that was to blow off his right leg seconds later, because, in emulation of Franco, he refused to duck or take cover. As his reward, he was to wake up in the hospital with a Military Medal pinned to the breast of his pyjamas; and in recognition of his daring raid through the Red-infested province of Jerez, during which he had brought dozens of terrorists to justice, an Order of the Day on his bedside table, signed by none other than Queipo de Llano y Serra, promoting him to general.

Herminia's eyes now fixed themselves on the photograph in the center. This one was bordered in black. Below it was a black wreath. It showed a man in high-waisted Cordovan breeches on horseback, reins held nonchalantly in the left hand, the long tilting pole used for the testing of calf bulls held out from the stirrup by the right hand, like a knight's lance. There, pasted on his face, was that handsome, vacant smile, which she had endured for three years.

Herminia rose from her chair. She went to the photograph.

Lifting it from the hook, she turned it over. The back held another glass pane, and the photograph of another man. He was a peasant, dressed in tattered shirt and loose pantaloons drawn tight at the waist by a string: a stocky twenty-five-year-old with a roguish grin and humorous eyes; Herminia's first husband; the man she had loved; one of the guerrillas hanged by the first Marqués de la Revancha de Jerez, Luis del Val, XIIIth Duque de Sacedón, father of Juan Luis.

Time passed quickly for those who had the patience to wait.

Everything was coming together. Herminia felt no need to telephone Número Catorce. There, preparation had been required; for if Nati was Herminia's peer in will and character, she was not in resolution and intelligence. Herminia was content to wait for the news she could be certain of; meanwhile preparing herself for the picking of a rose.

FOUR

Jacobo Rivas, Hidalgo de Sacedón

Atingle with the consciousness of his virility, head held high, eyes scorning the cobbles beneath his feet, Jacobo Rivas stomped his way down Calle Los Mancebos, his destination that back portal of Número Catorce against which he would pound the assertion of a revived manhood, pride of blood boiling in him anew, blood as ancient as any quartered in the neighborhood and in fact older and more noble than most.

The eyes of Jacobo Rivas flashed, scorching into cinders the people he went by, leaving behind him eddies of commotion. Preposterous the mantequero might be, a blowhard, puffed up, pitiable at the business of making ends meet, a blusterer in bars who, afterward, at home, ducked under the blows of his formidable mate. All that is of no importance. Almighty God in His mercy had granted him the boon of the morning's events, restorative, filling him with confidence. This showed in a face that was as hacked by a hatchet out of the haunch of a ham. It was a face of wondrous, meaty variety, puce at the brow, true gamboge at the scoop of the chin, ocher on the snout, and iron hat on the cheeks. Altogether, a strikingly florid visage, igneous, the front of a locomotive. As he advanced, he spilled people to either side.

The Almighty, however, enjoys His private jokes. Jacobo arrived at his destination. There, ahead of him, on the middle step of the stoop, loitered a sixteen-year-old boy.

"What are you doing here, chaval!"

"What's it to you, *Daddy-o?*"

Jacobo did not like that. He glared at the creature, a runty individual. Urchin. Street scum. Insolent gamberro. Smoking. Languid-lipped. Hair greased back in superabundant waves, smoothed into a duck-tailed dingleberry on the nape of his grimy neck. Dangling on a steel chain from an open, tubercular sternum, not a crucifix or Virgin of Pilar, but an Iron Cross.

A new generation. *What* a new generation! Worse than '36. Respect for nothing, nobody. Thieves. Muggers. The American influence. Midget church-burner. Baby bandit. Infant rapist. Embrionic murderer.

Jacobo spat a splat smack on the stone to the left of the boy's sandal-shod feet. "Get off the stoop, hijo de puta!"

"Cabrón, muéveme si te atreves."

Royal purple surged through Jacobo's cheeks. What *that* did to his normal coloration can be imagined. He raised a hand able to fell an ox. The boy looked up at him with unwavering, glittering, tigrine eyes. Jacobo lowered his hand.

What did it matter to him? Nobody, especially after this miraculous morning, could call him cuckold—and not pronounce himself a fool! What cared he for the insolence of scum; especially scum with one grubby hand in one grubby side pocket, and fingering a long, solid-looking something that easily might be a switchblade knife, that sort carried them about. And used them, mongrels that they were, festering meat from the gutters, the turds of society . . . Progress!

Spitting again (but this time circumspectly, into the street), Jacobo passed the boy, going up the stoop and pushing the bellbutton.

The urchin let flash a glance of amber amusement. Jacobo did not deign notice. He rang again. He waited. He rang again.

"Well!" He wheeled about, bellowing at the boy. "Is no one in?"

"You could have asked, *Daddy-o*."

"And you might have had the courtesy . . . shown the respect . . ."

"Don't make me laugh, blubber-king."

"I'll stomp you back into the gutter."

"Wouldn't advise trying it, *Daddy-o*."

"Who are you? What are you doing here?"

"Collecting—same as you."

"For whom? I've never seen you before."

"For the bodega, up the street."

"Viuda de José Blanes?"

"That's it, *baby*."

"What?"

"I said you're *real turned on, cool, baby, cool. Yeah, man*."

"Speak in Spanish!"

"Anything you say, *Daddy-o*."

Jacobo felt like booting the boy all the way down to the Manzanares River. He calmed himself. He was beginning to sweat. It was becoming very hot. Ignoring the boy, he jammed a thumb at the black nipple of the bell. He could hear the buzzing inside. He let it buzz thirty seconds.

"That ought to wake the dead!"

But there was no response. Up the street came Antonio Sánchez, the pharmacist—hunchbacked, pigeon-breasted, red-rimmed round astigmatic blue orbs blinking painfully on yellow-headed sties—a reader through the long nights of his insomnia, something of an intellectual in his class, the mantequero's good friend, nevertheless . . .

"Good day, Jacobo."

"Good day, Antonio. How are all the pains?"

"Some worse, some better." Sánchez merely nodded at the boy, who shrugged, smiled secretly, and gazed off down the street, bobbing his head like a cork on water, hum-mumbling in a thin, asexual voice, *"Ye-ye-ye-yeee, ye-ye-ye-yeee—if I had a hammerrr . . ."*

Sánchez glanced mildly at the creature, shutting his eyelids on their sore, sebaceous glands, which were being further irritated by the fierce sun. "Help is harder to come by every day," he observed to Jacobo.

"That's the God's truth. I suppose you're here to collect."

"Well, I don't like to be importunate, but I've sent a boy around ten times at least. Have you rung?"

"Nobody answers."

"Then Nati hasn't returned."

"Returned? Where would she have gone, with breakfast to get and cleaning to be done?"

"It's odd. Last night was my hitch on the emergency watch."

"Anything of interest?"

"Blasco's new baby swallowed a Miraculous Medal, but it caught in the throat, and I thumped it right out. Irujo checked with me at seven o'clock this morning . . ."

"Who?"

"Irujo, the sereno."

"And so it was last night, except for the cats . . . What's he got to do with Nati?"

"Nothing, except that he'd seen her slip out of Número Catorce around six."

"She's much too old for a lover."

"Good heavens alive, Jacobo!"

"And the hour's not appropriate. Two o'clock in the morning, even four, but not six . . . Get on with it, will you?"

"Well, it's just that Nati hadn't come back when Irujo spoke to me. At least, he hadn't noticed her returning. He asked me whether I thought there was anything amiss."

"Why should there be?"

"The Marquesa's not young, she's overweight . . ."

"You're not suggesting something's happened to her!" cried Jacobo, in sudden alarm about his 9,352 pesetas.

"Oh, I don't think so," said the pharmacist. "The house would be full of people by now."

Jacobo wheezed out his relief. Repeated punches on the bellbutton, however, raised no one.

Within minutes, the electrician from Calle Redondialla had arrived. The plumber's son-in-law then eased toward them his hopelessly deferential presence, utterly insignificant between the deformity of his ears, the stems edematose and the lobes like potatoes; followed by a manicurist (male) from a beauty salon in the Plaza de Independencia. And finally a slim, elegant youth from a fashion house sauntered up, shooting canary-yellow cuffs that flashed garnet and gold.

Each in turn tried the bell.

"Nobody in?"

"We don't know."

"They're hiding!" stated the manicurist.

"What fun!" giggled the elegant young man.

"Shall we come another day?" asked Sánchez.

"Not I!" said Rivas.

They waited with the patience of their kind. Only Jacobo, Sánchez, and the electrician were social peers, although the plumber's son-in-law hovered his amphitropous jugs close to them. Engaging the electrician in any sort of conversation proved fruitless. He was dressed in funereal black, wearing a long, mournful face like a deflated balloon with a stone weighing it down. "*Ye-ye-ye-yeeee, ye-ye-ye-yeee—If I had a hamm-errr, I'd hammer in the morning . . .*" "Mu-chachaaa!" shrilled the baker's wife at her wench (who was within half the decibel range). "Voy! Voy!" yelled a waiter at the café on the corner of Mancebos and Redondilla, below them, responding to the imperious *rurrRup!* of fingernails on a tin table top. "*I'd hammer in the eee-ven-ing . . .*" It was getting on to ten o'clock. Scurf flaked off the heated stones and pavement, disintegrating into a fine white dust. Baked bread, baked dung—the sun a wafer slipping between the parted lips of the sky . . .

Rivas had begun sweating profusely. Unaccountably, the tone of the morning had changed. How often had he waited for his due, an appellant on the stoop of success? He would not be cheated this day! Nearby, the flute of a scissors-grinder let fall its liquid glissando, poignant, hollow thrush's notes, a single, inconclusive theme, repeated and repeated, born in the hills of Navarre and brought like a cup of cool water to the plains of Castille. The Teddy-boy cocked his head, listening. "That's beautiful," he remarked to nobody in particular.

"Try it again, someone!" rasped an irascible Rivas.

The elegant young man sauntered to the stoop, depressing the button with a long, flexible index finger.

"Your nails need attention," muttered the manicurist—a squat, low-browed, sullen-looking individual, a Murcian.

"La, do you think?"

"Come around to our place," invited the first, pincering a business card out of his wallet. "We charge a lot, but to you it will be worth it."

"We're wasting our time," growled the electrician. He had come from the burial of his wife that morning, and he was upset.

"*Ye-ye-ye-yeee, ye . . .*"

"Oh, shut your mouth," groaned Jacobo.

"*. . . ye-ye-yeee—If I haihaihaihaiiiid a hammmm-errrrr . . .*"

"*Some*body stop that caterwauling."

"Not I," said Antonio Sánchez honestly, eying the bulge of the pocket.

"Then you stop him," cried Jacobo, wheeling on the plumber's son-in-law. "*Our* generation fought a war!"

"*. . . in the morning.* I don't think he wants to, *Daddy-o.*"

"I have a wife and two children," pleaded the plumber's son-in-law, twitching heterotropously.

"I don't believe it!" stated Jacobo flatly.

"Who cares, anyhow," said the electrician. "Nobody. Nobody at all."

"Maybe they're both out," suggested Sánchez.

"Like a pair of semaphors," declared the mantequero. "Oh. Yes. Or in the bathroom."

"Together?" asked the plumber's son-in-law.

"No, imbecile . . . !"

"Who's talking, *Daddy-o?*"

Jacobo turned from the stoop.

"You keep quiet! You shut your mouth! You . . ."

"*. . .* make me, gordito relleno. Yeah, you do it." —eyes glinting into the lead of the sky, shoulders loose, lips slack, cigarette limp, right hand nervous by his trousers.

"Pajudo! Crío mal sacado! A ver si te pillas el pito con la bragueta!"

The urchin scarcely glanced at the vat broiling above him. He said softly, "Pués pa' que te enteres, almondiguito, tengo una polla que como

me jodo de la puta de tu hijita se la saco por el culo." Adding, "What's
more, I've done it."

With a roar, a howl, a bawl, a bellow, a soul-shriek of "You lie!"
Jacobo hurled himself at the boy. The mantequero was upon him, fists
crashing down, when that hand flicked a bright, six-inch blade out of the
pocket.

Jacobo very nearly impaled himself. His heels dug into the pavement;
his body jackknifed over the point of the blade; but it was a dexterous,
even providential grab at the seat of his pants by Antonio Sánchez and
the plumber's son-in-law that saved him. Together, they hauled Jacobo
back. The boy gazed at his enemy with an evil, delighted grin. "I was only
kidding, *Daddy-o,*" he said, pocketing his weapon.

But it was not so easy to pacify Jacobo. To intimate what this filthy
little guttersnipe had about his daughter was more than her father could
stand. To the puce of his brow and the gamboge of his cheeks he had
now added a chin gone gossaniferous, his shaking countenance such a
kaleidoscope of furious reds that Antonio Sánchez feared an attack of
apoplexy. "Be reasonable," he implored, getting around in front, butting
his head into Jacobo's stomach while the plumber's son-in-law kept tugging on the seat of the mantequero's breeches. "Reasonable," Sánchez
muffled, mouth full of shirt. "My daughter is the soul of virtue!" Jacobo
brayed above his head. "Yef, yef! Yef, of courfe," whiffled Sánchez. He
spit the flannel out. "The boy said he was only pulling your leg . . . And
look, Jacobo, *look* who is coming this instant!"

None other than his apple of the eye, his rose, his single justification: swinging down from the plaza, a smile dazzling with its gladness
parting her plum-sweet lips. Jacobo ceased struggling at once. He gazed
at Soledad with that instant, ambivalent rush of joy and foreboding that
for the past two years she had not failed to wrest from him. She *was* a little beauty, with a gay bosom, the tiniest of waists, and delicate ankles
whose fine bones twinkled as she walked.

He glanced at his meaty hands, and down at the lump of his belly.
He envisioned Marisol's marbled corpulence. What mattered the slander
of scum! It was indeed a morning of miracles, and Soledad confirmed it,
a nymph, a blithe spirit, somehow distilled out of gross flesh. The sun
seemed to flare with revived brilliance as she drew nearer. The cobblestones winked and blinked; the stucco walls of the houses laughed. "Rocío
de la madrugada!" hailed the scissors-grinder, scraping his beret dangerously close to a plop of donkey dung. Soledad grinned at him—improperly
for a well-mannered Spanish girl. But it was all right. She had been cre-

ated to break the rules, just as physically she had confounded the genetical code. She was not yet twelve when she had metamorphosed as it seemed overnight from skinny stickiness to an almost frightening female precocity, disturbing Jacobo (even as he delighted in her loveliness) by an innocence (as he thought of it) so heartbreakingly vulnerable.

Every man of them gathered at the stoop had turned in her direction. Soledad spilled a smile equally over them all, harvesting with the faintest shrug the tributes she had become accustomed to. And then she ignored them, running the last few steps. "Papá!" she cried, breathless, brimming, "Say you will! Oh, let me, say yes, at once, please do, quickly!"

"To what, soul of my soul?" —gathering her up in his oaken arms, the silvery effervescence of her, and kissing her on one glowing cheek.

"Oh," she said, squirming in his embrace, "it's a miracle, Papá, a real miracle! She came this morning! *She* came to interview *me!*"

"Who, my dove?" —setting her down reluctantly.

"Doña Herminia, Papá! She said it was my letter, not a single mistake!"

"And who is Doña Herminia?" He was not so much forgetful as abstracted.

"The housekeeper for the Duque de Sacedón!"

Rigid did he suddenly become. "You're not to be a maid! You're better than that!"

"Oh, Papá, you don't understand! She wants help with the accounts, with the marketing and the ordering. There's the palace on the Castellana to manage, and the one in Sevilla. Papá, I'm one of *thirty* girls to apply! She examined *thirty* other girls and rejected them! She made me show her how I keep books. She tested me on prices . . . Oh, Papá, she was so thorough, she made me take my clothes off right in front of her . . ."

"What! What's that? Take your *clothes* off!"

"But of course, Papá, don't you see?"

"I do not! Where was your mother!"

"Still at church, but it's all right. Doña Herminia wanted to find out if I was clean, Papá! She said she wasn't going to have dirty girls with dirty drawers in the Duke's house. She's very strict!"

"Well, well," stalled Jacobo, not yet sure what to make of it.

Soledad pressed her advantage. "Papá, it's such an honor! Me—out of all the girls in Madrid!"

"Yes . . . that's so."

"And Papá, the house of the Duke of Sacedón, *our* town, *our* duke!"

"Yes . . ."

"And the wages, Papá. Food and lodging, and *four thousand pesetas a month!*"

That was indeed an impressive sum. He glanced over a shoulder at Antonio Sánchez; he glanced at the other men—anywhere for help. But they were every man-jack of them staring at his daughter, joy-filling feast that she was.

He said, "But will you have to stay overnight?"

"Claro! How else am I to learn, menus for grand dinners, the seating, the wines? Mamá got back in time to talk to Doña Herminia. She thinks Doña Herminia is wonderful. Doña Herminia tasted our cheeses and our butter and our milk. She candled the eggs. She said we have the best mantequería in Madrid, with the freshest produce, and reasonably priced, and she means to order here from now on!"

"Well, that is nice of her. . . . You say your mother approves of your lodging away from home?"

Soledad did not lie. She merely resorted to an ancient feminine wile, adoring her father out of the largest, sootiest eyes from Madrid to Cádiz. "Mamá said I must ask you. She thinks you're the most wonderful man in the world, Papá, you know that, and she wouldn't let me do anything without your approval. Oh, Papá, it's a *dream!* You will let me, won't you?"

Jacobo's lips smiled down at his daughter; but he was grieving, grieving to the base-metal nife of his soul. So very soon? To fledge her, his heart's beat?

He murmured, "You are very young, Soledad" —heavily, looking down on her scintillating eagerness with a sense of doom, knowing that he must lose her. She wanted to go. She did not mind leaving her home. He could only delay his capitulation, and to do so would be to wipe from her trusting, passionate face all the delight it had brought down the street, the radiance that lit up even stone and stucco.

He loved her too much to say anything but, "All right. When must it be?"

"This very day, Papá!" And then she herself was struck by the meaning of the occasion, her childhood in a single stroke chopped. "Oh, Papá!"

She hurled herself back into his arms. Again he lifted her, crushing her to his chest. This time she did not wriggle.

"Go," he said, setting her down. "And be a good girl. And work hard. And do us honor." He rotated toward the other men. "Eh!" he demanded, belligerent. "Are you dumb, all of you? What do you think of that! My daughter, selected out of dozens of girls in Madrid! Picked. Only fifteen, but already about to make her way, an excellent position, a high-paying position—one of the most important houses in Spain! Eh? Eh? Are you all dumb?"

Now the men pressed forward, swarming past Jacobo to surround Soledad. He stood alone. She laughed, swallowed up by congratulations, kissing Antonio Sánchez on one of his parchment-paper cheeks, and causing even that lifeless skin to flush. Jacobo Rivas watched from the stoop. So had his ancestors, on similar occasions and for similar reasons. Did nothing change, ever? Soledad disengaged herself. She blew a triumphant kiss at her father, pivoted, and went dancing back up the street.

The boy, the urchin, the good-for-nothing—Jacobo now noticed—had drawn off by himself. His head was bowed. His puny shoulders were held hunched together. A sob shook them!

It made Jacobo wrathful to see that. With a bound, he was at the waif, no longer the least cowed by the ready blade, grabbing him by the upper part of an arm, shaking him thoroughly and bellowing into his ears, "What's it to you? Tell me, what have you to do with this?"

"I . . . I'll miss her!"

"Miss her! What can you mean by that, eh? Explain, or so help me, I'll crack your spine right now!"

"I . . . watched her, every day. From the bodega, when she rolled up the persiana in the morning, and swept the mat. She . . . made me happy, just seeing her."

"How! What do you mean!" And he shook the boy again.

But the urchin was unable to utter it: like a candle in a window, he might have said, or a flute's fall from a minor key, or cobblestones when they're all washed down by a shower and laugh in their happiness the way she laughed when she caught him gazing at her. He managed, "Just that, happy! That's . . . why I took the job. I would have worked for nothing!"

"Oh," said Jacobo. His grip on the boy's arm loosened. It came to him, you see, with the clap of interior thunder. This was the meaning of beauty, its special privilege, the bloom of mortality. The one could never be possessed, nor the other denied. "Oh, that's it," he said in his turn. He remained motionless a moment, pondering the child. Then one massive arm went round the boy's shoulders, and he pressed that thin, suddenly stingless body to his girth. "That's part of it," he mumbled, patting the boy's back, "part of growing up, of life. And it never stops, hijo, it's never easy, a loss, a series of them from the day you are born."

Brusquely, he let the boy go, turning to the others. "Nobody answers at this door. We're wasting our time. They're either dead, deaf, or in the front of the house. I'm going around to the front. I mean to be paid!"

And he strode off. The boy glanced once at the other men, and followed. The others hesitated. It was a very daring thing, for a tradesman to present himself at the principal entrance of a palace like Número Catorce. But Sánchez, the cripple, said, "Rivas leads us, and we are within our rights."

Up into the Puerta de los Moros marched the mantequero; and then along a breakfront of small shops; and then down the crooked decline of Don Pedro, dogged by the urchin and trailed by the others; until they all arrived at the imposing portal of Número Catorce, coming to a halt under the immense granite escutcheon, whose visored helmet frowned mortally at them from behind its empty grill.

"Well," panted Antonio Sánchez, "what now?"

"This!" said Jacobo. He lifted the bludgeon of one fist, bringing it down on the lock plate of the double doors.

To everyone's surprise, the blow burst the doors inward.

"It's open!" exclaimed the plumber's son-in-law.

"What can it *mean?*" iotized the elegant young man.

The electrician, whose wife had sat up as they were about to screw the lid of the coffin down, growled out of his gloom, "You leave the doors open when someone's dead."

The elegant young man paled.

"I'm not going in!" declared the manicurist. "It's none of my affair, really. I'm not the owner, he wanted me to manicure the nails of Pidal last week, that Conde de San Martín, the dolt who fell down an elevator shaft, I said I wasn't going to do it, and what's more I didn't!"

"Cowards!" scorned Jacobo; and like his ancestors before him, he marched into the carriageway.

They found the inside entrance door ajar. Following Jacobo (the urchin glued as if to the electromagnetic mass of the man's posterior, the elegant youth mincing behind everybody, becoming distracted by a cherubim here or a seraphim there, and then pattering to catch up), they stumbled (the plumber's son-in-law; the manicurist also, cursing, being shushed at once by Antonio Sánchez) up the stairs. All was quiet. All was still. Through the portiere they pushed, and into the first vestibule. "Ouch!" bleated the elegant young man, whose wrist was slapped by the electrician when he tried to snitch a bibelot. The persianas were let down.

It was dark. With trepidation, quick looks over the shoulders, wonderment and thudding hearts, they made their way from one great salon to another. Finally they opened the doors into the rose parlor. There they found Nati, robed in her deepest black, bolt upright in the oaken rigidity of a Philip II armchair, and gazing on the sunken, simian, hooded countenance of her mistress, Odette Caro Pérez de Barradas, XVIIth Marquesa del Peregrino; who, shrouded in coarse gray wool, was laid out on a long table.

"Oafs!" snapped Nati. "Get on your knees."

They obeyed as one, raising their male antiphon to her female command as she intoned them into a rosary.

FIVE

Juan Luis Sacedón, Chairman of the Board

As fast as conditions permitted, Juan Luis maneuvered downtown, heading for Avenida José Antonio Primo de Rivera, known to everybody as the Gran Vía. He was late. Traffic was like the state of his plumbing: agonizing stoppages followed by convulsive rushes. Every honk reverberated in his skull, bouncing back and forth within it as a bullet is said to ricochet in a tank. There were moments when he thought his sphincter would never hold back the liquid importunities of his bowels. There were moments when he felt so nauseous—as when he sucked in the black diesel exhaust of a bus in front—that he nearly stopped the car to get out and anyhow *try* to throw up. It was getting very hot. Herminia had shaken him out of the bliss of his doze. Why? He began wishing again for death.

There was no place to park within six blocks of his destination. Wambling in gut and gait, he walked. Halfway along, he discovered that he had forgot his brief case. Never mind, he had not read the reports. Why should he? There was always Eugenio, in whom, after Herminia, he had perfectmost confidence: Eugenio, with every detail at his fingertips; who had let him know shortly after he had inherited his ambiguous position that he was required to read nothing; that, in fact, it would only be meddlesome, prolonging board meetings needlessly.

Befuddled by the crowds, buffeted by his thoughts, and bemused by the ominous gurgles in his gut, Juan Luis arrived at a steep tier of marble steps. He looked up. This imposing edifice was the executive headquarters of Utilidades Españolas, sole distributor of electrical power for the city of Madrid and its province, as well as for the cities and provinces of Guadalajara, Toledo, Segovia, Avila, and Salamanca. The building dated from 1917. Someone with a bad memory had thought of the Parthenon. It thrust into the sky a heavy façade whose masses of stone and marble were so begrimed as to have turned nearly black. Decorating the pediment were recumbent nudes of heroic proportions, each bearing a torch. As he climbed the steps, Juan Luis noted that one of the torches had lost its flame.

Through the portals he marched. A doorman, sweating in his dark blue serge uniform, epauleted and braided in gold, bowed deferentially. Pages in bright gold buttons jumped from their stools. He was convoyed across an immense lobby or rotunda whose domed and frescoed ceiling was supported round about by Herculean columns with massive Corinthian capitals. Juan Luis felt, as always, tiny. He might have been in a cathedral. He might have been in a railway station. There was a certain grandiose virtue, very Spanish, about this squandering of valuable floor space. He felt awed, and more insignificant yet, when he bethought that he disposed of it; that he *owned* this building and would come to command absolutely most of the capital structure sustaining it.

An ancient Otis elevator disgorged him into the fifth-floor private offices. "Señor Duque!" cried a middle-aged receptionist, leaping from behind her desk. She preceded him down a stuffy corridor, corkscrewing her sexless torso on its waist so as not to turn her back to him. They passed cubicles clacketing with typewriter keys. Juan Luis speculated about what all those busy fingers were up to. He had no idea what anyone did, nor how, in fact, it occurred to him, electricity was produced.

They were stopped by a pair of sliding doors. These the receptionist separated, stepping aside. Juan Luis walked into a commodious board room where, thank Heaven, Eugenio had finally consented to the installation of air conditioning.

Fourteen men sat at a long mahogany table. "Está!" someone ejaculated. All rose. Juan Luis recoiled. Eugenio had spun from his chair to come smoothly across the room, arms and hands outstretched, the protocol of welcome flashing gold dentures. "*Qué alegría!*" he wheezed in an orientally spiraling high tenor voice, and as though the last thing he had expected was such an honor. He clamped Juan Luis's right hand between his palms, murmuring through frozen lips, "After the others go!" Then he turned with his master to the board.

Juan Luis braced himself. At such moments, he felt more acutely than ever what an imposter he was. The directors ranged in age from their middle forties to their late sixties. Three were Juan Luis's peers; that is to say, nobles. These greeted him familiarly. The other directors, save the redoubtable Codina Moncó, verged on the obsequious. They came of affluent haute-bourgeoisie backgrounds. Juan Luis decided that the only person who felt as uncomfortable as he was the accountant, who, poor fellow, had dressed as though for a wake, pale puffy face sprinkled with sweat, chin tremblingly, crushingly aware of his worm-low standing in this high company.

He was seated at the head of the table, directors to his left and right in strict protocol, Eugenio near the foot of the table and the accountant at the very foot. Faces were now sorting themselves out. There was Casacorta, dour, dark, and tight-lipped, President of the Bank of Spain and thus courted by every major monopoly in the nation, so that he reputedly earned a cool 20,000,000 pesetas (then over $300,000) per annum in honorariums. There was Bravo Solís, brusque and bullet-headed, the Falangist demagogue from Valencia who had been named but recently Minister of Industry; and had therefore been nominated unanimously to the board of Utilidades. Next to him sat Codina Moncó, charming and benign, the wispy corona of white hairs on his pink skull shining like a silver halo. He was one of the tigers of Spanish finance, second (some said) only to Baltazar Blás, his importance to Utilidades being that he chairmanned a state-chartered monopoly whose special slice of the Spanish economic pie was the construction of hydroelectric dams. It was as natural that he should be on the board of Utilidades as that Juan Luis should be on his board, except that Codina Moncó, for all his grandfatherly mien, had unaccountably failed to extend this reciprocity.

Eugenio glanced at him. Juan Luis nodded.

Business began with a reading of the minutes from the last quarterly meeting, which were whizzed through by Eugenio with the singsong rapidity of a senile priest chanting early morning Mass. Don Indelicio, old, deaf, and cantankerous, and fussy about syntax, checked Eugenio every two or three hundred words. "What's that? Did we say the board *approved* the last minutes or merely *accepted* them?" "What's that? Eh? Eh? Did we *decide* on servicing Vega de la Carmen or *consider* it?" "Eh? Eh? What have you got there? *I* don't remember a vote being taken.

What? What? It wasn't a vote, a show of hands, let's be accurate, strike that, yes, correct it, not the same thing at all!"

The minutes were concluded when Don Indelicio's hearing aid developed static. Eugenio then had the accountant pass out the formal balance for the past quarter. Everybody was given a copy, despite which, in keeping with tradition, originating when most of the financial aristocracy was illiterate, Eugenio read out each item. Usually he did so with care, looking up through the cloudy concentric whorls of his lenses for comment. Today he hurried. It was evident to Juan Luis that he was uncommonly anxious to get done with the meeting. But now it was Don Gerónimo's turn to quibble. He was old, deaf, and cantankerous, and fussy about figures. He questioned every entry. Every entry had to be read to him twice and then explained. To Juan Luis, to whom all balance sheets were mumbo-jumbo (how in the world did liabilities and assets come out every single time to the exact same sum?), the discussions meant nothing. Some esoteric point had been raised. The whole table began wrangling, Casacorta dourly, Bravo Solís pugnaciously, Codina Moncó in an amiably serene manner. Juan Luis consumed cigarettes as if they were looped together like sausages. It would never cease. It was nearly noon. He was to meet Julio Caro for lunch at the Club Puerta de Hierro. There was something he had promised to do for Julio. He could not remember what it was. Of a sudden, his bowels would not be denied.

"Excuse me," he said, rising.

Nobody looked up. The argument raged, Don Eugenio's suasive nasal diphthongs weaving in and out the almost simultaneous vociferations of others. Juan Luis yawed his way to an executive toilet, whose bowl, it occurred to him, was a prince of its kind, having received only the loftiest of human excrement. His own ducal behind he tightened desperately. He had barely time to yank down his trousers and shorts. It was a long session. His anus stung with the watery stuff exploding out of it. His anus was sore at the touch of even the softest tissue. He wondered whether he were developing hemorrhoids.

Washing his hands, flushing the toilet a second time, he walked stiffly out of the bathroom, using another door. This opened on the hall. He motioned at a page, whose face and stature resembled that of a ten-year-old cretin, but who was actually a sixteen-year-old cretin. "Get me aspirin, two tablets. Then telephone my house. Ask for Herminia. Ask if there is any message from Don Julio Caro. Ask her to telephone him if he hasn't telephoned me and ask him at what hour we are supposed to meet for lunch. And ask him to remind her so that she can tell me what it was he wanted me to do for him this morning. Do you have all that?" Obviously, the cretin did not. Juan Luis wondered why he didn't telephone himself.

He walked turtle-stiff back into the board room, excusing himself again, taking his place and lowering his bottom gingerly to the chair, careful to separate the cheeks of his butt as little as his weight allowed.

Don Gerónimo, apparently, had been pacified; or perhaps the battery of his hearing aid had run down, because he was fiddling with the dial. The others were now debating the addition of a relay station somewhere south of Madrid. Juan Luis tried to listen. He assumed what he hoped was an attentive and intelligent air. He felt less crapulous, but that bronze clapper still bonged about in his skull. Did he want Herminia to rid him of Florita? At the moment, yes; perhaps later on in the day, no. He was condemned anyhow to perpetual torment. He had been serious with his father. Only a life spent in absolute devotion and chastity could have saved him. Herminia had been wrong; his father had not known him through and through, or he would have accepted his son's sincerity; and perceived that it was better for the line of the Dukes of Sacedón to end honorably with himself on earth than for it to perish everlastingly with Juan Luis. "Papá, I want to enter a seminary. I must. I want to be a monk." And he had received across his face, bloodying his lips and cracking one tooth, the blow of a steel hook.

What *was* it he had promised Julio? Don Eugenio was meliorating between antagonists. Wonderfully suave, always reasonable, he commanded anybody's respect. He was a rosy-lipped, gray-skinned, croup-chested, balding, shrewd, hard-working and thoroughly competent expatriate from Barcelona who had virtually run Utilidades Españolas for the past twenty years although his official position in the corporate hierarchy was modest. Why, Juan Luis asked himself, did he put up with it all? Eugenio not only carried the burden of two large and complex companies, but he acted as the family's agent in the most trivial matters, advising his mother on which chapusero to use for the remodeling of a salon, or arranging for his sisters anything from the purchase of an apartment to the hiring of a cook. In compensation, he received a ridiculous salary, 60,000 pesetas a month, doubled by Juan Luis from the almost immoral 30,000 pesetas he had been getting under the late Duke. Yet Spain was filled with such men; Juan Luis's class could not survive without the legion of able and honest administrators who serve their masters selflessly. It is characteristic of Juan Luis, misfit, that he, and not Eugenio, questioned the relationship.

Juan Luis drew on a fresh cigarette; his mind kept table-hopping. "Wie geht's?" What did that mean? "Est ist" something-something-something-something "geschlossen." There had been the two commissar types. And three or four months ago, he now remembered, he had encountered an Oriental. The elevator happened to be working then, and he was just stepping out on the sixth floor. He was so soused that particular dawn that he was scarcely astonished at this nut-brown, malarial little apparition in a business suit twice too large for him; who bobbed a series of bows like a sanderling drilling the rim of the tide; and who had clucked; and who had spread his lips apologetically back from a graveyard's set of stained yellow teeth, uttering as he sidled into the elevator, "Ahnyong! Nalssiga chokoonio. Keuronday moonul tadosio," or some gibberish of the kind, taped into his musician's memory. That, he recollected also, had been the day Herminia fired the prettiest chambermaid of them all, who, she said, filched cigarettes on the sly. He had been sorry to see the girl go.

"What do you think?"

The question curled around the back of his head, entering by way of his left ear. In an access of panic, Juan Luis realized he was being addressed by Codina Moncó. Every face in the room was turned his way. Impasse must have been arrived at. It was the Chairman's privilege and duty to break it.

Eugenio looked worried.

Juan Luis blinked. His mind raced. "I . . . agree with Don Eugenio," he finally delivered out of his mouth.

The administrator sighed, saying, "It's settled, then."

There came a knock. Eugenio whipped his head about. "Sí!"

The sliding doors opened a crack. The cretin's jug of a head poked through.

"What?!" wheezed Eugenio.

"El Señor Duque," pleaded the cretin. "A message . . ."

"Adelante," said Juan Luis.

The boy entered, terrified, hunched as though he were a badger expecting the blows of a farmer's stick. He scuffed along to the head of the table, nearing his tubular, rubbery lips conspiratorily close to Juan Luis's right ear; into which he then shouted, *"Doña-Herminia-says-to-tell-you-Don-Julio-is-still-asleep-and-cannot-be-disturbed, says-to-telephone-the-Señora-Duquesa-at-once-cannot-wait."*

Juan Luis groaned inside. His mother had worked up a second wind of indignation, he was sure, to be broken on him. "Thank you," he said, dismissing the cretin, who backed out of the room. "I beg your pardon," he said to the others, getting to his feet. But everyone murmured sympathetically. The only totem greater than machismo is mother.

Eugenio escorted his master into a private office adjacent to the board room. There, after the administrator had closed the door, the call was switched through.

"Mamá," said Juan Luis at once, "I am *truly* upset about this morning. I've thought about nothing else. I'll never, ever, forget again, I promise! I plan a novena starting next Monday, I'm going to call Don Emilio and ask him . . ."

"Never mind about that!" came her shrill, excited voice.

"No, Mamá, this time I mean it, I swear I do!"

"Will you please hush! This is urgent! Odette has been murdered!"

"What?"

"*Mur*-dered. Brutally, brutally mur-*dered*. With an ax!"

"Who?"

"*Odette*, you silly creature, your *cousin* Odette!"

"Dios mío!" exclaimed Juan Luis.

His mother spewed out the news. She had heard at half past twelve. She had been hot on the line ever since. Details were confused. Don Emilio was first on the scene. Plumbers and hairdressers were next. There had been a disgraceful confrontation between Ignacio Prades and a brute of a mantequero.

"A mantequero?"

"Yes, a mantequero!"

"Whatever about?"

"How should I know? What does it matter? Ignacio almost struck the creature. A goalkeeper from the Atlético de Bilbao intervened. There were signs of a fearful struggle, poor Odette, imagine it! Nati discovered her lying in the ballroom, in a *pool* of blood. It happened at night, or early this morning, no one is quite sure. Miriam Estepona says it was before dawn. But my Caridad called Consuelo's María, whose ankle is swollen again, what bothers they can be! Consuelo, of course, had rushed to Número Catorce, but she, María, *she* says it happened early last night, and it's from María that Caridad heard that the murderer chopped poor Odette into bits so fine that even the Commission of Bellas Artes will never be able to put her together again. How awful. Poor, poor Odette! I suppose now I'll never get back the shawl she borrowed last time she came over. There's no other sign of robbery. The police are all over the place. The police are questioning everyone. Nati, they say, is in shock. I've called Marisa Magascal. She's in hysterics, nearly blew me off the wire. She was playing cards with Odette last evening, she says she won, I doubt it. But listen to this! Marisa's new butler, a monster she found in Extremadura, *he's gone, he's fled!* I *knew* that sort of thing would catch up with Marisa one day, and now it has caught up with Odette, God rest her soul, the police are hunting for him everywhere."

His mother began repeating details. A Greek was conducting investigations. There were murmurings of a plot against the security of the Chief of State. Consuelo Orbaneja had collapsed. One of Jaime Orbaneja's buildings had collapsed. It was the peacocks all over again. Don Emilio had dreamt of them. C. O. Jones had had the audacity to leave his card. A scissors-grinder had cut a woman's throat . . . Juan Luis listened with his receding lower jaw hanging open. All he could think about was Sofía, who had loved her mother.

"The Smith-Burtons?" he interrupted.

"What?!"

"Where is Sofía? Have you heard about her?"

"Vanished! Vanished off the face of the earth!"

"What do you mean, vanished!"

How should his mother know! Under the circumstances, she wasn't sure whether one ought to appear at Número Catorce quite yet, although she was *dying* for firsthand information. That Greek, a fellow called Stepanópoulis Grau, was credited with having determined that it was a murder, although that didn't seem to be such a magical deduction given that there were chunks of Odette spread all over the ballroom floor. But . . .

"I have the board meeting, Mamá," Juan Luis reminded her. "I must go."

"Wait!"

"I really can't, Mamá."

"Wait, Juan Luis, don't you see what this means?"

He hadn't the foggiest notion: except that Sofía would be sundered by what had happened; except that gentle, darling Sofía, probably kneeling alone in some chapel, would be needing all the comfort God and man can give; and that she would receive the human consolation from her husband, the man who fascinated Juan Luis with such a passionate antagonism of emotions.

His mother said, "Now that Odette is gone, there's no reason left to keep everything secret. Ignacio is a prig and a pig. Since he married the Blás girl, there's no putting up with his airs. Well, his mother is dead; and the truth can come out."

"What truth?" he asked impatiently.

"Surely you know about Nacho!"

Juan Luis knew nothing.

"But *every*body does!" his mother cried. "He is *not* Odette's son! Ignacio is *Nati*'s son—yes, the maid, Nati! *Nati!* Nacho Prades has no more right to the title than the man next door!" His mother rushed into a complicated tale about a substitution of infants suggested by Marisa Magascal, who regretted not having followed her own advice with *her* son. Juan Luis now did dredge up in his memory some vague whisperings —a canard out of the past, as far as he was concerned, and of little interest.

"Mamá, I'm keeping everyone waiting."

"But this is of supreme importance!"

"Why? Poor Na . . ."

"Oh, you *are* such a dolt! *Fedi* would have seen it in a minute. If Ignacio isn't her son, *who* has more right to Odette's title than you? Now is the time to go to Nati and pry the truth out of her. *Now is just the time!*"

"You mean you expect me . . ."

"No, no, no, whoever mentioned you! You're the *last* person. Herminia, of course: maybe not today, but tomorrow, after the burial. Nati is sure to break down then, you know how devoted she was to Odette. *That*'s when Herminia can get to her and press the truth out of her. And then you, Juan Luis, you will have the title!"

Juan Luis lowered the cup of the receiver, to stare at it. This was, of course, his mother speaking; he had no business being surprised. He brought the receiver back up to his mouth. "Mamá, whatever for? Why do I want Odette's title? Nacho can have it, as far as I'm concerned."

"You can be such a *fool!*" his mother fairly shrieked. "Nacho has no right to it, none at all! It's a matter of principle. And a marquisate like Odette's is nothing to scoff at. You may marry and have children some-day!"

Florita's? he thought to himself. Wouldn't that surprise her! "Mamá, I already have more titles than I know what to do with, eighteen or nineteen . . ."

"You have twenty!"

"Well, I'm hardly likely to have that many children."

"But Odette's marquisate is the Imperial Marquisate, worth more than all seven of yours! It's worth more than a dozen nineteenth-century dukedoms, the *only* one in Europe with the umbilicus and the tripe!" His mother emitted what sounded like the groan of a woman in labor. "What *is* the matter with you that you can't see the importance of these things! I sometimes wonder whether your father wasn't right, that you came from nowhere, neither from him nor from me, a sorcerer's child, with about as much appreciation for important matters as some . . . some . . . some . . . some *peasant* from Sacedón! Your brother wouldn't be shrugging his shoulders. *Don't you believe our world is finished!* There are people about begging for even a *Papal* title. They try bribes, anything at all; they spend fortunes siphoning up and down family trees on the off-chance. And here you have a *jewel* practically thrown in your lap!"

"Mamá, I really must go. I'll call you again this afternoon."

Entrails slipping gears within him; head quaking worse than before; he stumbled back into the board room. The cretin had forgot the aspirin. He would try to hold out. He announced the Marquesa's death. Everyone was shocked, even the leftist, Bravo Solís, who said, "It's the end of an era." Old Codina Moncó shook his head doubtfully, gazing at Juan Luis and the three other nobles present. "Not until the last one fricassees in his arrogance," he murmured pleasantly, adding: "'They never change, and they never learn.'" The nobles (not Juan Luis) took heated exception, demanding Codina Moncó explain himself. He merely smiled, falling asleep. Twenty minutes of agitated discussion followed. Juan Luis felt extremely nervous. Eugenio began glancing at his wristwatch, and then at him. Raising his voice timidly, Juan Luis suggested they return to business.

He was astonished by the reaction. Everybody at once fell silent. There was undeniably something about being a sixteenth-century duke with Franco-Gothic warrior ancestors—one, anyhow, with an impressive block of a corporation's voting stock in his pocket. For a giddy instant, Juan Luis felt himself expand out of the mockery of his mortal frame, felt the heroic chainmail hot against a burly breast and in his two hands the salted iron hilt of the great ancestral broadsword. A visual collision, accidental, with the accountant's face sadly dissipated his daydream. Reality grabbed him by both ears. Plans for the new relay station, now agreed upon in principle, had been unrolled on the table. His approval

of a detail was asked. He approved. There was an objection to another
detail. He approved the objection. There was another objection, object-
ing to the first. He approved that. Finally they came to Eugenio's analysis
of the cash flow situation and general prospects for the next quarter.

Eugenio called on the accountant. This was the man's hour. He
rose to his feet and began reading from an intricate report that lost Juan
Luis with the first stuttered sentence. Gazing fascinated at this mirror, he
cringed inside. The sheaf of paper in the accountant's hands trembled.
His bloodless lips trembled. His chin all on its own trembled; and probably his knees were trembling also, because Juan Luis felt his twitch in
empathy. The accountant's puffy jowls in particular shook, atomizing the
drops of perspiration that came runneling off his forehead and down
along his nose. Juan Luis thanked God it was not he reading the report.

After repeated interruptions by Don Indelicio (syntax) and Don
Gerónimo (who challenged several of the projections), the report was accepted. The accountant dropped back into his chair as though someone
had yanked a string attached to his fanny. And now Don Eugenio rose
for the most solemn of the board meeting's ceremonies: the reading of
the profit-and-loss statement. Everybody drew his chair closer, leaning toward the speaker as if he were a magnet and they metal filings. Even
Codina Moncó had awakened, eyes sharp behind their caskets of flesh.

Soon it was clear that it had been a very poor quarter. On gross receipts exceeding 400,000,000 pesetas, net profits after deductions for
taxes, depreciation, debt servicing, the new relay station, and current operating expenses were less than 18,000,000. "Why!" came Codina
Moncó's rap of a query.

Eugenio revolved a full 45 degrees on his axis, shifting his feet so
that he fully faced the man. Don Eugenio, Juan Luis decided, really was
admirable. He made no attempt to defend his management, stating simply
that expansion carried out at too fast a rate in order to keep pace with the
rapid industrialization of the past few years had necessitated heavy borrowing (he glanced at Casacorta, President of the Bank of Spain) besides
creating personnel problems and unavoidable inefficiencies. Speaking,
he looked straight into Codina Moncó's eyes. "As His Most Excellency,
the Minister of Industry, is sure to agree, Utilidades has a social responsibility. In an effort to help attain the national goals of the Government's
Development Plan, Utilidades has laid in many lines that for the time
being do not pay." And he bowed at Bravo Solís.

Codina Moncó's eyes flickered in the direction of the Minister. In

Spain, business can be 75 per cent politics. And times were changing. Even such sacrosanct monopolies as the match-making industry had been opened a month or so before to competition.

The old man's face relaxed into benignancy. "All right," he said, "let's divide it up."

Of the available 18,000,000 pesetas, the directors voted themselves 4,000,000, the rest being distributed to littlefish stockholders. This may seem audacious, but corporations in Spain are run for the directors, and Devil take anyone else. Juan Luis received the lion's share, 500,000 pesetas, against which he had so many debts that he would be lucky to jingle in his pocket half. Master of millions, perpetually strapped, he was irritated.

Everyone rose and stretched his legs. Eugenio pressed a bellbutton. Waiters in black trousers and white, high-collared tunics brought in trays with ice, glasses, bottles of scotch and sherry, and hot canapés. It was nearly one-thirty. An inevitable half hour more had to be endured. No one was satisfied. Net earnings had been in decline too long. Codina Moncó, speaking within earshot of Eugenio, mentioned that Unión Eléctrica Aragona, a sister company in the North, had distributed 80,-000,000 pesetas in the past quarter. He said, "Of course, that company owns its power sources, and it has Blás management;" leaving the remark to dangle. Talk turned to Odette Prades. Juan Luis's three peers stole glances at him. He gathered what they were thinking: would he place a claim for the title? He had not realized the story was so generally known, although these men belonged to the older generation. A bore from the haute-bourgeoisie contingent cornered him and orated about the gravity of the Middle East situation. Spain, he said, whereas sympathetic to Israel, should not overlook her North African interests. Juan Luis nodded. Where would Sofía be? Could he not this once take her into his arms and melt with her in the caldron of his love? Good-bye, good-bye, until the end of time . . .

The last of the directors had been bidden out of the room, which was blue with tobacco smoke. Don Eugenio, wiping his eyes under the gold rim of his spectacles, went to the air-conditioning unit and pushed buttons so that a fan began sucking the stale fumes out. Then he turned to Juan Luis.

"I hope you have half an hour."

"I'll tell you in a minute." He rushed to the bathroom. When he came out, he said, "I think so."

Don Eugenio had sat at the table. He sat in chunky meditation, shoulders humped, left hand thudding and rapping the rhythm of a fandango de Huelva. Knuckles fell on the polished mahogany surface; as if released by a spring, square-cut fingernails flew out from beneath them. *Thud rrrup-rrrup, thud-rrrup. Thud rrrup-rrrup, thud-rrrup.* In a thin, high, true voice, Don Eugenio hummed the melody.

"Well," Juan Luis said, drawing a chair across from his administrator.

Eugenio kept humming. But now he gazed at the man who was his lord; and Juan Luis, the lord, gazed apprehensively back.

The extra-thick lenses of Eugenio's spectacles, hollowed in those concentric whorls, revealed his eyeballs as though through an inverted telescope. This had fascinated Juan Luis as a child. It fascinated him still. It was like looking into a pair of crystal cones. At their bottoms were tiny pits, black as basalt. Nervously, Juan Luis lit his fifteenth cigarette of the morning. A verse curled in cadence through his head.

> De varios pueblos de Huelva
> Y de Sevilla la llana
> Van tirando las carretas
> Al despuntar la mañana

With a final *thud-rrrup!*, Eugenio asked, "Do you still play the guitar?"

"Not as much."

"Lo siento. Once, you know, many, many years ago, I wanted to sing Flamenco for a living." He chuckled. "Me, a Catalán! You wrote poetry as a child."

"Yes."

"Why did you stop?"

"I ran out of things to say."

"That's too bad. We dream, all of us. What do you suppose happens to our dreams?"

"They dry up."

"Aaah, aaaaah," uttered Eugenio, lifting his little chin higher with each exhalation, and then letting it bounce on the air beneath it. "I don't think so. I think they hide somewhere, ashamed. We regret them, don't we?"

"Some of them."

"Juan Luis, do you ever wish you were someone else?"

The little eyes pinned their subject. The smile was not a smile: not friendly, nor yet inimical.

"I . . . I think we all have wished that. At times."

Eugenio bounced his little chin again; but now on the cushion of its dewlap. As if curiously, academically, he asked, "Juan Luis, do you have more than a remote intellectual apprehension of what bankruptcy is?"

Book Three

KINFOLK

(Or: Business Is Business, Even in Madrid)

ONE
The City

The hours between nine-thirty and twelve noon in Madrid impound an importance not readily appreciated by the rest of the world. At what about are the heirs of True Spain? The Duke of Sacedón, dressed for his downfall, whistles rhinitically in his sleep, still blissful in oblivion. Julio Caro y Prades, his playmate, may not arise at all. The alarm has rung, but his alarums are over. Diego Muñoz González, however, will be up at ten, oiling the slumber out of his muscles, anointing his pubis with perfume, and wondering whether he ought to risk telephoning Herminia or wait and merely dwell on the hours of golden sexuality in prospect. No sybarite Baltazar Blás. Nine sharp, and he has arrived at Customs in his chauffeur-driven limousine, frotting his fisherman's hands. Nearly as punctual is Deputy Inspector Stepanópoulis Grau, who bustles at his desk sorting last night's aberrations from yesterday's blasphemies, hoping for a crack at a homicide, or at the very least an insult against the dignity of the Chief of State. Jaime Orbaneja, still abed, has no real hopes, bankers may buy art, but they can't be expected to support it; and his buildings happen to require more support than most. Billy Smith-Burton would smash them. He slipped out of bed at the first crack of light, relinquishing the delicious warmth of his Sofía forever. And Ignacio Prades y Caro, Conde de Obregón, sits at breakfast, pale face drawn, large and handsome chestnut eyes striated red, trying to atomize out of his mind the golden succubus, who will shortly buzz her syncopated four times in the signal that she has awakened and that the real day may commence.

The lowly bodily functions of the city have been attended. That is, firemen have finished flushing dust and flyers into gutters, and traperos are already pitching their loads of refuse into the smoking aromatic dumps beyond Fuencarral or Vallecas. Pressure builds up in the great urban engine as the opening of the business day nears. Sidewalks throb. Avenues thrum. Policemen wade patiently through sargasso seas of immobilized traffic, paying not the slightest attention to the profanities pelting them on all sides, plucking out the dotty old lady who took it into her diddled old head to cross diagonally from a southwest corner to a northeast corner, indulgent with the inexperienced civil servant whose brand-new 850

(SEAT) has volleyed off someone else's brand-new 850 (Morris) and up on the greensward of the monument to Christopher Columbus, gently reprimanding the taxi driver who has just completed a hair-raising and wholly prohibited U-turn in the very teeth of the tide . . . despite which people eventually do reach their destinations, trolleys peapodful ring-ding-rattling along their rails and puffing out passengers, subway wells vomiting forth their hundreds of thousands of pedestrians in a seemingly inexhaustible flow that pours up and down avenues and streets. There is everything to be got ready. Waitresses in dozens of cafeterias dust stale flies off the stale cakes studded unsucculently in window fronts. Salesgirls all over the city busy themselves inking out yesterday's prices and writing in higher ones. Tellers in numberless banks slip into their pulpits and expertly tot up all those little chits, tickets, and stubs that help transmogrify the utilitarian chore of cashing a check into a rite only less mystical (and much longer) than the old Tridentine Mass, and probably devised by that supreme pontiff among paperpushers, Philip II, whose spiritual descendants, the functionaries of the State, are by now congregating in the dark corridors of their ministries and blinking with drugged stupefaction through the fumes of coffee held in waxed paper cups that at this moment are too hot to hold without scalding the fingers, but within a few minutes will cool, and become soaked, and drip sticky milky drops out their porous bases, themselves pondering with an emotion bordering on horror the moleholemountains of paper that they will be pushing across their desks during the day. Their counterparts in private industry are also gearing themselves for the travails ahead of them, punching out personal household accounts on office calculators and rummaging in file cabinets for lost combs, lipsticks, lottery tickets, and love letters, pulling out files to peer under them, and in the process shuffling a few Bs and Ts among the Ys and Zs. Executive secretaries contemplate their masters' thickly carpeted sanctums, on whose altars paper-and-ink are transubstantiated into the very flesh and blood of human destinies, wondering (in some instances) whether today their bosses may pay a visit to sign a letter or two, there is (at Confecciones En Ante, S.A.) that order for three dozen suede overcoats Model 72-A-*bis* six weeks overdue, nobody's fault, a shortage of skins thanks to unforseeable difficulties in obtaining an importation permit from Customs.

Such nits and nettles prick the peace of all those potentates for whose descent on the swatfields of life (between the hours of nine-thirty and twelve noon) Madrid has prepared since dawn. Ministers, bankers, high-level executives, by temperament and due course not necessarily trained or equipped but positioned anyhow (pater or pull) to do battle with dragons, they are many of them somehow seemingly forever doomed to flail at gnats, sufficient for the more feeble spirits to mull gloomily moping through their breakfasts, but which serves only to steel the resolution of such as Ignacio Prades y Caro, Conde de Obregón, and one day (perhaps? No, *surely!*) sooner than he expects to inherit his mother's very nearly ducal marquisate as well. He exists on three levels: the level of confidence, the level of doubt, and the level of fear. The level of fear is called Dorada; the level of doubt Baltazar Blás; and the level of confidence el Conde de Obregón, economist and sociopolitical progressive, whose treatise on "The Interdependence of Labour and Management in Pursuit of the Common Good" was once read by him before the Coordinating Committee of the World Confederation of Labor, which body acclaimed the work for its enlightened liberalism, and then recessed. Alas, Ignacio Prades y Caro is also Consejero Delegado (Chairman of the Board) of Confecciones En Ante, S.A. (known as CASA), and the nuisance of those three dozen overcoats Model 72-A-*bis* had been brought rather intemperately to his attention at eight-thirty on the dot, when no gentleman's rest is disturbed except by such as Baltazar Blás, who is no gentleman, but who happens to be his father-in-law. The story of the overcoats was not entirely clear to Prades.

TWO

Julio Caro y Prades

It all began nine months before, in July of 1966, when Galerías Pedro Puig placed the order after having scouted fashion predictions for the following spring. This was foolish anticipation to begin with, because anybody with executive authority ought to know that anybody else with executive authority is off on vacation, or about to go, and not expected back in Madrid until the waning days of September, when the partridge season compels an inodus. Galerías Pedro Puig were fortunate, however, in that the Director Gerente (Manager) of CASA actually processed the order in the last days of August, when he happened to be driving through

Madrid on his way from St. Tropez for a spot of dove shooting in Extremadura. His name is Julio Caro y Prades (de Borbón), first cousin (not that it matters) to Ignacio Prades y Caro through his mother, Ramona Prades, sister of the illustrious Ramón, late Count of Obregón, and further related through their common great-great-great-grandfather, Mauricio Caro, IIIrd Marqués de la Romana (*in excelsis*). He, Julio, shot 450 doves in six mornings and six afternoons, not that that matters either, although the experience proved excellent practice for the autumnal slaughter of redlegs, for which he also trained at the Somontes Real Club de Tiro de Pichón, where he won a cup. He checked on the Galerías Puig order and other business during the seven weekdays available to him in October, and on the thirteenth, fourteenth, fifteenth, sixteenth, seventeenth, eighteenth (poor week, that: three funerals and a wedding), and twenty-eighth of November, and also on the ninth, tenth, fifteenth, and twentieth of December; and it was on the twenty-third of December (torrential rains having aborted what had promised to be an outstanding shoot) that the plant manager in Barcelona (an excitable fellow whose name he could never remember) reminded Julio by telephone that CASA's supply of antelope skins would not be sufficient to fill all pending spring orders, and that an importation license was necessary. Of course, the Christmas holiday season (24 December through Twelfth Night) intervened, so that it was not until the morning of the eighth of January that the application reached Customs.

Tragically, the authorizing official's phlebitic mother-in-law dropped dead that very afternoon from what was diagnosed as a corte de tripa after having celebrated her saint's day with two glutinous plates of paella followed (incredibly enough) by two glutinous plates of cocido, so that he was absent a fortnight, partly because of difficulties in getting a coffin constructed of sufficient amplitude to receive the carcass, complicated further by protracted haggling with the director of the cemetery, who insisted that the family had bought just so much space and no more, and that he could not permit the overflow. The problem took on harrowing dimensions as days went by, the old lady fit into no known refrigeration vault in the morgues of Madrid, butchers and dairies wouldn't take her, the neighbors complained, the Department of Sanitation threatened the most condign fines, and the Church refused to sanction any chopping up of the sainted dead. He was a worn and weak official when he returned to work, only to discover that some underling had dribbled coffee over one pile of applications on his desk, which required sending the lot back to offices all over the city.

This was an unlucky moment for CASA. The company had moved to a new office building constructed by the romantic and distinguished Jaime Orbaneja, who happens to be Prades's brother-in-law (not that it matters), and by courtesy (marriage) Count of the Caribs. Befell the scandal of the peacocks. Presumably, the returned application for an importation permit was to be found in the molten mess of glass and metal and paper, and weeks more passed before CASA's Director Gerente (Julio) recalled that nothing had been heard from Customs; but by this time Spain was hung in the crêpe of Holy Week, and all business was suspended in reverent commemoration of the Passion and Death of our Saviour. CASA's Director Gerente commemorated these events in Marbella, on the Costa del Sol, where the single church's bells are no match for the tinkle of ten thousand highball glasses and the wail and thump of hard-rock pornograph records. He returned haggard and drawn from his seven days of spiritual exercises, only to realize that he had but seven days free before the commencement of feria in Seville, which would not be as glamorous as the year before, when Jacqueline Kennedy and Princess Grace of Monaco split the seams of society's columns, but to which he felt obliged by rank and position. He worked from ten to dusk all that week, signing and sending a new application to Customs. The authorizing official there, however, had departed on an inspection tour of the provinces, and no one, of course, was delegated to discharge his duties in his absence, which would have been tacit admission of his dispensability. The application sank beneath a drift of papers. CASA's Director Gerente returned from Seville much refreshed, but his secretary had been laid low by colic, as only colic in Madrid can, quite pulling the plug out of the executive suite. Julio Caro y Prades (not that his name matters) had no idea where anything was. He had no idea what to do. He spent most of the day in the Real Club de Puerta de Hierro, where between drinks, bridge, the wild and weird game called "mus," and more drinks he bludgeoned his brains trying to remember what business pended. Great good luck then descended. One of the archivists in the office reached into the very bowels of a file cabinet for a bottle of nail polish whose contents had providentially leaked out, cementing the vial to a copy of the new application. Ahhh! Julio ordered her to check the matter at once, himself rushing off to Galicia for a few days of salmon killing.

April can be a hectic month in Madrid. Kill a few salmon in Galicia, and one is likely to miss the best capercaillie stalking in Asturias, not to mention the bear hunting thereabouts, the trout fishing in Gredos, and the chance of popping at a few bewhiskered cock bustards on the plains to the southwest. CASA's Director Gerente squeezed everything in, but it was nip and tuck before the bullfights of San Isidro (15 May) were upon him, and he only arrived at the first corrida after a mighty battle of his own with back business. His secretary, recovered, had fielded ten telephone calls from Galerías Pedro Puig, two of them from Señor Puig himself. Señor Puig wanted his coats. He was exercised about his coats. If he did not hear at once from CASA's Director Gerente, Julio Caro y Prades, he would call CASA's Consejero Delegado, Ignacio Prades y Caro; and if he did not hear from him, he would call Baltazar Blás. Heavens! Don Julio mobilized his energies and went round personally to Customs. There he suborned one of the underlings into presenting CASA's application to his chief the very next morning, and on the top of the pile. It was thus expedited at last, in blue ink over the mauve ink of a stamp declaring that a license for the importation of three dozen antelope skins was categorically denied.

This fell news was communicated to Julio Caro by his secretary on the thirtieth of May, as he was setting off to assist at the christening of a Spanish infanta; along with the notification that Galerías Pedro Puig had canceled their order. He was at his wits' ends, a terminus he reached quickly. Galerías Pedro Puig was a major account; but during the past twelve months, CASA had failed to meet delivery dates on thirty-three (or was it forty-three?) out of seventy (eighty?) Puig orders. Nobody's fault. The cigar ash that fell into a wastepaper bin and started a conflagration. That whole batch of orders that had been held up a month in processing when the stockroom ran out of Master Comptroller's Co-ordinating copies, and the printer delayed and delayed in supplying fresh ones because the government, faced with a paper crisis itself, had pre-empted all production. This, however, was the first cancellation; and that sounded ominous. Driving to the Iglesia de los Jerónimos Reales, Julio Caro y Prades wracked his memory, wrenching out of it several dislocated but nevertheless now suddenly alarming impressions. Was not CASA also running late with orders for Corte Inglés; and for Galerías Preciados; and Almacenas Simeón? And did he not have the impression that there were a number of unfulfilled orders from the small boutiques? The record of deliveries was not good, not good at all. The company had lost money its first year, which was to be expected. He had not checked recently with the accountant (a puffy-eyed comatose puzzlefaced individual), but he had a queasy suspicion that CASA was running several more millions in the red this year, and as sure as the sun rose in the morning, Baltazar Blás would want to know why.

He arrived at the cathedral in a perturbed state. Throughout the impressive baptismal ceremony, he pondered what he should do. Everybody of any importance had assembled at Los Jerónimos. This failed to comfort him. There are times when even the fetus kicks within the womb. Julio Caro y Prades felt oppressed, hemmed in, a potential miscarriage in this ambience of what he imagined to be social and financial security. He mumbled responses; his attention roved. Up on the dais of the altar stood Su Alteza Real (S.A.R.) Don Escobosa José de Borbón y de Baviera, godfather of the little princess, and a majestic figure in his white tunic and golden epaulets. Not far behind the royal presence came Carlos Lapique, Duque de Centollos, despite his seventy-five years nearly regal himself in the furnishings of his rank, mouth shrunken perhaps and lungs keeping emphysematous time with the bellows of the organ, but the forehead still a noble dome and the nose a distinguished beak, even though a drop of something did glisten from its tip. Behind him came Nacho Pelau, appropriately Count of the Two Intestines and Colonel besides of the IVth Royal Howitzers. He sagged like a wineskin beneath his sash, but he seemed no less spirited for all that, remarking something to Marisa, Condesa de Magascal, who hulked hippically above him, and eliciting from her a snort that may have scared the Devil out of the infant as effectively as the archbishop's exorcism. At another pew stood Jaime Orbaneja, who was cocking fidgety eyes at the cornices and capitals of the nave, but who was elbowed into pious attention by his wife, Consuelo, Countess of the Caribs, who looked hot, dumpy, and cross. Beside her stood her sister, Sofía Smith-Burton, Condesa de Mil Lágrimas, lovely in the gentle folds of a pleated beige Berhanyer cocktail dress four seasons old but no less becomingly feminine. Notably absent was her mother, the Marquesa. Characteristically absent was Billy Smith-Burton, probably up to his scarecrow waist in gears and cogs and wheels, welding together whatever new monster of a contraption he was now working on. Julio Caro's listless eye went along cataloguing nobles, lesser and greater, and then stopped.

Near the communion railing, but partly obscured by the dazzle of candlelight, rose up the inquisitionally stiff black back of Cousin Ignacio. His presence was to be expected; but the actual sighting of him begot a gurgle in the gut of Julio, which by some sort of intestinal empathy generated a succession of gurgles in the congregation that concluded in a belch on the surprised countenance of the archbishop, who looked behind him and sharply reprimanded an acolyte. What was Julio to tell Ignacio?

He did not know. He tried to concentrate on the golden head, shining like a monstrance, of Prades's erotically compelling wife. She was dressed in an eye-popping pop-patterned canary-and-orange silk from Pertegaz, adhering to the strict Courrèges four inches above the knee, which was daring enough at a royal ceremony, but which adhered even more strictly and daringly to her luscious upper thighs, buttocks, and hips. He tried to console himself now with the Spaniard's favorite auto-erotic sport: slowly peeling off the dress and stocking tights, peeling her down to the nude voluptuous honeycomb of her flesh. It did not work. He was able to summon not a bubble of concupiscence. It did not help either to sneer at her as the daughter of Baltazar Blás. Nobody sneered, even in the intimacy of his soul, at anything belonging to Blás.

And then he was saved. He was attracted to the quite red quarter profile of Juan Luis Seguismundo del Val, standing to the left of the baptismal font and sweating like a mule in harness. Julio was attracted by the clatter of Sacedón's white-plumed helmet falling out of the couch he had fashioned for it in the crook of his left arm, and then by the commotion Juan Luis caused when stooping to retrieve it, the ferrule of his scabbard jerking up behind him to goose a duchess. Hope flourished in the Caro breast. Juan Luis was a cousin—although remote—of Ignacio. Julio's own kinship to Ignacio was closer, but there were differences. He, Julio, was not well off, the late Marqués de la Romana his revered father having shot to smithereens what remained of a fortune originating in the seventeenth-century slave trade through the marriage of the first Marqués de la Romana to the exceedingly wealthy Isabel de Frayle, a daughter of the distaff Bustamante descent. Julio, heir to the title, barely survived on the income from his modest portfolio in Financiera Sacedón; he had never managed to accumulate enough capital to pay the titular rights; and although he was commonly referred to by generous members of his caste as Julio "de la Romana," and although embroidered on his shirts and hankies were discreet (because not quite licit) crowns, it was *not* the same thing as being able to present himself properly as the VIIIth Marqués.

At the reception, held in the nearby Ritz Hotel, Julio Caro y Prades avoided Ignacio Prades y Caro, choosing a moment when Juan Luis stood alone and brooding beside a potted palm, at which he was staring, a glass of flat champagne held in front of his abdominal pouch. "Coño, que haces todo solo!" hailed Julio as cheerily as he could. He received in reply one of those moody gazes that so often disconcerted Sacedón's companions. But Juan Luis was a good fellow at heart. He listened attentively while Julio explained his problems. Encouraged, Julio then asked whether it was not so that his father had eased Pedro Puig through financial straits during the recession of '59? Juan Luis nodded. Oh, very good! Julio left the obliquity there. He looked about him. Ignacio had departed. Julio therefore asked Juan Luis whether he would be seeing their mutual cousin soon again, and Juan Luis replied that he expected to meet him that very afternoon at the cocktail party being given by C. O. Jones, the American oil tycoon. Wonderful! Julio now stated how grateful he would be if Juan Luis mentioned to Ignacio that the catastrophic order for three dozen suede overcoats Model 72-A-*bis* had suffered from a calamitous concatenation of the most incredible malefactions of fate, for which nobody (at least on this side of the veil) could be blamed. Juan Luis promised to do so. He promised while tilting the contents of his glass into the rich astringent soil of the pot, saying, "We're really of no use at all, are we?" Which made no sense, because Juan Luis was manifestly of great use.

The knots in Julio Caro's entrails dissolved. A native buoyancy returned to him. It was a fine, sunny afternoon. There was no pressing need to return to the office, the plant manager was always calling about something or other, a nervous type, his secretary could handle it, he would go to the swimming pool of the Royal Club of the Iron Gate and there bob away the hours with his peers.

THREE

Ignacio Prades y Caro

Thus (and through Sacedón first) had Ignacio Prades Caro, son of the Marquesa, been advised of the latest contretemps at CASA; and thus was the problem passed up to him for solution. Tall, spare, narrow-jawed; with gravely luminous eyes, a long straight nose, and pincered nostrils; his father's son, dignified of mien, irreproachable in conduct, and immaculately groomed; the VIth Count of Obregón broke his fast with the austerity he had cultivated. Half a glass of orange juice. One cup of black coffee. One soft-boiled egg. One slice of dry toast, thinly spread with apricot marmalade. He sat at the Queen Anne dropleaf table in his study, where he preferred his morning meal, brought in on a silver tray along with a rack holding his freshly steam-ironed *ABC* and the packet of last night's personal mail. It was a handsome, paneled study in a capacious, handsome apartment in a dignified building on the corner of General Mola and Juan Bravo. He enjoyed his matinal inventory of the furnishings: the maroon leather sofas, suitably worn, the leather-topped Sheraton writing desk on whose surface rested a silver pen-and-ink stand, George III, very fine; a silver paper cutter, also English, and catalogued by Sotheby's; a crystal, flowered paperweight, French, colorful, Linares of Madrid certifying its collector's quality; and—framed in sixteenth-century polychrome—a large photograph of his wife, from whose flawless and ironic features his eyes fled. He composed himself by concentrating on a 1765 Lowestoft bowl, overflowing with the last of the season's daffodils. He had a weakness for daffodils, their feathery, gold-yellow blooms, their joyous, springtime transience; saddening him, his features softening, his gaze introspective, too luminous, lips closing, lips whitening, turning down, and twisting . . .

That was indulgence! He bent his attention quickly to the *ABC*, which he made it his duty to scan every morning from cover to cover, as became a *philosophe d'affairs*. News from the Middle East was grave, and he frowned his concern. He read every word reported on the emergency session of the United Nations Security Council, nodding his approval of the American ambassador's statement that the Arab nations had no right, under the terms of the armistice, to occupy belligerent positions. Just so had he expressed himself last night, at the Ateneo, in reply to a question following his address, and with gratifying response from the audience. But now he frowned again, reading Torcuato Luca de Tena's exordium on the constitutional debate about to commence in the Cortes. Yes, Article XI was retrogressive, threatening to return to the Falange much of the power of which it had been emptied by Franco himself. Definitely an error on the part of an aging leader; which notwithstanding he read with keen interest the notice that General Franco had been named honorary and perpetual president of the Provincial Government of Tarragona. Prades was not one of those doctrinaires congealed in the antagonisms of the past. No indeed. On occasion he had criticized the regime, certainly, but the Generalísimo had instituted many commendable reforms in the social fabric of Spain, and if they were inadequate, well, a new generation of leaders would take care of that.

Less interesting news followed. There was a column and a half entitled "Capítulo de sucesos," recording foibles and disasters. A workman had fallen to his death from an eighth floor scaffolding, which had collapsed. A forty-year-old woman had created a scandal by walking about

Calle Madre de Dios nude. Three discreet lines dealt with the unmentionable scandal of Barcelona, involving more than a few prominent families. Ignacio skimmed through other such items (a multiple automobile collision, a stabbing), arriving at last at the financial pages.

They led off with a general report on the economy. Oh, the frowns! In the past ten years, the peseta had lost 51 per cent of its buying power (compared to 16 per cent for the dollar), and at a rate of 6.9 per cent per annum. The cost of living in Spain had jumped 28.6 per cent in the past three years alone, hourly wages 55.5 per cent between 1964 and 1966, and the balance of payments deficit was running at a staggering annual rate of 12,600,000,000 pesetas! He must speak to Baltazar Blás about this. It demanded grave thought, a profound and perhaps total reassessment of commitments (if Blás would *only* let him know what they all were!), and certainly the reprogramming of those projects personally under his (Ignacio's) direction.

He closed the newspaper. He felt better, having managed once more to dismiss the phantoms of the night as no more than that: lest they gnaw deeper into his self-esteem, and more profoundly into his self-confidence. Baltazar Blás. The level of fear burbled close under the level of doubt. At eight-thirty! Well, that vexing application of CASA's could wait. Far more urgent was the future of Armas Y Explosivos, S.A., a very major firm, keystone of the Blás industrial empire. He pursed his lips. He worried about AESA. His father-in-law may have been a brilliant manipulator in his time, but that time was passing; and Blás, like the Caudillo, was aging, and getting stickier with age.

Prades thought back to the golden days of his association with the financier. How hopeful had everything looked then! Baltazar chuckled all over him. It was Ignacio this and Ignacio that. Great things were in store. Society, he had feared, would be shocked by his engagement to the old pirate's daughter. Far from it! He was besieged with invitations, more than ever he had received. Bankers held special shoots for him, although he did not shoot, and their boards voted wedding gifts as high as 500,000 pesetas cash, so confident were they that depositors would be overjoyed at having the fruit of their savings used for this happy purpose. There was talk of publishing his collected discourses. Now when he gave an address people stayed seated through the very last of his multiple perorations, and the *Economista* began citing him as an authority.

It was an exciting year! The wedding was celebrated in fashionable Los Jerónimos, and the reception at the Palladian Blás mansion in Cuidad Puerta de Hierro, where 2,000 guests quaffed 110 cases of champagne, consumed 200 lobsters and 40 kilos of caviar. It was then, at the very end of the reception, as the couple stood poised for departure on the top of a cascade of marble steps, when Baltazar revealed (in a sonorous aside) that on that very day the future Marquis of the Pilgrim had been elected to the boards of AESA and Banco Blás, as well as to the boards of all other multifarious enterprises in which the bank held a controlling or substantial interest. "Now forget about money and go make babies!" he had shouted to everybody's embarrassment save his own, beaming that paternal, solicitous smile, clapping his son-in-law on the back while simultaneously bussing his daughter and signaling to the chauffeur.

Ignacio Prades had no intention of being a mere figurehead. The Monday following his return from the honeymoon, he walked into Banco Blás and asked to be taken to his office. There was none, he discovered. Blás seemed astonished by his appearance. But room was made for the Count of Obregón at once. And he applied himself. He studied balance sheets and production reports. He attended every executive meeting. He was appalled by the primitive organization of the companies. How they made money was difficult to conceive. Baltazar seemed to carry everything in his head. "Just let me know how much we've got in the till, how much we owe, and how much we've got coming in," he would say in his breezy style and with typical simplism. Ignacio Prades y Caro established monthly cumulative cash-flow projections. He demanded "moving" annual totals on sales, orders, and production. He installed a comptroller, with 1,000 square meters of office space on Calle Velázquez and a staff of nine clerks whose output, he was pleased to note, had risen in just four years from eight statistical studies a quarter to eighty-eight. He himself at least once monthly delivered to his father-in-law weighty analyses of corporate operations. Blás responded by giving him his own offices, away from the bank and its bustle, which was thoughtful; but Blás seemed less ready to promote him from a mere board member to Chairman of the major enterprises, which was strange. And then, toward the end of the second year of his marriage, something happened.

Ignacio did not know what, and perhaps he never would know. He had flown to Tokyo for an economists' symposium. He had left Madrid pursued by his father-in-law's blessings. Just four weeks before, Dorada had given birth to their second child and first son. Blás's celebration of this event had been monumental. As a special gift to Ignacio, he had funded the Fundación Baltazar Blás, and here he did put his son-in-law in charge of sprinkling Spain with good works from the 24,000,000,000 pesetas subscribed. Ignacio was delighted. This, he believed, was only the beginning. He returned to Madrid ten days later, on the twentieth of May. And everything—everything—had changed.

He did not want now to dwell on the more intimate aspects of this change: he never wanted to think about that, he spent every waking moment of his life trying to avoid the anguish of dwelling on that. But he dated the deterioration in his relationship with Baltazar Blás from that twentieth of May precisely. In public, his father-in-law remained deferent; in private, although he was still fond, he could be direct. And in strictly business affairs, he waxed secretive, more than ever autocratic in presiding over board meetings, where he would announce with his puerilely pugnacious grin that the bank had bought this or sold the other, moves about which a few of the older Blás associates seemed to have been advised whereas he, Ignacio Prades, had not been.

Since Tokyo, since Tokyo! What could be the matter? What possibly had he done to offend? Of course, one could not expect one's father-in-law to relinquish the critical corporate helms overnight, but now three more years had elapsed. Ignacio Prades felt himself no closer to the bridges of either Armas Y Explosivos, S.A., or Banco Blás. The situation, whereas not yet insulting, more closely verged on becoming so as time went by. He had felt its reverberations already. A slim edition of his collected *Thoughts on Social Order* was got out, but as a matter of self-respect he had had to purchase 1,000 of the 2,000 copies himself. He was beginning to feel like a prince consort. He simply did not understand what was going on. Blás unfailingly complimented him on his diligence. Blás, in fact, often said to him, "Nacho, why don't you relax awhile, take a trip to the Far East, go on a safari, tour the Greek Isles, take in the World's Fair in New York, or anything you'd like. It's not good to work too hard, m'boy." Ignacio had, of course, declined. The trips he did take were devoted to broadening his horizons. Just three months ago, he had attended a symposium of Christian Democrats in Rome. He had Caravelled back to Madrid fermenting with what he had heard and learned, and with how this new perspective might benefit AESA. During the fortnight that followed, he composed his major opus to date, a single-spaced eighty-two-page "Basic Plan for the Reorganization of ARMAS Y EXPLOSIVOS, S.A., Along Progressive Socio-Economic Lines." He had it bound in Avila of the finest Cordovan kid before presenting it to his father-in-law, only to note in Baltazar Blás's expression a peculiar, glazed sort of look, ever more frequently to be observed, and one which Ignacio Prades found as difficult to classify as the cognate expression that so often masked even

the daytime eyes of his wife. In the case of Baltazar Blás, it might be the
signal of senescence. Six weeks now had he had the Basic Plan. Not a
word about it! A few days ago, Prades had directed himself to his father-in-
law's office at the bank, to be greeted warmly, true enough. Baltazar was
in conference with an hotelier from Mallorca, who spoke the abominable
Spanish of the Baleares, half peasant, half (the cunning, cock-furtive
eyes suggested) bandit, not at all to the Count of Obregón's taste; and
also a thoroughly disreputable fellow by the name of Diego Muñoz González, but presumably of some importance to the real estate speculations
of Banco Blás, because Baltazar jumped to his Lilliput feet upon Ignacio's
entrance, came trundling around his desk, grasped him by an elbow,
hauled him to where his visitors were sitting (both now rose), and hooted
in his harsh tenor gravel, "Meet m'son-in-law, Diego, Eusebio, meet el
Conde de Obregón! Nacho, shake hands, Eusebio Zaforteza, Diego
Muñoz González, you'll be seeing more of each other, you three, Nacho's
one of our directors, he'll be analyzing your proposition sure as God sits
on His throne, an up and coming figure in Euromart talk sessions, I can
tell you, trained economist, graphs, pictures, reds and yellows, blues too
. . . now shake hands, shake hands, yes!" And the noble issue of noble
parents had been compelled to offer one of his diffident, attenuated hands
to the Mallorcan peasant, who had grunted a few gutturalities expressive
of his pleasure, and then to an underworld figure from the Caribbean,
whose clasp was offensively casual, and whose smile beneath the close-
clipped mustache hovered on the insolent. But when Ignacio had then
turned to his father-in-law, and mentioned the Basic Plan, he had been
told, "Yes, m'boy, very handsomely presented indeed, and I congratulate
you. How's my Dorada? How's my grandson? Got another on the way
yet? Don't slack off! Been telling you too much work's not good for a
man. Let's have dinner together soon. Yes? No? Fine!" And Ignacio
Prades, Count of Obregón, had found himself being bustled out of the
office with a belled volley of benedictions.

Sitting now at his breakfast, the son of Patroclus frowned sternly,
creasing more deeply the tuning fork between his handsome brows. He
would not permit himself to be treated—to be used—in such manner. It
was demeaning. His organizational talents were being derogated; and
only because the old fellow was really little better than a peasant and
bandit himself, shrewd, one had to grant, but limited, who could not
appreciate the exigencies of a new era. Eight-thirty sharp! A childish
display of vitality. No slouch himself as an early riser, and punctually at
his office by ten o'clock, Ignacio had been caught in the midst of his ab-

lutions, so that he was forced to speak into the receiver through the foam of his shaving soap.

Blás had not bothered with preliminaries. "What in Christ's good name is going on with those three dozen overcoats!"

"Excuse me?"

"Excuse my ass! Last night I ran into Pedro Puig. He was hopping mad. He needed those overcoats, three dozen style 72-A-*bis*. He says he's got a bunch of orders held up at CASA. Now what in the name of Jesus is happening over there?"

"The overcoats. Oh yes. You mean . . ."

"I mean the three dozen Model 72-A-*bis* suede overcoats Confecciones En Ante was supposed to supply to Galerías Pedro Puig six weeks ago. Angels and Saints!"

"I am aware of the matter. Precisely this morning I have it on my agenda . . ."

"What! What!"

"I have it on my agenda."

"You're muffling. Speak clearer!"

"It happens I have shaving soap in my mouth."

"What in God's name are you breakfasting on shaving soap for?"

"I am not breakfasting on shaving soap. I am precisely attempting *not* to eat it, it happens you telephoned just as I had lathered my face, and Rosa said it was urgent."

"Well, wipe it off, for God's sake."

"I haven't a towel; I'm in my study."

"Well, use something!"

Ignacio Prades used the skirt of his dressing gown. He said, "The matter of the suede overcoats is on my agenda this morning to analyze . . ."

"Yes, yes, yes, I'm sure it is, you'll analyze it in ten thousand words or more, Christ! But what I want to know is, what's gone wrong? What's going on?"

"It's not entirely clear. A number of delays were encountered in expediting the application for an importation permit out of the office . . ."

"Stop right there! What sort of delays? Why?"

"Here I must say misfortunes seem to have dogged the matter. First the coffin wasn't big enough, then the peacocks ate the application with the coffee stains, or so we must presume, and then Julio Caro's secretary came down with colic . . ."

"Colic? Coffee stains? Peacocks? Coffins? Jee-*sus*, Nacho, what kind of reasons are you giving me? Look, is Caro your manager there?"

"You know perfectly well he is."

"Well, crack down on him! *You*'re the Consejero Delegado. *He*'s your Director Gerente!"

"It's contrary to all modern business principles for the consultive and policy-planning levels to interfere with the day-to-day operations of the management level. Required here is a study-in-depth . . ."

"Oh, fuck that! Look, son, I don't mean to ride you, or shout at you, but if Caro doesn't do the job, fire him, get another man, but see that the job gets done. You're a hard-working young fellow, and nobody can say I don't appreciate Basic Plans and whatever other notions you may get out of all those conventions, there may be a lot of merit in them, I'm not saying there isn't, but this is Spain, not France, not Germany, not the United States, things work differently here, you can't hitch horses to donkeys or Christians to Moors, but meanwhile if you're bound and determined to take an active hand in things—and I respect you for that, I really do—if you can't be happy just going to board meetings like most of the others and listening and okaying and picking up your honorariums, then see that the job in hand gets done, and see that others get it done, hear? Hear me?"

"Yes."

"All right. Water over the dam. Now what happened once the application got out of the office?"

"It was denied."

"*Denied!* By whom?"

"Well, the authorizing official at Customs is a fellow . . ."

"Sure. Costa, Costa Ruíz, got to know their names, all of them, that's part of it. You mean *Costa* turned us down?"

"Just so."

"That son of a hosed down . . . What have you done about it?"

"Well, I was only advised late yesterday afternoon. I had my lecture on the 'Infrastructure of Socio-Political Trends Respecting the Revolution of Rising Expectations in the Third World' to pre . . ."

"Up the Third World's ass! We're talking business, here, in Madrid! We've got overcoats six weeks on order and no delivery, we've got a cancellation, we've got God knows how many other orders pending, and God knows how many other cancellations in the offing, and what about Galerías Preciados, and Corte Inglés, and Simeón, what about them?

Blás companies deliver. Blás companies don't foul up. I'll fix it with Puig. I'll do something about Puig. But . . ."

And now the Marquesa's heir, el Conde de Obregón, interrupted. "Puig has been taken care of," he said curtly.

"What?"

"Puig has been taken care of—or will be this morning. He won't cancel. Galerías Pedro Puig will not drop CASA."

"How? When? What did you do?"

"My selections of executive personnel are not entirely capricious. Julio Caro did lack practical experience before coming to CASA . . ."

"He'd never done a lick . . ."

". . . but he is a man of integrity . . ."

"Sweet Jesus save me from . . ."

". . . and taste . . ."

"I'll grant that. The new models show it."

". . . and breeding. He is well-connected. He spoke yesterday to Sacedón."

"The Duke? The Sacedón Sacedón?"

"Precisely. He happens to be a distant cousin of Julio—and myself, for that matter, not that it matters. It happens that Julio's grandfather, the VIth Marqués de la Romana, helped the late Duke of Sacedón, Juan Luis Seguismundo's father, form Financiera Sacedón and . . ."

A sharpened voice cut through. "Does Caro have any shares in Financiera?"

"Oh, a dribbling."

"Utilidades?"

"Not of which I am aware. Why?"

There was a ruminative pause. "I want to speak to you about that. Today. Eleven. My offices. Orbaneja will be there. Go on."

"Julio Caro spoke to Sacedón yesterday afternoon, at the christening. Then I spoke to Sacedón at the C. O. Jones cocktail party. I must say I have no personal brief for Juan Luis, but he seems eager to do anybody a favor, you will remember his help respecting the Obras Orbaneja note through . . ."

"Your brother-in-law's note with me matures today."

"I'm sure Jaime is deeply appreciative of your help also. But to wind up this CASA matter, Juan Luis promised to speak to Pedro Puig today, and I am satisfied we will hear no more about cancellations."

"Yes . . . Yes . . ." It was as though Blás's mind had wandered away from the subject. Then, "Now, that's more like it, m'boy! That's *just* the way to go about these things, *and just exactly where your real strength lies!* Read me? Get me? Look. Banco Blás and AESA; NICASA, BALESA, MALASA, SIQUESA, TICASA, RAPESA, PILASA, BABESA: Unión Eléctrica Aragona; the whole kit and caboodle, every last Blás business and investment, is going to be in your someone's hands someday, and I'm sure—I'm damned well going to make sure—that what I've built will be in good hands. But what you've accomplished here is only part of it, son. So Pedro Puig won't cancel. So maybe Puig'll use the overcoats for the fall. But meanwhile you are going to need those skins, so what have you done about Costa?"

"I tried to reach him by telephone . . ."

"*Telephone!*"

"What else? There's no procedure for this sort . . ."

"You should've gone there personally, boy, gone right down there to his office, and dragged Caro along with you, and showed him how to get things done!"

"I fail to see what good would have been accomplished. The global quota for the importation of skins has been exhausted, and there's nothing to be done about that."

"The Devil there isn't! You're a count, aren't you?—a grandee! Your father and brothers were heroes, weren't they? Oh, Sweet Virgin! I'll take care of it myself, don't worry, just don't go proposing any more Confecciones En Ante to me, it's all been costing Banco Blás too damned much money, not that I mind, if that's the way you want to amuse yourself instead of yachts and race horses even the nags win sometimes it's all right, but it can get too expensive, forget it, forget it, how's my Dorada, how're my grandchildren, I'll ring you back."

By observing his morning ritual—the inventory of the furnishings in his study, the methodically sipped and masticated breakfast, the scanning of his *ABC*—Ignacio Prades had managed to poultice the stings out of this conversation. There were positive elements to ponder. Baltazar had said (or had he?) that someday everything would be delivered into his son-in-law's hands. And he had stated that he wanted to consult with him at eleven o'clock. What the old fellow had in mind, Ignacio Prades could not fathom: something to do with Jaime Orbaneja's construction firm and Financiera Sacedón, probably one more in Baltazar's array of convoluted machinations, this was *not* the time for adventure, he certainly intended (and in most forceful terms) to impress upon Baltazar the unfavorable investment climate . . . Still, an advance, a definite advance, he was going to be consulted on a matter of policy, and taken into the old fellow's confidence, as he had not been in three years.

He shivered, suddenly. Any moment: the bell, the summons, the reality . . .

He stood up, walking to the Sheraton desk, gazing with deep, melancholic eyes at the photograph of his wife—and now it was Dorada, not business, not Baltazar, who possessed him. How—in what manner—had he offended her? How had he deserved the quotidian torment that had evolved out of his foolish, foolish surrender to passion?

He had met her in July of 1961, during the San Juan ball at the Royal Club of the Iron Gate. He was then thirty-eight years old, and sinecured to the Ministry of Finance. She was twenty-one. Ignacio had suffered previously from few romantic inclinations. But he was shaken by the beauty of this girl, the elder of the Blás daughters, reared quietly in the backwaters of a provincial capital, educated in France and Switzerland, and then launched like a bombshell into the society of Madrid. She wore a white satin gown, stitched with seed pearls. Her naked shoulders were Junoesque. Her bosom was regal. Her hair was a waterfall of platinum and gold.

They were seated at the same table. He asked her to dance. It was some barbarous rhythm from Cuba or Brazil, he could not remember, he did not know it. But his heart—the physical organ—throbbed under its influence. His pulse raced. And it was an unknown emotion, a sort of ague, that agitated the Count of Obregón's dessicated soul when in his stiff arms he felt the lissomeness of her body. He was exhausted by that one dance and went home.

He visited his mother next day—a rare thing for him to do—saying to her, "I met a girl last night. We talked about the *General Theory of Employment, Interest, and Money*. She's . . . very attractive. She is Baltazar Blás's daughter." And his mother had surprised him, replying in a level and matter-of-fact way, "It's time you thought of marriage. Remember, your great-great-great-grandfather, before he became the first Marqués de la Romana, happened to be able to afford two thousand Prussian mercenaries when his King needed them."

Yes, and Baltazar Blás happened to have had a fleet filled with munitions when Franco was so badly in need. But Ignacio persisted, skirting as close to the critical issue of his soul as ever he had and ever he would again. He said, "There . . . may be a question of her legitimacy. She and her sister are the issue of a second marriage—one of those Danish families brought to Málaga by the wine trade. Blás was married pre-

viously. That's known." He hesitated. "No one knows what happened
to his first wife." To which his mother had replied, gazing evenly into
his eyes, "I would not credit rumor, if I were you. And what is legitimacy,
Nacho? The sanction of time. And of money."

Staring still at the photograph, he sat at his desk; and fiddled with
the silver paper cutter in an abstracted way; and then shook his head,
shook sad unwelcome thoughts out of his head, dangerous and mortifying
thoughts; and stood up again, returning to the Queen Anne dropleaf
table; and plucked the first envelope out of the rack. It bore his mother's
crest. He was about to slice it open when Rosa, the maid, entered.
Baltazar was again on the line.

"That you, Nacho? I'm calling from Señor Costa's office. Yes, it
was all an error, you tell Caro to get another application down here
rightawayquick, this morning, and to ask to see Señor Costa personally.
Yes, and from now on, tell him to come directly to Señor Costa, yes,
Señor Costa will be delighted to receive him, I've told Señor Costa I'm
expecting him and his wife to visit the Mrs. and me this summer in
Marbella, and he promises to do so. How's my Dorada, how's my
grandson?"

Anger came to Ignacio's rescue. How ridiculous! Blás had evidently
raced out of the house in Puerta de Hierro, probably not bothering to
finish his breakfast. His voice was stuffed with satisfaction. Why? Because he had got "the job done." Yes—by paying the price of committing
himself to host Costa and his to-be-counted-upon grossly middle-class
wife, a social debasement that the Count of Obregón, having debased
himself enough already, would not and could not bring himself to emu-
late. Yes, there was something about being a noble, something no one
else had, something even a Baltazar Blás could not buy, nor his daughter,
no matter how viciously she tried, strip away.

He ripped the envelope open. The note was written in Nati's large
and nearly illiterate scrawl. He had not uncoded the spelling and syntax
of her first phrase when the four, syncopated drills of a bell in the kitchen
froze his eyeballs, catatonically freezing his muscles, so that even the
tendons of the hand holding the letter turned rigid, and his fingers
crinkled the sheet of paper into the palm, contracting in a spasm to crush
it.

Dorada. It was nine-thirty. Ordinarily, she would be ringing for
her breakfast at noon or later, but this was one of her golf mornings,
and sacred to her. He summoned her image as though they still shared
the same bed, and he were watching her. Eyelids clamped shut, she

would be arching her pelvis upward, bending her spine into a bow and abandoning herself to the pleasure of muscular distension, hips wriggling in estuous languor, breasts blossoming out of the lace-trimmed, coral-colored nightgown like magnolia blooms, nipples roused, plum-red, and erect, her head swiveling sensually on its base, stretching first one lateral rope of neck muscles and then the other, arms simultaneously seeking the air above and behind her, twining, wrists rotating, fingers unfurling from pink and dimpled palms. And then she would relax back on the mattress, and one cheek would nestle into the cushion of a shoulder, and she would yawn into the scented, amygdalate armpit, and partly close her jaw, and tongue her lips exquisitely, search and locate some nectar known only to herself, withdraw, and smile with nacreous delight; and only then would her golden lashes flutter open to reveal whites like rock quartz and pupils whose roral iridescence glinted citrine, emerald, and ruby darts, each a sliver in his imagination, slicing through his breast and lancing his heart.

He trembled. Since Tokyo, three years of torture. He feared her. He desired her. He hated her.

F O U R

Dorada Blás

She did not hate him; merely despised, which was sufficient, and more than he was worth wasting even that emotional energy on. She did feel for him physical abhorrence: the large black mole on his fish-pale belly, the sparse lank hideousness of the pubic nest from which dangled his pale and blue-veined phallus. The thought of it—the thought of the sight of him naked—wrenched the corners of her mouth back and caused her jaw to lock in a shudder. Her flesh crept as her bare instep might upon squashing a toad. Last night, flushed with the self-esteem that filled him after every lecture he pronounced, he had come into her bedroom. She had been about to turn off the light. He was in his dressing gown. She surveyed him with one, hostile, up-and-down sweep of her eyes. "What do you want?" she demanded curtly, knowing, contemptuous, noticing in his hands already that telltale trembling, noticing the anxiety that

was already chasing out the self-satisfaction that had precipitated him
into daring an approach. "It's . . . been weeks," he croaked. "And what
about it?" she had replied. "I . . . I want you." "Go want somebody
else, I'm going to sleep." "I . . . I must have you." "Oh, don't be a bore,
Nacho! You know it's no good." "But it's my right!" "Go make love to
your right, then." "But I need you, I must have you!" "Oh, God in
Heaven! Can't it wait for tomorrow?" "No! No! At once!" He had stepped
forward then, yanking the loop out of the fringed silk cord of his gown.
"Oh, you . . ." she nearly spluttered with rage. "All right, but be quick!"

She had tortured him. She enjoyed torturing Ignacio very much,
her spleen the only pleasure she could squeeze out of the horror of inter-
course with him. Play fair, her father had adjured her. Fair? She yanked
down the covers, rolled over on her back, yanked up her nightdress,
and flopped her knees wide, yelling at him, "Come on, then! Come on!
Stick it in and get done!" He was naked in a flash, skinny, corpse-pale:
she had almost gagged looking at him. She snapped off the lamp. She
permitted him (he was clumsy getting on the bed) to straddle and mount
her, that only. She did not permit him to kiss her anywhere, not even
her cheek, nor to touch her breasts (she crossed her arms over them,
fisting her hands), nor fondle her body in any way at all. She permitted
him only what precisely he could claim as his right, the entrance of
his organ. She was, of course, unprepared and unreceptive. He panted,
prodding her, doubling his thing against her. "Oh, sweet God you're
incompetent! You're hurting me, can't you tell? Don't push so *hard!* Wait
a moment! Give me a chance to relax! Are you really going to insist?
You're not even in the right place! Why can't you do it yourself? Can't
you find some dirty little gypsy girl who'd be glad to drop her pants
for you? Does it have to be me? All right. You're coming in, now. DON'T
PUSH I TOLD YOU! I don't want you. You make me feel like throwing
up, just the thought of it, like a worm in my body. Don't you
disgust yourself—having to rape your wife? Do you confess it? Is that
why you don't go to Communion, you don't dare confess it?" Taunting
him, taunting him, she achieved her objective: his collapse; his drastic,
crushing detumescence. His body, propped up on palms and knees,
swayed; as if to collapse on top of her. Oh no! "Stiffen those elbows!
Don't you *dare* touch me with your body, it's loathsome, I can't stand
the touch of your skin, like maggots, like maggots crawling all over me!"
She had him weeping above her; she felt the scald of one tear drop
on her left nipple. She laughed. The tear sparked her into concupiscence.
She envisioned Muñoz González thrusting through the pouch of her

pudendum and up deep into her womb. "You poor, miserable creature," she now muttered thickly at her husband, "come on, come on. You've insisted. Get it over with. Get done. Move!" And she gave a heave of her pelvis, an angry, impatient heave. And at this, the slightest token of encouragement, he blossomed inside her. He had no dignity at all, not the tatters of pride. He began to thrust eagerly, panting, panting out puling stale little love words, pale, plaintive, puling little love entreaties. He wanted love! He wanted what no hagfish of a man could ask of any woman. She lashed him with insults. She kept up estus, but the only contact she allowed was the necessary minimum conjunction. Because the image of Muñoz González had been dissolved by her husband's babbling, and only by an abstraction of the act was it bearable. And in six-eight-ten strokes, he ejaculated, his buttocks quivering, his thighs in spasm and causing the bed to quiver; and she laughed at him again, laughed hard between almost overpowering sobs of fury and outrage, crying, "Now get off, get off! And fetch a towel from the bathroom, and don't dribble all over the sheets and covers and carpet while you're about it, are you satisfied now, did you enjoy it, am I free for the next month?" And he had padded—crawled, if that was possible upright and on two feet—to the bathroom, and come crawl-padding back and proffering the towel, which she reached for with one hand after snapping the lamp back on with another, his eyes dumb-dog-pleading, dumb-dog-pleading in every line and feature of his long pedant's face. She tore the towel out of his hands, vigorously wiping at her brush, and then sitting up on the towel to permit his miserable, disgusting, viscous fluid to drain. She nearly wept then, but she barricaded back her tears. He drooped like a mortician at the foot of her bed, gazing on her, so utterly mournfully hangdog that she felt like rising up and slapping him across the mouth. "Don't look at me," she spit between clamped lips. "I won't have you looking at my body, it's mine, not yours, as if you'd eat it raw!" She chucked the towel at him, snapping off the light. She would douche herself later. "Good night!" she said—and heard him pad out.

An hour later, washed, she was still unable to sleep. Even during that first dance, she had been repelled by his flesh. She had not then understood why. He was not unhandsome. She had admired the intellectuality of his forehead, and had not minded its pallor, nor the swollen blue vein that forked like the Greek letter λ down to the eyebrows. His eyes were dark and liquid, really beautiful eyes. There was a priestliness about the mouth, but she had taken it for an austerity of nature consequent on intellectual dedication, and it rather attracted her. She had by now wearied of the run of vapid, well-fed, and lecherous escorts— the youths of her age. There was no incipient paunch on Ignacio Prades. The double-breasted tuxedo he was wearing, if old and out of fashion, hung with high-lapeled distinction off his spare frame. And the formality with which he asked her to dance; the circumspectness in the way he held her; even his opening conversational gambit ("Are you by any chance acquainted with the works of Lord Keynes?"), spurred by his evident nervousness, his unfamiliarity with the bossa nova and with (she suspected at once) women; and his surprise at her adroit reply (she had learned in France the art of extemporizing on anything at all without knowing pins about it): had intrigued and amused her. But she had not liked the touch of his skin.

She was, however, pleased to have been singled out by the Count of Obregón. At twenty-one, Dorada had been three years afloat in the froth of society. Gold diggers apart, offers of marriage had not been plentiful, and her father had said to her, "Wait for an honest to God count— that at least. And don't think of settling for less." Well, here was one; and his mother was the famous Marquesa, with a hulk of a palace on Calle Don Pedro. Dorada weighed values. She was flattered by the siege Ignacio Prades laid about her during the following weeks. He was correct. If she avoided physical contact with him, he did not press her. He took her to the theater. They attended together openings at art galleries. She was being introduced, moreover, into temples previously closed to the daughters of Baltazar Blás. Ignacio squired her to the Christmas dinner and dance at the Soto, the mense of the Albuquerques. He took her to an intimate Flamenco for forty held at Liria, the Alba palace, with Goyas and Zurbaráns tilting from almost every wall, as well as choice Riberas, Titians, and Velázquezes. That spring, Ignacio accompanied her to the fair at Seville, which she had attended before, but where she had never sipped cocktails at Las Dueñas (another Alba palace), nor danced at Los Pilatos, belonging to the Medinacelis. That night, he proposed to her.

It was actually four o'clock in the morning, in the patio of the Alfonso XIII Hotel, where she was nearly gagging anyhow from the cloying scent of tuberose. Dorada qualified her reply. As soon as Ignacio left her, she went to the night concierge. He was an Andalusian, lethargic by nature, and an old man besides. But Blás money spoke. In twenty minutes, she was changed, her seven pieces of luggage had been packed by a hastily aroused maid, and a car and chauffeur were waiting for her at the hotel entrance. She reached Madrid at three o'clock the next afternoon, having herself driven directly to the bank. She was at once recognized by the pageboys. A crew of them ushered her up to the private offices on the sixth floor. Doors opened magically. Within seconds, she was facing her father.

He sat in the crotch of his desk, which was shaped like a huge boomerang and fashioned out of blonded wood imported from Norway. He peered at her a moment. Then he said, "Well, you've had quite a drive."

"You knew?"

"Of course. Sit down, you must be tired."

An armchair, also of blonded Norwegian wood, was whisked up behind her by a flunky who was then dismissed with a nod of Baltazar Blás's large, benevolently featured but pugnaciously boned head. "Now tell me all about it," he said.

"You know I've been going out with Ignacio Prades y Caro."

Her father rolled his lips into a smile. With the nail of an index finger, he pried up and then flapped back the leather cover of a loose-leaf notebook that rested in front of him. He read from it.

"Eve of the Feast of San Juan, 1961. La Señorita Dorada was escorted tonight to the Ball at Real Club de Puerta de Hierro by Señor Don Julio Caro y Prades, a gentleman of no means but of noble antecedence. Seated at the table were . . ."

"Oh, stop it!" she interrupted. "Every single move!"

He gazed at her with his benign smile and lidded eyes. "When you're married," he said gently, "there'll be no further need. Until then, you and your sister are my responsibility—one that has to be exercised by remote controls since you both move in circles to which your father is not admitted."

Which was true, the curiousness of this striking her; and not for the first time. Her father had only begun dining at Jockey restaurant a few years before.

"And so you know about last night?"

"Not everything." He flicked the notebook shut. "Obregón proposed to you?"

"Yes."

Now he bounded to his feet. He whooped. He came bandy-leg bounding around his desk, and with his still powerful fisherman's arms, lifted his daughter right out of the chair, bussing her on both cheeks. Then back he went bounding to his desk, where he yanked open a drawer and snatched from its interior a long, leather jeweler's box. He stuffed it into her hands. "Open it!" he cried. "Go on, open it!" She did. Diamonds and emeralds sparkled up at her. "It belonged to María Luisa, the Queen! Oh, you've done it!" he said. "I knew you would! Oh, I felt sure you would! I've got a file on him—every detail of his life and character. No women in his history, Dorada! You're the first. It was inevitable, a man like that, when he falls he falls hard, and for good! And you've done it! You've made him fall!" He rushed to her again, grasping both her hands in his, kissing her hands. "Oh, Dorada, my Dorada, I'll give you a wedding they'll be talking about ten years from now! A count! My daughter a countess, *my* daughter, Baltazar Blás's daughter: and my grandsons peers of the realm! And just as soon as his mother dies, Dorada, it can't be too far off, you'll be the Marchioness of the Pilgrim, *the* Marquesa, the first in the land, and better than some duchesses! Why, you'll . . ."

"I didn't say yes," she cut in.

Her father's jaws closed slowly on a half-formed word. He stared at her. Then he walked back round his desk and sat down.

"He's a marica? Lot of 'em are that way, there's nothing on his record, or if there is and it hasn't been reported to me I'll . . ."

"No," she interrupted again. "It's not that."

"Well, what is it!"

"He's a rollo sometimes, for one thing," she said.

"Christ, girl, what man isn't—most of the time? *I'm* a bore when I get going on business. *You're* a regular pianola when you talk about clothes! What's that got to do with getting married? Marriage is the biggest rollo there is, but most people learn to put up with it, they . . ."

"Papá, last night when he kissed me . . ." She gestured in a perplexed fashion. "Maybe it's a question of pores, I don't know, I've heard of skins that are allergic to each other, Mireille, my roommate at Lyons, shuddered at the sight of freckles . . . Can a person live with that, Papá?"

She ended openly perplexed, her wide and nearly pulpy lips pursed in a sort of smile. Her father stared at her, saying nothing. When he did speak, it was with unusual care. "I fought my way up from the mud. It was not easy."

"I know that!"

"Wait now, listen to me, there's a lot you don't know, can't realize. It doesn't happen here more than once or twice in every generation, but I did it, I'm a power in Spain, I am able to raise up or throw down practically anyone—duke, minister, or banker—but there are some things no matter his wealth or power that Baltazar Blás can't do, he can't bull his way into membership in the Puerta de Hierro, he'll never be invited home to the decaying old palace of a grandee whose worthless financial skin he has maybe just saved."

"All right, that's your problem, I . . ."

"I asked you to wait a minute! No door in finance, not one in the Government, is closed to Baltazar Blás, but the hearth of Spain, the real Spain, that's shut from me forever, not if I live to be a hundred am I going to be invited to take my place there. And by God, Dorada, I *belong* there! Between the first baron of Spain and Baltazar Blás there's one difference, and one only: that baron had a son."

"And you don't. And because of that you expect me to sacrifice my happiness . . ."

"There's you and your sister, Dorada," he cut in. "Paz isn't like you, and she's not like me. She won't succeed on her own. Someone has to break the walls down for her, and that's you. You'll do it, because you're like me." He leaned forward over the desk, this peasant, this power, with his short torso and barrel chest and the monumental brow. "Listen, corazón de mi alma. I've had to do things in my life I did not much like doing, but if I hadn't done them, there'd be no Armas Y Explosivos, no Banco Blás, no house in Ciudad Puerta de Hierro, and not even you: not the way you would wish."

She said nothing. He stared at her out from under that bulging forehead. Easily could she have been his granddaughter.

"Is your car still waiting on the street?"

"Yes."

"Good." He pressed a button on his intercom. "Telephone Codina Moncó. Reschedule the lunch for next week." He canceled a factory inspection, two board meetings, and an interview with the current Minister of Public Works. He ordered his Commando to be got ready at Barajas Airport. "Let's go!" he said, jumping to his feet.

They arrived at Las Palmas that night. In the morning, they drove to a small fishing village across the island. It was a village of hovels—whitewashed, picturesque, the chimneys suggesting minarets and the cistern rooftops Palestine, but hovels nonetheless. There was no running water. There were open sewers. He showed Dorada the house in which he had been born. It was small and square, with a beehive-shaped abutment containing the oven. A woman sat on the stoop, staring dully at the distance, chewing something, perhaps tobacco. Several children were playing barefoot in the yard. Chicken dung squirted beneath their feet. One four-year-old girl, clothed in a colorless smock and nothing else, squatted suddenly, voided her bowels, and then ran off to play some more. "Those are your first cousins," he told her from within the leather-upholstered back of the hired Mercedes, "once—just barely—removed." On the return to Las Palmas, he said, "Dorada—love of my heart—listen to me, it's not so awful, the physical side doesn't last long, it's only minutes out of a whole lifetime, and what's that against becoming a countess, the Marquesa del Peregrino, a great of Spain?" He ordered the car into a middle-class section of Las Palmas. They parked next to a cafeteria. Dorada gathered her handbag to step out. He grabbed her by an upper arm, yanking her roughly down beside him. "Stay put!" he commanded. "Look through the window, into the cafetería. Do you see the cash register? See the woman tending it?" The sun slanted from behind them. "That's your half-sister," Baltazar said. "Her mother died last year. Oh no, I didn't sink her off the African shore, people are fools! Her father owned three smacks, and I needed them. She was his eldest daughter—and as fat and ugly as the girl you see there, our daughter. But I was faithful to her, even when she didn't give me a boy child, your mother hasn't either, I've had to live with that, and even when the child she did give me was that woman you're looking at now, who was born just as stupid and as sullen as she looks. But I put up with that too. All I asked of that girl's mother was that she grow with me. She wouldn't. When I made my first million pesetas, all she wanted to do was eat through them. When I made my tenth million, that was still all she wanted; and her daughter was just like her. It was only then, Dorada, that I showed her the proof that I'd never been baptized. The certificate I'd shown the priest was forged; but I'd never have opened my mouth about it—I'd lived with that woman twelve years, Dorada!—if she'd kept up her part of the bargain, and grown with me. She wasn't unhappy when the marriage was declared void. I gave her the cafetería, where she could eat to her heart's content. She married again, there's a trust fund for her daughter: they have no complaints."

He treated her to a lunch of stuffed avocado pear, grilled cigalas, baked sama, and that delicacy of the Canaries, small, round "wrinkled" potatoes in their brine-coated skins, squashed into the tongue-scalding peppers of a green "mojo" sauce. Dorada ate little. Her father did not eat at all. On the air ride back to Madrid that afternoon, he said to her, "You'll go through with it, Dorada. You will tell him yes, and tonight —cable him if he hasn't returned from Seville. And you'll play fair, hear?

There are a lot of stories about Baltazar Blás, some of them true, and many of them lies. Before Alburúa cleaned it out, the bureaucracy was corrupt. I used that. Sure I used that! I paid off hundreds of officials before the crackdown. That's how we smuggled in penicillin. That's how we avoided tariffs and sank our competiton. It was dangerous. I set up a jungle of corporate vehicles. Straw men headed them. Some of them went to jail. But not one of them talked, Dorada. No one pointed a finger at me—in court, anyhow. And you know why? Because *they* knew I play fair, I take care of my own. You may have to buy souls to get what you want, Dorada, but never sell your own, hear me? The morning they were let out, every last one of them was met by a messenger who handed them a savings account booklet, and that booklet had as much as sixty million pesetas entered into it, five per cent of all the profits the business made before it was dissolved. I've always played fair with my people, Dorada—and I'll play fair with the future Marqués del Peregrino, you'll see, neither of you will lack for anything."

Back at the house, in the library, he said, "But you, my dearest daughter, you have to promise me one thing. It's my fondest wish that you marry into the nobility. It has to be your fondest wish too. And if it is your wish, then you have to promise me—I mean get down now on your knees and swear by the Lord Jesus and all His Saints—that you will play fair with him, and never cheat on him, and never deny him his rights, it's a small price, Dorada, he's nearly forty, just let it last long enough for you to have children. But be my daughter, be a Blás, or say no, and forget him."

She had never admired her father so much as when he finished. He knew his commodities. She sent the cable. And during the first eighteen months of her marriage, she had been dutiful, enduring her husband's uxoriousness. She had even felt moments of tenderness, as when she first conceived, and told Ignacio, and saw tears well out of his dark eyes. She delighted in all the privileges of her new position. The subsequent wedlock of Paz to the Conde de la Madrugada filled her with satisfaction, because it might not have happened without her sacrifice. But then the charms, the compensations, began to pall. And rather than abate, Ignacio's intoxication with her body increased.

Dorada Blás had entered matrimony at least respecting her husband; his title foremost, consolidating her personal security; his seventeen years of seniority, placing him in a quasi avuncular position relative to herself, and permitting her, in the beginning, to transfer to him some of the feelings she had for her father; and his intellectual pretensions, suggesting to her an enlightened and demophilic student prince, a sort of Otto of Habsburg.

It was this last mantle of respect that frayed first. Dorada was intelligent, as Ignacio had observed. It was a mistake for him to have married an intelligent woman. She had never managed to bind his opinions with quite the reverence in which he himself bound them. Then they began to bore her. She picked up the meanings of his portentous vocabulary, idling through two of his source books; and from their heavily underscored passages coming to recognize, and anticipate, and grit her pearly teeth against, favorite sententions ("Just wages are those sufficient for labor to buy back the product . . .") that released the flow of other and more sententions ("The true measure of income resides in the quality with which it is expended . . ."), all borrowed. An original thought, Ignacio did not possess. She didn't possess many herself, but then she never claimed to. And she discovered before long that what she had taken as Ignacio's humanism was fussbudgeting in the abstract, which would not have bothered her much had he been candid about it, because she herself did not care for many individual human beings apart from Dorada Blás, and not even Dorada Blás excessively. His excessive love for her (and their children) irritated Dorada because she suspected that motivating Ignacio was a strong pulse of narcissism: he loved her in the mirror of self-esteem. His wife, being anyhow according to the Church united with him in flesh and spirit, and become part of him, had to be loved, just as the two products of their union, their flesh and blood, his flesh and blood, also had to be loved. For Dorada to be less than wholly worthy of his affections would be to question the worthiness of their donor. That was unthinkable.

Dorada might have learned to live with his failings had the respect she accorded Ignacio's seniority not begun to wear also. Every marriage, the most ideal, the most romantic, must survive the shock of cohabitation: the sight of a constipated husband groaning on the toilet, or his wife plugging into herself the tubes of intimate hygiene. Familiarity breeds at least perspective, and love, an unbalanced molecular state at best, can support little of that. In an avuncular relationship, perspective can be catastrophic, like an Avedon blow-up of the warts on Adlai Stevenson's face. Suffice here that the libido of Ignacio Prades, agent of his considerable ego; his lust, expression of a great and increasing psychological need; sapped, shook, and eventually tumbled Dorada's neodaughterly respect. She felt not merely her gender's ordained humiliation; she felt particu-

larly, individually, violated. The more Ignacio Prades rutted between
Dorada Blás's blissful thighs, the more she conceived within her, without
knowing why, and without any of the illicit pleasure, the guilt of incest.

This sense of physical sacrilege, and Dorada's dwindling intellectual
respect for her husband, worked one upon the other, so that by the time
she brought forth their son, she was ready to call it quits. (Her marriage,
not the child.) She now believed that her early sensual allergy to Ignacio's
skin had been an omen of her present reaction to his being. For nearly
two years, she had tried to conceal this from him. She played fair. She
submitted. Fortunately, in her husband's nature lingered something of
the chaste asceticism, or fastidiousness, of his long bachelorhood. He was
strictly orthodox in sexual technique. He never experimented. He did
demand the oscular rotundities of her bosom, the tugging of whose dam-
son teats incited in him paroxysms as feverish, or nearly as feverish, as
his ejaculations. She found this curious, plucking at her nipples herself
and wondering just what was so fascinating about them to Ignacio. (She
is not, you see, a sensual woman.) She thanked God that he never approached her during daylight hours, when it would have been difficult
to avoid seeing the loathsomeness of the mole-finched flesh that was
making free of hers. At night, after permitting himself one rapt survey
of the body he was about to feast on, he reached for the lamp cord
as fast as she did. But in the dark, as he commenced his pokings, pawings,
and pantings, her lips reared back from her teeth in the fanged grimace
of a car-killed dog; in the dark, she rolled her eyes up under their lids,
and tried to deafen her ears, and insensitize her flesh, and not grow
so very rigid that his burrowing bruised her. She might have gone on
suffering him forever had not Baltazar Blás snapped her tolerance.

Ignacio was due back from Tokyo on an evening flight. Dorada
dreading it, was preparing for his return. It had been six weeks since
the birth of their son. She knew there would be no further putting him
off. Then her father came pounding into the flat.

He pounded right by Rosa, down the hall, around the corner, and
into her dressing room, where she was sitting in silken splendor, long,
pale powder blue peignoir and negligee bouffant with pleats and tucks,
tweezers in hand, grimly, critically studying her eyelashes. She glanced
at him through the mirror as he thudded up behind her stool, thudding
at her, "Anybody about!?"

"See for yourself."

Back to the door he went. Right and left, he peered down the hall.
Then his torso jerked in withdrawal, he shut the door, turned, stared

at her through the mirror, and said, "You know what? You know what I've just found out!"

"Qué?" she plinked at him, leaning forward from the stool, cocking her left eye toward the mirror and the tweezers.

His bulging forehead was scarlet. He was in a grand stutter of rage. "I've just f-found out that husband of yours may not be the M-Marquis-'p-pparent at all! Just now! Just this afternoon, half an hour ago! I've fired my huh-whole fu-hucking staff of investigators! *Imagine! Imagine* leaving that out! *Imagine* IT!"

"You'll have a stroke," she said, plucking out an imperfectly curling lash, which she then blew from the steel pods of the tweezers, so that it fluttered away like a filament off the sun. "What are you talking about?"

Her father stooped until the furnace of his breath fell on the base of her skull. He pounded into her tympanums, "Nacho may be illegitimate! There was a story going round th-thirty/forty years ago he may not b-be the Marquesa's son. He may be her m-*maid*'s son, *her/maid's/ son!*"

Now did Dorada swivel about from her concentration on the mirror. Father and daughter stared at each other, the peasant, the fisherman, and the golden odalisque.

"What do you mean by that!" she said sharply.

"What I'm telling you!" He wheezed. His stubby arms, like spanners, rose and fell from his sides. "The story goes he knocked up that old witch of a maid the Marquesa still has hanging about, God knows why *he* musta had some taste in women, Nacho's supposed to be their son, the maid's brat, not the Marquesa's son, Christ, Christ God, my grandson son of a bastard and grandson of a *maid!*"

Dorada rocked back on her stool with laughter. She laughed, and laughed, and laughed. Her father's astonishment, his bewilderment, grew as she laughed, and as it grew, she laughed the more, until she began to edge into hysteria.

"Stop that!" he said sharply. "What's so godam funny?"

But she still hiccuped laughter. "You mean . . . these two years, everything—what I've gone through—may not count?"

"You're damn well right I mean it!"

Dorada nearly gave vent again to the geyser of comic, fierce exhilaration.

"*How* . . . did the Blás spy network miss out on this!"

His reply was testy. "I can tell you to the last duro what anybody of any account is worth. I can tell you who slept with whom, if it's important. But I didn't move anywhere near these circles until Nacho got me into Puerta de Hierro. By God, if something happens, if he doesn't keep the *only* godam thing he brought to this marriage besides his pecker and balls, I'll . . . I'lllll . . ."

"Get yourself another right-hand man, another heir to the Blás empire?"

Her father groaned. He stared at her as though he could not bear the sight of her face. "Nacho," he said, "couldn't make money out of the only waterhole in the Sahara Desert. He'd bury it under dunes and dunes of paper. He's cost me maybe thirty, forty, sixty per cent of what I'm worth with that sonofabitching foundation, and he keeps bleeding the rest of it . . . Jesus, Dorada, what a godam ass you picked to marry!"

And so her father, as well as she, saw through him. Dorada had wondered about that. She wondered now how many other people saw through Ignacio, but dissembled in deference to his rank, actual and prospective, and the might of the financial fortress supporting it. She would dissemble no longer. To be mounted by Ignacio Prades, perhaps never the Marqués del Peregrino, perhaps not his mother's son; to allow herself to be possessed by such a man; was humiliation indeed.

"Una huelga en amor," as they say, "es de piernas cruzadas." She greeted him at the airport as though nothing had happened. But that night she called her strike and crossed her legs. He was astonished. Let him be! She moved him into his dressing room. Thenceforth she permitted him use of her once a month, and no more. In the act itself she began by denying him her mouth, and then the breasts he seemed to crave so desperately, granting him finally no greater sensual satisfaction than what his dull corona, bungling into her orifice, could derive. And when this staged deprivation made him frantic, so that he wept, so that he begged for more frequent access even into her inert chamber, and then begged-pleaded with her to let him fondle just one breast, for just a moment, please, Dorada, why not? what's happened? why won't you let me? I don't understand! I want you and need you!—she had him stripped completely, she began to understand him herself, something must have happened during his childhood, a remark in the kitchen, an incautious flippancy overheard. At her paps, in her flesh, he sought reassurance. Her adamance sent him into frenzies of paper activity. He suffered, she now knew. But she least of all could pity his nakedness of spirit. She was Dorada Blás, Baltazar Blás's daughter, and her grasp on reality was unshakable.

Dorada had reached her mid-twenties by the fourth year of their marriage. Biologically, she was in sexual ascendance. The horror and frustration of her physical encounters with Ignacio left her nerves sizzling. If she was frigid with him; if with him coitus was a nightmare; she suspected it need not be so with a man whom at least in some way she could respect. After Ignacio slurped out of her, she imagined sometimes what it might be like with someone else, her fancy flipping male acquaintances like index cards. She hungered for a fit partner. And in this emotional state she met the man with whom, about an hour and a half from now, on this thirty-first of May, she meant to consummate a protracted dalliance.

It had begun on a sultry afternoon September past, at the Club de Campo, Madrid's other (and hoi polloi) country club. She was lazing on her back in a bathing suit, eyelids half shuttered, daydreaming about Billy Smith-Burton, her husband's virilely lank brother-in-law, who dominated her sexual fantasies. Her legs were spread out before her, parted slightly, exposing the poll they flanked to the pulsing warmth of the sun. His shadow had fallen across her toes.

Startled, she had looked up. He was the Santo Dominican, a recent guest-member. She had noticed him once or twice. People spoke of him as a gangster, she quite believed it, he looked it, the prototype of a thug-smooth South American underworld character, with mahogany skin, Indian-black eyes, and straight, Indian-black hair. He was nearing forty, she guessed—from lines etched like fossilized spines into the corners of his slanting, drooping eyes, as if a strain of oriental blood coursed also in him, and from the gouges spurring perpendicularly downward from his cheeks. He was partially backlit by the sun. He let gleam, let grow, let ripen, a smile. It glistened. It flashed like a row of white pebbles in a pool. One shoulder hunched slightly; a thigh twitched, as from the tickle of a fly. He was built like a fully matured pugilist, with strong, tight pectoral muscles, corded biceps, boll-like shoulders, and a washboard belly. He was wearing indecently abbreviated satiny white trunks, little more than support for his genitals.

On the instant of raising her eyes to him, she had thought about his potential in bed. Why not? She had "played fair" miserable years; even now, although in rationed manner, she submitted. She had given her father what he wanted: a grandson who would bear the Blás name as his second surname, but who would be a noble, a grandee of Spain—if nothing went wrong. She had completed her bargain, her side of it. And what was so terrible about taking a lover? Dorada inventoried the histories of several countesses and marchionesses and duchesses she had come to know.

There were affairs of such longstanding that they had become almost licit, husband, wife, and lover companionably driving together to the same parties. Even the Marquesa, her mother-in-law, was rumored to have been the mistress of Emilio Cortijos—and he a priest! Would Ignacio divorce her if she were prompted by these examples? Never. There is no legal divorce in Spain. And he was enslaved by his need of her. No: if he found out, Ignacio would lump it.

Waiting for her breakfast, she dwelled on the physique of Muñoz González—just as his Indian smokeholes on that first afternoon had dwelled curling over every exposed or adumbrated intimacy of her body. There was a moment when she had wished she wasn't wearing a bikini, vaunting as it did the gravidity of her breasts, pronouncing with its tight high hitch at the crotch the ample mound of her mons veneris. To that lode his eyes had traveled, after having examined the rest of her with almost palpable pleasure, resting immeasurably long moments there, until she blushed, closing her legs; and only after that finally raising his eyes, and smiling again his sapient gangsterish killer's South American Indian-blooded smile, smokeholes incandescent now, now taking a pantherpace closer to her, bowing a mockery of a bow, and presenting himself. What a chulo he was! Is there anything more chulo than Caribbeans? Diego Muñoz González, a common, vulgar name, befitting an ex-extortioner and ex-gunman, or whatever he had been. *What* a chulo!—a gold Rolex watch with a 24-karat gold strap, a gold-banded bangle of elephant's whiskers, and half buried by the stiff black bristles sprouting from the back of the fourth finger of his left hand, an embossed gold ring into whose bloodstone surface an improbable crest had been chiseled. And to him, the chulo, she had lofted the tiger lily of her right hand, wilting from her honey-colored wrist, and permitted those poisonously pink Caribbean lips to flutter there, feeling the prickle of his cropped mustache, and smiling back at him with a brazenness matching his own.

Meeting followed meeting. She conceived that passion for the game of golf that so astonished her husband. All through the autumn and winter, and all through even this chill and rainy early spring, she had risen regularly at nine-thirty every second morning of the week, and gone for her lessons, often lunching at the Club de Campo and not returning to her flat until late in the afternoon. Muñoz González had taken his time with her, and she with him. Putting off the sexual combat had been pleasurable. He was an easy conversationalist, and though he pronounced his Cs and Zs as if they were Ss, there was none of the nasal New World whine to mar the mellow chords of his baritone.

His French was impeccable. She enjoyed chatting with him in French. His family, she learned, originated in Santander. His father had been a sugar planter. He had fenced thoroughbreds and lanced wild boar. He spoke familiarly of "Jai" and "Radzi" and "Honeychild." She had been warned by her father that the business of charlatans is their professional plausibility, but she did not care whether what he told her was true. About herself, her background, her family, she realized he was learning much. And she intuited after a while that his primary interest in her was business. This upset her not in the least. She admired his single-minded pursuit of whatever goals he might have. He owned real estate in Ibiza. She suspected there was more to it than dotting dunes with cottages, because he questioned her about the AESA arms and munitions monopoly. Dorada had no compunctions about providing him with an introduction: her father could take care of himself. Meanwhile she enjoyed his indolent courtship. There was no question about their ultimate bedding of each other. But he was a sybarite. He delectated in every nuance of conquest, and the progression from one stage to the next: the distance they kept on the links during the early autumn months, the first linking of hands on a dark November day, his absence during the months of December and January, unexplained, unannounced, and his reappearance in February. She had greeted him coldly. He had smiled; and they had begun again, the accidental touch as he handed her a putter, the slow furring of her bare ankles and calves with his bare ankles and calves when the warm latter days of May arrived, and they were again in swimsuits, and lunching at the Club de Campo snackbar; and just yesterday, sitting together by the edge of the pool, and no one about, his calm lifting of her right wrist and placing the palm of her right hand flat on the wet latex covering his bunched male members, and his languid, insolent gaze, and his chulo's, insolent smile as she permitted her hand to tighten on the barrel, which was spongy at first contact, and then swelled hardening as she squeezed it. "Tomorrow morning?" he inquired. "Yes, all right, where?" "At my apartment on Calle Almagro__, sixth floor." "Not where you live, it's too dangerous where you live." "I don't live there. I simply rent it." And she had nodded her assent, rising then and moving three long strides away from him; and then halting, tilting her chin back over her shoulder, and calling to him softly, "When, at what hour?" —the long tendons on her neck tautening under the strain, her breath shallow and constricted, watching him hold up both hands, and raise his ten, fur-backed, pink-bellied fingers, and then obscenely, one of them.

Each stage oozing into the next, and leading inevitably to the time just an hour or so off when with savage and obscene lust he would fill his hands with her flesh and plunge his iron into the ocean of her womb. And he may have divined her purpose, which was, she hoped, the obscene match of his: to use him, his panther's body and his stallion's bag of equipment; and then, when she had had her fill of them, drop him. They both—she believed—looked forward to when they would weary of each other, and would seek to anticipate the moment when one would walk out on the other before the other was quite yet willing; a time when he, the experienced seducer, would tumble her on the bed, shred the clothes off her skin, and then perhaps spit contemptuously on her naked belly, laugh, and walk out; or the time when she, the novice courtesan, would sleek his clothes off, and sleek his prong into purple congestion, and then perhaps slap it with all her might, and watch the shock dilate his Indian eyes, and laughing at him, calling him a pig and a thug, walk out. They would jockey for the moment.

But that was possibly months off. This morning would see the first meshing of their flesh. He was ready. She was certainly ready, and had been for three years at least, more than ever since her failure with Sofía's husband. Just thinking about the surrender now set her loins to throbbing. She began winnowing them between the slick of her thighs. Her hands cupped, and then caressed, her breasts. Within moments, she was thrusting her pelvis upward, and recoiling, and thrusting again, and recoiling, surging to a sharp mock climax, and then relapsing fully on the mattress in mock completion, and giggling. She meant to defeat Diego Muñoz González.

Not many moments later, Ignacio Prades walked into his wife's bedroom—to catch lingering in her expression the molten residuals of passion. The abandon of her body on the bed was as though it had been tossed in spun gold and coral. Pain rived him at the sight, pain, the effect of Dorada's beauty on any man, the fundament of beauty, the hollowing of the breast and the filling of that hollow with yearning and regret. In an act of will that locked his every muscle, that squeezed tears into the ducts of his eyes and acid into his nasopharynx, and that quite finished crushing Nati's note, held before him in one pale hand, he summoned up that daytime ghost of dignity that in her presence alone supported him, announcing, "Mother is dead."

"Oh," she said lazily, "how terrible." She yawned. "When did it happen?"

"Some time last night."

"Then I'm finally the Marquesa. Well, that's something."

He looked at her aghast, or so Dorada interpreted his expression. "I'm telling you my mother just died!"

She thumbed the plunger of a bellbutton. "My God Rosa is slow this morning. I heard you. What do you want me to say? You never got along. You complained about her."

"But this . . . this is different." He was appalled by her attitude. The event had dealt him such an unexpectedly severe blow as never before had he received. "She's dead," he said. "My mother is *dead*. Just last night, she dropped dead, on the floor of the ballroom!"

"Well, I'm sorry about that . . . But she was seventy-something, wasn't she? It was bound to happen some time or other, you can't choose when or where."

"My mother is dead," he said to her.

And she thought then, yes, it was fitting: that the old lady should have died overnight, and that Ignacio was now the Marqués. The terms of the barter were completed. Neither he nor she had more to expect of each other. But watching her husband, she realized he was shaken—truly, sincerely. Tears glistened in his dark eyes, and they were undeniably handsome eyes, large and limpid, unlike the coal-smokiness of Muñoz González's eyes. In his severely cut dressing gown, standing there tall and spare and hunched against grief, his long, hound's face at least for these moments free of self, absorbed in something else, he reminded her of the scholar-prince she had once thought she was marrying.

"You *are* the Marqués now?" she asked him.

"What?" He seemed hardly to have heard her.

"There'll be no trouble about that, about the title?"

"The title? No . . . Why? I—I lectured Mother yesterday. Oh, she was being . . . ridiculous again, I had to tell her, times have changed, one . . . one can't keep . . . living in the old way. But I could have . . . could have . . . could have . . ." His voice thinned away.

"Could have what?"

He hesitated, as though unsure what to reply. "Could . . . have sent her . . . more than fifty thousand pesetas, I know she probably needed more. Could have . . . said to her, told her . . ." And he stopped again.

Poor worm! Poor slug!

"Have you called my father?"

"No."

"Your sisters?"

"Not yet."

"Go into your bedroom," she said.

"What?"

"Do as I say. Go into your bedroom. Wait for me there."

"I . . . don't understand."

"Do as I say, Nacho!"

He turned away from her as though wholly benumbed, passing Rosa, the maid, as she entered from the hall bearing a breakfast tray.

"Leave it on the dressing table," Dorada ordered the girl; and Rosa, obeying, went out.

Leaving Dorada alone, to think. Nothing at all had happened to cloud or challenge the title since her father had mentioned the rumor about Nacho's birth. There was no reason to believe that anything would happen. After a decent period of mourning, perhaps a year, they would hold an exclusive supper, and on the invitations would appear his mother's escutcheon. But he would be addressed by her title this very day, a servant was sure to make a point of it; and she, Dorada Blás, on the very morning when she could expect to be addressed as the Marchioness of the Pilgrim, hers by right of bed, intended to betray that bed, and with it her right; meant to cease once and for all "playing fair."

Dorada Blás hardened herself, which was not the most difficult thing for her to do. One last chance she would give Ignacio, doomed, she knew, because she wanted it no other way but doomed. But she would give him that.

She now exhorted the vision of Muñoz González's hard brown body.

She rose, walking through the bathroom that connected with Ignacio's sleeping quarters, locking doors behind her as she went. He sat sunken-shouldered on the edge of his bed. He sat bowed and bleak in the gloom of the shuttered chamber, barely acknowledging her entrance. Dorada let out a snort. She strode to the french doors, wrenching up the persianas. She drenched the room with light, wheeling, turning toward him, standing there a coral flame in the fire of the sun, standing there proudly with heated, heaving, and erected breasts. He recoiled, averting his eyes. She had chosen correctly his moment of psychological stress.

She ripped off her nightgown, flinging it behind her, striding forward and coming to a halt inches in front of him. She stood there wholly naked in a whorl of golden dust, grating at him, "Well, what's the matter with you? So your mother is dead. All right, she's dead. But your wife's alive, and she's feeling sorry for you, you poor worm—you poor, miserable slug! Did last night finish you?"

He flung his chin past one shoulder, behind him and away from her;

as if stung with a new kind of pain. "Take off your clothes!" He did not budge. *"Take off your clothes!"* He struggled ineffectively in his sitting position. She was out of patience at once, tearing at the lapels of his dressing gown, stooping to grasp the legs of his pyjamas and tear them up and off, dashing his trousers behind her, stepping back now to survey his nakedness. What a poor, pitiable sight it was; how feeble in its bush! Yes, he had been shattered by the old lady's death. He had not begun to fill.

She laughed at that. As a would-be man-eater, she had received quite a check from Billy Smith-Burton. Here, however, she was sure of her material. Leaning forward, gathering spittle in her mouth, she let it string out and trickle over his organ. Ignacio jumped.

Dorada laughed, straightening, pouting her pelvis at him. By looking up, his eyes would ascend from the gold-turfed mont along her rose-and-gold pelvis to the gold-tinted cupolas of her bosom. "Come on," she cried, "look me all over, everywhere, wherever you want. Look at my nipples. See? They're out, they're tough." She pinched them between the fold of her middle and index fingers. "Would you like to do that? Wouldn't you like to squeeze them?" But he cowered away, cowered whimpering away, lying back on the bed. Her option then wasn't graceful. There seemed to be no other. She clambered on her knees after him, straddling him, her thatch thicketing his thatch, her hot and swollen nether lips rubbing over his cold flatulence. She crowded his face with her breasts—so that, after moments, he lurched aside, trying to come up for breath. "What's the matter with you? Are you scared of them? Of me? Wouldn't you like to slobber all over them, pig on them, go on, go ahead, do it, what's stopping you, think of your mother's booboos while you're doing it, you've always wanted to be suckled by her, that's what you've wanted and why you never got along with her and part of what's wrong with you and why you're shocked about her now whose death you wanted also."

She was not actually aware of what she was saying. With a convulsion of his torso, he sat up, burying his face in his hands. "Stop . . . it," he begged her. "Please . . . please stop it." But she grabbed him by the hair, forcing his head back, forcing his eyes upward and open. "Stop, nothing! I'm your wife! You've never got over that, have you—selling yourself to a Blás, knowing your mother cared so little about you that *she* didn't object. But I'm your wife, and you need me. You need my body. You've got to push it back up there, push it back up my body where your father should have been. That's the truth, isn't it? You've needed me always, much more than ever I needed you, but it wasn't me at all, was it? And now I've got the last thing I ever wanted from you; now you're taking your mother's title off her dead body, and I'm taking it from your dead body, today!" She laughed once more at him. The sound was ugly. "It is dead," she said more quietly, "or will be. Get up," she commanded, "the bed is too narrow."

She made him lie on the floor, on his back. "Ahora," she inhaled, and she was upon him.

She practiced, and made him perform, every inversion of the natural act that frequent schoolgirl perusals of pornography recalled—and which needn't be detailed. Ignacio was so horrified that he became irredeemably flaccid, as she foresaw he would. His reaction intensified her concupiscence—that he could not keep up; that he was inhibited, a shell even as a sensualist. But he would never be able to claim that she had not offered him the most abject possession of her person. He would never be able to say that. And now she concentrated on getting her own back. It was Spain getting her own back, *his* body being ravished, not hers. Her revulsion rose to lustful extremes. Sucking and tugging and munching at the slimy slithering puniness of him really was like feasting on a corpse, and from this she derived necrophilic pleasure. It was increased by the certainty that the vision of what they were doing, and would never do again, would haunt Ignacio Prades to the end of his days, and eat into him, and corrode him, and finally rust out his self-esteem as a tin can is finally rusted out. She practiced on the blown, bleating sack of that nothingness that was her husband thirty minutes of unabated determination: learning what she would use to astonish Muñoz González, who would be her next victim. Conjuring up the full phallic potency of that gangster, Dorada achieved orgasm at last, auto-erotic though it was the first she had had with a man. At this, at her pelvic shudderings, Ignacio bleated—as if it were he who had induced them. She slapped him across the mouth. She rolled away and off and up from him. She stood up, pelvis streaming, lungs sobbing for breath, standing over him and hurling down at the devastation of his face, "Don't dream it was you! Look at you! I could tie a knot in it! For anything at all to happen, I had to pretend I was being cepillada by someone who can do it. This is the last time, Nacho, the last time ever between us. I've paid up now in full, and you'll never touch as much as my hand again, if I can help it." And she walked away from him.

She locked the bathroom door behind her, leaning back against it several moments, panting, panting ferociously. Then she straightened

herself. She had forgot her nightgown. Never mind. Ignacio would weep
into it. She stepped into the bathtub, whirling open the shower faucets,
raising her pointed chin and the perfect, supple, sinuous modeling of
her throat to the downward rushing of the water. She was hungry. She
had enjoyed every abomination. Nothing would conceal from Ignacio his
emptiness now. She had given him his chance, and he had funked it.
And he would not say boo to her. She would cuckold him with whomever
she liked, and wherever and whenever she pleased. Even discretion
would become less and less necessary. Nobody really cared any more.
She was to meet Diego Muñoz González in, now, less than forty-five
minutes at a sixth-floor apartment of the new Orbaneja building (God,
she hoped the showers worked there!) on Calle Almagro__, the same
floor on which goggle-eyed Juan Luis Sacedón lived. She might even run
into him, her primo político. She surely would eventually run into him.
She did not care. She felt strong. Her flesh tingled with the stings of ten
dozen tiny separate spouts of hot water. She was a Blás, her father's
daughter. She would win in the coming sexual war with the gangster
from Santo Domingo. She would win all her battles, and cower her lovers
as her father cowered his competitors. She smiled now with golden, rubied,
nacreous roral beauty, whirling the taps shut, standing there a moment,
a golden, iridescent shaft, a glistening, dew-drenched dryad who planned
to surprise her gangster lover by whispering into his ear at the moment
of highest sexual euphoria that just an hour or so before she had amused
herself by brutalizing her husband into permanent impotence.

F I V E

Diego Muñoz González

The bedroom is spare, nearly spartan. An iron cot. A framed photograph
of his parents. The wardrobe is large.

Luxury is expressed in the bathroom. Seven meters by five. A built-in
sauna. The tub is actually a small pool, lined in white marble and embedded in umber and blue floor tiles imported from Portugal. Heating
racks are hung with thick, terrycloth towels.

Naked, rubbed dry, almost clinically bathed and shaven (excess hairs pincered out of nostrils and earlobes), Diego Muñoz González stood tall and virile on a rubber mat, thighs flexed, rump tucked in, belly muscles tightened. He concentrated. Then he dropped like a falling oak on the ten stiff springs of his fingers, completing twenty swift push-ups before flipping over on his back for twenty sit-ups, twenty kneebends, twenty leg splits; a pop-up; and then, on an aluminum bar, twenty pull-ups. He finished with a selection of Royal Canadian Air Force exercises aimed especially at the chest.

Fifteen minutes, all this took. He was breathing easily but deeply. He was coated in light perspiration. A strong stud's scent issued from his armpits and crotch. It was not offensive. It mingled funkily with his lilac vegetal cologne. He let the sweat dry on his body, leaving its salty residue. Women—truly sensual women—like a touch of male rankness. They seemed to like his especially. They liked the salt of him on their tongues. He stood dreamily in the hard hot beams of sun shafting in from the window, drawing renewed vigor from them, pacing the tempo of his heart and lungs. He opened his eyes.

"Jesu Cristo!" He leaped back against a wall, flattening himself against it. Terror quivered from his smokehole eyes.

The cockroach squatted revoltingly near the base of the toilet. Then it scuttled out of sight.

Breath sobbed out of Muñoz González. He fought nausea. Since that landing in the fetid tropics of Santo Domingo—that terrible first night concluding the flight of his parents from Bilbao—he had feared and hated insects. They were his single phobia. The objects of his leisurely revenge, by contrast, had become impersonal, pawns whose characters interested him.

He recovered himself, went to the sink, unhitched the rubber contrivance from the towel rack, filled the two reservoirs with warm water, and strapped it on. While dressing, he thought upon, and was again able to admire, the calm with which Sacedón had greeted the first twist of copper coil around his throat. Had he had his choice, Muñoz González might have eschewed at least the indignities. The nakedness. The genitals filling the mouth where the tongue ought to have been. But all that had been necessary to bind the co-operation of Herminia. What haters women are! mused Muñoz González, wagging his head with a deprecatory curving of his lips.

He had chosen a black Italian silk suit. The shirt was of pale yellow silk with an especially high collar over which bushed the glossy hair of his nape. The tie and matching handkerchief were patterned in yellow and maroon silk.

He had spoken with Herminia a second, brief time, receiving the announcement that the Marquesa had been dispatched. He had ordered fresh roses for the Countess of Magascal, who amused him. He had an appointment with his tailor at four o'clock. He would school his handsome gray stallion at the Somosaguas riding club between five and six o'clock, and then meet with Scheel and Rougement at seven o'clock, when last details for the shipment would be determined; after which, the photographs wet and shiny, he would meet with Baltazar Blás.

He had played Blás well. Confronted by his record, he had shrugged, admitted to most of it, and permitted Blás to conceive of him as an opportunist, which was true, rather than a dedicated servant of the Revolution, although that could also be true. In this instance, the Party was not going to be pleased. *Tant pis.* He would come out of the venture satisfyingly rich. Tomás was waiting for him at Calle Almagro.

Content, Muñoz González strolled out of his modest bachelor's flat, one in the concave screen of tenements that, from far across a plaza, front the Royal Palace. Outside, he paused to gaze a moment at the double row of life-and-a-half-sized marble statues, set on pedestals along the center of the square's garden, some of them reputedly designed by Velázquez. They pleased him. The Royal Palace's wedding cake of a marble façade also pleased him. There was something exuberant about it. Scheel, Rougement, Hassam, Dong Thoc—almost all of his associates—had no aesthetic appreciation. After grub for their bellies, what they wanted was, crudely, meat. Muñoz González thanked God that sort of thing was behind him.

At Calle Almagro, he found plumbers up to their booted ankles in water, trying to stem back the leak in the fountain. A boardwalk, much used, had been lain. On it strolled Countess von Leddhin, a remarkable woman. Her back was straight. Her waist was tidy. The set of her chin was fearless. Cradled to her bosom was her huge, baleful, scarred old tomcat, which she stroked in her round of the courtyard.

"*Bonjour, madame!*" he saluted her.

"Ah . . . A beautiful morning, isn't it!" replied the old lady in that gentle and melodious voice, turning the dead beams of her eyes to him. She occupied the entire fifth floor.

"May I stroll with you a few moments, Countess?"

"That would be lovely."

He took her arm. She executed her blind steps gracefully. She had been a ballerina with the Comédie Française, and a memorable horizontale.

"How is the business going on upstairs?" she asked.

"Very well, thank you. Your check this month ought to run over
thirty thousand pesetas."

"*Arriba España!*" she chuckled, cello-toned. Then, in French again,
"What's that in old francs?"

"Two hundred thousand."

"Oh, that *will* be nice!"

The cat sprang from her arms, pouncing for the patriarchal old
carp, which had swum out with the overflow. But as its paws touched
water, the tom squawled, went rigid, arched its spine—hackles bristling,
hissing and foaming at the mouth.

"Oh! Oh!" exclaimed the Countess.

Muñoz González yanked his shoes and socks off, rolled up his cuffs,
and went wading after the cat. It leaped into his arms, but so frightened
it forgot to retract its claws, dealing him a bad scratch on the wrist.

"Tom hurt you!" the Countess cried, receiving the cat back into her
protection.

"It's nothing."

"But I scent blood!"

"Nothing at all, Countess, I assure you." Dorada, Muñoz González
suspected, would be excited by the taste. It was ten forty-five. He could
expect her within a few minutes.

Upstairs, he tinctured the tear. The medicine cabinet would have
done credit to a rural clinic. He now carried out an inspection of the
premises, starting with the central parlor, which was circular in shape.
There charter parties sometimes held communal sessions. Short, separate
corridors led to the bedrooms. Ordinarily not more than one couple, or
possibly a threesome, occupied them at a time. Mirrors faceted walls
everywhere—with taste, most of them a collection of "cornucopias" in
gilt, handsomely carved frames, the reflecting surfaces small and stained
to amber. The entire north wall of one love nest, however, was a solid
mirror: one-way; see-throughable from the adjoining room. This was
where Tomás generally performed. In the event charter parties preferred
the semblance of privacy while themselves both acting and watching
the activities of everyone else, there was closed circuit television. There
were oxygen tanks. Each bedchamber had its own period decor. Young
Inmaculada Urquijo, Countess of Cáceres, was romantically inclined
to the art nouveau room. Asunción Mendoza, on the other hand, was

eclectic. European and Asian salesmen, magnates, or whomever, she entertained wherever. Americans she sometimes expressed her contempt for
by insisting on the kitchen table. She was difficult; no less probably the
best of the fruits, if somewhat ripe, to have been plucked from the nightclub in Calle Don Pedro, which served Muñoz González as a show ring
for potential talents.

The room he selected for Dorada Blás was French, airy, enameled
in pale porcelain pastels. The bed was a revolving, circular altar, with
satin sheets and an avalanche of silk pillows. He checked the sound recorder. He checked the three 8-mm Canon movie cameras, the Nikon
35-mm with wide angle lens, and the Leica 35-mm with telephoto lens.
They were, of course, concealed. In Barcelona, there had been more
elaborate equipment. The exposure of that operation—nothing to do with
his own—might, Muñoz González realized, embolden a girl to exposing
this one. He was not perturbed by the prospect. Shortly, he would do the
exposing himself.

"Tomás?"

While he waited for his order to penetrate, he checked the bed's
ankle and wrist clamps. They might be needed. He did not think so.

Tomás hulked above and behind him.

"After the performance, Tomás, you will stay in the closet until the
pretty lights go on."

"Yes . . . master."

Through with the clamps, Muñoz González straightened. He did
not turn toward his servant. Except for glances, he looked away as he
spoke. Deformity of any kind grieved him with something like soul-
sickness. It was both an aesthetic and moral revulsion. It was in some way
connected with his phobia for insects; although he had admitted to López
Ibor, the famed psychiatrist, that insects are among the most perfect of
nature's creations.

"You will have an excellent time, Tomás."

"Thank you, master!"

"I regret having had to send you away last week, but the girl was
badly torn." Perhaps only Lady Hume and Asunción Mendoza were able
to absorb Tomás's highest rages of lubricity. Lady Hume paid extra for
them.

"I . . . I promise, master, I . . ."

"That one-eyed maid of la Señora Condesa, she served meanwhile?"

"Well, master."

The police would be after Tomás. He camped on the roof, where he chanced meeting little worse than a strayed plumber, since the outlet to the main drain had to be somewhere, everybody supposed; although acquaintance with Orbaneja's works made any supposition risky. Tomás would be safe for a while. He might have to be delivered up.

"You will take the edge off this morning on Petra and . . ."

"I . . . looked for her already. Petra . . . has been sent away, master."

"Embarrassed?" Spanish girls often were unable to resist tempting conception. Their maternal hunger could be a bother.

"I do . . . not know."

"Never mind. Has Doña Herminia found a replacement?"

Tomás's eyes contracted into terrified pits. The swiftest glance showed Muñoz González this. The man did not know how to answer. He was waging an excruciating mental battle.

"Never mind about that either," Muñoz González said soothingly. Tomás was an idiot. In panic, he might turn on anything, rending it limb from limb; even the man, who by servicing his incredible libido, had gained control of what little soul Tomás might be said to possess.

Soothingly, Muñoz González ordered Tomás to the roof, there to bathe and prepare himself. The plan was simple. Muñoz González would start Dorada in the central parlor. He would excite her and permit her to believe she was exciting him by compressing the rubber sacks between his thighs and thereby filling the thick-walled rubber phallus. Then, depending on her reactions, which he would gauge expertly, he would sweep her into the room with the one-way wall mirror, where, while he perhaps resorted to sodomy, she could watch Tomás on the second of whatever girls were this morning available. The sight of Tomás's really extraordinary organs would, if Dorada Blás followed the pattern of her temperament, as he appraised it, fire her into squeezing the rubber phallus so hard that flesh and blood might yelp. When Tomás was done—perhaps before—he would take Dorada into the French bedroom and undress her, permitting her to undress him down to his shorts. Now he would certainly resort to cunnilingus. When whole, he had found this for the most part unnecessary. Rarely had he enjoyed it. Lady Hume's blonde mont was unique in its downiness; her vaginal dew unique in its columbine's sweet freshness. Most women tasted of acid, rotten fruit. Once he had had to spend hours picking a wiry pubic curl out from between his close-set front teeth. There it had obstinately stuck, embarrassing him throughout an audience with Trujillo. But now sodomy had become his prime participation in the act. The pliers used on him had been less than surgical. Part of one testicle remained; there was vestigial seminal action. This induced, he would break two poppers under Dorada Blás's nose and have her inhale the gas. By this time the shades would be electronically drawn, the room nearly black. Stroboscopic lights would blizzard the interior, the signal for Tomás to enter. A third popper under her nostrils; and the substitution would be accomplished.

If she was aware of this—doubtful—she was not likely to object once impaled by Tomás. He would meanwhile set the cameras in operation. They were loaded for forty-five minutes of continuous infrared action; enough for two of Tomás's oceanic ejaculations. He would then substitute himself for Tomás, permitting the stroboscopic storm to subside. In their hearts, women knew by now what had taken place. Either they did not mind or they did not wish to admit it to themselves. The Jekyll-Hyde performance seemed to spellbind them.

He counted on it to intrigue Dorada Blás. He guessed she was the sort of female who would never or could never totally abandon herself— her rational faculties—to anyone or anything. He guessed her fundamental contempt for him. He guessed her purpose with him. He had anticipated, however. The tables were all but turned. When his flight was prepared for Mexico, with which Spain has no extradition treaty because Mexico is such an emblem of the democratic spirit and Spain not, the substitution would not take place with Tomás. It would take place with the Duke of Steel's sole heir, the incumbent, that poor puppy of a Juan Luis Seguismundo del Val. Then would Muñoz González grant Inspector Stepanópoulis Grau the great, undreamed of boon—to him exposing the vicious puttering in potted flesh among Spain's highest social and financial circles. On that day or night—perhaps within forty-eight hours— he would contrive to have present (and active) Lady Hume, the Countess of Cáceres, Asunción Mendoza, Julio Caro, Amontefardo, Beltrán, and several others.

A throttling sound. A warbling.

The new telephone.

Herminia, from the dukeling's apartment next door.

"Are you occupied? The red light isn't on."

"No." Glance at the Rolex. Frown. "She's late."

"Tomás told you I have replaced Petra."

"Yes."

"I have the Rivas girl for you."

His grip tightened on the receiver. "She's . . . ready?"

"I'd say she is splitting her stitches. She is a natural, if ever I saw one."

It was all ripening at once!

"When . . . will she be over?"

"Presently. Within an hour or so. She's clean, neat, and orderly. She will be a great help with the books. Will you start her right in?"

He would call on Scheel, Rougement, Hassam, and Dong Thoc. No charge tonight.

"Prepare her for one o'clock in the morning."

He hung up. His heart beat wildly. His throat was constricted. Tonight, the Rivas daughter—offered up as a feast. He would marry her in Acapulco. She would share his fortune. Nightly he would subject her to whomever he pleased.

The Duke of Steel had been executed just one year ago to the day. Twelve more months had passed in preparations. The Sacedón pup would be destroyed by Baltazar Blás at sundown, and Blás himself by Muñoz González not much later. The Rivas daughter would be the coup, the double. After the shipment, he would light the match to bring on the conflagration of personal reputations, destroying the corrupted world of privilege.

He glanced at his watch. Eleven-thirty. Where was the Blás daughter? Then he cocked an ear to the ceiling. Nothing. He lifted a cigarillo to his lips and began absent-mindedly drawing on it. Muñoz González should have listened more carefully.

For up on the roof, Tomás, naked, had stepped away from the pipe embedded in the cistern, his private shower. He had done this, releasing the lever that closed off the pour, because out of the corner of an eye he had glimpsed something thin and lithe slip over the roof's ledge. He turned to it. He was facing the Teddy-boy.

They stared at each other a goodly time, the one gargantuan and naked, the other rachitic and shivering in threadbare clothes, natural allies against God and nature and society. But Tomás blocked access to the elevator shaft's door.

The Teddy-boy took a step toward it. Ponderously, nevertheless effectively, Tomás covered the door with his bulk.

Another long moment they stared at each other.

"I . . . don't want to hurt you," said the Teddy-boy. The switchblade lay open in one palm.

Tomás did not budge. Perhaps the sight of that blade did not reach the brain. The blade itself, however, penetrated to his vitals; and he did then the only uncumbersome thing in his life, which was to slip almost soundlessly to his knees, and then slide forward and almost soundlessly on his chin and chest, and emit a single sigh.

S I X
Baltazar Blás

At just about this time, sitting at the boomerang-shaped desk of his Banco Blás office (which he dominated from bulbous bald brow to the sternum of his chest, a mushroom of pavement-buckling vitality) and dictating to his amanuensis of more than thirty years (Santiago Sert, a Catalán, and, not that it matters, first cousin of Don Eugenio Suárez y Sert, Juan Luis Sacedón's faithful administrator), that greatly feared financier, Baltazar Blás, also glanced at his wristwatch, a gold Rolex the mate of Muñoz González's and in fact presented to him by Muñoz González. Where was Orbaneja? In the architect, his son-in-law's brother-in-law, was the key to what might turn out to be among the slickest manipulations in Blás history.

"Sert, start calling the brokers. No! Never mind! I'll call 'em myself!"

Sert gathered up his notes, bowed, and shuffled his sixty-year-old steps out. Nearly a decade and a half younger than his master, he looked and probably felt as much older. Experience had taught him when Don Baltazar expected privacy.

Blás began his calls, jotting down figures in his neat, self-taught, tiny, and partially coded part-hieroglyphics. A thousand more shares bought by one broker, 500 by another; 800, 200, 900. Average price: 176 pesetas. Blás pondered. It was a joy to watch him ponder. The twin bulbs on his brow seemed to expand and contract. His pupils squeezed curling into nooks of deliciousness. He gave an undiminished love to any sort of lucubration. Power was the ham and hock of existence. Cunning in getting it was the spice.

He dialed the brokers back. "Enough for today." In the sluggish Spanish market, the price might jump.

Now he got out his abacus, rapidly strumming the beads. Nearly

750,000 shares over 250 days of buying at an average of 180 pesetas the share, for a total of 135,000,000 pesetas. Cheap! A plash out of his bucket. The Muñoz González shipment alone would plash back in several times that. He would build! Oh, *how* he would build!

Nevertheless, Blás frowned. He jumped up from his desk. One immense window looked out over the Retiro Park, from a height of six floors. The whole length of the sill had been planted to daffodils, gift of Ignacio Prades, who had touched his father-in-law truly by the gesture. Because Baltazar Blás also loved flowers. The simple hideaway he had bought on the isle of Lanzarote was a velvet black carpet of volcanic gravel, in which his roses and geraniums glowed like jewels. To Lanzarote, he slipped away for peace and thinking, himself smoothing the "picón" around the roots of his flowers, dressed in peasant smock and trousers, a straw hat with a wide, round brim protecting his flushed and happy face. Here, in Madrid, he could only dream of that retreat. He picked up a gilt watering can, gift of Dorada, sprinkling the base of each daffodil lightly while he stubbed the soil down with his fingers. He reflected. Bent over, tenderly moving along the blooms, he reflected on his Santo Dominican partner. Beginning in middle adolescence, the man's history seemed to be clear. Fatherless. Penniless. Son of an alcoholic mother. A brilliant academic record. Charged with molestation when he was seventeen. Charged with unlawful trespass at eighteen. Worked as a cane cutter. Boxed a few semiprofessional bouts. Worked as a stevedore. Foreman at nineteen. That year named corespondent in a suit of separation filed by a member of Ciudad Trujillo's haute bourgeoisie. Held (and released) on a stolen car charge. Convicted and sentenced to three months in jail for starting a brawl and causing "public scandal." Received his card from the Communist Party at twenty. Drummed out within months for misuse of Party funds and abuse of the Chairman's daughter. Joined the army. Switched to the police. A corporal at twenty-one. At twenty-three, a lieutenant. Married that year to the daughter of an American export-importer. Somehow single again at twenty-five; and wealthy enough to take up jumping thoroughbreds. Unclear whether he again joined the Party (questioned on this point, Muñoz González had shrugged his lazy shoulders, saying, "Anybody in opposition to Trujillo necessarily associated with Communists"), but he was charged on suspicion of smuggling enemies of the regime to Mexico in his sloop. At twenty-six, he had joined Trujillo's private security forces. Within five years, he was an officer in the caudillo's personal guard. He bought a plantation and brood mares. He bought a sixty-foot schooner. Half the brothels and casinos in Ciudad Trujillo paid him protection fees. Maybe it was that, Blás speculated, pincering a withered bloom off its stalk—too much of it. Or maybe Muñoz González was indeed simultaneously an agent infiltrating the inner circles of the Trujillo court. Whatever the motivation, he had been seized one night by former comrades in the security police, tortured, and nearly killed. The timely assassination of Trujillo saved him.

Blás put the watering can away. Codina Moncó was asking too much. He would make such a fuss over Costa in Marbella that the Customs agent would be grateful for life. That comptroller Nacho had fastened on the neck of Blás enterprises—a pest, and a snoopy one, and almost as much of a pedant as the man who selected him! Codina Moncó would get 20 per cent, no more. He stepped out on the terrace.

It was hung with wisteria. How he loved the scent! That other notion of Nacho's—the dogwood from Virginia—was a success. What blossoms! Like kisses—kisses of snowwhite beauty—being whispered. An unsalubrious history.

But Baltazar Blás had dealt often with the Muñoz González genre of adventurers. What he did not like were the Party associations. Recognizing the threat in them to such as himself, he feared Communists. But he did business with anyone: and this deal was manifestly unideological. The arms were destined for Israel, not the Arab nations, which latter would have been in the Party interest. And, curiously, in official Spanish interest, given Spain's stake in Río de Oro. Spain was trying to hold onto that stretch of Saharan desert while at the same time building herself as the Western nation friendly to Arabs—the nation whose culture and language are steeped in the Moorish tradition; the nation that had never recognized Israel. If Arab gratitude—a dubious reed—did not suffice to secure Río de Oro (at least permit Spain exclusive exploitation of minerals), Spain would still have a rôle as the logical broker between NATO and the Muslim powers. For these political reasons alone, Blás had been necessary to Muñoz González. Someone had to reason with certain officials. Wasn't Spain's thrust back into Mediterranean importance dependent upon recovery of Gibraltar? Was it sufficient that Franco descended of Jews and that he had saved many thousands of them from Nazi liquidation? Would not a confidential word about this undercover shipment dropped with the Jewish financial community in London's City incline them toward a sympathetic rendition of the Treaty of Utrecht? And, oh, that loan that Señor Blank had applied for. Italian soft ice cream wasn't the sort of venture Banco Blás ordinarily backed, but . . .

Temperamentally, the Spaniard admires Israelis. The arms, in any case, were putatively, if secretly and unofficially, destined for Algeria in exchange for gold, a commodity of supreme interest to Spain.

He grunted. He was satisfied. He had reason to be satisfied with himself. How beautiful the park of the Retiro, frondose under its gigantic trees. They formed a carpet of leafy green beneath him. They were at his feet.

Smuggling had come naturally to this descendant of roving Phoenicians. So had, it seems, his business instincts, and the qualities that distinguished him from the thousands of petty practitioners of contraband. He had been ruthless—there's no blinking the fact. Rumors persist that when Government launches set out to intercept a Blás smuggling smack, Blás sent out faster gunboats. The vessel disappeared off the face of the sea; and there were no survivors. By 1936—upon the outbreak of the Civil War—he had built up a modest flotilla whose principal trade was illegal traffic in arms. The Franco forces were short of everything at first. Blás gambled. Personally at the helm, he ran the Red blockade, donating twelve tons of munitions to the Nationalists.

The reward came in 1939, when he was appointed Spain's official broker for arms and ammunition, whose corporate expression became Armas Y Explosivos, S.A., a State-licensed monopoly that prospered during the troubled 1940s, and that boomed in the 1950s with the military base treaties between Spain and the United States. Banco Blás was the natural corollary. This is the way with Spanish business. Wealth quickly entrenches itself behind financier's syndicates or commercial banks, whose self-propagating walls corral Spanish commerce in happiest hegemonious harmony.

Curiously, whereas this sometimes gnawed at the conscience of the one-time filibuster, who in his day had had to bludgeon those walls down and plunder his way into the citadel, it in no way troubled the social-consciousness of his son-in-law, born as Nacho Prades was to the economic feudalism that has Spain trussed up like a turkey. Banco Blás gobbled up whatever came within reach, fair or fowl, and fattened gorgeously on the fare. Blás had never permitted legitimatized predations to dull the old rover's spirit. At a time during the 1940s when half of Spain was without shoes, and the Government protected a back-yard industry with the most rigid tariffs, suddenly; at the northwestern port of Bilbao; out of the Atlantic blue; hove a freighter laden with thousands upon thousands of inexpensive foreign footwear—in all sizes, shapes, and colors, but every last one for the right foot. There were, of course, no duties imposed. Some foreign entrepreneur had made a colossal error; and the worthless cases of leather were auctioned off to the first fool; who, as it happens, turned out to be a Blás agent. Within the same week, and out of the Mediterranean blue, there hove into the northeastern port of Valencia a freighter scupper-deep in shoes for the left foot only. These were similarly treated, Blás put two and two (or left and right) together, and Spain was shod as well as had. Years later—in the 1950s—I happen to have become involved in another of his gambits. This was a political putting together of two and two. India had an excess production of cotton and needed a market. South Africa had mills and needed the raw material. India (Third World socialist) and South Africa (right-wing racist) were not speaking to each other. So: some weeks later: a ship with Indian cotton arrived at Barcelona on the noon tide. The bales were off-laded into a Customs shed and there stamped SPAIN. By midnight, the "Spanish" cotton was being craned into the holds of a South African freighter. This venture in international hypocrisy continued eighteen months at a rate of two ships a week. What the Customs officials (the stampers) and I (the broker) got out of the arrangement is our business; but to Baltazar Blás it meant $80,000 the ship, for a total of $12,480,000.

Such as these comprised his extra-lawful capers since the founding of the bank. He had become, as a matter of fact, one of the voices of reform, among the first to lend his weight to sanitizing the bureaucracy; and in 1966 shocked the financial community by confessing to $50,000 worth of taxable income, an unheard of concession even though the sum represented less than 1 per cent of reality. He was altogether sincere: bureaucratic corruption and tax-dodging were in the long run bad for national morals. He had in any case solidified his position. But that his show of new-found piety wasn't cynical is attested to by the numbers of human beings in Spain living lives of leisure off rewards from Baltazar Blás for having refused to be bought. He genuinely admired them.

This side of him he never bruited. It would have been disastrous. It was essential for him to retain the image of a man who stopped at nothing once he set out after a business; a man who mobilized all his vast resources and a pitiless determination against a single target, to whom pleas were futile, and who, if resisted, resorted to terrifying methods. There had to be physical as well as moral fear of Baltazar Blás, as paralyzing to his prey as the shriek of a hunting owl to a mouse.

He had been lucky in this way. He was not unlike Franco, against whom enemies murmured such slanders as that he had paved the way for his pre-eminence on the wreckage of two air crashes that removed his most formidable rivals. Rumor feasted on incomplete truths. Yes, one of Blás's smacks was about to be intercepted by a Government cutter back in the 1930s; that smack did disappear off the face of the sea. Neglected in the accounting was that captain and crew had betrayed Baltazar Blás. No one betrayed Baltazar Blás. During the 1940s, when maquis still operated in the hills of Asturias, an industrialist was ambushed, robbed, and shot. It was known that Blás had been after his iron mines. Another time, when Blás was sucking many small, independent, and underfinanced credit institutions into his octopod Banco Blás, one chairman of a board who resisted his tentacles died in the Granada hills when a truck racing to Madrid with a load of seafood swerved into his chauffeur-driven vehicle and bounced it into a ravine. Again it was widely assumed that Blás had arranged the accident; the other board members quickly came to terms.

Happily, the worst was always assumed. Here, however, he was indulging in an extra-lawful venture whose consequence might be grave should matters go wrong (not that they would), and in association with a man whom instinct could not reconcile itself to. The lure was not only the fourteen-plus million dollars to be made on the delivered arms; nor only the prospect of future shipments; but also the substantial aid provided by Muñoz González in the planned financial coup. The stock being purchased for Baltazar Blás by brokers (using nearly half a hundred bogus names) was nowhere nearly so important as the pinning of Jaime Orbaneja to the wall; and with him that worthless figurehead masquerading as Utilidades's Chairman of the Board. Blás had no pity for Juan Luis Sacedón. Why should he? The pup was incompetent. He was an anachronism, injurious to the Spanish economy. Little more pity did he waste on Orbaneja—who was a concatenation of catastrophes that ought to be ended in the interest of public safety. Ignacio Prades's part in the plans did sometimes twitch Blás's conscience; because Blás, above all, expounded loyalty. Still, to set a man on his relations was buying his soul, not selling one's own. And possibly—*quite* possibly—Ignacio had not apprehended what was going on.

He churned a wake to his desk, flicking the intercom.

"Sert, *where's* the Count of the Caribs?!"

"I do not know, sir. But the comptroller of el Señor Conde de Obregón *begs* to see you . . ."

"Get me Caribs, Sert! Get me Orbaneja!"

SEVEN

Jaime Orbaneja, Count of the Caribs

Jaime Orbaneja
>naked cherub
>>courtesy Count of the Caribs

stood
>on two stocky sturdy legs whose fibers recollected faintly but pain-
fully the throb of city traffic. He
>>stood before the window of a bathroom
in which sink, toilet, douche, and tub announced themselves in the most
functional of white porcelain for what they were—hardly to his taste,
but apparently satisfying a rigorous cord in the nature of his wife, who
had selected this particular apartment in this particular building, and
who had prohibited him from tinkering with anything in it. What did
Baltazar Blás ultimately aspire to, he wondered? And what about antimat-
ter? Is it there that Heaven and Hell are hidden?

The window, whose panels were open, looked out over the once
elegant slope of Calle Antonio Maura, which falls east-west from Alfonso
Doce to Plaza Lealtad. Trans. (Transition.) Transit. There is a fascination in words (sounds spun to exigencies of thought). The Word *was*
first. (But before mouth ever groaned forth a syllable, thought had been
gestated in the breast,) (yowling in agony for light and air).

Light and air. (Juan Luis.) (Billy Smith-Burton.) Take a hammer
and crack an eyeball. Your turn first. Watch the veins in the white pop
with blood. Now look through that eye yourself. Is the world any different? He
>stood on the fifth floor of a poured concrete shoebox façaded
over by bricks baked to a vitreous vomit-yellow that nor time nor tempest
in two-score years or more would weather away, replacing what he supposed had to be accounted as the obsolete iron grills and fussy stucco
scrolls of the dowdy old stone house that had been pulverized by iron
balls so that this new one could rise. Is simple thermodynamic entropy
sufficient to explain an expanding and forever mutating universe? Who
is to tell? Below,
>all over Madrid,
>>streets and foundations shook under

the pneumatic compression of 2,400,000 round rolling tires, bearing burdens that in the aggregate weighed 1,500,000,000 pounds. Who—what—could stand it? "The surf is a formidable assailant. A storm wave may grow 40 feet high and 500 feet long and batter the land with a pressure of 6,000 tons per square foot. When such a wave crashes into cliffs, it compresses the air held within pore spaces of cliff debris. This bursts loose like an explosion, and takes entire sections of the cliff with it." (and a man?)

Because I was silent, my bones grew old. There is no health in my flesh, for my bones are filled with illusions. I, as a deaf man, heard not. I, as a dumb man, did eat ashes like bread, and mingled my drink with weeping. ("A whale has 1 tastebud, a cow 8, and human beings 32.") (Or was it 300?) Baltazar Blás was a whale. How

the traffic

whined down by the Paseo del Prado—like jets backed up on an airstrip, sucking sound into perdition. He shut, opened, shut his eyes. A lot of scurrying beetles: ants helpless in pits of fine white sand, the grains crumbling under their whirring filaments and tumbling them back to the bottom. But still they struggled, endlessly scurrying for the rim, endlessly being skidded back down. They sought footholds in Space. They thought to outrace Time. But Time moves with a measured, giant stride. Time outwalks existence, crushing the insects in its path. *Because I was silent, my bones grew old.*

Jaime Orbaneja opened his eyes. There was space in the Heavens, and timelessness there. But the sky, so spectacularly blue half an hour before, when he had been awakened by the blow of Consuelo's dream-driven foot in the small of his back, was now yellowing with the trapped fumes of industrial and automotive waste. Two deep breaths nearly asphyxiated him. Trans. (Transit.) The aphorism must include technology. "A major hurricane generates power exceeding the kinetic output of 150 atom bombs in continuous fission." He was not the first human being to question the blessings of his era. Certainly he was not the first Spaniard to do so. He grabbed the sill, hanging on. Down below, a green Renault risked destruction in a swoop across the street to parking space. Over in the Middle East, the Russians and the Americans might yet collaborate in concluding the Russo-American Age. Yesterday afternoon, after the christening, Jaime Orbaneja had had a final meeting with his accountant. He had then visited the bar of the Castellana Hilton and selected a whore.

He gazed out from the south side of Calle Antonio Maura. To his

left—to the west, down the slope of the street—he glimpsed the as yet
sacred oasis of Plaza Lealtad, ringed round and whizzed about by scuttling vehicles, but preserving still its green turf and shaggy chestnut trees,
and a grove of magnolias whose carnally effulgent blossoms never failed
to evoke the baroque bosom of Dorada Prades, so that whenever his nostrils filled with that faint astringent citrine scent, the Devil idled him
off into bathycolpian fancies. Obras Orbaneja was 60,000,000 pesetas
short. By contrast, the whore's dugs had hung to her waist, which may
have prompted his purchase of a two-kilo box of chocolates for Consuelo
afterward. He was a sinner, and the whole world with him; and the
world suffered from its wickedness. *"Turn Thine eyes of mercy again
toward the children of that race, once Thy chosen people . . ."* Once
Madrid had been a vast succession of parks and gardens. Less than ten
years before, residential areas like this one still drowsed to the stinging
siccative songs of summer, with children playing in their bowered tranquillity. By then, however, the city was doomed. The long-delayed postwar boom came rumbling over the Pyrenees, borne on the wheels of
millions upon millions of tourists, the pagans of the new era, and revolu-
tionizing Spain as nor the Republic nor before it Napoleon's legions had
been able to do. Spain, holy Spain!—panting for coitus with clay idols.
"Turn Thine eyes of mercy . . ."

He had not remained silent, old though his bones had grown! So
it was a functional sharing of space that the ten major banking syndicates
and their spawn wanted, the better to share the spoils. But he, Orbaneja,
in common with all creative spirits, possesses the power of alchemizing
dust into gold. Office buildings require vast mail bins to cope with the
masses of paperwork that make up the primary business of business, at
least in Spain. But he was horrified by the vision of drab metallic postal
boxes. He resisted the slovenly solution of stacking them in ells beside
elevators, or cramping them into the concierge's office. How to hide them?
How to forge their functionalism into the master aesthetic plan, and
endow them with special beauty?

It came to him one insomnolent night, when he was lying abed
timing the rhythm of his wife's snores and speculating idly on their decibel count. It was a galvanizing flash of inspiration, jolting him out of bed
and into his study, where, in pyjamas and slippers, he sat right down
at his drawing board. Of course! Using re-enforced concrete, he had
molded the exterior of the building into the shape of a huge, petrified
treetrunk, its gnarled stumps serving as platforms for balconies. This ex-

terior symbolized his deepest philosophical convictions: about business, Spain, society, and existence. The very thing! He would follow through on the metaphor, scrapping the present and nearly completed vestibule. It was going to be costly, he realized, but he would help make up for that by eliminating the service elevator and shaft (what did an office building want with one anyhow?) and by reducing the diameter of his plumbing (there were no baths; it wasn't as if everyone was going to flush all the toilets at once). Even with these economies, he suspected his firm was going to require a healthy cash infusion to allay the purchase of the materials he now planned to use.

That very next evening, he conferred with his accountant, a puffy-eyed comatose puzzlefaced individual who during the day labored in a bank for half a living wage and who after hours eked out the other half by hawking his services to several of many hundreds of firms that either could not afford a full-time accountant or did not condescend to the need for one. The meeting was not satisfactory. There were ledgers and ledgers and ledgers, from which in turn were refined three sets of books, the false set (designed to cheat the State out of as much in taxes as possible), the hopeful set (designed to keep creditors at bay and directors complacent), and the true set. But the accountant, overworked, who suffered beside from nightmares in which he added fruit preserves to automotive spare parts and got cookies for an answer, was months behind, and he was so confused between the hocus he prepared for creditors and directors and the pocus he proffered investigators from the Treasury that reality was lost in the muddle, and the only thing he could tell Orbaneja was that the company was somewhere between four flats short and two buildings long, and no cash in sight. Stunned, but by no means down, Orbaneja that night appealed to his brother-in-law, Ignacio Prades, persuading him to ask his father-in-law, Baltazar Blás, to advance a few million pesetas from the bottomless coffers of the Banco Blás against the collateral of the real value of the site and 26 per cent of the construction firm's stock—which did occasion Orbaneja some anxiety, because the bank was already in possession of 25 per cent as a consequence of previous moments of financial embarrassment, he was probably burning up whatever profits he could expect from the office building, and if he was not able to redeem this new note, Baltazar Blás would gain effective control.

But he was too excited to care. He had pioneered the revival of Gaudi and the art nouveau spirit: in defense of the human soul. This vestibule would be his chef d'oeuvre. He set his workmen at once to tearing out the old one. All that July of 1966, Orbaneja scoured Spain for the best masons he could find. Personally supervised by him, they built that fall and winter an immense oval room, with a midnight blue dome into which artisans hammered silver and gold studs in a pattern that emerged as the sweep of the Milky Way. The floor was paved with ceramic tiles baked to a black-green, suggesting a carpet of grass under a night sky. And then came the wrap-around walls. These were first blocked with black marble slabs. Into them artisans worked strips of sandstone, alabaster, and lapis lazuli; and into these an inlay of onyx, bloodstone, kunzite, tourmaline, rose and amethyst quartz, and quantities of enamel in ruby reds and sapphire blues and electric emerald greens, to fashion a tropical tangle of lush vines and leaves, and twenty royally gigantic peacocks, each with the jeweled fronds of its tail fully spread against the jungle dark.

It was magical, marvelous, a sensation; and Jaime Orbaneja's breast was decorated with an Isabélica, as the order is known for short. Outside was all the dust and bustle of newly industrialized Madrid. Inside was peace. One stepped through the portal shaped like a knot at the base of the treetrunk; and into a dell tenebrous under the star-studded dome, surrounded by forest and the grave majesty of the fowl. And in them did the splendor of Jaime Orbaneja's genius manifest itself. *The throat and breast of each peacock was a mail bin!* No keys necessary. No stooping to peer through dark slits to ascertain whether the post had brought anything. Because the bills of the birds were only open when they were empty, closing automatically fifteen seconds after their gullets were filled.

There was, unfortunately, a defect in the system, which transpired a few days after the tenants completed occupancy: namely, once the bins were filled, and the bills of the peacocks shut, there was no way of opening them again until their gullets were emptied, and there was no way discoverable to anyone including Orbaneja himself of emptying them without resort to a blowtorch; and when that draconian measure was applied, what came out came pouring out in a charred and molten river, setting back business in Madrid, as we have seen, by uncountable months . . .

But who was that below him! What puffy-eyed comatose puzzle-faced individual stared up at him from beside the green Renault, bulging brief case in hand! The accountant? But they had thrashed matters out last night, the worst was known! Yet the man gazed upward intently, as if he had some fresh disaster to convey. The forehead puckered further;

and then his knees buckled. He collapsed face down into the well between parked cars, brow striking flagstones with an inaudible rap.

Jaime Orbaneja's arms went rigid on the sill. It was like the face of the defeated officer in Velázquez's "Surrender of Breda." It was the face of the mourner in Greco's "Burial of Count Orgaz." It was the eternal face, eternally staring at one out of a crowd, an eternally questioning face, a face facing itself and the unanswerable question. And it remained in Jaime Orbaneja's retina, like a fading sequence in a film: while a concierge rushed out of his doorway to the curb, and a passer-by stopped, giving a slow, bewildered-seeming half turn. There could be no doubt the man was dead.

Jaime Orbaneja withdrew from the window. He palmed and pressed his pectoral muscles, as if he could thus stop the pounding in his chest. Ice water trickled from his knee joints. They gave, and he sat on the rim of the bathtub. He was shocked. He was frightened. Which goes to show what a foolish and ridiculous man Jaime Orbaneja is. Madrid was once a vast succession of gardens and squares. It was also a city of slums, with humanity packed in squalor. Fool. Romantic fool. He permitted himself to be affected by having witnessed the demise of a nonentity—as if he did not live in the twentieth century; as if he had not fought in one of its more sanguinary wars, and did not daily read the continual and compilating statistics of carnage everywhere, not even his accountant, that fresh statistic on the street: an illusion, a phantom, an accusation from an overwrought conscience. Time is no more than the endless skein of mankind's sins, stitch on stitch until Doomsday. *You* profess that, Jaime Orbaneja! He is a silly fellow: an anachronism in any Present with a nostalgia for an unreal Past. Look at him! What a spectacle he presents, middle-aged male bosoms heaving as he sits in rosy nakedness on the rim of the tub. Jaime Orbaneja is *emotionally upset*. Jaime Orbaneja *feels for* the balding young man lying out there. Need one wonder at the financial mess of Obras Orbaneja? Its founder and chief executive officer identifies himself with almost anyone he encounters. He dislikes no one, not even his wife, for whom, in fact, after twenty-five years of marriage, he retains an astonishing affection. Clearly, he is undiscriminate. He is a sentimentalist, who desires to bequeath to the world all that beauty (whimsical though it be) of which his mind and heart are capable of conceiving; and hang the consequence, or possibly the poor accountant. This is hubris, of course, the inflation of the romantic ego. Thus is he ever exceeding his budget; and thus is he incapable of dismissing a sloppy workman—not, anyhow, until well after he has heard that some tenant in an Orbaneja building was brushed by the feline whiskers of death. Even then, he must engage in powerful (anyhow portly) tussles with conscience, which he loses every time. The tussles. Because whereas he does end up firing the responsible parties, he rightly blames himself, knowing that in his engrossment with exteriors and decorative details he tends to skimp on the basics, thereby drawing negligence into the very blueprints of a building. And in almost every case, he was given prior evidence that a crew or individual could not be trusted. By nature easygoing, he failed to act on that evidence: which is another way of saying that he is a morally lax human being. Conscious of his failings, but unable to cope with them, Jaime Orbaneja is yet another one of the human herd, and no more than that, who suffers much.

The human being unable to cope with himself or his world invents shibboleths, good and evil, by which he lives. They are his answer to the imponderables of existence. They are his steppingstones in the dark rushing roar of the river. "Progress" has become such a thing to Jaime Orbaneja, this utilitarian and antipoetic age. "Less is *less!*" he hurls at Bauhaus. "Less is lack of charity, generosity, reverence for the creative gift! The ultimate *less* is the gibbet!" But the companion of his bed had scant interest in such matters. Nor did she comprehend why he, a true poet, one who composed in stone and concrete, bothered his head. But then she had never understood the creative spirit in him either, and why it was when the physical pulse of their union ceased, his poet's eye had started roving. He loved her all the same, they suited each other (he believed) admirably, even though she had become irritable of the morning, and frequently of the afternoon and evening too, and could be difficult, especially when she suspected in him the first heady rushes of a new romance.

It could not be denied that the poet was susceptible to female charms. Nor could it be denied that he enjoyed unusual success with women for a man his age, surprising him almost as much as it surprised Consuelo. On the whole, his amours were in the troubadour tradition. He mightily enjoyed sighing after a lady love. He reveled in the soulful interlocking of eyes, and in the not quite accidental touching of hands that sent sodium carbonate up and down his spine. On the rare occasion when these interludes transcended the merely romantic, he was the first to lose interest, actually offended by the odalisque's descent from taste and morals. But why Consuelo should mind was beyond him. He was rarely indiscreet. She knew that for all the raptures to which he was liable he would never abandon her or the children, so that her sometimes violent reactions—ragings and weepings—puzzled him. She ought to know that he valued their partnership in life. She took excellent care of the house, inheriting this talent from her mother. The household was her career, her profession, her art; as became a wife. That he appreciated Consuelo's competence, and sent her a dozen scarlet roses after every supper party they held, ought to satisfy her.

His profession, after all, absorbed him, satisfying his nearly every need. And those few times he gave way to thorough gloom were apt to occur when she failed to render him the professional appreciation he rendered her. Jaime Orbaneja's complaint was not, "My wife doesn't understand me," rather, "My wife doesn't care for my buildings." Herein lay the deeps of bitterness. Neither caring for nor comprehending what he built could only mean that Consuelo neither truly cared for nor comprehended his soul. He could never let her know how much she hurt him.

Jaime Orbaneja stood up. He had now managed to vitiate the shock of his vicarious brush with mortality. His legs were firm. He must think about Obras Orbaneja, the vehicle of his art. He stepped to the bathroom mirror.

He had given his personal appearance, which he personally deplored, more than usual attention. His mustache he had clipped to uttermost discretion. But no matter. He had been unable to rid it of its quicksilver tips, nor do anything about the gun-metal-blue roots that contrasted with such steely perfection. Withal, it was not a bristly, military, curt, commanding mustache. It swept softly over the lip, and it was like silk to the touch, a mustache that the most delicate of feminine fingers loved to smooth. He sneered at himself. Bah! No good. His lips were so gentle in their curve that pulling them down at the corners seemed to achieve no more than emphasis of their dreamy contours. He frowned fiercely. Not an iota of success. He knew no way of forcing his thick and still dark brows into convincing sternness, because beneath them eyes brighter than blue persisted in their frivolous dance, and the effect of frowning, despite his recent emotional perturbation, colored his suave cheeks.

Bah! Blast it! He glanced at his wristwatch. It was nearly ten o'clock. His appointment at Banco Blás was scheduled for eleven o'clock. What impended would never befall (no, no, it could not): he would redeem the note, the company, and honor . . .

Jaime Orbaneja hurried into his dressing room, donning a gray

double-breasted businessman's suit, permitting himself as the only dash
of color the rosette of his Isabela la Católica. Then, in the mirror paneled
into the doors of his wardrobe closet, he gave his appearance a last appraisal. It was no use at all. He could not help resembling a dashing (if
stout) (and somewhat underfinanced) visionary who could never be expected to manage his own firm.

Depressed, he walked back through the bathroom and into the bedroom, in order to bid his wife adieu. Should he, he wondered, confess to
Consuelo? She sat up like a costive Buddha in the center of their bed, a
region she had long ago pre-empted, so that when he turned over at night,
he had learned to revolve on his own axis. She seemed costive and cross—
munching away at her breakfast, a tray balanced on puffy knees, her
jowls jellying, her eyes still a little vacant, her coal-black hair rigged in
wirenet curlers and revealing highways of naked scalp. In the now wan
morning light, face and lips were drained of all color. She looked excep-
tionally toadish.

"I had a nightmare," he announced, glancing away fastidiously.

"Oh?" she said, pausing in a munch, and then munching again. He
could almost permit himself to become fascinated by the chomping rotation of her jaws, which was steady and methodical, mastication become
a technique.

"I had a nightmare," he repeated. "There stood the mayor, scissors
in hand. And there was the lintel above us—falling, falling . . . nearly
braining him. It kept falling all night long. It was horrible, you can have
no idea."

"It munched have been."

"It was a horrible experience. I saw a man just now drop dead outside the bathroom window."

"From which floor?"

"No, on the street."

"Of course, but from which floor? Pidal may have been pushed."

"No, no, no. I mean a fellow going to work, stepping out of his car."

"Everybody hurries too much. Nacho Pelau sprained his ankle on
the stoop of the Ritz."

"It was terrible—the nightmare. It looked as if the lintel were going
to crush us all. I *told* García that stone was rotten. I didn't find out until
afterward that he was buying shoddy and charging the accounts for the
best."

"Open the window a little," she said, twisting her lower jaw over to the left as she sucked at the crevice between molars.

He went to one pair of french doors, speaking as he placed a hand on the brass latch and lifted it out of its bracket. "I thought I was surely going to be squashed. It made such a noise! In my dream, I heard it again—a thunderous, dust-raising, crumbling noise." The latch came off in his hand. He examined it briefly. Then he took two paces and placed it on a marble-topped armoire. "I thought it might be you snoring, I thought that even as I dreamt. You weren't, though."

"I should hope not. Tum-tum rumbled all night. Chocolates. Try the other window."

He walked to it. "Things haven't been going very well," he said as this latch also came off in his hand. "I had to let García go—you can imagine, after ten years together. Where shall I put it?"

"By the other one, I suppose." She was still half asleep. Little more than her powerful digestive organs operated for at least an hour after her waking. He wondered whether like Louis XIV she had three times the tripe of normal human beings.

"I didn't build this building," he murmured, pairing the two latches. "It's distressing—the most carefully plotted plans, the care, the trials; and García, of all people, takes on a cabaret girl!"

"Is he married?"

"Six children!"

"You have seven. Ring for more muffins."

He reached for a velvet bellpull that dangled over the left shoulder of the headboard. "If you occupied your side of the bed, instead of the middle, you could ring for muffins yourself. Flora-something, dances. She's pregnant. One has such dreams—a whole new municipal principle, the solution to urban sprawl, to traffic, to smog: to the horrors of the megalopolis."

"A creature called Stepanópoulis Grau telephoned from the police."

"The lintel!"

"No, no . . ."

"The drain at Almagro!"

"No . . ."

"The peacocks, then, maldite be they!"

"No, no, no! Something to do with Billy Smith-Burton's permits. Sofía is not pregnant. Did she ever dance? Delicia Badajoz said she saw Dorada playing golf in the company of that Muñoz González. He makes holes in one, Delicia said, laughing, I can't imagine why." The rotor was beginning to purr.

He said:
"Residential edifices ought to be built underground. That would bring Madrid back to the garden it once was, everything gushing with fountains and towered over by trees . . .

She said:
"María never replaced them. My shoes are all curling. Why would Dorada care to play golf with that gangster? One of Marisa Magascal's American cousins—the Peruvian branch—says he ran scandalous establishments when he was in Santo Domingo. No one's got to the bottom of the Barcelona affair. *I* wouldn't be surprised if he *weren't* at the bottom of that. It's Amparo's saint's day, you've forgot of course, I've bought the presents . . .

"Only public buildings—theaters, libraries, museums, ministries, offices, banks,
                         would
be permitted above ground. And there would be no private automobiles:

            absolutely prohibited within the city.

"I did receive notice from BANESTO, I am *not* over . . .

"What would we do with Bartolomé, tell me that? What would all the chauffeurs in Madrid do?

There'd be a multipurpose vertical-dimension rapid-transport system: subways, monorails, and helicopters. Electric golf carts would be permitted for the elderly and infirm;

"What? What's that? Where would they find work *out* of the city, I'd like to know!

"Delicia's cousin's granddaughter may become engaged to Carlos Lapique's nephew . . .

"And what if it rains?

there would be buses
                    to the
zoned business and administrative
centers. For emergencies,
                    ambulances
and firewagons. For public order,
police cars. As for the rest, people
would walk, or bicycle,
                    or ride
horseback. Far healthier. No noise.
The fertilizer would be useful.

                    No smog,
and *faster* transport, one drove
through Madrid twice as fast in a
horse cabbie
            than in a motorcar to-
day, the automobile is a demon
that wastes natural resources, fouls
the air, encourages spiritual cal-
lousness, and massacres people.
Think of the moral turpitude

                    the auto-
mobile encourages! Anyone working in a corporation that produces
the demons must know that he is
helping produce instruments of
death—the cruelest agonies and
the sharpest heartbreak. He is
placing a bomb in the hands of
children . . .

        The producer of auto-
mobiles. He is abetting the as-

"There are never enough.
You *know* there would never be
enough of them!

"The doctor got there in time,
Sofía says. It was only a scare after
all . . .
    "In short skirts, I suppose!

    "Horseback!?
    "Whatever for? Madrid
would smell like a stable.

    "And froze to death!

    "When was the last time *you*
went to Confession?!! I saw Juan
Luis in his new Lancia the other
day . . .
    "Oh, he paid for it, you can be
sure of that, his mother quite
rightly exercises a tight control of
the purse strings, old Luis Sacedón
knew what he was doing when he
gave her that power in his will,
Juan Luis left to himself would
spend his entire patrimony in ten
years, Herminia has enough trouble with him as it is, she says she
never knows where he is or what
time he will turn up at night, dawn
more likely I've heard stories . . .
    "What's that? Children?
Death? Who? I haven't heard!?

phyxiation of the planet, and the end of mankind.

How many times removed must one's

actions . . .

be . . .

before . . .

one's responsibility ceases? When I build a house,

am I guilty of murder because García cheated on materials when his cabaret girl threatened to go off with a novillero? Is old Palacios—gone ga-ga since that stalactite hit him . . .

But tell me, am I responsible for that?"

"Whatever are you talking about?

"Oh, that's all right, Delicia's cousin's granddaughter is related to Carlos Lapique's nephew, but it's distant enough. Did you notice that drop of something hanging from the tip of his nose yesterday?

"Not for me you won't . . . and I will *never* live out in Somosaguas, twenty minutes out of Madrid at least and buried in the country!!!

"That was Countess von Leddhin's dog. It was the *door* that brought on Palacio's stroke."

("Am I not? Isn't the sin on my soul? Aren't all of us who drive art, technology, whatever, to extremes imperiling life guilty of each life lost?")

There was silence at his question. Only the dull roar of the traffic outside could be heard, and a thoughtful last munch from Consuelo.

"I shouldn't like it," she replied after that. She had paid uncommon attention to him so far, and he was grateful. The maid entered. "Ana, more muffins, hot, more jam, strawberry. Butter." Ana bobbed and withdrew. "I shouldn't like it," Consuelo said to him, moistening an index finger with her tongue, and with the pad of the finger dabbing up to her lips crumbs of muffin that had scattered around her plate and over the counterpane, "not one bit like living like a mole underground. I shouldn't think others would like it."

"That's an educable response," he told her, shrugging. "Who ever thought of spending months in submarines, at the bottom of the sea?"

"I, for one, never considered it."

"And what about speleologists?"

"What on earth . . . ?"

"Below it!" he said sharply. "We began as cavemen. They had the sabertooth tiger; we have the atom bomb. People increasingly delight in burrowing to safety. Boîtes and discothèques are in cellars. At night, one doesn't want a view. During the day, yes, while shopping or at work, then one . . ."

"*I don't work.*"

"Well, that's not the case with most people."

"I shouldn't like it," she repeated fretfully. "One would get claustrophobia. One would suffocate. It's stuffy in here, please put out your cigar . . . and if you should try *prying* open a window?"

He chose an onyx bowl in which to grind out the crusty glow of his Habana, walking to the first pair of french doors, digging square-clipped fingernails into the crack between doors, and pulling. With a modicum of effort on his part, they sprang open. In rushed Madrid.

"That's better," Consuelo said, raising her voice to a petulance above the city's metallic whine. "I can hardly breathe mornings. I really find it difficult breathing. I shall visit the doctor as well as the podiatrist this morning."

"Oh," he muttered, "we'd have air conditioning—foolproof air conditioning."

"I find breathing more and more difficult. When the elevator isn't functioning, I pant going upstairs."

"It would be functional . . . and so very beautiful!" Now he raised his voice, lifting arms and body so that he strained toward her on the tips of his toes, face flushed with excitement. "Do think of it, Consuelo! Madrid a gigantic park containing no more than lagoons of construction! Sculptures, not buildings! Wouldn't the petrified tree motif do? Of course it would, the very thing!" He took an eager step toward her. "I'll suggest it to Baltazar! Yes, this very morning, I'll *roll* the plan out before his eyes! We can't be so different, can we?" His tone had turned scornful now, as if the very notion of their being different was inane. "Men of vision are men of vision, whatever their spheres!"

"The elevators wouldn't work," she said, "the air conditioning would not work. We would all die like trapped rats, so put the whole idea out of your mind, at once, this minute! It's ridiculous, you'll make yourself ridiculous, I've suffered from enough of your calamities, I think *that's* what may be causing my respiratory troubles, I'm sure it is, we would all certainly suffocate, and if you go proposing a lot of nonsense to Baltazar Blás about turning Madrid upside down as if it's that simple a cake or something—where *are* the muffins!—your reputation will be quite ruined."

Ana (their María's niece; the lumbago in María's foot was worse this morning) entered with the muffins and strawberry jam, only the muffins were cold and the jam had been heated, so that she had to be sent out again. Jaime Orbaneja was dashed.

He said, "I have an appointment with Baltazar—at eleven."

"How unpleasant. I'm not sure I'd mention this business about Dorada and Muñoz González . . . What about?"

"The letra." Jaime Orbaneja began fiddling with his watch chain, a length of exquisite beauty fashioned and enameled in Jaipur.

"She may not know what she's doing," Consuelo thought aloud, "but people talk, and when they talk, *my* experience has taught me they generally know at least half what they are talking about, especially if it's unpleasant. *Which* letra?"

"The note I signed when I did over the vestibule."

She started in bed, splattering quantums of coffee into the saucer. "The dis*grace!* Those *mail* boxes! I shan't outlive it!"

"I need an extension."

Ana entered. The muffins were heated, and the jam had cooled, crystallizing, however. She had forgot the butter. "Never mind," said Consuelo Orbaneja y Prades, Countess of the Caribs. She jammed half a hot and thickly strawberried muffin into her mouth; chomped and munched with lateral converse mashing motions of her jaws; swallowed; stared at her husband; sipped a glass of water; and said, "Ten or eleven months ago, as I remember, you invested twenty million pesetas in Mallorca."

"Ibiza."

"It is a Blás development . . ."

"Part only. A man called Zaforteza . . ."

"A Blás development nevertheless, one that Nacho estimated would . . ."

"Triple—quadruple. Within six or seven months."

"Yes." A beat. "Well?"

"I . . . There have been problems. The development is nine months behind schedule. Sales have been . . . disappointing, young people called 'hippies' have . . ."

"What are they?!"

"Children with sad faces and very long hair. They have swarmed to Ibiza. Strands of their hair clog up wells and foul drains. On some beaches, one can't see a grain of sand for the beads. They are not very sanitary. For the time being, they seem to have depressed Ibiza's . . ."

"But you can't have lost very much! Land doesn't go down! Sell out your . . ."

"The money isn't mine."

Husband and wife stared at each other, he from the foot of the bed, she from its rumpled plains. He reeved his watch chain round sensitive fingers. She had ceased masticating. Husband and wife were, at last, in communication. There is nothing in the whole wide world like money.

"Has it finally happened, then?" Her tone was frigidly calm. "You've managed to bankrupt us?" The tone was stilling, so that even the sounds of the city receded. "How many millions did your father leave you?" she asked conversationally. "One hundred? Two hundred? And you've run through them in nine-ten-eleven years?"

Jaime Orbaneja fiddled some more with the chain and stared at the toes of his shoes, which twinkled. "Ninety million," he finally said, looking up, "and it was thirteen years ago, and I haven't run through it all, I *still* control Obras Orbaneja, I *still* own my five per cent of Financiera!"

But she, in some respects like her mother, had at least a practical grasp of practical affairs, even though her function as a Spanish wife of the upper classes was to spend money, not gather it in. Jaime was even now—she inferred promptly from his defensiveness—concealing the bottom of the berg. "Which," she stated, referring to Financiera Sacedón, "owns thirteen per cent of you; and the five per cent is bringing in less than ever now, *perhaps* because Financiera was foolish enough to accept thirteen per cent of Obras Orbaneja, what other brilliant transactions has the company made, I wonder, you can tell me, you *ought* to be able to, you *are* on the board, your father put you on it, *he* was a clever man to trade his oodles of Utilidades for that bit of Financiera stock, Luis dead just a year ago today and the company since his death falling apart—if it weren't for Utilidades, a *gold*mine since Madrid began to grow—that *worth*less Juan Luis with a ring in his puppy's nose being pushed and pulled this way and that his administrator running everything for him and probably pocketing the half of it himself, and you not paying the slightest attention, throwing everything you have or *had* down the Obras Orbaneja drain the only drain you've built that ever worked, and *my money too*, the little I had, and last night at that dreadful cocktail party given by that dreadful C. O. Jones there you were again don't think I don't know *why* you wanted me to accept the dinner invitation also *fluttering* all over that puta that ramera, that . . . that . . . that *fruit vendor's daughter*, you'd think *decency*, plain common decency, let alone your *position*, don't believe for a minute Blás will extend your note, Blás hasn't made his millions by extending notes, on top of disgracing and humiliating me *now you come to tell me that we will be out in the street with not a céntimo to our names*, oh!"

The telephone, which squatted on a table by her side of the bed, drilled out its self-importance. "Oh!" repeated the Countess of the Caribs, upsetting her tray as she lunged for the machine. "Oh, it's you, Nacho, I'm *livid* with Jaime, he has just this moment confessed . . . What! *What!* Oh, no, no, of all days! But how, what happened, I spoke to her only yesterday, at this very time of the morning? Oh, terrible . . . terrible . . . terrible!" And with coffee soaking through the sheets and covers, and percolating to her skin, she burst into tears.

Book Four

THE COUNTESS
OF A THOUSAND TEARS

In June of 1955, Sofía Prades y Caro, Condesa de Mil Lágrimas, celebrated her nineteenth birthday. For this particular occasion, her mother, the Marquesa, summoned the family to one of its rare reunions. Present were Consuelo and her husband Jaime, Ignacio, and—of course—Don Emilio.

The priest, who then resembled the father of the friar in the "Burial of Count Orgaz"—with the same incandescent mystic's face, the cadaverous cheeks, the wide and sensual mouth, and the long, trailing nose; but with every feature gentled and humanized by age—offered up Mass in the chapel of Número Catorce. The Marquesa always enjoyed this. The chapel is a cool Gothic enclosure within the palace, situated just south of the ballroom. It seats fewer than fifty worshipers, which is perhaps forty-eight more than have regularly worshiped there in the past hundred years or so, although there are hollows in the floor near the altar rail said to have been depressed by the devout knees of the XIIth Marchioness of the line. Fluted pilasters rise up to arch across the ceiling, as graceful and austere as the branches of elms profiled against a winter sky. The gray stone walls are unadorned, saving pairs of large, castellated "hachones," as they are called, whose staffs are sheathed in red velvet and set angularly into iron brackets, causing the wax of the thick candles they bear to dribble sootily on the flagstones below them. Behind the altar—a slab of rusted white marble resting on the wings of stone griffons—hangs a fine fifteenth-century retablo, with Christ benignly (for the times) crucified on the central panel, suffering it seems more from commiseration than from the torture, the side panels recalling those happy miracles of His Galilean days.

It was as if to suggest that God the Father could not bear not suspending His Son's agony with at least a few visions of remembered joy. This was the Marquesa's fancy, anyhow. But it was not only the retablo, the intimacy of the chapel, and its ancestral recollections that she loved. When Don Emilio cupped Host and Chalice in his attenuated hands, and raised his eyes to the Christ of the retablo, offering up Christ to Christ, Godson to Godhead; and when there issued out of the dark hollow of his open mouth that sepulchral *hostíam . . . puram, hostíam . . . sanctum, hostíam . . . immaculátam, Panem . . . sanctum vitae aetérnae et Cálicem . . . salútis perpétuae;* then the Marquesa felt always a sob roll up her throat, and tears well into her sea-green eyes, at which ever vigilant Nati, kneeling behind her, stuffed into her mistress's face the extra handkerchief she never failed to pack for the occasion.

After Mass, they gathered at an oaken board long enough for the seating of twenty-four people. The priest was silent, withdrawn. The Marquesa watched him fiddle with his merluza, which had cost her the earth. A glare deterred Nati from snatching his plate away (he would not have noticed it, she knew); finally losing patience herself and blurting at him, "Dios mío, Emilio! Put some of that fish inside you or I shan't ever invite you to lunch again!" Whereupon he gave his Knight Templar's head a good sacudo, opening surprised eyes at his hostess, begging her pardon and forking hurriedly into his mouth a few threads of white meat. The Marquesa grunted.

Twice in the past year had Don Emilio been carted to a clinic, where he had been treated for malnutrition. Oft had the Bishop, himself unlikely to suffer from the same sin, lectured Don Emilio on the perniciousness of ill-using the body God had given him. His Grace's reprimands had little effect. Emilio was as obstinate now as he had once been gallant— breaking with his King over Moroccan policy, breaking finally even with Ramón, his closest friend. They could both be burros, those two. It was Emilio, Conde de Cortijos, who abruptly renounced his title, severed his engagement to Marisa, gave away his property, entered a seminary, and emerged five years later as an apostle of the Republic. Perhaps only the Marquesa knew why this radical metamorphosis had been precipitated, but that was all many years ago. Passion had been humbled. There was scarcely a trace left of the old arrogance. Certainly, when matters of God were at issue, Emilio was still capable of jerking his head up in the old manner, and letting flash an eagle's golden shaft of scorn or reprobation; but his lips at once tightened with pain when that happened, and he forced his head down, lowering his eyes; and planned, probably, she always suspected, to freshly mortify the Devil in him that night, perhaps by slipping into the church after the last evening service, falling on his knees, spreading his arms wide, and turning himself into a stone figure of repentance until he dropped.

But it was Sofía, sitting in honor beside the priest, who at this moment caused the Marquesa most anxiety. Sofía was looking so very beautiful, and so desperately pale and resigned: the sight of her quite dissolving her mother's heart. Jaime, dear one, was doing his effervescent best to cheer her; and after a while, Sofía began to smile, and then a giggle escaped her, and then that silvery burble of laughter that came from God knew whom among her ancestors, but whose sound relieved her mother considerably. She looked across the table toward Ignacio, who was then thirty-two and still a bachelor. The way *he* fiddled with his fish . . . The habit of taking everything into his mouth as if it were offensive to the taste buds, or as if he were condescending to the fuel his body needed, had cropped up when Nacho was thirteen or so, and had never failed to irritate his mother, although now that he had removed himself to bachelor's quarters she had fewer opportunities of experiencing this annoyance. Ignacio sat wholly taciturn as though brooding over matters whose airing before this company would waste his time, and when another of Jaime's absurd sallies again wrung from Sofía that purling cascade, Ignacio's handsome eyebrows arched themselves into perfect ogees of wonderment and (his mother felt) disapproval. "Clear the table, Nati!" the Marquesa commanded, turning her attention to

Consuelo: her eldest: and scarcely an improvement on the scion of the family, at thirty-six more voluble than ever and all at once mushrooming over the tight elastic waistband of her girdle. Consuelo was blabbing at Don Emilio, who, the saint, now that he had recovered himself, bore with her as if she weren't a thorough bore, and even made patient efforts to elicit the logical or at least allusive links between the battery of non sequiturs; efforts wholly wasted because Consuelo was never interested in anything except emptying herself as rapidly as possible, and as fast as they popped into her mind, of whatever thought-morsels piled up pent there, as though her skull might shatter unless she unloaded the cargo.

The Marquesa, recognizing an aspect of her own character, was depressed. Observing her children, she was able to study several mutations of the human ego; and it rather dismayed her when she considered that they had all issued out of her loins. One could not broach the subject of Sofía to Sofía. Biddable as the girl ordinarily was, her self had become engrossed in the tragedy of that past November. She would deem anyone's interference, even her mother's, a breach in faith, a sapping maneuver aimed at the integrity of her love, whose memory had so swollen that it had become her sole reality. She fed that memory with devotion. She would regard any attack on it much as an alcoholic regards interdictions on his drinking. To the romantic, love and love's memory are similarly a matter of self-preservation. The romantic exists through love, and fights stubbornly to protect even its ghost.

The Marquesa sighed. The escaping sibilance of that sigh at once caught Don Emilio's attention. The priest, in a lightning glance, riveted his eyes on hers; but the Marquesa turned her head away. Was there a human being, she wondered, who went to the grave without having done irreparable harm to another? Were there mothers who had not failed? The priest kept shooting at her his penetrating looks. She rather feared them. Emilio was not like other men. Of late, becoming more and more apparent in the past decade, his spiritual powers had burgeoned, as if having grown beyond his control. "Forgive me, Father . . ." a penitent would begin, only to be interrupted. Before having heard its recital, Don Emilio would discuss and absolve the person of the precise sin weighing his soul. This did not happen always. The phenomenon was becoming more frequent. Now when he took his turn in the confessional, crowds queued.

Madrid had had its precedent in San Benito, of whom such stories are told. In Italy, there has been Padre Pío, who also read human hearts. Besides, Don Emilio *looked* a saint, his face and figure shouted of a tradition as old as Spain. He was the King's Warrior become God's. Age had bent the spine. Age and fastings and selfless devotion to the wretched of the parish had made gaunt the frame, etiolated the features, thinned to parchment transparency the skin, and crowned his head with a nimbus of white hair, the flesh so strikingly chastized that easily could he have modeled an Old Testament prophet for some contemporary Michelangelo. It was a scandal.

And an embarrassing one. Lifelong, he had been the equivocal spirit. He had veered so far à gauche as to have deserted the bumbling Catholic CEDA for the socialist UGT (which was to prove no less bumbling). True, upon the outbreak of the Civil War he had recanted, and his subsequent rôle in the conflict was nothing if not legendary. But he was no Falangist. He remained an outspoken Republican, and a preacher (until admonished by his superiors) against the Establishment and the economic hegemony it had not curbed. There remained sufficient ambiguity about his position to call for hierarchical prudence: he would never be entrusted with a parish. And as for people who had known the Conde de Cortijos in his youth, the latest evolution was unsettling at the least. Maverick noble, maverick hero: was it possible he had become God's fool? To acquaintances of yore, the notion was uncomfortable, even unacceptable; and many preferred harkening to the dark whispers of heresy being circulated among envious clerics. Perhaps only the Marquesa fully accepted Don Emilio's transfiguration, if so it can be called. He did not embarrass her. Ordinarily, he revived her faith and hope.

Once, long ago, at a ball in the Palacio del Oriente, he had confessed to her. Since 1939—sixteen years, now—he had been her confessor. Theirs was a rare relationship. Knowing the weakness against which he had waged a lifelong battle enabled her more freely to divulge her own transgressions. Neither realized how much honor this mutual respect did them. The blurted confidence more often than not destroys friendship. The soul that bares itself invites in ungenerous souls the edge of contempt. But at that time, the Marquesa had been in a position to forgive Emilio, Conde de Cortijos. And then, years later, Don Emilio, sacerdot, had earned the right to absolve her before the very throne of God. Because they had not dishonored themselves, love of a particularly beautiful kind held fast between them. Should she call upon him for help?

Sofía revered him. The Marquesa, however, was apprehensive about enlisting his aid. Emilio was apt to approve Sofía's alarming notion of entering a convent. What could be more wonderful, he might likely say, than for the girl to espouse herself to Christ? Of course, he was perfectly correct; but holy as he had become, he did not know her daughter the way she knew her daughter. Holy as he was, Don Emilio had never really known that daughter's mother, else himself he would never have plunged into a seminary.

Times such as these, the Marquesa missed her late husband. Experience had taught her that man's function in the lives of women is largely peripheral. Man is woman's epicycle, a ball rolling on the circumference of her ego, her affairs the real business (as she believed it to be) of life. She had once seen a flaming photograph in the Spanish edition of *Life* magazine. She had thought it was the sun, a vortex of hot orange gases spewing into space for thousands upon thousands of kilometers jets of unimaginable heat and ferocity. Looking closer, she noticed within the ball of this sun, near its center, a dark bloody nucleus, like a spot in the yolk of an egg. Then she read the caption and realized that she was indeed looking at an egg, a human egg, and that the blunt-headed wiggly things swimming into the fringes of this sphere, being trapped in those fiery jets, represented spermatozoa. This photograph struck her as the most explicit portrayal of life's truths she had come across. When begetting, a husband has an active function within the household: he penetrates then, if briefly, to the center. Otherwise his rôle is tangential. He provides. He protects. He makes seating arrangements easier (not always, to be sure, as when there are eight or twelve at the table). He is an

escort. He can be company. He is a convenient outlet for physical energies that may linger in the wife after a few childbirths, although he can
be more often a bother. It is not until children approach adulthood that
any real need of him is again apparent. Then (she now acknowledged)
his masculine presence can be a help, and his counsels of first importance.
Yes, on the whole, after due reflection and eighteen years of widowhood,
she could aver that she missed Ramón.

What to do about her darling daughter!

Sofía herself had not the slightest idea. By way of complicating
matters, she had been born with a certain inertia of the spirit that encouraged her to be content with things as they were, unsatisfactory as
they might be. Having staggered through the Spanish equivalent of sec-
ondary school, her formal education was completed. In 1955, only indigent young ladies of her social standing embarked on a career, and
although her mother was by that time feeling the economic pinch, the
situation was years away from crisis. Sofía's options were prescribed.

1. *She could resume the debutante whirl.*

Of her options, this one alone dismayed her. She was timid—unused
to socializing. Seventeen years separated her from Consuelo. Thirteen
years separated her from Ignacio. She had grown up almost alone in a
house governed by two aging women, haunted by the past, and stalked by
the future. This she did not mind. Before she was ten years old, she had
established a detente with Nati. Her mother, she loved. And for Sofía, the
many rooms and nooks of Número Catorce became her brethren.

Each possessed its character. Each had its secrets to tell, penetrable
only by long association, when the room became accustomed to her presence, began to trust her, and finally confided its history. At peace would
she wander through Número Catorce, mixing anecdotal fact with fancy
as she went. Passing into the rose room one dark winter afternoon, she
picked up and fondled the pierced ivory fan left there by Queen María
Luisa. From her mother, Sofía had learned the lore of the fan. Now her
imagination heaved with the wine-dark mysteries of souls long ago dead.
The exposure had not been accidental—she was sure of that. Two strong-
willed and sensual women, the Queen and the Duchess, engaged in a
no-quarter feud. Oh, no: the exposure was purposeful.

There sat Goya on the Louis XVI settee, summoned. Did he know
by whom? Sofía doubted it. He was a harassed man by this time. Queen
and Duchess imperiously arranged the sites of assignation, messages de-

livered while he was in a fury of creation, but which he dared not disobey. He must have been in a frightful temper, scowling as he stared black visions into the whorls of the Aubusson, hunched over and clutching with both hands the lapels of his cloak. His hands and fingers were spotted with paint, and smelled of turpentine. His fingernails were black with paint and grime. He was frothing over yet another portrait commission from the King, who did not seem to mind nor how often nor how savagely he was caricatured. It made the painter despair to think of reproducing once again that blank inbred royal visage. And he was sick to death of women.

But there, stalking his back, came the Duchess of Alba. She had slipped into the room through a portiere, one still in use, concealing a servants' entrance. How often had it rustled to such hands on such missions? Hardly a rustle did the Duchess's voluminous skirts make. She was dressed in emerald taffeta trimmed with velvet and ermine, a riding habit, with a tuck on one hip splitting the skirt in the front and showing tiny black boots. Her hands crept upon the painter's shoulders. He started, stiffening. She released a rolling chuckle, stooping to nibble his left ear, and then to nestle her smooth right cheek against the unshaven, unwashed swarthiness of his left cheek, teasing him with sardonically delivered endearments as with a shake he tried to free himself from her hands, to scowl more ferociously yet into the frenzy of demonic images that his burning, bursting brain had been gouging out of the carpet. But she did not let him go. She heard well-known steps approaching the double doors behind them. The Duchess smiled. Roughly, she twisted Goya about, planting her mouth on his lips and throwing her weight forward on him, so that they were both flung stretched on the settee, to be discovered thus by the Queen.

There was always some sort of intrigue in Sofía's fancies, and romance. She loved passionately the historical novels of the Marqués de Rivas. Valle Inclán's saga of the Carlist wars was a discovery for her, because it was in the last of these dynastic battles that her maternal grandfather had broken with the Bourbon tradition of the family, and had been stripped of his fortune. Sofía's favorite French author was Dumas. She delighted in *Little Women*, *Wuthering Heights*, and anything by Jane Austen. *Gone With the Wind* she read four times through, and *El Platero y Yo* she kept by her bedside, along with her manual of prayers. All through her adolescence, there was nothing she enjoyed better than to secret herself in one of the vast chambers of Número Catorce, curled up in a sofa, reading until even the dim light seeping through the cracks in the persianas faded away. Then would she rest the book on her knees, and dream into gathering shadows. And even now, at nineteen, she still found solace pouring her heart into the secret pages of a fat diary bound in blue calfskin and locked by a gilded clasp, composing gobs of sweetly melancholy verse, most of it dedicated to the Virgin Mary and St. Teresa of Avila. Her launching into society, taking place when she was just eighteen, had disillusioned her. Romance is by nature brief, an interlude. Romance is not raucous, nor loose lipped with intoxication, nor lewd: the parties, and the gallants attending them, affronted her one thousand years of breeding.

2. *Sofía could marry.*

    She had nearly achieved this second of her options. Late in August of 1954, at a wedding in Santander, she had met and fallen shatteringly in love with Fedi Sacedón, scion and heir.

    She knew it was no lesser attraction than love. In his presence, her heart leaped. Her bosom palpitated. Her cheeks flushed carnaline, and her soft doe's eyes glowed like chestnuts embedded in velvet. Federico was tall and fair, twenty-four years old, with a limber elegance and disciplined features. He was a doer, she knew—the pride of the old Duke, an honor graduate in law and first among his fellows in the stiff Spanish diplomatic examinations, a career for which his breeding admirably suited him. But it was the inward-looking streak in his nature that Sofía found so congenial. He had a poetic forehead, narrow and high, with deep-set dark eyes that rested on any object thoughtfully. His lips were thin, patrician, even severe; yet his special beauty shone in a smile that, after moments of contemplating whatever or whomever, spread slowly over the mouth, softening his entire expression; so that one felt signally honored. The memory of that smile was one of Sofía's treasures: how first his eyes had sought her out at the reception, and rested on her; how the unfolding of his lips had gladdened her whole being. "You are beautiful," had been his first words— "Eres bella," his simple, objective observation; and it was as if those vowels and consonants had never been strung together before, and as if her beauty had no reality and less relevance until he pronounced on it. Almost at once, they were talking books, and when she heard him trace rhythms in García Lorca back to Calderón, quoting fluently from their works, reverence was awakened in her. Sofía had been born to worship her mate.

    They were second cousins; generations of common alleles mingled in them. The Marquesa approved; the Duke was overjoyed. The Duchess, however, fretted, and precisely on consanguinous grounds, having re-

cently wept buckets over an historical novel dealing with the dolicho-
cephalic dolors and worse prognathic woes of the Spanish royal family.
But the Duke pounded down her objections with a paperweight,
declaring there was nothing the slightest bit awry with the skulls or jaw-
bones of either young person; and he sealed this affirmation right then
and there by giving Sofía one of his steely prosthetic hugs, having been
born with a pair of flippers in place of arms. It was agreed that an engagement could be announced on the first of November, with the wedding planned for some time the June or July following.

For Sofía, that autumn harvested happiness in an abundance she
could never have imagined. The engagement ball, held for various reasons at the Real Club de Puerta de Hierro, was a dream she floated
through as though somnambulant. Details escaped her. It was as if diamonds had been set into her eyes, dazzling her with their icy rays. When
the last dance was called, Fedi took her into his arms. He held her tightly,
to his heart, whispering, "If God struck me down now, I wouldn't care."
They were to meet next afternoon at Somontes.

The Real Club de Tiro de Pichón—Somontes—is situated on a high
northerly knoll commanding a view of the live-oak Pardo forest below
and the snow-capped Guardarrama mountains beyond. Sofía herself did
not enjoy pigeon shooting. The heaped torn bodies of the birds tore at
her heart. But the purpose of the jaunt this afternoon was to teach Juan
Luis, Fedi's twelve-year-old brother, how not to miss quite so often as he
customarily did. Fedi was devoted to his only brother; and Juan Luis
reciprocated with a puppylike adoration. Seeing them together filled
Sofía with special happiness. From her mother had she heard about the
bond between Ramón and Alfonso, elder brothers whom she had never
known. Ramóncito had been killed blazing his way through attacking
Loyalists, heaping them about him as he stopped a gap in the lines. Alfonso had been killed blazing a path to his brother's side, to fall within
a meter of him. For Sofía, it was as poignant as it was enchanting to
watch the del Val brothers. The elder, who had inherited a measure of
his father's impatience, was painstaking when anything concerned the
younger, whose failings, in the old Duke's eyes, were as copious as they
were irredeemable. It was Fedi who had taken Juan Luis's poems to Sofía.
When she praised them, and helped with a few cumbersome rhymes,
the boy was won over. She was now included in his pantheon.

The sun, descending, pulsed long, long shadows over the Pardo,
rusting the granite heaps of the Guadarrama and bluing its saddles of

snow. The sky was so oceanically blue, and the air so crystalline, that every rugged wrinkle on the immense lower rampart of the sierra stood out strikingly. The skins of Fedi and Juan Luis were chilled pink, over which the sun now cast a wash of gold. How handsome they both looked! She sat huddled on a painted metal armchair, in the open section of the spectator's terrace. The brothers stood in consultation about fifteen meters away, on the lower reaches of the concrete handicap ramp. Juan Luis had blundered down his first pigeon, and then missed nineteen in a row. He was crestfallen. He was humiliated before the helpers who set the traps. Noticing this, Fedi dismissed them. Now he was trying to put heart into his brother. Juan Luis stood in shooting readiness, at stiff (much too stiff) attention, a long .12 bore held to his right shoulder and trembling in the short-armed grasp of his left hand. His right cheek pressed tightly upon the comb of the stock, having been cautioned by Fedi that part of his trouble came from lifting his head just as he pulled the trigger. "Now remember, when the trap springs open, there's a *lion* on the pad, not a pigeon. You're alone, facing it. And if you don't kill it . . . why it's going to spring on you and gobble you up. All right?" He cuffed his brother on a shoulder. "Manitas, we'll try it again."

Fedi then stepped back a few meters, to Juan Luis's rear and right, placing him somewhat to Sofía's right also. In his hand, he held the electrical pigeon release panel. "Listo," quavered Juan Luis; and then, "Pájaro!" Sofía watched Fedi press the button, and heard the roulette whir of the bearings. The outermost trap on the right, the most difficult trap, fell apart in a flurry of thrashing wings. The pigeon rocketed into the air. But instead of driving for the barrier fence, away from the club house, it came back at them as if gale-blown, causing Juan Luis to pivot sharply. He missed the lion with his first barrel, and on firing the second barrel hurled two and a half ounces of burning lead into the breast of his brother.

3. *She could renounce all thought of love and marriage forever, stay home with her mother and languish into a virginal old age.*
    This had become the ominous pattern of Sofía's past seven months; even though the Duke of Sacedón, usually a stickler about the conventions, called personally to urge the young girl out of mourning and back into social life. But Sofía resisted any such idea for reasons more profoundly feminine than anyone except her mother suspected. With instinctual vision, she appreciated that the tragic romance of her love affair was unlikely to be repeated in life: that she had been granted at the

outset an episode of singular beauty. Never venturesome, that wisdom advised, "You are a figure of pity now as never again will you be. You are the true heart. Even as age withers your bosom, and wrinkles your skin, and fades your eyes, people will say, 'There goes Sofía, Countess of a Thousand Tears. She was lovely before. She is now more beautiful than ever.'" Thus was her poetic and literarily nourished nature tempted; and the Marquesa feared. She feared this tendency perhaps more than Sofía's notion about retiring to a convent, which was the last of her options, and dangerous because once inside a convent's walls, she was unlikely to summon the energy to walk out. But that sort of step—already a little out of date—was in Sofía's case especially ludicrous.

"Amor," she said to her daughter as they were returning from the evening Rosary at San Andrés, "you of the three are in many respects most like your father."

"In what way, Mamá?"

"You are physically passionate."

Sofía blushed, but the Marquesa trotted right along.

"There's nothing the slightest bit wrong with that. Peter was a passionate man—my favorite among the Apostles, by the way, I can't believe Our Lord preferred John, perhaps he didn't, we have only *John*'s word for that. Augustine . . . Francis and Ignatius: many, many of God's servants have been passionate, and the best among them. But you—my darling, my precious, gentle lamb—you lack one element in your nature they all possessed: a will of iron. Without which, you may not *dream* of the cloistered life."

Sofía was chagrined by her mother's directness. Unbeknownst to the Marquesa, she did seek Don Emilio's advice. He listened gravely as she spoke of her vocation and her mother's dismissal of it; and then smiled, lifting Sofía's lovely chin with one set of tapering fingers; and gazed mischievously into her pure, troubled eyes; and then threw his head back and laughed so heartily that she thought he might rock right out of the chair he sat in, carcajadas of laughter culminating in a hacking cough that quite paralyzed him, so that Sofía hastened off her knees, went to the shelf above his bed, decanted a gush of water into a glass, and supporting his shoulders with one arm, helped him drink from it. He apologized. He wiped his streaming eyes with a handkerchief; wiped his lips; and then blew his nose. All that time Sofía stood staring at him with a sense of shock and betrayal. Holy men did not kill themselves laughing when virgins who had suffered tragically from love offered their souls to Christ. Even now he sobbed for breath, and chuckles ruckled out of his mouth. "Child," he gasped, "God . . . created you to give some man happiness, and to raise . . . flocks of children!"

Matters were thus at impasse. But four weeks after the birthday luncheon, this was overcome, and Sofía's fate sealed: by the final in an exchange of letters consequent on a conversation between her mother and her mother's dearest friend, the Condesa de Magascal.

The Marquesa was then a vigorous woman of fifty-seven. Marisa Tamames de Magascal, approximately the same age, was already showing signs of the subluxation that would plague her later years and that even now was exaggerating the hippicness of her awkward frame.

They sat in the dining room, foraging through the remnants of a high tea. It had been served by a slatternly new maid, a dwarf nearly in the brachycephalic Velázquez style, who could not seem to keep her two-and-a-quarter thumbs out of anything. In such ways was Marisa Magascal very Spanish, after the Goyaesque fashion, although in other ways one felt that English corpuscles in streaming packs went tallyhoing through her veins.

"Sofía," stated the Marquesa between gulps, "simply can't go on shuttering herself up. That's a terrible temptation. I remember when I was ill in the early days with Ramón—losing children and so forth— how tempting it was to *stay* in bed, not get up at all!"

"It's a danger indeed," said the Countess, ginnling the last cupcake out from under the very cunning of the Marquesa's left hand. She had lost two columns blitz already that afternoon, and she was smarting. "Can you interest her in art?"

"Too sedentary."

"What about a course at the University on Tirso or Lope, or some other rollo who will bore her back into society?"

"I'm afraid Sofía has no head for formal studies. She changes facts to suit her sense of fitness. She won't have François Premier a scoundrel, for example. In her examinations, she had him keep every one of his promises to Carlos Quinto."

"Whatever for?"

"A paragon of chivalry could not be treacherous—not in Sofía's estimation. She knows very little about the world . . .

"I do not want her to go to France," ruminated the Marquesa. "Nor Italy, for that matter. America is out of the question. I can't afford it. Besides, there seems to be a reign of terror there at the moment, that awful senator's doing. I understand young ladies are scarcely safe in broad daylight."

"So you want me to write my cousins in England," said the Countess with her usual perception.

The Marquesa studied her friend admiringly. Marisa Magascal had managed to devour three slabs of cinnamon toast in this brief interval; yet, lucky woman, she never put on an ounce.

The Marquesa thought of Consuelo. Unhappiness, she knew, could express itself either in obesity or in tapewormish consumption. After Emilio chucked her for the priesthood, Marisa had permitted herself to be wrangled into a marriage de convenance. She should have known better; whispers are too often truth wrapped in shame. At once upon discharging the duty of begetting an heir, Magascal had returned to his other tastes. And Marisa had fallen in love with Ramón.

That had been clear to the Marquesa. Marisa, she believed, never suspected she knew. Love is blinding in that way. It is the most difficult of all aberrations to dissemble. When the loved man, as in this case, happens to be loved by his wife, as was still the case at the time, it is impossible. The Marquesa was aware at once of any change in chemistry, and any altering of atmosphere, concerning Ramón. That sensory reception center had not tingled to the warning of imminent crisis; and she wondered, had Marisa regretted, on Ramón's death, having strapped herself to honor; especially after she discovered her only son following his father's mincing footsteps?

She gazed upon her friend. Marisa had tasted few sweets in life, and had received from it few nutrients; and had now become gaunt, angular in mind and body, with a voracious desire to reassert the balance.

"It would be nice of you to write your cousins," she said.

And so Sofía was packed off to the Smith-Burtons, who had a country house not many hours from London.

Lack of any immediate communication from her daughter suggested to the Marquesa success. She was not deceived. After a fortnight, the post brought a missive several pages long over which Sofía had splashed her ardent hand.

"Mamá, this is a beautiful, beautiful place, and the Smith-Burtons are so kind to me. It rains as much as in Vizcaya, and the countryside is almost as green. But the light is silver, not gold. The hills are round and velvety. The woods are deep and dark and tall, the orchards a mass of apples that are almost ripe, and the fields filled with wildflowers, so that you *wade* through them. There is a pond with a rowboat. There are two lakes nearby, and many marshes. Why ever did we fight such a lot of wars with the British?

"There are sixty rooms in the house, *not counting the kitchen quarters and servants' wing!* And they call it a 'house,' just that, not a palace. It is built of stone and brick and wanders everywhere. Help is hard to find, Mrs. Smith-Burton tells me, and harder to keep, Mrs. Smith-Burton tells me, there is a young girl who won't stay long, a middle-aged woman who scolds her and tells everybody she won't stay long, and an ancient mayordomo who loses all his money betting in soccer pools, which is the reason he won't retire. About forty of the rooms— the center part and south wing, which faces west but is anyhow called the south wing—haven't been occupied since the Battle of Hasty, I'm not sure why, they've named a sort of pudding after the battle, I'm not sure why either. Mr. Smith-Burton has explained everything to me at least twice, but when he talks about anything historical the blood rushes into his face, and suddenly he is glaring and pumping his arms and even shouting at you, he writes articles for the local historical society and letters to newspapers four or five times a week, and Mrs. Smith-Burton wishes he wouldn't because he has to be put to bed when he reads the replies. Mr. Smith-Burton is a lepidopterist." The Marquesa paused here. Sofía had printed the word in English. It was a triumph of spelling. "That's a person," she read on, "who collects butterflies. Although he is very big, and quite heavy, and not young, he goes bounding over fields and meadows and bogs, thrashing with a net at the air. He never sticks pins into what he catches. He places them in little plastic flyboxes that he carries in a creel, and then, when he gets home, usually at teatime, he lets them loose. He loves to see them flying about the house. The young maid gave notice yesterday, but Mrs. Smith-Burton has promised to buy a vacuum cleaner.

"The eldest son, Egbert, is forty-six, and he is called Wiggles because he used to laugh such a lot and Waffles because he now puffs such a lot, and it took me ten days to learn that. He is very tall and immensely fat, and he collects stamps. I don't think he does much else. The second son is called Ogden. He is very tall, and very handsome, and he is in disgrace about a girl who dances. Ogden is thirty-four and works in London, I don't know at what and I don't think seriously. There are two sisters. They are both very tall, and one, Heather, is plain, and the other, Georgiana, is beautiful, but I like Heather. Finally, there is the youngest, Billy, who is twenty-five. Billy is as tall as Ogden, and very lean, and not one bit handsome, but I like him best of all."

This letter contained many satisfactory aspects. As if wellsprings had been released, a slew of communications followed. The Marquesa heard a good bit about Mrs. Smith-Burton, who seemed to be a woman of unshakable temperament. There was no further mention of Billy; but Sofía confided that she was no longer writing poetry, nor had time for her diary. At which the Marquesa pricked her ears. This was an excellent development!

Sofía was as a matter of fact drawn strongly to Billy Smith-Burton. Unlike Ogden, he was in no special disgrace. From childhood, his career had been distinguished by the wanting; and like those people who suffer from myriad minor complaints always—colds and hay fever and itches and stomach upsets—but live forever, so seemed Billy in the general pattern of his life, who did not become involved with chorus girls and leave them pregnant, but who also never seemed to accomplish anything quite satisfactorily. Billy did back into Cambridge. He was not sent down. But his "First" was in inattention; and although by build superbly conceived for an oar, he managed with very little help from wind, water, or fellow oarsmen to capsize the light blue scull during a titanic struggle with Oxford's darker blue. "It was not his fault, really," explained Mrs. Smith-Burton in a twilight hour of intimacy. "He is certain there was an American black widow spider in the boat. How it got there, one can't say, and no one else saw it. But Billy is knowledgeable about such things. If he *says* there was a black widow spider crawling up his leg, I am ready to believe there *was* such a spider, even if he imagined it only. His troubles, of course, began at the age of six, when the passion for taking things apart seized him."

Sofía was compelled to wait another week for elucidation. It was a drowsy, late August afternoon. They sat in the west garden, which actually faced northeast, watching cottonball clouds sail slowly across a ceramic sky. Mr. Smith-Burton had gone into the marshes with a snipe gun and his butterfly net. Egbert was cruising the woods with a contractor; he had come back earlier to fetch a rope, because the contractor had fallen into a cistern. Ogden was playing badminton with Heather, and from around a corner of the house, sounds of a heated argument reached them. Georgiana was away in Sardinia, on a cruise. Billy had disappeared as usual into the stables, engaged in a mysterious project necessitating two hundred packs of playing cards, which he had gathered after a door-to-door canvassing of every house in the parish.

Mrs. Smith-Burton sighed, stretching her legs on the floral mattress of her wrought-iron lounging chair. She seemed not to belong to her family at all. She was tiny, perhaps not quite five feet tall, and weighing certainly less than one hundred pounds. Her skin was English—that Dresden tone and purity that was so heightened in Georgiana—but she seemed otherwise foreign, perhaps French, with small, tidy features, small, delicate wrists and hands, and very black eyes. Unlike Heather, who was cardigan-English in style, or Georgiana, whose bold slacks and bolder blouses somehow always suggested that she had just stepped off a yacht in the Riviera and was on her way for an afternoon at the casino, Mrs. Smith-Burton dressed with chic silk taste timeless in cut and quality. Her movements were quick, and always appropriate. No fidgetiness is implied. Hers was a tranquil nature, like the slow meandering flow of the stream traversing a lower lot on the property. She had greeted Sofía, upon her arrival, as if they had met years before, and long had known each other, and as if she was a little surprised to see her on that particular day, but not the least astonished that she had come with luggage sufficient to spend the entire summer, although no one had advised her of the plan. This casualness, far from disconcerting Sofía, put her remarkably at her ease.

"He was a normal enough child," she said of Billy now, "until that time—a good child. He rarely wet his bed. He never fussed with the servant girls, as Ogden came to do, nor did he pig at the table like Wiggles."

"Waffles?"

"He was still Wiggles then. Billy was a bright little fellow, with golden curls I simply hated to cut, but Mr. Smith-Burton insisted they go. That was on the eve of his sixth birthday. Might it have been traumatic for Billy? One can't be too careful. Perhaps Billy felt like Samson, I wouldn't know, but his hair lost that beautiful golden color and turned straight and sandy almost at once after that. Are you chilly?"

"I am very well, thank you."

"The day is drawing on, and so is the summer."

"I am most comfortable, thank you."

"I feel the cold. I do wish Heather and Ogden would stop arguing. Ogden cheats, of course. Waffles used once to threaten . . ."

"He was no longer Wiggles?"

"Good gracious, no! He was already on his way to Ceylon. That autumn, Billy began picking things to pieces: his toys, his father's watch, our wireless. He did his best putting them back together again, but he was rarely successful. Then one afternoon—it must have been the following spring—he came home with a polliwog. He loved the creature."

"What eeze—*is*—a polliwog?"

Mrs. Smith-Burton explained. "He kept it in a pail, feeding it flour and yeast. To my surprise, it survived. It even grew. It began to sprout limbs. This was unfortunate. I should have surmised what was going on in Billy's mind. Often, I came upon him staring and staring into the pail. I should have guessed the struggle that was being waged in his little heart and head—between his love for the tadpole and his curiosity. Are you chilly?"

"No, I am quite all right."

"The summer is drawing on."

"I have my sweater."

"Now, I feel the cold. Mr. Smith-Burton never feels the cold. It's our only bone of contention, actually. Billy took it apart one afternoon; and he sewed it back together again very neatly indeed, but, of course, it was dead. Billy was not consolable. It required every sort of persuasion to get taddie buried. Three days later, Billy dug taddie up again. Ogden complained—they were rooming together at the time. Mr. Smith-Burton was upset. 'What does the boy want with a dead golliwogg, I'd like to know.' There was really no answer to that. I sneaked into Billy's room that night, and—ugh!—eased a *very* dead taddie out of his clenched right fist, flushing it down the john."

"Who?"

Mrs. Smith-Burton explained, wrapping more tightly about her the cashmere shawl with which she had prepared herself. "It did not end there," she said. "Waffles oafishly told Billy what I had done, and Billy at once turned his attention to the plumbing. I suppose there is some sort of Freudian connection, I couldn't say. We had just installed the plumbing. I don't know the state of plumbing in your country, but the state of ours is lamentable. Used you to have troubles in Spain?"

Sofía explained. Mrs. Smith-Burton had put the question as though Sofía had left Spain forever, and some years before.

"Well," she continued, "Billy crawled through cellars and tunneled into walls. He wedged himself in the attic, in a narrow passage between beams. Mr. Smith-Burton became wedged trying to extricate Billy. Old Hodges then became wedged, and Waffles was of course foredoomed. There was a moment I thought I might lose family and servants all at a

stroke. But Ogden, with Heather's help and Georgiana's less than help-
ful advice, extracted them all. Billy persisted, however. He tore out
lengths of piping. He disassembled a drying rack in Georgiana's bathroom
and with it made twins of the one in Heather's bathroom. It was rather
astonishing what his six-year-old hands were capable of accomplishing,
or destroying. He never found taddie, of course, but something astonishing occurred."

"Eleven-nine!" they heard Heather's clear voice call.

"Nonsense!" came Ogden's voice. "Twelve-nine!"

Sister and brother squabbled.

"The plumbing," said Mrs. Smith-Burton, "began to work. It has
functioned steadfastly since. True, it gives eloquent evidence of its functioning, I'm sure you have remarked on it, the whole wing shakes, but
nevertheless it does function. This may have been the most unfortunate
thing that could have happened to Billy."

"Boot why?" asked Sofía.

"*Butt* why, dear."

"Bu-hut why?"

"As I say, I have read neither Freud nor Adler nor Jung, and doubt
that ever I shall. Billy did not find his tadpole, don't you see? The plumbing became effective when he had abolished so many of its joints and
tubes. Taking apart taddie did not improve him. Putting taddie back
together did not revive him. But pulling apart pipes *without putting them
back* was just the thing!"

To Sofía, this explanation of the son by the mother seemed inadequate. Her sympathy nevertheless grew for the young man whom
everyone in the family treated as mentally disoriented, and who was
accorded by them—in an affectionate and tolerant way—little notice. As
the third son, he was unlikely to inherit much of anything. The caravel
of family finances, long a leaky craft, had foundered in an ill-advised
speculation having to do with the wholesale importation and breeding of
giant pandas, regarding which Mr. Smith-Burton was an enthusiast. Unfortunately, the new regime in China proved unco-operative; and the
only pair to be found in the Western world took an instant dislike to each
other, refusing even to chew on the same bamboo shoots. Mr. Smith-
Burton had been supporting the estate latterly by the improvident means
of wood-lot selling. They were down to the last four hundred acres.
Heather explained all this to Sofía. She had inherited her mother's san-
guine temperament. She did not seem to mind the slightest that they
would all assuredly become bankrupt. "Waffles," she said, "isn't likely to

inherit a bean himself, not that he cares, only the stamps interest him since he was retired from his post in Ceylon." These he stuck away in enormous philatelic volumes. "He collects them for what he calls their aesthetic appeal," said Heather. "Not one is worth two pounds sterling." The family was fast on its way to ruin, for which Billy was in no way responsible, but against which he was the least of defenses.

Some hopes were pinned on Ogden. Opined Heather, "He's as likely to marry a Soho harlot as an heiress. Still and all, he *may* catch an heiress, he has nothing against them. Are you wealthy, by the way?"

"No," said Sofía.

"Pity."

Ogden did not seem to mind. He teased her almost from the moment she stepped into the threshold. He had lewd, impertinent, ice-blue eyes. "Our little countess from Spain," he murmured, staring at her from his fixed position in front of the fireplace in the library. She did not like Ogden.

That very night, less than ten minutes after she had turned out the light in her bedroom, the door swung open. Ogden stepped in, closing it after him. It made no sound but the single click of the lock. She was very frightened, clutching in both hands her nearly completed rosary. He was dressed in a bathrobe of dark color. A pailful of moonlight spilled across her bed. Her dark hair, which in Spanish fashion for the young was worn long, reaching to the small of her back, had been brushed by her and twisted into two loose locks that parted around her neck and rested on the covers above her breast. Ogden eyed her, saying, "Charming!" And then, to her intense relief, he bowed and went out.

That next fortnight, he scarcely addressed an amenity to her. His rake's eyes followed her everywhere. It was Billy—distracted, abstracted, unseeing; awkward, brusque Billy—who put a stop to it.

"Stop being shitty!" he said abruptly to his brother, one evening when they were at coffee.

"I?" drawled Ogden.

"Yes, you!" snapped Heather in support.

"What's this about?" asked Mr. Smith-Burton.

"What's *this!*" wheezed Waffles excitedly, who was studying a new worthless acquisition with a pocket magnifying glass.

"Some more coffee, dear?" inquired Mrs. Smith-Burton of Sofía.

"Oh-*ho!*" said Georgiana, who was leafing through *Vogue.*

"Quite!" snapped Heather.

"My little brother!" said Ogden, smiling elegantly, but angry just the same.

"That's so," said Billy, withdrawing now in tone and interest. But that put an end to Ogden's pursuit. He sped off next morning in his Triumph for a London weekend.

Sofía was grateful. She was also impressed. The evening of Ogden's departure, she tried to smile her thanks at Billy. His rambling features were usually unexpressive. His irises—spines of gray, mauve, and gold, fractured glass marbles restless in their elliptical cages—were directed normally at the floor. He was moodily meditative, in the manner of a thoroughgoing egotist. But she caught him gazing long intervals at her, which was when she noticed that his eyes were beautiful, widely set and almost dazzling in their quizzical innocence. And then, finally, his lips spread away from strong, uneven teeth. It was much more than a smile. It seemed to leap from him, enveloping her in a candor and warmth that elicited from deep within her a leap of response.

Billy rose, bade a curt, general good night, kissed his mother on the cheek, and ambled out. Sofía's eyes followed him until a turn in the hall cut him from view.

Heather said at breakfast, "It doesn't really matter—your not having all the wealth of the Indies. Your English is remarkably good. Bih-lih, however, not Bee-lee. But that's not important."

Mrs. Smith-Burton said at lunch, "I understand you suffered a very tragic experience last autumn." Sofía was surprised by her hostess. She had not suspected her of any awareness, nor real interest, in anyone's affairs. She nodded in reply. Mrs. Smith-Burton said, "Coincidence is an extraordinary thing. Forty-seven years ago this coming September, my fiancé was killed in a grouse butt. I was there when it happened, beside him."

Mr. Smith-Burton said after supper, "You don't much care for dogs, do you? Well, never mind. My mother didn't. Wouldn't allow them in the house. Quite right, too. Spotted the rugs. My father was the second son of Lord Fenwyck. To put it more simply, my grandfather was Lord Fenwyck, the Fenwyck who sold Curzon all those eggs. Means nothing, of course. Don't know why I mentioned it. My great-grandfather was a greengrocer, ha-hah! House isn't mine. Belonged to Mrs. Smith-Burton's side. They were right enough with the Restoration; afterward they were debagged again. You don't object to butterflies, I suppose?"

Next day was hot. The younger Smith-Burtons went swimming in the pond. Georgiana looked Sofía over appraisingly. Sofía had donned a white, one-piece knitted bathing suit. She was very browned—egregiously so under the pallid British sun, as though her skin attracted all its bronzing rays, leaving none for anyone else. She had inherited her mother's once felicitous bosom, high, deep and full. Her legs were not long, but her thighs were sensuously modeled, and she had articulated calves and fine ankles. Her feet were small and arched, like petals.

Georgiana said, "I shouldn't wonder."

Waffles pondered matters another week. He intruded on Sofía in the library one morning, where she was studying her English grammar. He seemed taken aback to find her there, blinking his round eyes and exclaiming, "Oh!" He knew, however, that she would be in the library. Mrs. Smith-Burton was strict about Sofía's lessons: two hours every morning, and the household prohibited from disturbing her.

"Oh!" Waffles repeated, peering over her shoulder. "None of them *was*," he noted before shifting his weight into an armchair.

From which he announced, "Billy needs direction, of course. Not so unusual. When the Empire came crashing down about our ears, I was fortunate to discover stamps. Rum things, really. Don't know why I collect them. Saw one auctioned for three thousand guineas last winter. Wouldn't have given twopence for it. Queer lot, stamp collectors. *I* should go back to Ceylon. Poppa ought to be *letting* wood lots, not selling them. I was never happier, you know. It was an irregular arrangement, but she didn't seem to mind, and I don't know why anyone else ought care. I knew Alfonso—your brother. He was at Downside two terms. Remember him. Never met . . . Who was it, the eldest?" Sofía supplied the name. "Ramón, was it? Well, well. Raymond, Ramón. Sophia in English is the same more or less as in Spanish, brown-skinned or white . . ."

"Well," he said, heaving himself up from the armchair, "I just thought I would tell you I am heartily . . . heartily . . ." And, as if overcome by mortification, he waddled out.

At times, Sofía wondered whether all the Smith-Burtons were daft. This is not an unusual observation by foreigners respecting my countrymen, and it may be true about the English of a certain class. The Smith-Burtons did seem to speak in a special code. During a supper party held later that week, she remarked that neighbors, the Tuttles and the Holmeses and the Rutherfords, also deployed codelike phrases. She decided then that the Smith-Burtons were not wholly original. The mystery, if mystery there was, resided in Billy.

He paid minimal attention to her. He was, of course, busy in the stables with his project. He was looking drawn, now, and fatigued; and was more laconic than ever at mealtimes. When their eyes happened to cross, he jerked his away. But one night, pinned to her pillow, she found a sketch of herself. It was awkwardly executed, as if with haphazard, hurried strokes. They slashed down to the apex of the triangle of her face: to her chin. Within that triangle had been shadowed all that belonged to her, her dark eyes and soft full lips. She perceived that the author of the sketch loved its subject.

But when she thanked Billy at breakfast, he scowled, muttering, "It's no bloody good," and walked away. Heather said, "Poor stiff! He can't support a wife, you know, much less a countess."

That afternoon, Sofía decided to visit him at work.

The stables were vacant. The last thoroughbred to have thundered on the floorboards had been sold ten years earlier, after Mr. Smith-Burton heaved himself up on one side to topple off the other. The main building was a square well, flanked by corridors of stalls. There were lofts on two sides, and pulleys that had once upon a time lifted and lowered bales of hay or straw. Billy had made a trestle out of a plank and the pulleys. He stood on it now, fifteen feet above her, dressed in those loose, baggy, pleated knee shorts that make knobby long English male legs look so absurd. He wore a short-sleeved khaki shirt with torn epaulets. Later she was surprised to learn that he had volunteered to fight the Communists in Malaya. He was wearing a pair of dirty and tattered tennis sneakers, and no socks.

Filling the well was what might have been the molecular model of some complicated organic particle (in fact, its title was $C_{34}H_{32}O_4N_4Fe$ *in Fission*). The structure wavered on two long skinny stilts. These were built out of kitchen match boxes. From them grew pyrroles fashioned out of playing cards, all hanging together to form the walls, gables, and high roof of a ramshackle house. As she entered, Billy was reaching one very long arm—it seemed to stretch out from the shoulder with goose's neck elasticity—and placing near the center and top of his creation a king of diamonds. He paid no attention to her, save to murmur, "Close . . . the door . . . carefully. The slightest . . . breeze . . ." She realized then that nor glue nor staples nor any adhering element other than toothpicks held the construction together. He had built it as the Romans built the aqueduct in Segovia: without mortar, capitalizing on valences and stresses produced by the stones themselves to hold them in place. But Billy was doing this with the most fragile of materials. He placed the card successfully. Then, with utmost care—not at all in his usual, ungainly manner—he withdrew his arm and lowered himself to the floor, stepping lightly off the trestle to stand beside her.

"Like it?"

"It . . . it is *maravilloso!*"

"Marvelous, is it? The bloody thing has taken all summer. It's come down twice. The pulley rope snapped when I was working on the super-structure. The right strut gave way another time." He grunted the words at her.

She made her second decision of the day. "May I . . . come watch you work, Bih-lih."

"If you like. If you don't talk, don't move, don't breathe. Let's take a stroll."

Through beech woods. Down dales of hazel and silver birch. Over buttercup meadows. From the sedge of a marsh, with a hoarse cackle, shot up a pheasant. Under the obsidian surface of the pond, carp swirled. They arrived back at the house after dark, and Georgiana, who had returned from Sardinia that day, remarked, "You pair of asses! It's *pouring* rain!"

Mrs. Smith-Burton invited Sofía to extend her visit through September. Sofía cabled her mother, who cabled back permission. Every morning, after her bouts with English grammar, Sofía stole into the stables. She was absorbed by the thing Billy was making. Three, then two, then one pyrrole remained to be completed. Sometimes it took him half an hour to position a single card. More than once everything began to tremble, and she thought it would come down. She held her breath. She bit the bud of her lower lip. Billy had gone rigid. But his expression, she saw, was essentially calm. A light flickered from his eyes, a strange, cool, unconcerned light. One morning he met her at the stable door.

"I've been waiting for you," he said. "It's about over."

"Oh, Bee-leeee!" she exclaimed, throwing her arms about him, giving one of his cheeks a kiss. Then she pushed herself away, blushing furiously.

He did not seem in the least affected, nor to notice her confusion. "Want to see it?" he asked her coolly.

He led her inside. She looked at the finished whatever-it-was, and she thought it wonderful.

Billy seemed indifferent. He said, "Had enough of it?"

"It's . . ." No word occurred to her. But she breathed with an excitement she could not suppress. How ever was it to be moved? What art gallery in London would have a ceiling high enough to hold it?

"Had enough?" he repeated.

"Nunca."

"I want to be finished with it!" he said impatiently.

She turned her head. "What more is there to be done?"

"Watch."

He stooped. She saw that there was a length of string on the floor. One end was looped about the base of the right-hand strut; the other trailed toward them. Billy recovered this end, gave a yank, and the edifice came flapping down like a flock of slaughtered pigeons.

Sofía screamed. Clutching at her breast, she cried out at him in Spanish, calling him cruel, a monster among men. Then she fled, running into the house and up to her room. She flung herself on the bed, weeping until lunchtime.

Sofía descended for lunch. She was the Marquesa's daughter. At the top of the stairs, she set her dark head haughtily on its neck. With cold water, eye pencil, and powder she had erased so far as possible every vestige of her emotional storm. He did not love her. Naturally he would be unable to support a wife, and *never* the Condesa de Mil Lágrimas! He had courted her only in mockery, to once again tumble her dreams like a house of cards. She would weep no more. And she would show these English what sort of blood ran in Spanish veins!

Before she had reached the hall, a wail and fresh tears nearly overwhelmed her.

She fought them back. She took her seat at table with serene unobtrusiveness.

Ogden was back at work, in the City. Mr. and Mrs. Smith-Burton were present, and so were Georgiana, Heather, and Waffles. Billy came in late. He seemed in a foul temper. Heather glanced casually at her brother, and then at Sofía. She glanced as casually away, saying to Waffles, "You've spotted your cravat with the soup, near the knot." Waffles fished his tie up, raising it to his nose for a cross-eyed look at the spot while simultaneously reaching with his napkin for water. "Now you've slopped the whole tongue of it into the soup," observed Georgiana. Indeed he had. "Never mind," said Mrs. Smith-Burton, "it's ratty anyhow, and I wish you would get rid of it. Why do you men tend to khaki and olive-drab in the country, as though you were all still mobilized?" Elaborate variations were woven by the family on this and related themes. Sofía kept silent, eating with downcast blurry eyes. Billy was angrily silent.

"I say," he said to her, grasping one of her arms as they were drifting out to the terrace for coffee.

She yanked her arm free, hurrying two steps to catch up to the others.

He took two long strides that quite outmatched hers, wheeling to block her path.

"I don't want to speak to you, Beelee. I do not wish ever to speak to you again!"

"Come with me for a walk," he said in his peremptory fashion.

"No. Let me by."

He moved again to block her.

"Please come with me."

"I do not wish to!"

Billy swiveled his head about. The family was on the terrace. There was no one in the hall.

He clapped a hand over Sofía's mouth, and with the other arm swept her up and flung her over a shoulder. This was awkward, of course. Muffling her yells necessarily meant reaching with one arm uncomfortably behind his neck. But in this way he stalked with her out a back door.

Sofía nearly choked trying to scream. She wondered meanwhile whether it was so very terrible to be raped. But she kicked hard at his thighs, battering his back with fisted hands, and then raking it with long Spanish fingernails. The hand covering her mouth she bit until she tasted blood. She then became quiet.

Billy strode with her past lawn and gardens, through a copse of tall hickory trees, and up to a knoll on which the rye grass was still sweet. Then he dumped her.

She was on her feet in a flash. Bolts of lightning sprang from her eyes. Swinging with all her might, she slapped his face. His head was jolted by the blow. The skin of his cheek showed white imprints on strawberry red. Sofía slapped him four times more. Each succeeding slap was more weakly delivered. She sat down on a hummock and sobbed.

Billy watched her for a while, sucking blood out of the bite in his right palm. He lent her a handkerchief. When she had subsided to snufflings and coughs, he said to her, "I'm sorry about this."

"I am going home tomorrow!"

"I'm frightfully sorry."

"You are a beast, a bobo, I hate you."

"Oh," he said.

"I don't hate you," she said rapidly.

"Look here," he said, addressing her dead-levelly. "One has to sacrifice the living to bring back the dead. You have to understand that. I built it for you, for no one else, to show you that."

She stared scornfully at him, believing not a word.

He said, "One has to destroy to revive. One can't put the sick back together. *We* can't, living in the age we're living in. We have to tear the bones out of dead matter, and that way create new beings. It's quite the simplest truth in the world."

Still she was silent. But she no longer snuffled, and she was listening.

Billy crouched beside her, stirring grass, moss, and wet dead deciduous leaves with a stiff index finger. All the world around them was hung in low rolling clouds, and rooks called from the distance. He stared at the ground as he spoke, raising his eyes only for rapid glances at her face, and then boring back into the ground again. A mist of fine drizzle—*sirimiri*, as her mother would have called it—closed silently on their knoll, soaking them both.

"Nothing is real, don't you see? Only the suggestion of what is real. Our reality is all a set of baffling mirrors. We get nowhere looking into them. They confuse us. They distort images. They are all great liars. One has to smash them, I'm afraid. That's why I knocked it down. I should have warned you. I can see it must have been a shock. It was tactless— thoughtless of me, and I'm sorry for that. But you'll have to accept this if you want to accept me. One has, after all is said and done, one's class obligations. Both ideas—class, obligations—aren't particularly popular at the moment. Waffles understands. Everybody underrates him, even Father, although they're alike. Waffles collects stamps only because they are beautiful, some of them, which is the only excuse for collecting them, but which quite smashes the point of collecting them as other people see it. Ogden will never grasp that, not if he lives to bed Diana Dors. Ogden, of course, was born with a gross nature. He collects girls because he wants to sleep with them. That's the last thing one ought want a girl for. I'm not a faggot, don't misunderstand me. Look here, *will* you marry me?"

It may have surprised Billy Smith-Burton, but Sofía required more convincing than that. She was strongly conventional. They were now drenched, although the mist had passed on, but he realized that she wished to be kissed. The kiss, happily, was convincing. His lips found hers as bee the honey. And he was kind, he meant what he had said about Ogden. She would have struggled; she would have suffered through a devastating defeat of conscience; but had he pressed for more she would have given in at the last, because her whole being throbbed in a torment of desire, her passions aroused as never before, and a voice whispering the welcome seductive message that she must not allow herself to be cheated this time.

He calmed her instead, loosening his embrace, stroking her right shoulder with one hand, nuzzling her soft left cheek with his nose and fondling her closed eyelids with his lips.

"You're a Catholic," he said.

"Sí . . . mucho."

"We were once Catholics. I mean, my mother's family."

"I know."

"It would hurt you terribly, wouldn't it?"

She nodded. Tears leaked out of her eyes.

He kissed them. His lips blotted the tears off her cheeks.

"We'll get married," he said.

She nodded.

"I have no money," he said. "I don't know how ever I will be able to support you."

"We will . . . find a way."

"Your mother won't object—a pauper, a foreigner, a renegade Catholic?"

"No . . . creo. *She won't!*"

"I can't promise to reform. I love God. I love God with my whole heart and my whole soul. But I don't know whether I have a soul, and my heart may never be whole, and no matter how much I love God, I can't believe in Him. Can you understand that, Sofía? Can you live with it?"

"I will try to understand. I will pray, Bih-lih—with all my might!"

"It's a rum thing, I'm asking you to do; a rum chance you'll be taking. For me and my family, it may be too late."

"I thought . . . for me it was too late. But I found you."

He was silent a moment. Then he said, "I'll be true to you, Sofía—all my life."

She turned her head slightly so that her lips met his. They joined. To the west, a dull lemony glow appeared. It spread. The blue-black bank of clouds on the horizon lightened, and then whitened, and then were shot with purple and red. They kissed. They kissed to the receding rumble of thunder behind, and to the last quakes of lightning above, and to a rush of heavy warm air sweeping the autumnal sky all gold and blue. It was finally unbearable, and he whispered into her left ear, "I want you so badly!"

He rose abruptly to his feet. He stood above her, very tall, very lean, smiling his bony smile at her. "Let's go shock the family," he said, reaching for one of her hands.

Of course, no one was in the least shocked.

"But you are both of you mad!" said Georgiana, handing them full cups of hot tea as they straggled into the library, dripping water and sloshing in their shoes.

Heather said, "It's all fixed, then. Well, that's a relief, it's been a very long summer."

Mrs. Smith-Burton talked about dates, and wondered whether she ought telephone or write Sofía's mother.

Mr. Smith-Burton grasped both Sofía's hands the moment she set her cup down on a table, clapping them together as if they were toys and saying, "You'll learn to like dogs, I'm sure of that!"

Ogden wandered in from London, took the situation in, and said, "It's all as jolly as can be, but you will certainly starve."

"Don't be so sure of that!" huffed Waffles. And then he grasped the tub of his stomach and giggled like the old Wiggles.

Sofía and Billy Smith-Burton were joined in destiny three months later. The reception was held at Número Catorce, and it was the last grand occasion for the house. All the Smith-Burtons attended, except Ogden, who rather spoiled things by getting himself killed in a motor accident, when, as Heather said, he could have waited a few weeks. (Heather has never married; but there are no poets to sing of her love.) The Duke of Sacedón, with the sense of fitness for which he was renowned, gave his dead son's fiancée away, endowing Sofía besides with 1,000,000 pesetas in Financiera Sacedón bonds. This just about doubled her dowry. Billy ate a great deal at the reception. He was hovered over leerishly by Waffles, who for the past several months had been reverting more and more to the old Wiggles, although it had not helped his waistline. "It's a wonderful day, and all that," said Billy irritably, observing the fiftieth dashing young blood of Sofía's generation whirl her out for a dance. "What are you rubbing your tummy-tum-tum for? You'll wear a hollow into it." Wiggles giggled; and then became Wafflishly solemn, saying, "There's something I want to discuss with you and Sofía. Before you leave." Billy could not imagine what that might be, unless Waffles was aware that he had declined the position as a wrecking foreman with a London construction firm, for which Georgiana among others had deemed him singularly qualified; but he managed to snare his bride out of the lubricious embrace of an odiously handsome Julio Something-or-other, escape a converging buzz of her female contemporaries, and with Waffles huffing behind, duck with her out of the ballroom and into the velvet silence of the chapel.

Waffles, looking about him as though he expected Tirso de Molina's

Comendador to clank forbiddingly out of the shadows, fumbled into the vastness of his frock-coated bosom, extracting a ring box the size and shape of an English copper. With a ponderous bow, he handed it to Sofía.

"Wah-fools!" she exclaimed. "Not another regalo!"

He had already subscribed to the Smith-Burton gift of Royal Doulton.

"For . . . both of you," Waffles heaved. "I rather think it ought to be in your name, however."

Billy peered over Sofía's round, delectable right shoulder; and down the devasting contours of her bosom, which was bared in a square-cut satin bodice, and with which (the bosom) he was increasingly impatient to be off.

Sofía pried up the lid of the box. Inside was a scrap of magenta paper.

"Oh!" said Sofía. "It is . . . *very* nice."

"Yesss," sibilated Billy, puzzled. It wasn't a pretty stamp.

Wiggles giggled. He seemed to glow with larcenous glee. "Remember the night you put poor old Ogden down, God rest him? Remember how excited *I* was?"

Neither remembered.

"*That*'s when I discovered it!" puffed a portentous Waffles. "Bid for a book in a lot sale . . . Found this jammed under a vulgar Continental 1772. Couldn't be sure. Had to bide my time—look it up in the Royal Philatelic Society's library. There can't be the slightest doubt now. *That's a one penny British Guiana Number 13, 1856 edition!*"

Billy scrutinized the raspberry pudding countenance of his eldest brother, wondering whether the Moët had bubbled to his head. Wiggles —for it was he without doubt now—grinned at him. Owlishly. Gigantically.

Billy was more irritated than ever. Sofía wore a coronet of diamonds on her piled up dark hair, sparkling even more radiantly in the ghastfulness of the chapel. Her eyes were pools of mystery, in which tiny lights scintillated. Her lower lip pouted with purple cattleyan opulence —and his blood thundered.

"So?" he snapped.

Wiggles chortled. He clapped and then rubbed his palms, digging his elbows into his sides as if to hold the rib cage in place.

"A boy rummaging in an attic found the first one," he said. "There was at the time no . . . other. And it sold in 1940 for fifty thousand dollars."

"D-Dollars?" uh-uttered Billy.

"U.S.!" said Wiggles. "Since the War, there have been offers up to two hundred thousand. It has been insured for two hundred thousand Pounds Sterling."

Strains of "Smoke Gets in Your Eyes" seeped in from the ballroom. Billy and Sofía exchanged one of the glances that bound them ever closer. Carefully, almost tenderly, Sofía closed the box. Glancing once again at Billy, who nodded, she thrust it at Wiggles.

He recoiled from her, batting worlds of astonishment.

"Take it," said Billy.

"Eres un amor," said Sofía, eyes brimming.

"You've always wanted to go back to Ceylon," said Billy.

"This would make everything perfect," said Sofía.

"You could regularize the situation now," said Billy. "There are only ghosts and grave-watchers left in the Colonial Office, no one would care."

"We will never forget it," said Sofía. "I will ask the blessing of God on you for the rest of my life." And she went to him, grabbing him by the ears, lowering his head, and kissing him on the lips.

"I say!" said Billy.

But a roar rumbled over whatever he may have meant. Now Sofía and Billy stepped back, startled.

"You blathering babes in the wood!" quothed Egbert Smith-Burton, great-grandson of Lord Fenwyck, who supplied Lord Curzon with eggs from the greengrocery, nevertheless great-great-great-GREAT-great-great-GREAT-GREAT-GREAT-grandson (on the distaff vine) of the last unbeheaded purser of the last unbeheaded Catholic English monarch. "One can't ever go back, don't you know that? 'S all a dream. Leave it there, a might have been, where it belongs. I've thought and thought about it. Mother and Father, Heather and Georgiana, we can make do. But you're a pair of simpletons. With a future, though. You keep at what you're doing, Billy, and don't let anyone or anything sidetrack you. The stamp is yours. We'll lose Guiana too. It's an appalling thought, I know, but Britain will rise again, if ever it does, because of people like you!"

Madrid was a lovely town in those days—quiet, clean, unhurried. Rentals for spacious old apartments amounted to as little as 5,000 pesetas a month, so that the Smith-Burtons (Billy refused to style himself the Count of a Thousand Tears) were able to establish themselves on an upper floor of Espalter 2, commanding a view both of the Retiro Park and the Botanical Garden. By 1961, however, they began to suffer from the crush of the same vise that had been closing on the Marquesa. They had produced five children in as many years. Then they skipped two years and produced a sixth child. Three more years went by (there was a miscarriage) before their seventh child was born. Sofía now feared she was again pregnant; although she loved children, and she and Billy made love not only out of their joy in each other, but with the deeper, even primeval passion of man and wife, which is the desire to forge new life from their unions. But when they were first married, maids had been content with 300 pesetas a month. Twelve years later they could be surly at ten times the amount, and trained cooks, a haughty breed, demanded as much as 6,000 pesetas. Sofía reduced the staff to a minimum, accomplishing such feats as to combine a personal and drawing room maid in a single servant. The Marquesa complimented her daughter, telling her that she managed wonderfully within the limitations of her resources and the exigencies of her position; and later that day, while on her hands and knees, beside Nati, polishing freshly waxed parquet and relating Sofía's new arrangements, Nati had agreed with one of her disparaging sniffs, grunting, "There may be more to the girl than I suspected." Nevertheless, their income, once ample, now fell short by several hundred thousand pesetas every year. It was a terrifying deficit.

Billy's exhibitions, to which he sold tickets (he could not sell the works themselves, since he destroyed them), were infrequent. So far this year, he had held but one, earning 20,000 pesetas from it. It was Waffles, now most commonly referred to as Egbert, who tided them over. The change in him had been remarkable. Georgiana he had married off to the heir of an Italian automobile manufacturer. Their marriage was a successful storm of rages and infidelities, suiting both. Mr. and Mrs. Smith-Burton had passed away within a year of each other, peacefully and gracefully; and now Egbert, with Heather's competent help, ran the estate. It yielded a profit! Wood lots were repurchased. The forty rooms left to decay since the Battle of Hastings were put in order, and Mr. Smith-Burton's stupendously incorrect historical papers on the region were coolly collected into brochures and as coolly disseminated among travel agencies by Heather and Egbert, who meanwhile stocked the stables with thoroughbreds, the pond with trout, the marshes with mallard ducks, and the meadows and woodlands with pheasants. The place became a fashionable (and very expensive) resort for American executives whose interest in fishing and hunting was only exceeded by their delight in dining evenings with jolly Smith-Burton, grandson of Lord Fenwyck and descendant of the nearly Plantagenet descendant of a royal purser, but a most amiable

host for all that, with a sister whose every gauche angle and tweedy stride
absolutely bugled the Detroit executive's Wodehousian conception of
English gentry. Shrewd Egbert betrayed the Wafflish Wiggles lingering
in him only by the persistence of his belief (springing from who knows
what psychological compulsion) in Billy's genius; and every month he sent
money, tactfully representing the gift as Billy's share of profits. Billy was
grateful, but not deceived. "It's something, isn't it!" he said to Sofía, "—for
a thirty-seven-year-old father of seven children to be living off his brother's
charity." Yet there was inflexible agreement between him and Sofía on
one matter: come what may, Billy was to pursue the cataclysm of his
star; and that required of him every last ounce of energy and working
days that often exceeded twelve hours.

Sofía lovingly, happily, sacrificed herself to the artist. She entertained rarely. Perfume and all the unguents and creams so necessary to
the female she used sparingly. In clothing, she restricted herself to two or
three good dresses or suits a year; and year by year altered them with a
seamstress's skill to call at least a truce with the current fashion. Her dark
beauty helped. It had bloomed. At thirty-one she exuded what never
Dorada Blás would: an aura of feminine completion, intimate and allur-
ing in a way that permitted of male acquaintances nothing more nor less
than the deepest envy of her husband. Her only worry, which was not
economic, she let no one suspect; nor let surface by even the faintest frown
shadowing the peace of her forehead. It was Billy.

Twelve years after their marriage, he was further than ever from
peace of soul. Only in seepages occurring as infrequently as once in a
twelve-month did he let the lava inside him run over; words—a snatch,
a phrase or two—that poured hotly from his lips, and usually late at
night, when she had awakened suddenly to sense that he was awake, staring out of his shattered gray irises up into the darkness.

"Bih-lih . . . ?"

One of his hands would move toward her, and rest with comforting
warmth on her shoulder or breast, whichever it found. His touch, however, connected her mind to his. She would know that he had been awake
for hours, suffering in silence, and staring into whatever desolation it
was.

With a moan, she would turn to him, pressing hard against him the
balm of her body, imploring him to make use of it; and reassure her by its
use.

Afterward, she would lie on her back, her flank against his, her head nestled between the upper part of one of his arms and his lean chest. The hand of that arm would caress her waist and thigh; his other hand might lie still by his side, or might fondle her chin and throat and bosom, or press against her heart, as though its palm listened.

"I love you," he would tell her once more.

And she would sigh, her head revolving slightly to permit her lips to nip at the line of his jaw.

"What are you thinking?" he would then ask.

"That I am so happy. That I should take Marucha to the dentist. That I adore you, but we must both sleep, it is very late."

There would be silence. The fingers of his left hand would trickle from the firm center of her thigh upward. The index and third fingers of his right hand would curl under her left breast, along the ditch between ribs.

He would break the silence. "None of the children brushes his teeth properly."

"Bad teeth come from their English father."

"Disobedience comes from their doting Spanish mother."

"Spanish children are beautifully behaved!"

"Another myth. They are little savages. They make more noise than a rock group."

"I suppose you would have them silent—like all those poor, unhappy children I've read about in English novels! Were you brought up that way?"

"You have beautiful breasts." His right hand now cupped one of them.

"They are becoming too large, I am afraid."

"Not at all!" he said, giving his head a shake. "They're perfect."

"I would not want to be like Dorada. That is . . . too much."

"Possibly . . . I say, d'you know she wants to go to bed with me?"

"What!"

"Yes. At least, I think so."

"But, Billy, that is terrible!"

"I don't know about that . . . She might choose worse."

"No me gusta la broma!"

"Perhaps she was joking. But I don't want her. You're the only woman I've ever truly wanted, Sofía."

"I'm glad!"

"Well, I'm not so happy about it. S'pose I *am* queer?"

"Don't be silly!"

"You were prepared to marry Juan Luis's brother."

"That was . . . a long time ago."

"Do you ever wonder?"

"No. I was a child."

He cleared his throat. "What do you feel when we make love? I mean now, afterward."

She turned her head sufficiently to catch the lobe of his left ear between her lips, kissing it. "That you are . . . my lord."

"My . . . lord. How beautifully you say the words, Sofía. You're a goddess to me, you know. In the shed, I've painted three nudes of you."

She sat up as if sprung from a trap, twisting about.

"Billy! *What* are you saying!"

"I've painted you lying in bed, on your back, with a sheet trailing over your front and pelvis, and you with one hand at your mouth, sucking one of the sheet's corners, as you do sometimes."

"No es posible."

"I've painted you stepping out of the bath, steam rising from every pore of your skin, and the sun flooding through it."

"Bee-lee!"

"And standing, looking into a mirror, eight months pregnant."

"*Naked!?* PREGNANT!"

"Yes, of course."

"But you must destroy them, *at once!* Especially the PREGnant one!"

"That's my favorite. They're none of them any good, I can't paint, but that one is my favorite."

"Since when have you been doing this?"

"Started the first one about a year ago . . . Won't you lie back? You lift the sheet, and it's cold. Also, it tickles."

Her hair, which she had never cropped, came streaming down, its fringes whisking his bare chest as she jerked her head.

"I will lie back cuando prometes to destroy them! Oh, qué ver-güenza! La gente que habrán visto . . . *Who* has seen them, I shall die!"

She hurled those last words at him also in Spanish. He slipped into the language, which he spoke abominably.

"Nothing, I do think—with perhaps the exception of the (she) care-taker."

"The (*he*) caretaker . . . Me? Naked? Him? That awful old man with the crust on his eyelids?"

"But what does it import to you?" he asked in English—as sometimes happened, translating back literally.

"Muchísimo! To have people see me . . . Strangers, friends, one day the children!"

"You ought to be proud of your body, Sofía. Our children will be proud of having had such a beautiful mother."

"I do not care two whistles, not two peppers, about that!"

"You grow more beautiful every day."

"Mentira! I do not care. *Prométeme* to destroy them!"

"Never!"

The word was grunted at her. Sofía sat rigidly. She was very angry. She flung herself back now—but at a distance from him.

"You will not destroy them?" she inquired in a cold tone.

"Everything else, Sofía, the whole fabric of deceit; but not you, nor anything to do with you. I love you in every mood and in every shape—slim as a young girl, or gravid, with breasts and belly swollen in the bearing of one of our children. I dream of you, Sofía, all night and every night, and most of the day. Even when I'm working, thoughts of you rush into my head, and I smile, and my heart is lifted, and I cannot bear for the time to pass so slowly until evening. And, Sofía, when it becomes . . . too awful—working—I go into the shed, and . . . look at the paintings, which are *not* good. It saves me, Sofía my darling. Quite . . . literally . . . thinking about you, looking at those paintings . . . saves me. You really are my goddess."

She revolved rapidly on her axis, in the same motion lifting herself and yawing toward him until the upper part of her body rested on his chest.

Saying, "You must" (kissing his lips:) "not speak" (the crooked descent of his nose;) "that way about" (his chin;) "me. I love you for it" (and his eyelids, under which the eyeballs fluttered) "but you must not think like that. There are no goddesses, Billy. There is God."

"I found you," he murmured, stroking her back.

A phrase or two, snatches: mere fragments. Stroking and stroking her back, he fell asleep. She kept close, timing the rhythm of his diaphragm. Grimily, dawn percolated through the shutters.

On that particular morning, Sofía (first) made Billy swear that he would hide the paintings in the shed's locker, taking them out only when he was *positive* he was alone; (second) importuned him to burn the one of her pregnant, which he obstinately refused to do; and (third), after he had left, telephoned San Andrés.

Which was thoughtless of her. It was a long walk from cubicle to office. Don Emilio had been officially retired two years, now; yet he was besieged by visitors, some of whom left him dissatisfied, because he never fudged on the truth as he saw it.

Like most people worth getting on the line, he sounded curt, saying, "Now, if you are dressed. At half past twelve, if you are not."

He occupied a cell four meters long by scarcely half that wide. There was an iron cot; the bed was neatly made, but sans pillow or coverlet. A rude table stood by the head of the bed. Cupboarded into its lower half were a bowl and pitcher from Talavera. On its surface there was an adjustable reading lamp with a sinuous stem and a tin cowl over the bulb, black on the outside and silvered within. Centered on the wall against which the cot had been jammed was a black crucifix with a silvery, stamped-out metal Christ, the sort one sees in orphanages and hospital rooms. A shelf below the crucifix held a Bible in brown morocco, a crystal carafe half-filled with water, and two tumblers, one of them chipped.

The floor was tiled, with a hemp mat flung over it. There was no radiator. Sofía, as she spoke, kept her eyes fixed on the crucifix. She knelt at a prie-dieu that was too tall for her, and whose bare wooden slats were merciless on elbows and knees. Don Emilio sat in the only other furnishing, an ornately episcopal armchair, dragged in one day by His Grace himself (with the help of two young curates), because he complained that whenever he visited with Don Emilio he suffered from muscle spasms afterward. Don Emilio had offered the Bishop's seat to Sofía, but she had refused, insisting that he use it; whereupon he sat in it as if glumly, long legs crossed, chin and mouth clamped in the palm of one hand—staring at the floor while she unburthened her fears. Billy was in anguish. There was a caldron of anguish in his breast. She could do nothing. He would tell her nothing. And he was farther from, not closer to, God.

"Not necessarily," Don Emilio muttered. For a moment—for a fugitive instant—Sofía wondered about the priest: gone so very dry, it seemed, and since a recent synod of the Spanish bishops, to which he was invited as a sort of *starets,* in singular disfavor with the hierarchy. What—she asked herself—had dear Don Emilio said to shock them?

Nothing. His goodness and holiness shocked them, that was all. He was as ever her dear and beloved confessor. Billy! Billy!

Don Emilio kept nodding in yes/yes/yes wave lengths while Sofía elaborated on what she had come to tell. It was as though he recognized something in the story, something personal. Sofía kept repeating herself.

He did not interrupt her: he was an ancient, practiced listener. People in distress say the same things over and over again, until their tongues are coated with futility, and their throats choke with it, and finally, flatly, defeated, they stop.

"Do you love him still, Sofía?"

"Next to God, more than anything. More than Mamá. More even than my children."

He said: "I was thinking of them. Billy makes no objections that they are being raised in the Faith?"

"He supports it!" she answered, momentarily revived. "He wants them to be Christian. He wants God, padre!"

"Y a tí—te quiere mucho?"

"Sí . . . demasiado." She had been too ashamed to reveal the story of the paintings.

Don Emilio darted a look at her. He *grinned*.

"Everything that is loved under God's law," he murmured, "has God's blessing. Everything loved under God is beautiful . . . and we need never be ashamed of it."

And then: "I agree with you that his mother's explanation of her son leaves much to be desired. I don't think his early career of indifferent success matters. People do, you say, make fun of what he dedicates himself to now. That can wear on a man as he grows older. He becomes less resilient. The ages of eight, seventeen, and thirty-five are great watersheds. They are the ages of doubt, and self-examination, preparing one for the next stage in one's life. Yet, given what his mother told you about his early years, and what you have learned, there is a pattern in Billy—a kind of progression. He was born to a family with, at least on one side, high traditions; but a family that had lost faith in itself. He was born to a nation of high traditions, but also losing faith in itself; and at a time when all Christendom is corrupted with self-doubt. Billy has tried to break from that particular pattern. He marries an alien, from a country little understood by him. But his break is conservative. He selects a nation that is still fundamentally Christian, and a girl, you, who is a believer. In reaching forward, he is reaching back—or perhaps the other way round. But he comes to Spain to live. He seeks something here . . ."

And then: "When did we talk about this last?"

"A year ago, padre. On the Feast of the Assumption."

"Didn't you tell me he volunteered to fight the Communist insurrection in Malaya?"

"Yes."

"Why?"

"It's a very personal matter, with him, I do not understand why, but in Vietnam, he's for the Americans; and livid that we—Spain—don't support them there."

"But he left Malaya before that war ended."

"Yes."

"Why?"

"I . . . don't know."

"And when he came back, he buried himself at home and initiated his . . . his artistic career."

"Yes . . . I think that is when he began."

"Has he ever talked to you about Malaya?"

"A story or two, nothing much."

"By the way," said the priest, "I've absolved you of your sins. If you're guilty of anything it is of spoiling your children, not losing patience with them . . ." And he wandered away from her, sunk in thought.

Sofía waited. Her knees were numb. She would have runnels in them when she rose.

"I fought in Morocco," the priest murmured, "alongside your father. Those were the bad times, before Millán Astray and Franco organized the Tercio. We were under siege once two months, wholly isolated. Terrible things can happen in war. But they only confirm one's tendencies. A man is born with his nature like a tightly coiled spring inside him, which he spends the rest of his life unwinding."

Don Emilio lifted one of his hands.

Sofía helped him rise from the armchair. The priest shuffled a bit taking his first paces; he was getting so old. Eventually, as they traveled the long corridor leading into the temple, the coursing of his blood dissolved muscle knots, and his stride lengthened. Soon she was following his tall, bent back, and hurrying to keep up. In the temple, again with her help, the priest lowered himself to his knees before the high altar. The last morning's Mass had been said. The church was dark and cavernous; but costive nevertheless with an odor that thickened in the nostrils, of rotted velvets and brocades, powdering granite flags, and the fustiness of the human herd.

They prayed together half an hour, silently, elbows nearly touching. The faint glimmering of the scarlet sacramental light witched Sofía's eyes. She might have remained on her knees another half hour or more; except that she was pulled out of her thoughts. By a power, condensing beside her with all concentrated force. Startled, she looked up: and discovered herself being gazed upon; and felt herself being possessed, as if physically seized, by the serene beauty of Don Emilio's face; and she was prompted to the blasphemous notion that she was being rapt by Christ become the Father. "Ayúdame," he whispered.

She helped lift that huge but apparently hollow frame, light as air. His knees had stiffened. He rested lightly on the support of her right shoulder, hand cupping it. He nodded at the central aisle, and they began walking down it.

On the landing of the cathedral's steps, he said to her, "Vete en paz. God loves you . . ." And his face darkened.

Sofía was frightened by the change—as abrupt as if the sun had been sucked behind a cloud.

"Qué pasa?"

But he was deaf. She could tell he was deaf—to her. From his uncommon height, he looked down upon her. His lips moved, as though dryly. No words issued from them. Intently, now, he was studying her. Wells of sorrow rose in his eyes.

"Hija, tienes fé?" The voice was sonorous, compelling.

"Sí, padre." She bowed her head with the last word, and then raised it. She had faith.

"But do you have courage?"

She was at a loss how to answer. She did not have courage.

"But which one!" he asked; not of her. Then: "You know why we are here! Ask of God anything, anything—but never total happiness!"

Her dark eyes filled with mist.

"You believe," he said, "and so you understand that. Billy . . . your husband walked in the desert with Jeremias. He walked with the Baptist! He struggles against the conclusion, but one day he must come to it . . . Do you trust God?"

"Yes."

"Always, and in everything?"

"I believe in God, the Father, and the Holy Ghost, and in His only Son, Jesus Christ, our Lord."

The words came simply from her lips; an affirmation.

Don Emilio stared at the daughter of the woman he loved. He loved Sofía. Lifting his right hand, thumb and index finger crossing the air in front of her brow, he said, "Sí, querida de Dios, vete en paz. There . . ." He hesitated. "There is no power on this earth that can hurt you, nor anyone you love."

Sofía took Don Emilio's benediction home with her. And that evening, upon Billy's return from work, she found him cheerful; as though the words that had escaped overnight had relieved pressures within him.

But Billy's periods of relative tranquillity never lasted long. Lately, they had been briefer than ever. No matter how fervently Sofía prayed, those pressures built back up again. He fought them, but alone. Always, since childhood, he had fought his battles alone. The prescience of Dorada Blás surprised Sofía.

"Where's the genius?" her sister-in-law asked one evening in the powder room of the Hotel Ritz. A reception was being held for the new British ambassador.

"At home." Sofía had never trusted Dorada, who looked at her with gold-green flecks of envy, and at Billy in a tigrine, devouring way. She trusted Dorada less since Billy's words about her that night a year before.

"Does he never go out?"

"As little as possible."

"And you?"

"Sometimes, like tonight, when I think one of us is obliged to."

Dorada was lining her lips with a colorless stub of wax. She was dressed in a beaded and sequined gold-and-silver cocktail gown that hung from her marmoreal shoulders off two rhinestone-studded straps, basketing the opulence of her bosom. Rodríguez, Sofía thought: 30,000 pesetas at least.

Dorada slid her eyes along the mirror, observing Sofía through it. Sofía had her head bent to both hands as she fixed a sooty pearl in the lobe of her right ear. She was dressed in white, a simple thing draped at the back. Pertegaz, thought Dorada: memorized at a showing and put together by a competent seamstress.

"Is he that good?" she asked in a brutal tone.

"I don't understand you."

"I mean in bed!" Dorada said impatiently. She smiled into the mirror.

"I don't like to talk about those things."

"I bet he is," murmured Dorada. She swiveled on her stool now, looking Sofía up and down. "And I bet you're good too, and like it with him, and no wonder you stay home."

Sofía rose, retrieving her purse from the glass-topped table. Dorada laughed.

Glancing down at her, Sofía asked, "Qué te hace reír?"

"You think it's terrible to talk about such things."

"Yes, I do."

"Why?"

"They're intimate. They're between Billy and myself—and God. And no one else."

"You sound like your grandmother. Are you ashamed of liking to . . ." She used an ugly word.

Sofía blinked, obliterating it. She looked long at Dorada. With her dress, all bejeweled, and her spun-gold hair, she dazzled the eye. Her defiance failed to deceive it.

"Are you . . . very unhappy, you and Ignacio?"

Dorada picked up a brush and began yanking at one side of her head. The hair crackled.

"You don't like me to ask such things," Sofía persisted.

Dorada, as though clamping a pin between her teeth, said, "No, I don't; and I see your point."

"Can I do anything for you?"

"Like lend me Billy once a week? You have a man. Can anyone make one out of your brother?"

"You've . . . had children."

Dorada snorted, shaking her mane back into place.

Sofía stepped by her; but Dorada, catching her movement, swung about.

"Wait!"

"Yes?"

"Don't be so smug!"

"I'm sorry for you both, that's all."

"Well, worry about yourself!"

"Why?"

"Your husband's in trouble. I don't mean the police and the military authorities this time. Papá fixed that. I mean whatever it is that's chewing him up inside. You find out what that is. You had better find out before it's too late, and do something about it before it's too late!"

Sofía was alarmed. She went home directly. Billy was asleep. Even thus, furrows plunged from the corners of his mouth to the jaw. She slipped off her clothes and, naked, slipped under the sheets. He did not stir. She woke him with her lips. He muttered, turning away; which was when Sofía learned about terror.

Because he loved her, Billy, she knew, took special pains to conceal from her his struggles. Had he revealed anything to Dorada? (When?)

Had Dorada perceived his condition out of the empathy of unhappiness? (They met rarely in the course of social life. Could they be meeting privately? No! What nonsense! But could she be sure?) Sofía had an instinct for his crises when they were imminent. His eyes became especially translucent, their gray-blues and blacks hardening into flat metallic gray, in the same way as the sea when storm-haunted. He would lose pounds of weight off a body that was little more than whipcord to begin with. She pictured Billy as with his back to a precipice, an enemy, whatever it was, crowding him, and growing stronger as fatigue leadened Billy's arms; and Billy now yielding, fighting over every centimeter ceded, but being pushed inexorably to the edge.

Yet upon coming in from work, he made immense efforts to haul himself out of his interior life—efforts that reminded her of Don Emilio, when circumstances trapped him in social discourse too soon after Mass. It was the same sort of wrench for Billy. Despite which his bony, distracted smile never failed to greet her and the children. With them he played before their supper. They adored being lifted high by him, and then hurled into the cushions of bed or sofa; all except three-year-old Odette, named after her maternal grandmother, who was timid and whom he treated with special tenderness, lifting the child not quite so high and then simply lowering her (rapidly) to the cushions, and pressing her tiny body into them until she plumped with pleasure. After their supper, he read to the older ones, and when the time came for it, walloped them into bed; and then returned to the living room, to slump tiredly beside her on the couch, rest his head against shoulder or breast, and ask her about her day, and sometimes tease her when she opened her eyes wide and professed that nothing at all had happened.

There were magical evenings. Late, when the parlor maid had been dismissed for the night, a rage for each other might possess them. Then they could endure not even the short passage into their bedroom; and two children (by Sofía's reckoning) had been conceived on that couch. Mostly, they passed the hours reading, she a French or English or Spanish novel, and he books about paintings, sculpture, architecture, and science. Once a fortnight, they either dined with the Marquesa at Número Catorce or invited her over to Espalter; occasionally with Marisa Magascal, Billy's distant cousin, and twice a year with jolly old Nacho Pelau and distinguished old Carlos Lapique.

Billy liked his mother-in-law; and she, whereas convinced of his insanity, enjoyed him. When the Marquesa dined with them, neither Sofía nor Billy were burdened with conversational obligations. Her chatter, however, was always sprightly, glittering with swift shrewd insights. "His father made a mess of him," she said of Juan Luis, "refusing even to hear of his becoming a priest. And so now that Juan Luis is the Duke, one can expect him to continue making a mess of himself. You see, besides Financiera Sacedón, Juan Luis is the one monument to his father's memory." And of Baltazar Blás, "Of course he'll get the armaments for you. He is not the slightest bit interested in money. He despises people who are."

She made Billy laugh. Sofía was amused to see her mother coquette him with her dark eyelashes and gray-green irises. It reminded the daughter, child of the Marquesa's old age, that her mother had been considered one of the beauties of her time. The Marquesa confided in her youngest, "You could have done much, *much* worse; I'm sure he'll always be faithful, he's English. I am not so sure about Dorada; and Jaime, of course, is a scoundrel. But, dear, isn't Billy's infatuation with automobiles *very* expensive?"

Billy worked first in a studio, then in an abandoned garage, after that in a large shed, and now principally on new grounds beyond the Casa de Campo. The automotive period in his artistic evolution began in 1960 and concluded in February of 1965, with the American bombing of North Vietnam after the Gulf of Tonkin incident; and it was indeed costly. Billy became a ghoul at police sales of cars that for one reason or another had entered Spain illegally. At junkyards everywhere in Madrid, he went collecting bits and parts. Then, in the shed, stripped to the waist in the coldest winter weather, Billy hammered and welded and painted, achieving extraordinary effects. He might begin with the chassis of a Rolls. He would lop off the hood, attaching in its imperial place the proletarian snout of a Model A. Circling his subject, staring at it with eyes sometimes bloodshot from the ferocity of his concentration, he would commit further sacrileges, such as adding the grill of a Mercedes, the chrome extravagance of a late-1950 Chrysler, and horrific Cadillac fintails. The results often resembled armor-plated rhinoceroses, when they were not so incongruous as to resemble wildebeests.

Every working part, however, was hand-smoothed. The engines, which were also improbable collages comprising tidbits from several makes and periods, hummed when started and roared when accelerated. Mechanical monsters his creations might be, but their enamel (canary-yellow was his preferred hue) gleamed from hours of waxing and rubbing, and their chrome sizzled under the sun.

When a pair had been completed, perhaps after fifteen months of labor, Billy drove them through the streets of Madrid, stopping traffic everywhere. This was good advertising for his exhibitions, which he held in his (AESA's) new outdoor proving grounds. There ticket-purchasers were permitted to poke and finger his automobiles; to peer under their hoods and even (for an extra fifty pesetas) drive them a few feet. This was at a time of insatiable car-hunger, when some one million Madrileños dreamed every night of SEAT 600s, the tin matchbox that has put Spain on wheels and, as it is said, half the population in the hospital—to the extent that the more tender emotions suffered, the rate of wedlock falling off sharply. Having put in feverish morning hours preparing his finale, Billy would drive his creatures up a pair of ramps that faced each other, and that were shaped much like ski jumps. There, poised on the hummocks, engines running, the automobiles would be left.

Billy now motioned spectators back. Riot-arrayed Guardias Civil helped cordon them behind the circumference of a whitewashed circle whose diameter exceeded seventy yards and whose center was the ramps. Billy himself withdrew to a control station beyond the circle. He began transmitting electric impulses. The engines of the two cars revved up: the engines began to scream, and the automobiles to shudder. Their horns blared; each was mounted with a siren that from a low wail yeasted to a pitch so high that people rocked their heads between their hands. And then, at a culminating signal from the control station, the brakes were released, and the monsters jerked forward and went trundling down the ramps.

The actual velocity achieved was never much more than ten miles an hour, but with the first contact of bumpers, hidden explosives began to go off, and the automobiles would blow up section by section, flinging scorched metal parts high in the air, until finally there was nothing left connected with anything else, so cleverly (yet so discreetly: all debris landed within the circle) had Billy mined the cars that morning, and the ground about was littered by nuts and bolts and gaskets, and twisted shards of exhaust pipe, and tangles of wire wheel rims; and rockets now soared into the sky, to detonate in a shower of phosphorescence, and flutter for ghostly moments with the scarlet and gold image of the Spanish flag.

Spectators, frightened at first, gave vent to gasps of dismay as they roused themselves from shock or stupor and gazed upon the still smoking heaps of destruction; and at the first of these finales, three infuriated men jumped Billy and would have torn him to similar bits had not members of the Guardia Civil intervened. But individuals in the crowd, men and women both, were weeping. Their outrage was great. Spaniards, they plumbed intuitively Billy Smith-Burton's nihilism; and their reaction was violent. They hissed. They stamped their feet, waving fists at the author of this racial and religious insult, this profanity against Western Civilization, with respect to which Spaniards consider themselves the prime creators and the last defenders. They screamed for the blood of the Englishman.

The scandal leaped the Casa de Campo and went reverberating through the streets of the city. Oh, perfidious Albion! That evening, at the Puerta del Sol, there was a demonstration calling for immediate surrender by Britain of Gibraltar. Such resentment had been aroused that it invaded the highest sanctum of Authority, and the Smith-Burton affair dominated that Friday's State Council at the Pardo Palace. Camisas Viejas to a man insisted on the Englishman's expulsion; the younger ministers —the technocrats—were less certain. Would not repressive measures hold the State up to ridicule? And Don Juanistas within the Council reminded their Carlist and Falange adversaries that Smith-Burton was the son-in-law of the late noble martyr to True Spain, Ramón Prades y Caro, Marqués del Peregrino, Caballero Laureado, and intimate friend of Su Majestad, Alfonso XIII.

There were moments when it seemed that the ever-uneasy cohesion of rival philosophies within the Government, wrought over twenty-five years of ceaseless effort, would blow asunder. Then, as midnight tolled, an urgent telephone call was accepted from the Director of the *ABC*. A foreigner called John Cage, who happened to be traveling through Madrid, had witnessed yesterday's spectacle; and at a press conference at the University earlier in the evening had proclaimed it among the more significant and exciting advances in European art since abstract expressionism. This astonished the Council, and all Madrid, too, when people read their newspaper next morning, especially since no one had heard of John Cage. But Spain was then eager to establish her credentials as a fit partner in the contemporary world; and so with the sage caution—the *hábil prudencia*—that has characterized the regime, it (as they say) was decided nothing should be done.

Billy Smith-Burton's second exhibition, eighteen months later, attracted massive attendance. People knew what to expect, and there was less controversy. His third exhibition, held in January of 1964, drew fewer people; and his fourth and last exhibition, in December of the same year, was a financial loss. By then Madrid was filling up with automobiles, and disenchantment had set in.

It was when preparing for the finale of this exhibition that Billy received a visit from Dorada Blás Prades. It was a bitter-cold day, but Billy was as usual skinned down to his breeches, a pair of bedraggled Levi's stained nearly black and slick with engine oil. The white, English pelt of his bare torso was frosted pink by the gelid winds off the Guadarrama. Yet he sweated. There was but an hour to go before people ought to begin arriving. He had the whole rear end of one of his automobiles to mine.

Dorada had parked her Mercedes near the entrance of the proving grounds. He had not noticed her arrival. He noticed nothing when she walked up behind him, stopping to observe his labors. He stood as if uncertain, a wrench in one hand, a small stick of dynamite in the other. He was male-rank, the brown bushes under his armpits dripping. His back streamed with perspiration. As he stooped, muscles rippled from shoulder to waist. He was so lean that his bones showed.

"You chose an unfortunate week," she said.

He wheeled in surprise. Fury whitened his lips. "Get back!" he shouted at her, waving the wrench. "It's dangerous, you silly ass!"

She turned it to him in a leisurely manner, strolling to the safety of the whitewash. There she turned again. But he was studying the rear end of his automobile.

"You needn't have growled," she called in Spanish.

"Lo siento," came a low mutter. "Ambushing me like that, I might have banged a cap with the wrench." He squatted, and then began sliding himself under the car.

"It's freezing," she called again. "No one will come."

"Thanks," came a hollow reply.

"I dropped by to ask you and Sofía for dinner next Sunday."

"Why didn't you telephone her?"

"She said it depends on you."

"It's . . . a long way . . . to drive . . . to deliver . . . a dinner invitation."

He was lying on his back, and arching it. His hips squirmed as he struggled with something under the car. The Levi's tightened at the crotch.

She said in a tone as icy as the day, "I thought I'd see to what use you were putting the land my father lent you." She added, "The land I asked him to lend you."

"Why don't . . . you stay for the show?"

"It sounds stupid to me. Ten o'clock."

"I . . . work weekdays."

"Won't you be taking a rest after this?"

Using his heels, he shrugged his body back out from under the automobile. Then he stood up, looking at her. His forehead was smeared with grease. His face was gridded by fatigue.

"I may," he said.

She nodded. "And if you aren't eaten alive by the gallery today, drop over for a drink."

Her hands were stuffed in the pockets of her coat. It was mink, mahogany-colored. It reached to an inch above the knees, which were flushed under the sheathing of her stockings. Mahogany-colored boots, trimmed at the tops with mink, came halfway up her calves.

"I'm filthy."

She gave her head a shake. The hair fell like gold foil over the shoulders.

"It doesn't matter."

He frowned. "I may," he said.

There weren't twenty people to view the finale. Sofía was absent: she could not bear to watch him destroy his work. Juan Hidalgo and four or five other John Cage disciples had rallied to him. Their congratulations failed to cheer. Financially, it was a bad setback. Artistically, he was depressed. He was repeating himself. He had not advanced. He had spent fewer than ten months on this pair of automotive mutants. They had ceased to be meaningful; they had taught him nothing.

Hidalgo asked him over. He nearly accepted. He enjoyed the gentle company of that brilliant man. And Billy did not want to go home right away, where the effort of dissembling grew greater, and where he was ever more torn by Sofía's concern. "I love you," he whispered to her in his mind. "I love you with all my heart, and all my mind; and if I have one, with all my soul too." And he remembered Dorada's invitation.

Half an hour later, he was ringing the Prades's doorbell. His attire—the same grimy dungarees, a khaki shirt frayed at the cuffs, and a sheepskin-lined Levi shortjacket—provoked a minor sensation with the portero downstairs, who took him at first for a tramp. Wonderingly, he waved Billy to the elevator.

Dorada herself opened the door.

"Come in," she said—unsurprised, turning her back on him.

Billy stepped inside, shutting the door. He doffed his jacket, letting it fall on a vestibule chair. He then angled into a reception room that was paneled in authentic French boiserie playing dove-grays and -roses against chalky white. There was a tall, narrow door opposite, leading he supposed, he had never explored, to bedrooms and service quarters. Dorada had turned right through an aperture between the half-sprung sliding doors of an arch, disappearing into a nearly square parlor or card room that interposed between the dining room and a vast, formal living room.

He followed her, coming to a halt under the arch. To his right, there was a burled walnut table of rare quality. On it had been deposited a silver tray with glasses, ice and decanters. This was not Ignacio's study, but the far wall held bookcases flanking a pair of french doors, and the shelves were massed with volumes in fine leather. Along a gilt valence, floor-length satin draperies, burnt-gold, had been drawn.

The carpeting was wall-to-wall, unpatterned, mustard-colored, and thick. Off-setting the off-centered living room doors was a Pissarro landscape, dutifully lit from above and bearing on the base of the frame a modest gold plate that relieved the guest of any doubt. On the opposite wall was a Sisley.

Altogether, the room reflected its owners: rich, unimaginative, and impersonal.

"You desire it neat?" asked Dorada in English attractively curdled by French schooling.

She was poised by the tray, her weight allotted to one hip, upper body twisting on the waist so that her shoulders were canted unevenly toward him. Elbows hugging her sides, arms lifted and hands flung back from their wrists, she seemed to be saying, "Voilà!"

He assented with his chin. "No ice."

"The very thought!" She stooped, throttling a decanter by its neck and tipping its snout into a highball glass. "I have been . . . fro-*zen* . . . since seeing Nacho off at Barajas this morning." She tucked her chin in, glancing up at him from a fall of shimmering hair. "Do close the doors behind you."

He obliged. At once, his nose began to itch. On a coffee table set before a deeply upholstered couch, there flickered a stout green candle. Smudges of incense spurted from the wick. Crystal flue, sterling silver saucer . . . *Rigaud,* he thought, much the mode and without significance.

"Nacho is away?"

"In Paris for the night," she said casually, extending an arm across the table and at him. Taking a step forward, he accepted a glass that held four ounces of whisky at least. " '*La Justice,*' " she murmured, mixing herself a weak campari-and-soda, " '*et les Obligations Subsidiaires Devant le Nouveau Monde Economique-Social.*' A UNESCO symposium."

"Sounds fearfully important."

Dorada strolled with her drink to the couch, depositing it on a side-table before turning and flinging herself back into the pillows.

"It will shake the world," she stated, looking up at him blankly. She patted a place next to her. "Come sit."

Billy remained standing. Had he been alone with Dorada before? He could not remember. Certainly not quite so alone, cut off, as it seemed, from everything except the muffled roar of the city outside. He was tired. He was discouraged. And he was, he knew, uncommonly susceptible. In this womb of a chamber, Dorada's presence and proximity were overpowering. His skull pounded with an acute awareness of their isolation, as though she and he were pocketed in space and disengaged from the rhythm of time. Anything that might come to pass was without consequence. How easy it was to believe that. Cool, composed, she waited for him wide-eyed, fronds of gold framing rock-hard topazes that were centered in icy whites and faceted with speckles of rose, copper and green. Every breath she took reverberated in the rise and fall of her bosom. Her body compelled attention. Sheathed in a jump suit of emerald green velvet, the material hugged as if coveting the sumptuousness of its proportions, flaring below the knees to bell-bottom cuffs that slopped over slippers of vaguely Arab inspiration.

Six months ago, he had first felt the weight of Dorada's interest. Ignacio had returned from a trip to Tokyo. The Marquesa summoned everyone to a family dinner, no less depressing than most, although she did her gallant best to buoy the conversation. Billy was admiring her adroitness when he chanced to notice Dorada's gaze fastened on him. She had given birth weeks earlier to a son. She had had a bad go of it. Eyes glittered above drawn cheeks. Pain had deepened a dimple in her chin, so that it had grown to the size of a lozenge. He found himself returning the gaze.

At just about this time, Sofía mentioned that relations between Ignacio and Dorada had deteriorated, she did not know why; and during the next several weeks, upon the infrequent occasions of their meeting, he had become increasingly aware of Dorada's interest, expressed by an unaccountable flurry of invitations to dinners and cocktail parties, and at these affairs, when Sofía decided they ought go for her brother's sake, by seemingly chanceful tête-à-têtes. These scarcely advanced beyond civilities, but he had come to wonder about the cumulative indiscretion of the most trivial phrases. Words are always in character, and one after another profile the person uttering them, and one upon another expose his interior topography, so that by listening long enough to the most circumspect of people, someone bent on finding that person out can learn alarmingly much. Despite the conversational barriers he flung up against Dorada's inquisitiveness—obfuscations; even rude monosyllables—she plainly penetrated deeper with each meeting.

Just a month ago, at an Orbaneja dinner party, she had caught him alone in the library, where he was skimming through Jaime's collection of works on or by Gaudi, le Corbusier, Skeist, Heinrich Hertel, and other architects or theorists. He remembered nothing about the few words they exchanged until she popped into the air, and out of what he had supposed was the vacuum of her mind, "Do you believe in God?" He had answered that he did not. "How about yourself," she asked then, "do you believe in that?" To which, hoping to be done with her questions, he had replied, "Still less."

But she was not put off, a dog with a bone. "Then what about sin?"

"A philosophical quandary."

"Do you believe in it?"

"Yes."

"How, when there isn't a God?"

"I don't know."

He had begun to sweat. She may have noticed, because she laughed, saying, "How old are you?"

"Thirty-four."

"Aren't you ashamed, not to have answered these things by now?"

"If you like."

"What would you call murder?"

"A bad precedent," he told her, and in a tone as surly as he felt.

"And adultery?"

"A crime."

"Against whom?"

"The betrayed husband or wife."

"Why?"

"They're bound to each other."

"By what?"

"Love."

"And when one of them has stopped loving?"

"By honor."

"What's honor?"

"When do you suppose supper will be ready?"

"What's honor?"

"The oath you exchange at the altar."

"And if there is no God?"

"Explain."

Cream poured over the platter of her mouth. She said, "Then the oath is only as good as how you feel about each other at any particular time, isn't it? If there's no love lost between the man and woman committing adultery, who is hurt?" And she glided away, conscious, he guessed, of the unanswerable philosophy suggested by the susurrant recession of her rump.

Which was, at least, real. In his work, it seemed to him that he was reaching for galaxies that kept receding from his grasp with mounting velocity, so that he was up against something like a Hubble's Law for the arts. He had been absorbed the past thirty days; he had seen Dorada but once and had shunned talking with her. But as he stood during dull December afternoons in the shed, staring at his contrivances, he questioned with ever more uncertainty the value of what he was doing, and finally did not doubt that by repeating himself he was stalling, warding off the ineluctable logic put in motion by the special insight he had been granted.

He feared that logic. A fortnight ago, again at Jaime Orbaneja's, and after many too many drinks, he had let slip to his host something of his fear and its genesis; and had then covered, aborting the conversation. But he had been appalled by his weakness, and distressed by what such a slip might do to Sofía. Thought of Dorada had been preying on him since. There were different modes of self-destruction, the moral and physical. Resort to the one might prevent the other, or at least delay it. And when, as she said, no love is involved, who is hurt? He would be taking no advantage. Julio Caro had boasted often enough that only an improvidential interruption by one of Baltazar Blás's henchmen had prevented his possession of the daughter. There were other such stories, most of them of dubious authenticity, all distasteful to Billy Smith-Burton, who had never become accustomed to male braggadocio in these matters. Now they were frequent visitors to his mind. True, no scandal had been whispered in the three years since her marriage; but Jaime Orbaneja, rearing his Romanesque eyebrows, and touching a very pointed tongue to the lobe of his upper lip, had observed recently (with regret: he felt sorry for Ignacio, and he was not himself the lady's cup of tea) that Dorada had taken on the air of a Diana prowling for game.

She waited, face tilted, brow smooth, carriage almost prim, her invitation to sit next to her friendly without being remarkable. He was unsure of her, and less sure of himself.

"I'll soil the couch," he said.

"No importa."

"Crankcase oil is almost impossible to get off."

"Qué mas dá? I'm having the material changed anyhow."

He gave in.

At this, Dorada reclined back against the arm of the couch, hitching her knees up so that they rested on the middle pillow, right foot tucked under her left thigh, left foot planted on the floor. He sat stiffly. Large, roral glories speculated on him from behind their meshes of gold.

"How did it go this afternoon?"

"Rottenly," he replied in English.

"People are bored by that sort of thing."

"I think you have reason." *"What now?"* in fact, he had asked himself all day long. "How would you know?" he asked her.

The question was blurted in the curt, abrupt manner characteristic of him, as if framed with animus.

"I nearly died of boredom in Geneva," she said equanimously, "killed time in museums and art galleries. Look long enough, you can't help learning something. You get to sense what's worthwhile, what's . . . just a personal indulgence." She smiled.

His eyes wandered to the Pissarro, and then to the Sisley on the wall above.

Dorada followed his gaze. "Do you like them?"

"Yes."

"Would you like one?"

"Thanks very much."

"I'm serious."

"You're mad, then."

He continued in English, she in Spanish.

"Either of them could fix your finances for life. Neither you nor Sofía would have to worry about money ever again."

"I suppose so."

"Does it scare you to think of that—six hundred square inches of canvas daubed with turpentine and paint, a price put on genius?"

"A little."

"Papá gave them to me when I graduated. I picked them out. I told him I wanted a pair, so that later on I could sell the one I liked less and cover the cost of the first or trade it for something I liked better. Wasn't that clever?"

"I should think it depends on the market."

"Or on how you choose in the first place. Commerce is just a matter of timing, Papá says. Think how Impressionists have gone up in the past few years. They're hangable anywhere, that's why. One can't very well tack fifty or sixty million pesetas to the wall, but with a small Monet or Cezanne People Like Us all over the world can let other People Like Us know just who we are. Papá thought I was clever. He said it was too bad I'm not a man, I'd do well in business. I'd get what I'm after. Do you think so?"

He decided not to resent being tacked to the wall. Taking a swallow out of his drink, he studied the woman. There was something protogynic about Dorada. Her face was screen-star large. The forehead was like her father's, broad, and separated into two luminous bolls with a high plateau between them. Brows were wonderfully shaped, lyre-like, but her nose was too long, her mouth too wide, her lips too full, and her chin too heavy. Feature by feature, it was a bold, corsairing countenance, and it would vulgarize with age.

Taking her apart comforted him. He said, "You think like a man. Whether exploiting situations will always get you what you want is another matter."

"And you," she countered, "what do you hope to gain from exploiting your spectators?"

He was really surprised. "I never . . ."

She interrupted. "What gives you that right? Do you think some of us can't tell: that you are like a child who never had his cry, never threw his tantrum, and adopts a public pose, brusque, uncommunicative, but through his spectacles has his cry and throws his tantrum; and begs for notice?"

Whatever he had come expecting, it was not this. He drained the rest of his drink. She nodded at the table. He got up, went to it, poured himself another four ounces, returned to the couch, sat again; and now slouched back against the opposite arm from hers, drawing his legs up also. Knees nearly touching, they regarded each other.

Space, like silence, has character. On the ball of his left knee he felt a furry, tingling sensation. Perhaps, he speculated, electrons were jumping the bridge between them, the magnetism of living, heated, sentient creatures plucking from each other's flesh invisible particles of it, so that there was a precognizance of touch, a tactile suspense, an interlocking of space and a physical filling of it. Her eyes had deepened to amber, contracting on the pupils until they were mere dots. He saw himself reflected in them, trapped there. Her expression was candid with a sort of good-humored scorn, brows arched superiorly and triumph in her mouth. She had plumbed his conceit. She had identified one reason anyhow for the self-revulsion that had grown and grown and grown inside him.

Unless she sought what he sought, how did she dare? He was again acutely conscious of their solitude in this room. No sounds reached them from the rest of the apartment. Horns howled in agony outside. Their lowings came muted through the heavy draperies, and then were drowned by the ordinary rumble of traffic. With a lunge, he could clap a hand to her mouth and suffocate whatever cries he might startle out of her. Because one could deride Dorada's beauty all one wanted. One could isolate her every masculine feature, and call special attention to that bifurcated chin. But when looked at from a distance; when put together; framed by the cape buffalo sweep of her hair as it leaped up from the part in the middle of her brow, tucked back to the temples, caressed her cheekbones and then swept out again and away; shivering with light; gold's refinement of itself, hammered gold, spun-gold; eyes topaz or citrine, depending on her mood; or, as now, when roiled by ambiguous emotions, lynx-lambent: she dazzled: there was about her beauty cumulative shock, once arresting a man's attention holding it fast; and drawing it ever more powerfully; and tapping in him like odd amphigenous passions: antagonism; and rage; and a heady rush of peculiarly brutal desire. Decorum —not, as she had pointed out a month ago, moral fibrillations divorced from philosophical content—defended her. But by chucking truth at him, she had herself blown the thermostat of convention.

Yet he did not move. The mercury within him, boiling moments before with hostility and lust, subsided as suddenly as it had shot up. He granted her an ungrudging respect. Hers, he saw, was the self-possession of all desirable women. She managed the atmosphere with professional poise, by the challenge of what she had said and the mockery of her expression pre-empting action and rendering him impotent. All men, Billy Smith-Burton included, feared ridicule.

"Once," he confessed, rubbing his nose, "I thought you were brainless."

She laughed at that. "Like paintings, like anything, the more you think about whatever it is the more you're liable to learn. Women don't interest me. Men do."

"What interests you about us?"

"Your sex."

"That's . . . pretty limited, isn't it?"

"You're interested in death. That seems to me very limited."

"Wide of the mark," he told her.

"Qué dices?" They were still addressing one another each in his own tongue.

"Tienes," he now struggled, "la verdad por el . . . culo."

It was an unfortunate literalism. At least he should have used *rabo*. She grasped his general meaning.

"Then explain your spectacles! Tell me—I dare you!—tell me what they mean."

She had thrown her head forward with the words, lips curled as if in prurient expectation of prying from him some self-revelatory secret. He was silent.

"Light me," she commanded in English.

She had fished a long, filtertip American cigarette out of a basket-weave gold case he had not noticed before. "*Sanz*," he thought idly, searching his pockets . . .

"Behind you," she said.

There was a lighter on the sidetable, silver, scrolled and scalloped, and pleasant in the grip of his hand. A Ronson model, it had been a popular wedding gift when Sofía and he were married. With his thumb, he depressed the bar that ran along the top, and a weak flame spurted from the end.

He extended the lighter. She swooped over his knees, sucking the flame to the tip of her cigarette, hair cascading forward from both sides of her head and nearly covering her face.

She withdrew, giving her head a shake. He replaced the lighter, thinking hard. Dorada had in mind more than a physical adventure. He had noticed a tremor in her hand as he lit the cigarette; and he realized that there were fissures in her self-possession. Was he her first attempt? He gained composure from the notion. She puffed rapidly, nervously, although returning to the attack.

"You don't like me. I know that. Tell me why you came this afternoon?"

"You're Baltazar Blás's daughter, to whom I am indebted. As you reminded me this morning."

"Mierda," she said crisply. And then, switching into English. "Were you a virgin when you married Sofía?"

"That hardly concerns you."

"How many women had you known?"

"That's also none of your business." His nose itched again.

"Will you believe that when Nacho and I were married I was a soi-disant virgin?"

"Whatever that may mean. If you say so."

"That I never really . . . had? . . . a man before. That I have not been to *bed* with any man except Nacho Prades!"

"I congratulate you, or your father—observing at the same time that the Real Madrid soccer club won't find replacements for Puskas and Di Stefano easily."

But her face was flushed.

"Estamos baldadas!" she said angrily, falling back on Spanish. "A woman can't *budge* in Madrid. They have motels in America. There are motels now in Paris; and nobody cares anyhow. What *difference* does it make? Sex isn't a crime, it's something to enjoy, or ought to be! And that's another problem here. Who with? Juan Luis Sacedón? I'd scare him to death. Julio Caro? Worn to a stub! Oh, there's Beltrán and Amontefardo and two dozen others, but they belong to the same class, go after the same game, a gypsy whore, a visiting American college girl, someone safe and easy and a little drunk . . . I'm a Blás. Soft, spoiled, gazmoños en fondo, not different enough from Nacho, where do I look? Where do I find someone?"

"Let's," he suggested, "talk about something else."

"About how it would be like between us?"

She was very fast with those words. In a flash, she had changed, once again predatory, head thrust forward from the neck. Her mouth, parting with the personal pronoun, remained open, and he could see the pearly pickets of her teeth, and the pink underside of her tongue.

A long ash from her cigarette fell on the flats of her right thigh.

"I think not," he said less steadily than he wished.

"Then why did you come this afternoon!"

He failed, this time, to answer. She barked a laugh at him, twisting away to stub her cigarette out behind her. Then she faced him again.

"De verdad, os engañais? Not me! I can tell when I've stiffened the carne flaca. I can tell when a man wants me, and when he's thinking about trying for me. But there are things I don't know. How does it start? When does it actually begin? How do men and women know, instinctively, surely, that on *this* afternoon they're going to end up naked together on a couch or a bed, or that *this* night it will happen, the dinner and the dancing just preliminaries! Is it always uncertain? I mean the beginning, the first move, the choice between two actions that you take. You—Estás en un bajón! Is that how it begins with you, a crisis? You care too much for Sofía to tell her about it, don't you? Or do you distrust her? Do you doubt she's tough enough? Are you frightened of revealing too much about yourself? Are you frightened you'll find there's not much there, and that Sofía will find that out? And so you came here. Any *reason* will do, people don't *reason* things out. You want to explode, that's all. With what? Hatred? Despair? It doesn't matter. But you were hoping Nacho wouldn't be here. You wanted me alone. You came wanting that. *Why* not admit it?"

She had spoken so rapidly that he was still catching up with her when she had finished.

He said, "I admit . . . hoping I wouldn't have to struggle in conversation with Nacho. That's all."

A flame in her eyes declared the lie. She relaxed, wedging herself farther back into the couch with a squirming rotation of her buttocks.

"Well," she told him, "I've done more for you than that."

He looked at her inquiringly.

"I make up my mind," she said, taking refuge behind her eyelashes and regarding him as from a covert. "After you said you might drop by, I arranged for the children to spend the weekend with Papá at the finca in Ciudad Real. Silvestre is on the road with them now. He'll come back for me in the morning. Naturally, I sent the ama and Rosa along. There isn't a soul in the house, and there will be nobody to bother or interrupt us later."

It was she who was certain of him. He suppressed a sneeze. He had been outside all day, in the open air. The card room was clotted with incense. And he felt dizzy. He had eaten nothing since breakfast. He had drunk six ounces of whisky in less than half an hour.

"That's . . . efficient of you," he said, gulping another ounce and a half. "Very . . . Blás." He did not know what else to say. High up his nasal passages a dull itch teased. "Have you," he asked, worrying the septum of his nostrils with munching contortions of his upper lip, "figured . . . out . . . all the logistics?"

She grinned at that. It was gamin, malicious, attractive. "Nothing could be more perfect! You work odd hours, up at dawn some days, late into the evening on others. You never go home for lunch. You have the shed. There's a cot in it already. There's even a shower."

"And no heating," he reminded her. ". . . and a rheumy old caretaker who is always about."

She dismissed the caretaker with Papá's disdain. "He can be paid! He can even watch out for us."

"I haven't any money."

"I have more than I can use."

"And so I'm convenient."

"Yes, very." She grew thoughtful. "There's more than that," she said slowly, "more than thinking you'd be good, or at least interesting for a while. I want to explode too. Maybe not hatred, I don't hate you. I don't really feel anything about you. But disappointment; and the despair when I think that I'm stuck with Nacho forever. I don't want love. I don't want to feel a split second of tenderness, or even gratitude. That's all gone. I sold it, you see. I made a bargain, and that part of it I'll keep. I won't ask for, nor look for, what I can't give him. I want to take what I take because I like it, and give what I give because I want to. A different sort of bargain, no hopes, no illusions, no regrets when it's over; nothing but the act itself."

He was dismayed by hearing this. The words were ugly, even horrifying in their hard-edge conventionality, but a child spoke them. His mind cleared.

He said, "You're making a mistake. Solipsism destroys the host."

She did not understand.

"It's a disease. We're all infected. Years passed before I realized that even Spain isn't proof."

"Against what?"

"What I said." He was losing interest. "Maybe I have been exploiting spectators. It wasn't my intention. They were violent at first. They rebelled. But I've gone on persisting at a time when maybe another sort of sacrifice is the only one that will do any good. All the world is a walking ego, seeking and seeking, and seeking for the self in self-seeking. But it's the wrong way, the lesson is as old as time. The ego is everyone's enemy. The ego is an assassin. It's the ego you have to crush, not promote, or bit by bit, lover by lover, you'll destroy yourself."

"And you?" The question was sharp.

Dorada seemed excited; he, however, was overwhelmed by lethargy.

"Nobody is excluded."

"Not even Sofía?"

"From the effects—from the danger of the egos of other people."

"She never goes to your exhibitions, does she?"

"Never."

"Why! Have you wondered?"

"Yes."

"And have you found out?"

"She doesn't like to see me tear apart what I've spent such a long time putting together . . . No," he admitted, passing a hand over his eyes, "I haven't found out."

"Because she's always guessed or suspected, from the beginning leaped years ahead of you!" cried Dorada, leaping light years ahead of him. She went on in the same exultant tone. "Tell me, before you were married, did you show her one of your, your . . . ?"

"Things, call them. Yes."

"What was it?"

"A house of cards."

"Did you tear it down in front of her?"

"Yes."

"What was it you tore down!"

"One of the principal ingredients of life. Porphyrin IX. Heme. Of hemoglobin. Had I known about it then, I might have chosen DNA."

"But why?"

"To warn her."

"Did she understand?"

"She ran away. She cried. She may have, as you say, guessed. I tried to explain. I didn't know where it was all leading myself, then."

"You *are* a monster!" Dorada said eagerly. "Didn't you hesitate before asking her to marry you?"

"All summer!"

"When did you ask her?"

"The day I destroyed the house of cards."

"Because you were frightened and needed her?"

"I needed her. I feared for her."

"You'd already begun destroying yourself!"

"Trying not to by trying to."

"And it hasn't worked."

"No."

"Because of the ghost out of the jungles?"

He stared at her astonished. "What ever do you mean?"

"Two weeks ago," she said rapidly, "you started to tell Jaime about it. I watched you. I could tell it was important. I couldn't be sure about you until I knew. Jaime I got hold of yesterday. The only woman who can't handle him is Consuelo. But it was confused. You told him something about a man screaming for an hour."

"Qué tontería!" he snapped, roused now.

"You said it! You told him that!"

"Jaime misunderstood me. Or I'd drunk a lot, and I was speaking nonsense!"

"To get attention?" She gave a vigorous shake of her head. "Oh, no, not you, not in that way! You killed that man."

He sped a look at Dorada. Her hands were vised, the one in the other. Her eyes had expanded into globes, and her tongue, like a ribbon of Christmas candy, translucently pink, playing over her lower lip, as though it might dissolve from eagerness. Was it this she was after?

"Jaime started telling me about his experiences in the Blue Division," he said carefully. "I did mention some of the things I'd heard in Malaya."

But Dorada merely gazed at him.

"Don't be stupid yourself!" he hurled at her, wristing into his mouth a last half ounce of whisky.

"Would you like another?"

"No!"

"You're angry?"

"Naturally."

"Was it one of your own men you killed?"

"What bloody nonsense!"

"Then why are you so angry?"

"Because it's so bloody stupid!" he nearly shouted at her. "Sorry," he said then, looking away.

She murmured, "I'm stronger than Sofía. You can tell me. You can take it out on me."

He struggled to his feet. He blinked. His legs were not very solid. He sat down.

"Are you sure you wouldn't like another drink?"

"No!" he told her roughly. It wasn't the alcohol. She knew that. "I don't like being cat-and-moused!"

Dorada chuckled. Then, sobering, she asked, "What was your job?"

"I was rated a demolitions expert! Look here, let's . . ."

"But what did you do?" came the soft, persistent voice.

"Turned ambushes into counter ambushes, for Christ's sake!"

"And you killed many Malayans?"

"Chinese. Yes, dozens."

"And they prey on you?"

"I tell you this has nothing to do with anything!" He was furious, yelling at her. He could have struck her for insisting on the subject. "They were the enemy. They *are* the enemy!"

He lowered his head. His brain was swirling. He felt weak; and sick; and disgusted with himself. No one had provoked in him such heat.

"Am I the enemy?" he heard Dorada ask.

She was, at that particular moment, the most ravishable creature he had ever laid eyes on.

"Perhaps," he muttered. "No more than I," he said.

"While we make love," she asked him then, "would it give you pleasure to hear me scream?"

He stared at her.

She said, "You'll carry your experiments to a point from which there will be no turning back. Maybe I could save you from that? You could empty yourself in me. You could use me as you'd never use Sofía. You could . . . profane me, and pretend that I am you, and do to me what you'd like to have done to yourself." Her voice dropped to the lowest audible register; the words came as if filled with catarrh. "I—I want it that way. Will you telephone Sofía now and tell her you'll be late?"

He felt a river roaring into his loins. Yes, he would like to take her in the way she suggested, emptying into her entrails what she craved.

"Donde tienes el teléfono?" he asked; and let his head loll back on the arm of the couch.

Dorada allowed herself the briefest smile. Then her upper body began billowing over her knees and gliding toward him. One of her hands grasped the armrest on which his head lay. He felt the weight of her breasts on his chest, and their foam-rubberiness as they were compressed against him. Her face, seemingly shrunken, suddenly small between the waves upon waves of golden hair, descended, until her breath heated his lips, and her eyes, stark, wide, and rigidly open, drove his out of focus.

"I'll fetch one," she murmured, kissing him.

He wrenched his mouth away, jerked his head back, and hurled out a loud roar of a sneeze. Two quick sneezes of almost equal violence succeeded.

"That damned candle," he snuffled apologetically.

She laughed. Briskly, she swung her body off the couch, capping the flue of the candle with a silver lid. Then, walking to the doors of the living room, she separated them and slipped through. "With all my heart," he thought, "and all my mind; and if I have one, with all my soul." And again he sneezed, spraying the air with drops of incense.

Dorada reappeared, telephone clasped to her bosom and a long cord dragging behind her.

The apparatus she chucked in his lap; the cord she plugged into a socket, squatting on fluid knees to do so and then at once rising.

She turned to him. "Hurry!" she said.

He dialed his number. A maid answered. He asked for her mistress, waiting with eyes lowered until he heard Sofía call on the other end, "Bee-lee?"

"Yes, it's me." He spoke gruffly. "I'm sorry not to have called before. Hidalgo asked me for a drink . . . No, there weren't many people, but it's all right. Darling, listen, there's something I want to tell you." He paused. He looked up at Dorada, who, elbows akimbo, stood smiling at him. Without relinquishing her eyes, he said, "Dorado dropped by this morning to ask us for supper on Sunday. I'd rather not go, if you don't mind. Yes, and I'll be home in ten or fifteen minutes."

He let the receiver plop on its cradle.

Dorada flung her golden mane back. As he pushed himself to his feet, he noticed two things: the contempt in the curl of her lips, and the tears streaking the make-up at the outer corners of her eyes.

"Thanks for the drink," he said stiffly.

"You're a coward."

"That, I think, is so."

"You're lost!"

"I may be."

"You'll turn on what you love most," she insisted. "You'll end up destroying Sofía."

He now advanced a step toward her. "And where are you going?" he asked. She was silent. He said, "Will you put on a black wig, slip into some hole of a nightclub on the Gran Vía, and there look for a furniture maker from Valencia, or a potbellied businessman from Bonn?" She did not reply. He took another step closer, so that he was looking down on her. "You're new at this, Dorada. You were too sure, and you went too fast. But no man living with a brain in his head will take you on, I don't think."

"Why? What's the matter with me?"

"A lot. I'm not sure, but it's not our maleness you're after filling yourself with. Oh, it may be our balls you want—but to devour. Your papá, Dorada. In yourself."

The spirit drained out of her. Shoulders slumped, lips went slack, and her eyes dulled. He left her that way, standing there, alone in the card room, in her rich, unimaginative, impersonal, and empty flat.

Of this episode between Dorada Blás and her husband, Sofía never learned. She continued wondering off and on how Dorada had guessed that Billy struggled with some nameless interior enemy; she worried about Dorada's warning; but as time passed, and she observed an increased coolness between the two on social occasions, she dismissed as ridiculous and unworthy of her any suspicions she might have entertained. Sofía had not only been born with a store of wisdom about essential matters: in their personal relationship, Billy's tenderness grew. He held her more closely, and longer, and with a loving passion that penetrated to her bones, so that she felt sometimes like bursting into a canticle of happiness. But Billy seemed less and less inclined to follow up an embrace. He would whisper, "Just hold me, and let me hold you . . . forever!" And she, or he, would drop off to sleep.

Sofía's life evolved more and more into the sort of pattern that takes care of time. At whatever hour Billy rose for work—before dawn some days, and never later than seven-thirty—she insisted on being awakened. He kissed whatever part of her face was exposed, a cheekbone, her drugged, ripe lips, or the dark hollow of an eye, in that cave where it met the rise of her nose. "Qué hora es?" she would murmur. "Otra vez," she would say. Drowsily, half dreaming, she would listen to him wash and dress in the bathroom; and think of him; and would often desire him. When he had finished dressing, he would return to the side of her bed, stoop, linger with his lips tantalizingly close to hers (she kept her eyes shut tight), and then dip lower, and disappointingly touch her nose or forehead with them. Her round, warm, naked arms, sweetly odorous to the pits, would emerge from the covers and draw his head down to her soft breasts. "Qué mas dá si pierdes una hora?" she would murmur, her hands kneading the long muscles of his back. Gently, did he disengage himself. She listened to his steps until the hall door closed behind them; and then drowsed back to sleep.

She was awakened with breakfast: at nine-thirty normally, not later than half past ten if they had gone out for supper. The older children by this time were at school. When she was fully awake, after a cup of herb tea, the younger ones were brought into the bedroom. She fondled and played with them. On mornings of weakness, when there was nothing urgent to be done, she might drag little Odette into bed with her, and making a ball of the child's delicious body, press it to her heart.

Ordinarily, she was dressed by eleven. She had answered or put in half a dozen telephone calls. In her tocador, while brushing her black hair, or frowning at a silver gleam detected near the part in the center of her forehead, she received the cook, planning the menus for the day. By noon or earlier, she had gone out. Some mornings she took the younger children to the park, leaving the ama behind because she enjoyed being alone with them; which made the nurse jealous, so that Sofía felt half guilty and apologetic during the rest of the day. For the past five years, she had not taken her children to Número Catorce except on rare occasions when Nati approved. The old dragon, old in years but seemingly having cowered time, made it plain that the Marquesa was not built of the same stern stuff and needed her morning's rest. Sofía's mother, however, never ceased praising the diligence of two extraordinary asistentas it had been her good fortune to find.

Several mornings during the week, Sofía was involved in charitable activities. Her first concern was an orphanage, of which she was a benefactress (she raised money among her friends for it). These were illegitimate children. The sight of them depressed her. Some were the off-spring of syphilitic parents; others had suffered from rough midwifing or infant's diseases. Human eyes alone are able to escape such ravages. Their very extrinsic beauty in the skulls of even hopeless idiots pierced Sofía's heart. Their eyes convinced her that the soul is only casually associated with the body; and she found herself, despite herself, wishing for that child's body to die, an evil thought she was compelled to confess too often. Leaving the orphanage, she would call to mind her own children, every one of them handsome and robust; and although she could wish no less for her own, there seemed to be an injustice in the world that not even the teachings of her Faith could reconcile her to.

She preferred her hours at the hospital for the aged, where she helped as a nurse's aid, donning a neat uniform emblazoned over the breast with the Sacred Heart of Jesus and doing her best to cushion for patients the bustling efficiency of the nuns. Like most Spanish women of her class, Sofía was by instinct an excellent nurse. She emptied bedpans. She cleaned the bodies of advanced cases of senility, where intestinal control had collapsed. There was an impoverished intellectual whom she felt particularly sorry for.

He had suffered a stroke; and then another. She had not recognized him: three or four gray hairs plastered by sweat across a bald dome, with an unkempt corona of gray and black hairs around the base of the skull; slack-jawed, his set of false teeth falling into the bowl as he listlessly spooned the porridge up; white mucus leaking out of nearly blind eyes, and gummy yellow and green mucus running down from his wide nostrils, where it mixed with the slaverings of porridge that spilled over his stubbled chin and onto his chest. She was startled to hear his name, and discover who he had been—editor of a prominent literary monthly. She was very startled by one of his moments of lucidity, when he mumbled, "I . . . know you. You came to see me at the office, with, with, with . . . the young Sacedón, the one who was killed by, by, by . . ." The moment passing.

Until he died, several months later, she paid special attention to him. She tried reading to him, although he was unable to follow her. She tried capitalizing on his periods of relative clarity, and recalling things to him that she imagined might be of interest: poets, novels being published, plays of the past decade. A spark of interest she might ignite; then he would weep, blubbering, she never knew exactly why, going to him and mopping his eyes and mouth and nose. He gave no indication of recognizing her again.

Pity filled her when working with the geriatrics; she was not disturbed as she was at the orphanage. She listened patiently and attentively to long, long stories: about economic disasters, or ungrateful children, or faithless spouses; and, endlessly, ailments. Sofía did not mind. Life histories unrolled before her; she shared in hopes and alarums. This was her soap opera, ending only with a patient's death, sagas she related to her inquisitive mother during afternoon visits; more and more looked forward to as daughter and mother discovered in each other the affinity of like natures. Sofía's heart quite melted one day when, as she was about to go, the Marquesa reached for her hand, impulsively, and kissed it, her eyes filling as she said, "It's you I'll miss when my time comes, Sofía—you only of all the people I once imagined I loved."

Sofía tried to be back home by seven-thirty or eight, the hour Billy generally returned. On those gold star afternoons when he quit work early, she was overjoyed. It was a treat! She made him take her out for a stroll in the Retiro, for a look into the antiquarians on the Calle del Prado, or for tea at *Embassy* (budget allowing), which an English lady had made into an institution, serving wafer-thin sandwiches of lettuce, cheese, and chicken, and pastries as succulent as any to be found in Austria. When Sofía missed Billy's unexpected return, being out herself, she was crushed.

Their circle of friends contracted. They became less "social." Billy gravitated toward Madrid's narrow artistic world, an underground of ferment repressed by censorship and limited by mediocrity. Juan Luis Sacedón and Jaime Orbaneja developed into their closest friends. They would engage in discussions that became so convoluted as to lose Sofía and make Consuelo cross. With fervor, they pounced on the latest news about such mysteries as deoxyribonucleic acid, which had something to do with heredity, and which seemed to fascinate them. They would swing from talk of infinitesimal particles to such grandiose subjects as the nature of the universe. Billy opted for the oscillating conception, as he called it, arguing that the world must have begun as a thin gas, or a cloud of dust like the Coal Sack, contracting gradually under the force of gravitation into a superdense mass, and then exploding. He spoke of the colliding Galaxies NGC 4038 and 4039, which excited him especially for the ghostly nature of the collision, in which such vast spaces existed between the hundreds of billions of stars that it was probable the systems might pass through each other without a single crash between individual stars. "It's like walking down the Gran Vía or Alcalá during rush hours. You pass by thousands upon thousands of other human beings, and yet your lives never interconnect, you never see each other again, nor notice each other if you do. There's no impact between you, your histories and destinies remain a billion miles apart." The pattern, he said, was cosmic, universal: the world had begun an eternity ago in a state of almost absolute emptiness, contracted then into a "cosmic egg," blew apart, and is now going through expansion again back into an eternity of almost absolute emptiness. "Ours, in microcosmic form, is a paralleling of the universe. Galaxies are speeding away from us at two hundred and eighty-six thousand miles an hour, the speed of light—they'll fly right off the rim of space, and we'll be left alone; until our turn comes. We're in the cycle of destruction."

Juan Luis generally agreed with the Englishman. Jaime would argue back. It might be true, he would say, that galaxies are spinning out of the universe, and will be gone; but for every one that whirls over the edge of the known, another enters, and so the universe maintains a steady population always at the same density in space. "And that means that we are consequential, we do have impact on each other, and it's our job to build. Nature is symmetrical: for every loss, there has to be a gain."

How the two men related such things to their work Sofía was less than certain. But Jaime was good for Billy. His optimism soothed. Billy wanted to be proved wrong, she was sure of that. Billy wanted to build, and to believe in the worthwhileness and perdurableness of what he built. It was Juan Luis whose effect on him was bad.

Sofía had thought Juan Luis would resent her marriage. He had never entirely shaken the trauma of the accident. Afterward, his troubles with the old Duke were intensified. After the great clash between them, occurring when Juan Luis was eighteen, the boy frequented the Smith-Burtons. At first, he sought out Sofía, to whom he confided his troubles. She remained in many ways his sainted muse; and he became for her a younger brother, much in the same sense that he might have been had Fedi not died. But bit by bit, Juan Luis transferred his doubts and inquiries to Billy; and it was then that Sofía began to worry about them both, because they were too close in the very polarity of their natures. Thirteen years separated the men, yet Billy seemed to recognize in Juan Luis problems he had himself contended with. He gave hours to the young man. There were weekly visits until the old Duke was murdered, and Juan Luis inherited. Then had come a caesura. Contact was lost. Juan Luis toured the world. Upon returning, he abandoned himself all the more to a life that saddened Sofía. Now, once in perhaps a month would the telephone ring, and Juan Luis ask whether it would be convenient if he dropped by for supper. There was a change. The boy, in a thoroughly depressing way, had become a man. He lashed out at Billy one evening, "You yourself haven't gone far enough! You know it! When have you torn the bones out of dead matter, killed to bring alive?" This sent a chill into Sofía's veins, and from that day, she discouraged Juan Luis's visits. She had seen in Billy a darkness gather between the eyes: and guessed with terrified certainty that the younger man's half-bibulous ire had fired a wick already smoldering in her husband's mind.

These were her principal worries: on the one hand, their precariousness financially, dependent as they were on Egbert's monthly contributions; and on the other hand, more profoundly, a gathering in Billy of crisis. She saw it in him so clearly: the muscles of it bunching for a spring. She hoped to be there when the attack came, because if Billy, as her husband and lover, fully satisfied her, filling her with happiness, yet had she come to realize that for Billy she was a safeguard. When he came in evenings of late, he drew her to him, and held her long, unspoken periods; and she wondered with beating heart what had happened to him during the long loneliness of his working day; what leopard had stalked him, and what spring had been averted by what stroke of fortune. Because she knew that Billy had experienced a confrontation, and had escaped but barely with his life, and now clutched her to him, and listened through his breast to the warm beating of her heart, and whispered into her ear, "I love you so much."

This is a love story, you see, but a true one.

After the exhibition of December 1964, Billy had fretted for a month, accomplishing, Sofía guessed, nothing. Then he began building automobiles again, but without conviction. This lasted through February. The United States began moving troops to South Vietnam. New energy possessed him. He scrapped what he had begun. Billy became fascinated by the weapons of war.

He visited Madrid's military museum, which was practically next door. He studied offensive armaments from their earliest development. He frequented libraries. He appealed to Egbert for illustrated histories in English on the evolution of the use of gunpowder in China and then in the Italian city-states. Defensive armaments were his next object of study. He pored over Herodotus and Thucydides for descriptions of Persian and Greek battledress. The Duke of Infantado owned an especially fine collection of medieval armor, housed in his ranch near Madrid. Sofía obtained permission for Billy to visit. He spent days there, meticulously observing every detail of the armorer's art. Museums in every capital city of every province in Spain were roamed through by him.

This groundwork ran through the rest of 1965 and into the summer of 1966. As the American intervention in Vietnam intensified, so did Billy's research. He immersed himself in the development of modern armaments. In January of 1967, he began construction.

Acquiring official permission for this work was difficult in the extreme. Influence of every sort was used. The Blás land on which Billy had parked was situated beyond the Casa de Campo, and to the southwest, a leg of arid terrain near Madrid's principal military proving grounds. The road reaching it ran from the Extremadura highway to the hamlet of Boadilla del Monte. Except for some little distance at the beginning of the turn-off, where a row of cheap tenement buildings had been slung up, it was unpopulated territory, grazed by small herds of sheep when untramped on by recruits. Here he was less likely to blast anything of importance by mistake or set off forest fires; but there were army gunpowder deposits not so very far away, and the brass looked anyhow with jaundiced eye at paramilitary experimentations by an alien, and a Britisher to boot, and a person who by all accounts and past history was sick in the head.

Blás suasion prevailed. In February, he granted the Estado Mayor a lease to forty hectares long coveted by the Army. He paid the expense of a pair of sentries assigned to scrutinize what was going on. Billy acquired his parts through Armas Y Explosivos, S.A. A fence was put up, sealing in the area. Blás paid for it. Concrete bunkers were built. Blás paid for them. Underground storerooms were excavated. Blás paid for that. Many people, not excluding Sofía, wondered why.

Sofía began watching Dorada again. The few times Billy and her sister-in-law met, Dorada seemed no less cool to him. But Sofía, at a pre-Lenten dance, confronted her sister-in-law.

"That's a beautiful dress," she said, smiling.

"If looks could wither, my thighs would be sticks by now. Consuelo tells me it's shocking."

"I envy you. My thighs are too short to raise the hem much above the knee."

"You're clever," Dorada said, half-closing the shutters of her lashes—snake-eying Sofía from between them. "What do you want to know?"

"Why your father has been so generous with Billy."

"Why not? There's no water on the land. Until the canal is pushed through, he can't develop it."

"He's let the upper end for fifty years. That's a long time."

"Money in the bank. Whenever Papá gives something, there's a reason for it."

"What?"

"I don't know his business."

"What would he be getting from Billy? Why has he offered to pay for all the pits and bunkers?"

"Armas Y Explosivos uses most of them for storage. It's convenient."

"I thought AESA simply brokered the purchase of arms for the Estado Mayor."

"American aircraft. Special equipment. AESA itself manufactures small arms."

"The plants aren't in Madrid."

"No, but thousands of bird and big-game hunters are. AESA supplies the powder for their cartridges and the shot for their shells. There's a dump near Barcelona, and one in Valencia, and—I think—another in Sevilla. What difference does it make?"

Sofía wondered on several scores. In the manner natural to her, she did not press inquiries. She still permitted the rhythm of life to carry her along. She was wise. Billy had refused to tell her what he was doing, and tolerated no other visitors. She did not nag him. She waited, so certain was she that destiny is never hurried, and as unpursuable as it is unavertable. And one day in April he said, "If you'd like to take a look at things, you're welcome."

She went with him. She saw. She was not sure about, or would not admit that she guessed, what Billy was after in this newest development. She was thoroughly alarmed by it.

He worked in a pit that was ringed by a wall of concrete. There he had assembled a tank. To Sofía, it looked larger than a locomotive. It looked like a cross between a bulldozer and a peeling, blistered submarine. Its components were of French, American, British, Japanese, German, and Russian make, some parts, as he explained, dating back to World War I. The turret bristled with three cannons. Ugly, ventilated muzzles of machineguns poked out from perhaps a dozen apertures. But the tank was not an offensive weapon, a point later to be missed by a prissy little police inspector. It had no treads. Its weapons did not operate. And it was surrounded by every conceivable offensive contrivance in the history of mankind.

These were all mounted on concrete posts. Some of them were ridiculous. There was a peashooter. There were blowguns. There were spears, and bows and arrows, and slings with pebbles in their leather pouches. There were catapults, she guessed Roman in design. There were heavy Spanish arquebuses whose short stocks were ornately carved and inset with gold and mother-of-pearl. There was a set of dueling pistols and a revolver she recognized from movies as being a Colt, and a Lüger automatic. There were blunderbusses, muzzle-loaders, and lever-action carbines. There was something called an M-16, a new American rifle that spewed out she could not remember how many bullets in how many seconds. And there were machineguns, each with its long wrap of ammunition coiled beside it.

Every one of these weapons was aimed at the tank, and operated— even the bow strings—by ingenious remote controls. When Billy set them off, darts, arrows, stones, and bullets pelted the tank's armament from every side. "I start with the primitive things," he told her, explaining the details with pride. "Then I work up to the automatic rifles and the machineguns. It's a fantastic crescendo. Plates of armor fall off. The turret blows off when I fire the bazooka. Spectators are sure to think the whole tank is going to be riddled and collapse."

"Doesn't it?"

"No."

He looked away. Sofía tried to pry his eyes back toward her. This was very new, the only thing Billy had ever built not destined to destruction.

"Why?" she asked.

He was looking about him. His pit occupied barely a quarter of the enclosure. There were many sheds and bunkers. "I wonder what Baltazar is up to," he said.

"Bih-lih, why is the tank not destroyed?"

"Oh," he said, glancing at her and smiling, "because I get in it."

"Bee-lee!"

"It's perfectly safe. I've tested it twice—didn't set off everything, of course, a waste of money, but that's why the tank looks a little dilapidated. Haven't had time to fix it."

"Bih-lih," Sofía said in careful English, "I do not want *never* for you to get into the tank again."

He shrugged. But he looked away again, saying, "It's absolutely safe. In fact, it's soothing to be inside. The barrage sounds somewhat like hail beating on a tin roof. For extra consideration, I plan to take spectators in with me."

"That the authorities will permit *nunca!*" stated Sofía.

Now he turned his face fully to her. He was smiling. His English eyes were cool and clear, as though freshly dipped in the Atlantic.

"You are being silly," he said. "After the exhibition, I thought you and the children might enjoy the experience."

"The portraits," she said suddenly—walking away from him, toward the shack. "I want to see them!"

He reached out to halt her. She shook free.

"You won't find them there," he told her harshly.

She wheeled, facing him. "Why?"

"I burned them, a week ago."

"Why, Billy, why?"

"You asked me to—long ago."

She had never before seen Billy's gaze falter. But it now slid to one side.

He had not made love to her in several weeks. Another fortnight went by, and although he was as tender as ever, he initiated nothing more while eluding her advances. Sometimes now she shivered in his arms: his heart beat regularly. There was a calm in him she did not recognize. When she mentioned their ever-worsening financial problems, he listened, but he said nothing. When she told him that Marucha might have to have her appendix operated on, he nodded, asking only if it might wait a while. Only the progression of the war in Vietnam seemed to interest him. He read as if with satisfaction about the tons of bombs falling on and thundering in jungle valleys. He stared long moments at photographs showing human flesh seared beyond recognition by napalm, passing them to her afterward. He read to her about corpses discovered in hasty, shallow graves, and how quickly they rotted in the heat and humidity. "Don't any more!" she finally told him. "I don't want to hear about it!" Apparently unruffled by her attitude, he ceased. But he explained that his new work was no demonstration against the war. He celebrated it.

"How can you, Billy!"

"It's a purge."

"I know you think communism is evil—and hate it. But women and children are being killed. And men, little more than boys, Americans and Indo-Chinese both."

"Yes," he said as if there was no feeling in him. "It's curious. Locked in hate, in love, and in death. There's a kinship between us, between Marxists and me. We both feel nothing can be built before what is rotten has been dug out and destroyed. The Americans don't understand that. That's why they're losing, and a good thing too, miserable excuse for a war, they deserve to lose. They don't understand what this war is all about, and why they're being called on to die. And we Europeans don't understand it either. We don't realize that the Americans, God help us, represent our civilization—represent it there in Vietnam, and both for themselves and for us are testing it there, and have a chance of cleansing it."

"I don't understand. You're not against the war, you celebrate it, yet you don't seem to be very much for it, nor believe in it."

"Oh, I am and I do," he told her. "On all counts, strategic, moral, anything you like. Communism has to be crushed. What neither the Americans nor we Europeans seem to get through our skulls is that it's our historical duty, our destiny, to crush communism, to eradicate it from the world. Because communism was created for that. Communism was created to destroy our civilization, and to be destroyed by us. I'm against the war because it's an episode only. I'm for it insofar as it sucks America deeper and deeper, and makes us Europeans think harder. I'll be wholeheartedly for it if it leads to a decision, forced on the Americans, perhaps, and dragging us in the American wake, to declare total war on communism everywhere; and, if necessary, all-out atomic war. But I won't be discouraged if this doesn't happen through Vietnam. Whether or not we face up to our historical destiny, Communists will force it on us. Their dedication won't waver. They'll push and push and push and push, and finally it will happen."

Listening to him, relating these things so calmly, Sofía was horrified.

"And what will be left?" she asked.

"Nothing of the world we know."

"And you'd be for that—all of us gone, our children, you and I?"

"Yes."

"Billy! Oh, Billy, how can you say such things."

"Because sacrifice is called for—and the good, Sofía, you, Sofía, as well as the bad."

"And . . . And then will the time come for building again?"

He gazed at her, cool, Atlantic eyes, and bony, rueful smile. "I doubt it," he said.

"Not ever, Billy?" She could weep; what he was saying was too terrible.

"I . . . don't think so. Only simpletons, Sofía, can believe in humankind today. Did even Christ succeed in rooting out evil?"

He meant; he was saying; he was telling her; that there was no hope at all. Sofía refused to believe this. For the first time, she fought Billy and his ideas. She was outraged. His ideas were hateful. Christ had conquered sin forever. For that one purpose, He had come and He had suffered. Billy was now ruthlessly denying Christ.

He agreed. "And so has the world," he said.

"It has not!"

"Sofía, can you really say that?"

"I haven't!"

"Yes, and that's why you'll suffer more than others; and why it's so cruel."

He checked himself from saying: *talk* to your Don Emilio, *ask* him why the Synod was scandalized by him.

"What you say," she was insisting, "will never happen; and if it happens, it will be to begin again, God's not going to abandon us, He promised He never would."

Billy gazed at her. "You and a sprinkling believe that. And a sprinkling will always believe it, I suppose. But more and more of the world, and more and more all the time, has stopped believing it."

Jaime Orbaneja came to supper. They talked about these things. Billy was opening up as he neared the date of his exhibition, set for the first week of June. He was willing to talk about almost anything and with almost anyone.

"I wonder what Baltazar is up to?" he said to Jaime.

"Taking over Obras Orbaneja," came the gloomy reply.

"No," said Billy. "At the proving grounds," he said.

"What is happening there?"

"Through February and March, lorry after lorry began rolling in. They arrived late afternoons, always. I'd leave, but there would still be men unloading heavy wooden crates, hundreds of them."

"What was in the crates?"

"I'd guess munitions. What else?"

"For the Army?"

"I'd guess not yours. Blás is preparing to supply someone's war," he stated with complacence. "The question is whose? Yemeni? The Sudanese?"

Jaime Orbaneja's eyebrows were nearly touching the hairline of his brow.

Both men began ticking off possibilities. Billy pointed out that his proving grounds were located near the Boadilla road. From that road, driving west, there were any number of backcountry routes, many of them emptying into the Extremadura highway, which went to Portugal. "Yes," said Jaime, "it's probably for mercenaries in Angola or Mozambique. But the Government may not be aware of what Blás is about."

"Shall we expose him?"

Jaime jumped in his seat. "It would be the ruin of me! Besides, if Blás is doing anything sub rosa, you can be sure he has covered himself somehow."

"Well," said Billy, "he can supply all the wars he wants to, for all I care, and the more the better."

"How sanguinary of you! How immoral, in fact!" Jaime Orbaneja was shocked.

"It's merciful."

"I don't see how!"

"We're cerebralized apes, aren't we?" Juan Luis, who had called earlier, wandered in. Billy gazed at him hard, nodded, and turned back to the architect. "We're a complex of millions upon millions of cells produced by the squirming of an allele and the twist of a chromatoid."

"I object to that," said Orbaneja stoutly. "I don't believe in that!"

"Who cares what you believe!" came the harsh reply. "You, Juan Luis, I—we're anachronisms! The best we can do is lament the clanking of our biochemical chains, and hope that in the future we will all be begot and conceived in laboratories and turn out better."

"Billy . . ." said Sofía.

But he ignored her. "Have a drink, Juan Luis. Help yourself. No, you're unable to, aren't you?" Billy was overtly hostile. "Sofía'll do it.

ROSENDALE LIBRARY
ROSENDALE, N.Y.

Meanwhile something has to be done about people. Our welfare programs; our charitable shipments of food to perpetually starving Asians perpetuates their starvation and the agony of Asia. It's nonsense. It's an evolutionary crime. We, the civilized peoples, with our medicines and our excessive agricultural production, have helped to proliferate the masses in regions that by every measurable criterion are civilizationally inferior. Let them go! Let our own poor and diseased sink. If Darwin's law of biological selectivity makes any sense, then Hitler's gardens of love ought to be revived. I mean the notion of a master race. In the Western world, the most competitive members of society—evolution's best—are breeding less, and the least successful members, with flawed genes, are breeding most. From a rational point of view, this is intolerable. It's even more intolerable on the world-wide scale, with savages in Africa out-breeding, for example, the Dutch. Increasingly inferior human beings and civilizations have to result."

"That's not so!" again objected a gallant Orbaneja, popping to his feet. "The genetical bank is too immense for that!"

"You think so," came from Sofía's suddenly hateful husband, an Ogden-tone of sarcasm in his voice. "But there's no room for sentimental humanists any longer."

Jaime flushed. Sofía bit her lower lip. But Billy seemed to notice nothing—swept along by his argument. "People like Julian Huxley recognized what's happening long ago, but liberal thinkers for the most—obsolescent humanists like you—were and are still embarrassed by the Christian ethic. Well, we've knocked that on the head in our generation. There can be no moral compunctions, because what is morality? Morality is survival of the fittest; morality is to keep the human species from degenerating. What we want is the best for the most and the most for the best, and to eliminate the members of the species that drag all mankind down. Stalin eliminated the kulaks, Mao tens of millions of peasants. Forthright, those two. And logical. But we're still haunted by shibboleths that belong to a Christian world view. We won't face logic. In India, we preach sterilization and the loop. The successfully competitive classes will listen; the masses won't. Striking at inception is, besides, stupid. When you murder . . . sorry, wrong word, one of my atavisms . . . when you snuff out the life of a fetus, you are snuffing out an unknown quantity. You may be snuffing out the life of a Mozart or an Einstein, how would you know? Someone who might be the genius to solve all our problems. At this stage in the development of biochemistry, one can only hope that physical and mental fitness will be drawn to physical and mental fitness. But what about the fellahs all over the subtropical world? They eat and breed. They don't produce. They live miserable, wretched lives. Wouldn't it be better for demonstrably useless and suffering crea- tures to be extinguished—instead of the unknown quantity of the fetus? Why not? Shouldn't we therefore encourage all killing in barbarous places? Should we fear or should we foment the outbreak of hydrogen war, which will attack the greatest concentrations of the lowest com- ponents of the human species? The surviving masses, proportionally re- duced, will adhere to the surviving leaders, proportionally increased. No wonder the world-fear of the atom bomb! Power for the first time in centuries has been given to the few over the many. The masses, like a great beast, sense this instinctively, and quail at the thought. They fear that leaders in certain advanced nations may get together and decide that the best and even most merciful solution to Africa, for example, is to destroy in one apocalyptic stroke every wretched human creature on the continent, and then repeople it with the excess flow from the ad- vanced nations. This sort of thing should be the hope, the daily prayer, of the intelligent human being: that the Apocalypse comes to reduce the ever-increasing and unmanageable beast of the masses. Every little war leads us in that direction. Every little war succeeds in killing more and more of the inferior peoples, or the inferior classes within superior so- cieties, and each war is possible tinder for another, and for a world-wide conflagration. I rejoice, damnit, I rejoice!"

He had talked as though drunk. Sofía had never heard from him so many words. Unquestionably, he was serious. Jaime's face was now drained of color. Juan Luis, who had listened intently, said nothing. Sofía said nothing. Consuelo had fallen asleep hours before in the couch, and had snored through a proposition that almost certainly condemned her. "We must go," Jaime broke silence at last. He roused Consuelo. The Orbanejas left. Juan Luis, who, unknown to Sofía, six months before had initiated Billy's solution respecting himself, went with them. Billy wheeled on Sofía, and snapped at her, "Why are you crying! How can you be such an idiot!"

She cried for many hours that night. Billy's anger subsided. He apologized. She shrank from his touch. "I'm only carrying out the logic of our times where it drives us," he pleaded. She sobbed. Exhausted, she fell asleep.

Next morning she went to Don Emilio. She told him as much as she could remember about what Billy had said. She told him about the tank, and how Billy proposed that he and she and the children get in it.

Don Emilio was alarmed. He exhorted Sofía to bring Billy to him, and meanwhile to pray with all her might. "Your faith, Sofía," he said, "do battle with your faith!"

That evening, Billy entered with a basket of flowers and a tin of caviar. But, looking at him, Sofía could hardly suppress a shudder. A sudden, instant loathing leaped up in her breast. Billy was the enemy.

She turned quickly from him to hide the tears that again rushed to her eyes. She went into the bathroom. There she let herself cry. She ran icy water over her face. She told herself that this was the same Billy she had loved for twelve years. She told herself that this was not Billy, but an alien, evil spirit. She had to fight that spirit. She had to recover her Billy, save her Billy, bring her Billy back.

She returned to the living room. He was playing with the children. It was not possible, seeing him with them, laughing and jesting and tickling them, to conceive that he advocated the sweeping away of hundreds of millions of lives. But when he turned his face to her, in the midst of a laugh, she saw his stone cold eyes, she saw staring at her the hateful spirit that had possessed him and saw in his fondling of the children only guile, and in his contrition for having upset her guile also.

She was living with a murderer. She suddenly rushed to him, and snatched Odette out of his arms. She shooed the children away, into their bedrooms, leaving that evil, disingenuous Billy with a perplexed look on his face.

She stood in the hall. She did not know what to do. She wanted to take her children and flee. Her heart pounded. The maid went by her, bearing the opened caviar in a bowl of ice. Billy had ordered the preparations. He would be pouring vodka. She forced herself to go back to him, and when he raised those eyes and that bony, rueful smile, that worried face, that dissembling countenance of concern, she forced herself to smile on it.

She drank much of the vodka, more than she usually touched of any alcohol. She drank many glasses of wine at supper, and took sweet *Chinchón* anís after. Billy seemed amused by her sudden intemperance. He matched her glass for glass. In time, Sofía's mind and sight went a little fuzzy, and she saw only Billy's face, the loved irregular features of that face, and not the evil spirit dwelling there. The maid had long ago cleared the coffee cups. She was dismissed. They sat on the couch. Billy, in a playful manner, drew her to him. She responded ardently. Yes, on the couch, she thought, where two of the children he would doom had been conceived. Billy on this night was willing. The evil spirit was clever. The evil spirit had been found out, and wished to beguile her. Billy on this night was a lover for all the world and all history, and her senses reeled.

"Billy," she said afterward. "Oh my Billy!"

He began kissing her, chin, cheeks, eyes, forehead. His lips were wide and soft and nimble, nibbling here, nibbling there. "With all my heart, and all my mind," he murmured.

"What?" she asked him.

"I love you."

"Billy, come with me tomorrow to see Don Emilio. Please."

"It is a waste of time, Sofía, my darling, it won't help."

"But it may!"

"It can't change our world, can it? If he convinces me, what good will that do?"

"You could dedicate the rest of your life to convincing others!"

He was no less tender; he was no less stubborn. The arms that held her belonged to Billy. The person who loved her was Billy. But Billy had been hurled over the precipice. The enemy held his ground, now.

She argued with him, in low, pleading, desperate tones. He told her not to fret. He begged her not to. But she insisted. "Tell me," she said, "now tell me what happened in Malaya!"

And he spoke about it now, as he seemed to be willing to speak about anything at all, and to anybody—as though it no longer mattered.

"There were six of us in a lorry. We hit a mine. I remember the compression of the air under me, and then the feeling of suffocation, as though my lungs had been clapped flat. I don't remember hearing anything, but I landed about twenty feet away from the road, in the bush. Lay there looking up at the sky I don't know how long. Then I heard his voice. His name was Montagu, a sergeant, about fifty. He'd fought all over the empire. He knew enough not to scream. But he kept at it, in a high, yippering voice, like a puppy with its tail jammed in a door. I could not see him; but I could see them coming, three of them, hunting Montagu. I kept saying to myself, 'Shut up, Montagu—for God's sake shut up!' But he kept on screaming. They spread out a bit, rifles ready, moving carefully—very tense. I thought, 'If I blink an eye, they'll see me.' But they passed me, and their backs were to me. I noticed then that my pistol was still in its holster. I had an excellent opportunity. And then I thought, 'If I move, rustle anything, they'll hear me.' I thought, 'But they won't be listening; Montagu is screaming like a stuck pig.' I thought, 'If my hand is steady enough, I can certainly pick off the first, and surely the second, and I just might have a chance against the third; if I roll quickly; if I can move.' And then I thought, 'It won't work, I don't know whether I can move at all.' And when I had finished thinking that, one of them, the one in the middle, halted suddenly, raised his rifle, and aimed. 'That will stop Montagu,' I thought. But he lowered the rifle. The others had stopped in their tracks. He jerked his head at them, taking a knife out of his waistband. The three moved forward then, relaxing, letting their rifles sling along by their sides in the grip of one hand. They huddled together about thirty feet away from me, looking down. Montagu was still screaming. There was no change in his tone. The one with the knife stooped quickly, and then the screaming did stop."

He had stopped. "Go . . . on," murmured Sofía.

"There's not much else. I said to myself, 'You're a fool, William Smith-Burton. They'll surely look around now; they can't help seeing you.' But they passed right on down the road, talking to each other. I was found next morning by one of our patrols."

"And Montagu—the sergeant?"

"Oh, Montagu was dead all right. It was a good thing, for him, too. His legs were pinned under the lorry; his pelvis was crushed. They'd cut his throat. It was merciful. I doubt he felt the edge of the knife."

"And . . . you?"

"I was perfectly all right. Stiff and sore, a few bruises, and a small gash below the knee of my right leg."

"You would have been able . . . to do something: when those three men passed you."

"Yes," he said crisply.

"But Montagu would have died anyhow. You could have done nothing for him."

"I didn't know that."

"You said yourself Montagu knew enough not to scream. You must have known he was terribly hurt."

"I don't know whether that thought came to me then, or later, during the night. I may have incorporated it into the beginning of the story, to make sense of it to myself. Besides, even veterans can scream from shock."

They were both silent.

Sofía said, "That was . . . how long ago?"

"Fourteen or fifteen years ago. A year or so before we met."

"And you—you think you are a coward?"

"I know bloody well I am."

"Had something like that happened before—or again?"

"Like that, nothing. Do you mean had I been under fire before, and was I again?"

"Yes."

"And did I get along all right?"

"Yes."

"Yes."

"Then you are *not* a coward!" she said.

"Don't be silly. We're all cowards, we can all be frightened, that kind of thing can happen to anyone, and does. That's not the point."

She was bewildered.

"It's this!" he said energetically. "I made a choice. It was probably wise. I was likely too numb to have succeeded in getting the pistol out of its holster, much less shoot anyone with it. I was in a state of semishock myself; it's probable I could think, but not act. It's even probable one of the three did see me, and took me for dead, lying there without moving and with my eyes wide open. But I was thinking all the time, and I thought this. Montagu was divorced. He had no children. At fifty, he would get no further in his career. He had his pension to look forward to, of course. But that was all. And I thought, 'If I don't manage, and get myself killed trying to save Montagu, who is probably dying anyhow, what have I accomplished? I'm only twenty-three. I have my whole lifetime ahead of me. There are things I may do, and they may amount to much more than Montagu can dream of amounting to.' I thought this out as an intellectual proposition, I'm not sure whether right then, or later, after the men had gone, but I think before that. I thought, 'If a thirty-year-old man, father of three or four children, should see another child about to be run down by a bus, does it make sense for him to jump in the bus's way in an effort to save the child?' It makes no sense at all. In this case, he can have no way of foreseeing the potential of the child, who may grow into a genius, but as well into a criminal. Meanwhile he has responsibilities of his own, and his personal potential to further. It would be lunacy for the man to sacrifice all this for a strange child."

"But that's . . . don't you see that it is horrible, Billy?"

"Yes."

"You left the army then."

"It took another eight months to get out."

"And it was because of Montagu, because of what happened and what you thought, that you began making things to destroy them."

"Partly."

"You hated thinking what you thought."

"I disliked myself for the intellectual cogency of what I've just said, what I may have thought when the Chinese were approaching Montagu. It makes perfect sense, don't you see. And, as you say, it's horrible."

"But then, when you got home to England, you began building things, which was your . . ."

"Duty."

"I see that. And you tore them apart, which was . . ."

"My obligation to humanity. Call it that. A way of reminding myself that I am still human. A way of telling myself that I never really conformed to the intellectual cogency of my proposition, that it was simply fright, or the shock, that stopped me from trying to save Montagu."

"But you were not sure."

"I can never be sure, Sofía. There is no way ever of making sure now. One's never given a second chance, and even if it came my way, and I acted differently, it wouldn't wipe off how I acted before. It seemed to me that the only possible way I had of making up was to bury myself—to destroy it, you see, to leave nothing standing, nothing that could lead anyone into deluding himself that I am more important than, say, some waif playing in the street."

"You make me shiver, Billy."

"Yes, I shouldn't have told you."

"You make me feel so cold!"

"I'm sorry, Sofía. I am more sorry than I can say."

"But, then . . . When did your ideas change, how did they change?"

"For years, my love of you, and for our children, kept me in a sort of suspension. I kept thinking, 'Sofía is good, Sofía is worth everything, and our children too.' And I believe that. Then I came to see that my love for you and the children was a projection of my self: that I was indulging that self, and avoiding reality."

"What reality?"

"That my intellectual proposition, no matter how I rebelled against it, remained cogent. I kept hoping that with you, in you, I'd find God. I found in you a superior human being, a goddess to me. But only God, his existence, can counter my proposition. Only through God can anyone say, 'Every man, woman, and child has a soul, and that soul is precious to God, and it makes no difference if the man is a drunkard, the woman a whore, and the child a Mongolian idiot. Each is worthy of the sacrifice of my body and life. The Mongolian idiot's soul is probably purer than mine, and if I'm Bertrand Russell himself, to give my life for that child is to make at least partial amends for my sinfulness. God created that child, and gave me this opportunity, for that precise reason.'"

"And that's true, Billy!"

"If you can believe in God. I thought that here, in Spain, a Catholic nation, the belief would come to me. But I saw Spain changing. I saw Spain eager for, even lusting after, claptrap like automobiles. And so I made monsters out of them, and I blew them up, and everyone became angry, and it did no good. I saw then how even if a few people believe, it will do no good in any case: the overwhelming majority of the world doesn't believe; the overwhelming majority of the world seeks the projection of self, the golden calf, the idol, to replace the God that died. Without God, we're animals, nothing more nor less. And if that's so, and the world believes it, then it is time, as the Communists believe, as the Left all over the world in their way believe, to reorder the world along sensible lines; and to deal with animal-man as one would deal with horses and cattle; or, now, plagues of rats."

"What does that mean?"

"In part, what I said to Jaime last night. The self can't be destroyed when there's nothing greater in the universe. And if that's so, then only superior selves, superior individuals, can be tolerated. Superior individuals should band together to plan the elimination of the inferior. This is so sensible, Sofía, that it will come about because it has to come about, and people like you, the few that remain, won't be able to stop it. The masters, as we might as well call them, will establish minimum standards below which men and women forfeit their right to life. One would begin with the elimination of the mentally retarded, the helplessly aged, and the unproductive. And so on. As the diseased limbs are pruned—as the world is purified, and the race improved, and as it advances—then the standards will be correspondingly upgraded, until only the very best of the very best are permitted to survive, which biologically at least assures the survival of humanity. In this reordering of things along rational lines, there's even room for the return of slavery. A certain number of inferior peoples would be tolerated for the kind of menial offices that will always have to be fulfilled. They may even be bred down. They'll be treated, these new helots, decently; but they will have no political voice, that's obvious, and they must be sterilized. Their ranks would be replenished by one of our children, for example, one who for some reason or other falls below acceptable standards. Eventually, hopefully, science will master life, and the harsh measures that may be necessary for the next millennium can be one by one dropped, because mankind will have evolved into a superior creature making those measures needless. Meanwhile, I see no other way for the world to go; and, in fact, I see it either going that way or collapsing."

Sofía felt at this moment abandoned by God. She could think of no words to counter what Billy was saying, and no argument except the faith he could not accept and that he insisted the world had abandoned. She would have liked to have thought him deranged, but she knew he was not. She could summon against his ideas only the horror she felt, and that was emotional; that was, perhaps, as he said, a feeling that belonged to an age that was dying. She had to believe that what Billy predicted would not happen; neither the imposition of a scientific tyranny, nor the degradation and even extinction of the human species. Her religion did not permit despair. But her only resistance, the weak argument of her faith, was nothing to be put up against his implacable deployment of ideas.

"And what," she asked, "do you feel?"

His arms tightened about her. "Horror, Sofía."

Her heartbeat quickened. "You too! Then you don't, you can't believe it!"

"No, I do believe it: and I can't justify the horror I feel. But I feel it. I don't want to live in this new world, Sofía. I don't want you living in it, nor our children growing up in it. And maybe only an ultimate sacrifice, to show that the self isn't worth the means of improving it, can help. But I don't believe that either."

He wasn't evil! He simply could not find a way out.

"Why not come with me to Don Emilio," she begged. "For me, Billy, to talk to him. It may do no good. But it may help."

He kissed her. She could see his face now, ghostly in the light of dawn. "I'll go," he said. "But I'm sure we're in substantial agreement."

"Billy, he's a minister of Christ!"

"Which is why he sees things clearly."

"You've spoken to him?!"

"We've . . . communicated."

"But I can't believe Don Emilio . . ."

"He sees clearly. He saw through me, knew my story about Montagu is a lie."

"A lie!"

"Everything happened—the truck blew up over a mine, I was thrown clear, Montagu screamed—except for the Chinese coming. But, lying there half-stunned, I was terrified they might come. I wanted to stop Montagu's screaming, crawled to him with my bush knife between my teeth, but he was dead when I got to him. Would I have sliced his throat? Don't think so. No. No. But I imagined then the Chinese coming, and myself cowering on the ground and doing nothing. I imagined it, and it's all the same."

"The same! You call a nightmare spun out of your head the same thing as a real happening?"

"Christ said it. If a man imagines adultery with a woman, he has committed it. I betrayed Montagu. I've betrayed you."

The hurt for Sofía in those words was almost more than she could bear.

"Betrayed . . . me? With, with . . . ?"

"Yes, Dorada. Once. Nearly. Three years ago. Not in the flesh. But in my mind."

"In your . . . I don't *care* about your mind! You did nothing! You do love me!"

"Yes. Which is why I want to save you."

"From the evil it's possible for everyone to *imagine!*"

"From that evil. It's no less real, I told you once, reality's nothing but a set of mirrors."

"Billy, Billy, Billy—love me *less!*"

"How can I, my darling? You'll have to do that: for yourself, for the children, for me. Take the children. Leave me. Because we love each other so much."

He kissed her on the forehead. "Than hurt you, or see you hurt, I'd rather die."

They moved to the bedroom. Billy fell as if into drugged sleep. She remained awake for the second night. She prayed; but her head was numb, and her prayers mere dull recitations of formulas. Billy was contemplating the ultimate sacrifice. He would show his spectators the assault of all history against the tank. He would enter it, and they would fear for his life. He would invite others to enter it with him after it was seen that he escaped unharmed, and they would experience the din of ferocity beating on the armored walls of the womb. And on the last day, he would again enter the tank, and invite her and the children in with him, and this time the walls would collapse.

She thought numbly about the sacrifice he planned. For her the predicament was cruel. Believing, it was not suicidal to sacrifice herself and her children for the good of man, although Billy held out little hope that good would be done, or that their sacrifice would be understood. But he, the unbeliever, and she, the believer, would be laying down their lives for their fellowmen, and that Christ did, and Christ praised in others. She could not let Billy enter the tank the last time alone; she would not be able to bear that. She could not bear the thought of taking her children into the tank, nor of leaving them behind. She could stop Billy's sacrifice, by telling the authorities what he planned. That would be disloyal. Billy would never be able to forgive her that. And he would probably find another way. He would not choose some cheap form of suicide, because he was not a coward, and it would achieve nothing. But in some other way he would perfect his art, and in its annihilation annihilate himself, his self, the human self, the animal. As the alarm clock rang, and Billy struggled out of sleep, and wearily pulled himself out of bed, she fell asleep.

That was on the morning of 31 May.

When Ignacio Prades y Caro, Conde de Obregón, having first telephoned Consuelo, informed his thirty-one-year-old younger sister, Sofía Smith-Burton, Condesa de Mil Lágrimas, of their mother's death, she, as had Consuelo Orbancja, burst into tears. She didn't however, unlike her forty-nine-year-old sister, ask two dozen questions. She had been shaken out of a deathlike sleep. The telephone receiver was handed to her. She listened dumbly, trying to assimilate the news. Her lovely, troubled face went blank with the first words that entered her ears. Her face was emptied of content and animating rational power. Tears then began welling in eyes whose chestnut depth she shared with her brother; and as he finished speaking, she placed the receiver back on its cradle, as if tenderly.

And then the tears really ran, and she thought her heart would break, and she began to sob, pressing her face to her palms and rocking back and forth in bed, moaning, "Oh, Mamá, my poor Mamá!" Fully ten minutes she wept, racked by her grief, and slowly began calling not her mother's name, but that of her husband. Up she rose from her bed then, pressing the bellbutton plunger repeatedly, summoning her maid, advising her through a torrent of grief of the Señora Marquesa's death, and bidding her please to hurry, to fetch her a black dress and black stockings and a hat with a black veil, she would dress herself, the maid was not to let the children know yet, and the maid was to search for a taxi.

For Sofía, the time intervening was nightmarish. She wanted to rush at once out of the apartment, and to Billy. She was unable to. There are so many things to arrange when the windy gurgle of life quiets into carrion. All her spring clothes, not many, had to be sent to be dyed. The ama and the child not at school, little Odette, had finally to be told. And then the calls began. Everyone started telephoning, the news was out, maids in Ignacio's house had heated wires with their whispered excitement, an important death is such heady wine in their lives. Through their servants, all society was almost instantaneously aware, and the news spread so quickly that it was picked up by Radio Madrid and broadcast to the world at eleven o'clock, along with an announcement of the nation's grief at the passing away of the widow of the late Conde de Obregón, fallen hero of the Cruzada and father of fallen heroes. But by this time Sofía, nearly collapsing from exhaustion, had torn herself away from the insistent telephone and rushed out of the apartment and down to the street, where her taxi was being held. She gave the address, the outlandish locality to which she wanted to be taken, and then she huddled back against the tattered, tobacco-stale black leather seat, and lost her battle against a sob, and began crying once more, for she had loved her mother only less than husband and children, and needed her now more than ever, she could not believe her mother was dead, she wanted Billy's arms around her, she wanted the comfort of those long awkward fibrous arms, the comfort of his bony chest, his long irregular nose cold on her cheeks, and his wide warm lips pressing her lips, because she could support not another moment of this grief alone, Billy would support her through it, Billy would be washed by her grief, would change his mind, would be put off from his purpose, one sacrifice surely was enough!

The cabdriver had been kept waiting. He was surly at first. In the instant that he caught sight of the bereaved countess, he changed. His crusty Matritense heart, which had beat thirty years earlier with cold implacableness when he had assisted at the slaughter of dozens of aristocrats caught within the city at the outbreak of the Civil War, melted at the loveliness of this woman's face, which nor grief nor the black veil obscured. He jammed his right foot down on the accelerator, whipped U-turning down Espalter and toward Cuatro Fuentes, hurling his taxi into the traffic of Madrid with a ferocity that verged on glee, calling back to her, "No llora, señora, we'll get you there if it kills us!"

It nearly did. Looping a white handkerchief onto the stem of his outer rear-view mirror, he forged up the Paseo del Ateneo, horn blaring as he crashed lights and plowed through the crossing pedestrians at Neptuno and then Cibeles, skidding around that glorieta and cranking his diesel-drive shambles of a SEAT 1500 up Alcalá, right into the Gran Vía, through more lights and over the hump of the street and past Plaza Callao and down the funnel into the Plaza de España, hauling hard left at the monument at the base of the avenue, and gunning and hurling his car down Calle Redondo, el Paseo de Onésimo, to the very gates of the Casa de Campo before hauling hard left on his wheel again and throttling the engine up the two-lane avenue that skirts the great park and its commercial fair grounds, rising to the Carretera de Extremadura. There they encountered an interminable bottleneck, because the road was being torn up in the first stages of the construction of a four-lane western exit from the city; and cars and lorries and buses and taxis and motorscooters and three-wheeled motorscooter vans were strained out in a long, toffee-like lane that sometimes progressed not at all and for periods of well over three minutes at a time. The cabdriver apologized to his fare. He exploded at city authorities, whom he blamed exclusively. As nervous now as his passenger, he cursed the sindicatos, the traffic police, the ridiculous authorities who insisted that cabdrivers wear caps, a battle now several years old between authority and individualism. Sofía heard not a word of his tirade. They jerked along. She did not see the raw tenement buildings as they passed, nor the gullies being bulldozed left and right for the new highway. She kept thinking, "Oh, Mamá!" She kept thinking, "Billy will come back to me now." She kept thinking, "How I need him! How I need her!" At last, at Kilometer 4, they reached the turn-off to the Boadilla road. The cabdriver exulted. Jamming the gears from first to second and then to low, they went rattling down the slight incline of relatively traffic-free road, a narrow lane, ditched on both sides, the wall of the Casa de Campo to the right, more tenement buildings to the left. Fifty, sixty, seventy, eighty kilometers-an-hour they went. At the bottom of this lane there is a fork, the road to the right driving north and circling the park, the one to the left, across a very narrow bridge, leading to Boadilla. The cabbie turned his head around, asking Sofía, "Which one do I take?"

She screamed in reply.

An Army lorry was coming off the bridge, lunging wildly to the right. The cabdriver, after the custom of all drivers in Spain, was bestriding the middle of the road, with a very royal sense of possession.

He jerked his head back to the front at her scream. He saw the truck looming above him. He executed then one of those violent gyrations of genius without which motoring in Spain would be carnage indescribable. This time, however, it failed. There was no room to the right. The collision came with a combined impact of 120 kilometers-the-hour. And with the collision, the munitions-laden lorry exploded in a thunderous roar that shattered the glass window panes of tenement buildings half a kilometer away.

END OF PART ONE

PART TWO

The Pilgrims

Book One

THE COMMENCEMENT
OF A WAKE

And so, the first mourners to reach the bier of the great Marquesa were not her children, nor even peers of the realm. They were debtors, strangers, humble tradesmen from the compost of humanity.

Padre nuestro . . . It was Antonio Sánchez, the pharmacist, who interrupted Nati's orisons.

Doing so required courage, because he was compelled to lift those stied eyes toward a hot bright light that pierced the wall from behind the woman and seemed to X-ray right through her to land on the upper forehead of the Marquesa, tilting over the cowl and creeping like the process of putrefaction irreversibly down her mummy's countenance. But they had been hard on the balls of their knees over an hour; and Sánchez was a chemist; and it was getting hotter by the moment.

"Doña Nati . . . ?"

Santa María, madre de Dios . . ." Immovable: in the oaken rigidity of the Philip II armchair, gazing sightlessly at the sunken, simian, hooded countenance of her mistress, who was laid out in the coarse penitential wool of her shroud on a ponderous seventeenth-century table.

"Oye, Doña Nati?"

". . . *ruega por nosotros* what is it! *pecadores* . . ."

"Have you advised the family?"

". . . *en la hora de nuestra muerte, Amén.*" She stopped. She had finished—the last of the prayers. "I have advised . . ."

She turned her head toward them. There came a flashing from her diablera's eyes.

"I have advised the Marquis of the Pilgrim!"

Triumph. But almost at once, a dull film quenched her fires. She fell to brooding in her chair.

The tradesmen grasped this opportunity to slump back on hams and buttocks.

"My knees are raw," gasped the elegant young man from the dress shop.

"Better them than your culo," snarled the manicurist.

"Well," insisted Sánchez, hauling his rachitic body to its feet, "morticians ought to be here by this time. A doctor to certify cause of death. Nuns and the like."

There was no answer from Nati. She traveled somewhere else— maybe back to the farm, and her youth, when she and the Marquesa climbed the Moorish watchtower to gaze out over the meseta while rooks wheeled gabbling around their heads.

One by one, the tradesmen got to their feet: Jacobo Rivas with a heave and a grunt, the Teddy-boy tiredly, the plumber's son-in-law twisting one of his tuberous ears, and the electrician with eyes red from weeping. He went thudding across the length of the rose parlor, to stop before and loathe every feather in the mixed bag of a Flemish still life.

Sánchez was watching Nati. She seemed lost in her osteitic hands.

"May I summon a doctor?"

"There . . . is no need," she murmured. "I have washed her. I have used perfume against the heat."

"And talcum powder?"

"What's that got to do with anything?" asked the manicurist. He glanced at the crossed hands of the corpse. "No work needed there!"

Jacobo Rivas was gazing at the Teddy-boy.

"What's your name?"

"Joaquín."

"Joaquín what?"

"Never known."

"Where do you come from?"

"I remember a stone bridge, and a stream with rushes on the bank, rustling with water rats."

Sánchez had crabbed up alongside the remains. He was peering at the throat of the shroud, which reached the Marquesa's rigid chin.

He blinked rapidly several times. His eyes stung as though salted. What had Nati announced? A stroke, a heart seizure? Who would believe it? Purple had spread upward, reaching close under the lobes of those pierced, petite ears. Sánchez knew that if one were to turn the corpse over, the nape of the neck would show black from subcutaneously clotted blood.

"Are you going to put it to her now?" the boy asked of Jacobo.

The big man frowned at the question. But he had declared his boast before them all. He was hoist, so to speak, on his own peter.

He lumbered up beside Sánchez.

"A sad state of affairs."

"Yesss," said the pharmacist, studying the dead woman.

Jacobo was shy about looking at her. During the war, that was what had affected him most: the women, so often so obscenely sprawled by bombs, their skirts flung up over buttocks in a pantomime of lust. Jacobo had vomited—many times.

He obliged himself to look. Somehow, it seemed indecent to speak about the Marquesa's debts. He glanced nervously at the brooder behind them, whispering, "It . . . was my notion to demand our rights, I admit that. But . . . under the circumstances . . ."

"Vultures!"

Spat at their backs; spinning them about.

Nati had flung her torso forward from the backrest. She grasped the blunt arm ends of the chair so violently that it seemed certain finger-bones and knuckles would burst. "It's you who picked her to death!"

Jacobo and Sánchez both started. "Us?" Jacobo said, astonished.

"You!" cried Nati, pointing an accusing hand and arm. "Who put her on that table—instead of being with me, this instant, cleaning the ballroom!"

She flung herself to her feet, striding away from them. The ballroom —scheduled for today! She flung sliding doors open, stepping into that huge, dark rotunda . . . when she recoiled from it, a sort of terror seizing her, the heart beating violently in its bony cage.

She backed away from those shadows—back into the rose parlor, struggling to shut the doors. The terror was nameless. But she hung shaking to the brass handles of the partly closed doors.

"Jacobo, go to her!"

The mantequero reached Nati in three strides, grasping her, supporting her. Her whole body seemed to be burning with a dry flame. He led her to a couch, reclining her on the cushions.

"We've only come for our due!" he blurted out.

He had stepped back from Nati, surprised at himself. But this was all that anyone sought; and everyone had a right to it—to that minimum a human being can expect.

Nati's contempt was enough to scald. "The Marqués del Peregrino will pay you double!"

She withdrew into herself then, as if weary of vulgar matters. The tradesmen—all except Jacobo—glanced at each other. The promise ought to suffice. They should leave the woman to her grief, quit premises in which they had no place.

Sánchez touched Jacobo's elbow. But the mantequero flung his hand off impatiently. He was staring down at Nati.

He refused to be intimidated. He had assumed new dignity.

Nati did not notice him. From the couch, she gazed long, long, long: at the bronzes that shone and the silver that gleamed; and then at the silent, shadowy blind sockets of her dead mistress.

A floorboard groaned. The sound of a gasp reached them. "I remember!" cried out the boy excitedly. "Cortés. Joaquín Cortés! Born in Ponga! Bed in a straw stall, by the goats!" But no one listened. No one saw his suddenly rapt and glowing face, eyes lifted to the distance of infanthood. Everyone else—even Nati—had looked up and around. There behind them, halted at the entrance, gigantic under the neoclassical wicket, stood Don Emilio Guzmán y Stuart, Conde de Cortijos.

A spasm seized Nati, as though she meant to bolt up from the couch. The priest was very old. But at this his first sight of Odette Prades mummified in her sack, his heart had clamped within him in a mighty pump, sluicing a fierce rush of blood through his veins. He had squared those two-by-four shoulders, the hugeness of his warrior's frame beggaring even the by-comparison of Jacobo Rivas. And he was at that one moment the paladin of half a century before, or half the Christian era before, of Knights Templar and the Knights of Malta.

And then the breath seeped from his lungs. The groan that followed came like a grate closing on the coals of Hell. The tradesmen were transfixed. They felt a corresponding shudder inside them. Those great shoulders sagged forward. The back stooped. And Don Emilio shrank. Sinew and muscle were flayed from his bones; as it seemed, before their astounded eyes. He was enfeebled. His first step was as much a recovering of balance—a stagger—as an impetus in the direction of the Marquesa.

All eyes followed him. Nati was suspended in her servant's motor reflex, half risen, half still recumbent. "I was born in Ponga, in the hut under the bridge!" —came the wonderment, came the awe. Nati's eyes had gone unyieldingly hostile. "My father herded goats. He lost an arm in the war. He loved me more than anything in this world!" Nati was now in control. She refused to get to her feet, as she should have: obey the training of her half a century or more, conform—succumb—to those ten Christian centuries introduced back into the rose parlor by this priest.

Don Emilio came abreast of her. He was once more the Witness, the scandal, the saint, the celibate of the hair shirt and a back flagellated into perpetual sores. "My mother was . . . was . . . was . . ." The boy faltered. That pain was not to be visited on him. Don Emilio's eyes seemed to fall from dizzying height on Nati's face, resting there. Their sockets were shaped like almonds, and as huge as the rest of him. Their whites were crystalline, and their orbs of a golden hazel hue crackling with such intensity that one seemed to be gazing into the very pigmentation of suffering. Nati had overturned those ten centuries, smashing the cachepot to smithereens. An iris is composed of smithereens, jeweled darts of glassy refraction compressed by a hoop of blue steel. Nati was at this moment afraid.

"Daughter, why didn't you send for me?"

The voice entered their ears from everywhere—issuing from everywhere except the lips of the priest, which had not moved. Had he spoken?

They heard that rivering once more, rushing through the room—a roar, yet not loud: "Daughter, why didn't you arouse me?"

"At four in the morning?"

Earlier, much earlier—the room whispered.

"It was at four in the morning that she complained of a tightness in her chest!"

Nati had sat up fully. She was clenching her hands. Her face shone slick with humus. They had heard her speak. Had Don Emilio spoken?

His lips moved: they would have sworn for the first time.

"I keep the vigil until dawn. It's well-known."

"We had no need of crows!"

"You, daughter, have need of Grace."

He ruminated on her another moment; then passed by and with halting steps to the bier.

Gazing on Odette, Don Emilio forgot Nati. They were alone in the rose parlor, the dead Marquesa and he. This was the body that had saved him, the spirit that had restored his manhood; the flesh that taught him renunciation of the flesh. He searched the Marquesa's corpse. Odette! Odette! The Marquesa seemed to have been shortened to child's size. How often had he lifted her in his arms!

A finger that might have been borrowed from El Greco turned the wimple of the cowl down. Revealed was the throat and its powdered bruises.

Nati hissed in her breath. She began, convulsively, those sucking sounds that had so annoyed her mistress, clenching the joint of a fisted index finger between her teeth. Sánchez felt like a fly in still-oozing amber. The others were aware of nothing beyond the presence of Don Emilio, more legend than living.

He stared at the throat a long interval. He then did that unprecedented thing for one of God's eunuchs. A knee bent, searching for the floor. Supporting himself with a hand on the table's edge, he stooped that long torso forward and tenderly blessed the Marquesa's throat. Covering her wounds, he then kissed Odette on the blue-black shadows of her lips, kissed her on the tallow-cold brow, and finally, in last parting, on both sunken eyelids.

Lowering his forehead to the edge of the table, he began to pray.

"You'll send her to Hell!"

Nati had jumped up from the couch. She moved as though to fling herself on the priest—to tear him away. "Traitor!" she shrieked. "Filth! Hypocrite!"

Jacobo Rivas lunged toward the woman, wrestling her back to the couch without being able to seat her on it.

He was profoundly shocked. "You speak sacrilege!" he exclaimed, red-faced.

Nati struggled. Her features writhed with hatred. "Ask him if he can deny it! Invert. Traitor. Hijo de Satanás!"

"Hush, woman!" She twisted like a serpent in his hands.

"Ask him! Ask *him!* Will he dare deny it! The boy in Morocco, when to all Spain he was such a hero! Standing with Primo against the King! Defiling the house of his friend with his friend's wife!"

Her madwoman's accusations flabbergasted the tradesmen. They stared with dropped jaws at the priest. He seemed oblivious. Nati's struggles, her panting for breath, filled the room. Then, slowly, Don Emilio straightened his back.

He crossed himself. With his left thumb, he carved a cross on the Marquesa's brow. Now he braced against the table, winching himself erect.

He turned. He gazed first upon Nati, who stopped fighting Jacobo's grip, craning her neck toward the priest and like a viper hissing. Don Emilio next gazed upon Jacobo, and on Sánchez, and at the last on the boy called Joaquín Cortés, who had been born the son of a goatherd in Asturias, and whose mother, after her husband's suicide, had abandoned him in the rushes under the bridge, through which the water rats rustled.

He said, "Nati, you needn't fear me."

That rushing of an unheard river brought a gasp from the woman. The sacs were emptied, the sting drawn. She moaned, collapsing on the couch.

He turned to the others. "I confess before you, and before God, the truth of what this woman says."

"I know you! I *remember* you!" now cried out Jacobo. A terrible fear leaped in him.

"Hear me!" the priest belled at them all. These words they are certain he spoke. "The Lord sends his children saints from time to time. I am not one of them. God also sends his children condemned spirits. *Mene. Mene. Mene. Tekel. U-phar-sin.* I belong to Hell. My destiny is Hell. And it may be my powers come from Satan. The hands that touch the vessels of the Temple defile them. My lips burn at the Chalice. I am for you a sign of corruption. I walk among you as that sign, and before you and the Father profess my corruption. Hear me! Look at me! I am the condemned soul. I will burn. Yet I preach the Lord Jesus Christ, our Saviour!"

He gazed at them with crazed, steadfast, perfectly tranquil eyes. The men were appalled and dismayed and several of them besides Jacobo terribly frightened. Don Emilio—they insist—now disconnected from them. Rather, it was as if he had been unvolitionally disconnected. He was there, standing in the room as tall and as emaciated as a stone Daniel in a cathedral, yet he was no longer there. Sánchez tingled from head to foot.

Many moments went by. The return of animation was gradual. An elbow twitched. A short tremor ran up along the priest's spine. His eyes, which had gone as dead as the closed shutter of a camera's lens, seemed to open and fill again with intelligence.

He focused on Jacobo.

"You are . . . Rivas, the mantequero," ran again that river. .

"Yes, Don Emilio."

"Whence come my powers?"

"From Christ, Don Emilio!"

"No, no! From the bottommost pit of Hell. Believe that!"

"I believe, Don Emilio." His fear was so great now he thought his teeth might begin chattering.

"But Whom do I profess?"

"I . . ." He was confused, bewildered.

"Christ Jesus!" came the thunder.

"Yes, Don Emilio."

"Jacobo, pray. You will suffer, but you are saved. Thank your God, Jacobo. As the garrote snaps your neck, *thank* Him!"

Jacobo was terrified. The priest's terrible eyes now searched out the boy.

"Joaquín . . ."

"Sí, padre." In the boy's breast, terror also gathered.

"Find your heart. At once. Save it."

"Where!" exclaimed the boy, filled now with a different alarm; instantly comprehending.

"God is in your blade, Joaquín. Use God, go!"

"These are oracles, Delphic, almost useless!" came the clear shout from Sánchez.

The roached little man's indignation was white-hot. Alone among them, he had retained composure. His mind had raced. It had thrilled. Because the priest knew more than he was telling. Sánchez was positive of that. It was this that heated him. He met Don Emilio's eyes, fearlessly: and within the flash of an instant was shattered to perceive a gleam of satanic wickedness, a chilling, most awful laughter.

There could be no doubting the man was possessed.

Sánchez threw himself forward, turning his humpback on Don Emilio, spreading his arms as though to blot his presence out.

"Don't listen to him, none of you! He *is* evil! He is what he says!"

Silence hung in the room, a silence wrung with the tradesmen's horror. Then, from behind the pharmacist: "Thank you."

Sánchez pivoted. Don Emilio smiled gravely at him. He conveyed gratitude. In a natural manner, the priest now turned to Nati.

"I will prepare the chapel. Have the Marquesa brought in." And what walked slowly away from them was no more than a very tall, very old man in a stained and threadbare soutane.

Outside, a green Mercedes-Benz backed carefully into a perfect park along the curb directly in front of Número Catorce. The chauffeur, sweating in his black boots, gray breeches, tunic, and cap, dismounted and went round to the right rear door.

He opened it, stepping aside and to a slovenly sort of attention. Moments passed. Nothing emerged. Then a slim, long foot reached out of the car, tentatively pressing the sidewalk. A pause: and Ignacio Prades, Count of Obregón and heir to the Marquisate of the Pilgrim, stepped into the leathery glare of the noonday sun.

Tall, he was, and somber. He wore a winter's weight black serge suit, black shoes, and a knitted black tie. His shirt was of the finest linen, ivory in tone, with obsidian links at the cuffs set in gold. His pallor was extreme, *of* the bone. Bright fever-flushes burned at his cheekbones. The vein at his left temple throbbed.

For all that, he was nevertheless physically more—one searches for the word—*noble* than ever he had been. I have it from Marisa Magascal. "One was able," she neighed into my ears, "I mean very *nearly*, to pity Ignacio. There was a sort of *dignity* about him, I don't know quite how to express it, son of Ramón—Achillean, nearly—the very first image or thought that flashed into my mind was of a man preparing himself for execution, I mean to say he was evidently suffering more than any of us would have given him credit for. He was, in a word, striking."

Dorada might have acknowledged this. She might have found it possible to be moved by it, if fleetingly. Never had such depths of luster opened in those large, dark, gas-lantern eyes. The long straight nose was an aristocratic drop to his passionately contoured lips, which, although drained of color, were still swollen out of their censorial shape—no; say rather habit—by the predations of Dorada's teeth; and so seemed almost generous. In truth, dimension had been added to Ignacio through devastation. It was as though his long scholar's frame under that ascetic tuning fork between the brows had been granted sinew; as though fresh pints of blood—milk-pale though the corpuscles might be—had been pumped into his veins.

Ignacio was, you see, on the one hand engrossed no longer with himself alone and on the other hand engrossed with nothing less than the truth about himself. The dimension deepening him was cruel, that yes. He stood there on his feet a moribund creature. He was not a man; scarcely was he a being. His member was still stretched as limp and as stringy as a boiled asparagus from the brutal ministrations of Dorada. She had succeeded with him. By doing violence to an incorruptibly *fine* thread in his nature—the valid fastidiousness of soul cultured in his genes through generations of breeding—she had demonstrated to him his sexual . . . call it etiolation, if you will, or deficiency, or even cowardice; and he, being intelligent, had perceived in the metaphor what she had desired: the spiritual and intellectual emptiness that his genital failure suggested. He was in all ways a nonentity, a nothing; and when nothingness acknowledges its nothingness, what is left?

He swayed in the heat. Now, he actually stood as still and straight as a man is able, his chin raised and his eyes leveled directly ahead of him. It was the surheated thermal layers of Calle Don Pedro that seemed to eddy about his head, so that subjectively he felt the vertigo. He was, of course, compelled to enter Número Catorce. It was his obligation to arrange for the vigil—the nuns and the tapers and so forth—for the burial next morning, for the funeral Mass seven days later in los Jerónimos Reales, and for the novena of nocturnal rosaries. It was his obligation to stand up through all this, to sustain the sympathy of his acquaintances—he had no friends—all of whom viewed him, he now comprehended, as the congealed human absolute zero that he was, and whose condolences would be forced. It was meanwhile his obligation—as Ignacio Prades, Conde de Obregón, understood it—to tamp the shocking, almost uncontrollable, newly apprehended love for his mother, gushing this moment like a cataract from his entrails, and contain his heartbreak.

Of a sudden, sleepy Don Pedro was agitated. Carlos Lapique came creaking up from one end of the street as hurriedly as long stiff legs permitted, Dos Tripas limping along beside him. A short distance to Ignacio's right, a door rattled in its frame and was eventually blown open by Marisa Magascal, who looked as though she had been assembled, or perhaps bridled and saddled, by some hurricane originating in the River Styx and then passing through whole forests of Spanish moss, heaps of which it dropped on her in a profusion of widow's weeds. Down from Plaza Julio Torres began rolling a procession of automobiles.

The servants' underground had spread word. Mourners dismounted, among them the Countess of Estepona, the Infantas Don A. de O. and Don B. de C., the young Princess of Bavaria, a Holenhöhe, several Saoregueras, the consort Duke of Alba, Lady Hume (fresh, no doubt, from a janitor's or anyone's bed), the equally promiscuous Inmaculada Urquijo, Countess of Cáceres, two of the highest ranking officers in the General Staff, the Minister of Foreign Affairs, the portly, gentlemanly Count Rudi Hesselstein and his young kinsman, the stout Archduke Máximo, the jolly French ambassador, a host more; and, from a drab police vehicle, a short, spruce plainclothesman who fussily detached one of three uniformed officers to handle traffic.

Odette's death was a grand occasion, a sounding of the horn for Society. Anyone present thereby made public his status. She had been, besides, held in affection by her peers, which was all the nicer, because the professions of shock exchanged by people as they huddled on the street were fluent with sincerity, and the moistened eyes of a Marisa or Dos Tripas would not be subject to Spanish cynicism. "In her sleep," someone nodded, "heart attack." "I heard she was *murdered!*" someone else stated. "What? What? Who suggested *that?*" "Rosa, the Obregón's maid." "No, no, no, it was María, the Caribs' maid." "Wrong again," a third voice whispered, "it was Juan Luis's Herminia, who *told* María, who telephoned Rosa, who told my Amapola that the family doesn't know!" Julio Caro looked vainly about him for Juan Luis. People coalesced into bubbles of conjecture and began drifting toward Número Catorce.

Ignacio had remained standing there, suffering, suffering. He may have caught sight of Julio out of the corner of an eye. Ignacio had always faintly despised his kinsman. It was only clan loyalty (class loyalty, he comprehended now, along with increased estimation for himself) that had prompted his largesse in rescuing Julio from penury. Now: what right had he to place anyone beneath him? A charwoman, the lowest slattern or the most duplicitous of gypsy beggars, were not lower than the Count of Obregón. Oh my heavens, *how* Ignacio suffered there in the heat of his black serge suit and under the glare of the pitiless sun! Mourners had reached his proximity; they hung back. *Someone* should go to him, grasp one of his arms hard at the bicep, and help him into his mother's house. No one moved. Then, through the crowd—people making instant, respectful, and in her case (even) sympathetic way—came Consuelo, Countess of the Caribs, and her dashing, roly-poly husband, Jaime Orbaneja. Consuelo flung herself at once on Ignacio, bawling on his chest. He remained there with slack hands by his sides. He then tried to respond to his sister.

"O, Ignacio, Ignacio, pobre Mamá!"

His effort was real. "She . . . needed money, Consuelo. I . . . I sent her very little."

"And I!"

"Where is Sofía?"

"She rushed out to fetch Billy. O, Ignacio, no *es* posible que sea la verdad!"

Jaime now grasped one of his cold hands.

"I'm . . . so very sorry," he murmured. He kept murmuring it, "I am so very sorry"; and he was being truthful, he had been fond of his mother-in-law, but it was difficult for him not to break into a little jig, maybe a *sardana* or *jota*, snapping his fingers and lifting his voice in song. Because Odette—at least temporarily—had saved him. What a darling she was—had been! Not even Baltazar Blás would foreclose at a time like this (would the monster?). Death is the moment of truth, *olé!* God bless Joselito. God bless Manolete. God bless and keep and cherish dear Odette! An unsatisfied demand note, under the circumstances, surely would be glossed by the College of Notaries; who were, even though Blás might not be, human, and Spanish, surely hidalgos by nature if not by descent, true caballeros, and would permit the matter to hang at least until after the funeral Mass; when, if it was not instantly settled, they would clap down like the jaws of a trap. But Jaime and Obras Orbaneja were for the time being saved. Who knew what might happen in seven days? The whole world might be at war, God bless the Arabs also!

Ignacio had provided Consuelo with his pocket handkerchief, her own having become a soggy ball whose embroidered coronet scratched her septum, turning it quite red. The three now entered Número Catorce, followed at a decorous distance by Marisa Magascal, whose emotions required the support of Centollos and Dos Tripas, the one so tall and the other so short that her whole hippic frame was tilted askew, so that in ensemble they resembled a pair of delivery men struggling with an awkward wardrobe mirror. Behind these came the natty plain-clothesman, a man with a medical satchel, and two uniformed officers. Others milled about in the carriage entrance. Should they follow directly, given that the immediate family hadn't had the opportunity of, so to speak, picking up the remains? Julio Caro, being a closish cousin, decided to risk it.

In the rose parlor, Jacobo, the electrician, the manicurist and the plumber's son-in-law, were struggling with the ponderous table on which Nati had laid out the Marquesa. Nati was nowhere to be seen. The elegant young man fiddled hungrily with gi-gui-guis toward the rear of the room. Sánchez was attempting to direct the removal of the Marquesa, which was being carried out as awkwardly as the support of Marisa Magascal.

"Jacobo, you're lifting too high and pulling too hard."

"Give elephant-ears a hand, then! He's lifting too low and pushing not hard enough!"

"It's very heavy," complained the plumber's son-in-law, who struggled with his rear corner.

"If you let it fall," growled the manicurist, "I'll bop you so hard you'll grow cardinals on your skull!" He had the other rear corner.

"When we finally got her underground," muttered the electrician, hauling beside Jacobo, "the bricks caved in. Can you imagine that? The bricks caved in! And the mason, they say—fellow called García—used to be the foreman of one of Madrid's best-known architects."

"Doesn't surprise me in the least," huffed Jacobo. "No one puts his heart into anything nowadays." He gave a great heave.

"She'll roll off," warned Sánchez, "unless you, Jacobo, stoop a bit, or you," to the plumber's son-in-law, "lift higher."

Earlier, of course, they had discussed Don Emilio. The manicurist swore he had heard nothing of the conversation between priest, Jacobo, and the boy. The electrician admitted to having heard snatches, but could recall nothing. Jacobo remained terrified.

"The garrote!" he whispered to Sánchez. "*You* heard him. You heard him say that!"

"Pay no attention."

"Pay no attention? To Don Emilio? I knew him! During the War! When I was wounded!"

"Pay him no mind! Besides, he said you were saved."

"*After* the garrote!"

"That was not Don Emilio speaking."

"What do you mean, it wasn't Don Emilio?"

"It was Satan."

"You're an atheist! You don't believe in Satan!"

"I do in his case."

"I tell you, that man is a saint!"

"Not when he prophesies. He's a Devil."

"He only says that out of his humility. Think of the terrible, ridiculous things he admitted about himself. That's his saintliness!"

"No, he tells the truth. And that's his wickedness."

They had been interrupted at this juncture by Nati, who reminded them of Don Emilio's orders. She told them to cross the ballroom. To the rear of it was an alcove leading into the chapel. She left, then. It was then that they noticed the disappearance of Joaquín.

"Probably he had to pass water," said the electrician. "I've noticed boys of that type, that age, can't control their bladders."

"I'm worried about him," said Jacobo.

"Well, we've been given a job to do," said the manicurist. "Who's going to pay us for this?" But he was the first to position himself at the table.

They had reached the sliding doors. The Marquesa was tipping toward the back of the bier. In a moment, her head would protrude over the edge.

The plumber's son-in-law dropped his end.

"Idiot!" yelled the manicurist.

"She'll drip blood!"

"No she won't! Can't you see she's in rigor mortis? Grab her! Or she'll bounce and maybe crack her head right off."

Sánchez was already pushing on the Marquesa's shoulders. "Come on," he urged the plumber's son-in-law. "Try again. I'll help you."

"Who'd have thought a bag of bones could weigh so much?" muttered the manicurist; and it was on these words that Ignacio, Consuelo, and Jaime Orbaneja entered.

They came to a stunned standstill.

"What," said Ignacio, "is the meaning of this?"

Now the plumber's son-in-law and the manicurist both let their ends go, with a thud shuddering the tabletop; and since Jacobo and the electrician still held up the front, the cadaver slid fast on the incline. It would have slid off entirely had not Sánchez again thrown his puny weight against it.

Consuelo screamed, swooning back on Jaime, who neatly side-stepped her, so that she tottered with stumpy, rapid little steps halfway to the opposite wall. "Jacobo!" Sánchez pleaded. Realizing that she was about to fall, Consuelo lunged for support; and that turned out to be an ancestral portrait, by happenstance of Isabel "de" Frayle Guevara, "La Rica," whose galleons of slave trade loot fetched so many titles. The painting ripped off its silken cords, banging on the floor, Consuelo hanging to it for dear life. "Jaime!" she shrieked. "Jaime!" Jacobo and the electrician were meanwhile setting their end of the table down, Jacobo revolving on his bulk to face the dead woman's son.

Ignacio stood as though rooted. He could not bring himself to look at his mother, who was tilted askew and whose cowl had rolled under to reveal a bald spot on the crown of her head, one that in life she had been so anxious to conceal. Beyond him, his sister howled while teetering with the life-sized oil in its solid oak frame, Jaime finally hastening to assist her. Before him gaped strangers, intruders, men of a class never admitted to these parlors.

The Count of Obregón's emotions choked him. They demanded release.

"Who . . . are you!" he said.

"Antonio Sánchez, the pharmacist."

"Jacobo Rivas, the mantequero."

"Castillo, the electrician."

"Torre, the manicurist. Here's my card."

"Never mind that!" snapped Ignacio. He was nearly shaking from indignation. Marisa Magascal, Centollos, and Dos Tripas now pressed in, followed by the policemen and the doctor. "What are you doing here! Where were you taking my mother!"

Jaime had managed to remove the portrait from Consuelo, tilting it against a wall. She now rushed to her mother's side, gasping, flinging a palm against her forehead and collapsing back with a shrill cry; this time fortuitously into the arms of Marisa Magascal, who had hurried after her.

The plainclothesman stepped up to Ignacio—coming to a smart, heel-rapping stance, his card extended.

"Stepanópoulis Grau, Your Most Excellency, of the Brigada Policiaca. What's this—body-snatching? Do you care to press charges?"

Ignacio stared down on the spruce little man as though Grau were some sort of animated gargoyle. He ignored him, turning back to the tradesmen.

"Where were you taking my mother? Where's Nati? What's the meaning of this?"

Sánchez gimped forward. "You are . . ."

"The Conde de Obregón, who else!" He would not use the Marquisate—not yet, maybe never. To the rear of the room, half hidden by furniture from view, the elegant young man had lost interest in proceedings. He stared and stared at the most exquisite fan he had ever seen—pierced ivory, inlaid in gold; Queen María Luisa's fan.

"Well," Sánchez was attempting to explain, "we were taking la Señora Marquesa into the chapel. Don Emilio Cortijos is there, waiting for her."

"But you . . . !" Ignacio strode three paces deeper into the room, glancing from one tradesman to the next. "What *business* have you in this house, at . . . . at . . . such a time!"

Jacobo Rivas now came forward. Inside, he had begun to roil.

"If you want to know . . ."

"We have been here over an hour," interrupted Sánchez, cautioning his friend with a touch on an arm, "praying for your mother's soul."

"I should think you'd be grateful," put in the electrician. "This morning, at my wife's burial, there was no one but me."

"Grateful!" burst from Ignacio. He was by now trembling violently. "To such as you?!"

That was just about enough, for Jacobo. He planted himself. "I am a Rivas of Sacedón, hidalgo, and head of the clan. My right to be here is more ancient than yours."

"What nonsense is this!" Ignacio turned to the plainclothesman. "Remove them. Remove these . . ."

But the darkest anger possessed Jacobo. He had shed his blood and the blood of fellow Basques for such as this man.

He stepped toward the Count, until his eyes were mere inches away.

"We came in a body to collect our bills—months unpaid. And I, for one, am not leaving until they are settled."

Ignacio nearly strangled where he stood. It was so utterly sordid: his proud mother ringed round by jackals during the last of her hours above the sod. "You . . . will . . . all of you . . . depart this instant!"

And he wheeled, grabbing Sánchez's shoulder with a long reach and almost flinging the little man toward the door.

Grau and the uniformed police officers were already moving forward; but too late to stop what happened next. Because Jacobo Rivas's mutton-chop of a fist smashed into the Count of Obregón's nose, and Ignacio toppled backward, ramming the plainclothesman against the wall before sliding down along it to the floor.

The uniformed policemen drew their billybats, charging Jacobo. "Run!" Sánchez cried. But the doorway was by this time jamming with mourners, the van among whom halted amazed. There was really no escaping. Whether it was this, or a lifetime of buried rage, one doesn't know; but Jacobo stood his ground as once he had stood off the entire populace of a town, and as the billybat of the first officer to reach him arc-ed through the air, he grasped it with catquick goalkeeper's reflexes, twisting it out of the grasp of the policeman and whopping it on his skull. Simultaneously, the electrician neatly fouled the second officer at the ankles, sending him in a sprawl that smashed a rickety Louis XVI side-table. Stepanópoulis Grau, still partly pinned beneath Ignacio, from whose flattened nostrils gouted rich flows of blood, fished a whistle out of a pocket and began blowing shrilly on it. Several of the younger male mourners, Julio Caro and Amontefardo in the lead, were half pushed and half of their own accord went toward Jacobo, who had now backed to the center of the great parlor, legs spread in fighting stance and club grasped menacingly. "Not . . . until . . . our bills . . . are settled!" and *whop!* on the pate of Amontefardo.

Women shrieked. Men shouted. Grau—on his feet, now, but squeezing his knees against an imperative desire to go to the bathroom—kept blasting on his whistle. Consuelo swooned again. Jaime became entranced by a cornice. The elegant young man dived behind a Mudejar chest, clasping the fan to his bosom. The plumber's son-in-law tweaked his great ears in a misery of indecision. Sánchez sighed; and realizing there was nothing he could do here, slipped into the ballroom.

Electrician and manicurist stepped up beside Jacobo, whose leviathan belly heaved up and down, that sight of itself frightening many. Not Carlos Lapique, Duke of the Rock Crabs. "This is . . . outrageous!" he spluttered, moisture spraying off the point of his harrier's nose. Old that he was, he forthwith searched around him for a weapon, deciding on a carved, sandalwood sconce, which he ripped from the wall. Others followed suit, and soon people were scrambling for candlesticks, lamps, and vases. Police re-enforcements pushed through from behind. Jacobo shifted stance to face them. The manicurist tore an arm from a precious chair. The electrician yanked off one of its cabriole legs. The police charged. These were not, alas, or luckily, depending on how one views matters, the riot squad. They were principally traffic cops. The consequence was mayhem, with several mourners getting in the way of truncheon, fist, boot, or piece of furniture, and, in turn, more than one of the ticket-dispensers having his ears clipped by an eagerly but inexpertly flung bibelot. Partly thanks to this confusion, Jacobo and his flankers were not overwhelmed. One fellow sent flying by them knocked the Marquesa off her table and sent her like a boom head first into the bosom of Consuelo, who swooned a third time. Furiously, Marisa Magascal kicked the man in the scrotum, causing him to yelp like a hound-dog; upon which she recognized Julio Caro, who had only been trying to help.

Sánchez had gained the street through the kitchen wing. He went running as fast as his cripple's gait permitted to the Rivas mantequería. "Doña Marisol!" he cried. "Doña Marisol!"

Marisol Rivas was up in the bedroom, sprinkling the covers with rose water. She could scarcely wait for nightfall, planning a roasted unborn lamb for supper whose succulence would arouse in any man the most tender emotions. She had spent an hour in the confessional. There a young curate counseled that she had committed no sin in yielding to Jacobo's goatishness. In fact, he told her, she was a most fortunate woman to possess so uxorious a husband. She argued heatedly to the contrary; but in her heart rejoiced over the curate's verdict. She had hurried back with a smile that even consigning Soledad to her future in the household of Sacedón could not depress. The curate had told her more. It was *not* perdition for her to enjoy her husband. It was blessed by God. Oh, had she known this thirty years earlier! What a termagant she had been! How different their life might have been!

"Doña Marisol! Doña Marisol!"

She went lumbering downstairs to the shop. There, holding his sides, gasping, Sánchez panted out the alarm.

Marisol listened wordlessly. When Sánchez was through, she asked, "Has that tub of lard killed anyone yet?"

"No. He's more likely to *be* killed! He's surrounded!"

Those Cantabrian eyes darkened into twin stormheads. She

wheeled, going to the kitchen and snatching an iron skillet from the stove. Sánchez had followed her. "Doña Marisol," he cried, "don't blame Jacobo!" She dealt the pharmacist one subfusc glance, saying, "Blame him! That big kettledrum, I go to die *with* him!" And she strode out of the shop.

What a morning of miracles! This was the renaissance of the Jacobo with whom she had fallen in love. This was the man who on principle, great coward that he was, conquered his cowardice. Formidable was Marisol's aspect as she marched to the rescue of her husband. People glanced at the blackened skillet, flexed in one hand like a tennis racquet. People glanced at her bovine breastworks, thudding with every tread. Then people caught her eye, and they gave way before her, knowing nothing of the object of her wrath but nimble enough to escape the line of fire.

Near the portal of Número Catorce, a crowd had gathered. Police vehicles were scattered across the curb as though they were child's toys carelessly dropped there. There was an ambulance to one side. Stretcher-bearers were sliding a long rake's handle of a man into its rear. Weaving groggily out of Número Catorce came several casualties, some grasping their skulls in both hands while others cupped swollen eyes or chewed earlobes. Just as Marisol began pressing her way through, gray-clad riot police—Assault Guards—debouched from a paddywagon. She followed on their heels as they raced into the palace.

They reached the action ahead of her, where they halted, wide-eyed. The poor rose parlor over which the Marquesa and Nati had slaved twenty-four hours before was a shambles. Lampstands plugged through the canvases of paintings. The dust of crockery and the feathers of torn pillows fogged the air. Couches were overturned. Someone had swung from a chandelier, bringing it down like a great hoop skirt, smashing the crystals.

Both the electrician and the manicurist were out of commission, the latter being sat upon by Jaime Orbaneja, who had been brayed by Marisa into the fray. But Jacobo Rivas, back braced against the rear wall, panting like a locomotive, continued whopping lustily about him. Piled before him was a tumble of bodies. Two Assault Guards rushed forward with a weighted net spread between them. This they flung over Jacobo; and as he struggled in its meshes, their four companions rained hard rubber blows on his skull.

He was hit. He staggered. He was sinking to his knees when, with a banshee's cry, Marisol came springing over a settee. One glance at her

Vesuvian wrath, and Jacobo's attackers fled across the parlor. Marisol gave chase. Round the room they went, spilling tables, knocking over chairs, Marisol twice coming within skillet distance. The riot squad was reduced to three wobbly and desperate members when their sergeant whirled, seized the plumber's son-in-law, and, in a last-ditch effort, pitched him rolling under Marisol's feet. She tripped. She crashed on a magnificent Louis XV parlor stand, demolishing its marble and gilt. Quickly, another policeman scooped the net off the unconscious Jacobo, flinging it over his wife.

Thus began the vigil for Odette Prades; and it was, in a sense, a compliment from the living to the dead, for she had upheld True Spain to her last breath, as had, in her way, Nati. Marisa Magascal found the maid standing alone in the ballroom, a hand resting on the pedestal of the missing cachepot. She was staring at the smooth, marble back of the libidinous Leda, her eyes vacant. Plainly the poor woman was in shock, and near exhaustion. She moved leadenly under the impulse of the soothing arms of the Countess of Magascal, who grieved for Nati with a grief that for the moment subsumed her emotions respecting Odette. Marisa led Nati to her bedroom and made the woman lie down.

Outside the Red Cross had set up a field station at which came stopping a regular bus route of ambulances. This was when I arrived on the scene. My presence was scarcely noticed. I witnessed what seemed to be the unnecessarily rough handling of several men and an Amazon of a woman who were being packed into the paddywagon; only after to learn that they were Marisol, Jacobo, the electrician, and the manicurist. The elegant young fellow from the dress shop had escaped notice. The plumber's son-in-law was that evening to be transfigured by the tabloids into a hero who had fearlessly hurled himself under the feet of the maddened mantequero's wife, bringing her down at the cost of one of his ears, which was, alas, trampled and torn off. (No one remarked on the improvement.)

I was about to make my way through the babbling of excited men and women issuing out of Número Catorce when I noticed a chauffeured Bentley rolling slowly along the street. It was one of those silver beauties last manufactured a decade or so ago. There are only two such models in Madrid. One belongs to me, and the other to Baltazar Blás.

Police had blocked off traffic at the head of Don Pedro. Blás, of course, had been waved through. The paddywagon now lumbered off. The Silver Arrow nosed into its place, stopping. I was of half a mind to greet

Blás, when I held back, stepping behind the latest ambulance to arrive.

It was a convenient observation post. What I'm about to recount now comes partly from hindsight, partly by way of reconstruction. In some matters, I was already sufficiently informed to intuit what I was as yet unable to verify through investigation. Blás did not dismount at once. He spent five or six minutes viewing the commotion from the security of his chariot. Plainly, his secretary—Sert—had been unable to reach Orbaneja. Plainly, Sert had then telephoned his cousin, Juan Luis's Eugenio, who was also, but presumably from different motives, trying to track down the architect; and it was from Eugenio that Sert learned of the Marquesa's death, communicating this news to his master.

That notice must have affected Blás as nothing since the birth of his grandson. I would imagine he dismissed Sert. Perhaps he sat at his desk some moments, without moving. He may have got up then, going with that vigorous stride to the built-in liquor cabinet, fishing for a bottle of his finest brandy and drinking a shot down. One can doubt this. Blás is a temperate man. Still, the exception may have been made. He was, as of this day, father-in-law not merely of the Count of Obregón (decent enough title) but of the imperial Marquis of the Pilgrim. His daughter was the Marchioness. And Borja Baltazar Prades y Blás, the grandson named after him, would one day be the Marquis—and bear that title with a brilliance rare in this drab world, master of a fortune to be weighed on an international scale. Not even a Rothschild heir would bear comparison. What is a Rothschild? Do they descend from a fifteenth-century duke? Can they trace their line back to hidalgos of the eighth century? Little Borja would be able to—little Borja Baltazar Prades *y* Blás!

There's no wondering this man is among Spain's most fervent royalists, contributing 500,000 pesetas yearly to the exiled household in El Estoril. Blás had his old secretary pore over the stud books. He kept tabs on royal doings. Whom, after all, might little Borja marry? Why not a princess of one of the impoverished royal houses? Both money and blood are necessary. Then perhaps only an Alba or a Liechtenstein or a Devonshire or a Thyssen . . .

He frowned. What was that other element in social panache that distinguished these families? He did not have to tussle very hard. Art!

This is when he telephoned me. As usual, when anyone of Blás's category calls, I switched on the tape recorder. Our conversation is transcribed here verbatim.

"Carl," he began with his characteristic rush, "I've developed a passion for art. Suddenly. Grown on me. Stupid thing for a man my age. I mean, do you think it's stupid?"

"No, Baltazar, I don't think so. What . . . ?"

"Well, it comes pretty late in my life. I'm not going to be able to take my time about it. Have to assemble other people's collections, get a counselor . . ."

"There's no one better than Silvaramos. For any acquisitions in French art, I'd . . ."

"Carl, what would you take for your bunch?"

I happen to possess a choice collection of post-Goya painters.

"I'm not selling it."

"But what would you take for it? Thirty million? Sixty million?"

I laughed. "Baltazar, I've spent almost a quarter of a century . . ."

"I know *that!* The point. Don't have a . . ."

". . . and I guess it cost up to two hundred and forty million pesetas."

"Jesus! That much? Well, what would you take for it? Four-eighty?"

"I told you, I'm not selling. It's probably worth, besides . . . Oh, I don't know, two of the Picassos are major, the Berruetes are a complete set, I've picked up poor Edgar Neville's Solanas . . . Somewhere up around fifteen million dollars."

"*Jeee-sus!* That's one helluva investment you've put together! Well, they all tell me you've got the best. I want the best. What say twelve hundred million pesetas?"

There's a long silence on the tape. I was thinking, thinking hard. The collection is precious to me. When my beloved wife died, beauty went out of my life. But I had the comptroller's report—a photostat—at my fingertips, right there before me, on my desk. Not even a Baltazar Blás sneezes at twenty million dollars.

"Why are you so anxious for it, Baltazar?"

"I tell you I've got this sudden passion . . ."

"Stuff and nonsense. What's happened?"

"The Marquesa died of a heart attack last night."

That was when I had the news. It struck me . . . It struck me very hard. For the past several years, I've been one of Odette's ardent admirers, my discoveries about her sparking the study of the whole clan that has helped bring forth this chronicle.

"Yeah, I know, it's a shock," Blás said. He hadn't need of adding more. It required little imagination for me to trace the evolution of his thoughts, which I've reconstructed, as I say, or here invented for you.

I shook the image of Odette out of my head. Again I glanced at the report. This was a gold star day for Baltazar—the closing of the vise on Orbaneja and consequently Juan Luis Sacedón; and now the almost certain accession of Ignacio to the Marquisate.

"I'll want that twelve hundred million in cash. I'll want it today."

"Cash? Today! For God's sake, Carl!"

"Today, in cash—or there's no deal. I know I'll regret it, Baltazar. I'll change my mind."

A short hesitation. "All right . . ."

"In francs—Swiss—or marks."

"For the love of . . ."

"Swiss francs or German marks, and in my convertible Banco de Bilbao account by closing time this morning."

"You're a harder nose than I am!"

"I've learned something from you, my friend. And . . . I want more than money for my collection."

"You've taken an arm and a leg already! What else?"

I paused. "A piece of the action in Financiera Sacedón."

"No!" came his outraged yell; and almost at once after it, an astonished, "Hey, how do you know about that?!"

"I had similar notions. It wouldn't have been politic for a foreigner."

"What are you talking about!"

He was upset. He was angry. Whence the leak?

"Seven or eight months ago, Orbaneja came to me."

"Yeah! Yeah!"

"I wasn't about to bail him out. I couldn't have been more astonished that you lent him money."

"Favor. Son-in-law's brother-in-law."

"Fiddlededee," I snorted. "Your son-in-law's brother-in-law with a sweet packet of Financiera stock."

"Yeah, so?"

"You accepted another twenty-six per cent of his worthless construction company in collateral."

"So I am after control of Obras Orbaneja. Needs management, that's all—like most any other business, peanuts or toothpicks."

The faint hum of silence on the tape is the time it required for my cynicism to make itself manifest.

"All right!" came shortly from Blás.

I continued. "What you told Orbaneja is, 'That's not enough. You'll just be coming back to me again in six months' time . . .'"

"God's truth!"

"Oh, I agree. But you said, 'Now, I don't want to be hard on you. Go float thirty of the sixty million you need out on the market, Jaime. Somebody takes it, come back to me.' After which, you called Ignacio in."

"Where'd you learn this!" His voice was tense with anger.

"I've been in Spain a very long time, Baltazar."

"You still butcher the language!"

"I've made friends."

"You try godam well hard enough!"

"I brokered IBM into the country."

"What's that got . . ."

"Digits and zeros. Put them together, just as you once put together right and left feet."

I was teasing him—a dangerous frivolity on my part.

I said hurriedly, "Jaime came back to me for another try, that's how I learned. You were meanwhile dealing with Muñoz González."

"Christ!"

"He was on my payroll once, when I was hunting leases in Santo Domingo."

"Christ!"

"You helped him set up his Préstamos Cantábricos credit agency. You bought into his Ibiza deal, paying more than was strictly necessary."

"I suppose you got that out of a godam computer!" He was as nearly openly furious as I have heard him.

"No. From Muñoz González. In turn, he was to draw-trap Jaime Orbaneja for you. That's why you called in Nacho Prades. You told him that a new firm—Préstamos—was flush with cash, and just might listen to Jaime; but that Préstamos would probably want somebody to co-sign that half of the total note."

"Yeah, I told him that!"

"Was it your direct suggestion that Jaime contact Juan Luis Sacedón?"

"Don't remember . . ." He was nervous. "Came out in the conversation."

"I'm sure it did. Ignacio, in any case, got the message . . ."

"I'm not so sure about that."

". . . across to Jaime, who called Juan Luis, who of course said yes he would certainly help out the brother-in-law of the woman who once was to have become his sister-in-law, and who trotted right down to Préstamos with Jaime, where Rougement or some other Muñoz González henchman agreed that he would advance thirty million pesetas to His Most Excellency the Count of the Caribs on the strength of the signature of His Most Excellency the Duke of Sacedón; but, alas, a credit agency has to have something better than a signature, illustrious as it might be, and would not His Grace consider putting up some collateral of his own . . . say, some few thousand of the millions of shares he owns in Financiera?"

"You . . . bastard!" wheezed over the wire. Blás was resigned to my knowledge. Now he was after discovering just how much I knew. "That's about how it went. O.K., what else?"

"They settled on Juan Luis signing open bills of sale for two hundred and fifty thousand shares, forfeit tomorrow morning if Jaime does not satisfy the note. I congratulate you, my friend."

"Why me?"

"Because it's your money Muñoz González lent Jaime, they're your two hundred and fifty thousand shares, three per cent of the company. If you snare Jaime's five per cent on top, that's effective control—apart from any other stock you may have been snapping up through brokers."

"Yeah."

"And Financiera owns fifty-one per cent of Utilidades, so that control of the first is control of the second."

"Go on," came the man's high, impatient gravel.

"So you made sure of getting Jaime's Financiera stock. You had Nacho Prades sell him on your development in Ibiza . . . a brotherly tip. You manipulated Jaime into sinking most of the thirty million he came back and borrowed from you—the other half of his note—into that."

"It's a good property! It'll be worth billions of pesetas when I get through with it!"

"Oh, I'm sure it will. And knowing Jaime Orbaneja, I can guess he foolishly persuaded himself to believe that he'd double or triple his investment in six months, pay you off, pay off Préstamos, and pluck himself and Sacedón from the hook. But then you turned around to Zaforteza and Muñoz González, and arranged either a slow-down of sales or . . . yes, naturally! there's nothing one can't do with books in Spain! had it *appear* that sales were lagging."

"*I* didn't do that!" came an indignant protestation. "It's those damned hippies blew our schedule to Hell!"

"Fiddlesticks!" was on the tip of my tongue. But glancing down at my desk, I smothered the word. Baltazar indeed may not have been expecting quite such a slow-down.

"It makes no difference," I said. "You could count on the disaster of the peacocks; the collapse of the lintel the other day is just icing on the cake. Jaime's credit is ruined. You knew he'd be back, and on his knees. His notes expire at sundown, he hasn't got the money, Juan Luis is going to lose the Financiera stock he put up, and you're going to grab Jaime's bundle or threaten him with foreclosure."

"What then?" There's menace in the rap of those words, even over a tape.

"Oh," I replied, "I imagine you'll force Financiera into a series of murderous recapitalizations. You'll squeeze Sacedón management out; and then you'll have a free hand with Utilidades, that's your objective, that's the plum you're really after, which you and Codina Moncó will merge with your Unión Eléctrica into a major new utilities combine, a giant . . ."

"The biggest in southern Europe!"

"Yes, with a potential cash flow of fifty billions of pesetas. That much I have had put through computers. Which is why I want a piece of the deal."

"No!" came the instant refusal.

"I'll let you have my art collection for half. I won't ask for cash. I'll accept your note."

"You know I don't sign the damn things! I pay on the barrel for what I want!"

I was aware of that—one reason I made the offer. "Primitive of you," I murmured, lowering my eyes to the sheet on my desk. Then: "I could blow the whistle on you. I could bail Jaime out. I could bail Sacedón out."

"I said no, Carl! That's my deal—mine and Codina Moncó's. You're not getting into it, understand?"

"I understand."

"And as you say, I'm a primitive sort of person."

"You've made yourself clear. But" —because I also "play fair"— "there's something you ought to know, Baltazar. I've been working on a different angle months, now. I'm expecting notice by lunchtime. If it comes through, I'll be bidding for Utilidades myself. And, Baltazar, this time I'll have the guns."

The silence on the other end of the line did not surprise me. I

suppose nobody—not, anyhow, in the past forty years or so—has spoken
in this manner to Blás. He was at the moment occupied controlling himself. My challenge, implied, whether it would come to pass or not,
he would not forgive; not ever: and sooner or later, he would be coming
after me.

He is an admirable human being. The silence was brief. When
he spoke, his tone was jocular.

"You *are* everything people say about you, Balls. We can thank
God our interests don't often collide, or we'd have a battle that would
shake this little peninsula from its moorings. You'll have the money
before lunch."

"In hard currency," I reminded him, "—against guarantee of delivery
by the end of next week. That do you?"

"Just about does me in," he joked.

He rang off. I sat there thinking. I had . . . conned Baltazar. I
believed then that I had my man. Ambition is a fearful master. Servitude
to ambition is a form of murder, and sometimes suicide.

My reflections, however, are of no importance. I have intruded only
because I am unable to avoid it. We left Blás in his Bentley. On hanging
up, he may have smiled—I would imagine a gallows sort of smile, with
my neck in the noose. Then he dismissed me. Nothing was to mar this
day of jubilation. He, Baltazar, would track Orbaneja down to Número
Catorce, where he was sure the architect had taken refuge. But Baltazar
Blás was not going to be put off. Besides, he felt an irresistible compulsion
to walk into the palace, to view the dead woman whose blood flowed
in the veins of his grandson. He was deeply, humbly grateful to her.

Yet there, on the scene, he was as much cowed as he may have
been astonished by the hurlyburly. He had never set foot in Number
14, nor in any comparable establishment. The feudal weight of
centuries leaned suddenly on him. I could not distinguish his features
through the tinted glass; but I would imagine an expression of amazement
on Baltazar's face—amazement that this should affect him so forcibly
along with a clear analysis of what it was that affected him. He was,
you see, himself committed to that tradition. His blood mingled with
it now. To disrespect it amounted to a personal depreciation. When he
did step out, traces of that amazement were there all right, mixed with
chagrin. He was annoyed with himself: because he knew that he would
not be able to bring himself to close on his quarry. Not today. Perhaps
not for a week. He sighted Jaime Orbaneja, who was having a wrist
bound at the first-aid booth and who had magically improvised a sling

for it out of a glossy black silk handkerchief, somehow all the more dashing for his rumpled hair and split upper lip. It was at this delicate moment that Dorada came striding toward the portal.

"Hija!"

She halted. "Oh" —diffidently, uncaringly. "Papá, qué haces aquí?"

"It's proper that I should be here," I heard him say. I was jostled by someone at that moment. More and more people were crowding out of Número Catorce. Gawkers were emptying out of the surrounding houses. "I am the father-in-law of the Marqués del Peregrino. Where is the boy?"

"At the Clínica de la Concepción, nursing his nose."

"His nose? What's happened here?"

"How should I know?" She was impatient.

"But haven't you been here?"

"No."

"Dorada! Not here, with Nacho? It's your mother-in-law, the Marquesa . . . Where were you!"

"Home, if you want to know!"

"But . . . ?"

"Crying my heart out! I should have been dressing. I should have been . . . The police telephoned." I peeked. Her lips had tightened. She was angry. She was in a confused, very emotional state. "You'd have thought it was serious! Went to the hospital, waited there until he came out of the operating room, like a fool wouldn't accept anesthesia, fainted . . . I've come straight here. Why, tell me! I'm no Marquesa del Peregrino! Qué pinto? I'm off!"

Blás clasped his daughter by an arm. The pressure was slight, but authoritative. He glanced right and left. I ducked down, an undignified action at my age. I heard his strained whisper.

"Off? Where? You should stay here!" There was a pause. I risked another glance. He was studying his daughter. "Where," he said next, "were you heading when you were not here with Nacho?"

Dorada gazed at her father out of those dazzling, golden-lashed eyes.

"To fuck the balls of Muñoz González."

Few people, I imagine, have witnessed Baltazar Blás in a rage. He is ordinarily in iron control. But now he turned crimson. A thick, once callused fisherman's hand lifted. I believe he might have slapped his daughter's teeth loose had they been in private. Instead he scraped the heel of one shoe hard down Dorada's right shin.

He held her still by an arm, now squeezing it very hard. Their eyes were fastened on each other. I saw Dorada's eyes bulge with the pain. I saw red hatching shoot across the whites of her eyes as instantaneously as ice forms on salt water. The welt of her shin swelled up, pale and hideous. In places, her skin had been scraped raw. The blue-green yellow of the bruise was already forming.

Blás relaxed the pressure on his daughter's arm. He stepped back, gasping a bit.

Dorada had whitened, but that's all. She stared with a forbidding fury at her father, one that very evidently disconcerted him.

"Don't . . . dare touch me again, Papá. I warn you. I'm . . . not afraid of you. I'm not sure I care about your money. I'm the Marquesa del Peregrino now whether I want to be or not. Remember that."

"*You* remember it!" But he was shaken. Baltazar Blás was shaken by his daughter. Again he glanced right and left. Again I ducked. A child attracted by the commotion stared at me. I stared back at him. What was this old fellow doing crouching behind an ambulance? He opened his mouth as though to speak. I stuck my tongue out. I rolled my eyeballs. I snarled through my false teeth. Finally, I took them out and snapped them at him.

He ran away in fright. But now Miriam Estepona was staring, aghast. She was to lunch with me. I smiled—toothlessly, I'm afraid. She pivoted back into the throng.

People were speaking in loud, excited tones. I scarcely heard Baltazar Blás get out, "What's this . . . obscenity about Muñoz González?"

"You heard me."

"Wait, please!" came from her father. "My . . . head aches." In that voice, there was of a sudden great age.

"My shin aches," she flared back. "If I weren't grinding my teeth, I might scream."

"I . . . I am sorry, Dorada."

"Don't be. It's the peasant, the brute in you, that's all. It's useless to be ashamed of what you are. I've learned that partly thanks to you. And I thank you."

She must have turned to go.

"When did this begin?" I heard her father ask rapidly.

"It hasn't. It was to begin this morning."

"Since . . . when have you been seeing that . . ." Plainly, he could not bring himself to finish.

"Last September. He used me to contact you, remember?"

"You gave me no recommendation."

"Of course not. He's a gangster."

"And you . . ."

"I'm your daughter. Muñoz González and I share things in common. I repeat, by this time we meant to be sharing his cock and my . . ."

"Another foul word out of you . . . !"

I was watching them again. Baltazar could not bear it. He would explode. But she was now facing him with a tilted chin and that stunning golden head thrown back in defiance.

"What? Do what! What was it you sold Nacho? But it happens to belong to me, Papá, and I'll trade it for what I want, where I please!"

They stood there, toe to toe, so to speak. But she was stronger. There was no doubt. An ironic admiration grew in Baltazar.

"I could wish you were a son."

She was indifferent to him. Now she did make a definitive move away, turning on a painful leg.

"Wait! Take me inside!"

She glanced over a shoulder. "Afraid? You? To enter alone?"

He stepped toward her, plucking at one of her sleeves.

"Alone, it may be considered . . . insensitive, lack of breeding on my part. At your side, I am naturally there."

She was frigid.

Baltazar tried. "We must . . . talk, hija. You must not involve yourself with filth like Muñoz González."

"Maybe that's what I want my fill of!"

"But your position . . . !"

"On my back, Papá, with my legs spread!"

Tears had sprung to her eyes. I don't think Blás noticed. He was immersed in his own anguish. There was a resumption of wrath.

"I will have a bullet deposited in his brain."

She shrugged, wiping angrily at an eye. "After I have him, you can do what you like."

"If necessary," he now stated with great distinctness, "for the sake of my grandchildren, I will have you locked away. For their sake, Dorada, if it becomes necessary, I would have a bullet deposited in your brain."

The man seemed absolutely tranquil, now. Then, at this—for me—fascinating nexus, or impasse, Juan Luis Sacedón walked by, looking rumpled, hot, and distraught, his comparative chinlessness a portrait of futility and his nascent paunch sad and drooping. He passed within a few feet of me, sunk in what seemed to be more than his habitual lot of misery. He went as though oblivious to his surroundings, oblivious until, of course, being male, he crossed the hood of the ambulance and came upon Dorada.

I forgot to mention that Dorada was dressed in Pucci pinks and oranges, those vivid hues in themselves scandalous for a vigil, and that the frock was of a sheared silk that clung to every contour of her Juno-esque body, from her magnificent breasts to the wedge of her pudendum, at just about which height the hemline flirted.

Juan Luis blinked, dazzled. Next he saw her father.

He made as though to continue along—rapidly—when his mind changed.

He approached. "H'lo, Dorada. My sympathies."

"Thank you. It's been a profound shock."

"Not yet," came his curious reply. "Later, maybe . . . Oh, Señor Blás, how are you?"

"Very well, Señor Duque." Blás bobbed a short bow.

"Do I look pale, Señor Blás?"

"Why, a little." What an odd question, he must have thought.

"Do I look unnaturally pale?"

"I am not acquainted with your normal complexion, Your Grace. I do not have that honor."

"But you're looking forward to the honor of ruining my family, is that it?"

These words really startled Baltazar. Myself, I was wholly intrigued. Until this time, my personal acquaintance with Juan Luis had been brief, formal, superficial. I'm afraid I held him as lightly as Ignacio held Julio Caro.

"What makes you say that, Señor Duque?"

Juan Luis spoke as though explaining matters to a child.

"You see, it's not important. I could ruin," nodding at Dorada, "your daughter. Your grandchildren. Your power is very limited. I have nothing to lose. But you" —he giggled!— "have everything to lose."

And he turned from the astonished Blás, walking a pace to the door before revolving and saying, "Oh, Dorada, do people know yet what's happened?"

"Only that Ignacio lost his temper with a mantequero. The man hit him."

"Ignacio lost his temper?"

"And went down with one humiliating punch on the nose."

Juan Luis: "Still, it's something that he risked the punch. Who the Devil is this mantequero?"

Stepanópoulis Grau: "I have checked his record since birth. One Jacobo Rivas . . . of Sacedón, Your Grace. You may have known him."

The inspector had just that moment breezed out of Número Catorce. Stretcher-bearers appeared, hoisting a dumpy load covered with a blanket, a doctor walking along beside it.

I moved, permitting them passage. It was Odette, I was sure.

"I?" said Juan Luis, cocking eyebrows at Grau. "Oh." He pondered. "A burly man, bounced people off his belly in the fisherman's bar. Once a portero for . . ."

"The Atlético," said Baltazar Blás, surprising everyone.

Grau: "*You* are acquainted with the man, Señor Blás?"

Blás: "Stop the nonsense. So were you."

Grau: "That is a closed chapter in my career, Señor Blás."

Blás: "No chapter quite closes. They can always be revived."

Dorada: "What are you two speaking about? Who is this man, Papá, and who is this . . . ?"

Unnoticed by them, Odette was being loaded into the ambulance. Soon my covert would be revealed.

Blás: "An ex-agent. I fired him."

Juan Luis: "Yes . . . of course! Worked once as a handyman for my father. Now why would he clobber Ignacio? (By the way, probably I ought to clobber Ignacio—shouldn't I, Señor Blás?)"

Blás: "(Probably; given his conceit, you can't be sure whether he understood his mission.) Do you know the reasons, Grau?"

The doctor got in after Odette. The rear panels of the ambulance were being shut, one man already walking toward the driver's door. My hide would roll off in a moment.

Grau: "A discussion over bills owed by the late, lamented Señora Marquesa. The man is a lunatic."

Blás: "Wrong, Grau. You always were. Do you learn nothing? He is one of the rare men of honor I have known."

"And as like as not the true heir," noted Juan Luis. "El mundo es un pañuelo, and we're all snot blown into its pouch by a cosmic gale. Oh yes!" And he broke into another disconcerting giggle, which he scotched in half, sobering. "Say, it wasn't Rivas who murdered Odette, was it?"

Almost simultaneously, Blás exclaimed, "What! What! What's

that?" and the inspector exclaimed, "Why, how is it that *you* know about that?"

I was stunned. I heard Dorada cry out, "Odette . . . was murdered?"

"Well," said Juan Luis, "wasn't she?"

"Strangled," confirmed Stepanópoulis Grau; and he must have motioned toward the ambulance, although I could not see the gesture, because I had once more ducked. "We are taking her to the morgue now for autopsy."

"Oh, my God!" I heard from Dorada. The ambulance was starting up.

Grau: "Your Grace, may I inquire how is it that you know of this, and since when?"

Juan Luis: "My mother telephoned an hour or so ago. She got it, I think, from the Countess of Caribs' maid."

"I knew it!" came the almost triumphant shout from Stepanópoulis Grau. "Pidal," he stated, "Conde de San Martín, was *pushed* into the elevator shaft!"

I heard no more, retreating in pace with the backing ambulance, and soon out of earshot. A parting glance recorded the elation in the police inspector, the dumbfounded expression of Baltazar Blás, the aghast look on Dorada's face, and the pricked, inquisitive ears of Juan Luis.

I went straight to Muñoz González's flat, where I was able to corner him into a chat. The body of Tomás had been discovered. Muñoz González was a highly perturbed human being; especially after I advised him that Dorada had shown up at Número Catorce, and that a very frank exchange had taken place between her and her father—and also with Juan Luis. The strands of isolated information were finally being woven—or were of themselves weaving—into a choate pattern. A call confirmed that Jacobo Rivas had been booked into Carabanchel prison, and that suspicion of murder had been added to assault, battery, and a gaggle of other charges. I knew where next to pursue my investigations.

Book Two

HIDALGOS

ONE

Hidalgos of Sacedón

It is gracious of Almighty God (whose unique obligation to Spaniards must be assumed) to have granted Jacobo Rivas the boon of that early morning's events. For Jacobo is a soul of whom it can be said that everything had come too late. Everything he had been and done, he had done and been too late. For example, what malice of destiny had ordained his birth as the fifth son and eleventh child of a farmer who toiled a living out of scarcely 600 cloud-shrouded "carros"? Why had he been born so many generations removed from the glory of his race, nation, and town; and why, with all his pride, had he been doomed to disappoint this heritage?

Adam, you see, was Basque.

He chose a nice place to live: in the green and hilly crotch formed by the continental conjunction of France and Spain. This is spectacular country, especially below the border, where the northern shelf of the Iberian Peninsula protrudes more than 350 miles west beyond France and into that tempestuous region of the Atlantic known as the Cantabrian Sea. Here lies Sacedón, built on the bones of the Rivas family, most of which, alas, are scattered; although preserved in Bilbao's Museum of Archaeology there is a fascinating set that shows the mandibles of one prehistoric Rivas (it is presumed) still fastened on the kneepan of (the guess is mine) an Ybarra.

The hamlet itself is a conglomerate of roughhewn gray stone foundations above which pout second-story wooden galleries weathered like driftwood but gay with blooms of potted geraniums. Washing flaps bravely from these balconies, and young yokels in three-toed sabots go clonketing up and down the cobblestone streets staring at the blaze of snow-white female undergarments and from them measuring the charms of the flesh they hold. Their standards of pulchritude tend to have been set by the freshest heifer in the barn; happily, the womenfolk tend to live up to these dimensions. Despite which, suitors gawk at the merry voluminous *bona fides* with that melancholy precognizance of all ancient peoples, who are born with the essence of death in their mouths and aware of the ultimate insignificance of their march toward it; so that all joys are emptied before ever having been fondled, and weddings are only less gloomful than funerals. Farm dwellings hug the contours of the land, their squat, mansard, neo-Roman roofs plaited out of overlapping pink and orange tiles that spill beyond the walls and rest on stout gables whose undershot double chins are carved with the decorative solicitude once given to bowsprits and characteristic of any nation with too little to do and too much time for thinking and too long a history to brood upon and no hope, their brains as atrophied as their knuckles are rheumatic and their spirits as dull as the dank of their days.

There is much beauty. Sacedón is set in a landscape so moodily verdant that only Ireland or Brittany compare. If emerald is a color, the rich pastures of Sacedón can be called that. There is a whole spectrum of green involved—rye, apple and moss; scum and eucalyptus—greens glowing gold when the sun comes flooding over the back hills, but that when shrouded ripple like silver foil. All along the breadth of this coast sprawl the Pyrenees, tumultuous masses of which keep tumbling into the sea. On clear days, especially in the autumn, when the air seems to have been distilled in crystal goblets, their highest crags are sculpted against the horizon. More often, the crags are shut out; and clouds in rolling, rumbling herds press down and nearly snag themselves on the bell tower of the cathedral, and often blot out entirely the ruins of the castle. The whole northwestern flank of Spain heaves down to the Cantabrian in a front scalloped by coves and tidal lagoons, great bluffs studding the coast and forming amphitheaters connected each to each and within which vast sand beaches stretch like ligaments.

TWO

The Basques

God, in His Wisdom, decreed an historical agony whose consequence is that pastiche of irreconcilables called Spain; and—Don Quixote to the contrary—it is to be found here, in the Northwest; not on the plains of La Mancha, but here on the Atlantic rampart guarded and fought over by Galicians, Asturians, Santanderians, and Basques, none of whom much esteems the others but together constituting both the bulwark and the tragedy of their nation.

Which each of them appropriates. But the unparalleled pride distinguishing the Basques is that they antecede their neighbors, antecede the Franks, Visigoths, Vandals, and Celts (as well as the Carthaginians, the Greeks, and the Phoenicians, and even the most primitive of Iberian tribes, the Bronze Age inhabitants of Almería on the Levant); that, precisely, they are not Spaniards, not "Europeans," do not spring from any known Teutonic, Mediterranean, or Asian stock; that they reach farther back into the womb of time than anyone else.

Some believe they are the direct descendants of Cro-Magnon man, of the Upper Paleolithic period that produced the artists of the caves of Lascaux and Altamira, which would date them as a race from 15,000 to 25,000 years ago. If this is so, and if, as anthropologists conjecture, mankind separated from Tarzan prototypes 100,000 years ago, then to-day's Basques embody our closest link to the miracle of human emergence.

They superseded Neanderthal man, who was squat and low-browed, the Cro-Magnons by contrast being six-footers, with straight thigh bones, well-balanced skulls, high foreheads, large brain pans, and fully developed chins. The Basques have preserved these features. By fiercely resisting invaders, or any assimilation since at least the Magdalenian era (c. 13,000 B.C.), they have kept their stock pure.

Penned up in their mountains they may have been, but irreducible ever. Rome ruled them only nominally. Basques maintained their separate culture. Between the third and fifth centuries they did adopt Christianity, an immense event, the only major permutation in their recorded tradition: so stunning that the Faith has become for them a symbol of racial allegiance. Generations of fighting brought about their irruption north across the French border, back into the Gascony of their ancestors and even into proud Aquitaine, which, for a time, they dominated. Incorrigible individualists, however, and thus politically about as cohesive as a tin full of protons, they fell back before the might of Charlemagne, who claimed sway over them. So long as they were left alone, they gave two figs as to who purported to be their liege lord. Basque solidarity was their real interest; and in 824, at Pamplona, they founded the Kingdom of Navarre.

This union of the five Spanish and two French provinces lasted three and a half centuries. But the Basques failed to forge a state. One by one—in 1200, 1332, and 1370—they relinquished (respectively)

Guipúzcoa, Alava, and Vizcaya to the Castilian kings; and in 1512 lost their last independent strongholds—Pamplona and the Vizcayan port of Sacedón—to Ferdinand the Catholic. They retained, nonetheless, many special rights, or "fueros," continuing their famous racial assemblies at Guernica and more or less running themselves. At all times they kept trying to reassert their independence, joining the Carlist side in the civil wars of the nineteenth century, and suffering defeat with them in 1873, when their privileges were all but abolished. They never accepted this. When Jacobo Rivas was entering his prime, the Catholic Basque provinces—the people who produced St. Ignatius of Loyola and St. Francis Xaviar—made common cause with church-burning, priest-killing, nun-raping Anarchists and Socialists in one last try for independence.

THREE

Jacobo's Sacedón

About Basque history, Jacobo at that time knew not a notion; about Sacedón and his family, he subscribed to an article of faith. If the town had been treated badly, Rivases had been treated worse.

All along the Vizcayan coast there are any number of natural harbors. These are provided by the incidence of lagoons—rías—one of the deepest of which has helped make Bilbao the wealthiest and most industrialized city on the whole Cantabrian. For centuries, Bilbao's supremacy was challenged by a Sacedón whose Chief Councilor (or "agintari") was almost hereditarily a Rivas clansman.

The town is situated sixty miles west of the capital, a Vizcayan toe butting into the province of Santander; hence a certain doubtfulness about the absolute purity of its Basque blood—a slander furiously rejected by Sacedonese—and hence the suspiciously "montañés" sound of the Rivas surname. Never mind. Myth rules historical fact with fine disdain, so that history without its myths would hardly be history at all. It is true that until the year 1000 or thereabouts, shipping in and out of Sacedón actually exceeded the sea-borne commerce of Bilbao. Casting their bowers behind a breakwater in the lagoon, 500-ton brigs loaded ore from two rich iron mines or timber from vast hilly forests of oak and chestnut.

The industry of Sacedón was varied. Whalers brought in blubber to be tried. There were shipwrights, cordwrights, coopers, and tanners. A foundry produced pike blades, battle-axes, swords, dirks, and later blunderbusses. Expert armorers fashioned chainmail tunics for knights (the Cid's battle gear is said to have been smithied in Sacedón) and chastity belts for their ladies. The township's eighty square miles comprise thousands of hectares in valleys almost as fruitful as those of Galicia and much more industriously cultivated. And well into the middle of the sixteenth century, Sacedón boasted a fleet of 200 fishing smacks, which sailed northwest to the edges of the Gulf Stream for an illimitable harvest of tuna. In its prosperity, Sacedón counted nearly 6,000 souls, about one third of them living on the hills and slopes, and about two thirds—the fishermen, artisans, miners, and merchants—living within the walls.

There came the catastrophe of 1512, when those walls were razed and the town put to the torch. Shortly afterward, the mines became uneconomical; and then, with the Spanish empire's insatiable demand for ships, the forests were cut and cut and cut, until even the most remote of surrounding mountains began showing their bones. The Gulf Stream added to these calamities by shifting its course slightly to the west, favoring the tuna fleets of Santander and beyond; and the modulations of the currents began to silt in the opening of Sacedón's ría, so that larger craft were unable to traverse its mouth.

All this took a heap of generations, coinciding with the decline of Basque power generally and the crushing of the political power of Sacedón in particular. Responsible were the first Duke, Juan Luis Sigismundo del Val's great-great-great-great-great-great-great-great-great-great-great-grandfather, Diego de Bustamante, and the first Manú Riva, Jacobo's great-great-great-great-great-great-great-great-great-great-great-grandfather, hidalgo, chief of the clan. It was he who urged insurrection while King Ferdinand was busy with his attack on Pamplona.

When Jacobo was growing up, there remained but a handful of Rivas kin in a population of 1,500 Sacedonese. The mines served as cisterns, and only a dozen smacks still skimmed into port, using a channel that had to be dredged every ten years or so. His father, ill-named after the first Manú, a withered claw of a man, clasped the handles of his wooden plow, sweated, begot children, picked his nose, stared at the castle on its loft across the valley, did not deign a surly hello to any Ybarra, drank himself into a torpor on Saturday nights, never washed, mounted his wife from the rear, whipped the off-ox of his team to death one day, and stared stuporously at a strange sight, a foreigner, a woman, a brazen creature in what looked like underwear walking below on the beach; stared and stared at her, and spat to one side, and lashed the remaining ox, snarling at his youngest son to pull harder on his end of the yoke.

FOUR

Children of the Soil

Not quite nineteen, but two years now accustomed, six feet one inch tall, with oaken bolls for shoulders and an oaken trunk for a body. He pulled. The ox beside him pulled. The yoke weighed with an iron ache on his humping neck muscles. Horacio, the eldest son, had died in 1931 of a ruptured appendix, thus escaping. He had been twenty-six. The next brother, José María, had been hired out eight years before to the coal mines of Mieres in Asturias, and now at twenty-seven lay with rotted lungs in a company sanatorium. Patxi, twenty-three, had saved himself by joining the Navy, but Amadeo, twenty, was a hopeless drunk, giggling idiotically while their father, in one of his frenzies, pummeled him with small, knotted, bone-hard fists. Jacobo had not known an hour when his gut did not gurgle with a craving for red meat.

The family's twenty-eight acres—a pleated and wrinkled apron of land laced to the knoll from which the farmhouse braved bad weather— yielded just enough fruit, wheat, vegetables, and milk to keep everyone hungry at all times. Jacobo accepted that as so much else; the stink of liquid cow manure and urine that rose from the first-story stable and pervaded the living quarters; the mud and manure caking his body; the fleas; the bedbugs crawling out of the cornhusk mattress he shared with Amadeo; the grunts issuing from the partition behind which his mother and father rutted; the flies footing stickily over the faces of his sisters and brothers from April through October; the long, joyless winter evenings shuttered against the rattle of rain and the flue-sucking whoosh of the wind, hammering at the door in gusts or weeping through the brittle twigs of the orchard below, both floors of the house steaming with the tense, rhythmic exhalations of human and animal bodies, and punky with the smoke of olive oil lamps; the mounds of daily wash, summer and winter, trousers soaked to the knees in compost, socks sodden little balls of sweat, underdrawers stained yellow with piss and brown with excrement, and the shocking scarlet menstrual rags of his sisters flung on top (bringing the dread certainty that soon following their first few flows they would be leased as dairymaids or waitresses, two of them, one Jacobo's favorite, departing at fourteen never to return); the quotidian labor in the fields; the constant female scrubbing and scrubbing of chestnut floorboards no matter how scrubbed impacted always at the threshold with mud, manure, and goose or chicken dung; and the fact that he had never on any single occasion bathed his body entire, although he would have liked to.

It was the woman, the foreigner, who helped open his eyes to these things.

FIVE

Blackberry Juice

Sunday afternoon, some weeks later.

He was harvesting blackberries in the corner of the northeast lot at the bottom of the farm.

He worked with Jimena, his dwarfed, hunchback, twenty-one-year-old sister, whose daft and cunning eyes had always chilled him. He stooped for berries; she reached for them. When he was little, she had forced into his mouth a giant slug.

It was clear and hot. Over the hedge, beyond and beneath them, spread the yellow-white expanse of Sacedón's major beach, three blinding miles of it book-ended between the lagoon's southwest palisade and a promontory about a quarter of a mile west of the Rivas farm.

Jimena hissed. He glanced at her. She looked like a tortoise on guard, head drawn back between hunched shoulders, mouth open and tongue stiffly suspended between the jaws. She gazed upward.

He raised himself from his stoop. Smiling at him, across the hedge, was the woman.

She must have seen Jimena and him from a distance and come ambling along the beach. He had not noticed. He had been intent on easing selected berries from their barbed holds.

In Basque strangled by an alien accent, she asked him whether she might have a few. Without a word, he passed the wooden bucket over the hedge.

She wore a jersey swimming suit that reached from midthigh to her throat. As she raised both arms to receive the bucket, tilting forward on tiptoes, the material tightened over the wedge-shaped mound between her legs, depressing and squandering the contours of her breasts but also (she was wet) accenting the nubs of her sea-hardened nipples.

He jerked his eyes away. When Jimena was thirteen and he eleven, she had tried to play with him, backing him into the shadows of a stall in the stable. He had been frightened. He had managed to escape. But although Jimena had once immobilized him long enough for her to strip to her shift and then begin stripping that off, he had never seen a woman so revealed as this. Staring at the toes of his rubber boots, he blushed.

She thanked him, returning the bucket and strolling away toward the ocean.

The following Sunday he saw her again—walking by the farmstead on the steeply graded and rubble-strewn ox path that runs between head-high hedges of mixed lilac, wild rose, blackberry, and the deceivingly soft-looking spines of "hierba mala" (a species of bracken), zigzagging along the rill above the beach and then down into the valley behind Sacedón.

It had rained in the morning, cleared at midday, and now again was overcast. She was dressed in a yellow oilcloth slicker with a yellow hood. He registered little more than her eyes and dark spit curls. She carried a camera.

From the rill and its several knolls, each supporting or protecting a farmhouse, there are panoramic views of the ocean west and north, the church's bell tower and a few outlying village houses east, a splendid view of (at that time) the pentagonal sixteenth-century castle dominating Sacedón higher up, and to the south, sweeping about to the west, valleys, slopes, foothills, and mountains.

He was clinging to the pole of one of the three honeycomb-shaped hay crofts by the house, in the act of hacking out a block.

She waved at him. He did not intend to wave back—one ignored foreigners—but his right arm twitched upward.

He was not to see her again until June the following summer.

SIX

The Breeding Thereof

That autumn and winter, the vision of her body troubled him. Her legs and neck were short. Her torso had thickened at the waist. She was, he guessed, not many years younger than his mother; but of a different species.

He awoke one night from a feverishly erotic dream with a cold and sticky dripping on his belly. As luck would have it, Jimena stripped his bed next morning for the wash. She giggled, gazing up at him out of her erratic eyes and extruding an obscene tongue.

She was a growth, a fungus; as if impaled upon her deformity, evil, feeble-minded, and cunning. She would never marry. She would never find a location. Their mother was ashamed of her. Their father wished her dead.

Religion in Jacobo ran bone-marrow deep. Until Sunday, he kept smelling the fumes of brimstone. He walked on a thin crust. It would cave in at any moment, and beneath it there were the caverns of Hell.

Sacedón's church is mercifully underadorned. It is large and rectangular, God's fortress, with stepped and rounded Romanesque arches and a nave measuring exactly twice the length of its width. The smell inside is of stone dust; cool and penetrating, piercing the upper nasal passages as though one inhaled microscopic darts of stone. Wonderfully hewn and smoothed pale beige fieldstone pillars rise to a vaulted ceiling built out of cantilevered blocks of the same whitish material and shored up by an arabesque of high-arching ribs. It is an airy church inside, filled with light.

Upsetting Jacobo, who would have preferred stygian baroque shadows. There is, you see, nothing discreet about confessionals in Spain. Basically, they are tall boxes with apertures on two flanks and a large bay in the center. Women approach the flanks, where the church's wall and perhaps a low panel offer some illusion of privacy. Men traditionally kneel at the exposed center. Often and with candid salaciousness crones press up close behind the penitent male in the hope of being able to tuck into their moldering cuds some especially juicy sin of the flesh, on which they ruminate hours afterward with lewd pleasure. Jimena pressed up close to Jacobo.

He glared at her; but with a rap of his fingers on the dutch door, the old priest called his attention.

Jacobo was compelled to bellow out his sin: the doddering confessor's right eardrum had been shattered during the Spanish-American War and he had wax problems with his left ear. Getting up, turning, Jacobo nearly wheeled into Jimena. She dealt him a queer, savage glance.

That night, with Amadeo in his usual state of bliss, insensible, lying on his back and gurgling bubbles from between beatifically spreading lips; and with parents and two other sisters competing in a bullfrog's chorus; Jimena crept to his side of the bed, took one of his lax, dangling hands, and while pressing it up between her thighs and hunkering her crotch down on it delved for and began manipulating his member.

Jacobo awoke, ejaculating almost at once. Then, really coming to, he sat up and slapped his sister across the face, both mortified and furious. Jimena let out a howl that roused even Amadeo, bringing father and mother hotfooting into the room. Throwing herself on the floor, moaning and blubbering and writhing like a snake hacked in halves by the blade of a scythe, she denounced Jacobo, crying that he had enticed her to his bed on a pretext and then attempted to violate her. She pointed to the evidence.

Jacobo was dragged naked out of bed and beaten by his father and mother both until his face and body were a mass of welts oozing blood everywhere. His mother used the handle of a broom. His father used his fists and then, when Jimena scrambled to get it for him, his strop. The other two sisters wailed. Amadeo laughed and sang ribald ditties until a kick from Manú sent him sprawling across the floor, where he chuckled himself back to sleep. Jacobo noticed Jimena's tongue rolling out as the blows landed. He noticed the boom rising and swaying under his father's nightshirt. When half unconscious, he was dragged—late as it was, pouring rain that it was, naked as he was and nearly naked as was his father —out into the night and down the choked path where the barbs of rose and blackberry vines lacerated his skin and the spines of hierba mala punctured him and the rubble beneath stubbed and bruised his stumbling feet; dragged, yanked, and kicked along by Manú until they entered town and reached the priest's house.

The old fellow had been sound asleep; wax had nearly sealed off the hearing in his left ear. He seemed somewhat scandalized by the sight and condition of Jacobo, inquiring whether he had fallen off a cliff. When

Manú Rivas—dripping water and scattering spit—launched into a foulworded explanation of what had happened, cuffing and cursing Jacobo between phrases, the priest winced and then seemed confused. "Why diablos would he choose Jimena?" he asked Manú; who, at that irrelevancy, threw his hands up and screamed an almost incomprehensible general attack on the clergy, Jesuits in particular, which the priest was not, and fat bishops next, when the priest was little more than bones and His Grace in Bilbao very little more than that. But the old fellow finally plumbed the circumstances bringing Manú and Jacobo to his place in the dead of night, and he was indeed distressed by them, lecturing Jacobo roundly and telling him to go home, pray, repent, dress his wounds with one part iodine and two parts baking soda, and report next day for spiritual counseling. After which he asked whether they would both care to spend the night, as it was still sheeting rain outside; but Manú snarled that no Rivas would be caught dead in a priest's quarters—a subconscious allusion, perhaps, to a Rivas maiden who not so many centuries before had been caught very much alive in bed with a young curate. Giving Jacobo a final cuff, he shoved him out the door.

Thereafter, Jacobo was sent below, to sleep in the stable. Twice more—the compulsion seemed to grow with the new moon, clear or clouded—his demon sister attacked him, creeping down the ladder when the household slept. Twice more she shouted when encountering Jacobo's revolted rejections of her; and twice more over his helpless protests Manú Rivas came thundering down to beat his unnatural son until not even a whimper issued from the lump of contusions. And the second time, either truly or in the nightmare of his swooning state, Jacobo saw his sister creep up behind their still bludgeoning father (the blows now came in surreal slow motion; he heard but did not feel their thuds) and sneak one of her hands up his nightshirt; and either truly or in the delirium of his quaking skull saw his father whirl in what seemed first to be shock and anger, and then saw his father knock the girl into a crib of hay, fling himself after her, and squirrel his loins between her gaping thighs; at which point Jacobo shut his eyes.

The foreign woman had already done much to influence the young man's character. He was irredeemably disgraced in the eyes of his mother and two other sisters; a degenerate. Even Amadeo, in his sober interludes, glanced at Jacobo askance, wonderingly, half incredulously. On the other hand, Jimena ceased pestering him, as though subdued, desisting in her habit of dropping pellets of sheep dung into his boots and no longer sewing nettles into the pad he was saddled with when being attached to the yoke. The change in his father was less apparent. His viciousness, if anything, increased, but his eyes—those two charcoal pits at the bottom of which the embers of an unnamed and undirected but consuming rage at life and destiny burned—no longer seared the manhood out of his son's eyes but tended to jerk away.

During the rest of that winter and into the spring, Jacobo began his escapes. Given a few hours free of chores, he ran. He ran down the rill and into the valley and up the slopes on the other side and as far up into the foothills beyond as time permitted, on Sundays and feast days sometimes reaching the mountains, where a belt of woods still existed, and once in a while, when starting before dawn, leaving the woods behind and running and scrabbling up the highest ridges, where he entered a world of granite cliffs and gorges, and where the sea way way way below and beyond stretched illimitably. There, heart thudding and chest heaving, he drank the clear or humid air, eyes imploring Heaven. On one glorious Sunday morn, as he rested on an alpine meadow of moss, lichen, and wildflowers, a stand of stunted young oaks beneath him, he saw a yearling roebuck step daintily out of cover and—catching sight of him, head jerking high—freeze: staring at him out of eyes from which a whole world of wilderness and fear shone. Jacobo held his breath. All was still. The ocean was a distant plaque of frozen sapphire, the valleys and their slopes dewspun green, and the sky above limpid with an aqueous blue, fleeced with the softest clouds. Then—from one of the several small walled medieval cloisters scattered among the lower highlands—he heard the chant of monks at their matins, and distinctly the *Pater Noster,* dulcet off the sounding board of nature, the syllables like droplets of a mountain brook, ". . . *Et dimítte nobis debita nostra, sicut et nos dimíttimus debitoribus nostris . . .*" And the roebuck lowered its gentle muzzle to the grass.

He did not know what these escapes meant, nor what he could hope from them. He knew nothing more than that they helped him feel clean and pure and less of an animal, filling his breast with an ache of longings he did not understand.

SEVEN

The First Flooding

He matured greatly that spring of 1933. His runs helped develop an already broad chest and suppled his tree-trunk legs. At not quite twenty, he was a man in all but mind.

There had been bountiful rains. The rye rose sweet and thick and tall. By the middle of June, the first harvest began.

Jacobo enjoyed scything, especially when alone. The muscles of his bared upper torso rippled like marbles rolling in a chamois pouch. He loved the swing of the blade, and the scent of the fresh sap, its juices green and sticky and mingling in his nostrils with his own salty sweat and intoxicating whiffs of lilac from bead-clusters of white and lavender blossoms along the hedge. He did not notice the foreign woman, who stopped to stare at him from the beach below. All along his body the rhythm flowed, rising from the waist and pulsing through long cords of sinew that swelled and then recessed under a skin youth-smooth and still winter-white except on his arms and neck and in an inverted peak below the throat, where it was bronzed. He kept moving with fluid and unflagging exultation in his strength, his blade cunning as it undercut the ranks of green, downing a swath all the way across the broad lower lap of the farm. There, turning for the reverse cut, straightening, he caught sight of her; and this time, when she waved, he smiled and waved back.

They met later that week. Some two kilometers down the beach a spring of fresh water trickles into a rude cement trough and then leaks seaward across the sand. The two dozen farmers who work the precipitous bank of shore above the sand drive their cattle to this spring, which has never been known to dry. Jacobo had eight cows and a pair of bull calves in charge.

He saw her come strolling out of the waves, intercepting him as he was passing where she had speared her parasol and laid out her towel. She spoke to him. His brain went almost blank. He looked anywhere except at her. He found nothing to say, grunting those surly peasant grunts born of fear, pride, and a sense of cosmic separateness, and that sound churlish without intending to be. But she chatted with ease: about the haze in the sky and did he think another storm portended and the ring about the moon and hadn't they had a wet June so far; learning from her during the monologue that she taught school and came from Biarritz, which meant nothing to him. He felt a clod. He tried to conceive of something better to utter than his grunts. There was no one else on that entire scimitar of sand . . . Jacobo made a supreme effort, asking her whether she enjoyed getting all wet. She invited him to try it: and he looked up from his bare toes (he had shucked his boots) just in time to catch the puzzle of a fading smile.

Two Sundays later, having located after considerable searching an undershirt with no bad rents, and chopping off at the knees a pair of cotton trousers that had belonged to the defunct Horatio, he accepted the challenge. He shook with fear. He nearly drowned in the first roller, or thought he was going to. She was a strong swimmer and a strong woman. Laughing, she hauled him out, pummeling his back as he choked up salt water; laughing, she drove him back into the froth and helped hold his head up; strictly, she insisted he forbid his toes to grope for the bottom; taskmasterishly, she made him practice and practice the breaststroke, watching his powerful but awkward arms thrash at the foam.

By the third Sunday, he was fledged. She clapped her hands, burbling a series of birdcalls in a language he supposed was French, having discovered that Biarritz was a town in that country. Within a fortnight, he had surpassed her, braving the most awesome breakers from storms on the main, swimming dangerously far out and close to the inky edge where currents seize swimmers and bear them off. She was frightened, then, calling to him, shouting, "Pa' si loins! Pa' si loins!" —which he did not understand and did not heed.

He possessed the power of a bull. The sea curdled in his wake. He surged meters forward with every double-armed stroke. Never had he felt so clean and free, not even when having climbed to aeries deep within the State preserves, where oxygen was a vapor as thin and heady as the alcohol in Amadeo's breath.

Then a current bore him off. He was all at once puny, helpless as the whole ocean pushed mammothly against him. Because he had turned, trying with desperate flailings of his arms to heave himself clear of the current. It was useless. He was being swept farther and farther out to sea, tumbled by swells that could have swallowed houses. He fought panic. He stopped exhausting himself. She had taught him to float. Praying, he rolled over on his back, letting himself be taken—perhaps beyond the far horizon and over the edge of the known world.

How cold the water was getting! Beaded crests of it kept purling over the back of his head. And then, without warning, swells out of nowhere converged, clapping together above him. He was driven under. He churned for eternities in darkness and terror; until, with a kick and a thrust of his arms he shot back to the surface, limp with weakness as he coughed up brine and bile.

But now hope buoyed him. It had turned flood tide. Sacedón's parched ría was gulping the ocean into its funnel, creating a current that crossed athwart the one in which he had been trapped. And it proved stronger. He was being sucked toward the mouth of the lagoon, between the northerly and southwest palisades, passing the ruins of the two fortifications on their points. He rode in a smooth millrace. His vision cleared. On both sides there were reefs, as jagged and dark as the tusks of an old boar. He was swept between them. He was safely within the jaws of the lagoon. And now, to his right, not far—in a niche carved out of the southwest palisade's rampart—a rim of white sand beckoned him. It was a summons, an imperative. He bid for a last reserve of strength, setting himself crosswise to the current, pushing himself shoreward in a series of frantic, froglike leaps. Within minutes, his feet dragged bottom. At the instant of contact, weariness such as he had never conceived (fear of this order he had not known) sapped that final energy. He plunged stumbling along. He fell on hands and knees, crawling up upon that arc of heated white sand and there spilling over on his face.

EIGHT

Two of the Blood

"Struck him," said Julio Caro, laughing. It was a soft, cosmetic laugh. "Can you imagine Nacho's surprise! Can you imagine his astonishment! The impudence! The falta de educación! I got there just too late. I swear, I'd have given half a million pesetas to see it! I mean," he added with self-deprecating discipline, "if I had them."

They had met at the portals of Número Catorce, where Julio, recovered from Marisa Magascal's kick, hailed Juan Luis. Police cordoned off the premises from mourners and gawkers alike. Even Dorada was respectfully turned back; and with her Baltazar. Julio paled at the sight of the financier, but Blás, immersed in private thoughts, turned away. Juan Luis was also distracted. He had come at Eugenio's urgent bidding. There was nothing to be done now. He had encountered Blás by chance; and was astonished by his intrepidity. It was foolish not to fear the man. Everyone feared him. How was it that he, Juan Luis, the least of the least, did not?

His stomach heaved at that moment. His tripe knotted. Of course he feared Blás! He had been play-acting, that was all. He did not possess the courage of his instinct, nor the minimal power of intent.

Juan Luis had not forgot their luncheon date? No, he had not forgot.

They had driven in their separate cars to the Royal Club of the Iron Gate, beyond University City, Julio racing ahead to make sure of their table. Juan Luis lagged by a few minutes. Parking his Lancia in the shade of the southeast garden, he clambered out; and hit—rather, very nearly stumbled upon—bottom.

At his feet was a sparrow chick that had fallen out of its nest. It gawked up at him; he gawked down at it. Blind rage seized him. Stupid, altricial creature! He was shaken by a desire to step on the allotrope, to grind it out of existence. And then, deliberately, he had stepped on it, shuddering as the fragile bones and soft meat were pulped beneath his thin sole, leaving little more than a sticky smear of blood and feathers on the gravel. It was otherwise doomed to a protracted death.

Stone, brick and tile, Puerta de Hierro's handsome clubhouse backs against Madrid's Cuesta de las Perdices. Julio had selected a table apart, on that new deck of flagged terrace facing the northeasterly bowl of the Pardo forest, which unrolls in a succession of swales and low sandy hills brushed green-black with bushy live-oaks, humping gradually to the Guadarrama mountains. Just visible in the distance are the arms of the gigantic cross that soars from the Valley of the Fallen: *novi et aeterni testamente; mysterium*—oh, Lord yes!—*fidei*. And farther to the west, the rocky foothills behind which broods El Escorial, dour, ascetic seat of an empire such as never will be known again.

Philip the Second, Sole Sovereign of Portugal and Spain, of Sicily, Naples, and the Low Countries; Duke of Milan and Liege of Franche-Comté; Sword of Christ; Supreme Lord and Emperor of all the non-Christian world, Asia, Africa, and the New, and with a Bull to prove it; celebrated his coronation in Valladolid with a Solemn High Mass (*Qui tollis peccáta mundi, miserére nobis*) and the roasting of a heretic's flesh, whose scent he inhaled from his royal alcove like incense. *"An electrician, and a manicurist from Murcia."* Juana had been mad. *"Robbery seems to be the motive."* Charles V was not so very sane. *"Heard the police picked up a salesman from a dress shop, and they found a fan on him worth thousands of pesetas . . ."* Among the flower beds in the garden, hummed and droned honeybees. On the grass and along the terrace, chittered flocks of ragged, beggaring English sparrows, darting with reptilian voracity for tossed hunks of bread, tearing at them in a squabble of feathers, while under the awning hummed and droned and chittered luncheoners in the process of digesting a stock club menu: gazpacho, eggs a la Cubana, filet mignon with watercress, and a choice of chocolate chip cake or vanilla ice cream.

Juan Luis had practiced abstention. He sat in unrelieved distress, squeezing sphincter against juices that kept gurgling through his lower intestines. He felt he had surely soiled his underdrawers, the seam of which, thanks to the leotard fit of his trousers, was jammed up between the cheeks of his buttocks, irritating what he now diagnosed positively as hemorrhoids. He imagined he could smell the leakage of that excremental acidity, and that it was seeping through his clothes and rising to overpower even the lemony Gal toilette water in the club's men's room, which he had lavished over his hands. Awful thought. Lifting a crust of the club's straw-stale bread to his mouth, he sniffed surreptitiously at his fingers. Good God, they smelled still! Every pore of his skin conducted from the bowels.

The foulness of human flesh! Oh, this rotting, rotten state of fleshly perdition! The taste of the grave was in his mouth—sweetish, cloying. Oh, it was not right: that man should be afflicted with senses able to anticipate his end.

". . . Número Catorce is being searched from pillar to post for missing treasures. One of the four Charles III cachepots is gone from the ballroom."

". . . They meant to empty the house!"

". . . Yes, Stepanópoulis Grau, a crack member of the Force."

". . . What's this about Pidal having been pushed? Did you hear? Well, what's it got to do with Odette?"

And then: "A conspiracy, that's what! The life of every one of us is in danger! Tomás has vanished. Oh, Odette warned me! And on the very eve! But it was she who . . ."

Neighed by a still highly agitated Marisa Magascal, who was seated at a long table under the arcade, at the garden entrance to the clubhouse.

Centollos and Dos Tripas—the one with plaster above a brow, the other with a puffed eye—had apparently insisted on her lunching with them; on the club's reassuring atmosphere after the shocking and emotionally exhausting events of the morning. Juan Luis would have liked to overhear more, but politeness to his host forbade. Julio Caro—somehow unrumpled; soigné in a suit the color of scraped lead, with a neatly dimpled black knit tie and a shirt as fluffy as snowflakes; and sweetly talcumed, as though he had shaved not ninety minutes ago, which might be the case—chatted on.

Who was Julio, his host, his friend? Everybody knew him—the unmemorable man who knew everybody, but whom death quite terminates, that ten-years-later vaguely familiar face (what's his name?) ubiquitous in the snapshots of (what *was* his name!) tattered scrapbooks, the perennial bachelor on those plains of youthful middle-age, of blood and no means and no practical talent, proper in his formal relations with the fair sex, bonhommie-lewd among males, the somewhat amphigonous voluptuary with secrets of nastiness in his solipsistic bosom, suave and sophisticated, with a practiced wit but little real sense of humor, cruel, gossipy, and endlessly amenable, not yet having developed the scratchiness of his species (not yet old enough) (desperate enough), but on the way, his optimism a little less impervious nowadays although still resilient enough to float him through most straits. He worked his mouth now between Charybdis and Scylla, too much hope and the alarm of doubt, waiting for Juan Luis, who strove to remember what he had promised to do but meanwhile let himself be entertained by Julio's fund of forgettable tales: only Julio's hands betraying him.

There was that tremor in them. It had begun three or four years ago; and once last winter, it was whispered, just as the birds in an important shoot came hurtling over the line, he had shook and shook and shook so that he was unable to lift his gun, letting them all pass. The straits were closing on him. He had lived beyond the time when he could be deemed a desirable if impecunious match. There were now younger candidates . . . This afternoon the tremor was unusually pronounced. Julio became conscious of it. His expression darkened. He tried to master it, pausing in his circumlocutions, concentrating on bringing the flame of his goldcased Dunlop under the tip of a fresh Aguila cigarette. With scarcely a waver, he succeeded.

Coincidentally, a waiter shuffled up to clear dessert plates (Juan Luis had not touched his ice cream). Julio smiled, sieving smoke out from between the cracks of his well-spaced teeth. Now with the meal at an end, it would not be ill-mannered to provide his guest an opening.

"You are," he said expansively, "—I hope you know it—what Billy Smith-Burton would call a 'brick'."

"I doubt Billy would say that. Maybe his brother would."

"Waffles?"

"Wiggles. Sir Egbert, now."

"Yes, of course!" Julio Caro retracted at once. "But you are one nevertheless. Blás was a horror over the telephone. You wouldn't have enjoyed it. A miserable three dozen suede coats! As for Pedro Puig, I've never heard a fellow so heated about anything so inconsequential. *Thanks be to God* for Nacho, prig that he is. A buffer, Juan Luis. His shirt is so impenetrably stuffed it keeps him from being terrified of Blás. It's an immunity. I envy it. My tripa quakes at the sound of the bastard's name."

Juan Luis excused himself.

He returned ten minutes later; realizing that he felt somewhat better. Perhaps it had helped, the mushy rice (without the fried eggs and bananas and tomato sauce) and the steady nibbling of under-baked bread. Or that shot of Fernet Branca—that malodorous brew fermented out of artichoke hearts, chalk soaked in iodine—pressed on him by Julio out of his vast experience with hangovers. Julio had his uses. Yes, they were all indispensable, every member of the class to the other.

Fortified by this incipience of well-being, he confessed.

"Julio, I have to tell you. I forgot all about it. I haven't telephoned Puig."

The man's smooth, motherhenned face—mudpacks at night, foundation in the morning—sagged suddenly with every last one of his thirty-eight years, so that he looked all at once like an overboiled cauliflower head: not so much drained white as soiled brown, and not so much wrinkled as mushed, his neat to the degree of protandric features evanescing in dough.

"You . . . forgot . . . to call Puig?"

"Something came up this morning. I'll do it right away, after coffee . . ."

He trailed off. Juan Luis's mind, that forsaken third of him, shook alive. Suede coats and Julio's sinecure be damned! Of course he would call Puig—but not about retaining CASA on his list of suppliers. About the 30,000,000 pesetas that had to be raised by nightfall.

Julio Caro was stammering: his suavity, his sophistication, his every layer of defense peeling off; and his mendicancy like a green sickness rushing to the surface.

"You . . . forgot!" He had charged the lunch to his delinquent account! "How—how could you *forget?* Blás may have *acted* already! Blás never changes his mind! If Pedro Puig . . ."

"Odette," Juan Luis interrupted, reminding him. "Blás won't have anything else on his mind."

He gazed at Julio, whose mouth closed and opened and closed on a world of empty air. Yes, he had given his word: so often had he given it, the charitable impulse prey to the erosion of his moral drift. Would two petitions, one so trivial, exhaust whatever debt Puig might still feel to the late Duke? Would he answer to the large, *Impossible!* and then soften the blow by magnanimity to the smaller? That would be in the order of things. He, Juan Luis, was in no position to dissipate whatever credit he had lying about.

Yet he felt sorry for his companion of numberless debaucheries: not affection, because, as he recognized, people who join in the morally demeaning are unable to love each other; but a sadness, a recognition that he might be tomorrow the Julio Caro of today, and sans the redeeming virtue of proficiency in the partridge fields.

He said, "I'll telephone now. Order manzanilla for me."

He rose again, steering with the anfractuousness of his psychic state between tables, well-filled and a tight fit. A fine, hot day, and one becoming memorable to Society, people loitered, the sober dark suits of lineage mixing with the more relaxed garb of foreign residents, among the latter of whom (hosting a table for sixteen) Juan Luis noticed that couthless American millionaire with frenetic social ambitions, that Hispanophile who probably went to bed with the rosette of his Isabela la Católica pinned to the boutonniere of his pyjamas (earned for having drilled a pathological number of dry holes from Cádiz to Irun), C. O. Jones. He managed to avoid hearing when he was hailed by the man (who half rose from his chair), but in doing so—in his hurry—hooked the protuberant center (or belly-) button of his jacket in the nest of a lady's chignon, which he nearly ripped off. He apologized. Rattled, he snapped a flame under the lipstick of another lady at the same table as she was bringing what he mistook for a cigarette up to her lips; backing off in confusion and into a tray of coffee and liqueurs, which spilled with a very loud crash that attracted more than casual attention, fortunately with no damage to himself but unfortunately soaking Centollos, Dos Tripas, the Countess of Estepona, and several other luncheoners whom

Juan Luis hoped never to meet again on this side of the veil. He fled into
the saloon.

There, he set about putting in his call.

"How could you have done it!" had cried Eugenio, out of the depths
of his distress. *"Why, why, Juan Luis!"*

And this was the rub: what had caused him to dread this day, fortuitously the anniversary of his father's murder, not one of those many
things he had put out of his mind because he did not care to remember,
but an act whose deliberateness was evident to him at the very moment
when, six months before, he had watched himself rolling out name and
title with a ballpoint pen, conscious of the breaths being held back in
the lungs of the men behind him, his heart leaden with a sad, unwelcome
contempt. What had made him do it?

He was not even within his legal rights in pledging the 250,000
shares of Financiera stock to support Jaime Orbaneja's note. "I told that
bucket of iced blood at Préstamos," wailed Eugenio, "as soon as I found
out what you'd done, that what he has is worthless—that under the terms
of the usufruct all three trustees, your mother and I, have to sign. He
shrugged, telling me that it seems the Duke of Sacedón is guilty of fraud.
What happens, Juan Luis, if Don Jaime doesn't make good? You tell
me that!"

"Well," Juan Luis had said, raising his eyebrows, "I suppose . . . I
guess we'll have to find the money ourselves."

"Precisely! Thirty million pesetas! By sundown! Where is it to come
from?"

Juan Luis had blinked. What a question for Eugenio to ask! The
money was to come from . . . The money was to come from . . . Well,
where it always came from, the bottomless well; the vast Sacedón
fortune.

And that's when Eugenio startled him. "You saw Utilidades's profit-
and-loss statement this morning. I hope you survive the shock when you
see Financiera's next week. We can scarcely meet the interest on our
bonds. Juan Luis, your family's dividends this quarter won't top two
million pesetas—and there's your mother and your sisters to think of!"

And he had asked, "Why? Why has it dropped so much, Eugenio?"

The question provoked that rare phenomenon: a coloring of Eugenio's cheeks.

The man said stolidly, "You heard the explanation I gave Codina
Moncó. There's truth in it. Not a few corporations have expanded too

fast during the boom. Now there's a credit crunch. But it's also true that I've fallen behind. Technology has leaped leagues ahead of my generation. Companies like Utilidades can no longer be managed by people like me, who know the general rules of the game of business in our country but who aren't specialists. Our time is done. It's happening all over Spain." He flushed a darker red. "I've been . . . deeply concerned about the possibility of the Government chartering a rival; and that's why, at Utilidades, I've permitted the laying of so many unprofitable lines; lines, in any event, that I don't know how to turn a profit from. I've thought . . . I've seriously considered tendering my resignation: but that would leave your family to the wolves. Besides, I . . ." He paused. He drew in breath. Perhaps it was this that fogged his thick lenses. "I hate to think of someone else sitting in these offices, strangers taking over what your father and I built . . ."

He became heated again. "Juan Luis, how in the *world* could you have been so irresponsible! If we don't scratch up the money, there's nothing for it but to honor your obligation. Why in the name of God didn't you put up the palaces, or that heap of rocks in Sacedón, or the bull ranch that produces nothing but animals with Christian resignation in their worthless hearts, or anything, *any*thing else?"

"I did suggest them," Juan Luis had said humbly. "They insisted on stock."

"But why did you give them so much!"

"I . . . I guess I never counted."

Eugenio groaned. "They must have seen you coming all the way from Cádiz! Two hundred and fifty thousand shares! Three per cent! A pivotal, all-important block! Had you mentioned it to me; had I known even a month or so ago; I'd have had time to maneuver in the event Don Jaime defaults."

Incredulity, and the vague, inchoate suspicion behind it, had returned to the administrator's expression, who had begun by asking, "Have you ever wished you were someone else?" One did not "forget" about such things as 30,000,000-peseta notes on whose redemption hunks of valuable property depended. It was increasingly difficult for the business mentality to swallow that even Juan Luis had been wholly blind to at least some of the implications of what he had done. If that were so, then why hadn't he revealed his actions earlier, as the time for the payment of the note approached? Out of cowardice? This was certainly in his nature as Eugenio knew it. But if Juan Luis was afraid of owning up, the inference to be drawn had to be that he had been aware of what he was doing and had gone ahead and done it deliberately; and just as deliberately had concealed the matter until its consequences were close to being irremediable.

What probably deterred Eugenio from accepting such a chain of reasoning was the absence of motive. Why on earth would the young man choose to imperil the basic structure of his financial position?

And it was then that Don Eugenio told him Baltazar Blás was behind Préstamos, and that this had all the earmarks of a Blás raid. Juan Luis had got up wordlessly at the news, weaving to the executive bathroom. Sitting on the throne, right hand clutching the lid of the seat, left hand thrust between flabby white thighs and tamping down and out of the way a limp, diminished male member, he felt in the very flatulence of his bowels how genuine the jolt was: concussive, entrails shuddering and blowing into the bowl jets of liquified gas. Armpits rank with sweat, socks all spongy with fear, he sat there, doubled by spasm after spasm. He was a long way yet from shucking the old man and putting on the new, whom he did not know very well and couldn't be sure about.

An exceedingly pale young man resumed his seat in the board room, saying, "Baltazar Blás owns Préstamos?"

Don Eugenio shook his head at this simplicity. "A front, Juan Luis. Your tenant, Muñoz González, is the owner—but working for Blás. That bucket of iced blood I talked to this morning, that German . . ."

"Pate balder than an egg!" Juan Luis exclaimed, suddenly excited. "Porcine lips. Belly the boll of a tree trunk!"

"Yes, Scheel, you know him?" asked a surprised Don Eugenio.

"No, no—it's just that this morning—I dealt with a Frenchman, a Monsieur . . ."

"Rougement, another Muñoz González associate."

Juan Luis now felt a bit dizzy. "But what has Muñoz González got against me, and why was Scheel coming down the stairs at six o'clock this morning with a smile on his face as fat as though he'd just swallowed Countess von Leddhin's carp; and why did Herminia fire Pilar or Paca or whatever her name is, why does she go changing them about so often it seems to me if I remember generally after I run into NKVD types or some Oriental with great big teeth simpering and sing-songing 'Ahnyong! Nalssiga chokoonio,' and a whole lot else no Christian can make sense of?!"

He stared wide-eyed at Don Eugenio, on the brink of illumination. God is a great tease. But the administrator aborted the moment, inquiring, "Are you feeling ill, Juan Luis?"

"No. Nooo. Oh, very!"

"Shall I call for . . . ?"

"Not Herminia, not now, not at this moment."

"I meant a doctor," said Eugenio, thoroughly alarmed.

"Someday he'll bellow so loud, all the world will tremble!"

"Quinine? Was it malaria you contracted in Mozambique?"

"Worse! Worse! In the belly of pachyderm or dik-dik. But do I *now* possess the courage!"

"The humors, I gather, persist."

"That downy nape! Even Julio was impressed!"

"I can only answer the first part of your question, Juan Luis."

"Do! Do!"

"There's nothing personal in Muñoz González's involvement, why should there be? but Blás has used him in mounting his attack on Financiera. He's after Utilidades, of course: you heard Codina Moncó preparing the other stockholders this morning. In a stock fight, he'll drown us in the enormous liquidity of Banco Blás. Your family—I—we'll all be thrown out into the street. Unless we're able to inflict a set-back on him at the outset; now: unless we can ourselves raise the money Orbaneja owes, and keep a critical block of stock out of Blás's hands . . ."

Shiny seams of perspiration crossed the administrator's forehead. His glasses had fogged again. He unhooked them, blinking blindly as he blew on the lenses and with a finger in the linen scoured their concavities. Juan Luis stubbed out his twenty-fourth cigarette of the day, waiting for what had to be.

Don Eugenio hooked his glasses back on. "Are you prepared to take on the most powerful financier this side of the Pyrenees, Juan Luis?"

There was a pause. The ancestral broadsword waxed between the Duke of Sacedón's hands. "Oh yes!"

"Think, Juan Luis! This isn't a game."

"It's better when I don't think."

Briskly: "I've prepared papers for you to sign: most of your real property, even the palace your mother is living in. Understand this: you'll be risking everything you own. It will take just about everything to raise the enormous amount of capital we need."

The broadsword had wilted out of his grasp: and then, contradictorily, calm possessed the Duke of Sacedón. There was a certain logical imperative about the situation, consistent with the course of his life since that golden autumnal afternoon when there had been a split second of choice between the applying of tension to his right index finger, triggering

a combustion, a chain reaction of events over which he had had thenceforth, by having abdicated, little say. There had been the brief, futile,
twelve-month interlude of piety in that pattern, unreal, after which he
had abandoned himself to whatever destiny provided, permissive and
submissive. Or thought he had; and thought he was. "Jaime wants me to
back a note for him," he had told Billy Smith-Burton six months gone by.
"Should I? Is it an opportunity? Jaime will let me down. But is this my
chance?" And with the query, and with the maddened dancing of Billy's
eyes, he had become aware of that other person: the one who watched
with glacial passivity as he hazarded 10, 20, and even 50,000 pesetas
on the turn of a card, drinking himself insensible and smoking his lungs
out; the one nearly always present when he soaked his self-respect, or what
remained of it, in the juices of sluts; the phantom who looked on with
neither amusement nor opprobrium, a philosopher, when he himself
played the Mercutio with his cronies, the innocent with his elders, and
the unseeing with his inferiors; the man in the shadows, in the wings
of his being, who despised the Duke of Sacedón and acquiesced in whatever might lead to his destruction.

Don Eugenio was probably in Baltazar Blás's pay.

"Bring me the papers," he said in a firm peremptory voice.

He signed. The fight would be lost, but he would fight it. Because
it would be lost. Because he would be ruined. But he would go along.
Yes, he would go to Número Catorce and plead with Jaime to pay up,
and failing that, not to permit Blás any of his Financiera stock, whatever
the pirate threatened. He would confront his cousin Ignacio, and ask
him whether he had really taken knowing part in steering Jaime to the
Muñoz González credit agency, and plead with him to intercede with
his father-in-law for the sake of his cousins. He would keep his appointment that afternoon at the Financiera offices with Don Eugenio, who
perhaps after all was not purchased, and his mother, who would spiral
like her hair-do into hysterics. He would then say to Billy sometime during the vigil, "I've found the courage. I've steered my destiny, anyhow set
it in motion. What about you?" And he would meanwhile act his part,
and make his pitch to Pedro Puig, and continue the pretense of his helpless hopelessness until the blind collapsed and the naked, slimy little
creature within was exposed to all the world.

Puig was lunching: but the kitchen servant, upon hearing that the
Duke of Sacedón was on the wire, scuttled at once to her master for

help; and he, the butler, advised that he would advise his master at once.

Who eventually puffed, "Yes! Juan Luis?!"

"Do you think we'll last much longer, Pedro?" he asked the man. "I mean, the Puerta de Hierro, the polo fields, the trophies, kept artificially alive by the Victory, for which you and Eugenio fought under my father, God knows why?"

"Juan Luis, I have guests: a ministry and two banks. Have you been drinking?"

"Gall and womanwood."

"What's that?"

"I neglected to let you know I am delighted."

"Oh. Well. That's splendid. Maruchi and I were wondering. Is that all?"

"There's the *quo.*"

"The qué?"

"The *quo.* Was ever twat without one? To be quits . . . I have a favor to ask."

Not from the rationale he had provided himself, but from that deeper compulsion of which he had become aware, he pled Julio Caro's case. Puig bristled at mention of Julio, and then muttered something in the nature of oh all right Hell!—and Juan Luis thanked him.

"There isn't of anything."

"Still I thank you."

"You'll be there."

"With balls on."

"What's that?"

"The first waltz, if you have no objections."

"Objections! Maruchi will . . . what else do you want?"

"I'm in trouble." He would put himself through the paces: that much he owed Eugenio.

"What kind?"

"Florita. Little flower. Can flowers stalk one? Is it a pistil one needs for defense? Stay, men. Polly-nate a cracker. Money."

"Juan Luis, speak sense!"

"It's complicated."

"With your fortune, it has to be."

"I signed a bouquet of demand nuts amounting to thirty million seamen on a carouse. They're due back on board at sundown. We haven't got the money. Control of Financiera Sacedón is at stake."

Juan Luis could hear Puig's gasp.

"How on earth . . . Thirty million, you say?"

"Yes."

"*Control* of the company?"

"Yes."

"Saints! Who holds the letras?"

"Eugenio thinks Baltazar Blás is behind them."

"*Blás!* Holy Mother! I've been trying to catch up to the bastard all morning!"

"Who hasn't been? Poor, poor Odette. Can you lend me the money?"

"Thirty million? I haven't that much cash, Juan Luis. My own problems, Sears Roebuck on the wings, no reserves for an American-style personal credit system, unless I *do* sell, or the Germans *do* come through . . . I don't know what to say."

" 'Sorry' won't help much. Shouldn't Blás be grateful to you, now that you're sticking by CASA?"

"Blás? Grateful? What's Confecciones to him—a toy for Prades to play with—when he has a chance of grabbing Financiera? And with Utilidades behind that! Oh, oh, what a plum! *That's* behind the stock's activity on the market! Yes! Yes! The scoundrel. The coony old bandit! Always a step ahead—*two* steps!"

He ceased speaking. Juan Luis was puzzled by Puig's words, by the man's attitude. "I'm thinking," he finally said. Then: "Eugenio, has he had a stroke or something?"

"Not yet."

"Well, how diablos did he let you get into this mess? I've been meaning to talk to you—when the time came, when things were ripe—but why diablos did Eugenio permit you to mess around with Financiera?"

"I was playing grown-up. Sometimes I take my father's arms off the wall—stick my hands into them, see how long a reach they have."

"His coat of arms?"

"No, his arms. I've nailed them to the wall, crossed under his sword."

"What morbid nonsense! You mean you walked into this on your own?"

"With my eyes wide open." He admitted as much now.

"Oh, God!" came petulantly from Pedro Puig. Juan Luis imagined him stamping a foot, because he could not abide stupidity. "Your father," he said, "he tried to . . ."

"Tie everything up against just this kind of thing."

"Do you blame him?"

"He was prescient."

"Well, tell Eugenio . . . Tell him to call me later this afternoon. Tell him I'll get rid of Labor, but I'll try to keep Banco Peninsular and the Mediterráneo about."

Hope flared in Juan Luis, irritating him. (Was he not different from Julio Caro?)

"You mean . . ."

"No such thing. Told you, I'm up to my neck myself. But: there's something I've had on the fire. Know C. O. Jones? Not important. Just don't count on anything, hear? *What* a plum!"

Julio awaited Juan Luis with every sign of frazzled nerves. His tinted hair was awry. A fine frosting of perspiration decorated his upper lip. The face was now no overboiled cauliflower, but the ash leaf with all its veins showing. It was a topographical map of bared wrinkles and pouches.

Juan Luis sat down with a sort of contemplative reluctance. Never had he seen Julio so exposed. Poor fellow, he could bear the suspense no longer.

"Tell me, please!"

"I remembered. Good thing, too. I hadn't answered Puig's invitation to his daughter's put-at-a-distance party."

"Wha . . . What did you tell Puig?!" came the strained, cracked question.

"That I'm honored to accept," Juan Luis replied, sipping at lukewarm tea that tasted as though it had been squeezed out of a dishrag. He had ordered manzanilla.

Julio closed his eyes, his upper body declining in a long pivot from the waist back against the chair. Slowly, he brightened. He laughed for no reason. The world was not so grim. At thirty-eight, he was not so old, not too old. There were things one could count upon. He was, when all was said and done, a grandee of Spain, an estate no one could deprive him of. He might yet capitalize on it: Lady Hume of the downy nape and half a million pounds had promised to run before the bulls at Pamplona with him, and who knows what might eventuate from that!

Himself again: face smooth, skin firm, smile supercilious and voice condescending. "That bastard Blás! He's been after me for years. I told you, didn't I, about the time I came as close as anyone except Nacho to slipping the old whistle into Dorada?"

And Juan Luis settled down to one more rendition of Julio's favorite fantasy: in all the lewd eximiousness of its anatomical details; this—a flair for the obscene—being his other socially redeeming virtue.

NINE

The Birth of Pride

"Est-ce qu'il est mort? Bon dieu, oh, bon dieu!"

He opened an eye, looking up out of its corner.

She was standing above him, elbows clapped to her sides, palms clapped to her mouth; scanty plucked brows stretched in apprehension and eyes dilated with shock.

He tried to smile at her, although his mouth was half buried in sand. He attempted a nod of reassurance and thanks at the two fishermen she had summoned to his aid.

She had run very fast to catch up to him. She had had to run inland, up the high grade of the bank behind the beach, onto the road, nonstop down into town; and through Sacedón; and down to the port; and then along the broken edge of the lagoon.

He swam joyfully through the blood-red darkness of his brain.

Either at once or much later, he came to. It was late afternoon. The sun, sinking behind the westerly promontory, slanted a few last glances of gold at the sand, pouring with last loving intensity a flood of light on the flank opposite, purifying details, floating volumes, detaching each soft pale green patch of fresh-mown rye from the yellower green of pasture and the darker and lusher green of rising corn. He stirred. Beyond stretched a static, metallic sea, corrugated in the middle distance, flat and fading farther out, and banked against the horizon by a purple veil. There, immeasurable miles to the northwest, the horizon fulminated with racing dark sulphuric legions rushing to a phantom battle; while above—blue, blue, blue and pacific—reigned the great bowl of the sky.

How much time had passed? He did not know. He had been dragged up on a dune; he was wrapped in a woman's coat. It smelled wonderfully; of mothballs, talcum powder, rouge, female sweat, and perfume. She crouched beside him, shivering in her suit, which was banded in horizontal rings of orange and brown.

She had not noticed he was awake. She sat back on her haunches, on her shins, legs from the knee down folded under: staring past him. He studied her as he had not dared before.

Did he like her looks? He could not be sure. They were different, alien; not pretty. She had a small, narrow, fragile skull, with dark hair cropped close to its contours and teased into a tangle of graying curls. Her countenance was narrow, rather too long, like a sheep's in its convex descent, terminating in a delicately boned lower jaw that was spoiled by nascent jowls. Her eyes were round, and palest blue, with the enlarged irises and straining expression of the shortsighted. Their whites—never clear since he had known her—were now crosshatched by raspberry veins, dulling to orange down by the lower lids, which were also enflamed: he guessed from salt water and the watch she had been keeping. Her nose dropped like a slat from the forehead. It might have been attractive but for having been broken at the bridge, swelling crookedly there. This unfortunate knottiness was pronounced by a mask of brown freckles crossing from just below the cheekbones and up and over the bridge.

Her straw beach bag rested beside her. She had, it seemed, painted her face while he slept.

It was strange.

From the outer corners of both eyes sprang rusty crayon darts, their purpose to him incomprehensible, since to his sharp young vision they accented instead of dissembling the tracks of age. Nor did he understand why she had smeared on her upper eyelids a sort of paste of silvery blue that condensed in fine wrinkles, thus emphasizing them. Was this supposed to be pretty? Her upper lashes, by nature long and thick, she had smudged also with something sticky, soot from which in tiny tarlike motes had fallen to lodge between her sparse lower lashes. He wanted to blow the specks away. To him, used to the scoured faces and hands of his mother and sisters, the only parts of their bodies normally visible, these failures in the Frenchwoman's make-up suggested something unclean, something lax, a failure in hygiene or person, he did not know which, feeling only with a pang of disappointment that of her, who was not plunged unavoidably into mud and dung, he expected the purity of the sun and the sea and the sky. Scrutinizing her, he saw that not the rouge on her cheeks, nor even the month or more of sunbathing she had enjoyed, concealed the sallow discontent of her skin, large-pored and secreting a greasiness beneath the folds of her nostrils.

He felt a tug. Instantly, he screened his eyes. One of her hands—as though detached from her person—fumbled at the lapels of the coat; baring his chest. He felt her touch on the naked flesh of his left shoulder, electrifying him. He tried to keep his skin from shivering or shuddering (he was not sure which) as her blunt, tear-edged fingernails and an icy following palm traveled to the waistband of his shorts, moving back up over his navel and sternum and resting by his throat.

He chanced a look. She stared off still into the distance, across the ría: into shadows that were now leaping up the palisade, so that its sheer lower two thirds of rock was blackened, the loamy upper third a reddening and in places bronzed green. Her hand began kneading the taut length of muscle between neck and shoulder. He was unable to suppress a spasm of pleasure, squeezing his eyes shut as she felt his response and let her gaze fall on him. Her hand hesitated. Then it went on kneading the flesh where it was exposed by the low loop of his undershirt, descending in a munching motion down to his left breast, which, when she massaged it, stiffened involuntarily. He felt blood flow hot into his loins; but he kept feigning sleep or unconsciousness; he permitted the deliciousness of the feeling to soak through him; he who even when a child, as far back as he could remember, had never been fondled.

He risked another glance. As before, she stared away: into the leaping, creeping, pillaging shadows, rising now to the mound of tumbled stones on the point, bells tolling the Angelus and cattle lowing lost notes and the sky behind them a band of lemon. She was smoking. Two fingers of her left hand patted her lips and pulled away from them. He recalled now that she smoked incessantly, even as she went wading into the ocean. Again her left hand rose to the mouth. Chiggered though the light was turning, he was able to discern the amber nicotine stains on the first and second joints of her fingers: bothering him, cooling him. Her lips clamped the cigarette. Her lips had been painted also, but they showed a pair of pale parallel outer edges, no more. Her lips kissed each other. Their moist gumminess—whatever softness they possessed—was introverted.

This time when she glanced down she caught him watching her.

She snatched her hand from his breast.

Then she smiled—a parting of her lips, a slight lifting of the upper one.

"What's your name?"

"Michelle—Michelle Muñoz," she murmured with a certain thickness, drawing again from her cigarette and in doing so opening her lips wide enough for him to see the dark ridges of nicotine that scalloped her pebbly teeth. "Et tu, comment tu t'appelles?"

He gathered her meaning. "Jacobo . . ." He asked then, "Muñoz, that's not . . ."

"Seulement Jacobo?" she interrupted. In Basque, "Jacobo what?"

"Rivas."

Her spine stiffened.

"Hein? Hein?" she chomped at him, jowls quivering, cigarette snapped away from her lips. "Rivas, did you say!"

"Yes."

"Bon dieu, then there are some of you left!"

"Oh, there are lots," he told her. "We're supposed to have cousins in San Sebastián and Bilbao and down through Santander."

"But they don't count, those others! It's the ones living here, in Sacedón. Your father, what's his name?"

"Manú."

"*Manú!*"

She sprang to her feet. He sat up.

"Are you—c'est possible!—of the direct line, the agintari?"

"My father says so. He says he's the head of the clan, better than the Duke. But then he . . ."

"Mais c'est merveilleux!" She slipped back into Basque. Her excitement was nasal, twanging, contagious. "Do you *know* who you are?"

"Oh yes, hidalgos!" And he began to tell her about a legendary forbear who was supposed to have owned such a lot of good land; but she seemed uninterested by—even scornful of—that.

"No, no, not landlords! Victims of oppression, revolutionary leaders, fighters against despotism! You Basques formed the very first Democratic People's Republic! With you the State first withered away! And you—you Rivases—you are the heart and soul of Sacedón, the crushed defenders of a once free working class! Did your father never tell you that?"

"Not exactly . . ."

"But you, a Rivas, don't you *know* about it?"

"What?"

"The insurrection and siege, the sack, the centuries of struggle!" She looked down at him with a sort of wonder, or perhaps it was anguish. "Why do you think I've buried myself here?" she cried suddenly, in a tone so bellicose that he started. "Why do you think I chose this topic and this town for my cover?" Flinging an arm at Sacedón, "*He* came from here!"

She gazed at him out of glittering orbs. He gazed back at her blankly. He did not know to whom she was referring nor what she was talking about, conscious only that in her eyes he had acquired a new if disturbing significance.

She said, advancing a step, looming above him, thrusting out a hand, "No defeat is final, Jacobo Rivas, son of Manú! All over the world, the proletariat is rising out of the ashes. Come!" And she yanked him out of the sand.

T E N

The Archives

Sacedón's central square is spacious, thanks to Diego de Bustamante, who accomplished wonders of urban renewal with pick and torch. Who his Haussmann was I did not learn; but this was an era when the balancing of volumes and serene architectural homogeneity seem to have been bred into Europeans to the degree that they were incapable of building anything—cowshed or palace—that was not beautiful, faithful to its context and yet possessing unique personality. The square of Sacedón is cozy, picaresque with its huddle of houses and shopfronts, sagging galleries, and stepped slate roofs, and with miradors bubbling from the occasional corner. Here, across from the church, is situated the Town Hall, known as the Ayuntamiento.

And a handsome, proud seat for the deliberation of municipal affairs it is. Hanging from gables in a row across the whitewashed upper façade are polychromed chestnut boards proclaiming famous sons, among whom number a bishop of La Paz and the equivalent of a rear admiral. The Rivas and Ybarra surnames are remarkably absent; nor does an escutcheon honor any one of the fourteen dukes. In fact, the tourist can still discern the patch in the center of the façade where the arms of the family were at one time or another hammered down. They were supposed to have been replaced by an elaborate rendition of the town's coat of arms, which can be seen propped against a wall in the cloakroom, but no one in the past hundred-and-some years has dared climb so high when sober, which is understandable, nor cared to when drunk, which is prudent.

As one faces the Ayuntamiento, to the right, there is a two-and-a-half-story stone abutment that suggests a fortification. Certainly it antedates the rest of the building. Its blocks are immense. It may have withstood the rams of Bustamante. There are no parapets, however, its top peacefully meeting the tile roof that stretches across the whole edifice. Attached to this abutment, and half a story below the whitened façade, there is the traditional balcony. From here Juan Luis's father officially "liberated" Sacedón in 1937, a bullet denting his right elbow as it was bent in a salute to the passing colors. He never flinched, admirable man; and afterward it was decided he had been breezed by a spent ball (although spent from whose ancient ungrooved muzzle no one has ever explained). He and his fellow officers (including Pedro Puig, commissioned during the assault) were supported then as the gallery has been supported for the past four centuries, by three magnificent arches masoned out of the same beige stone used for the church, forming an arcade under which officials gather to chat and smoke and be noticed before filing into the building for their councils.

The chief agintari when I visited must once have been a man of startling good looks. His frame was still large, although it was bowed and his chest had shrunken. My notes read: "He squints on the left as though trying to grind a gnat out of the socket. His right eye is faded and rheumy, he has lost or chooses not to wear his upper plate, little warts bead along the ridge of his nose to a large comedo on the tip, and what drifts of hair remain on his scalp do not inhibit dandruff from sifting down in an almost continual fall." Later, however, after a tolerable supper, I wrote: "Yet if one sits back from José Ybarra and reconstructs his appearance of say thirty years back, when he was fifty or so, one can envision brilliant periwinkle eyes under thick curling black brows, a straight, fine nose, humorous and wide lips, smooth rosy cheeks, and a battle-ready chin." I might have gone on to say that between sojourns in jail he held Sacedón in fief for more than half a century.

He gave lordly assent when I asked permission to browse through the library. I thought it best to confess that my interest stemmed from the Jacobo Rivas case; but it may be that José Ybarra was too old to react to the name (he died three months later), little more than nodding, as though there could be no surprises for him in life, and natural that a septuagenarian foreigner with a driblet working knowledge of Basque should interest himself in the scandal.

I spent fruitless and bewildering days searching into cabinet after cabinet of parchment volumes, most gnawed at and some tunneled right through. Latin, Basque, and Castilian were used, which complicated matters. But at the last I came upon a folder whose blue had faded and was streaked by yellow.

Clammy sheets of paper inside turned out to be charts drawn by Michelle Muñoz over thirty years before.

A methodical woman, she had spent the whole of her first stay (1933) reconnoitering. I was at least able to direct myself to the pertinent volumes, which had not been touched since. What the Frenchwoman related to Jacobo about Sacedón and his family is, I found, essentially correct: when stripped of dialectical claptrap. In microcosm—in paradigmatic fashion—it reflects Spain, the seething rancors that helped ferment the convulsion of 1936 and perhaps the one of tomorrow.

ELEVEN

The Sack of Sacedón

When King Ferdinand, in 1512, fell on Pamplona, the first man through the breach was a montañés Visigoth, a cruel, ignorant and foul-mouthed warrior whose face and body were crosshatched with cicatrices collected over thirty years campaigning in the vanguard of the Aragonese army.

Three of the toes of his left foot were webbed, as were his right index and middle fingers.

I take this description of Diego de Bustamante (1462–1522) from the second Diego (born 1629), who inherited religion from his father, José de Bustamante Delamadrid, VIIth Duke of the line and first of the family, it seems, to get any religion at all. The second Diego—rather a mincing creature, judging from his style—had it from José that while she lived, Queen Isabel refused to admit their progenitor into her presence. He was a commoner. He was a lout. When he wasn't guzzling, he was wenching, and if he farted like an honest Christian, he burped with the resonance of a Moor. His savagery in battle shocked even fellow captains; but Ferdinand, less delicate in his sensibilities,* valued the man's tactical cunning and dogged fighting abilities, promoting him to

* P. 77, *El Cerco de Sacedón*, por Su EXCMO. Sr. D. Diego de Bustamante-Rivas, Marqués del Peregrino, *passim*.

the general staff just as soon as the good queen his wife had breathed her last. When he heard that Sacedón had risen (and for the umptieth time since the supposed pacification of Vizcaya in 1370), he assigned 2,000 men-at-arms to this captain and told him to humble the town forever.

Chief agintari was Manú Riva, a firebrand, who hoped by leading Sacedón into rebellion to spark the same Basque patriotism in Bilbao and Vitoria. He was little concerned when scouts advised that Ferdinand's troops were plundering their way toward Sacedón. He laughed when he heard their number. It was an axiom of warfare that it required thrice the defending force to storm a well-fortified town. He had himself 2,000 warriors manning the breastworks. He had besides 1,000 sturdy miners in forts on the promontories guarding the mouth of Sacedón's ría. The Visigoth would lay siege; but Manú had plenty of water, and the fleet of 200 smacks guaranteed fresh victuals for the 5,000 men, women and children gathered behind the walls. Let them come! The attackers would camp, lob cannon balls, eat themselves out of provisions, and go home.

Bustamante, however, took quick stock of the situation. He detailed half his troops to isolate the supporting forts, despatching most of his siege machines for the purpose. With his other 1,000 men, he occupied a meseta high on the slope above Sacedón, well beyond cannon shot. This perplexed Manú Riva.† He was further perplexed when the Visigoth set his men to chopping down hundreds of acres of woodland, stacking the logs in front of the encampment. And his puzzlement grew as the Aragonese began digging a deep and wide trench about one hundred meters uphill of Sacedón and right down to the lagoon on either side. All right: so the town was cut off by land; but the besiegers were still beyond effective attacking distance. Two weeks went by; the ditch was completed; the prepared logs were thrown into it, and pitch was poured over them. What conceivable military end was the Visigoth accomplishing?

Matters became somewhat plainer shortly afterward. The Aragonese had meantime foraged for meat. Cattle that Manú Riva had been unable to fit into Sacedón were rounded up and corraled. Goats were added to them: stag, roebuck, and wild boar were hunted. Still, Riva estimated,

† *Ibid.* See also *La Traición de Sacedón: Un Discurso Sobre Los Métodos ANTI-CRISTIANOS e INHUMANOS de la TIRANIA CASTELLANA,* por Rodrigo González González, HIDALGO DE VIZCAYA, 1861 edition, for a radically different interpretation of Manú Riva's state of mind.

there wasn't enough to last the attackers three months; and they had no fleet to fish with, landlubbers that they were! Yet it was then that he began suffering the first qualms. He watched as dozens of animals were slaughtered; and were not eaten; but were dumped below the trench and downstream of the two springs providing Sacedón with water. There they bloated and putrified.

Well, so the Visigoth was trying to poison Sacedón into surrender. Riva countered at once. To debouch out of the town and try to remove the cadavers from the stream would invite severe losses. Instead, he set everyone to making cisterns, catching the mercifully frequent rains. Still, the town's fountain stank, and some of the people began to sicken. And then something else was noticed.

A horrible rustling sound was heard at night. First hundreds, and within a fortnight, thousands of rats were scurrying over the walls to feast on the rotted flesh below the trench, from which they scurried back before dawn. The Visigoth made sure that there was no lack of edibles. Ruthless, certainly a pagan, he dug up the fresher corpses from Sacedón's cemetery, located on the shank of the northerly palisade, adding these to the pile. He spared not even his own few fallen, flinging them over the ditch. The population of rats quadrupled.

Now Riva must have felt the first icicles of fear. At that time, no one knew what connection there was between rats and the plague, but everyone knew they came together. High fevers began to rage; within hours, people began to die. Terror gripped every man, woman, and child. Now the nights of Sacedón were reddened with a continuous blaze; the Visigoth had ignited the logs in his trench. Smoke was deemed a protection against the plague (in fact discouraging the rodents from jumping his ditch and infesting his own troops with their fleas). It worked. The people of Sacedón grew weaker and weaker. Riva, desperate, led a foray out to remove the cadavers; he was beaten back by a storm of bolts and arrows, leaving 75 fresh corpses. Ten days of drought struck. People were forced to the contaminated town fountain. Now the dead within Sacedón's walls were so plentiful that rats no longer bothered going out. The Visigoth watched the funereal pyres loft their sticky black smoke. Judging the moment ripe, he left a few contingents to guard and feed the fire in the trench, moving his main body in a two-pronged assault on the supporting fortresses. They had been subjected to a steady battering for 74 days. In a single afternoon, both fell. The bodies of some 800 miners, all put to the sword, were dumped into the mouth of the ría. Once friendly guns now raked the fishing smacks as they tacked frantically in and out with their precious provisions. Manú Riva had been outgeneraled.

He surrendered. No need to describe how Bustamante sweet-talked survivors into setting torch to their own dwellings against the plague; nor the rape and slaughter that began as soon as the rats had dispersed and the epidemic waned. Every male over ten years old was decapitated, including Manú. The Visigoth watched approvingly as his troops ganged barely nubile girls and even old women, jesting, "How pure will Basque blood run tomorrow!" He spent the following weeks dismantling Sacedón's fortifications. He took the wooden effigy of St. Horacio, the town's patron, micturated on it, and then burned it. By way of culminating sacrilege, he used the very stones of the cemetery's church for the fortress-castle he erected on the meseta above the town, dominating Sacedón evermore.

King Ferdinand, advised of Sacedón's subjugation, ordered a *Te Deum* sung and named Bustamante absolute lord of the town, its lands, and people in perpetuity.

TWELVE

The Bustamantes

Diego Bustamante was, of course, despised with an unutterable loathing. Scarcely 400 Sacedonese survived the carnage. The raped women, with their priest's tacit consent, aborted or drowned the fruits of Aragonese seed. With the priest's blessing, thirty-year-old widows married their twelve-year-old nephews (Riva y Riva was shortened to Rivas). The blood remained pure; the racial memory intact. Fourteen generations in all has the feud between duke and town lasted; and this same stretch of time the more personal duel between Rivases and ducal descendants.

Diego himself spent little time in his fief, dying of a dirk's thrust ten years later in a Sicilian brothel. He was survived six years by his heir, the first Santiago, known as "El Glotón," who while at the oaken board of the castle one merry night rose suddenly, clutched his belly, flung himself to the floor, and, shrieking, rolled hideously to his death, having swallowed fishing hooks embedded in chunks of stew. His son,

Efrain el Feroz, next day disemboweled a hundred Sacedonese in the new town square, mostly women because there weren't enough men about, personally plunging his hands into the stinking abdominal cavity of Iziar Riva, Manú's widow and suspected authoress of the murder, who spat into his face as her entrails slithered out. Efrain ruled until 1539, expiring peacefully while drunk; although, when it came to the washing of his body, revenge (it was discovered) had been taken of his private parts, which were found later nailed to the gibbet he had built. His successor, Hernán (1523–45), seems to have had little imagination. He hanged a Riva youth for the desecration of his sire's corpse, and afterward chopped the adolescent into minute pieces that were fed to the fishes; but for that more or less understandable retribution he did not even earn a nickname. He was killed when the new portcullis—designed by an ingenious young page called Orbaneja—slipped gears and staked him to the dust; by which time the male population of Sacedón had recovered somewhat.

Thirty-three years had elapsed since the sack, and seventeen since the mass executions; but life in Sacedón was no bed of roses for the second Santiago (1540–59), known as "El Blando" (the "soft" one), who slept frequently in nettles and once in powdered glass. A placating, well-meaning fellow, he contented himself with reproachful glances at the townfolk, earning their contempt. When he offered to wed a Rivas maiden, he was scorned for his pretensions: duke he might be, but hidalgo never! It is said he died of the hiccups following a burst of tears.

It is said he died of hiccups; it is known that his younger brother, Luis (1541–71), did not much respect Santiago and dabbled in alchemy besides. Called "El Sútil," he gained his brother's political end that same year by seducing a comely Rivas girl (with the help of four men-at-arms). She, fatidically named Dolores, was the sister of Iñaki, the first Manú's grandson (from a posthumous son) and Jacobo's great-*to the seventh power*-grandfather. When Dolores conceived, the Duke carried her off to Madrid and married her; the shame of this event stinging for generations, although by Jacobo's time particulars had been forgot. Luis was drowned at the Battle of Lepanto. His heir, Don José de Bustamante Delamadrid (1560–1640), VIIth Duke, grew up puny of frame and heavy of conscience; and upon his accession (he was just eleven) crawled on hands and knees from Sacedón to the great shrine of Santiago de Compostela, where he pled indulgence for the sins of his forefathers. Impressed by this noble deed of penitence, the very devout Philip II conferred on him the Marquisate of the Pilgrim, an ancient Carolingian title he had received as a wedding gift from Charles V, his father, along with Holland.

Now: José became the first *Spanish* Marquis of the Pilgrim. Excluding a few generations when the title fell into disuse, Odette Prades was seventeenth in *Spanish* succession. She was actually the XLVIIth Marchioness of the Pilgrim, which gives some idea of the title's unparalleled antiquity. Besides, rare privileges were attached to it. Grandeeism confers on the bearer two exquisite rights: a male great may keep covered in the presence of the King; a female has a right to a cushion. But the Marquises and Marchionesses of the Pilgrim bear the exclusive office of the umbilicus and tripe. That is, at the birth of a prince, theirs is the pleasure to tie and cut off the umbilicus; and upon a sovereign's death, to receive the still steaming tripe in a golden vessel. Furthermore, since the titles and its rights are of Carolingian origin, the bearer may exercise these privileges upon the birth and death of any European prince. It is no wonder that True Spain drools over such a gem.

Sad to say, "El Beato"—as this Bustamante had been dubbed (he was first known by "El Pio," but this was dropped when irreverent Sacedonese promptly tacked on "Piojo," to coin "The Pious Louse")—was not otherwise favored by Providence. Two noble dames died on him without issue. The third wife, untitled but respectably born Meye de Riva-Herrera y Riva-Aguero, brought forth the clubfooted, harelipped, and flipper-armed deaf-mute second Luis de Bustamante (1628–1700), following which disaster she produced the holier-than-Papá second Diego (1629–1700), author of *The Siege of Sacedón,* who when offered the dukedom by his father shrank from it as though from Satan's kiss, opting to become the tenth Marquis of the Pilgrim and no more. Succession now fell on Beatitud, dwarfed and hunched of back though the poor damsel was. A dreadful thing happened to her. One afternoon when on an ill-advised jaunt through the woods, unattended, a drunken peasant snatched the reins of her palfrey, tipped her out of the saddle, and tupped her. The perpetrator was Jacobo's great-*to the sixth power*-grandfather, who thus avenged the rape of his aunt by Luis the Subtle. This occurred just days before Beatitud was confirmed in her Duchy by Madrid. Diego, her foolish and pious brother, learned of the incident. Shocked, he arranged a hasty wedding, having the groom hanged on the spot afterward. Beatitud's virtue had been salvaged. Alas, she had meanwhile conceived. This was unthinkable. Diego had his sister impounded in a convent, forcing her to relinquish the Duchy when a male child was born. It was upon this event that Diego hastened off with the Marquisate of the Pilgrim, removing to France. Beatitud took Orders, and Begonia, a younger sister (1639–1709), assumed the Duchy.

A rare beauty, one would have expected Diego to prefer Begonia over Beatitud in the first place. But Begonia was a feisty woman who, beginning at age fourteen, held a private sort of court in the castle. Through her hospitable gates were admitted practically every able-bodied seaman and cultivator in the township. She was not yet sixteen when she conceived a child conceded by her to have been fathered by any one of ten different men, all of them Rivases. Promptly was she married off to an indigent courtier, Pedro de Heredia Banantes Bazán, who, unhappy man, when the Duchess was able to spare him a moment, managed to get on her nothing but female infants, all of whom died of hiccups. It was the legitimized natural son, Pedro de Rivas y Bustamante-Heredia (1655–1720), known as The Bastard, who inherited.

Now not only on the distaff vine but paternally were the Dukes of Sacedón to be dukes of Sacedón. Their gobs of Rivas blood in no way mitigated ill-feeling; but under the venerable hidalgo tradition, the head of the ducal family was none other than Horacio, Iñaki's grandson out of Beatitud. And this, as I shall explain, was sweet revenge indeed.

THIRTEEN

The Order of

Hidalgo is a word whose philological origins are debated. Some say it means "hijo de algo," son of something, son of someone of account. Others say it means "hijo del Godo," son of the Goth, Spain's first nobles. And still others say it means "hijo de algos"; that is, son of a warrior whose feats in the reconquest of Spain earned him part of the booty, so that he was able to bequeath something—"algos"—to his descendants. It is a juridical state, denoting a free man of consequence, a squire. It is older than Spain, anteceding an imported nobility.

The story goes that when the first Bourbon King, Philip V, arrived in Madrid (1713), he proposed expanding the order by 5,000 new appointments. To which the Duque de Río Seco, Admiral of Castille (one wonders what waters he navigated) replied, "Sire, create all the dukes, marquises, and counts that you wish, but only God and time can make an hidalgo." One could not claim a place in the order unless one's grandfather had been an hidalgo, which meant that the Dukes of Sacedón, by this time splendiferously counts and marquises as well, did not gain this estate until the ninth of the line (Pedro the Bastard), whose grandfather was a Rivas. Most hidalgos tended to spring from the northern provinces, of course, the montañeses of Old Castille vaunting a great majority of them. But even in Basque Vizcaya was the order widely distributed; and until 1836, no one not a Basque was allowed to settle in the province unless he could prove his hidalgoship.

Rivases had resisted ducal stratagems to rise so high; but once done, there was secret satisfaction in the event. They remained patriots, sneering at the low origins of the grand folk in the castle. In their souls, they conceived sneaking pride in being related to what was evolving into a great noble line, close to the throne, and wealthy beyond (Sacedonese) measure. They were, besides, at muted loggerheads with their neighbors.

This erupted in 1718. The Bastard, a cunning fellow—worthy grandson of Luis el Sútil—had indeed mounted high in court circles; chiefly, it was bruited, by mounting high in the bedchamber of Elizabeth Farnese, well before she married the future Philip V. It was Pedro de Rivas y Bustamante-Heredia who along with Cardinal Alberoni urged the 1718 campaign to recapture Italy. In those days, a noble put his serfs where his mouth was. But all Bustamantes had had trouble with their unenthusiastic Sacedonese troops. Pedro therefore rode the 300-odd miles from Madrid to Sacedón; and from the balcony of the Ayuntamiento proclaimed a return to the town of its ancient democratic "fueros." All civil rights were restored, and Sacedón would once again govern itself.

He expected, as did the Rivases, Rivas rule. But the townfolk promptly elected a slate of Ybarras to the council: thus openly assigning blame for the catastrophe of over two centuries before, as well as letting The Bastard know what they thought of his wiles. Pedro's rage was great; he could not now renege. Horacio's rage can be imagined: against Sacedón for this humiliating rebuff, but even more against the Duke for his blunder. Pedro was to meet his death in the Italian venture; but Rivases henceforth took special pleasure in lording it over their lords.

It was the hidalgo institution that permitted them to do so. In its flower, heads of families called annual gatherings at which all subordinate relations pledged obeisance. This became a matter of acute embarrassment to haughty folk. The younger brother of the eldest son of the head of a certain clan migrated to Madrid, where he rose in the court hierarchy and where through ability, luck, or other means, he was granted a title with all its considerable material benefits. But when his thoroughly sophisticated sons happened to sojourn in their natal town, they were forced to show deference to their uncle, who might be a peasant hip-deep in manure. As time went by, the differences became more anomalous; and clan calls were when possible ignored. Nevertheless, Manuel de Mendieta, Pedro's son and tenth Duke, was subjected to this indignity, chief of Rivases at that time being Josetxu, first-born of Horacio and Jacobo's great-*to the fourth power*-grandfather. Following this one experience, Manuel point-blank refused to so humiliate himself again; and lived ever after dodging Josetxu during the summers, when he occupied the old castle. His son, the long-lived Diego de Mendieta, gave up Sacedón for vacations altogether.

FOURTEEN

The Decline

Spain *is* the empire. Nation and imperial might were born together. When, in 1825, the last of the Spanish armies was hurled out of South America, that empire was lost. The pressures of decaying power came to boil, discontent rife in a nation with only a few islands of its glory left. With the elimination of supranational purpose, so went national cohesion, inaugurating 150 ferocious years during which a people who were no longer able to sublimate their grievances in conquest, rule, and proselytizing the true Faith tore at their bowels. Josetxu Rivas's grandson, Sebastian, a tall and burly farmer in his thirties, determined to bring old Diego de Mendieta to heel.

He threatened descent on Madrid if the Duke did not respond to clan calls.

Nobles lived in fear and trembling of just such an event. An escutcheoned doorknocker would be pounded against its brass or iron plate. In entered a grinning country bumpkin before which the great

Marquis of This or That, Lord of the Royal Chamberpot, was forced
to drop on one silk-knickered knee, while servants giggled from behind
arrases. The institution was becoming a scandal.

The census showed 500,000 hidalgos listed in civil registers, full
9 per cent of the population. The fruit seller, the blacksmith, the butcher,
the barber, the lowly fisherman, the lowlier shepherd, and even locally
renowned poachers and other outlaws stared their betters straight in the
eye, and not only did not cede carriage space on the road, but actually
appropriated the center of it for their carts and ponies, plodding along
and forcing noble coaches into the ditch. Things got to such a state that
aristocrats everywhere rebelled. They breathed relief when, in 1836, Isabel II's regent mother, Cristina, abolished the order.

This happened by decree. And it was a major engine in the Carlist
uprising, for which the dispute over Salic law was an excuse. By the
stroke of a foreign queen-mother's pen, 500,000 Spaniards had been
stripped of a birthright.

Easy enough was it to decree that hidalgos no longer existed; something else again to convince them. Certainly Sebastian never accepted
it; nor did Santi, his eldest son; nor did Txomin, Santi's elder son; nor
did Patxi, Txomin's only son; nor did the second Manú, Patxi's heir
and Jacobo's father. To the Sacedonese, this was worse than the sack
of their city.

Sebastian took advantage of the general indignation to unseat the
Ybarra hegemony. He called for revolt. The Ybarras counseled prudence.
Sebastian, in an emotional address from the Ayuntamiento's balcony, reminded townfolk that the Navarran Carlists were fellow Basques.
"Zaspiak Bat!" he cried, "The Seven are One!" The Ybarra agintari then
rose as a man to remind their constituents what had happened the last
time a Rivas exhorted Sacedón to arms; but prudence was drowned out
in clamor. By resounding voice vote, townsmen hailed Sebastian Rivas
as their new prima inter pares; and it was he who led his fellow hidalgos
into Navarre; and almost at once into a cleverly plotted Isabelista ambuscade from which only an Ybarra escaped.

This proved the end of Rivas pretensions. None was to reach so
high again; and in the nature of things, families that do not rise decline;
and with very little help on their part, that decline becomes irreversible.
Rivases began vanishing from Sacedón. They sailed out into gales and
were swallowed up. They shipped to America as shepherds and were
swallowed up. They sought employment in the mines of Bilbao or the

kitchens of France and were swallowed up. Their lands were auctioned for taxes, to be purchased by Ybarras and Peredas and Petuntos. Michelle Muñoz had to relate to Jacobo his heritage. Not since Txomin had anyone in his family learned to read.

Book Three

CIVIL WAR

ONE

The Ancestry of Juan Luis

"Anyone who can *read!*" she declared. "Anyone with any memory *and respect for* such things at
                              all! It's as
                                        plain as the *nose* on your *face!*"
Juan Luis was aware that his nose lacked attraction, with its meaty moraines and the blunt shoat's stop of the nostrils. Still he thought it unnecessary for his mother to call attention to it.

He had been summoned just as Julio Caro (if one could believe the man) was on the verge of separating Dorada Blás's golden thighs: to Financiera's quarters in a run-down building on the lower slope of the Gran Vía, shared by a tailor, an exporter, two lawyers, a dentist, a chiropractor, a reader of palms, a bullfight ticket agency, and a ghoulish little firm vending tubes for hemorrhoids and belts for hernias.

A far cry from the Greek temple headquarters of Utilidades, but often so in Spain, the nerve centers of immense holding companies secreted within shabby milieus. Financiera occupies an L-shaped half of the fourth floor, the stem divided by pasteboard partitions into cubicles with access to a common corridor, the whole as dowdy and derelict as can be, pipes bulging in bundles from the main wall and cracks in the plaster suggesting abstract expressionist work by, say, Tapies. Don Eugenio's private compound in the rear contained a wooden desk, a slatted swivel chair, two telephones, a safe, a filing cabinet from whose jutting middle drawer a set of keys dangled, a fan, a Jacobean wainscot chair, a leather sofa and an elaborate gilt bronze-and-crystal chandelier from Valencia with two of five low-watt bulbs burned out and all its beads and bangles black with flyspecks.

The ducal bowels were finally quiescent. Juan Luis felt, nevertheless, unwell: leaden, ugly, the weight of his excessive bottom, the sag of his developing pot, all the slack and drag of indulgence beneath the self-deprecating hug of his shoulders depressing him. He sensed, with the anticipatory prickling of a rash, age and dissolution creeping upon his body, creeping like scurvy into his scalp, so that when he harrowed the browline with a furtive middle and index finger of the right hand he touched bare skin where he could have sworn only that morning there had been nap.

He braved his mother's eyes. Her vine of the Montijos and the Del Vals of Sacedón were not—Heaven knows—a handsome tribe. Her scant faded yellow hair was as usual spun into that high mound that undermined by overweighting her fretful little features, the mask of white powder (did she use the same base as Julio Caro?) ineffective against the bilious flushings of her skin. Stout she was, and gross of form and flesh, stuffed like morcilla into the eternal reprimand of her black weeds. She wore them neither for Odette nor in deference to the first anniversary of her husband's passing, but because she had relented not one moment all the long thirteen years following Fedi's death, since when the world had owed her its apologies. Her wounded and (perhaps more than that) *affronted* eyes now rejected this her second son: to challenge the skepticism she expected to find in Eugenio's gaze.

He was indeed peering dubiously from behind the whorl of his thick lenses, more gray-skinned than ever, his dewlap hanging bloodless, even his normally rubious lips drained by the crisis. The banks had not responded. "How could I risk revealing the true gravity of the situation? It would be ruinous—for you and for Financiera." Eugenio had been able to rout up no more than ten millions against Juan Luis's palaces and estates, forced to usurers who charged as much for their discretion as for their cash.

"I don't . . ." the administrator began.

"*Because,*" she interrupted him, "you are too sensible to *aspire!*"

The widow-Duchess had pre-empted the sofa, which, as also happens in Spain, was designed substantially deeper than the reach of the race from knee to buttock, so that she had the choice of sitting back and permitting her lower legs to sprout stiffly from the rim or squatting nearer the edge with her spine unsupported. The Duchess had elected the latter, jeweled hands crossed above the mass of her thighs, torso ramrod, knees pressed together and straight out, calves like a pair of cheeses curd-white inside the braid of her black nylons, phlogotic feet planted on the floor: an admirable pugnaciousness in her posture. She had met Eugenio's recital of catastrophe with only one clutch at where her bosom had in the past resided before descending to the comfortable support of her abdomen, calling for a glass of water but refusing salts. She had been told the worst before Juan Luis's arrival, dealing him no more than a single withering glance that summed up everything she had ever felt for or expected of him. He was surprised, having prepared for hysterics; but then he had noticed how sobering money matters can be.

"All," she stated now, "is *not* lost!"

Eugenio revolved his pale hands in a discouraged way, murmuring, "My sincerest wish would be to offer you some hope, but . . . !"

"Hope? Nonsense! *Certainty!*" She gave a snap of the pouch that hung from the corners of her mouth, in the lower center of which the articulation of her chin could be discerned. "If we cannot raise the sum, Eugenio, then certainly Juan Luis will have to move against Ignacio. Herminia will soon be at Número Catorce, to talk with Nati. I tell you, the mere *threat* of such an action will bring Blás about as *nothing else* will."

"Mamá!" Juan Luis protested. He should tell them about Pedro Puig. But would he?

She ignored him. "Eugenio, you do understand what I am talking about?"

"I am not certain, Señora Duquesa."

"Well, listen then!" She cocked her head, closing her eyes, lapsing into what seemed to be a spell. Then, in a strong, crooning, melodious voice she began chanting what sounded like an incantation:

Juan Luis
          son of Luis
                    son of Carmen
                              daughter of Diego
Son of Manuel
          son of Pedro
                    son of Begonia
                              daughter of José
José
     José de Bustamante
                    Duque de Sacedón
                              Conde de Patagonia
Hidalgo de Vizcaya
                    and
                    MARQUES DEL PEREGRINO!

On these final words, her eyelids sprang apart; and she gazed at her son and Don Eugenio from under lifted, coppery brows.

In turn, the administrator peered uncertainly at her, while Juan Luis writhed in his seat.

"Juan Luis!"

"Oh no, Mamá. Not now. You're confusing me with someone else."

"Kindly," she stated in a grand manner, flashing emeralds as she tipped over a hand, "provide me with pen and paper."

Bending to the desk with a grunt, the widow-Duchess began tracing a diagram whose genealogical clarity astounded the men watching.

DIEGO DE BUSTAMANTE, I DUQUE DE SACEDON
    c. con
LEONOR DEL VAL

Santiago de Bustamante del Val
("El Glotón")
II DUQUE DE SACEDON
    c. con
Cecilia Franco de la Fé

Dolores de Bustamante del Val

Efrain de Bustamante del Val,
("El Feroz")
III DUQUE DE SACEDON
    c. con
Paloma Sainz de Iturbi, II Condesa de Patagonia

Hernán Bustamante del Val y Sainz de Iturbi, IV DUQUE DE SACEDON
III Conde de Patagonia
    c. con
Humilidad "La Manca"

Santiago de Bustamante
("El Blando")
V DUQUE DE SACEDON

Luis de Bustamante
("El Sútil")
IV Conde de Patagonia,
VI DUQUE DE SACEDON
    c. con
DOLORES RIVA (hidalga)

José de Bustamante,
VII DUQUE DE SACEDON
("El Beato")
V Conde de Patagonia, Hidalgo de Vizcaya
IX MARQUES DEL PEREGRINO

"So that's where it comes in," breathed Juan Luis, who was leaning over his mother's right shoulder.

"Of course!"

"Where does it go?"

"You'll see, don't interrupt me!" And she hurried on.

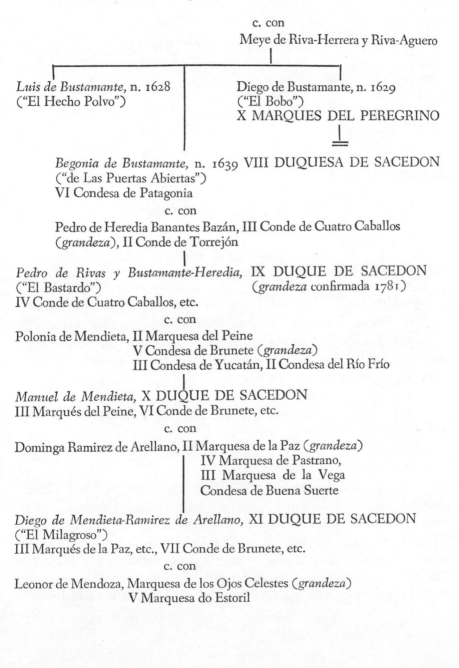

c. con
Meye de Riva-Herrera y Riva-Aguero

Luis de Bustamante, n. 1628
("El Hecho Polvo")

Diego de Bustamante, n. 1629
("El Bobo")
X MARQUES DEL PEREGRINO

Begonia de Bustamante, n. 1639 VIII DUQUESA DE SACEDON
("de Las Puertas Abiertas")
VI Condesa de Patagonia

c. con

Pedro de Heredia Banantes Bazán, III Conde de Cuatro Caballos
(grandeza), II Conde de Torrejón

Pedro de Rivas y Bustamante-Heredia, IX DUQUE DE SACEDON
("El Bastardo")   (grandeza confirmada 1781)
IV Conde de Cuatro Caballos, etc.

c. con

Polonia de Mendieta, II Marquesa del Peine
                V Condesa de Brunete (grandeza)
                III Condesa de Yucatán, II Condesa del Río Frío

Manuel de Mendieta, X DUQUE DE SACEDON
III Marqués del Peine, VI Conde de Brunete, etc.

c. con

Dominga Ramirez de Arellano, II Marquesa de la Paz (grandeza)
                        IV Marquesa de Pastrano,
                        III Marquesa de la Vega
                        Condesa de Buena Suerte

Diego de Mendieta-Ramirez de Arellano, XI DUQUE DE SACEDON
("El Milagroso")
III Marqués de la Paz, etc., VII Conde de Brunete, etc.

c. con

Leonor de Mendoza, Marquesa de los Ojos Celestes (grandeza)
                V Marquesa do Estoril

VI Condesa de Teruel (*grandeza*)
IV Condesa de la Garrapata, II Condesa de Guadarrama
|
Carmen de Mendieta-Mendoza, XII DUQUESA DE SACEDON
IV Marquesa de la Paz, etc., VIII Condesa de Brunete, etc.

c. con

Luis del Val Peir, Barón de Bataan
|
Luis del Val Peir Mendieta-Mendoza, XIII DUQUE DE SACEDON
V Marqués de la Paz, etc., IX Conde de Brunete, etc.
Marqués de la Revancha de Jerez

c. con

Mercedes Inmaculada de Montijo, X Condesa de Pilar, II Condesa de Irún,
II Condesa de las Arenas de Ibiza

Federico del Val, 1931–1955   *Mercedes Inmaculada del Val*,
V Marqués de la Paz   n. 1932, III Condesa de las
                                        Arenas de Ibiza

Carmen del Val, n. 1926
III Condesa de Irún

Here Mercedes Inmaculada de Montijo checked herself, curling back the sleeve of a black kid glove (never would she doff her gloves in an establishment of business), glancing at a diamond-cased wristwatch, and then peering sharply up into the bemused face of her son.

"We have arrived at you!" she declared.

"Yes, I can see that."

"Would *you* care to continue?" she then asked ominously, handing him the pen.

"The chart?"

"What else!"

"Oh." Juan Luis blanched. "Well," he said, drawing a little closer. "Let me see," he said raising hand and pen, thinking for some absurd reason about the grime he had once discovered in the niches behind Florita's ears. "I'm the fourteenth Duke," he offered brightly, smiling at her. "And then," he said next, wondering why well-born Spanish ladies like his mother did not have excised the moles on their faces (his mother's was of pinkish hue, growing out from under the fold of her left nostril), which tended to spread with age and sprout pig's bristles, "and then I'm the . . . the *eighth* Marquis of Pastrano, yes . . ."

"That does *not* come first!"

"Why not?" He was offended.

"The grandeza! Simpleton that you are, grandeur within its order of rank *always* comes first!"

"So it does. Yes, so it should! Let's see, of course! Marquis of the Peace!"

"Which!"

"I haven't the foggiest, there were so many, they never lasted very long . . ."

"Which *Marqués!* Which number! Oh, you are *not* believable. Here, give me the pen!"

She snatched the ballpoint out of his hovering right hand, completing the tree herself.

JUAN LUIS SIGISMUNDO DEL VAL, n. 1942, XIV DUQUE DE SACEDON
Seis Veces *Grande* de España
VI Marqués de la Paz, IV Marqués de los Ojos Celestes
VIII Marqués de Pastrano, VIII Marqués do Estoril, VII Marqués del Peine, VII Marqués de la Vega, II Marqués de la Revancha de Jerez
X Conde de Brunete, IX Conde de Teruel, IX Conde de Cuatro Caballos
XII Conde de Patagonia, VIII Conde de Yucatán, VII Conde de Torrejón, VII Conde del Río Frío, VI Conde de la Garrapata, V Conde de Guadarrama, V Conde de Buena Suerte
III Barón de Bataan

"*There!*" she exclaimed, leaning back with understandable pride of accomplishment and again glancing at her wristwatch. "Allowing for interruptions, fifteen minutes, forty-five seconds! Ten seconds less, and I would have beaten my record."

Even Juan Luis, peering at his long and high descent, was impressed. "You are a wizard, Mamá!"

"Astonishing!" agreed Eugenio, who was standing at the widow-Duchess's left. He genuinely admired her sureness and speed of hand. "Splendid, Señora Duquesa! I congratulate you."

The Duchess was pleased. There were not so many about nowadays.

"It really is not so remarkable," she said. "Naturally, I have left out all those marquisates and countdoms, vice-countdoms and baronies distributed along the way to younger sons and girls. It is really a shame! Manuel and Dominga had such a *whopping* big family that we lost *five* marquisates and *nine* countdoms all in a sweep. If I'd been Diego de Mendieta, I'd have taken some of the more important ones right back from his sisters and brothers, leaving them with such as Buena Suerte."

"I quite agree with you!" said Eugenio deferentially. He was now, however, becoming fidgety, bending back the winder of the gold pocket-watch in his vest.

But Juan Luis was moseying up and down his mother's work. "How did that come about?" he asked, pointing.

"How did what come about!" said his mother, at once on the defensive.

He glanced to his left, at her. Her nose twitched, causing the mole to blossom and hide, blossom and hide.

"Dominga's title, the Countess of Good Luck."

"Oh!" The mole rested, half in, half out. "She played 'mus' ten straight evenings with Charles II and never lost a hand!"

"Amazing!" said Eugenio, thumbing his watch back into its pocket.

"It was *exceptional!*" the Duchess reproved him.

"Wow!" said Juan Luis, stooping closer to the desk.

"What now!" bristled his mother.

"Leonor de Mendoza really *was* a catch, two grandeurs! You didn't bring so very much."

"I'll have you know the Countdom of Pilar is one of the most distinguished titles in the realm!"

"I'm sure that it is," said Eugenio, by way of making up.

"No grandeur, though," murmured Juan Luis: blinking, puzzling from this to that. "Tell me, who was Cecilia Franco—the first Santiago's wife. I mean," he added, again glancing sideways at his mother, "that's a Jewish name, she had no title, why did Santiago pick her?"

"She was rich!" said his mother, with a roll of her tongue enriching the very sound of the word.

"I see. And grandfather, Luis del Val . . . ?"

"Even richer!"

"Returning to which," began Eugenio in his high, spiraling voice.

"Just a moment," Juan Luis interrupted. "Sorry. I'm fascinated."

"And about time you were!" said the widow-Duchess; although with some apprehension. The catastrophic offspring of her late middle age had his shoat's nostrils within inches of the paper. What next was he likely to ask?

"Humilidad 'La Manca,'" he muttered, "Hernán's wife, 'The Armless One . . .' Is that where it comes from?" And he eyed her.

Just as his mother had feared! "I do not know," she said stiffly, "to what you are referring!"

"Well," her son persisted with that knack he had for the wrong thing, "what about Luis, José's son—'El Hecho Polvo'? If he was firstborn, why didn't he inherit?"

"*That*," his mother stated, "I prefer *not* to discuss."

"Would you prefer that I retire?" asked Eugenio.

"You stay right where you are!"

"Yes, there's no need," said Juan Luis. "All families have skeletons in the closet. It just happens that ours are incomplete."

"Juan Luis!"

"Mamá?"

She did not know what to say: unfortunately, because it gave Juan Luis time to scrutinize some more.

He asked her, "And why was Diego 'El Bobo'?"

"Oh, that! The people thought him an ass to turn down the dukedom."

"I don't call it so stupid," said her boob of a son. "He had plenty with the Marquisate of the Pilgrim. Besides, from what I've gathered about Diego—the first one; the first duke—he was a rogue."

"Who told you that!"

"Herminia."

"Herminia!?"

"That's what the people of Sacedón told her."

"I *certainly* don't think she ought to have repeated those calumnies to you! That kind of thing was always getting you into hot water with your father. And quite right, too! It's beside the point. A dukedom, Juan Luis, is *always* a dukedom—and no matter how it was earned."

"Like money?"

"When you come right down to it, *like* money."

"Which brings up Begonia," Juan Luis mused.

"*Madre* de diós, what *about* Begonia!" The hairs of his mother's chignon (or bouffant, or beehive, or whatever it was) were flying back out of their spiral, as though she had been caught in a propeller's wash. She was flushing purple and yellow, and her orangy lips kept twitching back from teeth that showed the gold of fillings and the black of decay and very little enamel that was not besides streaked with her peculiar lipstick: signs, these (the flushings and the twitchings; the collapse of her coiffure), that she was angry and distressed; but he had discovered long ago he was not truly afraid of her, she almost always came through firsts-of-the-month with cash he needed, and she had wanted to believe in that period of his piety. He was, in a way, fond of her, and not without pity: she for whom love had never blossomed and resignation (to that, to his father) not quite sufficed.

"Well, the 'Open Doors' about Begonia," he said gently.

"That is something else I prefer not to discuss!"

"All right. But how did she earn the cushion? I mean, her brothers . . ."

"Juan Luis, I choose *absolutely* to utter not a further *word* about that woman!"

"Come, Mamá! It's plain Pedro de Heredia wasn't Pedro de Rivas's father."

His mother lifted the ramp of her jowls and chin, shutting her mouth. Juan Luis went berry-picking elsewhere. "Now, the second Leonor, Marchioness of the Celestial Eyes . . ."

"*Even* to you," exploded his mother, "some things ought to be self-evident!"

"They were beautiful?"

"What *else!*"

"The King found them beautiful?"

"*Who* else!"

"Were they blue?"

"*What* do you imagine?"

"Mine are muddy. I've always been a bit embarrassed about being the fourth Marqués of the Celestial . . ."

"You have always been embarrassed about being anything at all! *And* for sufficient reason."

She had reached, he estimated, the limit of patience. Eugenio had finally resumed his swivel chair. "It is nearly five o'clock," he reminded them. His voice rose. "This has been most educational, but we are obliged to mundane matters: the twenty million pesetas left to be raised before tomorrow."

"But that has been taken care of!" said the Duchess.

"Begging your pardon, I don't see how."

"Juan Luis and Odette Prades are not merely distant cousins! As you can see, the Marquisate of the Pilgrim belonged to José de Busta-mante, from whom Juan Luis is un*questionably* descended."

"Well, what about Odette?" asked her son. "How did she get it?"
"Hah!" said the Duchess, reaching for pen and pad. *"Hah!"*

T W O

Mortal Remains

Poor Odette! Her remains cut up, scrabbled over, rummaged through, and picked clean!

Following my introductory (and brief) visit with Jacobo Rivas, I had César (my driver) take me to the Depósito—the police morgue, located near Carabanchel Penitentiary in a squat, flat-roofed building poured out of concrete and faced with that cheap vitreous yellow brick that so offends Jaime Orbaneja.

The vestibule is walled in beige glazed ceramics and decorated with a pseudo-Romanesque stone mosaic of the Resurrection, of about the artistic merit one finds in similar mosaics decorating Madrid's swankier cafeterias. I walked to a receptionist's bay, handing through my diplomatic passport. But a short while elapsed before Dr. Lucas Lachaise personally hurried out to greet me.

He was one of those singularly sweet old men, bachelors (usually) who have surmounted or simply outlived the turgid passions of the human soul, reaching in their seventieth or so year a sort of rosy resignation that is expressed in gentle eyes and gentle gestures and a kind, compassionate countenance whose every feature seems to be soft-spoken.

Dr. Lachaise is the Director in Charge of Forensic Investigations. Without ado, he ushered me into his private suite, which is a cozily furnished compartment with worn leather sofas, scarlet draperies, polychromed fifteenth-century ecclesiastical candlesticks converted into lamp stands, and on the wall behind his simple walnut desk of the same period, framed photographs of, presumably, his parents and long-departed kin. He interrupted courtesies to exchange a Monteverdi choral for *The Four Seasons*. My visit seemed to delight him. He insisted on offering me tea, catching, I imagine, English intonations in my otherwise correct Spanish.

I am lucky in human relations. People respond to me, I am not sure why, except that I myself respond to people; which is, I might add, a major factor in my financial success. Dr. Lachaise chatted amiably of the hot weather, of the Middle East crisis, and of flowers, about which I am also an enthusiast. After a cup of excellent jasmine brew, I ventured inquiries about his profession—and the man bounced alive!

He bustled me into an alcove off one corner of the office, where a Kodak carrousel slide projector beetled from a metal platform, and where with concinnous dexterity he set up a screen and then drew a curtain behind us, muting the light. Flicking the fan motor on, adjusting the beam, he began showing me slides.

I gathered quickly that these violently deceased—the buried, the no longer able to hurt, to give or receive offense, or to demand—are his phantom family: his children, his nieces and nephews, his true next of kin, kept alive beyond the grave through the rich dyes of kodachrome. When flashing the slide of an infant's drowned corpse, his gentle voice quavered. He could not understand—how, how in the world! had the mother of little Jesús been able to plunge and hold her pathetically struggling womb-fruit in a rain barrel? Upon showing me the terribly mutilated cadaver of a seventeen-year-old girl, that soft voice positively shook with emotion, because María Dolores had been a gay, open, joyous spirit, loved by her schoolmates and the hope of her aged parents, and this was the barbarity to which she had been destined at the hands of a sexual maniac.

In a Madame Tussaud way—in a strange, horrible way—the photographs were compelling. Some verged upon art. I asked many questions. I am interested in all human professions, and one of my delights is listening to an expert in anything, whether it be breeding of exotic freshwater fish or cabinetmaking. Dr. Lachaise was stimulated. He explained the origins and history of forensic medicine, and its rapid technical sophistication after the Second World War. I asked, "Were a body strangled, would you be able to deduce by what means, and at what hour?" Oh, certainly! I had certainly to see how his people worked.

Dr. Lachaise escorted me into the bowels of the morgue. These are long, air-conditioned—almost chilly—corridors into which the dewdrops of a Bach prelude were being piped. The floors are of a spotless, highly glazed white tile, which explained to me the rubber-soled sneakers everyone wears. (I very nearly came a cropper, caught at the elbow by Dr. Lachaise and steadied.) The main depository contains perhaps 200 storage vaults, stacked into the walls, where corpses are kept at a precise 33 degrees Fahrenheit. The pathologists are for the most part young men.

They scrimmage verbally with female technicians, cracking shop-oriented jokes that inevitably strike one's ear as ghoulish. But Dr. Lachaise insists on propriety. He is scrupulous about the modesty of his "guests," each of which is entirely covered in a white tunic. While I was present, one was being slid out of a vault on its pallet and lifted to a long, narrow metal table whose feet rolled on castors; whence, with a little rumbling sound, it was pushed toward the operating hall.

Nothing can be more up to date than this. There are six operating tables. Above each hangs a long, white fluorescent lamp of dazzling but cool intensity, attached to the ceiling by two aluminum struts. From every lighting fixture protrude cameras that can be manipulated on retractable extensions, like a dentist's drill. Each is equipped with three lenses of various degrees of magnification, operated by a shutter release pin conveniently suspended from a cord. The pathologists work with microphones cupped under their chins, into which they report continually as they cut and examine, this information being fed into a wall computer at one end of the chamber, where a technician monitors the information. "Reports filed after lengthy dissections," Dr. Lachaise told me, "are susceptible to mental lapses. This radically reduces error, saving time and conserving energies." He is justifiably proud.

I am, nonetheless, unable to express my horror at what almost at once met my eyes. Seared into memory is the image of Odette on one of those tables. At this point in the proceedings modesty cannot be maintained. There can be no pretensions of modesty. Neat, pretty, feminine, fastidious, and *private* Odette lay naked on her backside with her dumpy short legs spread wide, exposing her gray pubic tuft and liver-brown labia. From just above the mont on up to the throttle she was opened—sprung open like a wardrobe trunk, like the twin panels of a pouting French armoire, her rib cage separated and yanked apart to reveal the whole glistening spectrum of the entrails, heart, lungs, and tripe, scarlet, purple, and blue, with foam rubberlike subcutaneous fat gleaming clearest canary-yellow at the edges.

There is, inevitably, odor. I won't say more on that subject, but there is odor in spite of the air conditioning. One pathologist was bent over her innards, busily looping out the lower intestine, which he photographed while reporting into his microphone. At Odette's head worked a nurse and an intern. They had sliced her scalp in a circular incision that began at the hairline of the brow and reached around behind her ears. Slowly, they ripped the scalp back and down from the skull, permitting it to hang there off the table's edge like a mop, the membrane capping her head's dome pink and veined. "We exercise extreme care here," Dr. Lachaise explained. "We are as careful as plastic surgeons, cutting precisely along the hairline and then minutely suturing the scalp back into place. Fluff the hair forward a bit, and relatives suspect nothing." As he spoke, the intern briskly drilled into the brow of the dome, inserting immediately thereafter the teeth of an electrically operated saw with which he proceeded to top out the crown. "Not so long ago," said Dr. Lachaise, "we used hand tools, which required considerable manual effort and often damaged the soft tissues, destroying evidence. Now the brain comes out neatly and intact in its membranous sheathing. It practically pops out."

I had by this time managed to tear my eyes away. All around me I heard those terrible sounds, the whine of the drill burning through bone with a scent like that of a hot horseshoe when it is singed into the hoof, and the gunshot cracks of ribs being broken in other corpses, like pond ice. There was no place to look. My eyes swung wildly from wall to wall. At one table the rib-cracking had just commenced. "A linoleum cutter," Dr. Lachaise informed me. "Curious, isn't it, with all our sophisticated new tools, still nothing separates ribs more efficiently than a common linoleum cutter." Nearby, a child of six or seven—girl or boy, I do not know—was being sewed back together in a livid zigzag pattern across the front, what resembled wrapping cord being looped into a baseball stitch. "That, I'm afraid, is crude," Dr. Lachaise said, "but next of kin do not see it, we deliver our guests dressed for burial, their faces alone visible." At a trough near one end of the hall, organs were being washed in some sort of solution. "Antisepsis," explained Dr. Lachaise. "The dead can infect the living." Parts were being injected with other solutions. "Dyes," said Lachaise. He excused himself.

A heart was being held up for his inspection, large and rosy, with a purple, pear-shaped trunk. He took it into his hands, nodding at the words spoken to him, inserting an index finger into the stump of the aorta and thus returning to me.

"Are you squeamish?"

"I . . ."

He handed the heart to me. It was cold and firm, almost pleasant to the touch. Its weight surprised.

"Insert your finger where I had mine. The aorta, as you see, is calcified. Closing. A congenital infirmity. It belongs to the old lady over there."

I confess that I fainted.

Dr. Lachaise could not have been more solicitous, nor his staff more understanding and kind. Brandy settled my stomach. Dr. Lachaise was distressed. "It's entirely my fault," I said. "I came to inquire about her, the Marchioness of the Pilgrim, an . . . an old friend. You had no way of knowing that she would be on the operating table. What . . . what is your determination as to the cause of death? I'm particularly interested in how it was perpetrated."

We were back in his office. He buzzed for the monitor of the tapes, listened to the recording, and then interpreted the information for me. "She was strangled to death, after a struggle. Contusions show that the strangling occurred twice, the second attack, of course, being the fatal one, but against which the Señora Marquesa did not offer resistance. Time of death anywhere between midnight and 1:45 A.M. The manner of strangling was by hand, and the hands of the assailant possess long, thin, bony, probably aged, but unusually strong fingers. They left clear imprints. By the way," he added, "she would have died within six months anyhow. The aorta, shutting off the flow of blood."

Jacobo Rivas, it was plain, would be released. I did not then suspect Nati.

On my way out, I met—rather, I saw—Inspector Stepanópoulis Grau. He would be downcast by the post-mortem.

THREE

Deeds from the Dead

Ah! *Ah!* Aaa-a-a-aaah!

To the Keeper of the Seals! she had said, better by far: and off in her chauffeured Mercedes-Benz with Don Eugenio, leaving him to follow in his Lancia-a-aaah!

To the Ministry of Foreign Affairs: a cupolaed building in neo-Habsburgan style, ruddily façaded with brick and roofed over with slate, a rectangular massif appropriately situated in one of the more venerable (and therefore almost impassable) quarters of the city. Remaining to Asuntos Exteriores, nevertheless, a grandeur befitting the imperial past, hussars at attention by the portals in black kneeboots, white breeches, and scarlet tunics, their drawn sabers slices of silver. Inside, a splendid, crimson-carpeted staircase sweeps the visitor up to the more august chambers, which are nobly proportioned, of austere, high-ceilinged sumptuousness, showing that Spanish genius for eschatological pomp. Since on/about the seventeenth century, deliberations within these chambers have managed the almost incredible feat of reducing Spain from the mightiest power in history to a minor and penurious addendum. *Sic transit.*

In transit, Juan Luis was no longer: but foreboding-filled. At the head of those stairs, he had collided with a frock-coated undersecretary who staggered under the weight of Spain's Red Book on Gibraltar, jostling it out of the undersecretary's arms and down over the railing, where it fell on the breast of a frock-coated British undersecretary who had just entered under the staggering weight of England's White Book on Gibraltar, knocking the envoy as flat as his nation's case. Juan Luis was not sure whether patriotism permitted apology, but he called one over the railing anyhow, asking then of a hussar posted nearby where the sanctum of the Keeper of the Seals was to be reached.

His mother and an awed Don Eugenio were already seated. The room is a windowless rectangle. From its depths, across a leather-faced mahogany desk, the Keeper faced them. Behind this high priest—from floor to ceiling—blazed the complete royal arms of Spain, scarlet, azure, and gold.

Don Indelicio Salgado de Perrera has since died. I feel free to cite his true name and fully describe him. He was as bald as a billiard ball. He possessed no eyebrows and of lashes little more than whitish stubs. It was as though he had scraped off follicles from years of burrowing his way through the goatskin volumes massed against three of his chamber's four walls. His soul was pure.

He was the final authority. Although cases are tried in the Ministry of Justice, it is his word that weighs: yes, Don Fulano-de-tal *is* entitled to the Countdom of Such-and-Such, no, Don Fulano-de-tal is *not.* Bribes had been tried on him, munificent sums representing twice and three times his government salary of ten or more years. He, colorless, modest, but backed by the prodigiousness of the royal arms, lowered his gaze to the reflecting leather of his desk, looking down in mute reproach: until the new-rich shipping magnate from Bilbao or Valencia and his stout, ambitious wife withdrew; with, perhaps, burning cheeks.

Don Indelicio loved his work. He would have done it for less than the pittance he received. Having no pretensions—he was a poor scholar of humble background—the pretensions of others fascinated him. He knew the root-origin of every heraldic symbol; the difference between titles truly earned and those dealt out frivolously. He loved them all. They were (the parallel to Dr. Lachaise can't be helped) his romance. They were his children. He was always surprised by the respect that heirs of resounding suffixes showed him. He counted his probity for little. He would have been abashed, confounded, mortified, and overwhelmed by the pomp of his funeral, staged in the royal cathedral of Los Jerónimos and attended by most of the peers of the realm.

"I thought you would never get here!" said Mercedes Inmaculada del Val, widow-Duchess of Sacedón.

"Sorry, Mamá. Had to park . . . Fine day, Don Indelicio, how are you?" And he stretched out his hand.

Don Indelicio, who was doing badly; who had cancer of the abdomen, knew it, and kept it secret, retiring into the closet of his private bathroom when the pains became so vicious he could not suppress groans and even a high, whimpering scream; pushed himself to his feet and with a low bow accepted the honor of that ducal hand, overcome, as he was always, by this the great privilege of his office.

"Very well, Señor Duque," he said. "And you? I read of your attendance at the little princess's christening. It must have been an inspiring ceremony. Your fine gesture of casting helmet to the floor on the words of exorcism would have made your noble sire proud, certain as he would have been to recall El Cid's similar gesture at the christening of King Sancho's daughter."

"Thank you, Don Indelicio," said Juan Luis gracefully, blushing. The old man hobbled hurriedly around his desk, dragging up an ornate gilt chair into which Juan Luis fitted the ducal bottom.

"Tell him!" said the widow-Duchess impatiently. "Go on, Don Indelicio, tell my son how the Marquisate of the Pilgrim fell to the Pradeses. Tell him what you told me over the telephone this morning."

"We do not have very much time," murmured Don Eugenio almost inaudibly: meanwhile gazing with wonderment at the royal arms. They did not have much time: but here, in, as it were, the holy of holies, plebian matters paled.

Don Indelicio was now back at his desk. He bowed at Juan Luis's mother. "But you, Señora Duquesa, you know as well as I! In this sad, leveling age, you are one of the rare people who honors herself by doing honor to her honors."

Mercedes Inmaculada was pleased, showing it in her liverish flushings. Back her head went; pursed went her orangy mouth. She fell into the incantation while Don Indelicio nodded, eyes closed and dreamily, as though listening to chamber music; and while Don Eugenio and Juan Luis listened with varying degrees of astonishment.

Odette
> *daughter of Rodrigo*
>> *son of Rodrigo*

Rodrigo
> *Hidalgo de Castilla la Vieja*
>> *Conde de Casacaída*

and

XV MARQUES DEL PEREGRINO
> *son of Domingo*

son of Mauricio
> *son of Luis*
>> *son of Isabel*
>>> *daughter of . . .*

". . . of, of, of . . ." Panic! She had stopped. She had forgot.

"Diego Frayle," prompted Don Indelicio in as tender a fashion as possible.

"Of course, Diego *Frayle!*" blushed the widow-Duchess, purple and yellow. "Mil perdones!"

"No hay de que," murmured the gallant Don Indelicio; once again closing his eyes.

> *. . . of Diego*

son of Jorge
> *son of Juan*
>> *son of Antonio*
>>> *son of Dolores*

Dolores
> *daughter of Diego*

I DUQUE DE SACEDON. . . .

"I'm going back down, now!" she gasped. "I'm crossing over, siphoning!"

. . . father of Santiago
> *father of Efrain*
>> *father of Hernán*

father of Santiago
> *brother of Luis*
>> *father of José*

José
> *V Conde de Patagonia*
>> *VII Duque de Sacedón*
>>> and

IX MARQUES DEL PEREGRINO
> *father of Diego*
>> *father of Mamento*

father of Rodrigo
> *father of Luis*
>> *father of Roget*
>>> last, true

and
> XIV MARQUES DEL PEREGRINO!

"There!" she finished triumphantly.

"Excellent, excellent, excellent!" bubbled Don Indelicio. His mother—Juan Luis agreed—was a sort of genius.

He said, however, "The French are at Zaragoza."

"Yes," seconded Don Eugenio, brought back to reality; and somewhat startled that it should be Juan Luis to call them back to it. "I am, I'm afraid, still uncertain as to how this most interesting and admirable recital will help us."

"*Hah!*" said the widow-Duchess. "*Show* them, Don Indelicio! Go on, *do!*"

With a deprecatory smile, Don Indelicio brought out of his desk drawer a beautifully inked chart on vellum. It cannot be reproduced here, but every letter bore its distinguishing flourish, and attached to every name was the man's or woman's personal and family crest, drawn in minutely and colored with bright, waxy crayons.

Herewith a truncated version:

DIEGO DE BUSTAMANTE, I DUQUE DE SACEDON
  c. con LEONOR DEL VAL

Santiago el Glotón	Dolores de Bustamante
José el Beato, IX MARQUES DEL PEREGRINO	
Diego el Bobo, X MARQUES DEL PEREGRINO	Begonia las Puertas Abiertas, VIII DUQUESA DE SACEDON

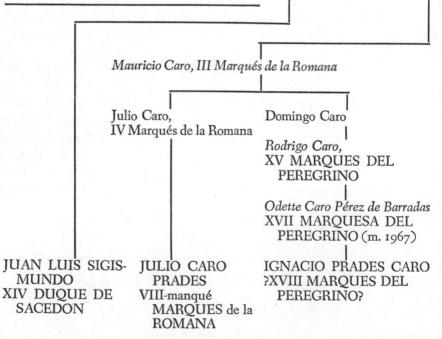

Mamento de Bustamante,
 XI MARQUES DEL PEREGRINO
     c. con
Mencia Camillo de Peralta
 |
Rodrigo de Bustamante,
 XII MARQUES DEL PEREGRINO
     c. con
Dorotea de Rohan-Chabot
 |
Luis de Bustamante,
 XIII MARQUES DEL PEREGRINO
     c. con
Denise Mireille de la France
 |
Roget de Bustamante (1735–1789),
 XIV MARQUES DEL PEREGRINO
     c. con
Marthe de Levis Mire-Poix (m. 1789)

Mauricio Caro, III Marqués de la Romana

Julio Caro,
IV Marqués de la Romana

Domingo Caro
 |
Rodrigo Caro,
XV MARQUES DEL
PEREGRINO
 |
Odette Caro Pérez de Barradas
XVII MARQUESA DEL
PEREGRINO (m. 1967)
 |

JUAN LUIS SIGIS-
 MUNDO
XIV DUQUE DE
 SACEDON

JULIO CARO
 PRADES
VIII-manqué
 MARQUES de la
 ROMANA

IGNACIO PRADES CARO
?XVIII MARQUES DEL
 PEREGRINO?

All studied the chart some little time—which, for its inclusion of
every individual in the various successions, was not as clear as the com-

pressed version I have reproduced here. Eugenio was the first to speak, pointing.

"Roget de Bustamante and his wife, both died . . ."

"During the Jacobin terror," explained Don Indelicio, "ending the direct line. There was no issue."

"Then how . . . ?"

"By siphoning!" snapped the widow-Duchess. "How else? How else are half the titles one knows perpetuated!"

"I've . . . heard of that," said Eugenio. His cherry-pit eyes shone with interest now. "How is it accomplished, may I ask? I mean, my grandfather's great-grandmother was the Marquesa de Bolivia. That is," he added modestly, "so family tradition maintains."

"And quite possibly it is so!" said the Duchess magnanimously.

"Quite," said Don Indelicio sadly. "Titles become lost, misplaced, abandoned: waifs."

"Take Julio Caro," interrupted the Duchess, "who can't afford the taxes on his father's marquisate. If he dies, Juan Luis, you should certainly look into that one. Lethargy has been the *end* of *no* end of nobility . . . lethargy and poverty.

"Poverty!" she repeated, clasping her bosom. "I shall not break down, never fear. The world began to disintegrate a century and a half ago, with the Jacobin madness, with the abolition of primogeniture. How many ended up without funds to validate their titles! How many titles fell into disuse! That's when siphoning came into practice."

"Too often, I regret to say," murmured Don Indelicio. "Relatives sometimes quite distant and not in the direct descent," he explained, "but with influence in . . . high circles, obtained the necessary signatures on their behalf and thus negotiated the concession of a title. The person with actual priority might be anyone—a servant, a shoeshiner—someone in the most humble of circumstances."

"Regrettable. Most deplorable!" stated the widow-Duchess.

"Few are the young today who appreciate the romance," Don Indelicio agreed regretfully. "The legitimate Marquis of Sonora, for instance, a title vacant many generations because the family lost all its money, was a fellow called Pedro Luis de Gálvez. I remember the man well. One could scarcely avoid him. He was a Bohemian poet who beat his wife to death and who begged about the cafés threatening to exhibit what he represented to be the corpse of a son, whose body he simulated by carrying a bundle of rags wrapped up under his cape. During the War

—our war—he personally shot literary colleagues on True Spain's side, saying, 'I don't kill you for being a Fascist, but for being a bad poet.'"

"Monster that he was!" said the widow-Duchess. "But back to siphoning, the Benamejí and Fuentes titles have been assumed by very remote relatives of the last Marquis of the line, who also went bankrupt and ended up—believe me—as a banderillero!"

"A picador," corrected Don Indelicio, "and an unfortunately poor one, at that. The rightful civil possessor of the titles—a legitimate Bernuy —is half gypsy on his mother's and grandmother's side, and a second-hand dealer in the Rastro—yes, here in Madrid, in our flea market."

"*That* Bernuy!" exclaimed the widow-Duchess, throwing her jeweled hands up. "He *terrorizes* the incumbent marquises—you know them, Juan Luis—threatening from time to time to sue. He says that if those foolish American tourists keep paying ridiculous prices for all those antiques-made-yesterday that he peddles, why, he is going to skin them down to mere 'Señor Dons,' as he puts it!"

"Siphoning," now murmured a long-silent Eugenio, treasuring the word.

"Yes," said the widow-Duchess, "a well-known but sometimes abused procedure. Much as I adored poor dear Odette, God rest her soul, her title *was* acquired by her grandfather Rodrigo—his wife was very rich and felt uncomfortable without a crown—by the most ab*struse* of siphonings, he did have *a* right to the Marquisate of the Pilgrim, but *not* such a right as you, Juan Luis, have!"

"Accomplished exactly how?" inquired Eugenio.

"By tracing descent backward, all the way up through Mauricio Caro to Dolores de Bustamante, daughter of the first Diego, and from there across and collaterally down to Santiago el Glotón, and down to Diego el Bobo, and from there down to the unfortunate Roget, who died by the guillotine shortly after receiving the tripe of Louis XVIth. It cost a packet, you can be sure!"

"I have put away savings," murmured Eugenio.

"Well!" said Juan Luis's mother, staring at him.

Her son was worrying a thought. "Mamá, the first Julio Caro, Domingo's brother, was the elder."

"What about it!"

"Nothing . . . except that if Ignacio isn't cousin Odette's son, then surely *our* Julio Caro . . ."

"Our Julio Caro is a no-account! I'm sure Don Indelicio will agree to that."

"Still, the principle of the thing, I mean after what you said about the way people pick up titles that don't really belong to them . . ."

"The principle of the thing," stated Mercedes Inmaculada, Duchess-mother of Sacedón, "is that Ignacio Prades, your cousin, is an accomplice with the despicable Baltazar Blás, his father-in-law, to ruin you and your sisters and your mother. That, Juan Luis, is the principle of the thing! And this is the one way to fight back: to put forth your perfectly valid claim to the marquisate, because you are by anyone's reckoning more entitled than anyone else!"

"Julio aside."

"*Yes*, Julio aside!"

"A suit would cost a fortune."

"The mere threat of one will *save* a fortune!"

"But, Mamá, there's the illegitimacy of Pedro de Rivas, The Bastard. There's the question mark about grandmother—Carmen—who was born in her father's ninetieth year, which is so miraculous who can believe it? They say—Herminia once told me—that a fellow called Sebastian Rivas helped great-grandfather Diego out . . ."

"Lies! If there is any germ of truth in that old canard, it was an Ybarra."

"Yes, Mamá. Nevertheless, some people could challenge my descendancy . . ."

"Are you suggesting that your dear, departed Papá was . . ."

"I'm saying, Mamá, that if we question Ignacio's right to the title because of *his* illegitimacy, Baltazar Blás will hire a battalion of lawyers to question my legitimacy, anyhow grandmother's; or even the legitimizing deed her great-grandfather Pedro received when Begonia his mother recognized him and Pedro de Heredia her husband adopted him. I mean, once you start throwing dirt . . ."

"*Who* is throwing dirt, may I ask? There is no question that Pedro the Bastard was legitimately just that, a true natural son of his mother—no question at all—and if Franz Liszt begat a child at age seventy-five, why shouldn't your great-grandfather Diego beget a daughter at ninety, even if he hadn't had any luck with three earlier wives! I resent . . ."

"But, Mamá," insisted her utterly exasperating son, "the marquisate was confirmed to the Caro line. If Ignacio isn't Odette's son, why shouldn't Consuelo Orbaneja inherit?"

"She might very well try! She might be thinking of that at this very moment, who knows? But it won't do her any good!"

"And why not?"

"The Marquisate of the Pilgrim is passed by strict agnation, *that* is why!" She produced this trump with triumph.

"What?"

"The concession, Juan Luis . . . Don Indelicio, *will* you please explain to my dunce of a child!"

"The concession is indeed agnate," said the old man. "Thus was it bestowed on Philip II, and thus did he bestow it on José de Bustamante."

"*Agnate*, Juan Luis," broke in his dam, "succession by the *male* line, *not* by the female. Actually, Odette herself wasn't . . ."

"But Philip II didn't bring in the Salic law, Mamá. That was the Bourbon, Philip V!"

"Makes no difference, Philip II received the marquisate under a deed explicitly demanding rigorous agnation, and he passed it on to José unchanged. That deed is in Don Indelicio's hands!"

At which point Juan Luis threw up his. "Mamá, we settled all that about male and female succession in three Carlist wars."

"We settled it for the crown. We did *not* settle it for individual titles of imperial origin."

"But it follows. Nobody since God knows when has ever challenged . . ."

"No? Do you think some of us are not challenging the right of succession to Alfonso Trece's crown by Don Juan Carlos! Do you think some of us don't believe his cousin, Don Alfonso, hasn't a better claim!"

"But please, Mamá! That has nothing to do with us! I don't care who gets the crown. I don't care who gets the Marquisate of the Pilgrim. I don't want to challenge. It's a great lío. It's a lío padre. It's the great-great-grandfather of lío padres. It would take the whole Ministry of Justice to figure this out, and gobs and gobs and gobs of money, which is what we don't—or shortly won't—have when Blás gets through with us."

"Exactly!" his mother said.

"That *is* the subject under discussion," ventured Eugenio.

The administrator was now rubbing his hands—whether from thoughts about looking into his family tree or from the battle plan suggested by the Duchess was difficult to determine.

But he said, "Señora Duquesa, you have, I think, a brilliant notion. Let us presume that sufficient doubt can be cast on the legitimacy of Don Ignacio to interest this office."

He glanced toward Don Indelicio, who seemed uncomfortable, perhaps because of his cancer.

"Yes," he agreed with reluctance, "such doubt would necessarily interest this office."

"Good!" said Don Eugenio. "Let us put aside the question of strict or loose agnation and simply maintain that on the one hand the first Julio Caro had greater right to the marquisate than his nephew Rodrigo, and then put forth the claim that, besides, Begonia Bustamante, VIII Duchess of Sacedón, and her descendancy (yes, by all *means* let us let the Salic law rest in its grave), have better (by being closer) rights to the vacant marquisate than anyone else through her fraternal relationship to the second Diego de Bustamante, X Marquis of the Pilgrim. Yes! That might very well do. It might indeed do just what we require. Juan Luis, I implore you, listen to your good mother; and this afternoon warn Don Ignacio that you are considering a suit."

Bidding Don Indelicio farewell, they rose and departed on these words—leaving a disillusioned old man who slowly circled on the chart, with his right thumb, the name of the ignored Bustamante, the ill-favored and ill-destined Beatitud.

FOUR

The Possessed

Truth, historical or other, lies in the telling. Mercedes Inmaculada, so exact to suit her purpose, ignored Beatitud. So did the Frenchwoman, Michelle Muñoz, when relating her version of truth to Jacobo. The Dukes represented Madrid, and both oppression. The Rivas family symbolized the Basque's agelong battle for liberty, which she described not inaccurately as democratic and egalitarian. To Michelle, hidalgos were not a petty squiredom but a primitive paradigm of Party leadership, a natural elite. She hewed to her late husband's great-grandfather's version of events (Rodrigo González González, the nineteenth-century separatist who wrote *The Betrayal of Sacedón* in French exile), which portrayed the first Manú Riva in heroic terms. Thus she limned him for Jacobo, in similar fashion glorifying the hot-headed Sebastian, who led so many Sacedonese into ambuscade.

All this she told him on a Sunday afternoon following his escape from the sea. Jacobo had resisted being dragged to the Ayuntamiento that late afternoon, embarrassed about walking into town wearing no more than shorts and undershirt. And so her discovery to him of his family's history was delayed a week. As she pulled out crackly records in which he saw cramped brown scratches that, to take her word for it, expressed his surname, his pride was excited. So it was all true! They were an important clan brought down by vicissitudes; and Rivas blood did flow in ducal veins! He was enchanted.

Not, of course, in the way she would have preferred, admonishing him, "You must look upon this as an obligation to continue the struggle for the rights of the proletariat. It is of no consequence that you and the Bustamantes are related; although," she sniffed with a flush of what seemed to him to be shame, "when it comes to that my late husband was an actual descendant, and I . . . I . . . *he* had a sword that supposedly belonged to the first duke, the shaft does bear the coat of arms, and I" —she was definitely feeling guilt— "have drawn a . . . I suppose you could call it a family tree, actually no more than a record of dialectical progression that proves conclusively how inevitable historical determinism is, from a tyrant's lackey through separatism and down to a fighter in the ranks of Marxist-Leninism . . ."

And she stared at him with a baleful sort of defiance, as though she had been caught in some sort of crime.

He did not question her. The intimacy felt (at least by him) the Sunday before had been dissipated. She called him Jacobo, but as older woman and pedagogue to a young disciple. He did not know how to address her, and as she gave him no clue, he called her nothing at all, clearing his throat when he wanted to catch her attention. Discovering his inability to read, she had clamped those self-pleasuring lips disapprovingly. Satisfying herself that his father indeed was chief of the nearly vanished Rivas clan, she insisted on being presented.

The prospect frightened Jacobo. He was looked upon as a monster since the accusations of Jimena, his humpbacked (from Humilidad La Manca through Beatitud?) sister; and when, lately, Manú Rivas discerned something in Jacobo's lowered eyes that suggested knowledge or suspicion of what had passed between father and daughter in the stable, the very sight of his son had become intolerable. To bring a painted woman and a foreigner to the homestead invited an explosion.

She prevailed on Jacobo. Nearly micturating, he led her up the zigzagging path from Sacedón. They reached the house. Before the woman could enter, Manú had blocked the front door.

Late Sunday afternoon, he was already sour with hard cider. He did not say he would answer no questions: in the beginning, he never spoke at all, gazing over the woman's head at Jacobo. She offered to teach his son letters. That brought nothing more than a splat of phlegm from Manú, spurting by her left foot and landing centimeters short of Jacobo's toes. She was startled, but she did not lose her composure: switching grounds instantly, explaining that she planned to memorialize the important Rivas contribution to Sacedón and Vizcaya; and adding that she was willing to pay for his and his son's time.

"How much for me?" muttered Manú.

"Four pesetas for every day you let me follow you about at your work. I promise I shan't get in the way."

"And for him?"

"Two pesetas every Sunday—for the afternoon, after the morning chores."

This was almost double the going wage for an adult hand. Her extravagance earned from Manú a nod of agreement; and saved Jacobo a hiding.

She spent the following week with his father. Privately, she told Jacobo how surprised she was at Manú's ignorance about his own heritage: he did not even know why it was that he detested the Ybarras, although he anathematized them all as usurpers. He possessed no more than the vaguest notions of Basque history, simplified to the single theme that his people had been swindled out of everything by Madrid and the Crown.

This pricked the woman's interest. Her pale blue orbs swelled slightly as she said, "So you are glad to be rid of that reactionary institution!"

Manú grunted.

"And quite right!" she went on animatedly. "The Church, the Army, the Crown . . . You support the Republic, then."

Jacobo's father squinted a glance at her. He was castrating the second of a pair of bull calves born a few days earlier. Jacobo was holding the victim down. As Manú pulled at the soft young scrotum with one hand and gave a twist of the knife with the other, the calf letting out a bawl, he said, "If they give us back our fueros."

"Perhaps not that bourgeois reactionary Samper," she said, apparently not the least affected by what she was witnessing; in fact, interested, peering into the skillet that had received the calf's parts, so that Manú, glancing at her, leered. She flushed, clamping her lips. "Not," she continued argumentatively, "with a Fascist like Robles and his CEDA behind him; but Largo Caballero would. You had Azaña for a president. Now you have Alcalá Zamora. You asked for that. Why did your deputies walk out of the national congress two years ago? Why did so many Basques turn about and support Robles?"

"We're Catholics, not burners of churches!" said Manú, spitting on the cauterizing iron, which sizzled. "Hold that becerra tight!" he snarled at Jacobo.

She watched distractedly as the iron was applied, the steer bawled piteously, and Jacobo fought its convulsions until the iron had scorched its flesh a second time; after which Manú nodded at Jacobo, who released the animal.

She was saying, "All Article 26 proposed was trimming the Church's political power, its stranglehold on Spain—not by burnings, that is the work of Anarchists, madmen, fools—but by ending the State subsidy to the clergy, by shutting down all those convents and monasteries that live off the poor, as well as the religious schools . . ."

But Manú had walked away, carrying his tools to the lean-to by the stable. She hurried on her short legs after him.

"Tell me," she insisted as he turned, "Samper has scuttled Article 26, Robles has seen to that. Does that make you support such men?"

"No. Jacobo, where is Amadeo?"

"I think in the orchard, with Mamá and the girls." Amadeo was actually visiting a notorious hut down the road, where a big-breasted, wasp-waisted girl serviced him for free, because even when drunk he retained a droll talent for storytelling.

It was a poor invention, blurted out. Manú squinted at the orchard, which was not far away. Then he aimed a kick at Jacobo, which landed on one thigh.

Jacobo's reflexes below the waist were not very much faster than those above his neck. But when Manú, unsatisfied, snatched up a cake of cow manure and hurled it at him, Jacobo easily deflected the missile with an instinctive, swift flick of his left hand. The cake, however, being dry, crumbled—sprinkling his head, face, and chest.

Manú laughed. He jerked his chin at the woman. "Born a liar," he rasped. "I know where his brother is. So long as he doesn't have to pay for it, that's all right with me, but not during working hours. I'll give him a thrashing he won't forget tonight. This one, though, this one wants to get it free, too—from his sisters!" He spat on the ground.

Jacobo felt the blood drain from his cheeks. "That," he said in a thin, far-away voice, "is . . . a lie!" The woman was gazing at him; he was conscious of this, but did not look at her, did not see her expression, kept his eyes on Manú, waiting for his father's fist to crash into his face—and the justification for at last retaliating.

But Manú Rivas blazed only—briefly, arresting his step forward and snuffing a choler in which doubt and then a peculiarly ugly furtiveness played. His son, he may have realized just then, was capable of breaking him in two.

He shrugged, addressing the woman, "Are the young like that where you come from?"

She said firmly, "They have rights too."

He scowled at her. "Rights? Who has rights any more? Us Basques?"

She pressed him. "You approved, then, when the Basque mayors last year held new municipal elections in defiance of the reactionaries who have taken over the Republic. You approved of the demonstrations for home rule."

"The demonstrations, yes," he said slowly. And then, with heat, "But who does José Ybarra think he is? He deserved to be locked up in the calabozo."

She told Jacobo later that there was no sense to be got from his father politically. Prejudices perplexed his viewpoint, such as his rigid fealty to the Church even as an anticlerical non-goer, which wholly baffled her. She spent the rest of the week pumping Manú about local customs. Jacobo saw that his father was flattered by her interest. With rising anger, he watched his father plant prurient eyes on the woman's buttocks, crotch, or breasts, from there glancing up at her face with a lewd, weasel-like sneer. She paid no notice. What Manú said all went into a notebook in tidy, fitful little letters.

On Sunday, true to her promise, she began teaching Jacobo. It was a fine day, and the lessons were carried on between swims. In the water, she was friendly, treating him nearly as an equal. On land, she was impersonal. These shifts in attitude confused him. He was nervous anyhow. He wanted to explain about his father's accusation. Midafternoon, when he stumbled stupidly through the first ten letters of the alphabet, missing three, she slapped his wrist. He started, face burning.

"I am sorry," she said. "You are slow. You're distracted, perhaps. What's bothering you?"

His face burned more fiercely yet. She gazed at him thoughtfully. Then her lips unclamped, he saw the encrusted nicotine under the gums, and he perceived that she was smiling.

She took his right hand. "Come, is it about what your father said the other day?"

He nodded dumbly.

Her voice was warm and compassionate. "But that happens, Jacobo. You are a young man, and living the way you do . . ."

He pulled his hand free. "I never touched her! It was my sister, she's wicked!" and he told her the story (leaving out what Jimena actually did and his semiconscious physiological reaction), not caring that her notebook had come out.

"Is that all?"

"Yes." He blushed furiously.

She gave him that disconcerting smile again. "I believe you. It's the Church again! The Church has *never* accepted the physical facts of existence!" She looked him over from toe to head, lips twitching. "A young stallion. A kettle at boil! Poor boy, why don't you go to the place Amadeo visits?"

"I . . . I have no money. Besides . . ." He could not finish.

"Tell me."

"It's . . . It's not right . . ." He was mortally embarrassed.

"You are very sweet, Jacobo," she said, once more taking his hand; pressing it, letting it go, and continuing briskly. "But you'll see! Free psychotherapy will take care of disturbed people like your sister. Free love will eliminate the need for prostitutes. Already, Jacobo, many of us are living that way: as progressive and liberated human beings! And it will happen here. But young people like you must help. With your name, you could be of great help."

But his mind had snagged on something he had been meaning to ask. "You . . . You married a Spaniard, a Muñoz."

"Yes."

"He . . . came from here."

"His great-grandfather, Rodrigo, I told you. What is it?"

"Nothing." He did not know himself: what name to give to those strong, blood-boiling emotions that attended the thought of her husband.

To her, Jacobo was spring water in a bottle.

She asked him, "Would you like me to tell you about Diego?" Her tone was grave and gentle.

"Yes."

"He was a good fifteen years older than you."

"Oh?"

"I met him in Toulouse, at a Party meeting. His smile—it made a woman shiver, Jacobo. Oh, what a man he was!" She looked at him. "Taller than you, not so broad, but elegant in his build and graceful in his movements, experienced, sensitive, intelligent . . ." Her voice thinned away, every word she had uttered lacerating him as she drew the comparison. She said, "We were married not for any bourgeois reason but because the Party advised it for technical reasons to do with my profession. Besides, it gave me a Spanish passport. Three years ago, he was sent to Santo Domingo. I was to join him there. But he was killed, betrayed . . . a martyr to the proletariat."

"I'm . . . sorry," he said.

She looked brightly at him, too brightly, eyes glistening. "Don't be. Yes, I was sorry, I cried, I still do. He died gloriously: for you, for me, for my child."

"You . . . have a child?"

"A son!"

"Where is he?"

"In Biarritz, with my father. I have important work to do here, Jacobo. My thesis on Sacedón is not just a cover. History has to be written so that its inner meaning transpires. You Basques must be shown what it really is you have been struggling for, so that you are ready when the call comes. Have you heard of Salvador Larrañaga?"

Jacobo shook his head.

"You will! A Basque, like my husband, and like Diego a Basque with good revolutionary Asturian blood in him. He is a great man, Jacobo. He was trained in Italy and Hungary, and he is now in Mieres."

"I have a brother in Mieres!"

"Yes, well, it will begin there."

"What?"

"The Revolution, Jacobo: which will free you in ways you never dreamed. Your father, as I've said, is hopeless. But no one is satisfied. We are sure of that. The Republic has served its purpose. I am going to Mieres myself, in October. You must tell me where your brother can be found."

All this was highly mysterious to Jacobo; but as Sunday after Sunday went by, he learned more about it. Much he thought wonderful. Nevertheless, like his father, he did not approve her hostility to the Church; and she, sensing this (he said nothing), modulated her attacks on it. She was prudent. Political indoctrination came only in spates between lessons. He tried hard to learn; she strove as hard to teach him. It was her task to overcome generations of illiterateness. Jacobo sweated as he clenched a pencil and let her bird-boned little hand guide his great paw into a vowel or a consonant. He knotted his forehead, armpits soaking as she plagued him for replies to phonetics. Then, after twenty minutes or so, she would rise. "Come, let's wash our brains out in the ocean." Eagerly, he would jump up, racing her to the waves. They played tag. Once, pounced on by a large roller, they were both toppled and churned about; and he felt the sliminess of her naked legs sliding between his, the cold woolen pack of her buttocks slamming into his crotch. She surfaced, spitting water and laughing. He swam away from her.

That afternoon, she asked without warning, "Have you found any-one yet?"

He blinked questioningly. She was relaxing on her towel, soaking up the sun. Her eyes were closed. He permitted himself the quickest glance at her body before averting his face.

At his silence, she said, "Have you found a girl?"

"Oh no." He felt himself reddening. It made him angry, to blush so easily. He was glad her eyes were shut. "I . . . don't have the time," he said defensively.

"Yes . . . I suppose I am taking up every free moment. Do you mind?"

"No, no! I'm glad."

"But does it bother you, not having a girl? I mean, of course, some nice clean girl your age."

He saw now that her eyes were opened: that she was watching for his answer. He did not know why, but he interpreted a certain rapacity in her expression, something vaguely analogous to what he had seen in Jimena—molesting as well as embarrassing him.

"Let's go for a swim," he said.

His father interrogated him a day or so later. Manú was up on a croft, stomping round and round the center pole, tamping the hay down while Jacobo pitched it up to him. (Finished, it would look like a beehive; it would cut like soft cheese.)

"Hot work," Manú volunteered, which was rare—the least uninsulting and unprofane comment.

"Yes," said the son.

"Hot work down on the beach?" Manú kept rounding the pole.

Jacobo hoist a fresh shock on the wooden fork. "On the beach?"

"With her—with that foreign cunt!"

Manú had halted. He was looking down at his son.

"You laid her yet?" he asked, pigging his eyes, pulling his lips back from rotting gums.

Jacobo had the fork half raised. He gave it a thrust forward, jerking it so that the hay was thrown instead of being spread on the mound by his father's feet.

"She teaches me," he said.

"What!" The word brimmed with nastiness.

"Reading and writing, what she promised!"

"She *pays* for that! Who are you fooling? Qué coño do you think these foreign women are after?" Suddenly, he raged. "I won't have it, hear? I won't permit it! You want the juice drained out of your big balls, you go where Amadeo goes. Hear me? Hear that?"

All his bantam body trembled with fury.

On the several overcast Sundays, they took shelter in an abandoned shed overlooking the beach, at the very bottom of the farm and well out of sight of the house on the knoll. He hated these sessions. Bad weather brought out the worst of her French temperament. She drove him mercilessly. Sometimes he thought he preferred one of Manú's beatings. She seemed now to take pleasure in humiliating him, staring at him with her pale, exuded eyeballs, smoking and smoking, blowing clouds of smoke into his face as she demanded replies, scolding him for his many errors and clamping the lids of her lips.

"You can be . . . so impossibly thick! It's not worth it, it's simply not worth it!"

"I'm sorry," he said, downcast.

But she railed at him. "How can you Spanish Basques hold your heads so high when most of you know nothing, *nothing!* Here I try to teach you a few dates, and you can't remember them from one week to the next. Here you still stop at the simplest words, and we've gone over them dozens of times! It's the ignorance of the masses that keeps them captive! It's plain, willful ignorance and plain, willful laziness!"

At that moment, a flash of lightning came quavering through the small window, and thunder cracked above them. She was always at grating edge when a storm threatened. This time she actually jumped in her chair.

"Close the window!"

He rose from the barrel they worked at to do so.

"No, leave it open. We'll stifle."

He turned back to her.

"I have such a headache!" she complained.

"Can I bring you some water?"

"That won't help. You can massage my neck."

He went round to her. He had strange emotions as he lifted his hand: distaste, as though he might grasp something unpleasant, he did not know what, and apprehension, nameless. But once taking hold of the back of her neck, at the pivot below the skull, he found the sensation pleasing; because although her neck was short and a little rough and creased by the thickening of middle age (she was thirty-four), it was also supple, and the muscles firm. She let her skull roll back on his fingers as he massaged her, moaning, "That's . . . delicious, delicious. It helps. A great deal. Oh!" She now reached behind her for his free hand, which he gave her. This she carried to her left cheek. "You are . . . good to me, Jacobo, I'm . . . sorry I shouted at you. Will you . . . forgive me?"

"Claro! You had reason to be disgusted." He kept on massaging her neck.

"No . . . never. Depressed. Feeling . . . useless. Larrañaga: he . . . he is my lover, you know that."

He had guessed as much. The term bore little more than abstract meaning for him.

"I miss him, Jacobo."

"I expect you do."

"I don't . . . miss him as much as I should. He's not at all like Diego, tall and strong and beautiful. He's . . . skinny, a bit like your father. But he's a dedicated man, he'll go far in the Party . . . Well, that's fine. Thank you. Back to work!"

By the middle of August, he had progressed. She rewarded him with tales about his family, for which he plied her. He learned how a Rivas forbear had made the Dukes bend the knee. Indulgent, deeming it also useful, perhaps, she overstated the Rivas rôle in events. His pride of family grew. She encouraged it, complimenting him on brushed hair and clean fingernails, filling him with dreams of his part in a millennial future. Of a sudden, he was reading and writing.

That memorable day—when it happened—they had picnicked in a special place he took her to, west of the large beach below the farm. One reached it by climbing first a spur of land that pushed arrogantly into the ocean, its sides sheer and its heights given over to gorse and loose rubble. Ravens rose up as they topped it, falling off the promontory and down-wind like black shaggy sacks with stones in them. "Mais c'est formidable!" she had cried, following the fall of the ravens. Across a diminutive cove stood another headland, equally bleak, swept on high by the wind and pounded at below by massive rollers that shattered themselves against the rocks at the bottom in blizzards of foam dashing skyward before disintegrating back into the wealth of sapphire from which they sprang. A sandbar had been built up between the points. Inside it the water was gentian, lavender, and the clearest and most translucent of aquamarines. The waves were gentled, surging shoreward in long, successive, exhilarating skeins of foam, tracing mesmeric rhythms deep, deep into the recesses of the cove, a grotto between precipices whose rim of rose-gold sand did not come into view until one had negotiated the ten or more switchbacks of an abandoned goat trail.

She was enchanted at every step. Once down on the beach, one had the impression of absolute privacy: one faced a sky and ocean feeling that no one else had ever been there and that no one would ever come.

She tore her tunic off. She went bounding into the surf like a schoolgirl fresh off a holiday bus, prancing as the first waves slapped at her thighs, calling to him to strip his outer clothing quickly and join her. One waded a hundred meters before the water rose above the waist. One swam another two hundred meters before reaching the bar and the depths beyond. Below, against a bottom of granulated marble, fronds the hue of grape juice swayed in silent orchestration. Above, against the ceramic sky, a solitary herring gull chalked its purity. "Ce n'est pas vrai! Ce n'est pas vrai!" She let out a call of unbounded joy, gamboling then in a burst of animal spirits, ducking and diving and shooting up to splash him, years dissolving from her skin and her cheeks flushing with the first really natural color he had seen.

Back on the beach, she chattered a torrent, telling him about her four-year-old son, who was so handsome, so like his father, telling him about her childhood in Biarritz as the daughter of a French-Basque pediatrician who corresponded with such important people as Codovilla and Ernö Gerö, who, she explained, had prepared the way in Spain for the Party. Oh, it was going to be wonderful: when all the toil and sacrifice of so many heroic men bore fruit! Suddenly she could not wait to go to Mieres and meet her lover, who was organizing the miners and who, poor thing, was probably worn to a shadow!

Jacobo listened to her. The mention of Larrañaga, and of leaving, saddened him, inflicting the sharp pangs of an emotion he could not identify. But as she burbled on, sometimes in French, sometimes in Basque, telling him how she had written Larrañaga about his brother and what a golden era lay ahead for such as him and all the world, her excitement infected him. He would take part, somehow! He would be a somebody in that new world! And perhaps it was this, the chiliastic contagion, that so vivified his mind: because, when they buckled down to work, he read her two whole pages out of the *Manifesto* without once stumbling, and wrote for her a page and a half of dictation in laborious but accurate enough scrawl. At that, she clasped him by the ears, pulling him toward her and lowering her plump little breasts to his face, kissing him on the head. *"There!"* she exclaimed, pushing him away. "I *never* thought we'd do so well! Oh, it's a wonderful day! Come, let's swim. No more work. We'll celebrate!"

She taught him a game: he was to try to catch her toes in the water while she tried to catch his. She laughed. They both laughed. It was ridiculous. They circled each other like spawning trout. When she lunged for his legs, he whipped them away. When he dived for hers, she somersaulted over him. But his hands were marvelously fast. He caught her by an ankle, and then by the other. He had won!

They dried themselves, running, snapping towels at each other. As if famished, they fell on the picnic hamper, cold Spanish tortilla and peppery chorizo de lomo. Between them, they squeezed a whole bladder of thin cool wine empty, laughing when she missed her mouth and trickled the pink stream over her chin.

She began packing away the remains. "Don't go!" he blurted at her. "Don't leave ever!"

She looked up from the hamper. Her lips twitched in that odd, repellent smile. "There are weeks left," she said softly, thoughtfully. Then she stretched out on her towel, turning her back to him.

He flung himself belly-down on his towel, couching mouth and nose under an armpit and drifting after a while into sleep. Once he roused, to see her sitting up on the rim of her bottom, hugging her knees to her breast and staring out into the ocean with a pensive frown. He napped again.

He came to with a start, the shadow of a cloud cold on his back. She was gone.

Flipping over, he jumped to his feet. Where was she? Bare and empty the beach on both sides. Her towel showed only damp half moons where she had sat.

Footprints led to the incoming tide. His eyes swept the horizon. Terror gripped him.

She had swum far, far out, farther than he had ever seen her go; beyond the bar, beyond the protection of the points. There were currents out there, as powerful as the one that earlier in the summer had nearly taken him. She knew that!

He smashed through the first hundred meters of knee- and waist-high breakers. Then he flung himself into the waves. For a while, he felt as if he were skittering over them, so violent were the thrusts of his arms and legs. Then, passing the bar, colder, denser water enveloped him. Sooner than he expected—not actually beyond the points—he reached her: to find her floating on her back, bone-white, painted little prehensile toes up, head turned to him with a faint smile.

He jerked his eyes away. But the scene had been burned into his brain cells; blue-black water, a porcelain sky scudded with small, static clouds, her legs browned to four inches above the knees, the incredible whiteness of her naked thighs and torso, the prickly bush of dark hair just surfacing, and her paps suspended by the sea, pink and white and almost as translucent as the sails of man-o'-wars. Her bathing suit floated beside her, trailed out by the tide, held by a little finger hooking one of its straps.

"Did you think I was drowning?" she warbled, apparently amused.

He tread water, unable to answer.

"You seemed . . . sound asleep," she called out then, the sea breeze whistling her words away. He sensed that she smiled; he did not look. "It's . . . a wonderful feeling, to float like this . . . dream . . . buoyed . . . sun beating . . . on your body. You . . . try it."

He was wearing, as usual, an ordinary cotton undershirt and a pair of wool trousers cut off at the knees.

The first of her next words were muffled by the slap and swirl of a swell and the distant pounding of breakers on the rampart points.

He caught, ". . . suit too. No one will see you here—no one but your old teacher."

He seemed to watch himself obeying, drinking brine as he kicked his trousers off. Trunks and undershirt he bunched in one hand. And it did feel good, the freedom of it, the swirling of the sea between his legs.

"Float on your back," he heard her command.

But he kept himself vertical, still looking aside, suffering from a torment of sensations.

He heard her laugh. "Come," she then called to him, "do what I tell you!"

Scant meters now separated them. "I . . . don't want to," he called back wretchedly.

"Do what your teacher says!"

"No!" A swell had washed her closer. "I *can't!*" he cried.

There was silence above the whine of the breeze and the thudding breakers. He heard what sounded like a chuckle.

"I see that you can't!" she murmured quite close to him. She laughed, a peal of merriment. Then one of her hands pounced on his bundle of clothes, tugging and ripping them out of his grasp.

"Give them back!" he shouted, revolving on his axis to address her.

She was no longer on her back; she was treading water also, bobbing inches in front of him, her shoulders—round and browned and freckled—naked above the sea, her breasts alternately submerged and exposed, her blue-white torso and legs ghostly.

"I won't!" She stuck her tongue out at him.

"Give them back! You must! Please!"

"Get them from me!" And she gave a kick away from him.

He lunged after her. She was quick. He was immeasurably faster. He caught and gave a mighty yank at his clothes: such a tug that he drew her over and on top of him. He sank beneath her weight, hearing her laughter as he went down, pushed farther by one of her hands and a shove of both her feet. Water sluiced into his mouth and nose and ears. He came up choking. She remained in possession of his clothes. Furiously, he went after them. They grappled. Their arms and legs locked. And then they were both sinking as his lips forced the clamp of her mouth open.

This occurred in the last week of August, when the finest weather comes to the Cantabrian. During the next three weeks, Jacobo sneaked out of the stable every night: no longer to run up into the hills. And then, between one day and the next, she was gone for good.

FIVE

Beached

She left Sacedón, as, from the beginning, she knew that she must: and as she thought, never to return; but pleased in the quick of her genital hunger by having feasted on the blooming staff and sap of her young peasant's virility, and eased in spirit by having conscientiously imparted to him the rudiments of learning, as well as having enlisted him in the service of, or at least predisposed him to, the great dynamism of the twentieth century. It was not within her to foresee his torment at her departure. She had initiated him into paradise, and then abruptly yanked it away, leaving him where he had begun: in a stable reeking with offal and buzzed over by flies, and bound to an existence (now intolerable) from which he would never escape. If she imagined his condition at all, it was romantically. Beyond her imaginative powers was the turmoil into which she had thrown him in body and soul: the harrowing nights he was to spend for many, many months; and, when receiving not so much as a note from her, his disillusionment.

She had fallen on his body as if it were her last opportunity. She was amazed, and then delighted, by the novelty he introduced her to (she had no way of knowing that from his father's example he assumed his way to be the orthodox one). It gave her convulsive satisfaction to be really mounted, releasing the strong currents of her masochism. She became as excited inverting the procedure, establishing her dominance by making him lie on his back while she rotated herself upon him. She exercised her sadism besides, so that by the end of the first week Jacobo was a mass of scratches and contusions.

Not since Muñoz had she feasted so well. A homely girl of petty bourgeoisie background and mediocre abilities, Michelle grew up the only child of a tyrannical father who exorcised his own mean success in life through rantings of a radical nature. A Jew, born and reared in hopelessly, eternally anti-Semitic Europe, the class he despised was actually that whose acceptance he most desired. He was unable to object when Michelle escaped into the Party.

At first, the Party gave her a sense of mission and importance. Under its auspices, she went to the Sorbonne. But after eight years of teaching during the day and distributing leaflets at night, she lost fervor. Or so I gather. From what I've picked up here and there about Muñoz, he was the Galahad to the rescue of her dreams, a swashbuckling sort of fellow, physically attractive in the matinee style of second-run movie houses. He was erratic, superficial, and a scapegrace—really an odd fish in the professionalism of revolutionary cadres, which was why he was indeed betrayed, but by his comrades. She fell under his spell nonetheless, as did most of the other female functionaries, whom he flattered, pinched, bedded, or promised to with cavalier unconscionableness. Michelle he gave a casual tumble late one night in the printing room of Toulouse headquarters. For her, it was a visitation from Zeus; for him, it was a surprise. He was brutal with women. The homelier they were, and the more obsequious, the more was he driven to mistreat them. She thrived on it. He put her through paces learned in brothels from Tangiers to Marseilles. He tried to outrage her self-respect but could not. Her readiness for perversion amazed him. Soon, with the logic of vice, he came to prefer Michelle to the cooler attractions of the prettiest secretaries or waitresses. And, when she suggested it (not the Party), he heard himself saying, "All right, if you want—we'll get married." There ensued, for Michelle, three months of bliss. Muñoz volunteered for Santo Domingo.

News of his demise came after her son was born. She received it as a judgment of God, or Marx. She accepted Maurice Thorez's letter of profound regret with all gratitude and humility. Because she was conscience-stricken. Not only had she wavered before Muñoz rescued her from doubt; afterward she had been lax in her duties and even sometimes failed to report for work, dallying in bed and demanding of her exhausted lover yet more. Her career since had been one of total dedication. Through the Party she would build a cenotaph to her husband's memory; and it was as much pride of connection as convenience that led her to suggest the thesis on Sacedón. She had by this time struck up with Larrañaga, whose Marxist purity she respected, feeling that to submit to his occasional needs was abnegation worthy of Muñoz's supreme sacrifice. But neither heart nor loins were ever to be satisfied again.

For her, Jacobo was an idyl, a last song to youth and passion. With him she practiced the many rites buried with Muñoz. When he refused to attempt anal coitus (her personal hygiene all over was as appalling as suggested by the nicotine encrusted on her teeth), she slapped his face with all her might; and when he reacted to her blows with enraged lust, throwing her on the warm sand or on the dank humus of the shed, and driving between her thighs in the conventional manner, she shrieked in a feigned frenzy of fear and pain that perhaps thrilled her beyond anything.

Many variations on the melody of sex she played. To satisfy booksellers I'll instance such as the Hindu *sakhr* and the quite preposterous *li-haing* of Cantonese origin, but I'm blasted (in preference to being damned) if I'll go into them. Jacobo did for the most part as he was bid, sometimes with wonderment, more often with growing moral qualms, and once (*li-haing*) with a dislocated hip he had to have secretly set to rights by the vet. She was, however, greatly tender between bouts, hugging him to her, pressing his face between her pouter pigeon breasts while with unwearying wonderment she tickled and fondled and re-explored his magnificent young body, murmuring every soft endearment. Toward the end, he became grateful for these interludes. After three weeks, he was as physically enervated as Muñoz had been, so that when at work he had hardly the strength to keep pace with the ox. He realized soon that his father guessed what was going on; and that avarice (she continued paying the fee for Jacobo's Sunday afternoons) only just overcame his jealousy. "What's a French coño like? Sweet? I *forbid* it, hear!" One more *cassus belli* between them.

Sucked dry of his juices he might be; but when she vanished, continence became at once unbearable. It was during that autumn of 1934 that two of the four sisters who remained at home married, straightening fences by doing so; but one couple came to live in the Rivas farmstead, displacing Amadeo, who was consigned with Jacobo to the stable below. This was a bad situation all the way round. Amadeo had easier access to the cider barrel; he was ossified nightly. Then, Jacobo was tormented by hearing the young couple quake the floorboards above him. His witch-like sister, Jimena the humpback, was also aroused, returning to her attacks. Amadeo put a stop to her intrusions the fourth time (he was coming in from his whore, half-soused only; he caught her slipping down the ladder to prey on the sleeping Jacobo), clamping her neck in his strong fingers and telling her in a soft, boozy, affectionate whisper that next time he would squeeze the life out of her. She believed Amadeo. But on All Soul's Eve, when he was out; when their mother was snoring in bed, drunk herself; when the other single sister was innocently in dreamland and the married sister and her husband had terminated an especially prolonged session of rutting and also slept; Jacobo, from his pallet in the eighth stall, next to the faithful old ox, heard the unmistakable rhythmic thumping start up above him from where he guessed was the kitchen. Had he known how, he could have wept.

He never resorted to onanism; it was a point of pride. Besides, all the young men who played on the scratch soccer team had been warned against it by the coach. The home atmosphere began to help after a while. He conceived disgust. Thinking back to the fading image of the Frenchwoman, an irreality inhabited her, and disgust here also entered. He began to perceive that he had been cannibalized. More clearly in retrospect did he find such aberrations as *sakhr* repulsive; and more and more did her stained teeth appropriate memory, so that he came to associate that sight with the vision of her inviting him unnaturally into an orifice whose taste and odor returned to him with a recollective retch. He could not help believing those things wrong, and that she had abused him. This belief grew with his moral remorse.

There is a worm in every earthly paradise, often a big one. After the very first go, on the beach of the hidden cove, Jacobo felt the gloom of damnation. He tried to ignore it the days following. But one moonlit night, when he had sneaked out to the abandoned shed below the farm, meeting her there (she brought blankets, wine, and cheese; he was expected to bring undiminished ardor), his melancholy was pronounced. With but little animation he performed *sakhr;* with no spunk at all, scarcely two hours later, he was pleading against a repetition of *li-haing.* When she proceeded to the trussing of *ho chi thieu* (the really detestable Indo-Chinese inversion of New Caledonian uterophagia, a subliminal form of cannibalism), he protested.

"But what is the matter with you?" she mouthful-mumbled.

He jerked away from her. He ripped off the cruel elastic band and with a yank released himself of the knouts.

She remained hovering near him—over him—still in demi plié. There was a most awful stink from the cabrales cheese, the Cantabrian Roquefort for which he used to salivate. It smelled of sweaty feet. It smelled . . .

"Come, Jacobo! I was just getting ready to . . ."

"No!"

She did a relevé. He felt better. But he could see her in the single beam from the hutch window: staring down at him, her sprung belly lurid above its dark bush, her paps opalescent, and her areolae dark and engorged.

The nubs popped. She was angry. "What is it! Have you been going to your brother's whore? Is that the low kind of thing you like? Or is it Jimena you want! Or . . . or . . . are you tired of me!"

"None of those things!"

Quickly, she squatted: intruding a hand where she so much liked to, caressing him, trying to revive him, her lips unclamped and her teeth agates, white and brown.

She had might as well fondled a dead squid.

"Are you unwell?" she asked, perturbed.

"No."

"Then *what* is the matter, cher Jacobo, mon petit choux, rêve de mon coeur. Tell your old teacher," she said coaxingly, "tell Michelle, who loves you so dearly, who could . . . who will . . . mmmmmmmmmmmmeat you like an éclair in one-mmmmmmmmmmmmm*bite!*"

"Ouch!"

"Sweet, sad, silly, squishy little wormmmmmmmmmmmm!"

"Please stop it! It's wrong, what we do."

She sat back on her haunches, astonished. "Wrong? Why, what-ever . . ."

But he had started now. "We will go to Hell, Michelle! We will burn!" A shiver quaked down his belly. "We will burn both of us forever!"

Michelle clapped her hands to her cheeks. She began to laugh. But she saw how serious it was to Jacobo. And so she took one of his limp paws, pressing it to the twin bubbles of her bosom, all motherly solicitude.

"Cher enfant, it is *that* which worries you! Oh, I *am* relieved. Only that."

"But it's enough, isn't it!"

"Shhh, now." She looked on him with profound commiseration. "Do you trust me?"

"Y-Yes."

"Am I not more educated than you?"

"Yes."

"Am I not more educated than your father and mother?"

"Oh yes!"

"And the curate?"

"I . . ."

"Jacobo!"

"I . . . I suppose so."

"And does not the Bishop of Bilbao live in a palace, surrounded by flunkeys, and do you not sleep in a stable?"

"Yes."

"And is Rome not the seat of reaction? Does not the Pope sit on a throne, covered with jewels, while the workers do not have enough to eat? Be scientific, Jacobo!"

"I . . ."

"Will you not believe your loving Michelle, who thinks only of your good, that religion is a plot against the poor, there is not a *scrap* of truth in it? Who saw Christ rise? Two hysterical women—saw what they called an angel (an *angel!*) who is supposed to have told them that he rose. They were lying, of course. If they were not lying, they suffered from hallucinations, what actually happened was that Joseph of Arimathaea, a member of the bourgeoisie, a rich man, stole the body and posted a young man dressed as an angel to impress the silly women. One *must* be scientific, Jacobo! Who is supposed to have seen him afterward? Why, his apostles, ignorant peasants and fishermen, like you, suffering from mass hallucinations. Oh, how superstition preys on you poor, ignorant, frightened . . . Tell me, when the current took you, were you not scared?"

He was ashamed to admit it, but he did.

"Why?"

"I . . . I thought I would drown."

"But would you not have gone to Heaven?"

"Well, I'd been to confession not very long before . . ."

"Then would you not have gone to Heaven?"

"I guess so—after Purgatory. After a long time in Purgatory."

"But you are not sure."

"Well . . ."

"Is Heaven not a good place?"

"Yes."

"Is it not better than here?"

"Much!"

"Then why should you be frightened of dying? I'll tell you why. Because you do not really believe in Heaven. You do not really believe in God."

"That's not true!"

She smiled pityingly. "Is God good?"

"Of course!"

"Do you love him?"

"What a foolish thing to ask!"

"Then why are you not in a seminary, studying to be a priest? If you *truly* love and believe in God, and God is good, should you not give up everything for him? Did not Jesus tell a young man that? If a person really loves the workers of the world, he joins the Party. It is the same thing, Jacobo. In your heart of hearts, you do not believe in God or you would not have been frightened of drowning and you would have given everything up for him as I have given up everything—everything!—for the Party. Because I *really* and truly believe in it. Nobody, Jacobo, but old women and uneducated people can do anything but laugh at the stories about Adam and Eve and Jonah in the whale—imagine! you know what happens to flesh in a stomach!—and the sun stopping for Joshua and all those fairy tales about Hell to scare children with. Not even the Jesuits believe in that."

"The Jesuits!"

She was amazed, genuinely astonished, by the depths of his ignorance. He was no more than an animal, when one came down to it: a great, dumb, magnificently hung beast—a bear trained for her pleasure.

One of her hands went a-berrying.

"What do you imagine? They are hypocrites, Jacobo! Your father would tell you that. They threaten the masses with Hell and dope them with dreams of Heaven to keep them in chains. But do you know something? The honest ones—a few high up in the Order—are with *us!*"

His eyes popped as though they would come out of their sockets; and she noticed, with satisfaction, that his member, around which she had sneaked an encouraging hold, gave a little lift.

"You are surprised?" He was dumbfounded: naturally. "They are our biggest hope, Jacobo. They are not only intellectuals but militant besides. Jesuits and Communists have the same sort of mind. More and more of them—secretly, of course—are joining us. Would it surprise you again, Jacobo, if I were to tell you that on the Pope's *Curiae*—that is his special council, his agintari—we have two Party members, both cardinals?"

"That can't be true!"

She smiled superiorly. (He had jumped again.) She did not actually know for a fact that the *Curiae* had been infiltrated, but it was reasonable to assume that the Party was trying. "Be intelligent about such things, Jacobo, I beg you. We infiltrate capitalist governments all over the world, do we not? Would we, Marxist-Leninists, not make a special objective of the Church, our greatest enemy? Many, many of your brighter seminarians and newly ordained priests are members of the Party. But enough of this! You are no longer frightened, are you my petit choux? Come, cher, cher enfant, just a teensy-*weensy* little *bite!*"

Despite her scientific arguments, and the superior intelligence he could no less than defer to, he remained stubborn in his superstitious ignorance, and unpersuaded that their Maker did not frown wrathfully indeed on what went on between them, especially on some of the things that went on and on and on between them, so that he was sometimes not sure which end was up nor which was whose. With the passing of time, remorse flowered into contrition. It was now the season of Epiphany. Christmas Eve approached, when even Manú attended the Cockcrow Mass and gave each of his children ten céntimos to spend as they chose. Jacobo could no longer bear it. He wanted to be cleansed. He wanted to receive.

The crowds at this Mass, by their coughings and shufflings, scraping chairs across the flags and creaking the pews, insulated sinners in cocoons proof against the cupped ears of most of the old crones. Still was his confession agony for Jacobo. Perhaps because of his jaws-of-Hell expression, he had attracted a hag like a burr on his back. Her breath came rancid over his left shoulder; an elbow as sharp as a fractured femur kept digging him in the kidneys. "Speak up!" "Yes, do!" said the doddering old curate, whose hearing was no whit improved by the hubbub and commotion. "Eh? Eh?" he cried incredulously. "Saints, what's *that!*" croaked the hag. "I said, Father . . ." "Speak up, boy! Curse the racket!" "This woman, Father . . ." "What woman? Speak up! Speak up!" *"Do,* por el amor de Dios!" chorused the hag "—*All* you young people mumble!" "I *said, Father* . . ." "We heard what you *said,*" she croaked again, "it's what you *did* we didn't catch." "Luz del Mar," exclaimed the curate, "be off!" "But he's barely begun!" "Be off with you, shame on you, I'll give you ten decades a night for the next two months!" She scuffled away. *"Now,* Jacobo, what is it you are telling me? What is all this about *sakhr* and *li*-what's-it?"

In the old way, in detailed fashion: exactly what and how many times. "You did this with a woman!" cried the old man, banging at the wax in his good ear with a palm. Jacobo had already been accused of attempted incest. Deplorable though that might be, the sin was not unknown. But the acts Jacobo now described wholly horrified the old man. And when he learned that Jacobo's partner had been—had had to have been!—an alien and atheist to boot, he wondered whether it were in his province to give absolution; whether these excesses of the greatest depravity would not have to be absolved by the Bishop of Bilbao.

Jacobo begged. His contrition was absolute. It had been an enormous relief to unburden his conscience. He longed now to be loosed. But the curate said he could offer no more than a contingent absolution. He warned Jacobo that to receive under these circumstances risked sacrilege.

"But when will I ever see the Bishop!" Jacobo cried.

"Hijo, I don't know. He's almost as old as I am, and he doesn't travel any more."

"But Don Alonso, you can't leave me this way!"

"Jacobo, it was your weakness and that woman who put you in this situation, not I. Don't you see what that she-devil was trying to do? That's what she was, an agent of Satan, perhaps Satan himself in abominable disguise! She was trying all the time to separate you from Holy Mother Church, from Grace; and she has partly succeeded."

The Goats

For Jacobo, his failure to gain absolution had two enduring consequences.

The first is this. Deprived of the Host, he was thus as a matter of fact deprived of Grace. And human beings are crippled without Grace, which is another fact.

Christians—Spaniards—will know what I am talking about. Since most of you whom I am addressing (my English and American brethren) are pagans, and therefore barbarians, and as a consequence unable to recognize reality when it smacks you in the face, I am obliged to explain. (Forgive an old man his share of pedantry; Victoria reigned when I was born). Namely: the common paradox of life is that we, in essential need of God, and all the more so when having sinned, are by sin separated from God and eventually come to feel in our worst real need no need; and slacken in faith; and fall off; and awaken one day with no sense of the divine within us, and no moral apprehension of sin; and may cling stubbornly to ethics for a while; but will with the most implacable inevitability lose that carry-over also; and end up begetting the civilization we know and almost without exception despise.

At least, how else explain the fixes Jacobo Rivas kept getting himself into? Why does he languish in a prison cell today, his mortal existence in the balance? His fall has not been all downhill, so to speak. He has skidded into the deeps across a . . . well, a sea of cordilleras. Jacobo's very blood helped prevent total separation. He clung to what now did deteriorate into (as Michelle Muñoz would have it) superstitious regard for the essential sacraments, but such regular obligations as morning and evening prayers and Sunday Mass lost for him their necessariness, which tolled for the future a loss of their meaning. This took time, of course. Just bear in mind that beginning in his twentieth autumn, the sense of God's quotidian indispensableness began weakening, so that if the ground beneath his feet seemed a little firmer than before, the sky above his head had lowered.

The second consequence was this: blaming the Frenchwoman for his spiritual halfway house, he held in ultimate distrust all notions coupled with atheism. He held her personally responsible for what happened to José María, his brother.

On 5 October 1934—some three weeks after that Sunday when Jacobo had hurried to meet his succubus in their private cove; and had waited for her all afternoon; and by sunset had known that she was never to come again—the Socialist workers' movement, the UGT, declared a general strike. Catalonia pounced on the opportunity to declare herself independent. In Asturias, all factions of the radical left—Anarchists, Socialists, and Communists—united in rebellion against the Republic.

Larrañaga had done his work. Miners 30,000 strong rose up. They seized dozens of towns and villages. They marched on the crucial ports of Oviedo and Gijón, investing them. A total of 1,600 Government troops defended. Clearly, they were doomed. The best the Government could muster was a relief column of scarcely 200 men.

In alarm, Republican leaders called upon a strange, quiet fellow, a Galician, reputedly a Monarchist, who from his relatively obscure post as chief of Spain's new military academy had been since 1928 the silent watcher of events; meanwhile, however, steeping himself in books on history and statecraft. He had been a hero, successively Spain's youngest major, colonel, and general, a brilliant tactician who during the Riff wars had proved himself an audacious and invariably successful commander.

But could even Francisco Bahamonde Franco pull his beseechers out of the fire they had themselves helped kindle? Where were his means? The Army had been disarticulated under Manuel Azaña's administration. Troops were untrained and ill equipped; most of the deserving officers had been retired or superseded by time-servers. Now how was the Republic to be preserved: before the Catalonians to the east and the miners in the west ignited also the curmudgeonly Basque provinces between them? The whole northern shelf of Spain, from Oviedo to Barcelona, with its precious natural resources and most of the nation's industry, was threatened.

One military unit the Republic had not scrambled: the North African corps, whose ferocious Moors had been disciplined by Franco himself. From Madrid, acting virtually as Chief of Staff, he called on these legions, placing them under the command of Colonel Yagüe, an old comrade. Ships were dispatched to bring the troops up from the Canaries, over a thousand miles down Africa's Atlantic coast. Patxi Rivas took part in the mission. Anxious days went by. The miners dynamited their way into the centers of the besieged cities. The wires to Madrid were piteous with calls for help. Redoubt after redoubt fell. Last defenders were massacred.

Franco sat stolidly at his headquarters desk: passive, imperturbable, exhibiting for the first time on the home front his total self-possession, by not so much as a raised voice betraying his concern, but all the while observing the Republican leaders about him, these political amateurs, these ideological fanatics ever jockeying for power, blundering, letting Spain go to rack and ruin while they plotted and counterplotted, so that even his beloved Galicia, his patria chica, was being put to the torch; who then, when the crisis of their own making flared up, came squealing to the Army they so despised, came helpless with frantic faces and leaking bladders to what survived of that glorious national institution whose officers they had humiliated and whose best regiments they had disbanded. Franco soothed them; what he thought about them he kept to himself.

At the eleventh hour, the first naval transports flung out their bowers at El Musel: the Alpine battalion, the 5th and 6th Banderas of the Legion, and a Tabor of Regulars, herded down the gangplanks. It was the tenth of October. Eight thousand rebels were already in Oviedo; in the Gijón area, "libertarian communism" had been proclaimed. But after a week of bitter fighting, the Army—mostly Moors, officered by Spaniards—crushed the miners, their last stronghold in Mieres being overwhelmed on the eighteenth, thirteen days after the start of the insurrection.

Franco was hailed as the Savior of the Republic.

There were reprisals. The Moors, accustomed to a tribal style of warfare, ran amuck. Yagüe did little to contain them. Churches had been burned. In a recall of Visigothic savagery, the miners had raped nuns and slaughtered priests. Blood-curdling stories abounded. Two at least are verified. A security guard was burned alive. Three little girls were trampled to death. The "center-left" British historian Hugh Thomas mentions other atrocities. The Nationalist (Franco) historian Joaquín Arrarias has admitted that most of them are not (now anyhow) verifiable; but in the hysteria of events, everyone had a tale of horror to tell, and Yagüe pursued suspects with indiscriminate vengeance. One of the men executed was José María Rivas, who had crawled out of his sickbed to take part in the final miners' defense of Mieres.

The Basques had refrained from rebellion. But to Manú, José María's father, he became a hero. José María had done honor to Basque-land's spirit of resistance. Even José Ybarra, the mayor recently released from prison, came to pay his respects; but he was turned away at the stoop. Manú was not about to bury the hatchet between the two clans. It was all these little hatchets, remote in time, perhaps, but buried indelibly in the brain pans of so many skulls, that in the great forge of history were being melted down and molded into the gigantic axes with which Spaniards were soon to clobber one another.

Franco was rewarded—by being named Commander-in-Chief of the armed forces in Morocco, with a headquarters base conveniently removed from Spain in the North African city of Ceuta. Grateful to him as the present Government might be, his words in Oviedo on the twenty-fourth of October may have struck something of a chill in their blood. He had said to a reporter, "The war in Morocco, with the Regulares and the Tercios, had a certain romantic air, an air of reconquest. But this war is a frontier war, and the fronts are Socialism, Communism, and any other forms that attack civilization to replace it by barbarism." He could have ordered Yagüe to restrain the Moors. He could have stopped the summary executions sooner than he did. General Franco was evolving the conviction that less than two years later would lead him into rebellion: in his mind, he stood for Spain and Western Civilization. To such as Manú Rivas, Franco was the Devil incarnate.

Jacobo did not project into national politics. His thoughts were of José María. His brother, lungs diseased, would have died eventually anyhow; the cause he had sacrificed himself for was good. But had he, Jacobo, helped precipitate his brother's death? He was by this time (November of '34) suffering from remorse. Not even a note! He had already begun to sense that for Michelle he had ceased to exist on the morning she boarded her bus for Mieres. It was not fair of her. She had fired ambition. She had told him he had a past to redeem and a part to play in the future. But what? Through the unending rainy nights of December and January he struggled with his frustration. He was a Rivas, an hidalgo: his blood the fresh sustaining wine in the veins of dukes. But what of that? Still the youngest son of an impoverished farmer; and no prospects.

As the twilights began to lengthen, he resorted again to his runs into the hills. Sometimes he did not return until well after the fall of night, to be abused by his father for shirking chores. He was now indifferent to Manú's opinion. The father no longer dared strike his giant son, who had entered into physical prime. Broad-faced, clear-eyed, stalwart, Jacobo would have been handsome save for the ready deferentialness of poverty in his stance and a sense of unarticulated disgrace in his expression; the sort of man who when casually offered an apple or glass of wine hesitates before accepting. That spring of 1935, he became known as an expert at "bolos," a tedious form of ninepins practiced all over the North. In pick-up soccer, played generally barefoot on the beach, he assumed his natural position as goalkeeper, his snake-fast reactions drawing attention. But the small triumphs coming his way merely fueled ambition. Manú Rivas resented Jacobo's absences and took no pride in his talents. Not for a moment did he suspect that his son might have the potential for professional play; although soccer, like jai-alai, was a Basque specialty, and the Atlético de Bilbao team a source of immeasurable satisfaction. A child of the poor in Andalusia might aspire to become a bullfighter; the Basque thought of "fútbol."

No more than his father did Jacobo dream he might qualify; nor envision how else he might escape the farm, the burden of whose work he again shouldered when Manú developed hernias. April and May went by. Haying commenced in the middle of June. At night, Jacobo was too exhausted to contemplate studies; he forgot most of what he had been taught, and his mental processes began to atrophy. More and more he wished for solitude. Sundays without exception he fled: to the mountains, where formless dreams would soar as he rested on some wild barren spine of gray-white granite, thinking back to the time when most of the land below had been owned by his clan.

On one of these afternoons, at about four o'clock, a storm drove over from the southwest—grinding out of its Asturian stronghold. It was a sudden, massive congregation of thunderclouds, accompanied by a mighty rush of cold wind. The hills cracked and then rolled with detonations. Lightning fissured the pall, purple and yellow, and Jacobo was drenched by a downpour. He clung to his perch. The wind howled. The wind sought to pluck him off and cast him into the heart of its fury.

There came an explosion of sound and a blinding river of light. Jacobo cried out. A bolt had struck ore in the pinnacle above. The whole cone of rock shivered with such violence that he thought it might disintegrate. He was terrified. He clung all the harder. And then, with the rain now like ten thousand driving needles picking the skin off his body and the wind shrieking about him and the thunder cracking cracking cracking as it smote the mountaintops with sound-splitting bundles of bolts, exultation seized him. He reeled to his feet. He shouted. He shouted above the frenzy of the storm. He sent the storm reeling away from him, driven by his bellows and by the waving of his balled fists.

Down, down, down it went, stampeding over Sacedón and rolling out into the sea. The sun had burst free above him, catapulted into the sky. The sun shone hot above him, secure in a sky bluer than ever before; and he was looking over the fleecy white anvil tops of a tempest in rout, marveling at their serene beauty.

All the world freshened. Never had he seen it so green. It sparkled. He felt as if he could pluck a crag off its base and hurl it as far as the world went.

Poor Jacobo!

In this mood, he started the climb down. Once on the slopes, he flung his legs ahead of him with long, joyous strides. The twin dull turrets of the ducal mense were just in view when he knocked into a girl.

At least, he very nearly did so. He was rounding a bend. She stood on the other side, peering away with a distracted gaze. She was tall and buxom, with wide hips and a straight strong back; and like him, soaked to the skin.

He knew of her: an Ybarra, one of the unlucky families of the clan. Her parents had run an Ultramarinos shop for years, and had thus enjoyed the status of burghers. He remembered seeing her, four or five years before, squeezing blood sausage into the intestinal sheath and expertly twining the spaced knots; and remembered thinking, though she was but twelve or thirteen, that she would grow up a handsome figure of a woman, able to hoist half-hundred kilo sacks of grain or he was mistaken. Then he did not see her again. Something had happened, the shop was auctioned, and the family had sunk to lowly tillers and pasturers of hilltop land.

She had come running out of her cottage and into the storm with no more protection than a shawl. She was searching for her brother.

Jacobo offered to help. She thanked him. They climbed together a hundred or more meters, where the bare rocks began. She spotted her brother first.

He was hobbling along a ledge that traversed a precipice.

"Salvador!" she keened with fear. "Wait! Stop!" And she began running.

Jacobo was transfixed. Now he remembered about Salvador. The boy was well known to all of Sacedón—because of his terrible affliction, a symbol of God's displeasure that prompted pregnant women on encountering him to cross themselves and then spit fiercely over their left shoulders; where, as everyone knew, unclean spirits lurked hoping to pounce on people unawares. But Jacobo ran after her.

Breathless, they reached the boy at just about the same time. His sister was already ordering Salvador back and out of danger. Above them reared a wall of granite; below was a sheer, dizzying fall.

Salvador had been looking for a lost ewe goat, sniffing, locating by a sort of instinct that pebble rolled out of place or that bit of lichen faintly creased by a hoof. The trail had brought him to this frightening ledge. His sister beseeched Salvador to turn back; he shook his horny head with a violent contortion, and out of his eyes Jacobo saw flash a ferocity of purpose. He hobbled ahead. The ledge narrowed and narrowed, reaching a bulge on the face of the cliff where it was less than half a meter wide. Here the girl grasped her brother, catching him by an arm. But Salvador, mewing nearly incomprehensible sounds and wagging a twisted, clawlike hand at the bulge, indicated that the ewe had continued around it. "But you can't follow!" the girl cried furiously, pulling him toward her.

Jacobo said, "I'll go." And he stepped carefully by them.

At the bulge, the ledge narrowed to centimeters. Jacobo worked his way facing the rock, spreading his arms and hands and searching along its surface for fingerholds. A glance down was sufficient to spin his brains. He shut his eyes several moments. Then he went inching ahead.

He negotiated the bulge. The hair on his nape rose.

Not twenty meters beyond, the ledge ended in a pilaster of rock so smooth that no creature—not even a goat—could proceed. With her back to that pilaster, stiff-legged, muzzle lowered and little horns hooking forward, stood the ewe. Between the ewe and Jacobo crouched a lynx.

Just as Jacobo sighted it, the cat wheeled, snarling with sudden fear. It was as trapped as the ewe had been.

And it leaped, coming to its decision before Jacobo could let out a breath. He met that spit of fangs and talons with a sweep of his left arm; and out into space the animal hurtled, screaming and clawing at the air.

Jacobo pressed his brow against the rock. Heart pounded. Not for seconds did he feel the pain of the long tear he had received in the forearm. Then he watched the dark blood welling out, feeling weak at the knees and a bit sick. He gasped. Time passed stilly with the plaint of a distant nightingale. He brought himself under control.

Her danger done, the ewe followed him back around the bulge. There, huddled in one another's arms, Jacobo found the girl and her brother. They were white-faced. They had heard the snarl, the hiss of the leap, and the high-pitched terror of its falling. Upon reaching safe ground, the girl tore strips from one of her petticoats and began binding Jacobo's arm. He, forehead knotting, stared at Salvador. Slowly the question formed on his lips.

"You knew the cat was there," he said.

The boy began slobbering.

"Why didn't you warn me?" Jacobo asked.

With a moan, the boy fell to the ground, arms and legs thrashing. Disgusted, angry, Jacobo swept up Salvador's makhilak and sent it cartwheeling down a ravine. Giving the sister a parting glance, he walked swiftly away.

In town parlance, Salvador was of course lumped with the several village idiots. But the veterinarian had once mentioned to Jacobo that the boy was something called a spastic, suffering from a brain injury that affected his motor muscles. His brittle hands, wrists, and arms were locked into the most grotesque positions, as though in rigor mortis. They shook at times uncontrollably. His claw-hammer-shaped head shook, his tongue was a lump, he slobbered, and brutish sounds—grunts and moans and hair-raising cackles—issued from between lips that writhed as he gasped for oxygen. He mocked—profaned—the human body, that image of God, for which he was as feared as, by some, hated. Pride had driven Salvador onto the ledge; and perhaps a desire to die.

On his runs thereafter, Jacobo took to drifting toward the escarpments and plateaus through which Salvador drove his charges. They sat together, watching the landscape in its perpetual mutations of shadow and sun, each passing phase with its beauty too big for any single soul, expanding chest and heart and spirit with a longing for God knew what, peace, goodness, immortality, rising to them in the sad, purling, thrushlike notes of a hidden ruiseñor, in the bells of sheep and the far-off lowing of cattle. Jacobo became accustomed to Salvador's infirmity; he began to understand the boy's distorted idiom, discovering a sensibility that surpassed his own. It lurked in very bright black eyes, wells liquid with meaning, shared (but not in the same degree; not nearly) by Salvador's sister. She, Marisol, was perpetually worried about her brother— that Salvador might fall from one of his chosen crags and snap the thin sticks of his bones—which was why she so often toiled up the hillsides to check on him. She seemed pleased to find Salvador in Jacobo's company, although she lowered her eyes modestly whenever they met.

August went by. More and more did Jacobo enjoy his crippled companion. Salvador was sensitive to the least mutation of mood; and when Jacobo felt depressed, one of the boy's icy, crooked hands would slip into one of Jacobo's great paws, and squeeze it, and there would come a gurgle of comforting syllables, birdcall tones, brookings, the cough-chuckling of a capercaille, that solitary giant grouse of the wooded mountains, itself so much like the soft low burble of a brook or the sweet musical pattering of raindrops on a canopy of leaves; and Jacobo would feel communicated to him a great tenderness, so that once he gathered Salvador into the brawn of his chest and held him tightly there, feeling surge through his arms a protective anguish as strong as any emotion he had experienced.

Which was why, when he heard the terrible news, he suffered so atrociously.

SEVEN

The Sacrifice

There is a tradition among the Basques, varying with the locality, but practiced still in remote hamlets. It is pagan. At the harvest, a festival is held, lasting as long as a week. Wild pigeons are netted, sometimes by the thousands. There is a stock fair. Teams of oxen compete pulling sledges weighted with boulders. A bowling championship is held, there are sometimes scratch jai-alai matches, and soccer games. Every evening there is dancing, and at midnight fireworks.

Itinerant carnivals roll into town. Booths are set up. Men and boys plink with air rifles at threads from which caramels are suspended. Children fish in troughs for trinkets, using little wooden lollipop sticks with twine and a hook. There are all sorts of rides: the merry-go-round with prancing steeds impaled on candy-striped poles; the Ferris wheel. Mellifluous barkers cadge women into the purchase of ribbons and combs, showing off an innumerable variety of tin openers and potato peelers that are magical in the hands of the demonstrator but never work at home. The men are all half tipsy; the women (in Jacobo's time) are dressed in their gorgeous and elaborate provincial costumes, with white cotton leggings, long and copious velvet skirts in scarlet, blue, or green, squeezed as tight as respiration will allow at the waist, and topped by equally tight but modest bodices that are heavily embroidered.

The festivities are opened in the central town square by officials of the Ayuntamiento, all looking flushed and portentous. If the town is important enough, an ecclesiastical dignitary—perhaps even a bishop— will celebrate solemn High Mass, assisted by the local curate and a bevy of red surpliced boys. From the surrounding hills come farmers and their families, who, during most of the year, live virtually isolated, driving their little milk wagons and towing cattle for display, trade, or sale.

The last day, the local saint's day, the day of the High Mass, is the climax. That is when the "king" of the festival meets his fate. All week long he has been paraded in a brightly painted cart drawn by a pair of white mules whose headbands and tails are braided with red geraniums, his royal way prepared by a court of the fairest lasses and the most stalwart lads. His scepter is a bullrush wreathed with the tassles of maize. His crown is a garland of marigold, and his hair has been sprinkled with the scales of sardines, so that it shines all silver and blue. For seven days, sweets and delicacies have been stuffed into his mouth. He has merely to nod for a mug of frothing cider to be thrust at him, and wherever he passes, people bow low, pelting him with nosegays— laughing boisterously the while. Because it is one of the village idiots who is chosen to reign.

In the autumn of 1935, this lot fell to Salvador Ybarra. There was no one except possibly the vet to distinguish between mongolism and cerebral palsy. The selection was by ballot. It was irreversible. No help that Salvador was a nephew once removed of José Ybarra, the mayor: Sacedón was poor in idiots that year, the new generation had produced fewer, and it was law that no king reigned twice. Marisol wept when the horseman in plumed black cavalier's hat and a swirling black cape galloped up to the homestead, rearing the white-eyed pony back on its shaggy heels as he cast the proclamation onto the mud of the stoop, reining hard about and galloping back down the mountain. She could not bear to look into her brother's eyes, which were ringed with fright and horror, because he knew all about the feast and the honor and what would happen to him. When Jacobo, later on that afternoon, heard, his heart—by far the largest muscle in his body—almost burst. He went pounding up the hills to the Ybarra cottage. One glance at Marisol, and a glance at Salvador . . . Uninvited, he intruded into the cottage, to find mother and father sitting near the hearth, heads bent in anguish and resignation. "Hide him!" Jacobo cried. "Let me take him into the hills and hide him!" They thanked the young man, Rivas that he is, but they shook their heads. It was the Custom. Custom was not to be denied.

All that week, Salvador presided. He managed his office with unwonted poise, ignoring cheers and jeers as he garlanded the team of winning oxen and handed prizes to the owners of the champion cow or bull or hog. Summoning what must have been a tremendous force from within, he managed to subdue most of his facial contortions. He drooled only every now and then, although whenever to the delight of children, whose peals of merriment and pointing fingers he seemed not to mind. Day by day, however, the terror masked behind his eyes mounted; and Jacobo, watching, felt his tendons swell and blood go rushing into his brain. As much as possible, he stayed away from the festivities, forfeiting his chance of dancing with Marisol; who, of course, whatever she felt, had to take part. Nothing could forestall, abridge, or abrogate the rites. From beginning to end, they were observed.

At sundown on the last day, Salvador was escorted to the town square. In front of the Ayuntamiento and across from the church, carpenters had hammered together a platform. It was in the form of a squat, flat-topped Roman bridge, with a landing to the rear for Salvador's throne. The structure was festooned with autumnal blossoms. It was hung with the fruits of the season: ripe red tomatoes on their stalks, plump pumpkins, leathery long-necked calabashes, mottled green melons, and large, round, luscious-looking apples. With all decorum, Salvador was seated. His court, after sprinkling him with flower petals, withdrew, dividing by sex down the stairs and posting themselves at the foot of the dais like sentinels. Salvador was looking very pale, now. He had begun to tremble, and his limbs to twitch. More than 2,000 souls had assembled. He looked down on 2,000 ruddy, smiling faces. The great bronze bells of the church tower began clamoring. One by one, led by the agintari, women and men, young and old, trooped up the stairs from the left, reached the landing, bent their right knee to Salvador, and then proceeded down the flight of stairs to the right. Not until the last person had paid homage did the bells cease tolling. There was silence. A river of expectation ran through the crowd, and a rumble of talk that grew and grew. Then, suddenly, at a signal, rockets streamed into the purple sky, exploding with hollow booms and showering the canopy with brilliant gold, silver, red and blue sparks. Battery after battery went up, in a gorgeous display, extruding gasps of admiration from 2,000 throats. Night fell with a clap.

All grew still. Above, bats and martins swooped. From the belfry, pigeons cooed. Little more than a murmur emanated from the crowd. Necks were craned to the balustrade of the town hall, above Salvador, where the council had gathered. José Ybarra, sweeping the multitude with his eyes, then glancing at the old curate (who smacked at the wax clogging his good ear in conformity), let a white handkerchief flap over the railing.

Salvador shrieked. His cry was scattered into atoms by the roar of the crowd. All surged forward. In mock panic, the king's court fled. Shouting, a pack of burly youths raced for the stairs of the dais, people massing and pressing behind them. Two reached the landing at just about the same time. Arms raised, they lunged at a Salvador now rigid in his sacrificial seat.

And that was when it happened. Skulking underneath the platform throughout the ceremony had been Jacobo. He had heard the boom of the last rocket; he had endured he knew not how the heart-stopping silence that followed; and he had felt to his marrow the famished bestial growl erupting on the signal of the white handkerchief. Lifting his hands to the rear edge of the platform, he swung himself up. At the very moment of the lunge of the two youths, Jacobo came at them from behind the throne, bulling them back against their fellows.

Everybody halted. There, in command of the landing, covering Salvador, Jacobo stood. He seemed to have reared up from nowhere, feet planted ten inches apart, oaken legs rooted—calling out of a strangled throat, *"Don't anybody try . . . Don't one of you touch him!"*

The shock of this rupture in ritual lasted moments. Salvador, behind Jacobo, struggled with his tongue, urging, "Go, g-go, they'll k-k-k-kill you!" Because the king had to be sacrificed, his crown torn off, his scepter dashed to the ground, his face spat upon, and his writhing body dragged through the multitude to be reviled and pelted by dung and kicked and slapped and finally dumped atop the other garbage of an abandoned quarry. Next year's crops depended on it. But the young men on the flights of stairs to Jacobo's left and right did not move. Below him, the crowd gawked. From above, mouths agape, hung the astonished heads of the town's council. The stench of cordite was thick in everyone's nostrils.

Then, from somewhere in the middle ranks of the mob came a long, quavering, "You ninny, get down from there!" It was Manú Rivas, mortified. His voice seemed to wake José Ybarra out of a daze, and he called from the gallery, "Jacobo, don't be foolish!" But Jacobo seemed deaf, his great chest heaving, mouth, nostrils, and eye sockets black hollows on a broad pale face. "Do what must be done!" José Ybarra ordered the youths on the stairs. They responded with a tentative advance, recoiling at once as Jacobo, come alive, dealt a massive stamp on the boards of the platform and bawled at them, *"No! Leave him free!"*

But he was no leader of men. There was appeal in this cry, mighty though the lungpower impelling it. Jacobo was rushed from both sides. A thickset butcher's son was first to reach him. Jacobo plucked the fellow up in his huge arms and hurled him into the faces of those below. The next four he grabbed and disposed of in similar fashion, and there was at least one crack of a collarbone. The people yelled in a crescendo of outrage. Above them all the voice of Manú Rivas pierced, shrilling obscenities. Now hordes of hardy peasants, young and middle-aged, went crowding up both flights of stairs. Jacobo was a bear, ferocious, looming above a pack of wolves, but they were too many. A club landed on his skull. He shuddered, buckling. With cries of rage and vengeance, his attackers swarmed over him. The man with the club raised it once more, high: and himself fell stunned to the floor of the landing.

The yokes used in the north of Spain are blocked out of dense pine. A yoke may weigh fifteen or more pounds. The yoke that landed on the head of Jacobo's attacker weighed at least that, and it was wielded by Marisol Ybarra. She had followed Jacobo's initiative, working her way under the dais and clambering up from behind. She had been followed by Amadeo, who was gloriously drunk, who pushed the yoke onto the platform after her and then struggled aboard himself, each hand armed with a fat wineskin. He swayed on the platform—behind the throne—rollicking with joy as he boffed the pig's bladders down on heads poking up from below. He was not seen by the people. It was Marisol who impressed them. She towered over most men. Under the torch lights, her black eyes flashed like gunpowder igniting. Her brawny arms bulged with muscle, and her bosom heaved with imperial and manifestly murderous emotion. With one sweep of her yoke, she cleared four men off the landing, fracturing a skull and smashing several teeth.

Her intervention gave Jacobo time to recover. He rose, shaking off an assailant who as much clutched at him for protection against Marisol as to fight. The moment she saw Jacobo on his feet, Marisol thrust the yoke at him. She stepped back. Amadeo thrust his wineskins into her hands. He contented himself with stamping on people's fingers and aim-

ing kicks at their faces, simultaneously gathering tomatoes and calabashes
and pumpkins and with rapturous howls lobbing them at anyone he saw.
Jacobo dominated the center of the landing, using the yoke like a boom,
in single swipes eliminating or knocking off their feet half a dozen or
more men. Those who were not wholly put out of commission were sand-
bagged by Marisol, who also traveled from wing to wing of the dais
and methodically repelled boarders.

Side by side and back to back the three fought. For a time, they
had the advantage. The very numbers of the indignant crowd worked
against them. But they were now coming from all sides. Amadeo was
the first to fall, uttering a reproachful little clucking sound as a rock
bounced off his forehead and he toppled like a trained gymnast over
the edge of the platform and under the dais, where he snoozed in comfort
and safety the rest of the night. Marisol was overpowered next: by her
own father, who managed to noose her in a rope, dragging her off the
platform with the help of fellow Ybarras, to whom this defiance of tradition was of particular shame. Jacobo lasted not many moments longer,
downed by the swing of a wine bottle. He was kicked and trampled.
Then over his body rushed the men, reaching the throne at last, where
Salvador, clutching his scepter, sat without a muscle quavering. And it
was consummated.

There were consequences to this affair. The "king" hanged himself
that night from a beam in the family's shed, using tough wire twine
that cut through muscle and bone, decapitating him. The Ybarras as
a clan suffered a blow to their prestige, which should have comforted
Manú, but which did not, because the blow Jacobo had dealt the Rivas
name was irredeemable (Manú did not learn until some months later
that Amadeo had participated in the outrage; by which time both were
past caring, because Amadeo succumbed to hepatitis). Half dead, Jacobo
was dragged back to the stable and dumped in the straw. He bled profusely from head, ears, nose and mouth. Two ribs were broken. He could
hardly breathe. The veterinarian presented himself at midnight. Manú
bid him begone. But the vet, if not especially competent, was a kind
man. He reminded Manú that he had two cows fresh that might be
needing professional assistance; and thus gained entrance to the stable,
where he dressed Jacobo's wounds, stitched his scalp, finished removing
a loose incisor, and bound his chest. It is likely, however, that this attention would have been unavailing, infection set in, and Jacobo died: because he was given no care at all by any member of his family except

Amadeo, who did his best to pluck the maggots out of his brother's flesh.

Three mornings after—following the burial of Salvador and dressed in deepest black, bruises still a livid green-and-yellow above one brow and below an eye—Marisol Ybarra showed herself on the Rivas stoop. She demanded to see Jacobo. Jacobo's mother told her to go away. The demon humpback and the other unmarried sister backed their mother. One of the married girls went at once to fetch father, husband, and brother-in-law from the lower lot; because, young as Marisol was (scarcely past eighteen), she had overnight achieved the reputation of a she-bear.

Manú and his sons-in-law came hurrying up the hill. He wasted not a moment with Marisol, shouting at her, "You and Jacobo between you have brought enough shame to your families. Get back to your house where you belong!"

Marisol tucked her chin in, uttering a low call. From behind a hedge stepped two strapping young men, her older brothers. This was a surprise. They worked in the Duke's coal mine near Bilbao. They, too, were dressed in black. In their hands they carried the one a three-tined wooden pitchfork, the other a scythe.

Manú did not blanch. He wielded a hoe. His sons-in-law were similarly armed, and one had a sickle besides. There was a moment when both families stared at each other. Blood was welling up the neck of Manú, and a large vein on his forehead was swelling and throbbing with it. It had taken many centuries for the showdown.

Just as Manú lifted his hoe, the voice of Amadeo came from a window above and behind them. "Everybody stop."

Manú wheeled. Amadeo's flushed, merrily besotted face grinned down at him. Wavering dangerously in his hands was a muzzle-loading fowling piece.

"What do you want with Jacobo?" he asked Marisol in a polite tone.

"Take him home. Care for him."

"Does your father approve?" Amadeo inquired.

For an answer, she glanced at her brothers, and then back up at Amadeo.

"Then take him," he told her, swinging the gun on his father.

One of the sons-in-law made a movement. Manú barked, "Stay still! That loony will shoot." And he was right about that.

Marisol drew a pony and cart from behind the hedge. Her brothers walked into the stable and between them hoist Jacobo, depositing him on a blanket that had been spread over fresh, clean straw. Nodding at

Amadeo, Marisol grasped the reins of the pony, turned the animal's head, and led the cart away.

Salvador's suicide had struck Señora Ybarra hard. The boy's affliction had never been a source of shame with her; it had cored depths of love. And so it was she, over her husband's objections, who had sided with Marisol and her brothers in the notion of tending Jacobo; who, as they heard from the vet, was being left by Manú to rot. Marisol's mother personally cleaned Jacobo's infested flesh. Leeches were applied by Marisol, and the vet came to pack him with new dressings. Jacobo had never experienced female spoiling. It was a wonder to him. Señora Ybarra was almost as large in frame as Marisol; but her big hands possessed the same sensitivity as Salvador's. They were healing hands; and Jacobo mended quickly, so that within three weeks he insisted on taking over the dead boy's old job of goat-herding. Within another ten days, he was sound. There was no thought of returning to his father's house. But there was no room for him on the tiny Ybarra farm; and no work for him, of course, in all of Sacedón. What was to be done with Jacobo became a quandary: strangely resolved.

A message reached the hilltop holding, delivered by an ill-natured footman dressed in gray livery and sweating profusely from his long climb, to which, as a house servant, he was no longer accustomed. He carried a note from the Duke. It read, "I was an unhappy witness to your courage. I have arranged for you to be apprenticed at Carbón Industrial. You must report to Señor Don Alvaro Sastrústegui de Figueras." He had added the address—a street in Bilbao—enclosing one hundred pesetas.

There seemed to be no option.

EIGHT

Brothers at Arms

At the zenith of his young manhood, condemned to dig for coal.

Never mind his horror of the dark, nor the claustrophobia that panicked him, nor the chokedamp in the poorly ventilated shafts that often killed men before they were forty. He endured. He had igneous fortitude. His lungs he tried to protect by breathing through a handkerchief. On Sundays and Feasts, he pumped them full of fresh oxygen, playing soccer with his companions until dusk halted the games.

A scout from the Atlético de Bilbao spotted him one afternoon. To his astonishment and joy, he was signed. In painful letters, he wrote Marisol about this wonderful event; and she, by way of Sacedón's scrivener, an ex-seminarian who had been dismissed because of an unconquerable stutter, wrote back her joy in the stilted and somewhat florid style then still in usage. He trained with the scrubs that autumn and winter, conveying to Marisol his every triumph, as when the coach remarked that he had progressed rapidly; to which Marisol replied with congratulations and a stern reminder that all gifts come from God. By spring, he was a regular substitute on the second squad; and veteran "hinchas" (fans) of the Atlético, watching practice sessions, began to talk about the giant new portero with heavy legs but hands as fast as the dart of a trout. He wrote Marisol. She responded with congratulations and a stern reminder that all gifts come from God, adding that their heifer had died. He sent her money, receiving in reply a distant letter of thanks with a stern reminder that it was improper for him to have made this gesture, since, so far as she knew, there was no understanding between them, adding besides that she and her family were not mendicants. A postscript, however, in somewhat more natural Spanish, and hinting at excitement, communicated that her parents had persuaded her of the propriety of treating his gift in the form of a debt discharged for the care they had taken of him, and since they had been able to purchase a weanling at a good price, it would not necessarily compromise her if she used the small change to invest in some linen. Jacobo pinned this letter under his shirt, close to his breast, taking it out now and then to kiss the postscript.

Fortune heaped her favors on Jacobo in the middle of April. The first-string goalkeeper splintered two fingers of his left hand. On the following Sunday, his substitute, the second-string goalie, lunged after a ball and cracked his pate against one of the posts, giving him a concussion. *Faute de mieux*, the rookie was used.

Jacobo was unable to contain himself, telegraphing the news to Marisol. Either because the scrivener himself was becoming excited, or because Marisol was no longer able to restrain her delight, the answering missive was a straightforward canticle of happiness, with only a prudential aside reminding him that the misfortunes of others ought not to be the occasion of unlimited rejoicing. Jacobo slept with this letter under his pillow.

There were three games left on the schedule. Jacobo excelled. Bilbao buzzed about his performances. Madrid's solemn *ABC* featured him in action against the Real Madrid on the cover of its magazine-like daily, streamering across the bottom, *Qué Es El Atlético de Hoy? Rivas, Rivas, y Rivas.* He was the sensation featured in the May issues of sports magazines, and sporting goods manufacturers solicited his endorsement of their products. Jacobo mailed clippings to Marisol, formally proposing marriage. The old curate warned her that Jacobo's soul was in grave need of repair, but then burst out, "Christ and His saints, *seven* saves in the second half against Real Madrid! THAT taught them!" The wedding was set for July. On the eighteenth of June, Francisco Franco rose up against the Republic.

Many Basques were uneasy about the Popular Front that had taken over the Government. Overwhelmingly Catholic, they were disturbed by its Jacobin tenor. Autonomy, however, had been promised to them. This long cherished objective was too precious to forfeit; and the provinces of Vizcaya, Alava, and Guipuzcoa took up arms against the rebellion.

It was a blow when the delegation of bishops they sent to Rome to explain their stand was given short shrift by Cardinal Pacelli. The Basque clergy nevertheless insisted that Franco's insurrection was morally indefensible, failing to satisfy the four conditions established by Thomas Aquinas. Defiant priests marched with fighting units. And, at first, it was the separatists who ran affairs. Anarchists and Socialists were in the minority: only two churches were burned; by August, persecution of the rich and middle classes had virtually ceased. Enthusiasm roared to climax when, on 1 October, a rump meeting of the Spanish parliament approved the Statute of Basque Autonomy. This was followed by a gathering at Guernica of municipal councilors. There, under the Oak of Liberty, symbol of their nationhood, they declared the state of "Euzkadi," forming a provisional government and electing a president.

Almost at once, control began slipping from traditionalist hands. Ideologues of the extreme left infiltrated, Socialists devouring anarchists and in their turn being devoured by Communists. This became the pattern all over Loyalist Spain. For the Republic, it was mortal. Having alienated the professional officers' corps, the central Government was compelled to rely on second-rate or politically appointed commanders who too often blundered their troops into bloody disasters. Jacobo and his comrades were marched back and forth along the Cantabrian shelf fighting sharp, savage, and wasteful actions. Captains bickered among themselves. Logistics were a nightmare. And then, on New Year's Day of 1937, when Jacobo, wretched under a downpour, was dreaming of Marisol, a commissar attached himself to the unit.

He was a squat, balding, blunt-headed Albanian with cold inky eyes. Speaking an almost incomprehensible Spanish, he subjected the men to hours of indoctrination that might better have been spent in military training; and what he said recalled to Jacobo's mind the Frenchwoman, Michelle Muñoz, whom he had not forgiven. But soon it became apparent that this man was boss: the officers deferred to him; they seemed to fear him.

There was a change in atmosphere, and it was chilling. On a gray and mournful dawn in January, one of Jacobo's closest companions was executed. His offense had been to get up the day before during a political lecture and tell the commissar to his face that he personally did not give a damn about the dictatorship of the proletariat, what he wanted was warm socks for his feet. And then, on an afternoon in late February, Jacobo and his battalion were marched by a horrifying sight. Five nuns from a humble cloister, one of them a woman in her seventies and another a girl scarcely out of adolescence, had been dragged out into the plaza, stripped and impaled through the vagina on thin sharp stakes that protruded from their collarbones. As Jacobo passed, he noticed that one of the nuns twitched still.

Up to that moment, he had performed creditably. His guts writhed with fear before an attack. Once in motion, nothing stopped his charge; and he was recommended for a decoration. But as he trudged to the defense of Guernica, where there was a small but important ammunitions plant, he was filled with doubts.

On 31 March, the Nationalists launched their offensive against Bilbao. Slowly, implacably, 50,000 Carlists from Navarre closed in on 10,-000 Vizcayan Basques. The fighting between these near kinsmen was ferocious. Men died in droves. Torrential and incessant rains compounded the horror as trenches became quagmires in which the dead bloated and the dying drowned. On 29 April, Guernica—a short distance east of Bilbao—fell.

Jacobo and his platoon were crouched behind a street barricade stretching across the rear of the central plaza. They were exhausted, a cadaverous group, the cumulative fatigue of months of battle and now unrelieved days of fighting hollow in their cheeks and leaden in their limbs. "No pasarán!" their commissar barked at them in a voice grown hoarse. They did not hear him. Their brains were clogged as with the viscosity of the mud through which they had marched and countermarched, attacked and retreated. Directed by the commissars, especially selected cadres had been busy all night flitting in and out of buildings on some mysterious mission. Now the commissars had retired behind the barricade, pistols drawn. Mortars exploded with dull, repetitive thumps on all sides, splintering wood and mincing human meat. Bullets zinged overhead or whined ricocheting from stone walls. It poured rain. Jacobo and his comrades watched as the stench of gunpowder thickened and the rising torrent of war roared toward them. The outer perimeters of defense had disintegrated. Soldiers, at a run, were falling back to the barricade at the head of the square, diving headfirst over it. Then, under the massed assault of red-bereted Carlists, howling their fearsome warcries, that line crumbled. Blasting their way through gaps, the enemy burst into the square—maniacs who with set bayonets drove right into the spluttering muzzles of machinegun nests, hurling themselves forward until in instances their legs were riddled through, and then literally severed from their torsos, not even this stopping them as they writhed a little farther along in their death throes to fling a final grenade.

The difference between the Basque defenders and the Carlist *requetés* was not courage. It was not even a matter of mere numbers. It lay in total conviction on one side and doubt on the other. Jacobo's platoon broke—flinging rifles down in panic and stampeding to the rear. The commissar, shrieking, shot two of them. Jacobo halted, turned, let loose a bellow, and flung himself on the Albanian, slapping the pistol aside, reaching for the throat with one hand while shoving the butt of a palm up under the commissar's jaw. At the junction of head and neck, the man's spine snapped.

At that moment, a slug tore into Jacobo's upper thigh, shredding its way out through the gluteal muscles. He fell. He lay there on the wet cobblestones, the tide of battle sweeping over him while blood kept gushing out his wound as though the femoral artery had been cut. Then, suddenly, his body was shaken by the concussion of dynamite charges going off, a concatenation of explosions that blew out the walls of buildings everywhere in town. Astonishment and outrage seized Jacobo. He raised his head. With black waves washing across his eyes, he lowed like a bull, like a bull in the arena with the sword thrust through its shoulderblades—with the fury of the betrayed.

"Rivas . . . Jacobo Rivas," someone murmured, "the star portero of the Atlético."

"I know."

He opened his eyes. The biggest man he had ever seen loomed above his bed. The pain of Jacobo's wound blurred vision. It was night, and there were shadows. But the man was a priest.

"*You've come to confess me. I am dying.*"

These were Jacobo's first, very natural thoughts.

"*Neither. They want to amputate your leg.*"

Jacobo shut his eyes. There is no one, he says, to describe his feelings.

"*I would rather die,*" he told the man.

"*I understand you.*"

"*Intercede for me!*"

"*If that's what you want.*"

"*Who are you?*"

"*That is of no consequence.*"

"*I can hear your voice in my mind. I'm speaking without moving my lips.*"

"*Don't fret about it.*"

"*You know that I am in mortal sin. You know who brought me to it.*"

"*You sinned against her, Jacobo.*"

"*I!*"

"*Who else?*"

"*You're . . . a traitor. How do I know that? You ranged yourself against the King. You broke with the Royalists and the traditionalists, and you preached the Republic. What are you doing here?*"

"*I am a prisoner, the same as you.*"

"*Did you see what I saw? Tell me! Did you see what they did to Guernica?*"

"*I was not there. It doesn't surprise me.*"

"*Then why are you a Red!*"

There was silence.

Jacobo reared up on his waist. He shouted, "*Why are you a Red!*"

"*I am a Republican. It has all gone badly. But it has been necessary. There won't be a victory, not as some dream of it. It will never be the same—and thank God for that, Jacobo, do you thank God for that. True Spain is dead.*"

"*Then what should I do?*"

"Pray for the soul of the man you murdered. Wash your soul."

"Give me absolution!"

"Not yet. For you, Jacobo, not until the end comes. When we meet again."

And he vanished. Jacobo awoke—when again he awoke—to find himself still sitting up, and interns on either side bending him back against the iron of his arms, trying to make him lie down.

He was surprised to awaken at all; and more than astonished to find himself in a clean, efficiently run Nationalist field hospital. One thing only ran through his thoughts. The commissars had mined Guernica, the town that is holy to his nation, the Basque's rallying ground for over one thousand years. It was the atrocity convincing him. The "rojos" were Red indeed—murdering scum to whom nothing was sacred. Once more had treachery been dealt to him and his people.

When strong enough, he asked for paper and pencil, scrawling three notes. The first was addressed to Patxi, his mariner brother, who, like most of the Navy, had mutinied on the outbreak of hostilities, assassinating officers and rallying to the Republican banner. In this letter he told Patxi what he had seen, urging him to surrender. He then wrote to Marisol a long letter detailing his experiences. To his father he directed a simple announcement that he was alive, a prisoner, and, if given the chance, a convert to the Nationalist cause.

The censors were delighted with what they read. Propaganda mills had ground Guernica into a symbol of Nazi-Nationalist (Franco) bestiality. Here an eyewitness Basque soldier averred to the contrary—that it was the commissars who had blown the town up. Jacobo's three brilliant appearances with the Atlético gave his testimony counter-propaganda value, at least in Spain. A pastiche of his letters was air-dropped wherever Basque resistance continued. Three months later, he was accepted into the Nationalist files.

He fought for Franco with the benediction of Marisol, the curse of his father, and silence from Patxi. Two more years the war dragged on. Jacobo took part in the offensive on Alicante. His platoon, belonging to a brigade commanded by the Duke of Steel, Luis del Val of Sacedón, was among the first to tread the streets of Barcelona. Then, in March of 1939, Madrid surrendered. Peace came to the Peninsula.

NINE

The Rubicon of Honor

For Jacobo Rivas, peace ushered in fifteen years of sorrow and privation. Everything he did was done too late, and whatever came to him came too late. His switching sides earned the contempt of former comrades (a traitor) and little credit from his new comrades (a suspect Johnny-come-lately). Patxi was executed as a war criminal. Jacobo had known his brother too little for deep grief. Nor was it within him to extract solace from the astounding fact that he, the eleventh child and fifth son, now stood to inherit his father's position as chief of the Rivas clan. Without money, without distinction, robbed by the war of what might have been years of stardom on the Atlético, the bauble was as empty of meaning as for generations it had been of content.

When he showed up at Sacedón for Patxi's funeral, the townfolk nodded at him with reserve. And Manú, grown withered beyond recognition, and more bitter and venomous than ever, told him that if he crossed the threshold again it would be to meet a bullet in his chest. Jacobo was not likely to test the challenge. Sucking at one of his humpback sister's long, oblate, she-goat paps was a half brother, Manú's son.

Jacobo turned his back on the door forever. His heart lightened—and his stride lengthened—as he passed the charred remains of the ducal castle, put Sacedón behind him, and went climbing up to Marisol's farm. He came upon her scything.

At the sound of his voice, the sweep of her arms and shoulders stuck in midswing, as though the point of the blade had rammed into a tree trunk. She straightened slowly, turning slowly. At the sight of him, one bare arm went up, and all along its length, from the pouch of her bent elbow to the plane of her hand, she wiped the sweat from her eyes.

The war had emptied her of joy. Her face was hollowed, her shoulders were sloped forward as though unequal to the matured weight of her bosom. The hand she gave him was roughened, chapped, with broken fingernails under which black grime had become embedded. She had developed muscles too massive to be womanly, and when she led him to the cottage, walking ahead of him, he noticed that she lumbered on hips that had grossened.

OSENDALE LIBRARY
OSENDALE, N.Y.

For three years, alone, she had sought to support herself and her aging parents from the meager produce of that hilltop farm, hiring herself out in the evenings at a nearby Nestlés dairy, where she stripped the teats of fifty cows for a token fee and one liter of milk. Her elder brother had been killed. The younger had been returned with stumps where there had been legs and a ragged hole where once teeth, gums, and lips had constituted a mouth. Marriage was for the moment at least out of the question.

Greatly depressed, Jacobo bid the family farewell and set off for Bilbao—a two-day march—where he rejoined Atlético.

The team's glory was on the wane. So were his reflexes. He was only twenty-five, but the wound and three years of combat had taken toll. He gained a berth on the second squad, primarily because Basque manpower was decimated. During his first appearances, he was hissed. His slightest error drew howls, and his saves silence. But after two years, scrimping put enough by for him to take on a wife; and finally, in the autumn of 1941, Marisol and he were married.

It may be irrelevant to question whether they then loved each other; to both their union seemed in the order of things destined. Physically, they were fit mates. According to the custom of her time and class, Marisol stretched herself on the bridal bed without having received a word of even veiled information or advice from her female relations. She had led the bull to the cow, of course. It was a disgusting necessity. The lewd ruttings of sheep and goats had done little to raise her esteem of sexual contact; and when once she had seen a panting bitch and dog ligamented back to back, as though they were Siamese twins, that low esteem was depressed beyond measure. For all she knew, this was to happen between herself and Jacobo.

Original sin, to Marisol and her sisters throughout Spain, meant sex. (It is disobedience.) The Immaculate Conception meant the absence of sex (confused with absence of sin, the true meaning), and sex was therefore non-immaculate and by extension foul. Besides, full five years of supporting herself and her family made her independent. She was not about to surrender her intimate parts, her being, to the lust of any man: not without a struggle.

And combat it was, with Jacobo roaring and then gasping his frustration while a grim smile of absolute defiance rolled across Marisol's lips. He, of course, expected a battle. His wife was a decent woman. But that smile was an intolerable challenge. He returned to the attack, this time exerting every last ounce of his exceptional strength, achieving for moments from his wife stunned respect, which, low creature, Man, he took advantage of at once to slam home his charge, eliciting from her a shriek of pain and outrage. They were both much satisfied with each other, although Marisol wondered whether she had not been split in two, and Jacobo wondered whether he would be able next day to lift an air bubble.

The pattern of their physical intimacy was thus established. Jacobo took his wife when he felt it was better not to burn; he was as brief as possible, and he expected a fight. She learned finally that compliance saved energy and bruises, although she wondered what earthly pleasure Jacobo derived from it all. Marisol's existence soon centered not on Jacobo, nor on herself, but on the children she hoped they would produce. By seeding pure new souls for Christ, she would in some measure absolve her soul (and perhaps Jacobo's also, if that were possible) of the unmentionable they committed together.

Marisol did not actually portray her condition as a martyrdom, although she felt it came close, because she had been taught from infancy that all life is that, and any sensible woman put trust in the hereafter. Similarly, Jacobo rarely wondered whether he was happy, because that estate pertained only to the rich. He and Marisol lived hedging extreme poverty; half Jacobo's salary went to Marisol's parents, paying for a hand they had hired in her stead and for the medications their advancing years required. (Mercifully, their mutilated son succumbed to pneumonia during the winter of 1941-42). Marisol's fecundity was an added strain, and for a time a cause of deep sadness to them both. She had costly miscarriages. Harsh were the postwar years, and they lost four infants in a row, only one of them surviving more than six months. Marisol prayed fervently. God was punishing them. Jacobo was too lustful. And had she not, in her weakness (searching her heart for the truth) permitted herself to enjoy a few moments of their last encounter? Perhaps, she wondered, there existed another way of conceiving children.

She had no women friends with whom to consult: and this was one more cross for them both to bear. Jacobo was no less unpopular in the mid-1940s than he had been right after the war. His teammates scarcely concealed their dislike for the turncoat. He was justified in wondering whether the coach was wholly justified in confining him to the second string, because the other portero, although quicker in the legs, was not so fast with his hands and did not give to his rôle the unflagging concentration of which Jacobo was capable. One Sunday in the autumn of 1944, this fellow seemed to come apart, helping to convert a 3-0 Atlético advantage into a 3-5 loss. The fans were furious, the coach disgusted. He turned to Jacobo, saying, "You will defend the posts against Barcelona."

That was a big game. Barcelona was developing into the strongest team in the Spanish league. Jacobo might have jubilated. He did not. He was now thirty; the wound in his left thigh bothered him increasingly with the dank of Bilbao's climate. No matter how brilliantly he might block goals next Sunday, it would be, he suspected, in the way of an ember on which hot oil is dripped; a last, self-consuming flare of faculties growing cold.

There was a young fellow called Eixaguirre lusting for the position. The boy had no experience, superb reflexes, and courage.

Which was the other thing. Jacobo had emerged from the war with a horror of physical contact that was almost craven. He had a fear of being damaged. He dreaded his rages, such as the one that had murdered the commissar. Everybody, coach and teammates, sensed there was something amiss with the giant. By this time, it had begun to evolve into a moral cowardice, noticed by Marisol, although she said nothing. Jacobo turned finances over to her. Poor as they were, he would not haggle. He refused to face debtor and creditor alike. As much as I have grilled him, he has been unable to provide me with a clear description of the late Duke of Sacedón, whom he met with daily for several years every summer; mentioning no more than the steely glint of the man's arms, matching a steely glint in his blue eyes. There is mystery about this. You may have noticed not a line of description about Jacobo's mother. She does not exist. She exists somewhere in Jacobo, but in a layer I have been unable to fathom. Suffice that Marisol's authority grew during this period. Jacobo's declined. And as it declined, he began drinking; and drinking induced blustering, the boastful might-have-beens of the never-to-be, so that Marisol's eyes darkened with a disappointment that in its time would conceive disdain. The syndrome of failure had picketed Jacobo.

It was in this frame of spirits that, on the Saturday before the game, he received a mysterious summons.

Jacobo sat in the steamy locker room of the Atlético, having come off the field from a light practice session. The name meant nothing to him. The fellow delivering the message was a nattily dressed, slim, dark, and bouncy youth, announcing himself as Stepanópoulis Grau with an air implying that his name ought to ring bells. Sniffing fastidiously at the rank aroma of male armpits and sweated male genitalia—not unpleasantly spiced by the acrid, sticky resin that helps harden the soles of feet—Grau stated that his master would be pleased to receive Jacobo in his suite at the Carlton Hotel; and that he was authorized to say the meeting could be of very particular interest.

Bowing as though he had completed the mission of a plenipotentiary, the young man turned to leave; and then came hurrying back to ask where the urinals were located.

Jacobo studied the visiting card that had been deposited on the bench beside him. On the back of the card, crabbed in light blue ink: "One o'clock."

Jacobo frowned. He suspected what this was about.

He was thirty. He felt aged to forty.

Dress though he did with the urban formality of Spaniards, in a suit and tie and a starched white shirt, there was no concealing the shine at the seat of his trousers, nor the fraying at cuffs and sleeves, nor yet the skillful reweaving at the bulge of the left elbow. The Carlton's concierge —in frock coat and winged collar—measured him with experienced eyes, sending Jacobo around to the service entrance. Jacobo went humbly, with the acceptance of any European of peasant background, no more humiliated than, say, an American Negro of the time and generation; and no less aware. But he was met by the self-important youth who called himself Stepanópoulis Grau, and by him, with an aura of portentousness that enveloped Jacobo, was ushered four flights up the service staircase and into the elegance of a corridor whose wainscoting and creamy parallel rungs of Victorian plaster awed him. He envied the seesawing self-assurance of the fanny he followed.

At the paired doors of a suite, they halted. The young man rapped with firm, feminine rapidity on a panel, turning to smile at Jacobo beneath the plucked whisper of a mustache as he revolved the bright brass knob of one door, pushed the door open, and stepped aside.

Jacobo walked into a vestibule. Toward him advanced an astonishing person.

The bulbous forehead impressed him first; and then the outthrust barrel of the chest. He watched as thick, short forearms shot forth in welcome, synchronizing with the motion a rubbery stretching of lips. A small fist clamped his large one with bone-crunching power. As though the man's legs were struts sunk to the very foundations of the hotel, he yanked Jacobo into the parlor; and with a more than amiable slap on the back sent him stumbling toward a tray that sparkled with decanters, glasses, and ice. Hardly had a glass of whisky been screwed into Jacobo's right hand than he was yanked away and nearly flung—Jacobo felt, although in the same, hearty, compulsively irresistible fashion—into an armchair. Nearby was a sideboard heaped with delicious-looking seafood. Reacting to the graveled command, Grau jumped to serve Jacobo helpings of juicy cigalas and a whole shoal of hot and crackling sardine fry, chanquetes, that were as tasty as though they had been sizzled just moments before in the skillet.

Jacobo stuffed his mouth between sips of scotch, which he had not tasted before and did not much enjoy, but which he assumed was expensive and an honor to be offered. Meanwhile this fellow surnamed Blás—this fifty-year-old of plainly fisherman stock, who had to be a very important man, who perspired mightily in a white linen suit but whose fourth finger was weighted with a blindingly large canary diamond set in heavy gold—sat in front of him like a bright-eyed, benevolent troll, beamed at him, and with the most astonishing memory quoted to Jacobo details of his seven incredible saves during the second half of that memorable encounter with the Real Madrid eight years before. The financier (as Jacobo further assumed) claimed to have followed Jacobo's career with the keenest interest, his praise so fulsome that Jacobo at first suffered from embarrassment. "Not Ricardo Zamora in his incomparable prime had ten afternoons like yours against the Real!" exclaimed the man, wound up to hyperbole. But it was pleasant to be reminded of now irrecoverable glory; it made a person glow to discover that someone at all remembered, and that a body of such consequence as this Baltazar Blás must be should invite him to a luxurious apartment in the best hotel Bilbao boasted and have him stuffed with the costly fruits of the sea and plied with exotic liquor.

Less than natural for Jacobo not to have responded; not to have warmed to this person. Asked what his emotions were when first he manned the gates of the Atlético, Jacobo felt rise in him a surge of articulateness, once again twenty-two years old and in love, and braving the reserve of 20,000 spectators who, with his second leap and deflection of a rifle-like shot from the enemy forward, rose in a roar of acclaim. Blás was an intent listener. He interrupted only to offer Jacobo a third highball, which he, mindful of the game next day, refused; and then more appetizers, which Jacobo thought it safe to accept.

Blás now inquired about his personal life. "You are married, Señor Rivas, are you not?"

"Four years."

"Children?"

Jacobo shook his head sadly.

"God has not yet rewarded you with children?" asked the financier in an incredulous tone.

"Not one to survive."

"Oh, I am sorry to hear that!" said Blás. He seemed genuinely upset, genuinely sympathetic. He lowered his eyes a moment; raising them suddenly. "But you are young," he said. "I . . . Señora Blás and I . . ." He halted. Then he blurted the words out. "We have two lovely daughters, but a son we do not have. For me, Señor Rivas, this is a great desgracia. I am a simple person. Some call me a very lucky fellow blessed with every good a mortal can desire—but I share with you and all other men the wish for a son to follow in my footsteps."

Jacobo was moved by this confidence. He exhorted his host not to give up hope, *he* wasn't giving up hope, Blás seemed to him to be an energetic and manifestly potent fellow, his prayers would be rewarded; and he, Jacobo Rivas, along with his wife, Marisol Ybarra, would intercede with the Almighty on his behalf.

The financier seemed exceedingly touched by this. "That is very generous of you," he stated solemnly. "I admire your faith; and I respect the man who is not easily persuaded of defeat." He sighed. "Alas, I fear my wife is beyond all that now. Our daughters . . . I should not complain. When all is said and done, a man has to face facts, his age, his condition, and learn to bear the truth in dignity. Do you agree?"

"I do!" said Jacobo, admiring the financier's resignation.

"And what about you?" Blás asked.

"Me?"

"Aye, you."

The man was smiling—in a sorrowing, compassionate manner.

"Well—as you've mentioned—Marisol is still young, and I . . ."

"Your wife is young. You are too old."

Jacobo's mouth fell open with astonishment.

"When are you going to confront the truth?" the financier persisted in a gentle, chiding tone. Jacobo remained dumbfounded. "Oh, I don't mean too old to beget sons!" the man continued. "I mean," he said, delivering his next words with a dreadful sort of realism, "too old ever to come back, too old and worn from the War ever to become again anything better than a substitute . . . and perhaps too old to hold on to that much."

The words engendered silence. Jacobo fought on several fronts: not to register their meaning, to deny their utterance; and, both defenses crumbling, to grasp at a straw.

"I . . . I am playing tomorrow. I . . . I will show them!"

The financier wagged his head in pitying fashion. "Do not say to me—one who will treasure forever the privilege of having seen you in your great days—what you cannot convince yourself of in your heart. Whatever may happen, tomorrow means nothing. You know it. The public knows it. You must face this as I must face that God, for my many sins, has denied me a son. Are you big enough, macho enough, Señor Rivas?"

Jacobo was astonished by what happened to him now. He felt tears sting their way over the rims of his lower eyelids. He sat immobile, shocked by the phenomenon: but the tears came. His host's gaze of instant commiseration caused them to flow all the harder; because it was true, he was finished, the man had no more than articulated what he, Jacobo, had already conceded.

The financier motioned with his large head. His minion, who had been standing behind Jacobo, retreated to the vestibule and out of the suite, closing the door after him. Jacobo was grateful for this show of delicacy. Now it seemed less shameful to cry—somehow, alone with a man like Blás; and he permitted the torrent its way.

"Yes," the financier murmured, eyes steady and comprehending, as though he had traveled a similar route, "let it come. Let it out. There is a time for us all. We are called upon to face what we are—and the little that we are. Sometimes we need help, more often than not from a stranger."

He leaned forward abruptly, stuffing his own handkerchief into Jacobo's hands. Jacobo wiped his eyes and face, blew his nose, cleared his throat—emptied of emotion, the world gone bleak, and even the understanding of such a personage as this Señor Blás unavailing.

"May I ask," his host said now, "what plans you have made?"

"None." Jacobo had never considered the question. He was to have become a legendary goalkeeper, like the great ones of old, like Zamora. He had promised Marisol . . .

"May I help?" the financier asked.

"How?" Jacobo's voice was dead-dull. When, after all, had reality measured the leap of dreams?

"I have purchased an iron mine not far from Bilbao. It has been abandoned. I am reactivating it. You have a position there as foreman whenever you want it."

Jacobo shook his head. "The mines . . . Not again. That I promised myself."

"You start as foreman. You may rise higher."

Again Jacobo shook his head. Spreading his outsized hands, he scrutinized them. "It . . . can never be as it was, and I am not good for anything else. I am stupid. I cannot manage men. I am worthless."

"No one can take from you what you proved before the War," said the financier sternly. "Remember that: you can never be less than what you once rose to." He paused. "On the other hand . . . It is sad!" he let out indignantly. "Fate—a terrible, stupid war brought on by anarchists and Communists—tricked you out of your destiny. Perhaps, as you say, you will never rise higher than foreman. Men are born to do one or two things in their lives, and usually just one; and if by chance that thing is taken from a man, then he has missed his chance."

Jacobo wanted very much to cry again.

His host continued. "It is unfair. You have been cheated. Why do you imagine I asked you to come here?"

"To bribe me," said Jacobo: without thinking. He blushed.

Blás grinned at him. "What was to be your answer?"

"That . . . the last day I play, I play not for money; not for any amount of money."

The financier seemed delighted. "You're a fine fellow, Señor Rivas. I plan to wager on the Atlético tomorrow. If the Atlético wins, for every stop you make I will reward you with twenty thousand pesetas."

Jacobo's lower jaw dropped as though yanked open. As well it might, 20,000 pesetas at the time commanding the purchasing power of, say, $2,000 today.

"Then . . . What is it you want from me?"

Blás hitched his chair closer. "I am in the business of exportation and importation. There is an official in Bilbao, in the Customs, who is not co-operative."

Jacobo was alarmed. "What has this to do with me?"

Señor Blás sat back. He studied Jacobo, the twin bolls on his bald dome glowing. "I read your statement—the flyer put out by the Army. You are Christian. You are Basque, but a patriot. Have you since changed your thinking?"

"About what?"

"Reds. Communists. Real ones."

"No."

"They are to you . . . ?"

"Filthy deceivers!"

"Who should be . . ."

"Run off the face of the earth! They corrupt. They promise paradise, and then they vanish, leaving one in a hellhole."

Jacobo meant what he said. But now he drew in his breath, regarding the financier fearfully.

Blás sprang his trap. "I agree. This fellow in Customs is a Communist. I have, however, no hard proof. His record is masterfully doctored. I need one credible and unimpeachable witness to at least one link in the skein of circumstance. I believe this man helped organize the miners' rebellion in '34, but we cannot be sure of it. He has committed no common crime. He is involved in no atrocities. Naturally not. This fellow is one of the Party's long-term plants. He is an incorruptible, efficient bureaucrat with an excellent standing among his superiors here and in Madrid. *Credible* doubt is sufficient to have him exiled—or simply removed from his position, which is all that I am after. It's a question of shoes, the right and left of it. I want him out of the way. I do not want to know about it. I want nothing to do with it. I propose to give you his record as my agents construe it, and let you judge for yourself. He goes under the name of Ortiz. His real name, we believe, is Larrañaga. His common-law wife is a Frenchwoman called Michelle Muñoz—she was married to a Red from Santander or Asturias who disappeared in the early '30s, we are not sure. We are certain that she visited Sacedón during the summers of '33 and '34. We are told by your father, Manú Rivas, that she—as he put it—made a bigger fool of you than you were from birth."

He smiled, rising. "I wanted to be sure your sentiments had not changed since you wrote your brother Patxi urging him to repent and surrender. What is needed is a patriot who will attest to the truth. As you know," he added with a comradely shake of Jacobo's left shoulder, "failure to volunteer information about True Spain's enemies is a crime against the Fatherland."

Jacobo was ushered back down the service stairs by Stepanópoulis Grau, who handed him a sealed brief. Jacobo accepted the package with a hand out of which sensory consciousness had seeped, so that twice on his way home he dropped it. That night—slowly, murmuring the words aloud, causing Marisol to complain that she could not sleep—he read the brief. The evidence was weak. Clearly, he was needed—someone who could honestly swear, for example, that he had known Michelle Muñoz, that she had admitted to him her allegiance to the Party, that she had told him she was meeting Larrañaga alias Ortiz in October of '34 to help organize the miners.

He had not forgiven Michelle. José María had been a victim of

Yagüe's reprisals; it was the many Michelles and Muñozes and Larrañagas who had helped deceive the thousands of Patxis to their deaths.
And—if he refused to testify—there was the threat.

Jacobo slept little that night.

Next afternoon, as he walked with heavy legs out on the field, he
was as usual hissed. Within two minutes of play, the Barcelona had scored
a pair of goals, one a fair shot, but the other a high, looping rebound that
he sprang after too late. His muscles had not responded in time to the
alarm flashed by his eyes. The thousands in the stadium screamed for his
blood. Atlético's three defensemen turned their backs on him, their disgust eloquent. Not five minutes later, Barcelona came pressing back down
the field, passing long, deep, and with marvelous precision, dodging
Atlético's defense, and zigzagging into the lap of churned-up mud and turf
in front of Jacobo. A kick was deflected. The ball dribbled to the right.
Jacobo should have been out of his cage already, to throw his bulk on the
peril. But he stood as though frozen between the posts. A Barcelona
wingman bulled out of the pile-up, tripped, slid, and yet managed to boot
the ball. It came at Jacobo's unprotected left flank. Now he hurled himself in its direction; but again too late.

There was outrage in the stands. Jacobo heard curses. He heard
threats. The chant began, *Ei-xa-gui-rre, Ei-xa-gui-rre!* His team captain
stalked up to him, glared, picked up the ball, handed it to him, and then
stalked away. *Ei-xa-gui-rre!*

There was no further scoring that half. During intermission, Jacobo
sat in a spreading pool of silence. The no substitution rule was in effect,
or he would have been sent to the showers.

The second half saw an Atlético out of the past; forty-five minutes
of unrelenting, slashing attacks. The team scored in the sixth minute of
play, again in the fourteenth minute, and then a third time in the twenty-
second minute, tying the score. The crowd was delirious. But stunned
though the opponents were, they stormed back. Both teams now played
the wide-open game, leaving just two men in defense. Shots pelted either
cage. Barcelona's goalie leaped for save after save. Even the highly parti-
san Basque crowd applauded. Jacobo was doing no less well. He was
fired up. The blood in his veins boiled. He felt in his muscles the old
fluidity; in his arms the eupractic speed, and even in his legs a long forgot
lightness. There was, besides, a resolve in him such as he had never
known. Atlético scored. Jubilation shook the stands. Four to three, the
home team in front, and only twelve minutes of play left.

For a while, those twelve minutes seemed to be more than Barcelona needed. In a ferocious, sustained reaction of overwhelming superiority, Jacobo's gate came under continual siege, fired at from all angles and with bewildering rapidity. Atlético's defense became disorganized. Jacobo was as good as alone. Eight savage boots sent the ball whizzing at him. Eight times he flung himself into the air, hands snaking out of space what seemed to be certain goals. He had never been better. And the crowd chanted, *Ei-xa-gui-rre!*

Atlético committed a maximum penalty foul. The free shot was kicked with cannon-ball velocity: low, curving, and true. No one could have stopped it. *Ei-xa-gui-rre, Ei-xa-gui-rre!*

The score was 4-4. The time: five minutes to play. Barcelona was satisfied with the tie, recoiling in a rampart against which Atlético's forwards, center, and even defensemen flung themselves fruitlessly. The clock clicked off seconds. There were fewer than three minutes to play, then two, then one. Atlético's attack continued. The referee was raising the whistle to his lips when an angling ground ball with a fierce spin bounced off the left Barcelona goalpost and skidded in.

On the field and in the stands there was tumult. Teammates swung themselves on the neck of the scorer, some running up to jump on his back. Both teams were awarded a standing ovation. No sound of the chant. In the locker room, the trainer nodded at Jacobo; but he turned then to speak at length, and privately, with the eager young Eixaguirre. Jacobo took a satchel out of the upper compartment in his locker, packing personal belongings into it.

Half an hour later, as he was leaving the stadium, he spied Blás's man across the street. Grau wore a double-breasted pepper-and-salt suit with lapels peaked so high they nearly protruded above the padded shoulders. He raised Laurel and Hardy eyebrows at Jacobo, turning into a café.

Jacobo waited for a trolley to pass. Then he crossed.

Grau stood in the shadows at the far end of the bar, a round-bellied glass of cognac in one hand. The fellow's black hair had been slicked flat over his narrow skull; as Jacobo approached, he inhaled the aromas of a pungent hair oil, nearly as pungent shaving lotion, and talcum powder. Grau quaffed his cognac when Jacobo was a stride away from him. He then dropped fifty céntimos on the counter, walking by Jacobo as though not recognizing him. Jacobo felt a thick, heavy weight being slipped into his satchel.

In the trolley, on the way home, he fingered the brown paper wrapping. He did not remove the parcel to examine it; nor, when home, pull it out. After supper, while Marisol was clearing, he managed to slip it into his worn military knapsack. Marisol had offered no comment when she saw that he had brought his satchel with him. When in bed, she said, "This morning, I threw up." She then rolled away from him.

When Jacobo felt positive that she slept, he eased out of bed. He adjusted behind him the blanket-screen that served to partition sleeping quarters from the rest of the single room. The parcel was tied in twine. First trimming an oil lamp, he picked the parcel's knot apart. His hands were shaking. His fingers were clumsy. Perhaps a minute or more passed before the wrapping fell away.

There were the bank notes: crisp and clean, strapped together in twenty-eight bundles by broad black elastic bands, under the last of which was a note.

Jacobo counted the bills carefully. He had never seen so much money: 280 1,000-peseta notes. He thought his heart would stop.

Then he puzzled over the pile. Altogether, he had blocked eighteen shots. That came to 360,000 pesetas.

Now he read the note:

Agreed: eighteen saves in all, and eight of them extraordinary. The second and third Barcelona goals, however, were inexcusable. I have therefore penalized you 40,000 pesetas for each. You should be more than satisfied. But if you feel my deductions are unjust, then let's meet again to discuss the matter.

The note was unsigned.

What a strange man! thought Jacobo. He paid a fortune promptly, without having received so much as a promise. Within this generosity, he quibbled—although leaving the matter open for protest. A lure? Another snare?

Jacobo gazed half an hour more at the money. Then he wrapped it up, put it away in the knapsack, went back to bed, and tried to sleep.

Next morning he was late rising. Marisol massaged a sore muscle in his back, after which she brought him a glass of aguardiente, the newspapers, and a flimsy blue envelope.

It was rare to receive a letter; rarer for Marisol to volunteer offering him alcohol.

He looked up at her from the bed.

"What do the newspapers say?"

"The brilliant attack in the second half saved the game you had lost in the first half."

"And . . . no one mentions my saves?"

"They are mentioned. But what you let through is emphasized."

He rested his gaze a long time on the envelope.

"From . . . the Atlético?"

She nodded. "By hand."

"You know what it must be?" he asked her then.

Marisol got heavily on her knees. She took his face in her hands, kissing him on the lips. And that, too, was a rare thing.

The severance contract offered three alternatives: field work within the organization; a lump sum payment; his earned pension. Marisol understood him when he told her that he could not bring himself to remain with the team as anything but a player. What he had earned in the way of a pension was little, and every day the peseta bought less. She agreed with him that he should elect the lump sum. He perceived the worry in her eyes. He felt an impulse that was like an ache to let her know about the 280,000 pesetas: to tell her about the financier called Blás, and what Blás wanted from him, and how perhaps doing what Blás wanted—which would be no more than attesting to truth—might imply the man's protection. But he held his tongue.

When Marisol had gone to market, he rose, dressed, hoist himself into the straps of his knapsack, and went for a walk.

It was a heavy, overcast day, sprinkling moisture. He walked down to the ocean front, and then along the wharves. He passed the Customs building and warehouses.

The sea moved with leaden monotony beneath the steady pelting of rain. The clouds turned blacker above, some hanging like sacks with boulders in them; and presently it was pouring. Dressed in shirt and trousers, Jacobo was soaked. He was indifferent to this. He turned his steps back toward the town and the address he had noted in the brief.

It was a street less squalid than the alley in which Marisol and he lived, but not much more prosperous; and in the rain, with the gray cobblestones and the gray stone blocks of the houses, gloomy. He passed a cutlery, a barber shop, a fruit stall, and a bicycle-repair establishment; above which the Larrañagas lived. His feet came together.

He was undecided. Did he wish to go up?

He pondered as the rain plastered his shirt against the skin. Across the street was a café.

He walked to it. Inside there were several tables set by a window.

Men sat at them, playing dominoes. One table was free. He ordered coffee.

He sat there two hours. A trolley, the shambles of a pre-War truck, a drove of sheep, and mule-and-cart carrying a tarpaulin-covered piano went by. Women huddled in black shawls and shielding themselves under black umbrellas trotted up and down the sidewalks. Card players at the table in front of him called for the bill and left.

It was nearly noon when he saw a woman emerge from the doorway adjacent to the bicycle-repair shop. She stooped, raising her arms to spring an umbrella open. It was a decided, even petulant and somewhat sullen gesture. He recognized Michelle Muñoz at once.

What was he to do? Why had he come?

Only life's unimportant decisions and actions tend to be planned, thought out. What followed was decided for him.

Michelle Muñoz came directly across the street and entered the café.

At first he thought she had recognized him; had somehow found out that he was sitting there, waiting to see her. Because, as he regarded her with crushing nervous and muscular tension, she walked directly to him, turning only at the last moment to sit at a chair left vacant by the card players. A waiter approached her familiarly, bringing (without having to be told) a little white saucer on which a tall glass rested. A single cube of ice bobbed in the clear liquid, sharing the surface with a rind of lemon.

Jacobo studied her with ferocious concentration. She was dressed in a shabby black wool coat, which she slipped from her shoulders, revealing a styleless black wool dress beneath it, buttoned close up under the chin. Eleven years had passed. She was now in her middle forties, and her hair had gone the coarse gray of a plowhorse's mane. She had grown stout, not in Marisol's muscular manner, but in lardish fashion. Her jowls were especially swollen; her nose remained as thick as ever at the bridge, although the mask of freckles had paled, possibly from infrequent exposure to the sun. Her skin seemed exceedingly sallow and unhealthy, the pores larger and oilier. A few teeth had now rotted to their stumps, and those remaining were more heavily encrusted by nicotine. She smoked as feverishly as ever, fishing a cigarette out of her handbag even before the drink was deposited on the table, and puffing at it in the same rapid, nervous manner between lips that had tightened even more forcibly into clamps.

Aware that she was being stared at, she turned her slightly popped, faded blue eyes at him. The silvery mascara was gone from the upper lids, but those clumsy darts of rust-brown still spoked out from the corners. Her stare was cold. She turned her face back to the window, gazing out into the street.

Jacobo was having difficulty with his emotions. Was it possible that he had pleasured in this aging, slatternly, somewhat repellent-looking woman? Had he permitted her to exploit his body during hour after hour and day after day, ravaging him?

Finally: was it possible that, having joined in depravity, she was able to stare at him without the slightest flicker of recognition?

Jacobo felt like throwing up. He was scandalized. He was incensed, indignant, flushing with an emotion that bordered on the homicidal. It could not be tolerated. She was evil. She deserved to be destroyed.

What Jacobo might have done next he will not conjecture and I can't divine. He knows only that he sat there in a fulmination of wrath and outrage, and also in a bile of disgust and self-disgust. Might he have leaped at her and begun choking her? Might he have snapped her skull from its base as savagely as he executed the commissar? Or might his self-disgust have prevailed, and Jacobo Rivas slunk out in unresolved misery, having gained no more than partial insight into the core of his weakness—that rotted melon of a core, that slushiness inside whose occasional fermentations to the surface were to make him wretched for the rest of his life, perceiving of himself (when he permitted it) that he was anything one cared to call him except a man, everything except virile, a gigantic husk like those great crustaceans trapped in fishermen's nets offshore near Sacedón and when hauled up discovered to be swarming inside and eaten out by an invasion of pulpy sea maggots against which not even the lobster's formidable armor is defense?

The option was not granted him. A youth entered: a tall, lithe young man, perhaps no more than thirteen or fourteen but looking two or three years older; a youth who carried himself with excessive and somehow malignant maturity, as though all too fully aware of his handsome dark features, his smoldering eyes, his berry-red lips, and that sort of feline male sexuality manifest on occasion in earliest adolescence and to women of all ages vanquishing.

He stood a moment by the entrance, looking about him, eyes then landing on the Frenchwoman. His gaze rapidly shifted to Jacobo, fastening on his eyes; and Jacobo received the very strong—remarkably strong—impression of icy contempt.

He then stepped up close to Michelle Muñoz, speaking in a tone just audible to Jacobo, and in a patois, words of which he was able to interpret.

"Come home," he said.

She glanced up at him, then jerked her face away.

"C'est bien, Maman," he insisted. "C'est assez."

Without looking at him, she mumbled, "Leave me alone."

Flashing a glance of—as it were—warning at Jacobo, the youth stepped closer to her.

"Father does not like you drinking alone," he murmured in a tight voice and from nearly motionless lips. "Father will be home within an hour. He will want his lunch."

"Then go to him," she said in Spanish, loudly, sullenly, still gazing out the window. "Vas à ton père. Dites-lui que je vais me saouler là geule." And in Spanish again, "Tell him I'm remembering."

Casting another glance at Jacobo—this time as though apprehensive —the youth shut him out by turning his back on him. When he spoke next, there were urgency and pleading in his tone.

"Please, Maman. We need you."

Jacobo's view of her face had been obstructed. Only from the shriveling of that part of her brow visible to him could he tell that she had shifted her gaze from the window to stare up at her son. Then she rose, her son paid the bill, and the two walked out together.

Jacobo watched them cross the street, the youth's arm around his mother's back.

He paid his own bill and rose, quitting the café, wandering along through the drizzle and gloom, and thinking, "If she is evil, how can she be needed?" And, "Why does she drink herself to death? What is the disappointment that has crippled her?"

Running water oiled the cobblestones into goblets of lead, red, and marmoreal light. His shirt had fastened to his pectoral muscles, which themselves hung as though sodden. He passed a church.

Stopping.

The doors were open: in Spain an unusual thing after morning services, when doors are ordinarily locked and the temple and its Presence barricaded away from human beings, so that if it is the last refuge for the hounded or tormented it is as often the least accessible one.

Jacobo trod up the flight of stone steps and entered.

It was dark, tenebral. He stared across a range of empty pews at the vacant baroque altar, its high retablo of shrouded and meaningless allegorical symbols—angels, prophets, and nameless saints, polychromed on wood panels—and at the brooding cruciform impaled on blackened timbers. The place was unhallowed, empty, a ghost forgot, the blood-red jewel of the sacramental light flickering in the distance like a dying pulse.

Jacobo trod the stone flags of an aisle, passing a confessional. Inside sat an ancient priest, reading his breviary with the help of a pocket flashlight, chin trembling and silver-thatched head wagging as he murmured the psalms.

Jacobo knelt before the man.

He told about his relations with Michelle Muñoz. He told about his failure to gain absolution and his gradual indifference to the sacraments. He spoke about the ghostly priest who had appeared to him in his delirium, and whose words he did not at the time understand nor yet plumb, and how he had committed sacrilege during his wedding Mass, having accepted Communion while in a state of sin for Marisol's sake—and out of cowardice. He told then of his growing fear of human beings, and of all traffic with them, relating each of Marisol's miscarriages and the loss of their infant, and how she was again pregnant; asking whether God punished on earth as well as in the afterlife, to which the priest replied that "spiritual disorder is echoed always in material disorder," an equivalence Jacobo was disposed to accept.

He said, "I am Jacobo Rivas, substitute portero for the Atlético. I was released this morning."

The priest, who had stoppered off his beam, now flashed it an instant at Jacobo's face, saying, "However did you let in that third goal?"

"I couldn't get myself moving in time. It was one of those things."

"That's no excuse. You gave me heart failure. I can forgive you the penalty shot in the second half."

"I'm sorry. There is a man who sent me two hundred and eighty thousand pesetas for the saves I made."

"What on earth for! A child could have blocked half of them. Oh, yes, there was a racha there of . . ."

"I know. He wants me to denounce a Communist, the husband—the lover—of the woman I told you about."

"Are you asking me whether you should do that?"

"Yes."

"Do you believe in Christ?"

"Yes."

"Do you love Him?"

"Not enough. She pointed that out to me."

"Will you observe His Commandments and the rules of His Church?"

"I am weak, I have told you."

"Piff! Last night I sneaked down to the pantry and stole a slab of butter—fresh butter, a gift to the Monsignor."

Jacobo was horrified. "Aren't you ashamed?"

"Yes . . . but not sufficiently. That's why I'm here—praying for an attack of indigestion. The butter was delicious. I ate it greedily, sinfully. When I told the Monsignor about it this morning he laughed, telling me I am incorrigible. That's the trouble. I *am* incorrigible, I've had a weakness for butter since my childhood in Galicia."

"You are not a Basque!"

"No—but I still have the power to bind or loose you, young man, and don't you forget it!"

"What do I do?"

"Your wife is pregnant again?"

"Yes."

"You have no job in the offing?"

"No."

"Communism is evil—the anti-Christ. You are aware of that."

"Yes."

"Two . . . hundred and . . . eighty . . . thousand . . . pesetas, he gave you."

"I am not giving it to the Church."

"I wasn't about to suggest it!"

"Then what should I do?"

"What Christ would have done."

"What is that?"

"That's where I'm stuck, I can't tell you. *Technically* the money needn't be considered thirty pieces of silver. On the one hand . . . On the other hand . . . I am getting too old for spiritual counseling, no doubt about it, I ought to retire, I am actually retired, you caught me here fortuitously, that slab of butter curdles whatever little left of moral insight I ever possessed, once I could have advised you, once upon a time I would have known just exactly what to tell you."

"You mean there's no answer!"

The priest seemed to rise in the confessional. "No answer?" he cried. "You expect an answer, pat, a decision? Christ God, man! Christ God!" He seemed to sit down again. "Do you imagine any of us receives an answer all our lives long? Do you think this soutane and the miraculous powers in my hands give me answers to the Chinese box of Justice? Come! Recite the Creed. I am going to absolve you, and pray for you, and try to forget you. My bones will lie under yours, and on top of your bones there will be generations more all having asked for an answer and all having rotted out their miserable existences of doubt and despair. Cephas! Cephas! Let us squat together and draw on the sand, Jacobo Rivas. Let us pray!"

Jacobo Rivas walked out unelated. He did not doubt the priest was mad. He did not doubt the man's power of cleansing souls. But he had imagined relief to follow from having finally closed some of the distance between himself and his Creator. There was nothing of the kind. There was the knowledge only that if God could understand and forgive, he could not. Chill comfort that he had been born as he was.

Blás was not in. Jacobo had to wait in the service entrance half an hour. Then Stepanópoulis Grau descended, announced importantly that Señor Blás would be pleased to receive him, dashed into the cook's urinal, returned, and escorted Jacobo up the stairs.

The financier looked tired; and older in the dull, midafternoon dimming of the wet day. It was plain to Jacobo that he had been reared in the African south, where skies are monotonously blue and their sun a predictable terror. Blás was friendly, but less affable.

Jacobo returned to the man his brief. He also searched out of the knapsack the bunch of pesetas, setting that down on the marble top of a coffee table.

"Then you are not in agreement?" said Blás inquiringly; speculatively; bald right eyebrow crooking up above a less flexible bald left eyebrow, so that the furrows on his promontoried brow formed in a meaty, uneven ripple.

Jacobo said nothing.

"You've read the brief. It did not convince you?"

"I knew the woman."

"Intimately."

"Yes."

"You went to see her today."

"Yes." He spied a snicker of satisfaction on the prim lips of Grau.

"You feel sorry for her—tenderness—nostalgia."

"I feel responsible."

"The priest absolved you?"

"Yes."

"Advised you?"

"No."

"Confound curates!"

"He is old, maybe insane."

"And God? What do you think of Him? To have created us."

"I ask, 'Why should I be one of the unlucky ones, one of the weak ones?'"

"Indeed, why should you?"

"We aren't like one of those plants I've seen growing in the sea, all needing each other, all doing a special service for each other, some of them the tentacles that sting and bring the prey to the mouth, others the mouth and stomach, and still others the ones that reproduce for the whole colony: all different, all a whole, you can tear parts of them away and the rest will continue to thrive, I mean the colony, the individuals within it do not matter."

"But we are not like that," emphasized the financier.

"No. We feel. We are complete."

"But we are a community nevertheless, we each have our function— the dead and the living, unless my memory fails me, the saved and the damned."

"Were you a priest?"

"A contrabandist."

"Stolen goods smuggled, small bales of truth sneaked from shores you can't imagine and pitched out at midnight on the sands. Is there a difference?"

"Their job is more difficult, their crimes greater. Snatching a slab of butter is as inexcusable as being an accomplice to the concealment or protection of an enemy of Spain."

"That priest . . ." There was sudden fear in Jacobo's voice. "He was . . . real?"

"Reassure yourself."

"He had the powers of Peter?"

"Somewhat disused, somewhat decrepit, but effectual nevertheless."

"He did not send me to the Bishop!"

"You are not worth the Bishop's time."

"My sins are heavy."

"They are redeemable."

"You opened the church doors. You planted him. How? How did you lead me down the street and into the temple?"

"Everyone follows the path he began cutting with his first teeth."

"Are you Satan?"

"I hope not."

"Are you Gabriel, then?"

"Decidedly not."

"Should I detest you?"

"You will have a legion for comfort."

"Who are you?"

"A power."

"For good or evil?"

"They do not enter the terms of barter."

"Am I dreaming?"

"I think so."

"Are you within my dream or directing it?"

"You summoned me. None of us can resist."

"Take me back."

"To start over?"

"Yes!"

"Not all the way, I'm afraid. That is given to no one."

"As far as possible, then."

Blás rose, grappling with inertia, stomping gravity beneath him.

Jacobo walked down the street, losing his way, but finding the church again at last, and the old priest with the mesmerically wagging head thatched thinly over by hair granulated with mercury. He repeated everything he had to say, receiving absolution, walking then unelated and undecided back to the Carlton, waiting for Grau, waiting for the pompous little man in his checkered suit and incontinent bladder, son of a government functionary, he guessed with unreal clarity, who used to wet his bed and be punished so severely for it that once he tied his penis tightly in twine and nearly died of peritonitis; and being escorted by him up the service stairway and into the financier's suite, where he placed a brown-wrapped parcel of crisp green thousand-peseta notes on the veined marble top of a coffee table.

Blás said to him, "Suppose we threaten denouncement—that only. Would you agree to it? He will consult the Party. He will be removed, probably posted somewhere outside Spain, which is all I am after."

Jacobo said, "He loves his God. He is a sort of priest. There's more to be said for him than for us. If it is because of his faith that you move against him, then have him shot, don't stop at less."

The financier said, "You are not so indispensable that I need remind you what your refusal to co-operate in a patriotic and in fact legally imperative action could imply for you."

"If his faith is evil, or you believe it is, put him to death. I broke the neck of a commissar once. I could break your neck."

"Eventually, I'll find some other witness. The money, meanwhile, belongs to you. It has nothing to do with this other matter. If you feel I have been niggardly about the goals you let through, fine, I will restore the eighty thousand pesetas I deducted."

He signaled to Grau, who stepped forward, handing Blás an attaché case; out of which Blás extracted a packet of bills, counting out eighty green notes in reams of five each and placing them neatly on top of the parcel.

"There," he said, returning the case to Grau, "take them, put them back in your knapsack, and good luck to you."

"No."

"You need do nothing about my problem at Customs." This was said with some exasperation.

"All the more reason," Jacobo replied.

The financier stared at him. "Would you like to work for me?"

"Day before yesterday, perhaps."

"Now?"

"Never."

Jacobo retrieved his beret from the carved, curving arm of a little chair, over which he had draped it.

"Thank you anyway," he said, going to Blás and offering his large hand.

The financier cocked that bulbous head at him. The bulging frontal lobes shone.

He stated with some care, "I'll have the money deposited in your name in a savings account at the Banco Bilbao."

"Don't do that."

"It's my pleasure, Señor Rivas." He rose before taking the hand of his visitor. "Good-bye. May you succeed in begetting many sons."

Jacobo reached home after dark. He was never to be sure what he had dreamed and what he had not. Not for many years did he dare inquire of the Bank of Bilbao whether there was a savings account in his name; by which time he had begot many sons and many daughters too, losing the last of his self-respect.

TEN

Rivas at Bay

Having turned down Blás, there was no recourse for Jacobo: the Rivases retreated to Marisol's family farm in Sacedón. The hand was let go. Jacobo enlarged the cottage by digging cellars out of the hillside, shoring the ceiling up with cement pillars and façading these quasi-caveman's quarters with stone and rubble. The damp was extreme.

Marisol, freshening yet once again, suffered in the spirit. For a Spanish woman, to work the soil is only less low than mendicancy. She had imagined herself rescued by Jacobo. Now she was hopelessly back where they had begun.

In 1949, Primitivo was born, earning his name not from being the first son but the first to survive. He was quickly followed by Serenidad, Antonio, and Celestina; and then, between miscarriages and another infant death, by two others. To his despair, Jacobo noticed that Marisol successfully conceived and bore after she had dragged him to settle his accounts with God every Eastertide. These were about the only accounts he was able even fitfully to meet.

These were the years of the great famine. I remember. I had first begun visiting Spain in the mid-1940s, reluctant to return to money-making and feeling at a loss after five years of active battle command for my native England. The triumphant Allies spewed Fascist Spain out of their mouths. France, Great Britain, and my adopted America, along with that other notable democracy, the Union of Soviet Socialist Republics, joined in anathematizing Franco, excluding Spain from the chaste United Nations Organization and spiting her from international commerce. Being an English recusant, with gobs of French blood, I understood at once that fascism had nothing to do with the case. Spain was being made to pay for her Catholicism and three centuries of empire, neither of which has ever been forgiven by her historical rivals. Let alike Loyalists and Nationalists, the true Reds with the true Fascists, and all those multitudes who were neither, starve. And they did—by the thousands.

Jacobo scoured the countryside for the odd job, leaving the farm to Marisol, who would scythe away in the broiling humidity of August even when immense with the next child. Jacobo milked at the Nestlés factory when the chance was offered. He quarried. He fished for crabs in seaside lagoons; and under the rocks below Sacedón's sea wall poked a hook with a white linen lure attached to it, hoping for an octopus to scuttle out. He filched plums and apples. He plucked blackberries. He snatched at the teats of stray she-goats, draining half a pint of watery milk; and whenever a compassionate deity gave him the occasion, he poached roebuck or wild boar from the State preserves.

God seemed to be rarely bothered with Jacobo, His fickle, weak, but faithful servant. Thirteen full years, Providence forced him to the trough of defeat and gave him gall to drink. The children kept multiplying. In vain Jacobo's efforts; in vain Marisol's untiring arms and back; hunger emaciated them. Finally, although they sacrificed their own appetites as much as the necessity for maintaining their strength permitted, he and she both began glancing at her parents.

Marisol's father was far gone in dotage: he slopped up whatever was offered, and as much as was offered, seemingly unaware of circumstances and the needs of his grandchildren. Marisol's mother, although almost as old and almost as weak, was in possession of her faculties. One evening she murmured to Marisol, "There is no reason for you to take the goats to the high pasture. The climb is not good for you so far along as you are. Your father and I can manage."

Then she looked down. Jacobo looked away. He had seen in Marisol's face the awful understanding. He could not bear to meet her eyes.

He went to bed as quickly as he was able. Marisol lingered half an hour more; then joined him, speaking no word.

Next afternoon the goats wandered back down alone; Jacobo climbed to the high pasture—where he had first met Marisol and the spastic Salvador; where he had killed the lynx—in search of the old people. They had apparently slipped and tumbled into the ravine, shattering their old bones almost precisely where the cat had met its death.

Their absence scarcely helped. Marisol suggested that Jacobo swallow pride and appeal to his father. Jacobo would not hear of it. Marisol, past caring about dignity, then prompted him to approach his brothers-in-law for part-time work. Again Jacobo refused. He had been, for a brief period, the begrudged success of the family; that family had refused to have part of him, and he would not now crawl to them. His obduracy on this score was the first difference between them to really bring out the rage in Marisol. She struck Jacobo across the face. It was his incompetence, his cowardice, his vanity, and his low lust that had driven them into their desperate plight. He was a failure as a Basque and a Christian and a husband and a father. He had managed to antagonize in some way or another almost everyone, so that when relief work was organized by the Ayuntamiento, he, among the neediest, was never a candidate.

Now that she had discovered its use, Marisol's tongue was as untiring as the rest of her. She even accused him of having been stupid in his defense of Salvador, her brother: in his defiance of tradition. This last accusation she did not really mean; but she had been strained beyond endurance. Body and spirit were exhausted.

The year was 1950. Jacobo turned thirty-six. He began suffering from periods of impotence. He would desire; he would importune. To his wife's disgust, he could not perform.

He consoled himself with periodic drinking bouts. Down at the port, with the lowest of the farmers and fisher-folk, he imbibed quarts of nearly pure grain alcohol, boasting mightily, sometimes fighting, every now and then ending up at the house his brother Amadeo had once frequented, where another in a seemingly unending line of sister-whores received. With this woman, he rediscovered his potency, but he was always deeply ashamed afterward: of his betrayal of Marisol, of his viciousness, and because of the money he had spent. He regarded himself in a very bleak light. He did not attend his mother's funeral.

One late night, stumbling away from the whore's cottage, down into the ravine and up the zigzagging path that led by the ruins of the castle and thence on to Marisol's farm, he encountered the Duke.

There was a clear moon; its light flashed off the stern aristocrat's steely appurtenances. He was walking alone and stiffly through the grounds, a tiny figure with an authoritarian military spine, gazing up at the twin turrets of stone between which the charred central portions of the great house still seemed to smoke.

He spun about at Jacobo's approach, peering at him across ten meters of spilled silver and blue with almost murderous antagonism. Then his features relaxed, just slightly; disdain entered.

"I know you!" he snapped, taking a decided step forward.

Jacobo wavered a bit as he came to a halt, getting out a slurred, "Sí, señor."

"The Rivas who tried to stop that savage spectacle," said the Duke. "The football player. The Johnny-come-lately into the Crusade."

"Sí . . . señor." He remembered—managed—to sweep off his beret.

The Duke about-faced on his prosthetic leg, staring back at the ruins. "Just look at that!" he exclaimed. "I watched it from the sea—

ROSENDALE LIBRARY
ROSENDALE, N.Y.

watched them blow the place up and set fire to the rest; watched it from the ship, barbarians, looters, vicious animals! Our infantry wasn't half an hour away. Not even the Tiepolos were spared."

Jacobo swayed, saying nothing.

The Duke jerked his chin at Jacobo, showing half a thin, long-nosed profile, startling Jacobo by the sudden resemblance he perceived to his father. "Eh!" the aristocrat snapped again. "You heard what I said? I walk out nights to look at it—and then," pivoting, pointing, "to look at the cemetery. Those ruins were left by Sacedón as an eternal reproach to my family and me. They were the first sight we saw when we got up mornings and glanced out our windows. Well, the first thing you people are going to see for the rest of your existences when you look out your windows and up toward the hills for the weather portents are these ruins—an eternal reproach to you, to your brutishness. It wasn't the Reds—strangers—who did it. I know better than that!"

Jacobo swayed on.

The Duke turned to him abruptly.

"You fought in my brigade during the last of the War."

"Sí . . . señor."

"Then you went back to the Atlético."

"Sí . . ." He hiccupped. ". . . señor."

"You failed there, came back, squatted at the farm of your wife's parents and . . . What? Besides drinking yourself sodden!"

"I . . . I work . . . where I can find it." His shame oppressed him even through the stupor of his drunkenness.

"How many children!"

"Five . . . No, six."

"You can't even count them?"

"Six . . . señor."

"Half starved, I suspect."

"Sí . . . señor."

The Duke turned from him, staring ferociously back up at the turrets. The family now summered in what had been stable and servants' quarters.

"No," the Duke muttered, "so long as I live, never will I clear the place. I'll leave it as it is . . ." He wheeled once again toward Jacobo, saying, "Do you realize that when that evil and decadent and half-demented man—your father, Manú—dies, you will be chieftain of the clan?"

Jacobo nodded. It meant so little.

But not, apparently, to the Duke. Tradition had its claws in his entrails. He had followed Jacobo's career.

"Do you consider yourself worthy?" From his eyes flashed scathing blue-white beams. "Pah!" came contemptuously from the Steel Duke. "A . . . worthy . . . representative of True Spain! A worthy head of the clan indeed! Report to me tomorrow."

"Sí, mi General!" And Jacobo actually came to attention, saluting: but it was a grotesque gesture, since he nearly fell forward and upon the Duke, whose lips merely tightened.

Jacobo's meeting with the Duke of Steel may have saved his family.

The choice for Jacobo was not easy. Taking the job in the Duke's mines had not bothered him. To work as a servant, on the actual grounds of the enemy, was different.

For Jacobo, the choice was continuing penury, or this, or the blood money—if it existed.

He loved Marisol. He loved his children. He decided that to accept was the lesser of the dishonorable alternatives; that, in fact, to swallow some pride for the sake of wife and children was the honorable, if distasteful, thing to do.

Having made that decision, he by and by discovered that he was proud to work for General Luis del Val, XIIIth Duke of Sacedón. Were the Dukes not kin, blood of his blood, flesh of his flesh? Shortly, he had taken his place in this Duke's camp as against the town. It was, in its way, a strange reconciliation of historically embattled bloodlines. Manú was so outraged that he sent an emissary offering to settle past differences if Jacobo would leave the Duke's provenance and come work on the parental farm. Jacobo sent back a profane no.

His handyman's job, bringing little more than subsistence, helped nevertheless to restore self-respect. He was much pleased when the Duke grunted his approval of a chicken pen neatly patched or manure spread meticulously over a flowerbed. With a will, he built under the Duke's direction a gigantic billboard, which the noble placed on posts between the turrets, and on which was painted: TO OUR EVERLASTING SHAME. He liked the heir, young Federico. He was tickled when the boy jested, "Maybe the hidalgoships will be revived when the King returns! That would be amusing, Jacobo, wouldn't it? Will you oblige me to kiss your hand?"

He recounted this to Marisol, but she merely went on basting the night's meat. If no more than tenuously, they had been members of the middle class. Now her husband was a Jack-of-all-trades.

Her attitude angered Jacobo. He was the "etcheko juan"—master of the house, who, if he cared to, wore his beret at the table. He wheeled right around, stomping out of the hut and down the mountain to the seaside tavern, where, after many drinks, he recounted what the boy had said; and when meeting with smirks, rose up in thundering fury (his cowardice sent to flight by it), and smashed three or four of those smirks into a pulp of blood and dentine before he was overpowered; for which scandal, after nearly three and a half years with the Duke, he was dismissed.

This was a formidable blow. Jacobo recognized the justice of the action. Severity was the Duke's principal trait. He himself lived a rigorous upright existence, free of even the whiff of moral delinquency, and anyone associated with him was expected to meet the standard set. During the War, he had used the firing squad liberally in cases of insubordination, funk, or rapine following the conquest of a town. (It was said by his troops that theirs was the only brigade in the Army that never harvested what it had sowed and never sowed after a harvest.) There was no appeal.

This happened in 1954. Soledad was a year-old tot. Jacobo despaired. How alchemize subsistence out of a few overgrazed hilltop acres and the odd job? Five long years rolled by in terrible, losing struggle. Poverty —dirt, most grinding poverty—pounded, broke, and ground to pieces the last Rivas resistance. Jacobo aged. He was dulled to brutedom.

There was now a medical doctor in Sacedón, a young and dedicated man. And there was a young curate, filled with newly ordained zeal. Although the doctor professed atheism, they established a working team, disputing their philosophical points as together they climbed the most remote hills of the parish and each in his way tended to the needy. It was the doctor who advised Marisol and Jacobo that their infant daughter was suffering from such a syndrome of malnutrition that her bone growth was seriously endangered. Soledad had already become Jacobo's favorite child. In the quicksilver spirit of this one daughter, with her bright trusting eyes and the ardent swift impulsive huggings of her thin little arms, he could for moments coat present and future, take joy in a father's love, feel happiness again, and sometimes even loose his booming basso in a song. He was shattered by the diagnosis; and during his confession, conducted in the cowshed while the curate scatted off hens that mistook him for a perch, begged the curate to tell him what he should do. The priest, searching for a flea or fleas in his right trouser leg, admitted that he had no idea for the long term, although he had been able to scrounge 10,000 pesetas from His Eminence the Bishop of Bilbao with which he was supposed to relieve more than forty destitute families. But he was rather taken by the large appealing eyes of Soledad himself; and after debating in his mind whether it was really necessary for him to consume six tablets daily against his various allergies (it was: he sneezed with percussive force; this was the rye grass season), told Jacobo that he would divide 10,000 by 40, which came, he assured the slow-witted man, to 400 pesetas; and having for the moment dispensed with practical matters, lectured Jacobo about his patronage of that unmentionable family of sisters in the portside cottage, giving him absolution while gently removing the nibble-minded muzzle of a goat from his fly.

The money helped. Vitamins were purchased not through the pharmacy but directly from the doctor (who halved the wholesale price while persuading himself that he really did not absolutely require the new stethoscope); but a decision of some sort had to be made.

There were three Church-run foundling homes within a two-days' walk. Upon mention of the fact, Marisol tore open the top of her faded brown blouse, exposing her still magnificent breasts, and cried, "Kill me! Go on, drive the blade of your knife into my heart!"

That was when Jacobo went to the local subsidiary of the Bank of Bilbao and asked whether there were a savings account in the central house ascribed to him. He insisted on a telephone call, for which he had to advance the small charge; and then waited the several hours it required for the call to come through. When it was announced, he further insisted on himself speaking; and after many delays and many switchings from one department to another; and after being instructed on how to hold the new-fangled receiver, whose compact smirking black perforated smugness intimidated him so much that he barked angrily at it, pulling it down from his lips to stare at it and thus catching very little of the crackles that kept coming out the other end; heard—it sank in finally, he comprehended—that there was indeed an account credited to Jacobo Rivas y Echevarría, domiciled in the town of Sacedón, and that with accrued cumulative interest it now amounted to nearly 650,000 pesetas.

Jacobo fainted.

The sprawl of his body on the floor stopped the manager of Sacedón's Banco Bilbao as he was walking out of his office for a meeting with the town council. "Who is that!" he cried at an underling. Jacobo Rivas, he was told: the one-time portero for the Atlético. The manager —a balding, intellectually featured fellow in his late fifties—stared at

Jacobo. He stared and stared. It had not been a dream, then: not a nightmare.

He stepped over his rival, walking home instead of to the town hall, where he redeemed his and his wife's honor.

This inexplicable and shocking murder-suicide engrossed Sacedón for weeks; it did not penetrate Jacobo's consciousness. He brooded in the hilltop cottage. Marisol's tongue was unable to pry his great bottom off the milking stool at which he sat, which failing she applied to his head the solid oven-baked crockery of a water jug; but this had little more effect than to wrinkle the now oft-scarred brow. Of course, inflation had robbed the peseta of truth, but this was a day when a laborer was grateful to be handed 30 pesetas at sundown. Domestic servants earned not more than 400 pesetas the month. On the mere interest from his fortune, he would be able to support as many children as God saw fit to give Marisol, and live in idleness.

"If you are merely to sit there," Marisol shouted at him, ". . . if you intend to sit there forever, do no work, let us all die of hunger; go, go to your drunken friends and your whores, but get out of my house!"

He rose.

No cross had weighed so heavily on Jacobo's shoulders than the knowledge that at any time he need do no more than order the money transferred to Sacedón and draw on it at will. He reached town in a sweat of indecision, his steps leading him to the bank, which was locked tight, and whose window grills were crêped. He had heard from Marisol that something important had happened; that a special contingent from Madrid's Bureau of National Security had been summoned. Because, among the bank manager's private papers, subversive material had been discovered. All this had been recorded in the now nearly muscle-bound furrows of his brain without his having noticed it. That entire week he had fought the almost overwhelming temptation of telling Marisol about the windfall; fought it not merely because she would adduce highway robbery to his other grievous sins, but because she would have no doubts at all as to what to do with the money; and no compunctions.

He was turning from the bank, and with the intention of proceeding just as Marisol had suggested, to the portside tavern; when a black official Citroën limousine chugged up over the cobbles of the square and stopped, steaming from the radiator. Four men in dark city suits, white shirts, and florid ties, dismounted.

One of them exuded authority. Two inferiors walked to the chained bank's door and began unlocking it. The chief meantime surveyed the square while a third underling brushed dandruff from his broad shoulders.

This was that prissy little fellow Jacobo had last seen in the Blás suite at the Carlton Hotel: fifteen years—a lifetime—ago.

He was older. There were flecks of gray in the shiny black hair and on the cutting edge of his pencil-stroke mustache. He seemed less conscious of his importance—humbled by life's vicissitudes—walking at the left and slightly to the rear of his slow-moving chief, treading the cobblestones as though in deferential fear of displacing them. As he passed, Jacobo reached out an arm, grasping him by his flabby little bicep.

"Excuse me!" pipped the little man; startled; casting an uneasy glance at his superior, who described a half turn toward them.

Jacobo said, "You are the one, the person responsible."

"I . . . I do not have the honor . . ." stammered the little man. He was in his early thirties now. His hair had come to a widow's peak, its defenses caving in at the sides. It still reeked of oil. He had preserved his wasp's waist, and that faintly androgynous narrowness of hip and over-all birdness of bone that one sees in Mediterranean gypsy youths, Puerto Ricans, and some Orientals.

"I'm not sure I have any longer," murmured Jacobo, his great paw remaining clenched on the man's bicep; inflicting pain, apparently, because he began squirming.

His superior intervened.

"Here, there, you, fellow, take your hand off my officer!"

Six feet tall, the chief had a blunt, no-nonsense set of features, the nose pug, the eyes well protected beneath a low brow, his chin solid.

Jacobo did not release the arm. "You are responsible," he repeated.

"Are you raving?" cried the little man.

"Release him at once!" barked the chief, authority in his voice. Then, as Jacobo obeyed: "Responsible for what?"

"This situation," mumbled Jacobo, with a gesture that took in the world but happened also to embrace the bank.

"What!" The superior now addressed his deputy. "Stepanópoulis, what in God's name have you got to do with this! Ortiz's just about the only person in the whole kingdom you failed to mention in your dossier!"

"I have nothing to do with it!" Grau bleated, knees collapsing toward each other. He could feel the burning sands of the Sahara. He could smell the prison of Carabanchel. "This man is a maniac."

"You worked for him!" Jacobo spoke up accusingly. "It was you put the money in the bank."

"What's that?" said the chief, now fully facing Jacobo. "What's this about money!"

"He put it in the bank," Jacobo muttered. "He worked for him."

"Stepanópoulis, did you hear the allegation? You put money into the bank. You worked for him."

"I don't know what he's talking about! Sir, believe me, I don't even know what you are talking about." His knees gripped each other.

"What are we talking about?" said the chief, addressing himself once more to Jacobo.

"The money."

"Whose money!"

"The Blás money."

"*Who?*"

"Blás."

"*Baltazar* Blás?"

"Of course."

The chief now turned menacingly on Grau. "Stepanópoulis, were you ever in the employ of Baltazar Blás?"

"I . . . I . . ." His knees rubbed each other; then both knees began wagging desperately in a lover's clinch.

"Stepanópoulis Grau, are you, an officer—God help us!—in the Bureau of National Security not aware of the gravity of this?"

"I am not going to touch it," said Jacobo. "It's not mine."

But neither agent paid him attention. They were staring at each other: on the chief's face a rock-hard expression, on the inferior's face anguish.

"Answer me!" the former said.

But Grau only moaned. His knees now flapped apart and came together and then flapped apart again, as though he were dancing the Suzy-Q. "Please . . . a bathroom . . . !" And he rushed by his chief and into the bank.

Jacobo was about to turn away when the big man detained him.

"You, fellow, what's your name?"

"Jacobo Rivas."

"You live here?"

"Not in town."

"Pretty countryside."

"Yes."

"Oh, so you prefer the countryside, you don't like the town."

"Only in the summer."

"The fishing good?"

"Not very."

"I've . . . seen your face before."

"Yes, I have too."

"My face?"

"No, mine. But I don't recognize it."

"Are you daft?"

"My hearing is quite good. It's my eyes, I think, that were strained, not the reflexes."

"Are you drunk?"

"Not yet. I hope to be quite soon."

"What makes you think my sergeant worked for Baltazar Blás?" The chief spoke these words indignantly.

"He wore a white suit."

"Who? Grau?"

"Señor Blás."

"What has that to do with it!"

"I've done nothing. I will not use a penny of it."

"Of what?"

"The money."

"*Whose* money!"

"The Blás money."

"But who are you! How in the world did you know the bank manager is connected with Blás?"

"Oh, I know nothing about that." Jacobo was all at once worried. What—in his witless, spoken musings—was he getting himself into?

"Come out with it, now! The murderer-suicide was a known revolutionary. Señor Blás denounced him fifteen years ago, as was proper. But he escaped. He slipped back into Spain, we're not sure when. He came here at his request six months ago from the Valencia branch of the Banco Bilbao. Now, if you are intimating that Señor Blás, in some form, subsidized Larrañaga, I want to know about it, and I . . ."

Jacobo sputtered, "Larra . . . Larrañaga?"

"Yes! The deceased. His true name. Why?"

But Jacobo fainted.

Upon reviving, he found himself in the library of the Ayuntamiento, which he had not visited since being introduced to its treasures by Michelle Muñoz. His mind revolved slowly as he came to. It could not be that the dead bank manager was the same Larrañaga, alias Ortiz, alias (as he called himself before his death) Zárate; it could not be that she had been in Sacedón for the past several months; and that she was dead, murdered by her husband no one knew why.

When the security force entered—all four, led by their chief—Jacobo had wits enough to ask no questions and to plead illness and hallucinatory seizures induced by undernourishment. The young doctor, summoned, stated that it would surprise him not at all to hear such things of Jacobo, who was indeed in wretched physical condition and who had swooned, in fact, on the morning of the murder-suicide, and in the bank. While he spoke to the chief detective, Jacobo stole glances at the fellow called Stepanópulis Grau. Grau yanked his eyes away, but Jacobo noticed the man's relief when he again denied ever having met him or known anything about him. The police chief was satisfied. The doctor called upon his friend, the curate, to testify to Jacobo's character, which the curate did with a silent plea to his Creator for indulgence; and then the Duke of Sacedón himself gimped in on his tubular prosthetic leg, by his authority diminishing the chief detective's authority to the weight of a speck of dust, declaring that he had known Jacobo Rivas many years and that the man, although mentally retarded and of lamentable habits, possessed no malice.

Jacobo was released. He walked aimlessly down to the port, very much in need of alcohol; and at ten paces from the tavern door, encountered his father.

The man was a mummy: blackened leather and tendons sticking to a scaffold of bones. He was no less furious and no less intoxicated.

"You!"

He blocked Jacobo's path, eyes a fierce orange.

"Again!" he said.

"I had nothing to do with it," Jacobo stated, stepping forward. "Get out of my way."

"Stand where you are!"

Jacobo halted. He was prone to obey even the ghost of authority.

"You had everything to do with it!" Manú screamed at him.

Jacobo was thankful there was no one about.

"To do with what?"

"It was you who started it!" Manú shrilled in hopping, skittering fury. "Twenty years back it was you who took her to our house, you who fed her starved foreign cunt, disgracing us! But no wonder she came back: the dirty old sow! No woman ever had a Basque between her legs forgets it. So she came back! So she trapped, seduced, raped my darling little boy, your brother! And now he's gone! Now he's left me, gone I don't know where!"

Manú, dribbling tears, swatted Jacobo across the face, turning and stumbling back into the tavern.

Jacobo felt earthquakes in his skull. He went stumbling up the path to the whore's cottage. She was entertaining, he was told by her parents, who offered him a thirteen-year-old they felt was old enough to "feel the bit." He declined. He waited. They asked him whether he would have some wine. He declined. The old lady was weaving a garland of flowers; the old man was busy sewing up a pigeon net; the thirteen-year-old sucked a thumb and stared at him out of eyes as big and black as coat buttons. Up from the cellar ladder climbed his half brother: whom he had not seen since just after the War; whom he was shocked now to see, his twin in appearance.

Except that he was nineteen, not forty-five; and with a trace of his mother's simian expression on an otherwise handsome set of features.

They stared at each other. "You next?" his half brother asked.

"Yes. Do you know who I am?"

"Jacobo. You're older than I expected."

"And you. Your father is at the tavern. He's crazy, looking for you."

"My father or my grandfather?"

"That's a poor joke."

"It's been a poor joke on me."

"You speak disrespectfully."

"I will speak as I like."

"Not about our father: not in front of me." The blood had rushed to his face.

"Then I will speak about my grandfather!"

Jacobo hit him.

When the boy got up off the floor, he attacked. Jacobo was weakened. Still, he was surprised by his half brother's strength and quickness. His hands were flashes of light . . . and his legs: his legs were also fast.

Jacobo received many blows before he managed to put his half brother down again. Then he helped revive him. Both washed their mouths out in the wine offered by the old people.

Jacobo said, "The bank manager's wife, was she French?"

"Yes. God, what a bull you are!"

"She must have been in her fifties!"

"I needed the money."

"What for?"

"Our father's right. I've escaped. I'm leaving."

"Where do you plan to go?"

"I don't know."

"What will you do?"

"I want to play football."

Jacobo gasped.

They walked out together, parting on the lower slope of the town, having taken an overland route in order to avoid meeting their common father or anyone else. They never saw each other again. (Jacobo's brother, a star, uses an assumed surname.)

Jacobo climbed back up the mountain to the cottage. He had failed in both resolutions of getting drunk and defying Marisol with the whore. He trudged slowly. One resolution alone had been arrived at: not—not ever—to touch the money.

At the gate, he stiffened himself against what he knew would be the storm. He was astonished when a weeping Marisol flung out of the cottage and flung her considerable weight into his arms.

"I am so sorry!" she cried.

News had been sent to her by a fisherman's son that Manú Rivas had collapsed in the tavern of apoplexy.

Marisol, of course, deemed Manú a wicked man. She wept anyhow, because a family death was a family death whatever the merits of the case; and if one thought about Manú, his unshrived death was ample cause for weeping. Jacobo was much bemused to learn after the burial that he had been the proximate cause of his father's stroke. A fisherman, thinking to give Manú condolence for his runaway son, said to him, "You lost the best, one after another. Now you only have that worthless Jacobo."

Manú had jerked a besotted head up at this. "No Rivas is worthless!" he had cried, springing on his erstwhile friend; and falling to the floor with his lunge.

Jacobo did not know why this story consoled him. He did not love his father. He was baffled that he valued even Manú's negative defense.

He was now chief of the clan.

Manú Rivas died in August of 1959. His estate was quickly settled: rumors attending it at once displacing the murder-suicide as the prime topic of town interest. Because he died a comparatively wealthy man.

The farm was valued at 250,000 pesetas. But under Manú's mattress his humpback daughter-mistress found a sack of gold pieces dating back a century or more. Their value was estimated at 380,000 pesetas.

One third of the total 630,000-peseta assets came under the "legítima": a net total of 210,000 pesetas in gold and property. This was shared by Jacobo and his six sisters, 30,000 apiece in cash and value. All the "mejora" and all the "libre de disposición" had been left to their half brother.

Jacobo and three of his sisters sold out their share of the farm to their humpback sister and the two farmer brothers-in-law, whose property adjoined.

Marisol had a long talk with Jacobo. They were clearly doomed in Sacedón. They would have to move to a city and he would have to apply for a job as a laborer.

They discussed the matter with the doctor and the priest. Both suggested Madrid as the answer. There was more opportunity in the capital city. Marisol, in private, gave her forceful approval to the idea: there Jacobo would not be haunted by his past. But what to do in Madrid? They would have to find lodgings. What trade could Jacobo adopt?

"There is much construction," said the doctor at another meeting.

"True," agreed the curate, "but the really remunerative labor is skilled."

He removed a tick from the crevice of one ear. It was big with his blood. Marisol was big again with her seventh child.

The doctor pondered. Then he said, "You both know your milk, cheese, butter, and eggs. Jacobo certainly knows his wines! And you, Doña Marisol, your parents once owned the Ultramarinos. Could you not find a location for a shop—a mantequería—with living quarters upstairs?"

It was merely a suggestion; but Marisol seized on it. Jacobo abhorred the notion of leaving Sacedón. He loved the hills. But he had not the will to resist. Marisol began searching out a buyer for her little farm.

The best offer she could get was 50,000 pesetas.

They met a third time with curate and doctor.

"A total of eighty thousand pesetas . . ." the priest murmured dubiously.

"It's not nearly sufficient," said the doctor. "You will be spending time and money looking for a location."

Jacobo stated, "I have six hundred and fifty thousand pesetas in the Banco Bilbao."

His words stunned priest, doctor, wife and progeny.

Marisol took two steps toward Jacobo and wrapped him in her huge arms. But nothing would ever compensate for his renunciation of honor.

(Later, Marisol was to add this secret hoard to her grievances. Why had not Jacobo told her about it years before, when it could have done so much good and stretched so much further? Why had he not drawn on it when they were—those terrible, dark, despairing years—down to the boiling point of leather for soup? Had he not, in a manner of speaking, caused the death of her parents; and the loss of how many infants!)

(Jacobo accepted her point of view. I was to argue this with him over several meetings in his cell at the Carabanchel prison. "You held out as long as you were able!" I said with some degree of passion. "No more could be asked of you. You *earned* that money—you didn't pay blood for it." He shook his great head with the stubbornness of the unsophisticated, who can be cursed with a truer moral sense than our own. "If I used it at all," he said, "I should have used it for the children. That is why God has turned His face from me." "But" —I argued back— "you did use it for the children, for the children and for Marisol!" He wagged that head again. "I used it for myself.")

In Madrid, Jacobo was late again. The ten-year boom from scarcely one million inhabitants to well over 2.5 million had begun, gestating inflation. Rent control did not help: three fourths of Madrid was decaying into squalor as a consequence of the law, and now speculation pushed shopfront prices into the stratosphere. Arriving, searching, they were forced into the old quarters, where their clients were the poor, the lower middle class, and the mostly impoverished nobility, who bought little and paid late. Jacobo and Marisol knew their milk, cheese, butter, and eggs; and she something about tinned foods, and he something about wine; but neither understood business. He was hard put to support his interest payments on the locale. Alone among his fellow tradesmen, Jacobo was unable to provide his family with telestatus, nor his wife with the electric iron he was forever promising, not to speak of the categoría of a SEAT 500 runabout. To bolster his battered self-respect he did two things: ate hugely (of food now they had plenty), developing in eight years a monumental avoirdupois, so that he now walked back on his heels in a rather stately manner; and boasted unconscionably at home and in taverns—maintaining the fiction that it was Marisol's fertility that had fobbed him out of potential stardom as an athlete, a fable accepted by many of his neighbors, who each lived his private myth, as do the poor and disappointed everywhere, but one that stuck like a bolus in Jacobo's throat; that himself he could never quite swallow. A voice kept whispering, "Jacobo, you are now fifty-three years old and a nothing; and you have never been anything else but a nothing."

It was merciful indeed of Almighty God to have granted him the great boon of the morning. Although, of course, and as we have seen, He who giveth, taketh away.

Book Four

THE EXPOSURE OF INSURRECTION

Herminia

"Señora Contesa."

"Oh!" let out Marisa Magascal, startled by the door that had opened so discreetly behind her. "Oh," she said, her long features lifting with relief, "Herminia! Thank heavens you have come!"

It was still the forenoon. Herminia had slipped into the rear of Número Catorce. Solemnly had she viewed the wreckage of the rose parlor, where the police were taking everyone's name and address before releasing people. The folly of the human herd! The sheer spendthrift-ness of undirected passions. She had sighed: sorrowfully, this faithful servant of Justice, this patient angel of retribution. Now she took three of her rolling little steps into this austere servant's bedroom, glancing at the grim figure on the cot.

Nati gazed at the ceiling, motionless, a counterpane tucked up under her chin.

"A sad, sad day!" observed Herminia, shaking her white head, her normally cheerful countenance clouded. "How is she?"

"I've given her a sedative. She wouldn't permit me to undress her. Oh, Herminia, it *is* a sad day!"

The Countess nearly broke down, this gaunt heap of bones. "There!" said Herminia, going to her. Marisa let herself be comforted in the old ama's arms, pressed to her starched maternal bosom.

"There, there," Herminia crooned, patting the Countess on her spavined column. "The time comes for us all, it is in God's hands, we can only resign ourselves."

"Oh, that's so, Herminia, that's so!" weepily agreed Marisa, "but Odette—la Señora Marquesa—she was so, such a wonderful, the disgrace of that terrible brawl . . ."

"There, there, there," said Herminia, each with its pat, bringing her nanny's white apron up to gently pinch and dry the running Magascal nostrils. "Now you must take care of yourself, and show strength. Get some rest. Leave Nati to me."

"Dear Herminia!"

The Countess went. Herminia tested the door on its latch before turning to examine Nati, whose expression of dull suffering had not changed.

"Are you all right, Nati?"

From Calle Don Pedro, the tremolo of another ambulance siren rose, reaching this still back room—the saddest of all city sounds, the pain and grief of stricken persons, who are never again so alone, so disconnected from their fellows. Nati's lips moved.

"I'm cold. I am feeling . . . very cold." A shudder rippled down her long form.

"Shock, natural. That will pass." Herminia drew a slat-back chair up beside the bed, taking one of Nati's bony hands out from under the coverlet and chafing it. "You will be feeling better soon."

"I feel nothing."

"You have avenged yourself, Nati." Long ago, Herminia's soul-stricken wail at the foot of that gibbet from which the stiff trussed body of her lover swayed in the broiling Andalusian breeze had transcended the Sacedóns in malediction against the whole of the old order.

But Nati turned her head to one side, away from Herminia.

"Have I?" she muttered. "Why? I have done nothing. It is all for nothing."

"Now, now, that is foolish talk. Think of the years of humiliation, the drudgery—the thankless, hopeless, empty years."

"There were some . . . beautiful years. Once—once long ago, when we were girls—I loved her. She loved me."

"Tsk, tsk, tsk! Sentiment, Nati. Out of place. Unworthy of you. There can be no love between them and us, between servant and master. We function or we do not function, like donkeys. The unpardonable thing is for us to become a human nuisance to them."

"But it was *I* who wronged *her!*"

"That is not possible. Now," she went on briskly, drawing her chair a bit closer, "I am here at the request of the Duchess of Sacedón. She wants you to publicly declare that the Count of Obregón is your son."

"What else!" murmured Nati; wearily, to the wall.

"But I have come," continued Herminia firmly, "to say that you must deny that nonsense. It is time you admitted the truth to yourself. You took the life of the Marquesa in just retribution for centuries of abuse. You must understand truly what you have done, and why. You never submitted to the lust of that wicked class, Nati! Obregón is not your son."

Nati's long form stiffened under the counterpane. She jerked her face back from the wall to stare at Herminia.

"What are you saying!" she whispered fiercely. Then, more loudly, "What other reason!" She went up on her elbows. "Don Ignacio . . . !"

"A myth," stated Herminia, pressing the woman back on the bed, "that you imagined out of your need."

"No!" said Nati, struggling up again. She had strangled the Marquesa for less.

"All right, have it another way. The late Conde de Obregón shamefully took advantage of you—and then discarded you!"

"Never!" Nati's tendons bunched. Her eyes burned dangerously.

Herminia spoke on with imperturbable authority. "Do not lie to yourself. When you were called to wetnurse the Marquesa's brat, it was your infant son who died. Out of your torment at this injustice; out of the deepest, most passionate sense of justice to yourself—I know, Nati, I know, I went through something not unlike what you went through— you made yourself believe it was the other way round, and that your boy was substituted for the Marquesa's infant."

"That . . . is not so!" came now weakly from the bed. "Nacho is mine. Why, why *else* kill the Marquesa?"

"We've gone through that. You had ample reason."

"But it was you . . . You *agreed* it was necessary, to protect Don Ignacio . . ."

"I agreed because it suited me. It suits me whenever one of us strikes back. But whatever you prefer to believe, Nati, whatever suits *you*, do as I recommend. If you love him, confess that Don Ignacio is the true son of his mother—else he will inherit neither the title nor Número Catorce. The Sacedóns, you see, plan to challenge his rights."

Nati flung her cheek back over to one side. In order to protect her son (not her son, who really knows?), she was faced with the choice of confessing to the truth (who knows that?), and thus renouncing her myth (the entire rationale of her life these past forty-odd years), or telling an untruth, and by this false renunciation making monstrous what she had done to her mistress.

The tears came slowly to Nati, each a searing squirt pressed from a boil of agony; then faster and faster, rolling down her harrowed, once beautiful cheeks.

Herminia got briskly to her feet. Nati was a broken human being, done for, anyone could see that. What a pity! What a terrible pity!

She said gently, "Try to get some sleep. If my weary old bones don't fail me, I'll come back this afternoon and heat you a cup of manzanilla."

In Herminia's infusion of revenge, bankruptcy of the Sacedón tribe would be the culminating ingredient. If she was able, she meant to deny her little boy the remotest weapon with which to fight back.

T W O

The Detective

"Well," said Baltazar Blás to his daughter, "what are your plans now?"

I had—you will remember—slipped away behind the shield of the very ambulance carrying Odette to the morgue. Father and daughter were gathered still near the stoop of Número Catorce, thronged about by half a hundred jabbering people. "Murder!" now spilled from everyone's lips. Representatives of Spain's polite press had by this time gathered. At the request of eminences, Stepanópoulis Grau (reluctantly) forbade picture-taking. He forbade interviews, announcing his availability for a press conference at one forty-five, in time for the important roundup radio and television broadcasts at two-thirty. He was—as Baltazar presumed acidly—already composing his statement, fussing from personage to personage, wild with delight to be scooping into his notebook a catch that included ministers and ambassadors, nobles the most exalted and even Princes of the Blood, not to mention the very pride of the ruling financial community. He had forbade all entry into Número Catorce until his men were done with it.

Blás doubted not that he could intimidate his former minion into admitting him; but he saw no point in this at the moment.

He was watching Juan Luis Sacedón, who spoke briefly with that other quintessential worthlessness, that Julio Caro (whose neck Blás would have liked to wring), both turning up the street toward the plaza, where their cars were parked.

Baltazar's eyes narrowed on the unprepossessing rear of the Duke. He had shown himself unexpectedly—remarkably!—cool. By God, Blás exclaimed to himself, he had been threatened by the pup!

"Well?" he rasped at Dorada.

"I'm . . ." She checked her wristwatch. ". . . *over* two hours late for my appointment." And with a swish of that indecent skirt, she limped away from him, following in the wake of the señoritos.

The day was disintegrating for Baltazar Blás; as indeed it had and would continue to for so many of my acquaintances. He did not care to risk a scene on the spot. But he would never permit Dorada to prejudice the future of his grandson.

He whirled—abruptly and with the decisiveness characteristic of him —marching to his Silver Arrow.

Deputy Inspector Stepanópoulis Grau was questioning the dignified Duke of Centollos, Carlos Lapique, who had—as you will remember —struck out valorously in defense of the proprieties, only to be (this I neglected to mention) butted in the ducal belly by the electrician, so that he was shoved back with the emphysematous wheeze knocked out of him, and compelled to sit down near Dos Tripas while the battle raged. He was at this moment having his noble brow treated for the lump raised by a flying piece of crockery (Sèvres, he noticed), inclining his patrician old head to within reach of a stumpy Red Cross nurse who doubled off-duty as a sausage-stuffer.

"You, then, Your Grace, were the first to raise an arm against the madman!" said the ecstatic Grau, ballpoint hovering like a blue darter over his notebook.

"Not at all!" snapped the Duke. "It was de la Romana and young Amontefardo who went for him first. And it wasn't an arm I raised. It was a sconce."

"A sconce?"

"Carved, wooden, fifteenth century, 'less I'm mistaken. 'Fraid I broke it. 'Fraid quite a lot of valuable stuff got smashed."

Grau scribbled away. What wonderful luck! The Inspector, his chief, had a bellyache that confined him to bed, as only colic in Madrid can. No one would whisk this case out of his hands . . .

"But you witnessed the aforementioned Rivas strike His Most Excellency the Marquis of the Pilgrim."

"Ignacio is not yet the Marquis," came the tart reply.

"But," persisted Grau, "you did see the suspect strike His Most Illustrious the Count of Obregón?"

"Most Excellency the Count. Get matters straight. Obregón carries the hat—Ferdinand VII, true, but decent enough despite that. And no, I did not see him strike Ignacio. I entered with Two Intestines and the Countess of Magascal after it had begun. Count and Countess of the

Caribs were there, dancing around an oil painting for some inexplicable reason, shocking! one can expect anything of him, not at all in the character of her . . . But weren't *you* there?"

"Oh yes, Your Grace!"

"Well, why in thunderation are you pestering *me?*"

For corroboration, Grau might reasonably have explained.

Blinking the whole truth. Behold the little man: as excited as a lower-middle-class up-until-this-moment frustrated nonentity can be: to mince his scared self-important way into such an explosive affair when he had expected a routine certification of natural death; to happen to be in charge of at least the preliminary investigation of the murder of the great Marquesa; and to have thus endowed (as he viewed it) with plausibility his much scorned thesis that Eugenio Pidal de Estrada, recently defunct noble, had been pushed into the elevator shaft.

A rebellion of the lower orders was in ferment. Else: how had all those servants known the Marquesa was murdered a full hour or so before he, Stepanópoulis Grau, brilliantly spotted the bruises on her throat when assisting the doctor in raising the corpse from the floor; where, as you will also remember, it had rested during the better part of the row? Behind everything—he was certain—there was an infamous plot, with the object of embarrassing the Regime and bringing about its fall. Oh yes: he was convinced of this. His every instinct trembled with the certainty. His sensitive little penis twitched with it. All his (up to now) mortifying career had he dreamed of cracking such a case. He had even hatched several in his imagination—nefarious, subversive schemes whose deft dismantling would catapult him into public fame and official favor. He, the lowly Deputy Inspector, would finally show up his chief, who for the past eight years had treated him with open derogation. He wanted to stuff his notebook with as many depositions attached to as many resounding names as he was able.

But the Duke of Centollos, now neatly plastered on the forehead, was staring down at him along the droop of his haughty harrier's nose, from whose tip a drop of moisture glistened. Grau bowed, excusing himself, turning to spot his sometime employer yawing in that purposeful, fisherman's manner toward the Bentley.

Stepanópoulis had been sixteen when, in 1943, he attached himself to Blás. He was at the time running errands in Málaga Customs, where his father held a sinecure. Blás had needed a signature on a certain license, and in a hurry. Stepanópoulis scurried with it to his daddy.

Although from the outset the youth's manner annoyed Baltazar, he had been handy for minor assignments. He was acquainted with the ins and outs of officialdom. Of gossipy bent, he was quick to spy out the venalities in people. He achieved successes encouraging him to aspire to something like diplomatic status in Blás operations, entrusted with matters of note. He splurged his first bonus on an MG roadster. Contemptuously, he swept his Spanish hair oils off the bathroom shelf, restocking it with imported American oils. He purchased a set of golf clubs and a pair of natty, size 5½ spiked two-tone oxfords to go with them. One day, he would stroll the links of the Royal Club of the Iron Gate.

Alas, Blás soon perceived that Grau's obsequiousness occulted vaulting ambition, his fussy energy incompetence, and his vanity a self-esteem that habitually colored reality with wishful thinking, so that he was forever acting on unwarranted assumptions. In ferreting out a substitute witness for Jacobo Rivas against Larrañaga—whom he did eventually come up with—Stepanópoulis comported himself with such weighty mystification that shortly all Bilbao knew who he was and who his master, and the shoe caper as a consequence very nearly came to grief. He was sacked.

Grau was bitter about this. Competence allows its errors, vanity never. He sold the MG. A bullfighter's tailor bought his golf clubs. He was rescued by a cousin, who wangled a job for him in Madrid with Security.

This was a bright new chance. Grau was eager to polish it. He studied hard. He learned much about the operations of the Russian NKVD (today's KGB), and their astuteness in planting or cultivating agents. Indeed, they became an object of inverse worship to him. Their skill, their sapience, were as he liked to conceive of himself. He assigned an almost mystical omniscience to them, and an ubiquity to their operations, that rivaled the faith of Michelle Muñoz. Why, surely! he thought to himself, Moscow would not overlook the opportunity of infiltrating the Church. He chanced one day upon the ferocious anticommunist diatribes of Segura y Sáenz, pre-War Archbishop of Toledo. Hmmmmmmm. Did not the man protest too much? Segura had returned after the War, promoted to Cardinal of Seville; and from that pulpit his bituminous rhetoric frequently irritated the Chief of State himself, denouncing the Falange (as it did) for being "irreligious," and speaking (as he would!) of "exaggerated nationalism." What an incongruence. To people of Stepanópoulis's mentality, the loathing of one form of authoritarianism necessarily implies uncritical adoption of its current political adversary. Anything less is suspect. Could it be that His Eminence's strident anticommunism of the past was a brilliant reverse-propaganda ruse, establishing him on one side of the fence while at the same time, through that very fanaticism, undermining the cause of anticommunism? *Hmmmmmmmm!* And was not his present deploring of "Nazi influence" in the Falange admirably suited to the purposes of Moscow?

The world is a transparent place to such as Stepanópoulis—and a frightening one. He is in fact to be numbered among the rare people on this earth to perceive that the late Senator Joseph McCarthy of Wisconsin was an NKVD plant, with the mission of discrediting all measures of internal security in America through his bumbling offensiveness. Respecting the Cardinal, were there not palpable grounds for suspicion? A Prince of the Church! Stepanópoulis shivered.

He asked himself, was True Spain safe in any quarter? He spent the feverish nights of four long years assembling a dossier. In every case study, the logic was as ineluctable as here above suggested. He named half the prelates of Spain, a third of the General Staff, and two out of three Ministers. Absurd? Hardly. Was it not the property of genius to conceive of the inconceivable? At the very least, shouldn't such people as Cardinal Segura be placed under surveillance?

With a scarcely containable chuckling of inner pride—with a joyful bleating of his bladder—Stepanópoulis submitted his dossier to the Director General of Security himself. He went above heads in doing so; and howling heads above him everywhere rolled. *Hélas,* the property of mediocrities is to belittle genius. Grau was sentenced to dessicate in the almost uninhabited Spanish Sahara, where only goats, gazelles, and stray Berbers on their moth-eaten camels were around to feed his fantasies. Eight years was he condemned to this alkaline exile; and then, when recalled—upon his tearful oath never again to commit his speculations to writing—he lasted just two years before Fate summoned him to Sacedón, where calamity in the form of that mad ox, that maniacal Jacobo Rivas, had again hit through the revelation that indeed he had been once in the employ of Baltazar Blás; and he was sacked a second time.

How the injustice rankled! It befell another cousin, his present chief, the Inspector, to take Grau into his office out of family obligation, where he was appointed Deputy in order to be kept the better under eye. Grau was aware of this. He resented it. He was given paste to paste paper with, and clips to clip paper with, and staples to staple paper with, but only *in extremis* was he permitted to sally forth after evildoers, and then his temperament tended to get the better of him. He arrested the innocent because clearly they were too innocent. He let go the guilty because, for example, who would be so foolish as to publicly trim his fingernails with the dripping dagger he had just used in carving up his landlady? Released, that fellow promptly drove the self-same dagger into the back of the janitor.

Even had Fortune favored Stepanópoulis in such matters, the apprehension of common criminals would not have satisfied him. He was a patriot. All Spaniards are. Someday, he knew, he would be justified. The British hadn't thought to suspect Fuchs, had they? and look what that got them! Nor Americans the cultured, well-born Alger Hiss, and see how this had paid them! What he was stumbling upon now could make up for everything. Domestics, it was clear, were being organized against Society. How infernally clever of Moscow! How natural that Moscow should move on this front! (Who knew their masters better than their servants? Who but Pidal's domestic staff would count on the absent-mindedness of the man before eleven o'clock in the morning, aware as they were how he had twice nearly stepped into the way of a bus on the Gran Vía, tipping his hat both times?) Naturally allied would be the front of petty tradesmen, fed up with having their bills ignored, and thus easy marks for subversion. There was that Murcian manicurist. Who could trust Murcians? There was that electrician, who had no doubt conspired with a mason called García to inter his wife alive. And there was Rivas, his nemesis, who as a youth had entered into intimate relations with a French female Communist, whose love for the man, as it turned out, was so great that it had driven her back to Sacedón.

Who could hazard how thoroughly Rivas had been indoctrinated? He and two brothers had shed blood for the Reds. One had been killed by the Generalísimo's Moors in Asturias. The other had been executed. What rancor roiled in the surviving brother's breast? There had come his suspiciously sudden conversion to the Nationalist cause. But had he not refused to denounce Larrañaga?

A cunning individual. A crazed, cunning man, the mantequero. A moment more, Stepanópoulis stood by watching while Baltazar Blás mounted his imposing Silver Arrow. The detective's brain throbbed in its fragile case. Exaltation lifted him to his tippy-toes. What was the old bandit up to—stockpiling munitions in that lot on the southern flank of the Casa de Campo? And under the maniacal transparency of that other lunatic, Señor Don William Smith-Burton, consort-Count of a Thousand Tears? Every decent, tax-evading citizen of Madrid had reason

to despise Don Guillermo, destructor of mankind's dreams. He, a Briton—
as little to be trusted as Murcians—had probably on his part cultivated a
detestation for the people of Madrid. What was that contraption—that
monstrous war machine—that Don Guillermo had constructed? Art? Art!
Nonsense! Who could be expected to swallow such stuff? It was a fearsome weapon, that's what it was. And for what purpose? Why, the Army's
principal powder magazines lay right next door.

Yes! That was it! (Up and down on his toes went Stepanópoulis
Grau.) Rebellion was planned with selected assassinations designed to
sow terror and confusion. The powder dumps would be blown. Then the
survivors in his dossier (Cardinal Segura had died) would take command
of a mass uprising of the rabble. Mighty and resonant names would
emerge among the leaders. Yes! Yes! Ever in Spain had the nobility produced its turncoats. Often in Spain had aristocrat, priest, and peasant
joined in unholy alliance against Order. A Montijo or Romanones once
upon a time. Perhaps today an Albuquerque, Alba, or Centollos!
Why . . . !

Grau was seized by an imperative desire to relieve himself. Would
he be able to accomplish both necessities—pass water and detain Blás—
in time?

He rushed into the carriageway of Número Catorce. He could make
it no farther. Neck burning, he pivoted toward a wall.

That neck turned scarlet when the last of the high born to be questioned by his officers—the tall old Countess of Magascal—emerged from
the palace to balk, halt, stare, and then exclaim, "OH, this is the *limit!*"

Grau dribbled to a piteous end. He zippered up as fast as he was
able. That is, he lost another precious forty seconds, because the teeth of
zippers in Spain tend to stick as though cemented, and often it is wiser,
if one is able, to wriggle out of one's trousers entirely than risk the consequences. This befell Stepanópoulis. He pulled, he yanked, he wrenched.
He ripped the toggle right off! What was he to do!? When in distress, one
can borrow the time, matches, cigarettes, neckties, and even shoes from
one's fellowman. Zippers one cannot borrow. Zippers one daren't even
ask to borrow. Stepanópoulis could have cried.

But he was a patriot. He bunched up the trousers at the fly, and in
a Groucho Marx sort of stoop, went darting out of the carriageway and
down the sidewalk and out into the street, just managing to block Blás's
limousine as it was swinging out of the curb.

"Stop! Stop!" he yelled, hopping up and down like a goblin in front
of the hood.

Blás thrust his formidable dome out a rear window. "Get out of the way! I'm in a hurry!"

"Stop!" cried Grau once more, rushing round to the open window. "Some questions . . ."

"I haven't time, Grau, I . . ."

"I must ask you about the munitions license you arranged for Señor Smith-Burton!"

The chauffeur, uncertain, had not quite halted the Bentley. It rolled slowly along in a U-turn back up toward the plaza, Grau scrambling along beside it.

"What about the license!" shouted Blás.

"Señora Grau and I," gasped the little man, "drove by the Casa de Campo two Sundays ago. The explosions, I heard, I saw, I . . . wish to ask you . . ."

"None of your business!" Blás shouted into his face. "You're no longer in Security, and Security cleared it. Pepe, push that pedal to the floor!"

And the Silver Arrow rocketed up the street, leaving Grau in a whirl of dust and a cloud of dismay, because something had popped out of his fly, and who should notice it but the widow-Duchess of Sacedón!

THREE

Father and Daughter

He had faced a ludicrous trial in getting away. And it was never wise to short-shrift even a Stepanópoulis Grau. But he had to stop Dorada. He glimpsed the tail of her Corvette skidding out of the plaza and into a street at its head. He gave Pepe rapid orders. At a stoplight near the Plaza Mayor, they had caught up with her. Blás signaled for his daughter to pull over. She flashed an angry glance at him, gunning the Corvette forward and as fast as she was able the moment the traffic light winked.

But this was Spain's midday rush hour, two o'clock. The congestion frustrated escape. And Pepe was a veteran helmsman of the old days, with a slug embedded in one thigh. He thundered the Silver Arrow after her. Jaywalkers jumped as though squirted out of the way. Hearing that majestic horn, catching sight of those two tons of gleaming gun-metal behind the snarl of the flashing silver grill, even taxis beetled aside. Dorada ran one light at Plaza Cibeles, but before an indignant policeman was able to place whistle to lips, a sudden vacuum similar to those produced by the rush of an express train nearly sucked him off his feet. "That's it!" cried Blás, exhilarated, "don't let her slip into a side street!"

Because she had doubled back by this time, making a run for one of the lateral lanes—when a bus held her behind its lumbering bulk. "We've got her!" exulted Baltazar. Deliberately, Pepe rammed the rear of the Corvette up on the sidewalk and against a lamppost.

Dorada was badly jolted. There was Blás fight in her, nevertheless. Furiously, she kicked her door open. A goggle-headed patrolman on a motorcycle came sirening into view. But Baltazar was quicker than anyone—out of the Bentley and by Dorada's side before she was able to react, whispering, "Get in, and say nothing—or I swear I'll tell the officer where you were heading and for what!"

He then faced the patrolman (whose countenance was a very angry red), saying as he bundled Dorada into the back seat of his car, "Terribly sorry. Baltazar Blás. My daughter, Marchioness of the Pilgrim. May have heard. Mother-in-law murdered. Upset. Sudden stop. No avoiding. Kindly summon a tow. My card. My address . . ."

Dorada seethed in silence during the drive to Banco Blás. One moment there, in the Retiro, as they circled the statue of the Fallen Angel, she verged on tears. Her father noticed. He said nothing. They arrived. But Dorada planted her feet on the sidewalk. "I'm not going in. You'll have to drag me in!"

She was more gloriously beautiful than ever in her anger, blond hair blazing across the bright pink flushes of her face, eyes blazing their golds and greens against the leafy backdrop of the park's woods.

"If you want to make a spectacle of yourself, that's up to you."

"What are you going to do? Lock me up? You won't be able to do that forever. I'll escape. I'll get away. You'll just be putting it off."

He grasped her under an armpit. They entered the bank. Dorada limped badly. "Accident," said Blás to the pageboys and officers who pressed forward to assist. "Nothing serious. Call Sert."

The old functionary had already been advised. He hobbled into an elevator behind father and daughter. On the way up, Blás asked whether the 1,200,000,000 pesetas had been deposited to my account in Banco Bilbao.

"Not yet, señor."

"I promised the money'd be in his hands before lunch!"

"We . . . we routed the order through the Comptroller's office. Calle Velázquez, señor. Terrible traffic. And then the Comptroller . . ."

Blás was incensed. "What in Christ's name was the reason for all that!" The elevator had stopped, its hatch sliding open. Blás barged out into a hall, dragging Dorada with him. "When I give orders . . . !"

"But you yourself, sir," pleaded the frightened secretary, scurrying along behind, "you agreed to channel everything above five millions through the Comptroller. You remember, sir, when the Señor Conde— I mean, the Señor *Marqués!*—became so upset . . ."

"Angels! Yes! I remember!" growled Blás, flinging a dining room door open. That damned paper office, another of Ignacio's costly whims. "Come on, Dorada!"

He was about to slam the door on Sert's face when the man again raised his faithful old voice.

"Señor?"

Blás wheeled. "What now?"

"Señor Puig has called."

"Not those suede coats again!"

"No, señor. It concerns Financiera Sacedón. He would like to meet with you this afternoon."

At this, Blás jerked his chin up.

Now the businessman, the manipulator, the buccaneer thrust to the foreground. Instinct spoke to him of trouble. It was definitely broadcast, then: his move on Financiera. That was bad. He could expect the stock to double or even treble in the morning. There would be a run on that stock. Sacedón might then be able to buy his way out of his own notes, and retain control.

"Sert," he said, enunciating clearly and calmly, "telephone every brokerage in Madrid, Bilbao, Barcelona, Valencia, and Seville. Tell them, Sert: tell them that whoever tries to outbid me for Financiera stock will regret it. And tell them that they are to execute no orders for that stock tomorrow at all."

Fear would grip them, Blás was confident of that. There wouldn't be a one to dare.

He added, "And call Señor Puig. Six o'clock, here, in my office. Anything else?"

Sert gulped. "The Comptroller . . ."

"Devil take the man!" roared Blás. And now he did slam the door on his servitor's face.

"You're in a pleasant mood," Dorada remarked icily. Her father's discomposure had returned to her some of her own. He did not answer, jerking a chair out for her and then seating himself at the head of a long, blond-oak table, stomping for a buzzer. A waiter bowed in and bowed out. Within minutes, the first course was being served: brine-plump scampis grilled in garlic salt.

"I'll buy you a new car," Blás said, heaping his plate.

"You could have killed me!"

"Pepe knows what he's doing behind a wheel. Stove in a cutter, once—neat as can be. I was prepared to take chances."

"I loathe you. I don't even know how to telephone Diego. My shin aches. I'm still shaken. I'm not even," glancing at the bruise, "in fit condition!"

"I could tell you that I regret everything," said Blás, pincering a shrimp between finger and thumb. "But I do not approve of promiscuity and never have. Contracts are made to be honored. And the partner you picked is out of the question. Now, do you want to pamper your emotions, or can we talk business?"

Once again he had occasion to respect his daughter. Visibly, she brought herself under control. What a shame she was not male!

"What do you suppose that puppy meant?" he asked, slurping a meat into his gullet. "That he could 'ruin' us?"

"Juan Luis?"

"Me, you, your child, my grandson." He swallowed.

"You're not paying attention to Juan Luis, are you?"

"I pay attention to everyone! Aren't you hungry?" Dorada was staring at her plate. Blás shrugged, cracking a second shell, lopping the piteous, prayerful head off and with a square-cut thumbnail splitting the soft underside of the belly. He stuffed the morsel into his mouth, gesticulating with a greasy hand. "Suppose he suspects you and that gangster?"

Dorada grimaced fastidiously. "Him? When he couldn't pull up his trousers without help?"

"He knows I'm after Financiera."

"So I gather."

"Eat, damnit, they're good!"

Dorada began fiddling with a shrimp.

"His Eugenio," her father went on, "he's fitted the pieces together. Adm'rable man, by the way. Had Codina Moncó call him this morning after the Utilidades board meeting, make him an offer. He hung up.

So Sacedón knows I'm after him, and what's his one defense, tell me that?"

Dorada discovered that she was hungry after all. The meats were firm, delicious. Her father personally went to the market twice a week and picked the seafood. He was forever the peasant!

"You must have it figured out," she said.

"They're cousins," said her father, holding a scampi by its tail and bouncing it in the air in front of her, "Sacedón and the Marquesa. My guess is the Sacedóns plan to challenge Nacho for the title."

Dorada's eyebrows lifted. Before she could speak, the waiter entered. They both guarded silence. Dishes were cleared. Finger bowls, quartered lemons, and fresh napkins were put before them. They washed and dried their hands. Cold veal was served.

"Said I had everything to lose," mused Blás the moment the waiter had left, "he had nothing to lose." He reflected, those bulges at the brow gleaming under the pulse of his brainpower. "I've underestimated the pup, Dorada. He knows what's dearer to me than life itself—you, my grandson . . ."

"Leave me out of the list."

"All right," he confessed, nodding. "My grandson. I have everything to lose if we lose that title. And he . . . ?"

"Lose it?" came sharply from Dorada.

He ignored her. "Thought him a perfect fool. Not at all. Knows his class is done for. Merciful thing would be to put them all out of their misery. Lost their function. Used to be the governors, ambassadors, generals, and admirals of Spain. Thought victory would bring all that back. But Franco wasn't about to snatch Spain out of the fire just to dunk it in the sea. Two generations of 'em have waited at the bar of Puerta de Hierro hoping for a call. They have nothing left. That's why they need us! He knows this—that pup! Knows he's not able to cope. He played along. Has nothing to lose. He's been committing a sort of suicide, Dorada. Yes, that's it. He's a noble. Sees his duty: to himself, to his class, to Spain. The destruction of himself: the turning over to me and people like me what only we have the vitality and talent and brains to handle."

Dorada was astounded by her father's monologue. "Aren't you giving Juan Luis too much credit?"

He wagged his head stubbornly. "No, that's it, I'm sure of it."

"Then why fight you at all?"

"He's scared. Natural. Still not quite up to acting on his convictions. Often a person has the voice of his convictions, not so often the courage. Or maybe it's his breeding too. They've always known how to die, Dorada. They were lions during the War. In the pup's way, could be he wants to go down fighting . . . If he has a case."

Dorada put her fork and knife down. "Does he!"

"The point's moot. I don't make a practice of worrying until there's reason for it."

"You were angry enough when you burst into my dressing room that day!"

"I calm down quickly."

"You'd better *back* down on Financiera. You can do it gracefully, turn the matter around: You've been preparing an attack—in the event they planned one. You're willing to see reason if they are."

Her father stared at her. He was angered.

"I want Financiera," he said. "Most financiers in our country are simple manipulators, Dorada. Let innocents do the work, then strip 'em. Just five banks in Spain, girl, own ninety-five per cent of our major industry, and Spain suffers for it, bankers are the worst *do*ers God ever bred. But I'm a builder. I create things. I make them grow. I'm not backing down. I've never backed down. You and I both want the title. That means—first of all, whether you like it or not—you are going to drop Muñoz González."

He received his own stare right back in his face. "I told you that I do as I please."

"There can be no scandal at this juncture, Dorada!—not until the marquisate is legally confirmed to Nacho. Then sleep with anyone you like, I won't object. But today you're returning to Número Catorce, there to act like a Marchioness. And you will do so until this is settled."

"In return for which?" She was seething again.

"I'll guarantee you the title."

"How?"

"Through that other mess, that Julio Caro. He's another cousin."

"With better credentials than Juan Luis?"

"Maybe. His great-something grandfather was the elder brother in the Marquesa's line. This afternoon or tomorrow, I'm going to put a million pesetas in his hands—an outright gift. Then I'll supply him with cash for making his claim. If it's solid enough to discourage Sacedón—a court case could run into the millions, Sacedón may not have them to risk— and if Caro then quietly drops it, satisfying himself with his father's title: he'll never have to worry about money again."

Dorada thought on this. She curiously resembled her father when she thought deeply.

"Will Julio dance for Baltazar Blás?" she asked after a while. "His fathers," she reminded him with malice, "were greats of Spain when your fathers were picking their noses on the stoops of hovels."

Blás snorted. "He'll be able to shoot all he pleases, and strut around the Puerta de Hierro, and probably land some stupid daughter of some rich provincial merchant or other." He paused, reading her thought. "You're not stupid—at times."

But Dorada did not dismiss contingencies. "Just what if for some reason Julio doesn't go along?"

The answer came blunt and brutal. "He's panted after you for years, now, hasn't he?"

A moment lapsed before the implication penetrated.

"You . . . make me sick."

"Puke in your plate, then, but don't be a fool. That's only a last resort. Now, after lunch, I want you to take me with you back to Número Catorce."

Dorada smiled. "Never," she told him. "You'll never see the inside of it, Papá. *My* price is that you never come near me nor my son again."

There should be no need to dwell on how cruel a blow Baltazar Blás had been struck. It was evident to Dorada. She felt justified.

"That's . . . a very hard condition," he managed to utter after a few moments.

"Accept it—or whistle after your dreams!"

She did not tarry for dessert, getting up and leaving her father hunched over his plate.

FOUR

Carabanchel

The moment consciousness returned to him, Jacobo asked himself: what had he accomplished?

He lay in the paddywagon, which went bumping over cobbles as it rolled through the southwest outskirts of Madrid. He felt sick. The elation of battle was gone. What—over a lifetime of muddled intentions, some not ignoble—had he to pride himself in?

He felt a warm gritty-wet dropping steadily on his cheeks and sliding to linger in ticklish suspense on the edge of his jawbone before flowing down to the neck. Marisol: leaning over him, couching his battered head against her blessed bosom, and weeping! Weeping—for him! Jacobo kept his eyes closed. In the presence of the electrician, the manicurist, and two edgy Assault Guards (one of whom nursed a lip split by Marisol's fists), she keened over him such words of tenderness and admiration and love as never had he heard during the most intimate moments of their courtship. That anyhow was something, and for a time it comforted him.

But then the paddywagon halted. Then had his still groggy bulk been half lifted and half dragged out into the blinding refraction of a flagged courtyard, which was pounded by sun and compressed by imprisoning walls of masonry that bellied like stone sails in the heat. There they had been separated—Marisol, howling like a she-wolf, wrestled away to the women's adjunct of Carabanchel prison. Alone, stumbling on feet that were as though stuck in buckets, he was shoved in the opposite direction, taken into a grim chamber and there arraigned, benumbed brain bonging to charges specifying every particular in which mayhem consists, sufficient (he suspected) to keep him behind bars a decade or more.

He nearly collapsed upon hearing the final charge. Murder? Brute that he was, had he killed anyone in the melee? No. No . . . He was charged with suspicion of murdering the Marquesa!

Jacobo trembled in the arms of the guards supporting him. Don Emilio's prophecy was coming true! Surely nothing less than the garrote would do for the monster base enough to strangle an old lady—and such an illustrious one! His mind prickled under the ice-cold clamp. The flesh on the back of his neck raged under the iron bolt he could feel winching into his occiput. His neck snapped!

He sagged at the knees, dead weight hurling his guards forward and against the desk.

In the infirmary, trustee nurse and orderly treated Jacobo. She, pert and pretty, with the boldest of prostitute's eyes, chided him. "Shame on you, brawling at your age! Now, now—the needle won't hurt!" "The Devil it doesn't!" chuckled the orderly, a smug, rotund young pimp who neatly picked the dentine out of Jacobo's knuckles with a penknife. Complacence began percolating through the frightened man's veins. Franco had all but abolished the death penalty for civil homicides. In most cases, the maximum was thirty years . . .

He started. Thirty years!

He had not murdered the Marquesa, of course. But what had fact to do with the case? His luck being what it was, he would be found guilty. Should he confess? He dozed.

He awoke in a stone cube with a steel door, two bunks, toilet, washbasin, crucifix, and a grill through which the blue of heaven poured. Thirty years! (A co-operative attitude?) (Yes, under the circumstances.) (If he confessed to the killing, they would hardly pay attention to the lesser charges.) (He would be doing them a favor.) (He would be humble, contrite, beating his breast, pleading his combustive temper, his pressing need of the 9,000 pesetas, his nine children, his not even a half-hocked SEAT 500 bug-on-wheels to show for a lifetime of hard work . . .)

Perhaps they would mete him the minimum, twenty years and a day. With good comportment . . .

Prone on his bunk, Jacobo began to sob. Given the best comportment, he could not possibly expect to spend fewer than fifteen years cooped up. Let out, he would be sixty-eight years old, as good as carrion, no good whatever. And now, when he had managed to renew Marisol's respect! When the future—what little remained to them—could have been so different! What, but *what* had he harvested from the vineyard?

I was admitted to Jacobo's cell at this breakdown in his emotions. The hulk of him shook with sobs. I had come with an offer of legal backing. He scarcely listened. I doubt he saw me. Blubbering from his swollen lips came exclamations of grief and self-reproach, of devotion for his wife and his children and especially that rose, his Soledad, whom never would he clasp to his bosom again. I left him to his grief.

FIVE

Drawing the Net

A shut fly and the press conference helped revive Grau's spirits. The auditorium was packed. Always had he imagined himself where he was now, at a raised lectern studded with microphones, and at his feet, a hundred or more newsmen tilting forward on their seats for his least scrap of information.

He had rehearsed the scene so often that he handled himself with aplomb. His replies were brisk and clear. He understated—as people with the wildest fermentations in the head so often do. Yes, he had been *among* the first to arrive. Yes, he had experienced the *premonition* of foul play. Reason? A certain instinct, gained from years of experience . . . Cause? Strangulation, probably, but the cadaver was at the morgue now: there would be an official report later in the day. Why had the maid concealed true cause of death? (Grau hesitated here. Smoothly, he replied in circumlocutions:) She was in shock. An ancient retainer, she may also have been attempting to protect the family. And the mantequero, did he do it? The mantequero had been booked on *suspicion* of murder, nothing certain. Interrogation would take place within the hour. Motive?

"Gentlemen, let me confine myself to this. I do not believe this case began with the murder of the noble Marchioness of the Pilgrim, and I do not believe it ends there either." An assistant appeared at his elbow, whispering. Stepanópoulis Grau would have liked to cock an ear down to the man; unfortunately, Isias is tall, and Stepanópoulis was therefore compelled to strain an ear upward. But he nodded with suitable condescension. "I'm off for the interrogations now, caballeros. Let me assure you that I will personally advise of any developments . . . consistent with the security of the State."

With that bombshell, he walked off the platform.

He had impressed, he knew it. He had appeared on some six million television sets throughout the nation. He had probably appeared in Portugal, France, and Italy as well—or would that evening. Had he known how to whistle!

Unfortunately, the foregoing is all in the imagination of the Deputy Inspector. He had watched too many American television dramas. Press conferences aren't the custom in Spain. Terse communiques are issued by the *Director General de Seguridad;* and in matters of this delicacy, that terseness can be extreme. Still, he was satisfied with what he had composed for Security. He would not repeat his error!—confide in the present Director General. Oh no. Until he was ready, he would stuff his intuitions into his breast pocket. He would meanwhile prepare blank warrants, to be sprung on people at the opportune time. He thanked his buttons for the Napoleonic Code, under which one is guilty until one proves oneself innocent. Because then, with the charges registered, the inexorable procedures of Spanish Justice took over. No authority from on high would be able to suppress them. Full examination of the "denuncias" would take place: willy-nilly. He had meanwhile tipped off a few reporters as to who had been treated by the Red Cross after the brawl —and that was quite a roster. He had slipped his card into their hands. Accounts would mention that the case was being investigated by Deputy Inspector Stepanópoulis Grau. Journalistic imagination would fill in the rest. "A slim, restless individual of the historical national type denoting keen intelligence." "A man whose acute powers of observation and deduction are evidenced in mobile features and flashing eyes." With the case in his hands, he disposed of numberless functionaries, legmen, and officers. Pertinent information would flow to him from countless archives. Tips would stream across his desk from underground agents. Already were neat index cards being slipped into his hands. Several dozen plainclothesmen had been deployed throughout the city, questioning individuals and collating the information. Oh, how the belly of his cousin, the Inspector, must ache now! There was nothing the man could do. Empty as the title had been, Stepanópoulis held it: in his chief's absence, Deputy, and thus commander, of investigations for the Barrio de Latina.

Yes, he would have whistled had he been able. Trailed by Isias, he hurried to Carabanchel.

S I X

A Vision and Interrogations

When Grau and his beanpole assistant were let in to Jacobo Rivas's maximum detention cell, they had a spat.

Actually, a falling out. Better put, a falling apart.

"Clumsy!" snapped the hopped-up little man, recovering his balance by catching at the upper bunk in the cell. "You knocked into me!"

He was prickly with subordinates, being frightened of them, but: "No, sir, I did not!" expostulated Isias, recovering his balance by clawing at the stone wall on the opposite side. "You, sir, if you please, knocked into *me!*"

"Nonsense!" Stepanópoulis glanced about him, sniffing. "I smell *in*cense!"

"Smoking coals," contradicted Isias.

"I am your superior!"

"My nose is longer. Coals, sir, anthracite."

"It's much the same thing, but what I smell is sweet."

"What *I* smell is acrid, like the cinders in the boiler room of our apartment house." He giggled. "Like brimstone."

"Isias, there's no time for quibbles. The point is: from where does the smell originate?"

Isias, also sniffing—tweaking his supersonic needle of a nose from side to side—stepped toward the door.

"It concentrates here."

"So it does," agreed Stepanópoulis.

"But it's getting less strong by the second."

"Yes."

"It's faint, now."

"I smell nothing at all."

"Your hair oil."

"My what!"

"Excuse me, your cigarette. Black tobacco, pungent, a bullfight's scarcely a bullfight without good, rich, traditional black tobacco . . . But you're right, sir, it's gone."

"Make a note of it, Isias." Grau flashed a gilt wristwatch. "Odor of incense in suspect Rivas's cell at 2:46 P.M., 31 May. Strong. Concentrated by cell door. Dissipated by 2:48 P.M. Do you have that, Isias?"

"Yes, sir."

Grau now turned to the prisoner. "Señor Rivas, have you been burning incense?"

("Or cinders?" murmured Isias.)

"Where did you obtain the combustibles?" continued Stepanópoulis, shooting an irritated glance at his subordinate. "Señor Rivas, do you hear me? Where did you get the matches and the kindling and so forth? It's strictly against prison rules, I'm sure!"

But the prisoner was mute. In fact, like smoke, he was vanishing— there where he sat on the bunk!

"He's escaping!" cried Isias, leaping forward to catch at the fading substance.

"Never mind," said Stepanópoulis superiorly. "He's pulled much the same sort of foolishness before—in Bilbao, once, at the Carlton Hotel. But he'll be back. There's no such thing as escape."

Jacobo's was a radically transmuted psychology: which is the only way I am able to explain these matters, for whose account, of course, I am dependent upon the protagonists. No longer was he sobbing, as he had been when I left him half an hour or so before. This was a man sunken, or perhaps shrouded, in gloom. This was a Rivas sitting listlessly on his prison pallet, paws clasping the iron limbers. This was a beast of many burdens, a pondering peasant, a meditative Jacobo who had confronted ghosts.

Grief, remorse, contrition—such emotions were a waste. His life had been a waste, had been a shadow. Marisol he would never recover. Soledad he would never see again. A fresh, culminating torment awaited him, and then the garrote. And it was all his doing. Accurately, it was all his *not* doing.

Suddenly had the sobs dried in his throat, and the heavings in his bullocky chest ceased. Because suddenly did he admit that he had accomplished absolutely nothing with his life. Do dice wail in each other's chameleon faces as they are rattled in the cup? Do donkeys bray for the pity of their condition, and oxen low in lament of their yoke? (*When I grew old, my bones cried out.*)

All his life, purpose had petered like sand through spread fingers. Rather than grasping his destiny by the spine, and cracking it across one of his oaken knees, he had permitted Destiny to shackle its bit on him, and like a plowhorse had he plodded its rows. He had been gelded. By his mother? By Manú? By Manú and the Frenchwoman between them? No, by none of them. By Almighty God.

His fear had become apparent to Jacobo on that afternoon, when the ocean current swept him toward the empty horizon, and he had noticed Michelle Muñoz's carnivorous lips and jaw, like a moray eel's. Craven fear has possessed him on the ledge, when he came upon the lynx; and it was this that had so angered him with Salvador, who had seen through him and had perceived his fear and who had for that reason not warned him. But it was by that time too late for anyone to help. He was already craven in the spirit, cowered in the heart, and sick with the fears in his brain.

And this was why his resentment against the Frenchwoman had abided: not because she had deserted him so ruthlessly, but because in her predatory ruthlessness she had elucidated to him his moral quandary, pointing out that fear of death meant absence of faith.

There was no faith in him: whether in God, himself, family, traditions, or nation. Yes, that was it: she had shown him that at bottom he was not a believer, fearing not to be one, and he resented her all the more because she, at the time, proselytized a powerful *atheology*, *was* a believer. The War had then fallen upon them both. Years after, at the bar in Bilbao, resentment flared into outrage, because he perceived in her face and figure a loss of faith similar to his own. Yes, that was what he had seen in her, without understanding it. That was why she had not recognized him. Had she begun to doubt the inevitable triumph of the Party, which in Spain had failed so miserably? He did not know. Something had happened to that ardor. Aging, a slattern, she was left with a consort she did not love, shabbily clothed and in a shabby apartment: left with gin and a son who mourned for her. Finally she had been driven back to Sacedón, where once she had still been young, and doxologies to her belief possible; and to that simulacrum of himself (from whose fresh sap she had drawn strength to allay her doubts) in the body of his young half brother.

It had made him ill to think of. She had made him ill to think about. He resented her, loathed her, because she had lost faith. He harbored his grudge against her because, while herself probably beginning to doubt, she had meantime demonstrated to him that he affirmed nothing whatever, and had offered him a sham to take Faith's place. With a myth, she had destroyed myth. She had left him weak, confused, defenseless, bereft of Grace, in which he did not at heart believe, while at heart with all his heart longing for it. And with the departure of Grace had he lost the freedom of his will; and thenceforth had been the dumbbell of Chance, the plaything of events. And had not had the will to keep his clutch on the last tatters of honor—had used the blood money. He was that crustacean hollowed out by the lice of the sea. He had become that animal-plant of many parts, any one of them expendable. He was a handle. He was a coat hanger, and the cloak draped over it. He dangled in space without existing in it.

Had all these things been revealed to Jacobo through a willed writhing of the sueted coils in his brain? Naturally not. After weeping, he had fallen asleep. In the black caverns of Hades, Don Emilio appeared to him, a much younger, still forceful man—as he had appeared to Jacobo when, wounded, delirious, he first experienced vision of the priest. That height and those shoulders pre-empted space. The eagle burned in his severe eyes, there was might in his long jaw, and battle in his stained soutane. He held a cross, raised on high. From his bunk, Jacobo looked up at it, transfixed by the pale ivory cruciform with one arm missing from shoulder to wrist, so that a disembodied hand clutched at the nailhead of its agony.

"I've come again, Jacobo. For the last time."

"Thank you. I was calling for you. I need you."

"You won't thank me when you wake."

"You will tell me the truth?"

"You were told it in Bilbao."

"It did not help me. Help me now!"

"Listen to your heart. You are pure of heart, Jacobo."

"I am broken. My heart is broken. The blood spills from it."

"Molten gold, Jacobo. The heart must break. Salvation lies in the impaled heart."

"*My bones ache. I have grown old among all my enemies. Because I was silent, my bones grew old, whilst I cried out all the day long. Save me!*"

"*Rebuke him not, O Lord! in Thy indignation, nor chastise him in Thy wrath.* You must save yourself."

"I do not believe!"

An attenuated index finger, white as a beam of light, pointed to the pierced side of the Christ.

"Believe."

"I can't."

The finger jabbed at Christ. "Believe in your Creator."

"I can't! I can't! I don't! *And I want to!*"

"Therein your cowardice, Jacobo. Christ comes to the mad only. Christ is the courage to go mad. Listen, Jacobo, listen to your heart."

The priest stood there silently, and in silence they communed. Jacobo listened to his heart. The blood spilled from it—a golden liquid torment through his veins, so that his whole being became incandescent. "The Frenchwoman held on more fiercely," he heard himself silently stating. "I wronged her, in body and mind. Was it my fault, Don Emilio —was it my fault! I was the beast in her loins, the serpent in her womb. She was defeated, crushed . . ."

"Do you know how," came the apostolic voice, "can you see her?"

Jacobo shuddered. "Cockroaches scuttle across the floor. A suitcase is opened on a cot. It's night. It's terribly hot. She flings clothes on the floor. She weeps. She blazes at her lover. The boy, awake, listens through a door. Her lover turns suddenly toward her. He cups his face in both hands. Now he flings them aside, he says something to her in a low voice, she cringes, she cowers, she wails, she shakes her head in a no, no, no! She collapses!"

"What did he say to her, Jacobo! Can you tell me that?"

"No!"

"Listen, Jacobo—listen to your heart!"

"No, I can't, it goes—my brain burns, there's a light in it that blinds me! Ohhhh!"

He clutched at his eyes. The pain was as though flat, white-hot blades were being pressed upon the balls of his eyes. He screamed.

"Open up, Jacobo, open them!"

"I was too weak," he whimpered, rolling his head, "too weak-willed! I should not have clutched at belief when I did not believe. I should have believed *despite* not believing! She sinned, but mine was greater, I had truth in my hands, the Light of the World was in my soul, I could have saved her, but in my weakness did not and forfeited Grace. I am doomed, Don Emilio!"

Lowering his hands, he had managed to spring apart his lids. The pain was gone. In a dazzle of exploding stars he saw the sepulchral figure staring down at him.

"In Time's dissolution, you are not doomed," the priest said. "This moment is of no account, Jacobo. You are a meshing, motivating cog in the destiny Christ God has decreed for the world."

"It ends soon!"

"For such as us, yes, very soon."

"In fire?"

"Just so."

"Is that why you betrayed your friend, your class, your King, and now your country? Is that why you've become a Communist?"

"A revolutionary. A secular, ranked with the hordes of my liege lord Satan."

"But you, a priest . . . !"

"I believe in Almighty God, Creator of Heaven and Earth. I believe in His only Son, Jesus Christ, true God of true God."

"Yes, yes, *I* want to!"

"But I believe also in my lord Satan, Prince of this World, who comes into his kingdom."

"No! *No!*"

"His legions advance over the earth and will rule it. They will bring Satan into his dominion. For that was *I* born. To aid in that was I conceived in the beginning of Time, when Yahweh first warmed the void with His breath and willed Creation."

"Not so!"

"My saber hacked a Bedouin woman in half. My gender pierced the dunghole of her son, scalding his excrement with my seed. What exists is corrupted. What is to come is the purest evil. Ordained priest after ordained priest will wield the Cross in its service. We are the ministers of Christ. We therefore bend our knees to Satan. This is ordained."

"Sánchez—he was right about you! You, a man of God . . . !"

"Priest after priest will hope to rid the earth of the old and then rid the new of its evil, sanctifying it in Christ. But that is a fool's dream. Christ our Redeemer decreed the coming to power of Satan, and to aid that is our duty. I am a sign of His Will, stranded between genders, between evil and good, nobility and shame, commiseration and contempt, power and helplessness. *You* are a sign of that. My knowledge has doomed me. Your innocence saves you. I, who loved Odette, could not warn her. I, who loved Sofía, knew her fate and could not —*would* not!—turn her from it. Because innocence must end. Because to be innocent in this day is to have suffered corruption of the soul. I did not want to know! I would that I hadn't known, that I do not know!—out of weariness, out of despair, out of my pride of rebellion against a God who bids us work for good but tells us that we are condemned to become Satan's vassals. Who can be saved today?"

"Please, please . . . !"

Contempt replied to his writhings for mercy. "The evil of twenty centuries befouls us, engendering greater and greater evil, and who will be saved, Jacobo Rivas? The saint? The blitherer who opposes with his clown's goodness the consummation of the scheme of the All Good? Better for the immanence that it come quickly, before thousands more innocents are lost, and thousands more condemned. Better is it to bare our necks, as you will do, and speed the acceleration of the end to the end, so that finally God is able to loose His laughter, and in a mighty child's fist crush the tin and all the scurrying beetles caught in it, and hurl it and its contents into the outer darkness."

"I wish to die."

"First, tonight, you will atone. One suffering is reserved for you, so that you may believe. You will make amends to the Frenchwoman, whom in your innocence you wronged."

He began leaving then as he had come, fading through the steel door like a ghost in a dream. Jacobo sat up sharply, stretching a hand out to detain him. Quickly, he brought it back, lowering chin to chest, staring at the floor—as the key turned, and the police officers entered, knocking into the burly insubstantial mist of the departing saint, and ricocheting off it against the walls.

"I told you he'd be back!" crowed Stepanópoulis, biting at a hang-nail.

"Right you are," said the admiring Isias. "There he sits, big as life!"

"Mantequero, do you hear me?"

"Wherever it came from," noted Isias, "the scent is definitely gone. There's nothing to account for it in the cell, no fire, no . . . Oh, wait a moment."

He stooped by a far corner. "Didn't notice this before, did you?" he asked, poking in a small heap of char.

"Naturally," said Stepanópoulis, watching as his assistant raised fingers to nostrils.

"You're right, sir," Isias said, straightening up. "Incense." And he thrust his fingers under Grau's nose.

"Anthracite," opposed the Deputy Inspector. "You happen to have been right."

"No, it's incense."

"Don't be impossible, Isias. What's that I see there?"

Stepanópoulis now pointed at the mound. Something gleamed dully in it. Isias stooped again. He came up with the remains of what evidently had been the crossbeam of a crucifix, a singed yellow hand clutching at the nail.

"Sacrilege!" cried out Grau, recoiling, terrified, shocked to the roots. He wheeled on Jacobo. "You add sacrilege to your crimes!"

"The last ordeal, maybe," came Jacobo's muttered response, absorbed as he was still by his vision. "The one that awaits me."

"Isias, call the Holy Office. This monster has burned the crucifix in his cell. He has committed sacrilege—on public property, moreover! What we need here is an inquisitor!"

"But sir, this hand, it's ivory. The cruciforms in Carabanchel are made out of alpaca."

"What does that matter! Call an inquisitor, I say! You were right from the nonce. What we smelled was brimstone. The mantequero has made a pact with the Devil. They are all engaged in an unholy union, the lot of them!"

"But sir, there hasn't been an inquisitor for over a hundred years!"

"No, no, no—right again, don't say that you're not! don't contradict me now! there hasn't been, the world misses them. Spain hasn't been the same since, our Fatherland would not be a cadaver quivering with maggots if only we had the Holy Office still, and burned our traitors at the stake!"

"Meanwhile, what should I do with it?" asked Isias, holding out the remnant.

"Put it in your pocket. Tab it. It's evidence."

"But of what?"

"Of derangement, of course, of the hellfire in a spirit given over to the Accursed. You are looking at a madman, Isias, never doubt that, the mantequero is as mad as Joan."

"He doesn't seem mad. He just looks depressed."

"Ask him! Ask him! Rivas, confess it, you are possessed, a lunatic, a homicidal maniac!"

"I may be," Jacobo replied slowly, scratching his head. This was all punishment for his sins. He was as good as a murderer, having used the blood money. In fact, he had murdered.

"Yes," he said now, more deliberately, scratching his balls. "I am a wild beast who should be locked up. I have killed."

With that, he again dropped chin on chest, gazing at the blunt toes of his shoes. He and this Stepanópoulis Grau, perhaps everyone, executed a long mountain jig to the tambourine of God's will. Hand in hand would they go to the banquet of the Lord.

But the Deputy Inspector was hopping with excitement.

"You admit all!" he cried out in triumph. "The maid let you in. You strangled the Marquesa. You confess to the plot, to the rebellion, to the . . . !"

"I killed," Jacobo interrupted him, losing interest, "but not the old lady. It was during the rebellion, that much you have right. There was a commissar attached to our unit. At the defense of Guernica, I saw him shoot two comrades. I broke his neck."

"Won't help us," said Isias, scratching his crotch—the itch having leaped across from Jacobo. "I mean, killing a commissar—he could get a medal for that."

"Confess to strangling the Marquesa del Peregrino!" Grau nearly screamed.

But Jacobo had turned stubborn. He would suffer for truth, not lies.

"I," he said, "came to the defense of my friend, Antonio Sánchez, a cripple assaulted by the Count of Obregón. Then, attacked by your men, I acted in self-defense."

"That's true, you know," offered Isias. Seeing his superior's face: "I mean, as far as it goes."

Stepanópoulis exploded. "Clever, clever, clever, too clever by half!

You aren't helping yourself a bit! I am thoroughly acquainted with your character, remember that!" He brandished a batch of index cards handed to him by an agent in the lavatory of a cafetería near Calle Don Pedro, where a garage mechanic had managed to zip up his dignity with a pair of pliers. "The Bureau has checked your record. It's a Chinese firecracker of violence. Before the War, you ignited a riot in Sacedón, smiting townsmen with the jawbone of a yokel. At the fisherman's bar back in Sacedón, you bounced on the bellies of innocent folk. You are a madman, clearly, turning Señor Blás down when he had taken a liking to you, turning all that money down! Confess! Confess! You are possessed by Satan, an infernally clever mongoloid criminal, plotting the overthrowal of the State!"

But Jacobo kept a sullen silence.

"Isias," Grau said grimly, "we'll see what we can get from Señora Rivas!"

"Watch it's not more than you bargained for!" came from Jacobo; but Grau had stepped out, a turnkey slamming the bulkhead shut.

Marisol had also been placed under maximum detention. She was merely defiant—weepingly so—until ordered to strip in the presence of female wardens. That lewd command touched off gunpowder. Not her sainted mother since infancy, not her husband in twenty-eight years of wedlock, nor even midwives during bloody labor had seen her wholly nude. "I prefer death!"

The first warden to approach her was flung like a sack of flour across the cell. Shouts for re-enforcements went up. Four of the brawniest female wardens in the women's compound were soon struggling with Marisol; but it was only through needle and syringe that they were able to change her into a prisoner's smock.

By the time Grau and his subordinate entered, Marisol had revived—magmatic enough to melt the very bars. Stepanópoulis kept slightly behind Isias and two wary wardens as he began his questions.

"Madam, where did your husband spend last night?"

"Where all decent men ought! Where were you?"

"I? Why, I was home too."

"Well, that's something. By the looks of you, your wife must be a terrible cook."

"The fact is, Señora Grau is allergic to heat. I do the cooking."

"Poor man!"

"Oh, I don't mind it a bit, I rather enjoy it . . . Madam," he said in a sharper tone, "from what *hour* was your husband at home?"

"He never left the shop, the whole day long! In the evening, he took inventory with Soledad. Then he went to bed."

"Do you share the same bed?"

Marisol erupted from her cell's bench.

"Please!" begged one of the wardens.

"Do sit down!" pleaded the other.

Grau had retreated three rapid little steps. "Señora Rivas, I only meant to inquire . . ."

"What you meant is all the same to me!" exclaimed the Amazon, towering over everyone except Isias. She gasped, "Is there no decency in this place? Only to a confessor would I . . . !"

"I simply want to know," Grau inserted as fast as he was able, "whether he might not have slipped out early in the morning. The maid found the Marquesa dead just after dawn . . . or so she alleges. I am simply trying to determine . . ."

"Jacobo was with me the night through! Do you think I would not know that, with his great weight? When he gets up, all the bed quakes. When he takes a step, the floors quake, the windows rattle, the cat leaps howling out of the larder, and the little ones pop up to kiss him. Once only did he arise this morning."

"Ah!" Out came the notebook. "When was that? For what?"

Marisol blushed crimson. She sat down, struggling terribly within her. But Jacobo's life might be at stake. "To make love," she finally murmured, hanging her head. Then, jerking her head back up, eyes subfusc: "I married a *man*, worth twenty pressed flounders like you! To make love!" she repeated proudly, grasping her breasts, "twice, this morning, within forty-five minutes! Now you know with what sort of person you are dealing! An hidalgo, a nobleman, a lion! Get out! Get out! Leave me alone!"

Stepanópoulis was relieved to go. He had to relieve himself anyhow, this time wisely wriggling out of his trousers. He perspired through the lotion slicking his thin hair back. He chewed on the cropped stubs of his headwaiter's mustache. Of course, a spouse's testimony did not count. Still, if the children and neighbors corroborated that Rivas had not quit the shop, this portion of the case would be more complex than he had hoped. His cousin, the Inspector, just might arise out of the ashes. He had to determine the murderer of the Marquesa quickly. Only then

would it be safe to elaborate, demonstrating to his superiors how everything obeyed a sinister design.

"Isias," he asked as the man helped tug trousers back up over his
hips, "the names of those maidservants I gave you—are they being questioned?"

"Yes, sir. One's pregnant. Another smokes marijuana. A third . . ."

"Never mi . . . !"

"Oh, and by the way, a scissors-grinder is accused of raping the
wife of the baker on Calle Los Mancebos this morning."

"Bother that! I want transcripts of the interrogations as soon as they
can be copied. Now," belting himself, "off to the morgue."

But there, as you know, Dr. Lachaise gave Grau what, on the surface, seemed to be bad news. The Marquesa had not met her fate at
the dawn hour. Time of death was between midnight and one forty-
five in the morning. (Of course! thought Stepanópoulis, irritated with
himself: she had been in rigor mortis.) Therefore the maid's tale was
at the very least confused. And: very thin, long bony fingers had left
distinct marks on the Marquesa's throat.

Grau now rejoiced. The maid! Clearly, that witch of a skinnybones!
Much, much better than the mantequero! Oh, this was wonderful! *Pidal
had been pushed!*

But a telephone call was announced from police headquarters. Grau
trembled. His cousin!

He accepted the receiver. Numbly, he cupped it to his ear.

Yes, it had to do with his cousin: who, hearing of the events, and
in the greatest alarm, had stumbled up from his bed of pain, dressed
as quickly as intestinal seizures permitted, and gone lurching into the
street . . . only to be hit at a crossing by a Vespa! The call was to advise
Grau that the Inspector had been taken to the Clínica de Loreto, with
a concussion and three cracked ribs. "Splendid!" said Stepanópoulis.

He borrowed Dr. Lachaise's facilities, where he pondered hard
as a merry tourmeline stream sprinkled musically against the porcelain. He had leeway, now. He would not precipitate matters. He would
inhibit his genius from those leaps of clairvoyance that had so often been
his undoing. He would personally interrogate the nightwatchman, Irujo.
He would interrogate the electrician and the manicurist. (Might they
not have all held the struggling Marquesa while the maid throttled her?)
He would . . . send Isias to interrogate the Countess of Magascal, and
diagram the movements of the victim on the previous evening. He would
learn as much about Nati's history as possible. He would study the reports

on the other maidservants, that María who worked for the Count of the Caribs, that Rosa who worked for the Counts of Obregón, that What's-her-name who worked for . . . Yes, and others. And then: he and Isias would drive out to the proving grounds, where Guillermo Smith-Burton labored on his fiendish inventions. And he would enter headquarters with his case all but complete by nightfall. And they would believe him!

The stream ended.

He checked his wristwatch. Three ten. He had a great deal to accomplish!

SEVEN

Florita

"Go directly," the widow-Duchess of Sacedón admonished Juan Luis outside the Ministry of Foreign Affairs, "to Número Catorce—don't dally for a moment—and corner Ignacio at *once!*"

Well, Herminia's little boy walked sadly the twelve blocks to where he had left his Lancia. What was the matter with him? Why did he not tell his mother right out? Or, if not, with a good will lend himself to the imposture of a position for which nature had never intended him?

Juan Luis was irritated. And that—his irritation—of a sudden made him feel good. The dreadful hangover had passed! God, in His mercy, had mercifully terminated punishment. He was able to experience emotions unrelated to knots and seethings in his intestines, to nausea in his stomach, or to hammerings in his head. Oh, health! As he ignited the engine, he renewed acquaintanceship with the world. It was a baking, glorious afternoon! How to savor its last hours? *Go* at once to Número Catorce, and yes/no corner Nacho? A very large—a gloomy, even fatidic —decision to make. A last toast to decadence was in order, no? A last whinnying between muscular thighs. A last pull on the teat of indulgence!

Had Herminia paid Florita off yet? If so, a pity—today, on this splendid thirty-first of May. Florita would be curled up like a fetus in the double bed of the little flat on Dr. Fleming. Her work did not begin until just before midnight. It was five-thirty now, she would be rousing, she'd want a cup of thick black coffee, a glass of anisette, and something else sweet to release her tender feelings . . .

He stopped off at Gales to buy half a kilo of her favorite chocolates. One last go together! He was bored with Florita, but she did love him in her way, and he was fond of her, and she was very, very good. And he was in much, much better fettle on afternoons—oh yes, it was evident at this moment—in really excellent fiddle. He would strum the guitar for her. With his steely fingers he would pick out a pertenera, inciting in her a suspense with the Juegos Prohibidos, cool her with a Bach prelude, and then thomp abruptly into a rich atonal malagueña whose rhythms never failed to stir the gypsy passion.

Twenty minutes later, box of chocolates tucked under an armpit, he was slipping into the flat. The shades were still drawn. It was dark. The musk of her tuberose perfume drew thickly into his nostrils. He sure-footed his way to the bedroom door, there halting.

He was puzzled. Disconcerting sounds seeped through to him. He opened the door. "Florita?"

In that gloom, his eyes were startled by an eruption of buttocks. In panic, his mistress flipped over and away from the man straddling her. "Juan Luis!" came her shriek.

"Oyyy-*ye!*" came the indignant honk of the interloper. "Not now you don't . . . !" And he grabbed for her, yanking her over on her hindside and thrusting through the windmill of her resistance.

"Juan Luis!" Florita shrieked again.

"Juan-I-don't-give-a-fart!" bellowed the interloper, whopping his sweaty nakedness into the concave sounding board of her sweaty nakedness, producing the fat smacking thumps of tuna being ganged into a boat.

Juan Luis went to the window and hauled up the persian slats, flooding the room with sun.

"Wow!" went the interloper. "Oh, oh, oh, oh!" went Florita. "Wow, wow, wow!" went the interloper. "Oh, oh, oh, oh, *ohhhh!*" groaned Florita. "Uggeruggeruggerugger-UG-*grrrrrrrrr!*" came (from) the interloper; and he let himself topple forward on her, like spilled noodles.

Florita squirmed out from beneath him, burying her face in the bedcovers.

"Who," asked Juan Luis, feeling foolish, but courteously allowing for moments of recuperation, "is this man?"

The interloper was still breathing heavily, but he managed to grunt, "García, at your service. Who are you?"

"Sigismundo del Val," said Juan Luis curtly.

The interloper craned his head about, screwing up an eye. He was a man in his early forties, dark of visage, unshaven, with broken teeth.

"Well, I'll be!" he said. "Fancy!" he said, turning over and wiping spittle from his mouth. "To meet you—here—again."

"I'm afraid, the pleasure . . ." murmured Juan Luis.

"At the works," prompted the interloper, scratching his ribs, "at the unveiling of the tree trunk. I used to be Orbaneja's chief mason—until I got fed up with slave wages."

"Oh yes, I remember now," said Juan Luis, who didn't. "Did you come here to fix something?"

"I'm what you might call in residence, most afternoons, when my hitch is over at the cemetery."

"In . . . residence?" He ought to sit down, not simply stand there looking—as he felt he must—half-stunned. But the only available chair had García's blue mason's smock and trousers flung over it. "Is that so, Florita?"

She kept her head covered. García slapped her sharply on an olive rump.

"Speak up! The Duke asked you a question. Tell him. Sure I'm in residence here. You must be . . . oh, sure, the moneybags. What do you know! Sharing the same ass with a duke! What do you know!"

"I think . . . maybe I ought to leave," said Juan Luis.

"Why?" exclaimed García, thrusting himself off the bed. He stood there in all his naked laborer's paunchifying muscularity, filled with bon-hommie. "Stay a bit and chat. I put coffee on a few minutes ago. What do you know!" —and he went thudding around the perimeter of the bed, stooping wide-assed (hairy and black too) here and there in search, presumably, of his underdrawers.

"You're the one," said Juan Luis slowly, on to something, "who was cheating the Count of the Caribs." García was not wearing a contraceptive. Florita, Juan Luis knew, possessed none on religious scruples.

"Oh, that!" García tossed over a shoulder. "*Here* they are!" he exulted—a grimy cotton truss that he retrieved from the polka-dotted puddle of Florita's Flamenco costume, which lay where, last night—just before dawn this morning!—Juan Luis had flung it. He began thrusting his feet through the leg holes. "The dumbskull, never examined an account, couldn't understand accounts anyhow. What could he expect?"

"You . . . have children," Juan Luis now stated. "I remember he was upset—Jaime telling me. It's five, isn't it?"

"Six!" cockcrowed García, patting the white bulge of his equipment.

"Potent fellow," mused Juan Luis.

"You can say that again! Florita, how about it?" He laughed, reaching to deal her another whack on the rump. "Good and firm," he said, "I won't waste the time of day on flabby ones."

"And you've been . . . in residence . . . how many months?"

"Six, seven."

"Florita, *are* you pregnant?"

There was a whimper from the bedclothes. Why she buried her head and not her nether parts, Juan Luis was at a loss to understand. In his opinion, her buttocks were a shade scrawny.

"He's asking you!" said García, stinging them with the tail of his undershirt hard enough for pink to compete with the olive.

"Yes," sobbed Florita.

"You can't be more than three months pregnant."

"Almost five," sobbed Florita.

"I won't be coming here when it shows," said García giving a deep, appreciative sniff at one armpit of his smock. "You understand that, I warned you about that."

"I was away on safari then!" exclaimed Juan Luis.

"Get anything?" asked García.

Juan Luis shook his head at a sad memory. "Missed an eighty-pound tusker, hit the gas tank of the Land-Rover instead. Blew up. Stampeded the herd through a village."

"What a shame!" said García.

"Did Herminia come here today?" asked Juan Luis. "Has she spoken to you?"

"The little old dame?" said García, searching for his sandals. "Couple of hours ago."

"I'll pay it back!" sobbed Florita, now whipping her head about sufficiently to provide him with a poignant glimpse of that stunning Semitic scythe. There was a tug in his heart. "I don't want any of it!"

"The Devil you don't!" declared García, straightening up with a sandal in hand. "*I* upped it to four hundred thousand, half's mine. And when you sue through the courts, like she said, I'm getting ten per cent."

Moments were required for this to fully register in Juan Luis's mind. But he knew. Now he knew—and now he admitted—everything.

He had been in possession of the knowledge all along; just as he had been aware of what he was doing when he signed those demand notes, leaving it up to destiny, even hoping for the worst. Herminia was his enemy. She had known of Florita's pregnancy, and that García was responsible. She had suggested the blackmail. She had devoted twenty-five years to undermining his manhood and morals, to encouraging in him every vice; until he was all but helpless, and under her dominion. Out of that growing—perhaps innate—desire for self-immolation, he had acquiesced, veiling the truth from himself. He wanted nothing so much than to be destroyed, to have ended for him—because he was too great a coward to act on his own—the useless ordeal of his existence. Billy Smith-Burton was correct.

His mind reeled. Herminia! His loving, beloved Herminia!

"Oh!" he whimpered, dismayed. He had pressed a heated arm too hard against the box of chocolates. Sticky, vanilla-scented mocha had squished through cardboard seams and wrapping tissue to smear the fabric of his suit.

He would have to change. It was this that determined him to seek out Herminia and face her down.

EIGHT

The Financier

Long after lunch, Baltazar Blás sat brooding at his desk. Not the daffodils, nor the dogwood on the terrace with their burden of soft, white, whispered kisses, were able to vivify him. Two long hours—more—passed in this heavy, suspended, uncharacteristic state. The red jewel on the intercom glowed. He flicked the switch.

"I said I wanted to be alone!"

"Señor Puig, sir!"

Was this, for Blás, the second knock? Would there come, for this great man too, a third?

Blás drew on bottomless reservoirs of strength. "Send him in"; and he rose from his desk to greet the merchandiser personally.

They sat at a hutch of white leather armchairs occupying an ante-

room attached to Blás's office, a blonded coffee table separating them
on the level of their knees. Blás forced upon himself the heartiness so
useful to him. It was as important that people believe in this jovial
exterior as that they believe in his capacity for ruthlessness, the latter
being the complement of the former. He spoke business in general. He
joked earthily. He let drop a note on the pervasive fear of American pen-
etration in Spanish markets. "But they don't stand a chance!" he declared.
"Too soft. Soft-hearted, soft-headed, teams of lawyers and all that, but
always eager to believe what they want to believe. Eh, Puig? Found
that too? All they really have is capital, no? Plenty of that, of course!"

Puig was less ebullient. He was the younger man by nearly twenty
years. The difference was more than generational. His background was
petty bourgeoisie rather than peasant. Energetic, sure of himself in his
own milieu, he possessed a somewhat more smoothed person than
Baltazar Blás. Otherwise, one would suppose them to be related. Spaniards of the self-made merchant class share tribal characteristics. They
seem to issue from the shortest stock of the population. There is a cocki-
ness in their posture. No eyes are quite so beady, nor so distrustfully
and shrewdly lidded. When at social functions, and standing side by
side, they face out from instead of toward each other, conversing in
low, machinegun-bursts of speech, faint smiles ever ready on their lips
as they gaze at the crowd, but continually sizing one another up with
darting, lateral whipsaw clicks of their eyeballs.

Whisky was brought in. Baltazar Blás's attitude I am able to relate.
He was the patriarch. It was he who chose graciously to assume a
benevolent but plainly fictitious equality with his guest. Puig he was
scarcely acquainted with, and held in limited esteem: a hard-working
individual who had fairly carved out his second-rank position. No more.
What Puig's initial attitude was as they shadowboxed I am less able to
relate, because I know little of the man. I would hazard that a prickly
imminence of fear was not absent in him. Baltazar Blás, after all, was
made of legendary stuff. He had chewed up and spat out dozens of
Puigs, bankrupting half of them. But it may be—and again I am guessing
—that the merchandiser gained in confidence as they chatted. He may
have noticed how very old Blás was suddenly looking. He may have
detected false notes in the heartiness. Puig is a florid, sandy-haired man
of considerable girth. Quite soon, he stated his purpose.

"Young Sacedón telephoned me lunchtime. He tells me you are
after him."

Blás nodded. The lids narrowed imperceptibly the space over his eyeballs.

He said, "His company. I have nothing against the Duke. There is, in fact, a great deal to respect in the young man."

This must have surprised Puig. "I am in debt to the late Duke his father, you may be aware of that. Juan Luis asked me for thirty million pesetas, which I gather he needs to keep you from taking control."

"Have you loaned it to him?" inquired the imperturbable Blás. He added, "I respect loyalty, Puig. But I warn you that I mean to have Financiera."

"Why pick on the boy?"

"I've said it's not personal. Well . . . I suppose it is. Spain can't afford them any longer, Puig. Now, did you advance him the money? If so, you have made a mistake. You'll lose it."

"Can Spain afford any of us?" Puig asked with a naturalness that disconcerted Blás. "One could argue, wouldn't it be best for us to sell out to the Americans? They possess, after all, more than capital. As a retailer, I can tell you that we don't begin to comprehend their techniques."

"Ah," said Blás, steering for waters he preferred. "Sears Roebuck. Woolworth at the door. Frankly, I think they are going to lose a lot of money, at first anyhow. Techniques are applicable only to societies that have something like the same technological base. Still," he added brightly, "I can imagine they have . . . less capitalized operations worried."

"Not I," Puig retorted. The man felt—Baltazar perceived—that he was dealing from strength. "I've been locked up with ministers and bankers all week. I have an offer from the American May Company for my three stores."

"My congratulations. But will the Government permit the sale?"

"It's been approved."

"Wouldn't it be better for Spain if the middle-sized department stores banded together? I mean, pool factory sources, marketing, deliveries, and so forth."

"Yes. Preferable. Commerce showed me your proposal."

This checked Blás. Since when were his communications with the Government disclosed to third parties?

"A mere notion, Puig, not a tender. It occurred to me when I began looking over Financiera's assets. Noticed its position in Galerías Pedro Puig."

"And this morning you dictated the memorandum to Commerce."

"Yes, this morning."

"And the moment I saw it, I called other owners. Met with three of them before lunch."

"You move rapidly."

"You encourage that, Señor Blás. We're considering syndication. And we're willing for you to finance it."

"Well, now, that may be of interest. Yes. And it's the patriotic thing to do."

"All the easier for you to wholesale financing from the Bank of Spain, an advantage not so available to us. No bitterness, Señor Blás. Fact, that's all."

"And you've weighed the fact that I won't touch your proposition without control?"

"Yes."

"And you're willing?"

"Yes."

"And you're not frightened I'll replace you?"

"Not personally. I'm a good manager. Your memorandum frightened the others so much they'll accept just about anything. I'm offering you something you want, Señor Blás. I'll help you get it. But I want something in exchange. I want a position in Financiera—as an elementary protection."

Blás was now openly startled. For the second time this day had such an impertinence . . .

"Impossible. I have all the partners I need."

"I want a position in Financiera—and I want the Sacedóns protected."

"That's also impossible."

Blás smiled. His expression regretted the decision. Puig was silent a moment. But he was not perspiring, which by this time he should have been.

"I'm just fifty-eight," the man said. "Worked hard all my life. I could sell to the Americans, enjoy myself. If I decide to do that, all I have to do is cable—and two point four millions in dollars will be released to me at once. In which event, I am perfectly able to advance thirty million pesetas to Juan Luis. I discharge my debt there."

"Able, yes. As I've mentioned, you will lose it. And you'll have incurred my displeasure."

What followed was flabbergasting for Baltazar.

Puig said, "That doesn't worry me, Señor Blás. When was it last anyone challenged you? Twenty, thirty years ago?"

"These are matters I don't intend to discuss, Puig."

"Juan Luis's time is up, Señor Blás, true. But so is yours. You've kept going on two pillars—capital and reputation. But some of us can't be bullied so easily—not now when we're able to protect our flanks by alliances with foreign firms. This is no longer the Spain you grew up with. Several months, now, I've been in contact with West German interests. They're as intrigued by the possibilities of Utilidades—your target —as you are."

"Their name!" Blás snapped.

Puig supplied it. "They're powerful," he added unnecessarily. "They need me, a Spaniard, in order to obtain permission to operate a utilities firm here. They've agreed that fifteen million dollars from me will represent fifty-one per cent of the stock . . ."

Blás came down hard. "Within two years they'll do to you what Chrysler did to Barreiros. They'll squeeze you out!"

"For what Chrysler paid Barreiros, Señor Blás, they can squeeze, cuddle, or pinch me, and they're welcome! I've consulted with Labour and Commerce. They don't view the notion hostilely. What I mean is, we may get permission to break the utilities monopolies all over Spain, which includes Utilidades and your Unión Eléctrica Aragona. You see, they've been smart enough to set aside an ultimate sixty per cent for INI," by which he referred to the State's development corporation, "which Labour especially likes, because it's a step toward nationalization. And that's popular, today. As an alternative," he concluded, "we can begin at any time purchasing Financiera stock ourselves."

"You'll make me richer in the process!"

"That's beside the point—for you. It's the company, the power, you want."

To say that Baltazar was flabbergasted is by way of understatement. Here was impertinence verging on insolence. This fellow from the second rank meant to contest the sway of the Blás empire.

Blás now spoke in a tone that had chilled many a man.

"Do you seriously propose pitting your influence in the Government against mine?"

"The ministers are a new breed," came the reply.

"And you propose pitting your and your German partners' financial resources against Banco Blás?"

He was genuinely incredulous. And that finally affected Puig. The man was very nervous, now. There was no way of estimating the hugeness of the Blás fortune.

But he said, "The prize is worth the risk. We will, naturally, be thinking it over." He rose. "No one in Spain, Señor Blás, would choose to take you on. I hope you give my earlier proposals some consideration."

Blás got to his feet. He accompanied Puig to the door. There were parting courtesies. They bowed at each other. They smiled. They shook hands. Both were aware of what a battle might be engaged.

Blás was watching the elevator engulf Puig (and perhaps thinking of Pidal) when, suddenly, to his right—near the door of his office—there appeared a tall, sepulchral individual, at whose elbow Sert was vainly and in a kind of panic tugging.

"What . . . ?" began Blás.

"The Comptroller!" squeaked out Sert. "He . . ."

"How *dare* you!" Blás exploded, wheeling on the man.

"You don't," said the Comptroller, "have the funds to cover the paintings you just bought."

"WHAT!"

It may surprise fellow entrepreneurs among you that Baltazar should be surprised. He had handed $20,000,000 over to me. This is a very substantial cash outlay. I am myself wonderfully rich. Yet if someone should ask me to set down a million dollars in ready money, I would have to make arrangements. We are modern businessmen. We put our resources to work at once. Spaniards of the old school tend to hoard liquidity. Blás was used to being enormously liquid. He was scarcely able to comprehend what Ignacio's Comptroller told him.

Now, this young man was of the dispassionate breed of Spaniards, something like those new Opus Dei technocrats alluded to by Puig, who today have taken over the Government. The wrath of Baltazar Blás did not phase him. "If you shout once more at me, sir," he stated with utmost respect, "I'll walk back out that door and permit you to bankrupt yourself as fast as you please. It's all the same to me." Blás blinked.

The Comptroller continued, tonelessly and to the point. Need I detail the story of eclectic expansion? It's much the same sort of thing Eugenio explained to Juan Luis respecting Financiera Sacedón, compounded by such occulted outlays as the millions in spot cash paid to the French for the paralegal arms transaction, which Blás had not run through AESA's books (this was a private deal) and which the Comptroller had had to infer from a study of half a hundred bank balances. In short, he related to Blás what I knew from the photostat of his summation, filched for me by Julio Caro after my dinner two nights before, when I buttonholed him about a debt; that his (Blás's) cash receivables amounted to $25.6 millions, but that his immediate liabilities came to $7 millions—before payment to me of $20 millions, for a net cash deficit of $1.4 millions.

Baltazar was financially embarrassed! To his ineffable shock and astonishment (in this day of astonishments and shocks), what the dreary Ignacio had been telling him all along had had truth in it: the time is past when a single human being armed with an abacus can go free-wheeling along at the head of a vast and complex maze of interlocking corporate structures; primitive bookkeeping no longer suffices; and it was Ignacio's highly automated office that knew what was going on.

Baltazar reacted very much like Odette on the morning before. Why hadn't he been advised! Why hadn't anyone told him!

But, you see, he had been told—in report after meticulous report, to which, book-ended as most of them were by Ignacio's discursive comments on social obligations, he had paid cursory attention. There was no actual crisis, of course. He would be able to sweat out what he needed —dispose of some properties. "But," warned the Comptroller, "it's my duty to make clear that any other unanticipated, unprogrammed pressures will be serious in the currently restricted money market. I need not dramatize the effect should word go round that Banco Blás is pressed for cash."

Blás, as I say, felt much like Odette when she was faced with her trivial household accounts. And he felt not unlike Juan Luis earlier during the day when Eugenio confronted him with his situation. He was stunned.

There are, I suppose, lofty observations of a philosophical nature to be drawn from these parallels. Of the common human condition, for instance. Or of mankind's common hubris. Maybe you care to draw them. I am not up to it. Suffice that now nothing could be permitted to go amiss with the arms shipment. Baltazar was at the mercy of Muñoz González. He needed those extra millions. Should he be put under pressure by Puig meanwhile, to whom could he turn?

I hoped, to me.

NINE

The Conspirators

Driving to Almagro from Dr. Fleming, Juan Luis felt misery. He had adored Herminia. He loved her even now. How often had he soaked her bosom with his childhood tears! How often had she wiped his infant's bottom for him, or stood by him nights with cough syrup ready in a spoon! But she had deceived him with Florita. It was plain she had been deceiving him all along. Why? Why?

He had to find out. Infinitely was he depressed. His one ally and confidante apart from Sofía of the Thousand Tears, and privy to his soul as never could he permit Sofía to become, must loathe him, must despise him! To Herminia, what had he done? How had he hurt her? Or was he to accept that no one in the world could love or in some small manner esteem Juan Luis Seguismundo del Val, unhappy Duke of Sacedón—that in the eyes of all the world he was in fact as he deemed himself, the belly of the worm.

He underwent his customary, hunching scurry under the stalactites. The flood in the courtyard had been brought under control, but only by the banging of a wine bung into the fountain's nozzle. Under a lily-pad glistened the bronze scales of the indestructible carp.

The elevator was functioning. He was rattled up to the sixth floor. Instead of ringing, he used his key to enter the apartment.

Stepping inside, he all at once felt like crying. He felt something akin to what he imagined must be the emotions of a young husband returning home for the first time with the certitude that his wife is unfaithful. He would have to fortify himself for the confrontation.

He went to the living room, stepped behind a handsome brass-ringed bamboo bar, and filled a tumbler with whisky. He drank it neat, slowly, savoring it. There seemed to be no effect. On the shellacked surface of the bar was a set of three hand-cut rock crystal decanters with chased silver stoppers into which had been engraved the ducal arms—Herminia's Christmas present. One of the many things she knew about him was how much he loved beautiful objects, especially those worked by hand . . .

He rang for the parlor maid.

No one answered the summons.

Perhaps it was her afternoon off, he never could keep track. He rang now for Paca or Pilar or Petra, or whatever that luscious young personal maid was called; failing also to raise her.

Was there a short in the circuit? No, he could hear the buzz in the kitchen quarters. Once the circuits had become crossed, and when the Countess von Leddhin below rang for her butler, Juan Luis's cook came hurrying to his bedroom, and when he pressed the bell four times for Herminia on a midwinter morning, the central air-conditioning turbines roared to life, the janitor's new oven began baking, the burglar alarm howled, and the heat went off. But this was not the case today. Exasperated, Juan Luis walked out of the living room and down a corridor to the service area.

Pantry and kitchen were as strange a terrain to him as the backside of the moon. But they were vacant, that he could tell. They were, in fact, evacuated. This he surmised only after a while—from the stripped neatness of counters and, when he opened it, the stripped nakedness of the refrigerator. It was an eerie sensation. It was like boarding an abandoned ship in mid-ocean.

He pushed through to the service quarters. This, to him, was an exploration into Mars, or even beyond our solar system. The plaster in the narrow hall was gouged in places. Four flimsy doors faced each other. One was ajar, and from it came a foul smell.

Juan Luis looked in. His eyes met the open bowl of a toilet. There was no cover. To sit upon, it offered a plastic oval that had come loose from its hinges. An elementary sink. A curtainless showerstall. The bulb above the sink had been left burning, but apart from a few long black hairs coiled near the drain, there was nothing to suggest recent use— nor a jar of hand lotion on the glass shelf, nor even a smear of toothpaste.

He entered a bedroom. A chair, a bureau, a ribbed length of rug covering the linoleum between two iron cots. The rug was askew. The cots had been stripped to their thin mattresses. The door of a closet had been left open. It was bare, with several of a swept-aside bunch of wire hangers hooked to the rungs of their fellows and dangling like mobiles.

The next bedroom, a single, had also been denuded. Juan Luis went to a bureau, pulling out the drawers. Empty. Empty. Empty. Emp . . .

What was that? He peered into the recesses of the fourth drawer. A long, black velvet case had been overlooked. A necklace? He reached for it, unsnapping the lid.

Inside was a flesh-colored rubber object with straps. Beneath that lay a pamphlet.

Juan Luis had already begun to feel a burning in his cheeks. He extracted the pamphlet. The text was in Scandinavian, but the glossy photographs were sufficient to instruct the dullest mind in every conceivable use of the dildo.

He was shocked. Hurriedly, he put the thing away, slamming the drawer shut.

Juan Luis's brains were scrambled with shock. This was an afternoon of revelations. Now he understood the men staggering out of the apartment next door as he came staggering in, and the high rent Muñoz González had been willing to pay. Now he understood Herminia's fury over the maid he tumbled, and her constant firings and hirings. Oh, this was depraved! This was terrible! How could his kind old ama—whatever she thought of him—stoop so wretchedly low!!

Upset that he was, he very nearly neglected the third bedroom, another double. But a glance inside showed him that the apartment was not quite evacuated. Here there was at least one occupant, the cheap dresser holding a set of pink plastic-backed toilette accessories and a snapshot of a broad, burly man with, presumably, his wife, who was a woman of heroic proportions. A Bible topped a neat stack of other books on the bedside table. There was a hand-stitched rose coverlet, and on the pillow rested a picture of the Virgin.

A fresh arrival, he guessed—and this one probably some innocent being prepared for sacrifice.

He was by this time again more puzzled than anything else. Why had everyone but this girl, whoever she was, been sent away?

Juan Luis walked back through kitchen and pantry to the corridor, turning a corner before reaching the door to Herminia's suite. There he hesitated. He had to compel himself to knock.

There was no reply. A sharper rap. Still no reply.

He tried the knob.

Herminia's door was locked.

Juan Luis pondered. He then nerved himself to one of the rare sneaky actions of his life—because, for whatever one takes Juan Luis, there is this to be said of him: he does not possess the mean vices. Juan Luis determined to enter and search Herminia's quarters, into which he had never trespassed uninvited.

He went back to the pantry to look for tools.

Some six hours earlier, at around noon in the morning, an increasingly impatient Muñoz González had gone springing up the service stairs to the roof. Dorada Blás was late. What could be delaying the brutish Tomás!

Stepping from deep shadow to blinding sun, he blinked: and then almost instantaneously reacted to what he saw, dropping into a crouch and glancing sharply left and right.

There was no blood visible, and no wound, but the giant sprawled forward on his face was unmistakably dead.

With that panther's grace, Muñoz González reconnoitered the premises, moving swiftly around the perimeter of the roof but careful to keep below its parapet and out of sight. There were the service elevator shaft, chimney hatches, and a storage shed. No one lurked in their vicinity.

Eyes darting back and forth, Muñoz González deduced. The position of the corpse suggested that Tomás had been defending access to the elevator. The assailant, his master now guessed, was somewhere in the building.

Maintaining his crouch, he circled back to Tomás. He levered up one shoulder, uncovering a sticky mass of blood. Shoving harder, he saw where the blade had been thrust into the man's gut. The weapon had been withdrawn.

Once again, Muñoz González swept the roof with his eyes. No one moved on the roofs of adjacent buildings. Grasping Tomás under the arms, he attempted lifting the body. Muñoz González was a muscular man, but it strained strength to drag that colossal cadaver even a little way. He would not be able to carry it alone.

He cursed. Struggling, he half rolled, half shoved the corpse into the shadow of a ledge, out of direct view of a strolling janitor or some repairman who might be summoned to fix a next-door television aerial. He was nevertheless worried. Plumbers were still in his building, working on the flood.

He now backed his way into the shaft, shutting and bolting the door before straightening up. He stood there a moment on the tiled steps of the stairway, thinking. Then he moved on cat's feet back down to the service entrance of his flat.

A warning from the Party? No, he thought, he was on good terms with it for the time being. Then who? Why?

He stopped in the kitchen to telephone the dukeling's flat. He got the control tower of Barajas Airport instead. He dialed again, but he had

failed to wait for the *click, click-click* of the first three digits. Upon a
third, furious attempt, he connected with the cook. Her voice shrilled
through the wall as she shrilled into the receiver. Herminia, she told
him, had trotted out on an errand. Where! Oh, she thought to Número
Catorce, she was not sure. The widow-Duchess of Sacedón had telephoned
her half an hour before about something to do with . . .

Muñoz González hung up. The cook's voice continued shrilling
through the wall as he stood there and chewed savagely on his mustache.
Where in blazes was the Blás daughter? Had she had misgivings? If she
showed up now he was in a fix, with Tomás up on the hot roof putrefying
and no one to service her, no one for the substitution. Rougement might
do . . . Later. Later. The corpse had to be attended to first. What it sig-
nified had to be discovered.

He dialed Dorada's flat. This was risky, but there was no help for it.

A weepy domestic answered. No, the Countess had not gone out.
She had locked herself into the bedroom with orders not to be disturbed.
Who should she be told was calling her? The phone hadn't stopped ring-
ing all morning. The poor Señor Conde had . . .

Muñoz González swore soundlessly. What was the matter with
Dorada! Had he misgauged her? *Had* she winded his design?

The day was coming apart. He meant to move the munitions after
midnight. He had to have something to wield over Blás—just in case,
not merely as a matter of personal revenge for the hounding of his parents to their deaths in that miserable little town. The shipment depended
upon the man's trucks and his organization.

Muñoz González cocked an ear. Was there someone moving in the
pantry, in the dining room? Cautiously he stepped to the swinging door.
He listened. In the dining room, was it—light treading of feet?

Rapidly, he glanced behind him. There was no fear in Muñoz González, but whoever had managed to knife Tomás had been good, had
been quick.

He plucked a roast carver from a rack. He eased himself through
the door and into the pantry.

He stood there seconds. No sounds came to him. On the deepfreeze
he had imported from America, a large pot rested. He lifted its top by
the handle, holding it before him like a shield.

He eased through the swinging door that admitted to the dining
room. No one. Perhaps what he had heard was one of the girls in the
dukeling's flat. Sounds carried far through any walls built by Orbaneja.

He now walked quickly to the circular reception parlor. There he cantilevered aside a fine, Flemish rendition of Susanna and the Elders, uncovering a wall safe. He twirled the combination. Inside were mint-new bundles in several currencies. Inside were the demand notes Juan Luis had signed at Préstamos Cantábricos, along with the all-important collateral pledging Financiera stock. And inside was an automatic with a bulbous silencer attached to the muzzle. This he slipped into his waist-band, closing the safe and sliding the canvas back over it.

Behind the settee there hung a curtain. He went to it, reeving it back with the yank of a cord. Here, embedded in the wall, was the master television screen for his closed-circuit system. He switched it on, waited for it to warm up, and then began flipping toggles on the control panel. Room after room came into view. Most of the cameras were aimed at the opulent love couches but he was able to control them remotely, scanning the interiors. If there was an intruder in the flat, he was in hid-ing—at least for the moment—under a bed or in a closet. Muñoz González was therefore comparatively safe.

He set the system to automatic. Every few seconds, bedrooms and bathrooms gave way to each other. Only corridors went unscanned, an oversight he now deeply regretted. But, backing away from the screen until his shoulder blades met the opposite wall, he reached for a tele-phone that was supported by a gilt, wrought-iron trolley; and began track-ing his associates down.

Scheel he finally located in his favorite gymnasium, where a sauna baked out of his flesh the nights he spent buggering and being buggered by girls. They spoke in French, Muñoz González fluently, Scheel with a thick tongue. Yes, the West German turncoat said, he knew where Has-sam was to be found—at the Embassy of the United Arab Republic, praying. Where Rougement and Dong Thoc might be he did not know . . .

"Look for them!" ordered Muñoz González, rapping the receiver on its cradle. The art nouveau room faded from the screen. It was replaced by the chamber decorated with feminine French flair (courtesy of the Countess von Leddhin), where by this time he had intended to watch Tomás split screams of agony and joy out of Dorada, photographing her every convulsion.

Next door, it was a happy scene at this half-past-noon hour. Soledad Rivas, clutching a cardboard suitcase in one hand, girlish heart thump-ing, had arrived.

A pretty young cook smiled at her. An even lovelier, dusky, green-

eyed waitress smiled at her. And Doña Herminia herself, recently returned from Número Catorce, came hurrying in on her bowed old legs
to greet her.

"Cariño!" she said warmly, pressing both Soledad's blooming cheeks
between her palms. "So your father saw reason?"

"Yes, Doña Herminia! Isn't it wonderful?"

"Well, I knew he would, he's an intelligent man. Come, now, dear,
I'll show you to your room. You've met Julia? You've met Magdalena?"

She was turning with Soledad toward the service quarters when
Julia, the cook, spoke to her.

"Oh, Doña Herminia, I forgot to tell you. El patrón called half an
hour ago. He seemed very anxious to see you."

"Even at my age!" joked Herminia. "Men can't wait a minute, can
they?" All the girls giggled. When Doña Herminia was in good form,
the sun seemed brighter, the air exhilarating. And she was in high good
form at this moment, having trapped Nati in her logic, and thereby snared
Juan Luis, and now having successfully plucked this rosebud of a Rivas
girl. All there was left to do was arrange for the paternity suit against
her little boy. "Get him on the telephone for me, that's a sweet girl. Oh
dear," she said to Soledad, bustling her along. "I have to go out again. We
need fruit and vegetables. Some days I scarcely catch my breath!"

Having a cot to herself almost brought from Soledad a whoop—she
who was used to sharing beds with sisters in common sleeping quarters
with her brothers. For the time being, Herminia told her, her duties were
to mend linen and help tidy the main living quarters, but mostly to be
available to Doña Herminia, who would bit by bit instruct her in other
matters.

Doña Herminia then left on her errand, permitting Soledad to pack
her belongings away and change into a freshly pressed uniform that
fitted her as though made to measure. She was becoming a little bored
when an hour went by; and quite bored when another hour went by. But
she had been bidden by Doña Herminia to stay in her bedroom, and on
no account was she going to displease that great lady by disobedience.

Muñoz González was meanwhile sweating out the wait for his associates. He did not actually sweat, perspiring very faintly. His thirty-six
years had seen him through many unpleasant moments. Watching the
television screen, he collected his thoughts. The assailant might be anyone. It could be an innocent—perhaps one of the plumbers, surprised by

Tomás, frightened by him, and acting in self-defense. This was a rich apartment house. It could be a thief.

But as fast as he hypothesized, as fast he doubted. A gnawing instinct —one with which he was familiar—told him Tomás's murder had to do with him: that he, personally, was the objective.

Scheel was the first to arrive. It must have been a relief for Muñoz González to see the man. He was thoroughly professional. His very brauhaus burgher's bulk inspired confidence. He was dressed still as Juan Luis had seen him that dawn, in a Dacron gabardine suit, white silk tie, and perforated brown and white shoes. He remained tranquil through Muñoz González's résumé of events.

"Blás," he said in his disagreeably accented French, "is it certain he does not know what you intend with his daughter?"

"As far as I know, he's not even aware that we've been seeing each other." Muñoz González shook his head negatively. "Say he found out. Say he's confined his daughter to her bedroom. He wouldn't act until the shipment is on its way—nor until I deliver the Duke's collateral, the Financiera shares."

Scheel agreed. "They are our guarantee, our protection . . ." He lifted his bulk from the chair in which he had been sitting. "Well, shall we bring the body down?"

"Too heavy, even for you and me. We'll need to post the stairway anyhow."

The telephone and doorbell rang almost simultaneously. Muñoz González jerked a chin at Scheel, who nodded, accepting the proffered automatic and moving ponderously toward the vestibule with it. Muñoz González picked up the receiver.

It was Herminia. "We have problems," he told her.

"Big?"

"Over two meters long and weighing more than a hundred kilos."

"I do not understand you."

"You will when you drop by."

"There is something I must do first."

"I want you to come right over."

But Herminia had her own fish to fry. "I won't be longer than an hour or so."

She clicked off. Scheel was returning from the vestibule with Rougement, who was followed closely by Dong Thoc and then by the tall, melanistic, soberly suited Hassam, their contact with the Israeli authorities.

Scheel handed the automatic back. "I have told them."

"Oh, I say!" exclaimed Hassam in his stilted Oxonian way, "this is very bad news indeed!"

"I suppose you've checked the place out," said Rougement casually, looking around him. He was a French Algerian, a veteran of Vietnam —one of those raw-boned, brawny ex-opponents of De Gaulle now soldiering in anyone's army.

"We'll do that now," answered Muñoz González. Dong Thoc was assigned to watch the screen, a precaution against surprise. The four others were thorough. Their search completed, they gathered again in the parlor, where Muñoz González said, "Rougement, have Dong Thoc watch the staircase." Rougement nodded. He spoke in a burbling tongue to the Korean, who twitched the wide corners of what seemed to be a perpetual graveyard's grin. Muñoz González leading, they left Dong Thoc posted at the servants' entrance, climbing to the roof. Between them, they managed to lug Tomás down, spreading a mattress cover on the floor of the reception room and laying him out on it.

"What now?" asked Rougement, staring at the huge corpse. Unlike other people, Tomás seemed even bigger dead.

"We may have to keep him here until . . ." Muñoz González addressed Scheel. "The trucks are set for tonight?"

Scheel nodded, mopping the fleshy rolls of his forehead. "The weight of a dray horse! They begin loading at eleven; they should start rolling by not much later than one."

"The ship?"

"Docked this morning in Valencia."

"And the money?"

"Half at the landing," said Hassam, "the rest upon receipt of merchandise."

"Or I shall empty out your skull," mentioned Rougement. "Thong Doc and I shan't leave your side a moment, *vieux ami.*"

"Should you attempt raising the Blás girl once more?" inquired Scheel.

Muñoz González was already dialing. Busy signals. He rang again, connecting. The butler. Something had happened to el señor Marqués. The police had called. La señora Marquesa had dressed suddenly and gone to the hospital.

Muñoz González swore audibly.

"Well?" inquired Scheel.

"At a hospital. Husband's hurt, or something. She can't call, I didn't give her the number, it's unlisted. She may come later. Rougement, how about asking your sidekick to fix us something to eat?"

"Ah, yes!" agreed Scheel, "he is a genius in the kitchen."

"Meanwhile?" asked Rougement. He gestured at the corpse. "I can think of pleasanter company."

"I quite agree!" said Hassam, who was distressed at finding his suit spotted with Tomás's blood, and who was busy rubbing at a sleeve with a handkerchief.

"If the Blás daughter doesn't show up by nightfall, you, Rougement, go after her . . ."

"Dong Thoc and I," Rougement corrected.

"You both go after her, bring her here, and if it's necessary, we'll do it by force."

Scheel's tongue rolled over his porcine lips.

Muñoz González, frowning, viewed the German with distaste. The man's concupiscence, however, recalled to him the orgy he had planned, with the del Val puppy planted on Dorada, and all the other high-born guests taking turns with each other. And there was the Rivas girl.

"We . . . are going to advance everything," he announced. He was thinking hard and fast. He spoke collectedly. "In fact, it's better to do so —create a diversion, keep the authorities busy with a morals scandal."

Not bothering to explain himself, he strode to the kitchen.

He was half an hour on the telephone. Dong Thoc entered during one call, performed magically at the stove, then went out with a tray on which delicacies were heaped. Trying to reach Lady Hume, Asunción Mendoza, young Amontefardo, Julio Caro, Suisa, and others was frustrating business. Everyone was out. Everyone was at the house of the deceased Marchioness of the Pilgrim, and if not there, lunching. Yes, well, he thought, they'd have their fill of death. Some of them were likely to be erotically aroused by its presence, and all the more willing. He would feast them first, caviar and smoked salmon and shellfish, that delicious-smelling soup Dong Thoc had concocted, a meat course . . .

He left messages: a very special celebration for a selected few. Most would rise to the bait. He would drug the champagne slightly. The moment he knew the trucks were rolling, he would summon that Stepanópoulis Grau.

He returned to the parlor, where his associates lounged in the chairs and sofas, eating, and where, arms crossed under her bosom, Herminia stood registering the body of Tomás. A flexible reed shopping basket rested on a table near her, showing a head of lettuce, carrots, and strawberries.

"I don't like this one bit," she said to Muñoz González, who accepted a cup of soup from Dong Thoc. It tasted as delicious as it smelled.

"We are none of us pleased," he retorted, sipping. "That party I mentioned, I'm scheduling it for tonight."

Rougement raised his eyebrows. "We invited?"

"You'll be busy. But I want you for something else. Herminia, I'm advancing the Rivas girl also—to this afternoon."

Studying Tomás, the old woman nodded. "We decamp . . ."

"Tomorrow morning."

"Sooner for me. I will be the first under suspicion when you advise the police."

"Police!" exclaimed Scheel, spitting breast of partridge from his mouth.

"Oh, I say!" said Hassam, broiled mourning dove stuffed with dove pâté and a sweet-sour sauce of prickly-pear jelly sticking in his throat.

"I'll explain, I'll explain!" Muñoz González brushed over them. To Herminia: "Getting away is your affair."

"I am making it yours," said the little old woman.

He smiled. "Only if you admit your passion for me."

"I despise you."

He laughed. "You can leave with the trucks—tonight, when everything is arranged."

"My money?"

"You'll have to wait until we get paid."

"No, I'll need it now."

"There's not enough in the safe."

"One million pesetas you can lay your chulo's hands on. The other two million I will trust you for."

He was grinning. Even under the circumstances, he could not help flirting with Herminia.

"Are you sure?" he asked in his laziest drawl.

"No nonsense," came her reply. "*When* I have the two million in my possession, my lawyer will send that envelope to you."

"All right," said Muñoz González. She was a remarkable woman. Had he a child, he would entrust it into her care.

"Now," she said, "how are you going to dispose of Tomás? You can't leave him here. You can't leave him lying about, not with guests expected and a banquet to prepare. And he is much too big to sneak out of the building."

Scheel wiped his mouth. "The incinerator?"

"Much too small," said Herminia, "even cut up. It would take all day and the next to consume everything."

Muñoz González conceived of an idea. "Dong Thoc, just how good a cook are you?"

"Superb," said Scheel. "Aren't you having anything besides the soup?"

"We serve the butler tonight," stated Muñoz González, grinning at his private joke. "Dong Thoc, will you need anything special?"

"Perhaps origanum," answered Rougement for his friend. "The slaughtering will be the hardest job, but I'll take care of that."

"Good fellow!" said Hassam.

"How many are we to plan for?" asked Herminia.

"I'm not sure. Twenty at the most."

"Well, ten kilos will be ample." She studied Tomás again. "The rump, perhaps a thigh. The rest is gristle. Bones and tripe into the incinerator," she said to Rougement, "or as much as possible, and the rest . . ."

"In the freezer," said Muñoz González.

Rougement nodded, reaching for one of Herminia's strawberries.

She said, "I will go and prepare the girl. You won't be needing the others?"

"No. Dismiss them."

"I am hardly going to do that," she told him. "Julia has served faithfully the whole year. Magdalena . . ."

"Is a marvel," said Scheel, smacking his lips.

"I will try to place them, but I should think fifty thousand pesetas each is not too little for them to expect. No," she corrected herself, "seventy thousand pesetas for Julia; cooks always get more."

"Agreed," said Muñoz González.

Herminia left, then, content that she had provided so generously for her girls.

This is when I knocked. I feel myself creeping into this tale much too often. Apologies. But I was intrigued by the gigantic cadaver, although, to my knowledge, Muñoz González never claimed to be tidy. Suffice that I informed him about the conversation between Dorada and her father, and in return for this information—this warning—requested the privilege of purchasing Juan Luis's blank bills of sale at 100 pesetas the share, or 25,000,000 pesetas total, 5,000,000 less than the Orbaneja note but a discount I felt fair under the uneasy circumstances. (I was a bit tickled by the thought that I would be using Blás's own money for the payment.) Scheel—notably nervous—was for accepting, Rougement not. "That collateral is our guarantee," agreed Muñoz González, glancing at Scheel. And so I left him my card, saying that I could be reached at Puerta de Hierro, where I was giving a luncheon, until four-thirty or so.

When Soledad finally heard Doña Herminia's footsteps in the hall, she jumped from the cot to her feet, smoothing the covers and then, turning as the door opened, presented herself demurely.

"Very neat," said Doña Herminia kindly as her eyes roved the room. "Were you reading?"

"Yes, señora."

"What, may I ask?"

"The Bible. I . . . I also read love stories." And she gestured at the books by her bed.

Doña Herminia smiled. "You look as pretty as fresh apples, my dear. I am sorry I was delayed." She inspected the drawers of the little cabinet over the cot. "Yes, very neat. Now: I know you must be excited—it shows in those cheeks, my dear—so I want you to rest. Yes, no work today, a long nap."

"But I can't sleep now, Doña Herminia!"

"Can't? Tut, tut, willful with me already!"

"Oh no, Doña Herminia. I just meant I'm . . ."

The old lady nodded. "I understand. Excited! So was I, at my first location, oh, so many long years gone by! While I step out, you undress and put yourself in bed, and I will be back presently with a tranquilizer that—you will see—will make you pop off to sleep just like that!" And she snapped her fingers.

Soledad sighed as the old lady went out the door: but she did as she was told, putting on her cotton nightdress and getting into bed. Doña Herminia returned moments later with a pink pill and a glass of water, which she held for Soledad as Soledad drank, just as a mother might hold a glass for her daughter.

"Sleep tight, my dear. Dream lovely dreams."

"Thank you," answered Soledad; who knew that this was one order she was going to be unable to obey, despite the pill; and who ten minutes later was breathing soundly in the deepest of sleeps.

"Well," said Rougement, glancing at his watch, "time I got started." It was past five o'clock.

"The meat will be very fresh," observed Scheel.

"Can't be helped," said Rougement, stooping to Tomás's shoulders. Scheel gave him a hand, Hassam and Dong Thoc dragging Tomás's feet. "Watch out, he's leaking again!" said Hassam, huffing. "We all had better examine ourselves carefully before going out," muttered Muñoz González, who was at the safe, sorting papers and packing the most necessary items, including Juan Luis's collateral and notes, into a brief case. The telephone rang.

Muñoz González strode to it.

Herminia: "Send someone for the girl."

Rougement was despatched. He arrived dressed in a surgeon's greens, which he had found in the masosadist's parlor. He looked quite smart in it, like a television doctor.

"You haven't begun yet!" whispered Herminia, as they entered Soledad's room.

"No. I'm asked to do just about everything."

The ex-Legionaire lifted Soledad's slightness easily in his strong arms, noticing the firm contours of her full young breasts under the cotton.

"Who gets this?" he asked with interest.

"I believe all of you," said Herminia. "Don't bang her head against the door, please!"

Magdalena opened the door for them into the servants' stairway, Julia slipping ahead to reconnoiter the coast. She beckoned. Herminia and Rougement walked across the landing to the door of the adjacent flat, which was being held open by Dong Thoc. As they passed, Julia whispered, "For the patrón?" Herminia nodded. "Oh, the lucky girl!" said Julia.

Herminia thought it fitting to place Soledad in the peasants' chamber, one she had helped decorate, including the straw pallet, the rick, and other authenticities. Yes, Soledad's cotton nightdress went well with the decor. Herminia dismissed Rougement, tucking Soledad in and then bending to kiss her forehead. "I am sorry, my dear," she murmured, "truly sorry. But you were part of my agreement with that chulo. It can't be helped."

Sighing, she withdrew.

She found Muñoz González in the central parlor, closing the safe.

"Did you bring your basket?" he asked her.

"No."

"Well, there's the money." He pointed to stacks on a table—one thousand one-thousand-peseta bills. "The million."

"And the money for Julia and Magdalena!"

"That's there also," he said, smiling at her. "The Rivas girl?"

"Breathing peacefully, the little lamb."

"The sedation can't be too heavy!"

"Within half an hour, she will be rousing—in just the right state."

"Not earlier. Dong Thoc has to start cooking, and he must be first with her."

Herminia nodded. "He is delicate—and kind, all the virgins have said so."

"May I ask you where you went this afternoon?"

"To my little boy's mistress."

"Ah, that. Were you successful?"

"Of course."

He smiled. "We ought to celebrate, Herminia. The ruin will be complete. You've been waiting much longer than I for this. I want to tell you something. I admire you very greatly. You are, I think, the only woman I've ever respected."

"Compliments from a gangster do not impress me."

He laughed.

"Well," she sighed, moving toward the vestibule. "I have to pack my poor possessions, break the news to Julia and Magdalena—that will be trying, they become so hysterical—and *burn* this ama's costume. I have hated it these twenty-five years."

She paused at the door. "I will be back for the money. But tell me, your mother, you did not respect her?"

Muñoz González looked up from the brief case. The vestibule was narrow, opening almost directly on the parlor. Herminia was not far away, one hand on the doorknob.

He gazed at her. He was solemn, suddenly. "I could not respect Maman," he said, using the French inflection. "I could only love her with all my heart, and feel it break over what happened to her."

There was a short silence.

"Well," came from Herminia as she opened the door, "there's something to be said for everyone, I suppose. You have surprised me for the first time."

He laughed as she went out.

Soledad slept; and then fluttered her eyelids. The covers were pulled down from where Herminia had left them, under her chin. The modest nightdress had been unbuttoned, and one thrusting, pink-tipped breast was disclosed. Her lips twitched into smiles as she dreamed: of pink castles on fairyland hills and Prince Charmings on horseback with huge phalluses bulging their doeskin trousers. Had anyone removed the paper wrappings from her love stories, they would have seen imported Argentinian editions of *Candy, Fanny* and *Justine*.

Her eyes opened. The hayrick. The pitchfork stuck into it. Was she back in Sacedón?

Her eyes dilated. Lurid figures, animal and human, pranced across the ceiling in diabolical postures. She was terribly frightened. A pair of eyes watched her. She wanted to scream. Her nipples were being thrummed and plucked between sausages. Murmuring, she was at once asleep.

When she again opened her eyes, she was aware of being bent over by someone, and of those same eyes, and of a hand reaching for her bosom, and of that hand lifting the sheet to cover her.

She had a moment of clarity. Her fear then was too terrible for a shriek. Because a ghoul—a corpse—stood over her, with moss growing on his face. She fainted.

"No, wake up!" Joaquín Cortés whispered fiercely—the urchin, the Teddy-boy who had knifed Tomás at (as he understood it) Don Emilio's direct command. "You must wake up, now!" he again whispered, grasping her shoulders and shaking them. "Find your love," the saint had ordered. "Save it." And he had run as fast as legs could take him to the mantequería, and there learned that Soledad had left minutes before, and asked of young Amadeo his sister's address, and had been told, and had hopped buses to Calle Almagro and inquired of the janitor after the Duke's flat, and had received the answer that it was on the topmost floor, and had decided then to enter by way of the roof from an adjacent building, and had, since the knifing of Tomás, hidden in the air-conditioning shafts (out of order since midwinter), where, unbeknownst to him, he had crawled through ropes of lint over the water main whose whereabouts so mystified plumbers.

By chance—it was God's will—he had found his way to this precise room: scrawny that he was, able to worm through the sheet-tin shafts; and there had waited, thinking he was in the Duke's apartment, peering through the baffles of an outlet and deciding with a patience born of purpose to nestle there and watch until Soledad chanced in or some course of action occurred to him.

He had reached his lair about half an hour before Muñoz González ordered the search. He had heard men's voices. He had watched while a tall, raw-boned man entered in the company of a dark-suited Arab. They examined the cupboards at two corners of the room. One stood guard while the other looked under the outsized pallet. They lifted the lid of a heavy chest, and then the raw-boned one took the wooden fork and thrust it hard and repeatedly through the large mound of hay in the rick.

Joaquín was in danger, he knew that. Rougement held a .45 automatic in one hand. Once he looked up at the baffles, and ice-gray eyes seemed to pierce right through them. The boy held his breath. The men left. But now he noticed in an opposite corner—placed high up by the ceiling—the moonstone malevolence of a camera lens, roving the room on an electrically operated swivel. He was trapped. He did not know what to do. He could not turn around in the shaft. He could only slither forward through more of that furry lint; and now he dared not risk the noise.

The ensuing three hours were torment for him. Where was his love? What might be happening to her? He had by this time registered the ceiling. He was just sixteen years old, but it required little for him to realize that he had blundered on a brothel of some kind. Soledad and he had never spoken; but she had smiled radiantly at him when passing the wine shop, and his whole being had responded. He was about to accept the risk of moving on when the door was kicked open (he heard— he could not see—that), and in entered the raw-boned man, carrying her!

His heart leaped with fear. Was she dead! No, no: she was lowered with considerable tenderness to the pallet, and then a very motherly sort of woman, by her dress an ama, dismissed him while herself bending over the girl: who, he now realized, was in the deepest of sleeps.

He did not know whether to look or avert his eyes when the old lady unbuttoned the front of Soledad's nightdress. (He did both.) He saw her fish a perfume bottle out of the voluminous pocket under her starched white apron. She anointed Soledad's soul-shattering bosom, whose naked glories he was simply unable to tear his attention from, although this filled him with shame. Next he saw the old lady fish a tube of what looked like unguent from that pocket, squeeze a blob of it into one hand—up high by the four closed fingers—and then, and then, and then . . .

He now did jerk his chin to one side, but tardily enough to comprehend that this monstrous old woman was reaching down between Soledad's innocent lower limbs and . . . and . . . inserting the unguent in a part of the girl that he refused even to mentally name.

Completing the ministrations, the ama tucked Soledad into the covers, spread her raven locks in streamers down both shoulders, and then stooped to kiss her, murmuring something about regretting the circumstances.

He was in anguish. He was more than ever at a loss. Harm was plainly intended. Soledad had been drugged, obviously, and was being prepared for . . .

They had to escape! (How?) She had to be awakened! He heard a thumping from somewhere, an occasional whacking and a cracking. He pressed the button of his switchblade. The stained blade flashed from its case. The baffles were set into an aluminum frame. This frame was screwed—top and bottom, and on the sides—to the wall. That he ascertained by slipping fingers through the openings and feeling with their tips. Now, awkwardly, blindly, he slipped the knife out through those openings, and, inverting it, probed for the painted-over heads of the screws. The tips of his fingers fed the pointed blade into a screwhead's indentation. There was danger at every moment of losing his grasp, of the knife falling from his hand—in which case they were lost. He could thank God—had he known—that this was an Orbaneja building, or never would he have been able with that sharp point and in that awkward position to loosen even one of the four screws. Half an hour went by. Two screws fell to the rushes of the floor. He had about decided to attempt pummeling the frame out—and hang the noise, hang that roving camera lens—when he heard a guttural voice calling in French.

A heavy tread approached. The door was opened. A bald, corpulent, brutish man moved into his view.

Back turned to Joaquín, he came to a momentary stand in front of the pallet, gazing down on Soledad. Then he raised his eyes—the red rolls of fat on the back of his neck bulged—to the camera lens; and Joaquín saw that it had been switched off.

What followed was torture for him. Because this horrible, gloating, goat of a man—more monstrous by far than the old woman—drew up a milking stool, crouched his fat hams down on it (and his crotch unnecessarily hard against the stool's upright), and with both hands began kneading Soledad's defenseless breasts, raising his eyes to the ceiling as he rolled their fullness under his palms and going "Ahhh, ahhh, ahhhhh."

Joaquín almost screamed at this point. He wanted to kill—to smash, to obliterate! There was nothing he could do.

The door opened. No more happened for a moment. The satyr continued his kneading and his obscene sounds, pressing his crotch more tightly against the upright. But then the raw-boned man stepped into Joaquín's view. He was a grisly sight, the green tunic he had changed into drenched with blood from the waist down, with splinters of bone and chunks of raw meat adhering, and a dripping butcher's cleaver dangling from his right hand.

He came to a spread-legged halt just behind the satyr; who, jerking about, almost tumbled off the stool.

"So you were checking on whether she was asleep, still?" came Rougement's disgusted voice.

Joaquín did not understand the words. Their tone he was able to interpret.

Scheel lumbered to his feet, embarrassed. "Checking on the merchandise, you might say."

"Dong Thoc suspected as much. He's first. He's particular." He jerked a thumb toward the door. "Out!"

"You do not give the orders," said Scheel, pig's eyes squinting.

"Out."

"I will remember."

"Out."

Scheel stiff-legged his way by Rougement, who glanced once at Soledad, and then followed the German out of the room.

The breath seeped from Joaquín's tightly compressed lips. He thanked God for the intervention. He thanked Don Emilio for sending him. If Soledad did not wake up, he knew what he must do.

She moved. Eyelids batted open on unseeing eyes. He had loosened and freed the top screw. Now he was able to force the panel out and down. Legs first, he dropped from his covert, hitting the rushes and falling on cramped bent knees. He moaned on the floor for a moment. Massaging the circulation back into his legs, he managed to rise, approaching her unsteadily.

It was then that he covered her nakedness. How, how to get her out!

He heard voices. As rapidly as he was able, he dodged behind the hayrick.

The door was opened. He did not see, but Dong Thoc entered, followed by Rougement and Muñoz González.

"Explain again," Joaquín heard a deep baritone voice say—still without understanding the French. "He's to be as gentle as possible. I don't want her ruined. You're to follow. Change and wash-up first. Make it businesslike, she'll be more awake. Scheel can bugger her then, as long as he wants so long as she doesn't bleed too badly, and then Hassam can give her the Egyptian works, front and back, top and bottom. I want her tamed. I want her shamed to her soul. Then I take over."

Rougement repeated this for Dong Thoc—who spoke flawless French, so that there was no real need to translate into Korean. But since teaming up, they had discovered utility in the ruse.

It's a pity Spanish wasn't used. It's a point for Esperanto, the Mangold Languages Institute, and universal education for all classes in polylinguistics. Else Joaquín might have waited until the other two men departed, and killed the Korean—with perhaps some chance of escape.

But he was ignorant, the expunged scum of society, a snot-nosed guttersnipe destined for nought of good and much of evil. He attacked from behind that rick with an adder's deadliness. The nearest person to him happened to be Rougement, and between his shoulder blades Joaquín buried the switchblade. Faster than an adder was Dong Thoc, whose left foot drove up high in a karate kick, slamming Joaquín in the crotch. Before even the cobra-quick Muñoz González was able to react, a hissing Thong Doc had flung himself upon the boy, wrenching the knife from him and driving it into his puny breast.

It all happened in less time than it takes to pronounce Hamlet. With Joaquín slapping the rushes in his death throes, grasping the hilt of his own knife and spitting bubbly blood from the lungs, Thong Doc turned to Rougement, his friend, and lifted the Frenchman's head to his chest, tears cascading down his withered brown cheeks.

It was at this stage of affairs when Juan Luis began looking for tools with which to crack Herminia's suite. Rougement—in my opinion the best of this nefarious gang—and Joaquín Cortés had been dragged to the central parlor, stood over and gawked at. Nobody, not even Hassam, gave thought to the blood staining the carpet and the blood on their clothes.

"Who could he be?" inquired Scheel.

"I've no idea," came from Muñoz González.

"I suggest we forget everything but the shipment," said a highly upset Hassam. He extended a comforting Third World hand toward Thong Doc, nevertheless, but was ignored by that broken-hearted little man.

"We do as I order," came Muñoz González's silky voice, "until I order differently."

"Much as I esteem you," said Scheel, "I personally resign." He bowed, as though taking his departure.

Muñoz González whipped out his automatic.

"No one . . ."

But the German had been prepared, and a Beretta spoke twice, the first .32 slug creasing Muñoz González's left shoulder while the other, with Muñoz González springing to one side, sizzled through the gap between his right bicep and side, boring into the wall. Muñoz González's silencer kicked back and up in his fist, and Scheel fell thudding to the floor in a heap over Rougement.

"Goodness gracious!" exclaimed Hassam. "What are we to do now?"

Three corpses, in addition to the giant hunks of Tomás in the kitchen.

"Matters," stated Herminia, who, dressed in a modish silk summer suit, had returned for the money, "are getting out of hand."

When they all heard the yelp from next door.

Juan Luis was bent over the lock of Herminia's door, struggling with the retaining screws inexpertly, when he heard the two reports from the Beretta and felt heat nearly sear the top of his head as a projectile passed over his doubled body from behind and whomped into the door's wood.

He reared up, blinking. He saw the hole of the nearly spent slug, an untidy crater edged with streaks of glistening lead. Vaguely he registered the *poof-poof* of the silencer going off. In muffled manner came the thump of Scheel's body from behind him. He turned around, seeing the hole from which Scheel's slug had emerged. It occurred to him now that there had been gunfire, and that had he been standing erect at the volley, he had been likely dead.

That was when he yelped, racing down the corridor for the hall door.

He reached it and burst through to the landing at just about the time that Muñoz González flung his door back, also stepping out.

Both stopped and stared at each other an instant. Juan Luis took in: the automatic in Muñoz González's right hand, the blood on his clothes, the dim figures of a woman and two or more men behind him, and beyond them, a crimson heap of corpses.

"Señor Duque. Is . . . there anything the matter? May I be of help? I imagined I heard shots."

"Me too!" said Juan Luis; and with his steel-strong guitarist's wrist, he snapped the long screwdriver he had been using as hard as he was able at Muñoz González's face, so that it came cartwheeling directly toward the man's eyes with blurring speed and force.

This obliged Muñoz González to duck aside, exposing Herminia. By sheer bad fortune, the beveled working point came flipping about to pierce and lodge and drive right through her right eye into the brain. With a cry, she flung up her hands and fell backward on Hassam.

Juan Luis did not see this and did not hear her. He had not recognized his old nurse in the modish suit. He was leaping down the first flight of stairs. Muñoz González lunged after him, raised his automatic for a chance shot, and then thought the better of it.

He cursed in soft, dulcet notes, long and fully. There was now no help for it. He would have to quit the premises—and Madrid—at once. He would have to supervise the shipment himself.

He made his arrangements as speedily as possible, slapping Thong Doc into coherence, ordering a humble Hassam to dress Soledad, and then going to his safe and whirling the lock open.

He extracted a thick pile of glossy photographs, rifling through them. There was Lady Hume, with a mouthful of Tomás. There was Inmaculada Urquijo, Countess of Cáceres, with a mouthful of Asunción Mendoza, who had a fannyful of Scheel. There was Amontefardo, being tickled into a tower of Pisa by Petra, and young Magascal humped up for the thrust of Magdalena's dildo. More. Many more.

Well, this would keep the authorities busy enough, along with the chopped up body of Tomás in the kitchen, a ham of him roasting in the oven, and the four bodies in the parlor.

These he arranged in the form of a starfish, heads to heads, with a bundle of photographs placed in the center.

TEN

Brothers in Arms

"You can't mean you actually know the animal!" exclaimed Ignacio Prades y Caro, Count of Obregón, stepping forward to receive a mourner.

He did so stiffly, with a refractoriness that neither the humiliation trussing the bridge of his long patrician nose nor even the loss of his mother quite managed to fissure. But, as best as he was able, he complied with the form.

It is peculiar. Spaniards, as virile as they are demonstrative, freely engage in the rite of the abrazo.

First comes the sighting. They bring their feet together in a sudden stop. They stare as if incredulously, drawing their heads back from the chin and popping their mouths open. "It can't be!" cries the silence of the one. "But is it possible?" declares the gape of the other. Their countenances light up in a dazzle of recognition. And then, already hugging empty air, left arm raised high, right arm held low, they rush together.

A more solemn display characterizes vigils. The bereaved may take but one or two steps forward. It is up to his friend to close the gap between them. He comes clucking, arms advanced, face dissolving in sympathy; and it is he who initiates the embrace, patting the back of the bereaved in consoling fashion and murmuring, "I am so sorry! I am so very sorry!" This is a tender sight.

Billy Smith-Burton was having none of it. Earlier he had muttered, "Rather like crabs pickpocketing each other."

"Not so!" Jaime Orbaneja had objected. He huffed, "We're more romantic than that!"

"The only true and consistent romantics in human history," put in Juan Luis, surprising Jaime by his sincerity.

There was that something unsettling about the boy, this afternoon more pronounced than ever. His hair was mussed, his tie pulled down from the collar. He looked ill. Was that *chocolate* staining his armpit?

"Well," said the architect, "we are people who still love people, preferring them to poodles."

"We're warriors," Juan Luis said then, pouty cheeks blushing like Christmas bulbs as he took stock of his words and how incongruously they came from his round little mouth. But he braced himself. He sucked in the sag of his belly. Had he not hurled a screwdriver at the fearful, blood-stained figure of Muñoz González, with that heap of corpses behind him? Had he not made good his escape? "Caballeros," he stated, "right out of the Middle Ages. It's the kiss of peace between knights. Look at the posture. There's an element of wary reserve. Our legs are firmly planted. And see how our chests never touch! There's armor still upon them, separating us the one from the other." Abruptly, he shuddered. "How long has it been since we were at each other's throats?"

He had raced down the six flights, across the courtyard, through and under the fangs of the tunnel, and into the street. Like a rabbit leaping into its burrow, he had leapt into his Lancia, gunning away from the curb. Had what had happened, happened? Had he truly seen those bodies on the floor, and the blood, and Muñoz González with the pistol in his hand? He stopped at Balmoral bar for two double shots of scotch, which he took straight. His pulse raced the more. What had all that to do with Herminia? And why, why Herminia's treachery, and her unholy alliance with the Santo Dominican gangster, and the callgirl arrangement, and the unexplained evacuation of his flat? He did not know. He could not puzzle the mysteries through. He knew only that he was more than likely in danger, that he ought to report matters to the police. He would be, however, and this he knew also, embroiled. *His* premises had Muñoz González rented. It was his chatelaine who supplied the girls; and they were quartered in his very own flat. Who would credit that he had been unaware?

Somewhat more composed after a third whisky, he decided to proceed to Número Catorce. There, among his kind, he would be physically safe. He would gain time to decide what to do. And if he decided on telling the authorities, there would be that Stepanópoulis Grau handy.

Juan Luis took firm hold of himself. At Número Catorce, he engaged Jaime and Billy in conversation. Policemen had been stationed by the entrance, plainclothesmen were evident near the doorways of each room, but the Deputy Inspector was nowhere to be seen. Juan Luis was present when, helped by his chauffeur, Ignacio Prades entered. The Marquesa's son nodded stiffly at his wife, gazing at the crowd of other people without seeming to individuate any of them, those glow-worm eyes gone dull. His contusions spilled well beyond the bandaging. It was as if Nacho had been staggered by the succession of blows; staggered out of sleep and into a waking reality more terrible in its reduction to zombie-like paralysis than any nightmare.

So, in fact, as we know—as we can easily infer—felt the man. Partly because he was so tall; partly because his spine was locked with suffering while threatened with the deliquescence of fear; and partly, too, because his broken nose throbbed with pain and he therefore averted his face; and overwhelmingly because he was Ignacio Prades y Caro, whom no one could love nor feel truly sorry for no matter how hard a person tried; his abrazos did not quite come off, both halves disengaging abruptly, the sympathizer feeling somehow rebuffed, and Ignacio perhaps feeling more than ever the haplessness of his state, of his invariable but involuntary offensiveness, that coldness in the core that seemed to jell all human feelings. More than ever before had he been made aware of his inability to establish contact between himself and other persons. Gladly, with his own two hands, would he have ripped his chest open and torn that block of ice out. The cry had welled in his throat, "Does none of you see? Can't one of you understand? *I can't help it! I cannot help being what I am!*"

His shoulders slumped: against his will. He tried to straighten them. But it was nearly seven-thirty in the late afternoon of a day that ought never have begun yet would not end. The sun outside held a prodigious grip on Madrid. Número Catorce raised loaf after loaf of heat. Every parlor, excepting the chapel and the cordoned ballroom, seemed to swell with the yeast of those three hundred and more tribal representatives. En masse had Society gathered—which would have pleased Odette had she been there to see it. The scandal of the circumstances, naturally, had attracted curiosity-seekers; and there had been unacceptable people— persons on the social fringe—who had tried crashing the portals. In this at least Dorada had been efficient. She had provided the police with a list of names, scanned and approved by Consuelo. Ordinarily, most of the sympathizers would have come and left by this hour, with only members of the family and their intimates staying into the evening. But there was an atmosphere of suspense at Número Catorce. People—several of them veterans of the morning, limping or with arms trussed up by slings or with swollen lips—excused themselves by thinking, "At least I ought to stay until Ignacio gets out of the hospital." And then, when he came, ". . . until Odette is returned from the morgue." They tarried, Nacho Prades knew, out of morbidity. This angered him. He would have liked to throw them all out of the house! But with that fatidic incapability of expressing the natural emotion, he released instead the irascible in him.

"You say . . . you are acquainted with the brute!"

"My father was. I've seen him, I know *of* him, I can't remember very well. He did odd jobs around the place. He bounced people off his belly."

"When?"

"Oh, when they laid bets in the fisherman's bar."

"I mean, when did he work for your father?"

"After the War. We're related, you know. Which means, by the way, that you are too."

"What!"

"One of my ancestors was a Rivas: two of them, in fact. Come to think of it, Father once told me that this fellow's father headed the clan."

"What the braggart said is true, then!"

"What *did* he say: I mean, before punching you in the nose. Sorry."

"That he's an hidalgo."

"Well, yes, I suppose so. Who isn't, from the North?"

"Animals! At this time, on this very morning, to present himself, to come demanding . . ."

Ignacio's words faded into the heat. He and Juan Luis had been crossed by the moving figure of Dorada: as by a shadow. Ignacio stiffened, looking after her. Juan Luis followed his gaze sharply. Dorada was exceedingly pale. She was no less beautiful, and (he thought) no more likable. She and Ignacio were matched, in a way. Death did little for some people. Perhaps not actually seeing the toadish, jowly little face of the Marquesa peering up all waxen from her cowl made the difference. He, however, Juan Luis, could smell the fetid presence. He felt again that sparrow chick that he had crushed under his thin Italian sole. His naked instep crawled once more with a babosa he had in childhood mashed into a gelatinous quivering on a back road in Sacedón, close to the cemetery.

Again he shuddered. In that cemetery, a stone wall the height of a man's head had been bracketed to the remains of the old church's apse. Standing on tiptoe, one was just able to view the contents: bones, human bones, leg bones and arm bones, skulls that had lost their mandibles and mandibles that had lost their skulls. Two meters high, three meters long, and a meter and a half wide, or deep, was this raised charnel pit, filled to the overflowing with broken, jagged, colorless shards of what once had been human beings. They were the overflow. They were the intermixed paupers and princes when, in 1936, trenches had been gouged through the cemetery, the blades of shovels and the points of picks crack-

ing ribs or piercing craniums and scattering them about. Perhaps that
pelvis on top had belonged to his grandmother, whose flesh had churned
in moist concupiscence as she received seed into her womb. That jawbone, with strong, yellow cuspidors still firmly attached, might have belonged to some Rivas forbear for all anyone could tell or now care: but
some human being had ground those caps against their mates, had masticated meat, had felt in the gums that rinsing action of fresh wine. Death
was the only incontestable fact: and not the beguiling sophistry in the
Crito, nor the promise of the Resurrection, nor, certainly, frantic contemporary flight from the subject, dulled its impact, dispersed its shadow,
kept at bay its inevitability . . .

Número Catorce reeked of death. Everyone had come to do it homage: the shattered Countess of Magascal, the courageous, stoical Duke
of Centollos, and poor Nacho Pelau, Count of the Two Intestines, who
was little able to control his emotions, a poignant reminiscence causing
him to squeeze his eyes shut and blubber shamelessly. Juan Luis's eyes
happened to cross those of Billy Smith-Burton. Billy jerked his head
aside: but Juan Luis had caught the same awareness there. Yes, he was
doing the right thing, the correct thing, accepting the course of truth.
He would confess—anyhow report—to Deputy Inspector Stepanópoulis
Grau, the moment that dandified little creature showed his officious,
obsequious face. What mattered whether the Sacedón reputation (and
fortune) were destroyed? What mattered the extinguishing of the ducal
line? What had mattered victory or loss in the Civil War, the triumph
at Lepanto, or the disaster of the Armada? Between great and little events
there is no essential distinction; and they share a common irrelevance.
Among the actors in these events, the exalted and the humble, the doom
is common.

He looked about him once more. Daylight had finally begun to fade.
Gloom filtered into the chambers, wrapping mourners in a common
mood. With the possible exception of Dorada, they seemed metamorphosed back into subaqueous jelly. They moved like fish in an aquarium,
in a sort of stately, silent pavane. But in the golden flesh of Dorada a
fire of some kind raged, and there was agony within the stiff silhouette
of Ignacio. Billy Smith-Burton presented a brooding, violent, apocalyptic
face to Jaime Orbaneja, who now with the sun descended could not
repress a rabbity nervousness. Consuelo, his wife, had sat her dumpy
torso on a chair nearby, skirt hitched up, knees gaping wide, head lolling
in the moronic, tongue-protruding catalepsy of exhaustion following
shock, her outstretched arms supported as though on the crossbeam of

a crucifix by a pair of fat female ravens roosted on either side and garrulous with fans and smelling salts. Consuelo's grief was probably real,
although it showed as much too much as the flabbiness of white flesh
above the black ribbing of her stocking tops. Was there redemption even
in death?

Where was Sofía?

"I shall take him to court," said Ignacio suddenly, savagely, turning
his most frigid stare back to Juan Luis. "I am going to persecute that
man through the courts and break him!"

There was no redemption, not anywhere.

ELEVEN

Potentates

As Dorada recounted, Ignacio had refused anesthesia when they set his
nose—and had promptly fainted. He came around half an hour later.
His nose was packed under ice. There were tubes in the nostrils, draining
pink fluids.

"I . . . I must get up!" he had muttered to a nurse who hovered
pneumatically at the foot of his hospital bed.

He had been dressed in his own pyjamas—brought, as he learned,
by the Señora Condesa, his wife, who had departed minutes before
his regaining consciousness.

Mention of Dorada had produced immediate depression. He felt
tears in his eyes, and a renewal of anguish. His nose throbbed almost
unendurably.

For long hours, he lay silent. They were excruciating hours. Few
of the fleshly vicissitudes man is heir to hurt so acutely as a crushed
proboscis. No wound is so terrible as mashed love. And, of course, the
most atrocious of all hurts is to self-love.

For Ignacio Prades, Count of Obregón, Dorada had been the golden
incarnation of self. Between, within, the delirium of her thighs, he committed autoadoration. It was masturbatory. It was the repulsive narcissism
Dorada perceived. Which was why her spirit had never been engaged,
had been in fact most intimately violated, in that her being as an individ-

ual; a person; a woman; had ever been irrelevant to her husband. Dorada existed for the tickling into tumescence and burst of his ego. She existed for the sick oozing of the pus of self-love, for the pleasure and contempt of his rod, in whose ruthless and ultimately insensate metastasis only was he able to obliviate doubt.

Of such things, in his bed of pain, the pretender to the Marquisate of the Pilgrim was becoming aware. His pilgrimage would be long. How he fought it! What onslaughts of tears and anguish he was to loose! She had shown him that morning that what he worshiped was as empty as a bank on Sunday. It was a church in which the sacramental light had been doused. It was the shell Jacobo Rivas had come to recognize.

He rebelled. The cry was born in him, *I can't help being what I am!* He had never been so correct. His cry is a philosophical exactitude. It is the deadly truth.

He reached for the bellbutton, squeezing it. That slight movement produced a dizziness of pain.

"Yes?"

"Call the doctor."

"He's operating on a lung cyst."

"Call . . . him, as soon as he finishes. I must get up."

The surgeon arrived half an hour later.

"It's out of the question," he said. "We were able to do little more than pick splinters out of the nasal passages. Tomorrow, when the swellings have receded, we will set your nose properly. You probably face cosmetic repair later."

Ignacio reached for and tore the tubes out of his nostrils. In terms of pain, that must have been the near equivalent of wrenching a ganghook out of one's gut. He fainted, reviving almost at once. (There is iron in all Spaniards.) (They remain conquerors.)

"I . . . must attend to my mother's vigil," he stated, sitting up.

"Nurse!"

"Do . . . not dare . . . interfere!" And he lurched to his feet—just as the nurse came billowing forward, his knees liquifying under him, so that he clutched at the proximate support, her voluminous breasts, tearing the clothes off her to the waist.

As he might have explained, he was obliged to suffer the fullness of humiliation. ("Doctor! Doctor! I've been *attacked!*" "Miss . . ." "Doctor, the Count is a sex maniac, you *witnessed* it!") Ah, yes, his duty. For he had come to see: he had been at fault, shoving the crippled pharmacist. He had deserved his pulped nose. All Society would be mocking him, and would be collected at Número Catorce: and he would return there to endure that mockery.

Entering his mother's house was an act of superior courage for Ignacio. (Worthy son and brother of Laureados de San Fernando!) To the bone, he felt the silence when, supported by his chauffeur, his intrusion into the throng became noted. Within him, a jaw froze into a grimace . . . as the low, rushing, murmuring sibilance of reaction agitated the mourners. At the entrance to the wrecked rose room, he dismissed his chauffeur, assaying tentative, unsteady steps alone. (Yes, Ignacio belongs to the breed that mounts the scaffold unhelped, with all the dignity of mankind's solitude of soul. Yes: he is a nobleman.) He felt himself stiffen —inside and out—and he defeated the waves of vertigo on that high scaffold, blinding himself to the cruel jeers and raucous scatological insults of the holidaying villagers. There, by the chopping block, stood the mini-skirted executioner. He faltered. The shut-off din of the multitude roared into his ears, sight of Dorada lacerating the shreds of his heart. She scarcely acknowledged him. Ignacio nodded. He thought, "I have wronged you in ways I can never remand." A paunchy, pouty, tallish, young, chinless, scared, irresolute, stained-under-an-armpit curate approached him, breviary in his embarrassed little hands. "Do you repent, my, er, son?" Juan Luis, of all people—of all the peers of the realm!— struck up conversation with him. And Ignacio plumbed why. Because: no one else was doing so. And this commiseration from the somewhat disreputable friar or monk or curate or whatever he might be with the murky red-veined whites of promiscuous indulgence and the mussed hair and the now glazed beeswax stain under one armpit sparked a sort of rage in Ignacio, and he had burst with rage against the mantequero. *I am going to break him!*

He turned away from Juan Luis then (who may or may not have muttered, "There is no salvation," and, "Where's a telephone?" —puffing away on his pigeon's toes without waiting for a reply). In an almost surreptitious manner, lamps were being clicked on. In an almost surreptitious manner, people were drifting to the dining room and back again through the library with highballs clinking in their hands. Who had arranged for that, and for the solemn caterers in white ties and ghoulish black tails? Where was Nati? He should seek her out. He dreaded doing so. His mother had rejected him. Bewildered, inconsolable, he had rejected Nati the moment boyhood verged into puberty—when, as Dorada guessed, he had wandered into the kitchen in Biarritz, and overheard his father's bibulous old boob of a Percival fracture in his cockney to the cook that Nati had usurped a deal more than a valet's duties, and who knew whose brat the young master was?

Thirteen years old, Ignacio had faded back up the service stairway.

But he should search out Nati. It was his duty. Whatever ghastly revelation might come from meeting her at this emotional time, he was obliged to confront it.

"Here!"

A chilled tumbler of whisky was being thrust into one of his hands. He looked up. His soul leaped with the anguish of love.

Dorada. "I'm sorry about this morning."

"You . . . mustn't be."

"I am . . . prepared to continue as your wife—to fulfill my obligations. Up to a point."

"That would be unworthy of you."

A golden eyebrow arched. She was called from him by the head caterer. More guests were at the door, among them Baltazar Blás.

Blás had telephoned me, with his call exciting my hopes. Would it be convenient for him to pay a visit?

Is the spider welcome in the fly's net? I've outwaited Getty in a taxi until he paid the fare. I've winked financing out from under the keen clever long nose of Guy de Rothschild as neatly as he winked the staircase out from under the noses of the U.S. consular service in the Paris mansion he sold them. A man my age is thrown back on infantile pleasures. Now for Baltazar!

I was struck by the age on the man when he was shown into my library, where I received him. He is seventy-nine, and I seventy-seven years of age. I felt young by comparison.

I offered him a drink; which, to my surprise, he accepted. He tossed the Haig & Haig off much as a peasant tosses off a thimbleful of cheap cognac. He asked me for a cash loan. He suggested, as an alternative, that I return the 1,200,000,000 pesetas to him, accepting notes in their stead.

I was able to appreciate how much in pride this was costing the old bandit. It was time to be candid. I confessed that I had become aware of his cash shortage. I confessed my position in the West German combine that had contacted Pedro Puig.

He smiled. There's a world of grit in the man. He bowed acknowledgment at me before sipping at the second whisky I prepared for him. "You've outmaneuvered me, Balls! I congratulate you."

"For a position in Financiera," I mentioned casually, "you can forget the twelve hundred million. We can amalgamate with the West Germans."

He wagged that enormous skull slowly, negatively. "No."

His stubbornness was irritating. "Warfare could hurt you very badly," I stated pointedly. "It could ruin you, Baltazar, unlikely as that may seem."

"I've grown old, and fat, and maybe senile. Too much prosperity. Bad thing for a man. I need a fight. I need to become lean again. No, Carl," he said next, his smile sorrowful for me to behold, "I'm an old fighter. That's the way I'd rather go to my grave."

"My God," I exploded, "the pride of you Spaniards!"

"Do you disapprove? Does it arouse your contempt?"

"My sincerest esteem."

"Drink to that with me," he replied, raising his glass.

"I drink to your virtues, not your faults."

We drank.

"You have a nice library. You read a great deal."

"I started as a public schoolteacher—a master."

"I've never had the time to read. In fact, never learned how. Old Sert takes care of it all for me . . . Is reading valuable to you?"

"Less and less. Since my wife died, I've taken to sitting here and staring at the books."

"Silent companions?"

"Yes, I suppose so."

"I find that sort of thing gardening, at my place on Lanzarote. Visit me sometime."

"I'll be happy to."

"Your grandchildren?"

"I live for them."

"How many?"

"Three. Two girls and a boy." *My* pride expanded. "Charles is in Yale graduate school, Far Eastern studies. Third in his class! The East, the Orient, there's the future, Baltazar. Mary—the eldest—she has two children of her own, now. A graduate biochemist, married to the nicest young Canadian you ever met, petroleum engineer. Eleanor . . ."

I stopped. He sat there staring at me, the glass as though about to be shattered in his grip.

What ensued—a painful, piteous spectacle in this childlike giant—I have given my word never to detail. But I learned then of his conversa-

tion with Dorada, and her ultimatum. "What should I do?" he asked
me. "I want the title for little Borja. But I know Dorada, she's harder
than diamonds, she'll never let me see him again."

I rang for my Silver Arrow, thinking as I did so, Belshazzar. MENE;
God hath numbered thy kingdom, and finished it. TEKEL; *Thou art
weighed in the balances, and art found wanting.* PERES; *Thy kingdom
is divided, and given to the Medes and Persians.* But whose: Holy Spain's,
our all of us, God's?

Baltazar gazed at me questioningly. "We're going to Número
Catorce," I announced. "Together. I want to pay my respects to Odette.
Buck up. You have every right to be there. Dorada can't cavil. But it's
time you and the Duke of Sacedón had a talk. It's time for you to swallow
some degree of pride, Baltazar."

"Time for me to retire to Lanzarote?"

"Perhaps."

"And putter about in my gardens."

"Why not?"

"Dressed in a peasant's smock, with a straw hat on my head and
a trowel in my hand."

"It's a rather touching picture. *ABC* is sure to run it."

He laughed, suddenly, banging his glass down on my Jacobin bench
table.

"Let's go!" he boomed, jumping from his seat with depressing vigor.
"Caca, Carl, ca-caaa! *that's* my answer to you—and a balls-busting corporate battle that by God *will* blow this little peninsula off its moorings!"

Ignoring Dorada's astonishment, Blás plowed straight across the
room to Ignacio, "My boy!" he crooned, flinging his arms wide; and—
alone among them all—enveloping Ignacio in the true warmth of an
abrazo. "She was a wonderful woman, son," the old shark said, stepping
back from the startled count. "I'm sorry as I can be!"

Dorada was at his side, like a lioness in all the tawn of suppressed
fury.

"Qué haces aquí?" she whispered fiercely.

"Lo que hacemos todos, hija—mourning a great lady."

"I told you . . ."

"Somos de la misma sangre—y de la misma leche. Now go cosset
your guests!" He now turned back to the recovering Nacho. "My boy,
my boy! These things pass. Time heals. My God, you certainly have

everyone here who amounts to anything. A credit to Odette. Poor Odette! Damned if I couldn't blubber like Dos Tripas over there."

Ignacio stared at him. "All you ever wanted was the title."

"Yes, that's so," Blás readily admitted, eyes batting back and forth like billiard balls. He caught Jaime Orbaneja slipping from the side of Smith-Burton and fleeing to the refuge of an adjoining parlor. Hah! he thought, didn't believe I'd show up! He said to Ignacio, "Still, I can be sorry, you know. Just about of an age. An era. I am. I truly am sorry!"

"You . . . can't be. You scarcely saw Mamá after the wedding. You never . . . felt anything for me. I am—I, I know it—not a practical business mentality . . ."

"But you were right all along!" the old man interrupted, clasping Ignacio by the biceps. "Your Comptroller's office, it's saved me from a serious situation! Anyhow, warned me about it. I'm grateful to you, my boy! I've treated you shabbily!"

Ignacio was flabbergasted. This was his father-in-law, Baltazar Blás —owning to error, apologizing!

He reddened. "I'm . . . no manager," he said icily. "The Blás empire needs a topflight manager, but I'm not the man."

"Of course, of course," Baltazar agreed heartily. "You're a thinker, Nacho, a programmer. Cut the crap you lard the reports with, there's sense in them. Managers we can hire! We'll find someone. Right now, I'm in a bind. Need those brains of yours, boy, need your advice. Want to discuss it with you . . . later, of course!"

With that sidelong flick of his eyeballs, Blás espied Juan Luis, who, emerging from an anteroom, was hurrying toward Smith-Burton.

He said abruptly, "You know I'm after Financiera Sacedón?"

Ignacio raised his eyebrows.

"All has to do with Orbaneja's note. Complicated. Details unimportant, used him to trap the Duke. Used you to dangle the bait."

Ignacio gazed uncomprehendingly at his father-in-law.

Blás sighed. "Nope, guess you weren't aware of it. Look, suppose we walk over to him now, you and I. I'll explain you didn't know what was going on. That'll clear you. Then we'll see what accommodation we can arrive at—Balls, that son-of-a-bitching hijo de la putísima Gran Bretaña has a point, lose one, win one, give a bit, gain a bit . . ."

"Not now, Baltazar!" came from Ignacio. Emotion wrenched the next words out of his mouth. "Not now, business, financial dealings, the whole world Mamá couldn't understand and couldn't bear, not now, here, under the roof she fought so hard to hold up—when we're waiting for her!"

"Course not, course not!" came from an instantly abashed Blás. "Half a brute still, just as Dorada says . . . But, you do know the Sacedóns plan to challenge your right to your mother's title, don't you?"

And there it was for Ignacio: the long, long buried being exhumed, as it had been for Odette.

He paled, visibly. Blás moved forward an inch, fearing Ignacio might faint. But with an abrupt gesture, Nacho fended the man off.

"I can't expect less," he said. "And . . . I accept it."

Blás's lower jaw sprang open. "You mean, you won't fight it?!"

"I'm almost certain I won't."

T W E L V E

The Return of the Marquesa

Juan Luis had reached Billy Smith-Burton by the time Ignacio uttered these words. He stared at his mentor a moment, a loathing of the dried, angular Englishman overtaking him. He glanced then at Blás, who stood near the center of the rose room beholding his son-in-law as though Nacho were—as it were—a mule who had just kicked the wind out of him. Earlier in the day, for moments, he had not feared Blás. He had stupidly not feared Blás. And now: he gazed on the financier, and what he saw was little more than an aged tyrant whose helplessness had been exposed; and realized that in truth he did not fear the man. Billy was turning that quizzical face to him, eyebrows rising slightly and creasing faint leathery seams in what mind's memory always recalled as a youthful skin. Billy, diabolical Billy, who had dared him, who had softly into his ear one midwinter night six months before planted, "Do you have that much courage—to speed the end of it along?" Billy had aged. Billy was worn out. And Billy he no longer feared either—no more himself the trespasser concealing his guilt, the beggar for crumbs at the foot of the shrine and from the careless intellectual largesse of the lawful keeper of that shrine. Strength comes from renunciation, just as Billy had been telling him all along. Yes, renunciation. Ignacio was learning that. Juan Luis had finally come to it. (Fedi was dead, *dead!*) There had grown in him an urgency to speak with Sofía, to have her confirm his decision, applaud his acceptance. And he realized now that he no longer needed her. The sparrow was fledged.

"I've telephoned your house," he said abruptly. "Sofía hasn't been home since this morning!"

The Englishman gazed at him. "So?"

"Where is she!" He glanced left and right. There was Consuelo, being brave in a roost of jackdaws. There was Ignacio, turning his stiff spine on Blás and stalking on uncertain pinnings away. He would speak to the Deputy Inspector the moment the man showed up, tell what he had seen, confess about the girls Herminia staffed his apartment with. He would not go after Ignacio's title, not fight the raid. "I've been at Número Catorce now nearly two hours. Sofía wasn't here any time this morning, Jaime says he hasn't seen her all day!"

"Is it the pudendum only, Juan Luis? Hairy catch-all of lice, zygotes, and zippers. Can it be that?"

"What?"

"No one knows of Sofía's whereabouts since she heard the news this morning."

"But . . . ?"

The Englishman's lips twisted, exposing for an instant the gleaming irregular bones in his mouth. "She's left me, Juan Luis." He lifted and let drop a shoulder. "Es mejor," he said in Spanish.

Juan Luis shook his head violently. "Sofía wouldn't go without seeing Odette! She *loved* her mother!"

"You have a point, there," Smith-Burton mused, slipping back into English. "Sofía possessed an abundance of love. One could say she had a genius for love, I mean as distinguished from fucking and sentimentality. Yesss, that was the trouble! Sofía made *love*."

The once a puppy-dog stepped forward. The once a puppy-dog snarled.

"Tell me what's happened, Billy! Tell me what you've done to her!"

His small clenched fists were sweating. The keeper of the woman he adored looked him up and down.

He rued his lips, saying softly, "I'm not obliged to tell you a thing. Or am I? I mean, that you're in love with my darling Sofía also—does that imply a proprietary right? That is," he went on, blinking, thinking, "is love, whether centered on the spitcurls of the pudendum or not, licit or not, reciprocated or not, assumptive? What do you think, Juan Luis?"

"Where is she?"

He was breathing heavily. He could not control his breathing.

Smith-Burton seemed amused. "You're not quite there, yet, are you? You've only stretched the umbilicus."

"Where is Sofía?"

"Gone," he said with another shrug, "God grant forever." He stooped forward, so that twitching lips clapped inches close to Juan Luis's eyes. "Safe," he stated with a flickering smile, "out of my reach."

"Why! Why! She worshiped you!"

Nodding, the man straightened from his stoop. "Precisely," he said. "My obligation was to destroy that, no?" His expression turned whimsical. "Within my madness, oh fideus fool, I retained wisdom and love enough still to betray her—with breath, Horatio, heated to the fumes of rarest liquor, with lips as nectared and as slick as the insides of the peels of bananas, with nipples the clearest amber and tangier than butterscotch, and with loins in which whole seas of passion foam over the shores of wildest, most undreamed of lust. In short, sirrah, the plain of it, with the golden odalisque, Dorada Blás."

Juan Luis's hands shot forth, clamping on the throat of the Englishman. "Here, there!" I let out, leaping between them as fast as my years permitted. Smith-Burton's swollen eyes were fastened on those of Juan Luis. "Do . . . it!" I heard him utter. From across the room came the cry, *"Odette, they are bringing Odette!"*

I shoved at Juan Luis. His hands wilted off Smith-Burton's neck. He trembled violently, reaching for support, which I supplied him. "Odette!" arose in an awed, mounting murmur, everyone in the assembly revolving toward the double doors. And there she came, aloft in a plain black casket, a military honor guard marching her into the room. The interest of her arrival extended to the street, where hundreds of the curious had gathered at the portal of Número Catorce, floodlights playing on the aisle formed between parallel ranks of helmeted policemen, up which all afternoon and evening had kept flowing the flor and nata of Madrid. Up that aisle had Odette's gutted cadaver been borne, past the snouts of television cameras and past the batteries of amateur and news photographers—borne on the epauleted shoulders of the purple-sashed caballeros of the Order of San Fernando, into the carriageway and up through the rose room and into the domed ballroom with its granulated marble floor and its ghostly dancers and ghostly strains of the waltz and the smooth gleaming back of the Leda, and from there into the low rounded arch of the chapel, where a Don Emilio prostrate before the stone altar in his threadbare soutane labored to his feet, turned with demented eyes, and gestured at the prepared catafalque four smoking torches at the corners wrapped round with fringed crimson silk royal-blue velvet mantel reaching to the floor on all sides front crusted with gold thread heavy as nuggets proclaiming the quasi-ducal arms of the Marquises of the Pilgrim emeralds and rubies the size of walnuts sewn to the great crown on top and a crucifix in hammered silver rising above it. There on the ancestral sheet was Odette's coffin deposited, and the hinged upper peek-a-boo dutchdoor lid raised by one of the bearers to expose the waxy puckered pouch of her face, nuns gathering near to raise their rosaries and renew their ceaseless rustling of the sorrowful mysteries. And there now into the vault pressed in as many mourners as would fit, at last able to discharge their obsequies.

THIRTEEN

The Tightening of the Net

In life, Odette had often wondered what servants did with their time. She would have been intrigued by the information presented to Stepanópoulis Grau as he scurried through reports culled from personal interrogations and recourse to the superlative Security archives. Rosa, for example, the Obregón's moronic maid, had managed to conceive and bear three illegitimate children under the very roof of the Counts, all healthy and all farmed out with relations in her native Córdoba. María —which would have astounded Consuelo and Jaime—their dear old faithful, complaining María with the lumbago in her foot, owned several low-cost apartments and letted them at scalping interest rates to the country bumpkins leaving their farms for the promise of the capital. She in fact was titleholder to Jacobo's shop-residence, this coincidence thrilling Stepanópoulis. But it was the dossier on Herminia that dizzied him. The woman had been a *Red*, an Andalusian la Pasionaria, her terrorist husband executed by the late Duke of Steel! It was *this* woman who had anticipated the news to her peers that the Marquesa had been murdered. She worked for . . . "Give me the file on the incumbent Duke of Sacedón!" HMMMMmmmHMMMMMMhmmmmmm! A dissolute, unworthy heir! Killer of the true seed and squanderer of ducal semen in sluttish purses! A moral weakling, the easy prey of any strong-minded woman. An intimate of Smith-Burton!

By this time he had learned the story about Nati and the late Count of Obregón. He knew that Herminia was Nati's one confidante in the servant class. How all these raw data fitted together, he was *not* sure; but that somehow they did, of course! Little further digging was required for him to discover that Pidal's butler was Herminia's first cousin's nephew, and that Tomás, the monster who had vanished from the household of the Countess of Magascal, was Herminia's step-son by the man she had accepted after the execution of her true love.

It was now nearly six o'clock. "Isias," he declared, jumping up from his desk, "we are off!"

At the time, we have to recall, there was a great deal of construction on the Extremadura highway. It's one of the principal routes of ingress and egress for workers from Villaviciosa de Odón, and as far out as Móstoles. There was a lot of military traffic besides, the main barracks of the Army being situated on both sides of the road, just beyond the turn-off to Boadilla del Monte. Many drab lorries lumbered along ahead and behind Grau's police sedan.

"We'll lose them when we come to the turn," predicted Isias, who drove with the abstraction of thin persons, intellectuals, and lovers, while his superior chewed furiously at the stubble of his mustache.

"Yesss." Stepanópoulis thought aloud. "The pup was in revolt against his father. Yes, that has to be it! And she, his nurse, fostered that revolt, filling his head with subversive notions, just as the mantequero's head was subverted by the Frenchwoman. Yes! Yes! That explains part of it, the motivation . . . *Watch* what you're doing!"

Isias almost ran down a peasant woman who, hobbling along under a load of faggots, crossed in front of the hood at the juncture of the Boadilla road. A fast yawing of the wheel avoided her: but they did not lose the lorries. Over two dozen of them preceded and followed the police sedan into the turn-off. There was no passing the convoy, narrow as the road is, with crumbling shoulders and a buckled bed.

"They're headed for the powder magazines," asserted Isias. "Their weight has made migas of the tanbark." He thudded into a pothole.

"You are making migas of my bladder. You jostle my brains!"

"Sorry, sir." And he hit another one.

"Idiot!"

But this time it was not Isias's fault. The whole convoy had shuddered to an abrupt halt, forcing Isias over. Grau—exclaiming "What can it be!" in the mounting of his impatience—craned his neck out the side window. Just beyond the little bridge one humped over before the road forked, left lane to Boadilla, right lane circling the Casa de Campo, a deep, round crater smoked, workmen digging in its pit with shovels. Motorcycle policemen in black boots and belted cavalry jackets were directing traffic in a cumbersome detour off and then back on the road. Drawing nearer, Isias exclaimed, "It's as though a bomb went off!" Grau's scalp lifted at the words. Just so! Scorched shards of metal, peeled rolls of paint, the stuffings of a seat—every nut and bolt and every working part of whatever this had been lay scattered about, tortured, disjected, as though by explosives.

"Pull out of line, go by the trucks!"

Isias did so. An angry trooper stepped forth with raised whistle.

"Deputy Inspector Grau!" Stepanópoulis shouted, flashing identification. "What happened here!"

He received a salute, and the words: "This morning—a munitions lorry, from the powder depots—hit a taxi. We'll be digging for remains until we reach China."

Had it then started! Grau pounded on Isias's shoulder. "Move! Go! We may be too late!"

A few minutes later, they bore right onto a dirt track and went jouncing toward the Blás property.

Signs announcing Smith-Burton's forthcoming exercise in sadism were plastered to the stone wall of the compound. The date was next day, Grau noted with relief, the first of June. Plainly, 1 June was the date of insurrection. Plainly, he had arrived in time.

"But we are here none too soon, Isias," he murmured while a security guard at the gate checked their credentials.

They drove through. "What," exclaimed Isias, "are Army vehicles doing here? Look, sir!—the ones we left at the fork are following us!"

Grau glanced at his assistant with contempt, the emotion he preferred for underlings. Isias was empty of imagination. He lacked the least power to observe. These neat squares of olive camouflage were not Army trucks. Because they resembled Army trucks in every detail made it the plainer that they were not Army trucks. They were counterfeits.

Stepanópoulis dismounted, surveying the scene; joined in his silent scanning by a perplexed but faithful Isias. There, toward the depths of the property, was the war machine put together by Smith-Burton. It resembled a Krupp nightmare, an iron brontosaurus. It brooded in its death-dealing hideosity, waiting there for the night and the dawn and morning to follow, when masochism would draw the sick-in-mind to yet another flagellation at the hands of Smith-Burton, and when in the confusion it would shudder to life and aim its triple nine-inch cannon barrels at the powder magazines, not five miles distant. Everywhere about there were concrete bunkers, in which munitions and arms were stored by AESA, Blás's monopoly. Would armed commando units issue from them on the morrow, each a highly trained cadre with each its specialized mission, one unit to blow the bridges across the Manzanares River and capture communications, the other to raid and gain control of the nearby national television networks in the Casa de Campo, a third to corral the general officers in the war ministries, and a fourth to lay siege to the Congress and the governing palace? Of course! Of course! The two dozen or so lorries already parked in the enclosure were being loaded with crates carted from the bunkers. Arms caches were to be planted throughout Madrid under the cover of darkness. Men purporting to be sergeants directed the operation. The weapons were real enough: stenciled letterings on the crates ranged from M79 .40-mm grenade launchers and M20A1B1 3.5-inch rocket launchers all the way up to such heavy anti-tank systems as the M29 David Crockett with its M2121 tripod mount. Oh, this was extraordinary—and directly under the Government's nose!

As Stepanópoulis watched, more of the lorries came rumbling through the gate, parking neatly beside companions. A "sergeant" bawled at one of the drivers, "Where in Christ's name have you been! We roll by midnight!"

"Isias," Grau murmured, "do you have your sidearm?"

"Yes, sir!"

"Well, prepare it. Loosen it in your holster."

"I left the rounds on my wife's dresser this morning!"

"For heaven's sake! Here, take mine. Have it ready, but out of sight!"

Stepanópoulis stepped up smartly beside the "sergeant," identification palmed in one hand.

"Yeah," said the fellow uncivilly, "wait a minute! Hey, you, there, *watch* that crate, that's white phosphorous in the rifle grenades!" To Grau: "Whaddayouwant?"

"I would like to see your identification."

"This is Army business . . . Hey, no, *blockheads!* The M67s load on trucks twelve and thirteen!"

"I insist on seeing your identification."

"That's right, twelve and *thirteen!* It's the .66-mm *rockets* load on eleven . . . Civil police don't have any authority over the Army!"

"*If* you are the Army."

"Goddamnit . . ." A crate had been dropped, splitting open 3.5-inch rocket launchers. The "sergeant" released a roll of obscenities, finally pivoting back on Grau. "Here, look at it, Sergeant Alfonso Dávila, IVth Engineers!"

Grau took the identification and studied it carefully. As was to be expected, it was a brilliant verisimulation of the real article. There were all the stamps. There was the man's photograph—realistic to the length that he was pictured some ten years younger.

"Your orders?" he now said, handing the identification back.

"You go stuff your ass with a bung! Want to know anything, call the CO!" The man strode off, yelling at crews that had bungled the weight loads on two trucks, so that they listed heavily to starboard.

Grau smiled grimly. An excellent actor. A professional imposter. Even the clumsiness of the onlading was in brilliant imitation of a military operation, with malingerers sneaking smokes, and a confusion of contradictory commands being bawled by non-coms.

He strode back to the sedan.

"Where to?" asked Isias, loping along beside his chief.

"Headquarters, IVth Engineers."

"Sir, will you confide in me?"

"By and by," said the by-the-moment grimmer Grau.

The interview half an hour later with the commanding officer of the IVth Engineers absolutely confirmed Grau's suspicions. The man refused to say anything more about the operation than that the arms and munitions were due to be delivered by dawn next morning at Valencia, and that Security had approved everything. Naturally, this was all a tissue of falsehood. Being prepared was civil war. The commanding officer of the IVth Engineers was undoubtedly either a stooge or a traitor. Whoever in Security had approved this AESA "shipment" was probably a traitor; and not inconceivably that man was the *Director General de Seguridad himself!*

Yes! Yes! That would explain the scorning of his dossier ten years ago. Who could surmise how deeply the infiltration had penetrated? Franco was aging. There was impatience in the Government. Had the Chief of State been encircled and isolated by a wolfpack of ambitions? Would he be able to succor the Caudillo, get through to him personally and warn him? How? How!

He must be prepared. His brief had to be incontravertible in every respect.

Isias was bucking the cinema traffic back toward the center of Madrid when a notice crackled over the sedan's radio.

"What is it?" Grau snapped, taking the receiver.

"An outside call, sir. Says it's important, for your ears only. I'll switch you."

"Yes?" shouted Stepanópoulis.

A Caribbean baritone lazed over the radio waves.

"Deputy Inspector Stepanópoulis Grau?"

"*Acting* Inspector Stepanópoulis Grau!"

"You did the research for Señor Baltazar Blás in connection with the Larrañaga case back in the forties, correct?"

Grau was silent. He did not like to be reminded—especially over official wires.

"Come," purred the voice, "admit it, you served the State well, ridding it of subversive scum. Admit it, and I am prepared to give you the kind of tip police inspectors dream about."

"Who are you!"

"A victim of Señor Blás, like you. Don't ask more."

"What does your information relate to?"

"Horror, Inspector, corruption, Inspector—on the highest tax-evading level."

"I . . . I handled the Larrañaga investigation."

"My congratulations! I suggest you drive to Calle Almagro—. Go to the sixth floor, which is owned by the Duke of Sacedón. There you will find your reward."

There was a click on the other end. Grau hammered on the receiving set.

"Yes?" said the operator.

"Trace that call!"

"Oh, I have, sir. It comes from the sixth floor premises of the Duke of Sacedón, Almagro—."

Everything had something to do with everything else! This thirty-first of May was to be remembered in the annals of Spain.

"Sir," asked Isias, "do we follow it up?"

"It . . . could be a diversion," murmured Stepanópoulis. "There's . . . so little *time!* It could be a trap!"

"Should I radio for auxiliary . . ."

"Nooo. No!" How deeply had infiltration penetrated? "Isias, are you prepared to sacrifice your life for the Fatherland?"

"Well, I mean, I haven't really thought about that. I mean . . . Uh, yes, sir."

"Good! Now give me back my pistol, switch on the siren, and drive to Almagro as fast as you are able!"

FOURTEEN

The Gangster

Diego Muñoz González turned from the telephone to watch Hassam and Dong Thoc carry in a half-conscious Soledad Rivas.

She was wrapped in a raincoat. Dong Thoc kept a tender palm over her eyes, so that she would not see the corpses.

"She'll need clothes!" Muñoz González reminded the Korean.

"They'll be in the Duke's apartment," said Hassam.

"Get them." Muñoz González flicked over his wristwatch. "Nearly eight. I'll . . ."

"And the money, sir?" inquired Hassam, glancing at Herminia's basket with its crisp packets of 1,000-peseta notes.

"Bring it along . . . No," he corrected himself as he lofted brief case from desktop. "We'll leave it for the police." He strode toward the vestibule. "I'll warm up the car. Now fetch her belongings. Leave this note on her cot. We'll dress her at the proving grounds."

He opened the door into the hall, waving his confederates by him. The girl was reviving. Muñoz González glimpsed the mound of one naked breast before shutting the door and returning to the parlor.

He cast a last glance at the neatly arranged cadavers with a pile of glossy photographs at their heads. Well, the discovery would rock Madrid —that was sure. It might very well bring down the regime, certainly hurt it. The CP would thank him for that. It would mitigate the Party's predictable anger over the shipment to Israel. The Party would stuff it! He had suffered torture for the Party's sake at the hands of Trujillo's police. He had given enough, his very manhood! He'd be rich, after the shipment —a dollar millionaire several times over. He knew how to handle himself.

The Party was getting old, cumbersome, soft. Long ago he had conceived contempt for the timid, bureaucratized CP, he who had inherited revolutionary blood with his Basque genes, generations of it, each more radicalized. He took the corruption of the West as axiomatic—and he had made it his business to thrive on that corruption. He had determined in adolescence that he would never permit himself to be ruled by dogma, as had been his mother and stepfather. Blindly obedient, faithful as a hound, what had been his stepfather's reward? What had been his true father's reward?

Muñoz González admitted his cynicism. He had grown up under the shadow of treachery, betrayals and counter-betrayals.

The pale face of the urchin stared up at him, open-eyed. "Poor kid," thought Muñoz González idly, lifting the boy's skull with the toe of a foot to study the face better. No, he did not recognize it. Who was he? Was it probable so young a person had been sent on a killer's errand? By whom?

He frowned. The puzzle nagged at him.

He gave his head a shake. No time for speculations.

Long lithe strides took him down the back stairway to the garage. Nothing must interfere with the shipment. He had waited a long time, for fortune and vengeance. But . . . Dorada Blás. He had missed there! Thought of it angered him anew. How was he to get back at the father, who had hastened his parents to their sorry end? By diverting the munitions from Israel to Egypt, and pocketing the whole payment? No. Money meant little to Blás. And Muñoz González had a score to settle with the Party.

He remembered: the dismal night of their arrival in Santo Domingo. The heat, the bugs, the hole in a wall provided for them. His mother's weeping, reaching him through a cubicle's thin partition. The way her weeping turned into abuse of Larrañaga, her tongue lashing the gentle idealist, telling him that their life was a failure, that the Revolution would never succeed, that he was a dried out raisin, that she had never loved him, that when she compared him with her Diego, martyred on this very island, why, she could throw herself into the ocean. She went too far, and she carried on too long. The patience of the foster father he had come to love snapped. "Your wonderful Diego," he had said, "volunteered for assignment here to get away from you. Your wonderful Diego was such an irresponsible and undisciplined fool that the Party was compelled to liquidate him."

He had that score to settle against the Party. It was filial duty, scant affection though he felt for the shadowy figure of his true father. But he was a Basque, after all, an Ybarra, son of agintaris. He would someday avenge the wrongs done to his mother. "Promise," she had said to him, sobbing and sobbing. "Promise you won't forget," she had begged him on the gangplank of the freighter that was to carry her and his foster father back to Spain. He would join them when he completed university studies. But he was never to see them again.

No, this shipment of anti-tank weapons, perhaps crucial to Israel, would go to the Jews. And Blás . . . ?

As he waited for his associates, engine running, the solution came to him. First, he would burn the Duke of Sacedón's demand notes. He would burn the collateral—the open bills of sale of Financiera Sacedón stock! Yes, that would hurt Blás, bollix his plans. But more. After the shipment, he would post letters to foreign news agencies detailing the entire operation, further embarrassing the Franco regime (another point gained there with the CP), and implicating not only Baltazar Blás but his son-in-law, the Count of Obregón. That poker-up-the-asshole would be locked up, even though Blás himself used his enormous wealth and influence to somehow escape consequences. Prades would be jailed, his titles maybe even stripped from him, he . . .

Claro! Muñoz González slapped a palm on the dashboard. This would be the final twist of the knife. His mother had shown him a genealogical chart once, in boyhood. He was a direct descendant of the Basque patriot and historian, Rodrigo González González. Through the Ybarra connection, he was a descendant of the Dukes of Sacedón, first Spanish holders of the Marquisate of the Pilgrim. From safe refuge, he would slap a claim on the title. He'd have plenty of money to finance it. For all he knew, he might turn out to be the true heir!

He flashed the flame of his lighter, bringing it close to his signet ring. Over generations had it come down to him. Maybe there was substance in the bloodstone!

Muñoz González loosed a chuckle. Oh, that would be a twist of the knife indeed!

Hassam and Dong Thoc appeared in the garage's weak lights, supporting the Rivas girl between them. "Get in! Get in!" snapped Muñoz González, thwomping the side of his Mercedes' door.

They wheeled into Calle Almagro, descending to the Castellana. Expertly, he maneuvered the big car through dense evening traffic. Heading into the Gran Vía from Calle Alcalá, he saw a police sedan, siren squealing like a bitch being spayed, the globe of bloody warning on its roof spilling its scarlet across them as it hurtled by. Stepanópoulis Grau? Muñoz González crinkled the right-hand corner of his upper lip, in that feral ambiguity between a grin and a snarl. The former Blás agent who had helped fling his parents into exile. Well, he was in for a surprise. Oh yes: his discovery of the corpses, and the photographs, and the cooking chunks of Tomás, would be his undoing. Everyone involved would face trial—Spanish Justice was as independent and impartial as Her Majesty's the Queen of England—but Grau would not be thanked for it. The Establishment would turn on him and devour him; leaving only the mantequero, that Jacobo Rivas, to settle accounts with. And the final entry in that book was secure, huddled between Hassam and Dong Thoc.

Muñoz González now lifted his baritone in a bossanova.

FIFTEEN

Officialdom

Upon Grau's departure, the CO of the IVth Engineers—a colonel—rang his superior, a brigadier general, who rang his superior, the Governor General of Madrid, who in turn rang his old comrade, the Director General of Security.

"Whozzit?" this man asked.

"You answer the telephone yourself these days?"

"Oh, Miguel. My girl's down with the colic. Pandemonium without her. Can't locate the files on *Tito*, for God's sake! How's the little woman?"

"That had better not be a crack!"

"No, no, no of course not!"

"She's up in the Pyrenees, taking steam baths. Says she's lost ten kilos, won't believe it until I see it. Look, José, I'm a little uneasy over this AESA shipment. You sure it's all right?"

"Well, officially it's unofficial, but it's unofficially officially O.K. We need the gold."

"But has The Boss approved this personally? That's something I want to know."

"Well, Miguel," temporized the Director General of Security, "you know how The Boss is these days, getting along, listens, doesn't say much —oh, it was mentioned to him, all right. But it's O.K., the Council of Ministers individually approved. Not in session, naturally."

"I'd be happier if I saw The Boss's Fulano-de-tal on the orders."

"What's bugging you, José baby. Tell your old messmate!"

"There's some big-nosed police inspector running around asking my Engineers what's up. I mean, say this got out? We're neutral—neutral in favor of the Moors, may God incinerate the black-souled heathen!"

"Won't get out. Who is this fellow?"

"Stepajópomus Frau or Brau or . . ."

The hair on the nape of the Director General of Security rose.

"Grau? Stepanópoulis *Grau?*"

"That's it."

"Oh, God, no! Had him in my section fifteen years ago. Don't worry. Sit tight. I'll dump him back in the Sahara, this time until the sun bleaches his bones!"

SIXTEEN

The Scandal

That exchange took place at eight-forty, just a few moments before Grau and Isias, having first searched Juan Luis's flat (and found the dildo in the maid's room, and identified the occupant of the only room that hadn't been evacuated as a daughter of Jacobo Rivas through the contents of her purse and the photograph of the mantequero and his wife, that deduction being somewhat simplified by the note on the pillow reading, *Rivas! I have your flower, and I will drag her through Babylon!*), eased open the door into the adjoining flat.

There should be no need to elaborate on the shock and horror at what met their eyes. There should be no need to describe the boil of the Deputy Inspector's excitement. The brothel bedrooms, the sexual perversions documented in the glossies, the cannibalism, the brutal killings! The basket heaped with bank notes. That evil old wetnurse with the screwdriver driven to the hilt through one eye and the brains oozing out around the shaft. (An internecine struggle? Were the leaders aware that he, Stepanópoulis Grau, was panting on their tracks?)

"Jesu Christo," let out Isias.

No less awed, Grau said, "Touch nothing. Call in the fingerprint squad, photographers." He reached out a hand, grasping his assistant by a wrist and pressing it. "Isias, Isias," he whispered, "it's turning out exactly as I foresaw."

Meanwhile, however, the Director General of Security was telephoning his counterpart in the civil police, and he in turn began tracking down the Inspector, Grau's cousin.

SEVENTEEN

Proofing the Pudding

At the proving grounds, Muñoz González had Soledad carried into the little hut Smith-Burton built against inclement weather. He occupied himself reorganizing and spurring the loading. Twenty minutes later, he ducked into the sheet-tin shelter, where he found a bound and gagged Soledad sitting up on an iron cot with affrighted eyes.

"This won't do at all!" he exclaimed.

"We requested that she not scream," apologized Hassam, "but she began to anyhow. Thong Doc has offered her coffee . . ."

"Dong Thoc," corrected the grinning little graveyard digger of an Oriental, asserting himself for the first time in anyone's memory.

"Excuse me. Dong Thoc. But she won't touch a drop. She would not dress herself."

"Just as well."

Muñoz González stepped up to the girl. He cupped her soft chin in a brown, muscular hand, raising it. Her eyes were a kaleidoscope of amber, topaz, and chocolate, set in moonstone whites and fringed by the darkest of lashes.

She was frightened. Her deep bosom rose, swelling in a sigh-spasm of fright. She was a little beauty, the most voluptuous piece her age he had seen.

This surprised Muñoz González. In halcyon days, how many lush, tropical fruits had he speared? Unrememberable dozens. What was it that so disturbed him about this Rivas chit? What brought those tiny beads to the brow of Dong Thoc and the pink pointed tip of his tongue to Hassam's purple lips?

Ah, yes—the quality of innocence in the girl, the frighted innocence of her expression coupled with the unself-consciousness of her sexuality. Yes, that was it. Did anything tantalize men more than the prospect of ravishing a rose in its first bloom?

Moments more, he stared at her, eyes smoking under the brows.

"Soledad," came the deep chords of his voice, "no permanent harm will come to you if you are tractable. In Mexico, we will marry. You will live in idleness the rest of your days. But you must obey me."

She snatched her head back, clamping on one of his fingers through the gag.

All she managed was to pinch the flesh.

Hassam said, "Do you wish us to tame her for you now, sir?"

Muñoz González gazed at him. He hesitated. If only . . . but no, with the little remaining of one battery, he could not trust himself. And she was the mantequero's daughter, he had to remember that, daughter of Jacobo Rivas, the memory of whom had finally consumed, had totally degraded, his mother—her brains at the end rotted with gin, her mind drifting back in time to the peasant who, she had once in drunkenness told him, had betrayed both the Revolution and herself. "How?" he had asked her. "By changing sides during the War." "But how did he betray you?" he had pressed her. "He wiped out the memory of your father! He compelled me to loathsome, terrible acts! He brutalized me, corrupted my soul!—so that, so much so, that I knew I could never love a man again! But he would never come away with me, that I knew also. Oh, he was vile! For him, I was a summer adventure, nothing more, alien flesh to despoil." She had wept then with self-pity, breaking her young son's heart. "*He*'s the reason I drink, and why Ramón and I suffer! Oh, I *tried* to save myself, stole away one morning, without telling him—stole away on a golden September morning in a bus, leaving happiness forever behind me."

That myth Michelle Muñoz had constructed for herself. (Perhaps she believed it: she had not recognized the real Jacobo in the bar.) Her son believed her. He had no reason not to believe her. Flesh of Rivas had despoiled his mother's flesh. Flesh of his mother would despoil Rivas flesh.

Muñoz González nodded, stepping back from the girl. "Thong Doc first. Then call for me."

He ducked his sinewy length back out the hut's door, shouting orders.

E I G H T E E N

Nati

In the chapel at Número Catorce, Ignacio slowly rose from the prie-dieu at which he had been kneeling, Consuelo at a prie-dieu on his right and an empty prie-dieu for Sofía waiting on his left. One rosary had ended. People shuffled out of the pews behind him, fresh mourners taking their places. After a pause, a second rosary would begin, and then a third, and a fourth, continuing through the night and into dawn, attendance diminishing to a few intimate friends as midnight drew near, and then to just those members of the immediate family not thoroughly exhausted, and at the last to the three nuns, who would remain on rooted knees until the hour arrived in the morning for pallbearers and burial officials to take up the coffin.

Where had Sofía been all day? Ignacio wondered. She would need comforting most of all. How very tired Consuelo looked, with the cross and petulant fatigue of the overweight. Close behind her knelt Marisa Magascal, her hippic cheekbones, nose, and jaw gone the color of bone, in shape as bleak as a Picasso cube.

He seemed to be noticing people as never had he. In a single sweep of his eyes, he noted the absence of Jaime, who had probably toddled out for a drink, the incongruity of the presence of the American, C. O. Jones, and the awful reminder of the soberly dressed plainclothesman in the rear. Yes, his mother had been murdered, had been strangled to death.

He shuddered. There was a press at the low arched entrance to the chapel, its oaken, iron-studded door obstructing the available space, so that people entering and leaving had to squeeze by each other, and anyone as tall as Centollos had to stoop besides. He turned now to gaze upon his mother. "Are you?" he asked in his heart. "Please, you can't have gone yet, not until the twenty-four hours are consummated—please won't you whisper to me that you were?" The torches flickered, and their sooty flames bent as though a wind were passing over them. Nothing. One of the inexplicable drafts that, in childhood, during winter mornings at the private daily Mass, used to chill him; drafts, as he had been told, caused by hidden and now forgotten passageways. A gigantic shadow crossed him: Don Emilio, moving from one Station of the Cross to the next, lips patting each other penitentially as he sloshed holy oils over the marble bas-reliefs, dripping oil on tapestries, pews, and whatever else he came near. He had crossed the border of senescence, it seemed all at once.

It was time for the Count of Obregón to find out.

He stepped to the head of the coffin. "You won't tell me," he whispered, stooping and kissing the Marquesa on her cold brow. Then, blinded by tears, he strode back through mourners and out of the chapel.

In the ballroom, he panted for breath. An ever more sultry night, many people milled in the huge domed chamber, which was less close than the parlors. No one came near him. He caught himself staring at the sensually modeled back of the Leda, twisted slightly as she embraced the swan to her loins. His mind crowded for some reason with every shameful or furtive action of his past, as when, in early puberty, he had attempted one dark evening to mount and spill upon that shining marble, feverish palms clutching the splayed, beautiful, oversized breasts. He thought of Dorada, his Leda come alive, a Helen for him, a Clytemnestra, a daughter of that stone-coldness against which even his fifteen-year-old lust had been unavailing.

He looked up suddenly. Dorada stared at him from across the dance floor, Julio Caro beside her. Nearby, under the bust of Augustus Caesar, Juan Luis smoked in long, unsteady draughts, gazing into space. Ignacio shook his head. He would search for Nati.

It had been twenty-five years since his steps took him to the servants' quarters of Número Catorce. He lost himself in the labyrinth of dark corridors, footfalls creaking the ancient floorboards. He was frightened by the shadows. Eventually, he found his foster mother's door.

He stepped close to it. "Nati," he whispered. Then, more loudly, "Nati, I'm here, I want to see you, I . . . your . . . Nacho."

There was no response.

He tried the knob, pushing the door back and into the room. He stepped in after it.

And he screamed—falling back against a wall, covering his eyes with both arms.

Nati's elongated sparseness swayed like a drooping vulture from the cord of the overhead lamp. A chair had been kicked to one side.

Ignacio lurched to the open sink. He thought he would vomit. The pain helped clear his head. *Oh, no!* thundered in the brain. *No. No. No.*

He managed to straighten from the basin, turning.

Nati swayed ever so slightly, from the draft of the open door. One cheek rested on its shoulder, almost as though she slept. Her mouth was open, but the tongue did not protrude. Her eyeballs had turned up under the lids, as in so many crucified Christs. Her gray hair—still luxurious— had been let down, and it reached to the small of her back.

There was a note on the dresser.

Nacho stumbled to it. The scrawl was difficult to make out in the light reflecting from an outdoor street lamp on Calle Los Mancebos. He murmured the words to himself: *"I killed my mistress at the Devil's prompting. May her son, the Marquis of the Pilgrim, forgive me."*

He crushed that note in his hand much as he had that morning crushed Nati's note announcing his mother's death. Ten, fifteen, twenty minutes he stood there. He had lost both women, one of them—which?— his mother. He knew no more now than before. He would never know . . .

"My God!" came a gasp from behind him.

He whirled, as though to fend off attack.

It was Dorada, a spindle of flax in the frame of the door, friezed there by the vision of Nati, citrine irises glowing against the diamond whites.

Those eyes lowered to him, finally: flares. They stared at each other. It was he who shook the spell, stepping forward and handing her the note. Dorada spread the wrinkled surface out, reading attentively, glancing once at the hanging dead woman with her long black skirts and the gray cotton stockings on ankles and feet that dripped like withered cornstalks.

"Nati . . . calls you the Marquis."

"It doesn't answer the question."

"It's enough."

"*I* need to know!"

She shut the door behind her, turning to him. How self-possessed her voice: "Once in possession of the title, why should you care?"

He slapped her with all the surprising force of a palm, knocking her sharply back. The sound of the slap rang in the room, in his ears, within his breast. She swayed like a poplar under an autumnal gust, righting herself slowly and staring at him.

He breathed heavily. The thumping of his heart was audible to him. He did not retreat a step, as one so often does after violence. They were utterly alone, together as never before. His strong long fingers curled until the nails bit into his palms.

"I . . . I want you to forget about this morning," Dorada said, holding her cheek. She tasted blood in her mouth.

"When . . . the mourning period is done, I'll be suing for separation."

"You can't do that! There's no cause! I've never been unfaithful!"

"I'll ask for it on the grounds that you refuse to submit to your conjugal obligations."

"And make yourself a laughingstock!"

"That's no longer important."

"Nacho," she said, limping close to him, bringing her marble bosom upon him and pressing her swan-feathered pelvis against him. "Whenever you want, from now on, wherever you like, and however you want it, and with . . . with . . . with affection, Nacho, I won't lie, I won't say love, maybe that'll come, but with . . . with . . . respect! Yes, respect! I can respect you! Your willingness to leave me, when I know how very much you want and need me, I'll be yours, yours forever, Nacho, my Nacho, kiss me, kiss me now! I want you now! now! now!"

He pushed her from him.

"I'll place a countersuit," she raged, flinging her hair back, "alleging your impotence!"

"You would be justified. This morning, you may have lost your arsenal."

"All right! We'll separate! But *after* the title is confirmed."

He brushed past her in walking by.

"Wait!"

He halted with the door's handle half twisted in his hand. "Yes."

"Don't leave me here alone! Walk back with me."

"You found your way here. Find the way out." He opened the door, walking through and away.

"No, wait!" She ran three steps after him. "I . . . I came to fetch you. The Police Inspector—he wants you about something urgent. He wants everyone in the ballroom."

NINETEEN

Treason and Stupidity

Earlier, waiting for the photographers and the fingerprint team, Stepanópoulis Grau paced back and forth in a state of the most acute excitement and anxiety. He had found out the premises were rented by the Santo Dominican who ran a nightclub in the building that adjoined Número Catorce. He had called for a briefing on the suspect career of Muñoz González, and learned of his connection with Blás. Oh, it was all coming together!—all of it a dream come true! He should at once contact headquarters. This was too big for his department. He ought to report it to a higher echelon for mobilization of the entire force. But he was not so stupid as to be ignorant of the consequences. Yes: he would have discovered the most sensational deck of monstrous crimes in recent Spanish history. And he would be taken off the case—but at once! His cousin the Inspector would never forgive him for the discovery. The Authorities would not forgive him. His choice had might as well be exile.

And then . . . and then . . . and then—but, oh! they would bungle it! They would not connect these crimes with the insurrection being prepared in the Casa de Campo. Those in authority who remained true —*were* there any!—would not credit the plot. He would have to do something with what he had discovered, something drastic, something that might cost him life and liberty, but something demanded by his patriotism. And . . . before treason or stupidity stopped him!

He had good reason to fear. His cousin had been tracked down in the hospital. At first, doctors refused to permit the telephone call: "The Inspector has a serious concussion." "If you don't put me through to him," rasped Madrid's police Commissioner-in-Chief, "why . . . !"

Grau's still groggy cousin listened to the Commissioner's heated voice. The Deputy Inspector was bungling matters, nosing about where he had no business, interfering with Army affairs, messing into areas belonging to Security, bringing half officialdom down on the neck of the department. He was to be yanked off the case at once—*at once!* Personally, by the Inspector his cousin, or by the Saints the Inspector would answer for it!

God, groaned Grau's even groggier cousin. He had begged their common great-grandmother, matriarch of all the Graus, "Please, don't do this to Spain, don't force me to take Stepanópoulis in!" The Inspector was a chubby, devoted, hard-working veteran of twenty-five years on the force. He had never taken a bribe. He had solved a respectable number of cases. Just the other day he had placed a down payment on a cottage for his blind wife—on the flank of the Guadarrama mountains, where she could listen to the music of the wind and inhale the resin of the pines. Now . . .

He had a nurse dial his headquarters. The officer on night duty said that Stepanópoulis hadn't been in since six o'clock or so, but half an hour ago he had called for the Triple A check-out squad. The address?

The Inspector ordered a car.

Meanwhile Stepanópoulis was fussing the fingerprint specialists into the most rapid activity. The photographers were done. They had shot the bedrooms. They had taken ten angles of Tomás's severed head, which had rolled out of the refrigerator when they opened it; and several of a leg they found in the deepfreeze; and more of the pots bubbling on the stove. They had panned the circular parlor with a series of wide-angle frames, closing on the corpses arranged in starfish formation, head to head, and on the pile of pornographic snapshots in the center, and on Herminia's benign face with the screwdriver's hilt protruding like a cork from one eye. "I want blow-ups within half an hour!" shouted Stepanópoulis. "I want twelve by twenties rushed to me, at Calle Don Pedro, Número Catorce. Go!" He wheeled upon the fingerprinters. "Concentrate on that screwdriver for now! Dust a preliminary!" They did so. Grau had called for the prints of suspects in his thick file. Every Spaniard carries an ID card; the pods of the entire population are on microfilm. He was handed a talcumed sheet. The doorbell buzzed. "Check it out, Isias!" snapped Stepanópoulis, striding briskly to the vestibule.

He flung the door back, shouting, "Yes!" —and his battered, ever more groggy cousin and superior, with a head bandaged like a mummy's and a chest plastered up to the neck, almost fell into his arms, croaking, "Stepanópoulis, you are to . . ."

Credit Grau for fast thinking. This was the first of his bold measures. Slamming the door shut behind him, he slapped a hand over his cousin's mouth. Arching his bantam body, he then drove head-on into the round of his cousin's belly, doubling the man back out into the corridor and against the surprised police driver. Hesitating not an instant, he flung his cousin through the open door of the Duke's apartment, yanking out his automatic and ordering the driver in after him. There, using bedsheets, he had the driver bind up his cousin, and then himself bound the driver, tapping the man on the skull with his own nightstick for good measure.

Grau's bird-sized heart was racing when he got through these violent exertions. He barely made it to Juan Luis's bathroom. He was scarcely able to piddle. As an afterthought, he went round the flat, pulling telephone wires out. He was obeying higher duty: preserving the State, the Spanish nation, perhaps the person of the Caudillo himself!

He rushed from Juan Luis's flat, banging on the Muñoz González door. Isias opened it for him.

"Who was that calling? Why . . . *Sir,* you're all *mussed* . . . !"

"Never mind! Did you check out the prints on the screwdriver?"

"Yes, sir! You'll never believe it. They . . . they belong to the Duke of Sacedón!"

"I knew it!" Stepanópoulis pealed, tippy-toeing in an arch of glee. "No one at all is above suspicion! Come! They can finish up alone!"

Taking over the wheel, he drove as fast as two accidents and a herd of sheep permitted to Número Catorce. He had recognized faces in some of the photographs, featured as they were almost weekly in *Hola!* and other picture magazines. There he would surely find most of the culprits still gathered. He would corral them all. Earlier he had telephoned orders for the mantequero and his wife to be brought to the palace, and for the other tradesmen besides. He would confront them everyone with their crimes. He would confront them with each other. And he was prepared for his most audacious and desperate of measures. He knew the press would be covering the entrance to Número Catorce, a legitimate news event. Well, he would bring them into the palace. His charges would become public property, so that no traitor be able to interdict them. Yes indeed, he *would* hold his press conference, and in the very heart of subversion!

He arrived with fever on his forehead. A technician from the police laboratory was at the portal, waiting for him with a folder of large, damp 12 x 20s. Grau gave orders. He invited television crews, reporters, and gazette photographers to follow him. He buttonholed the first plainclothesman he came upon, in the carriageway, whispering that he wanted all guests and family—with no exceptions!—in the great ballroom. A procession formed behind him. "What's up?" asked a TV technician, struggling in the stairway with equipment. "You'll find out soon enough!"

snapped Isias, long-legging after his chief. Grau marched into the rose room, steering straight across it, acknowledging glances neither to the right nor to the left. "What's a-foot?" asked guests vainly as plainclothesmen began herding them in the Deputy Inspector's wake.

The babbling under the starry rotunda of the ballroom grew as from every salon in the palace people gathered. "There's a rosary going on in the chapel," Isias mentioned tentatively. "*Everyone!*" he got for a retort. Grau had come to a halt in the center of the dance floor. A golden flame accosted him. "Inspector, what's the meaning of . . . ?" "Madam," he said peremptorily, "kindly fetch the Count, your husband." He scanned the huge, circular chamber. Where should he set up? Where would be the architectural center of attention? The camera crews had finally made it, trailing cables with the care fishermen give their dragnets. A uniformed policeman snapped to attention, saluting. "Sir, the prisoners from Carabanchel have arrived. They're coming up the front."

"*What!*" exclaimed Grau. "Turn them back this *instant!* They are to use the servants' entrance!" Anybody would think he was ignorant of the proprieties! "And Sergeant, when all are accounted for, *bar the doors!*"

TWENTY

Vengeance Is the Lord's

I was still in the chapel when the beanpole assistant of the Deputy Inspector entered; saw him shyly edging his way between pews toward the altar. The sanctum was at capacity, with some half hundred people chorusing the fifth rosary of the night as though in rhythmic decompression of gas pains. The stone walls sweated. I was newly impressed by the sweatiness of plump female feet. There was a low layer of that acrid leathery odor in the crypt-sized chapel, spiced with the rank aroma of those not infrequently to be observed Spanish women who grow beards from their armpits with pride; and, in a layer above that scent, the more wholesome smell of moth-balled and cedar-closeted wool under male arms. By way of topping that—at least where I knelt—were gusts of garlic from the nicotined lungs of Inmaculada del Val, Juan Luis's dam, who depressed a pew several grades of rank beyond me, but who, although bent to her devotions, still managed to swivel that wasp's nest of faded orange hair in time to note every fresh arrival into the by now fetid premises.

These were becoming more humid with the minute as Don Emilio continued saturating just about every icon in the place with his holy oils, an (as it seemed to me) excessive sanctifying that presumably had to do with the new liturgy, most of which is incomprehensible to the average old sinner like me. But watching the holy man through the better part of an hour, I was struck by strangeness in his behavior. His grief, I readily understood. It glowed in that wasted face with luminous intensity. It was manifest in the extra burden that seemed to bow his gallows' frame, and in steps that seemed ever less certain, as though the bones were powdering into dust. He had led not one prayer since my arrival. Approached by some noble lady with a jeweled rosary to be blessed, an impatient gesture escaped him, accompanied by a most awful mottling of his cheeks. One can't blame the poor woman for being frightened. Don Emilio Guzmán y Stuart, Conde de Cortijos and sainted servant of Almighty God, was angered. Why? Roughly, did he grasp the beads from her. Harshly, did the beautiful long plane of his right hand slash the Sign above them. Abruptly, did he then turn from the woman, resuming his solitary rounds.

He was stooped over the catafalque, dousing the velvet, when Isias reached him. Kneeling as I was in the rearmost pew, I could not hear what the beanpole said; but I saw Don Emilio's expression again cloud with wrath, and the policeman's long larynx gobble in agitation. Then the priest seemed to undergo a change of mind. He gazed up past Isias toward the exquisite retablo above the altar. Slowly, he nodded.

Stretching out a hand to hush the chanting nuns, Don Emilio faced us. We fell quiet. "Children," he stated with that peculiar, penetrating dulcetness, "the authorities want you in the ballroom, and without delay. You, too, good sisters. We will suspend orisons." And he turned to the altar, collapsing on his knees.

"Father," came from Isias across the intake and expellations of our fifty-odd pairs of lungs, "the Deputy Inspector said, uh, everyone. That's to say . . ."

I heard no more in the general interrogative murmuring and the creaking of weight being lifted from pews. I was myself one of the first into the ballroom. Suffice to suppose that Isias backed away from the coals in the sockets of Don Emilio's eyes. Most people would have; but Isias is nevertheless responsible for the one exception to the Deputy Inspector's order.

TWENTY-ONE

Babylon

At about this time—just past ten o'clock—Muñoz González was reading from the munitions inventory sheets under one of several bright arc lamps that blazed with cynthian chiaroscuro and bleakness on the proving grounds, pitchblack shadows from lorries, crates, and soldiers waging implacable warfare with blinding reflections.

"Four thousand M67 recoilless rifles," the Santo Dominican said.

"Check," confirmed a sergeant, pencil ticking the item on his duplicate list.

"Two hundred fifty thousand rounds 90-mm ammo."

"Check."

"Twenty thousand M25 antipersonnel mines."

"Yes."

"And five thousand M19 antitank mines."

"That's it, sir."

"For the American weapons. Start on the French small arms, trucks thirty-four through fifty-two."

"Right away, sir!"

The man saluted smartly, about-facing and marching off.

Muñoz González grunted with satisfaction. It was clear to him that he had organizational talents. By backing lorries to the mouths of bunkers, more had been loaded in an hour under his direction than under the military Engineers all afternoon. Non-coms no longer caterwauled emptily at indifferent recruits. Squads of eleven men each chain-ganged the munitions quietly and quickly. Two hundred thousand pesetas in a woven basket hanging from one of the arc lamps had put a stop to malingering.

Yes, he thought with another grunt, panther-pacing toward a bonfire, he possessed talents he had scarcely exploited. With the stake he could expect, he would do famously in South America. What money might be unable to buy, the body of the Rivas girl likely would. As he hunkered at the fire (he collapsed on his hocks—in the sudden swift spring-muscled manner of the big cats), a bolus of laughter rumbled up from his chest. Yes, the money, the girl, and maybe the title too! He mustn't forget the title! Was there a mongrel from the Río Grande to

Patagonia who did not in his breast house awe of noble Spanish blood? He would go far!

From his dispatch case, he extracted Juan Luis's notes and bills of sale, feeding them one by one into the flames. There, igniting and then curling to ash, went the control Blás had panted after. Muñoz González gazed meditatively at the documents. Up in flames went youth, lust, love and the ambitions of men. Into ashes disintegrated desire. Oh, he would get richer and richer. For what? For whom? Did the woman exist who could induce a sufficiency of seed from his mutilated parts?

His Indian's eyes glistened like oiled basalt. The live-oak faggots sputtered and crackled. A soldier walked by casting a bundle of thyme and rosemary into the pile, bringing about a leaping of flames. The Santo Dominican's head jerked up. What was that fellow doing . . . !

He relaxed. It was all right, the odd squad rested ten minutes every fifty minutes. The boy—a bronzed, fresh-faced peasant's son—walked on to a knot of his fellows who were lounging in the shadowy outer circumference, one of them softly yodeling a fandango de Huelva. What a beautiful, saddening lament! What richness there was in the soul of the race, what genius for the tragic! The smoke was now spiced with scents common to the plains and mountains of all Spain. He breathed them in deeply. He would never be back. He would lose Spain. How much he would like to have begot a son of the land, his seed's fruit from a Spanish womb . . .

Hassam stood beside him. The Egyptian was pale beneath the dark pigmentation of his skin—sallow, as malarial as the Nile. His limbs trembled.

"Go all right?" asked Muñoz González, rising in the same swift, big-cat manner.

"Rather! Thong Doc is reviving himself with poppers. I am nearly done in too, if I say so. Never, never, never . . ."

Muñoz González was taken aback. "She . . . but she's a virgin, just fifteen!"

"Virginal after a manner of speaking. She was born to be on her back, sir. *Sakhr* and *li-haing* and improvisations thereof twice each with Dong Thoc. *Ho chi thieu* with me, and eagerly, relentlessly, indefatigably!" Hassam saluted, Sandhurst father that he had had. "Congratulations, sir. In that girl alone, you have a fortune."

And wobble-kneed, he began walking off.

"Rest awhile if you must," called the astonished Muñoz González after him, "but then both of you start checking air pressure, fuel, oil and water. We roll in ninety minutes!"

What nonsense! he thought, himself walking to the hut. She was of course a virgin, a properly brought up Spanish girl. If they had hurt her! If they were trying to excuse themselves . . . !

He ducked through the hut's door, coming to a stop just inside.

Soledad lay on the spartan cot to the rear. She was naked except for the wool Army blanket that draped from her waist in a fold down between her separated thighs, the flesh of which gleamed like fine handsmoothed ivory in the light of the oil lamp. In her nakedness, she curiously resembled the portraits-in-the-nude of poor Sofía, Countess of a Thousand Tears, Soledad's remote cousin, which Billy had not destroyed. Her chin was tipped up at the ceiling. Her eyes were closed, thick lashes screening her round, high cheekbones. These were flushed. Her breath was shallow and ecstatic, sipped in between swollen lips. Her breasts rested laxly on the high barrel of her ribs, but even in their abandonment they were of an exquisite perfection, the convexity of their lower hemispheres tilting the upper hemispheres into a shallow, delicious concavity.

Muñoz González's black pupils contracted. In his loins, he felt a nearly forgotten stirring.

She opened her eyes, gazing at him. "Are you next?" she asked sweetly.

He took three more strides into the room, standing over her.

"I will marry you in Mexico—as I said," he barked at her in the harshest tones. "But I will use you like a prostitute, as your father used my mother. And I will have you serve anyone I choose—humpbacks, lepers, sadists, anyone!"

"I love you."

"What rubbish! You're to be my harlot."

She stretched her arms toward him. In the act, her breasts swelled, their nubs hardening.

"You've done for me what I've wanted always, since I can remember, since my flows began and my brothers started noticing me and I watched lovers in a parked car and my hands discovered my body, and I began letting men who owed Poppa money off half if they helped me in other ways and then—as I learned—paying people Poppa owed money to in ways they liked almost as much as I. But like Dong Thoc, no one! Like Hassam, nobody in the world!"

She had been drawing him toward her. Her fingers were like iced eels at his waist, tugging at his shirt, reaching inside.

He drew back, dismayed—furious! "There's no pleasure in you for me. There'll be no pleasure for you from me. In five years, so many men will have passed through you that your paps will sag like bladders and your gender will be hollowed out like a cave and your womb will be sterile."

"Come," Soledad said, sitting up. She smiled, like a child. She had reached his loins. A hand had discovered the deception. "Is this something new?" she asked curiously.

Muñoz González unbuckled his belt, letting trousers fall. As he stripped to his mahogany skin, he spoke to her.

"You will learn every indignity. With this contrivance, I will pierce you in a way Nature herself prohibits. You will scream. You will want to tear me with your teeth. I will laugh at you. I spit on you. I sprinkle you with my contempt. But I am beyond your powers."

"We'll see about that!"

Brutally, he flung himself on her. As he had promised, he had her biting through his hide in spasms of sheer agony, and when he entered her from the rear, her shriek split the air. But she enjoyed it! She was enjoying it! This was a terrible thing. This was the lower-middle-class Spanish virgin whose spirit he had meant to break! But oh, he had forgot. Spain has been raped throughout the centuries, the youngest virgin and the oldest harlot in the world. This was the niece of Begonia and daughter of Beatitud. But she is unconquerable, is Spain. Soledad's whole being consisted in sexual hyperphagia. Each climax pitched her into a more famished ardor; and soon his body was oiled in his sweat, and her body wriggled oilily beneath him, and she was ripping the contrivance off him, and all the steaming flesh of her, the engorging lips of every orifice, the whole bitchwoman's hummock of whoredom, the very furnace of ravening female coital lust concentrated on his tortured parts, rousing into regeneration the seminal sac; until suddenly his brown blue-veined phallus sprang erect, and its bulging corona ached for the planting, and he was within her driving with a sweet anguish he had thought forever lost, and what burst from him was a miracle.

"Oh my God!" he let out hoarsely, collapsing on her. "Oh my God, my God, my God!" he kept repeating. This had not been the thin ejection of a few drops from a quarter-filled tube. This was full sexual potency, so that the fluid burned in him from the root and surged burning through the entire thirst of his barrel to explode within her in a scalding broth of virility.

Her loins shuddered on his gender. Her sweet wet warmness contracted in peristaltic progression the length of him from base to borehead, drawing the last of his milk with a sort of excruciating itch. "My God," he breathed again willing now to die. "Where—how!" he gasped, "did you learn *that?*"

"Oh," she panted, "I'm a great reader. Poppa always encouraged our reading."

He raised his head. He grasped both her cheeks in his hands. "We will marry."

"Yes, we'll marry."

"I want a child."

"I will give you one child."

"I want many children! I want sons!"

"I will give you one chance at having one son."

"You'll be mine, mine alone. No one will separate us."

She smiled into his eyes, crinkling her nose mischievously—nipping at his nose with strong little teeth.

"You'll have to share me," she said.

"What? Never!"

"If I see an amputee on the street and want him, you will fetch him for me. If my fancy calls for six men at once, you will hire them, and watch us, and I may even feel pity for you, and invite you to be last."

"No, no, horrible—*never!*" he cried.

But her heat was at him, and upon him, and within him. And he was soon begging for deliverance.

TWENTY-TWO

At Número Catorce

My schematization of events that evening has it that it was some forty-five minutes earlier—just past ten-thirty—when I stepped into the ballroom from the chapel, coming to a stop under the arcade while others who had been attending the rosary pressed from behind and around me, the heavy oaken door shutting the last of them out with a solid slam and the thud of iron bolts being shot.

I must say I was impressed—freshly impressed—by what greeted my eyes. Heretofore dispersed among the several great salons of the palace, the three hundred-odd illustrious mourners were now goldfished under the star-speckled dome of this single chamber; and it's fair to hazard, I think, that not since Odette's wedding ball had there been such an assembly, nor such expectation. But it was a dark, nervous thing that thrilled our bosoms. ("The police have identified the killer!" I heard muted from more than one pair of lips.) Stepanópoulis Grau stood like a midget stone Avenger behind the filigreed Mudejar balustrade of the choir built for violin orchestras, raised sufficiently above us to command attention. Uniformed and plainclothes police blocked every exit. Other lawmen were politely organizing the multitude ("Your Grace, over here if you please"—for a duke; "Your Excellency, this way"—for a Minister of State or an ambassador; "Señor"—in reverential understated simplicity for a Prince of the Blood). Professional military men congregated to the extreme right of the choir, generals, colonels, majors (of noble lineage), and captains (also of the nobility), the mailed fist of Imperial Spain, the Army, upholder of tradition, bulwark of order, and glorious over a millennium of mostly victorious campaigns, presenting despite the mustard-colored drab of field uniforms a brave spectacle in their crimson epaulets, stars, crosses, sashes, black armbands, and swords. Next to them grouped prelates in full-skirted purple and crimson, three monsignors, three bishops and a cardinal, large silver crosses swaying on their breasts. Behind and to one side of them came Government, along with the deans of the Diplomatic Corps, prominent among whom the gallant old ambassador of Free Hungary, the sash across his front weighted with a jeweled decoration dating from the Europe of Franz Joseph. Occupying the center were nobles and their ladies, mostly dressed in the austere black hanging over Spanish taste since sixteenth-century sumptuary edicts, a severity that quite knocked the cheer out of the popinjays in the courts of France and Flanders at the time; respect for rank here propelling the exiled Queen of Bulgaria, the bearded young King of Albania, and grandsons of the Spanish royal vine forward, dukes, marquises, and counts mingling behind. The extreme left was held by industrialists and financiers, many of them disposing of riches beyond the ken of their counterparts in other nations, but lack of refinement in feature and mostly peasant statures vividly reminding me of their parvenu status in the structuring of my adopted land. Nevertheless, and on the whole, no such brilliance is possible elsewhere but in Spain; not in burgher-ridden Germany with its swarms of penny arcade princes, nor in the so often louche France of risible restoration fantasies, and no longer in the kingly island of my birth, the lament for whose dismembered Empire is whined nowadays by knighted insects.

Brought together just under the choir, or dais—directly before Grau —were family and intimate friends of the Marquesa, among them Consuelo and Jaime Orbaneja, who twitched his upper lip in rabbity fashion, Billy Smith-Burton, who drooped from thin shoulders in deep depression, Marisa Magascal, Carlos Lapique (Centollos), Nacho Pelau (Dos Tripas), and slightly to one side, manifestly feeling like a comedo on the smooth cheek of beauty, Baltazar Blás. These and all others stood. But on folding chairs near the center of the dance floor—a sort of plebeian square inset among the nobles—sat several dozen newsmen, including representatives of the foreign press, sent for by courier; because if doom was to fall on the Deputy Inspector, and doom on Madrid, he had determined to have it broadcast.

I confess that dignity robed the nervous little man (I remained, of course, under the arcade to the rear, but my septuagenarian eyesight is as sharp as a young mariner's). I saw Isias come up behind, whispering. Grau nodded curtly. Other aides mounted the caracol staircase to confer with him. He nodded again. Nearly everybody was present. His eyes roved us. The lenses of television cameras positioned at both ends of the upper gallery roved us. We were expectant. There was tension now. Heat rose in the room, so that shortly everyone sweated in discreet trickles down the backs of necks and (in my case anyhow) down ribs.

I spotted Juan Luis, not far from me, introspective under the bust of Caesar Augustus, absent from the ranks of his peers. I had last left him in an armchair of the rose room, much agitated. He was more than mildly concerned, I imagine, as to whether he would have indeed throttled Billy Smith-Burton saving my intervention and the arrival of Odette's cadaver. It was shortly after, as I was to learn, that he was accosted by Jaime Orbaneja, who had indeed slipped away from the chapel, but for several whiskies, not one.

That romantic soul perspired freely on his debonair little feet, standing chubbily above Juan Luis, gesticulating with the hand holding his drink while the fingers of the other plucked at his silvered mustache. He was nervous.

"Juan Luis," he opened abruptly, "I have something rotten to confess. I never dreamed that old barbarian, Blás, would follow me to Número Catorce on such an occasion! Any minute, now, he's likely to . . ."

"I know all about it," Juan Luis cut him short, tone weary.

Jaime blinked. "You do?"

"You conned me into backing your note. You don't have the thirty millions."

"Oh," said Jaime, not precisely understanding what he meant by that oblate sound. "Juan Luis," he said next, "I can't ask you to forgive me. I can't forgive myself. I am a poet!"

"Yes, that's so. I wish I were a poet. I've always wanted to be a poet."

"But I'm a bad poet! The verses of good poets scan, hold together. My buildings fall to pieces."

"That's so too. But interestingly, everyone admits."

"Inexcusably, Juan Luis," said the architect, tears in his eyes. "I'm morally culpable, I understand that now. I wish that lintel had hit me on the *head* instead of chopping the toes off the Mayor!"

"Why don't you go stand under the stalactites in my apartment building? Sooner or later, you're bound to be impaled."

"I'm too much of a coward!" moaned Jaime pathetically.

"Well, I guess I am too. The Deputy Inspector just came in, see him? I should be talking to him right now. Thought I was freed. God damn Billy showed me I'm not."

"How *ever* will I explain things to Consuelo?"

Juan Luis lifted his eyebrows. "Consuelo? I'm taking matters serenely, Jaime, you have to admit that, but it seems to me there are others you ought to worry about explaining things to before Consuelo! I mean, after all . . ."

"You're right. I'm a scoundrel. But it's Consuelo I love. Do you laugh at me? You think it not possible, anomalous of me to claim when my knees tremble and my blood races at the sight of any pretty lass to cross the Castellana?"

"I think I've learned that everything is possible, and anything. Character traits don't necessarily come in mutually antagonistic pairs, the positive and its negative, matter and its anti-matter. The anomalous is just as often paired."

"I've learned my lesson," said Jaime, who rarely bothered to listen. "I'm not up to managing Obras Orbaneja, no, I shan't hide from the fact. I'm a *lyric* poet. I need someone to provide the structure. I've been talking to Julio Caro. He's unhappy at CASA . . ."

"Unhappy? He'll be fired any day, now."

"Just so. What difference does that make? He's unhappy. He's done wonders restyling CASA's outfits. If I wangle my way out of this fix, save something of Obras, why, I'm going to invite Julio to manage the firm while I devote myself to designing!"

Juan Luis gazed at the architect in amazement. Jaime beamed good will. He *believed* in his plan of reform.

"There is," Juan Luis said slowly, "no salvation."

"Except that which we seek in ourselves!" retorted a revivified Orbaneja, draining his whisky and turning as though to go for more.

He rotated directly into the face of one of the plainclothesmen, who requested their presence in the ballroom.

Juan Luis had been standing under that Roman bust several minutes when I espied him, smoking. Now he dropped his cigarette, grinding the orange glow on the bright granulation of the marble floor, much as earlier he had ground out the life of a sparrow chick. He began filtering his way through the financiers, toward the choir, his progress impeded by the self-demeaning attitude that triggered in others the instinct to obstruct rather than let through. I was watching him when a whispering arose from the ranks of the nobles to my right. They, by contrast, were readily giving way to some presence that was blocked from my view by the dewy back of Leda: until, with a ripple, the center of the assembly opened to disgorge a ghostlike Ignacio Prades, his swollen-faced golden idol of a wife limping after.

They stood there before the dais, gazing up at the Deputy Inspector, Ignacio tall and stern and two paces in front of Dorada, who avoided the eyes of her father.

Television cranks whirred. Photographers' bulbs quaked.

The Count of Obregón stated in a clear, strong tone, audible everywhere in the rotunda, "My mother was strangled by her maid. I've just now found the woman in her room. She has hanged herself. She left this note." And he handed it up to the startled Grau.

Consuelo promptly swooned, Jaime just catching her by the waist before she brought down a skinny young policeman. "Nati?" came shrilling from Marisa Magascal. "No, I can't believe it!"

From everywhere, now, voices vent their astonishment. "Nati? The indispensable Nati?" "That marvelous woman? Odette's most faithful companion?" "Her childhood friend? Impossible. Impossible!"

Grau raised his hands, Nati's note clutched in one of them. The voices subsided.

He said, glancing over heads at two subordinates, "Benjamín,

Eusebio, go to the servants' quarters at once." The men detached themselves from beside columns, converging on one of the exits. A television camera swung its snout in their direction, then rapidly back to the Deputy Inspector.

Who said, "I, for one, Ladies and Gentlemen, will not be astonished if," slapping at Nati's note with the other hand, "this is as stated—the maid murdered her noble mistress at the prompting of the Devil. But we will investigate. The servant called Nati may have been murdered herself. This note may be a forgery. Anything at all is possible, and that is why I have . . ."

"A moment!"

It was Nacho Prades who raised the interruption.

The presumptive Marquis of the Pilgrim said, "The mantequero, he has nothing to do with my mother's death. I want him released. I want him brought here."

Grau replied, "The mantequero is *not* yet exculpated—perhaps of being the immediate instrument of the death of Her Most Excellency, your late mother, but not of other and as serious charges. I have already summoned him."

And he gestured to his left. There, under the lacy arch of an inconspicuous servants' entrance, behind a screen of guards, stood Marisol and Jacobo Rivas, the electrician, the manicurist, and the foppish young fellow from the dress shop, who had been picked up during the afternoon as he sat on a foam rubber toilet seat playing with the precious fan.

"Bring them!" ordered Grau.

Television beams trained on the pathetic group while male and female guards shoved them forward, Jacobo at once alarmed and dejected, Marisol proud and fiery, the electrician lugubrious in gray prison pyjamas twice his size, the manicurist scowling, and the elegant young man smirking. None had a notion as to what portended, but Jacobo felt cowed as he had not during the hugger-mugger of the morning—to be facing such an exalted gathering in these premises while dressed in convict's garb and with irons on his wrists. Was this the torment Don Emilio had promised?

Reaching the choir, he squared his shoulders. If so, he would face it with as much dignity as he was able. And, in so doing—in squaring those bullock's shoulders—his chin went up and his light blue eyes met the solemn gaze of the man he had struck.

Not six feet separated them. Centuries like a chasm opened between them.

"Strike those irons off the man's wrists!" said Nacho Prades, Count of Obregón.

A warden glanced up at Grau.

"I regret . . ." began the Deputy Inspector.

"Do as I say!" insisted the son of the Marquesa.

The handcuffs were struck.

"Come forward, Jacobo Rivas!" commanded the Marquis of the Pilgrim.

Jacobo obeyed in a clumsy, bear's waddle.

The two men now stood face to face, alone in the center of perspective and in the down-focused cross fire of television kliegs, the noble as thin and stiff and tall as a gibbet, the lout broad and corpulent and like a dismayed ox.

"I'm . . . sorry about your nose," Jacobo managed to get out. "Didn't mean to hit you so hard. When you pushed Sánchez, why, I guess I lost . . ."

Ignacio now sprang all our jaws open—by taking a quick step forward, dropping his left knee to the floor, and simultaneously grasping the mantequero's meaty left hand.

"I acknowledge you," came from stiff lips, "chief of all the Bustamantes, hidalgo of the Reconquest, to whom I swear anew my allegiance and of whom I humbly ask pardon for my offenses this morning."

Jacobo's gasp was only one of several hundred.

"This is too . . . much!" I heard in Mayfair from the not nice Lady Hume.

"Una barbaridad," agreed Julio Caro. Had Dorada been suggesting to him half an hour ago a . . . closer relationship? Could it be? And had the surprising Nacho swatted her in the meantime?

The ex-goalkeeper of Atlético de Bilbao recovered more quickly than the rest of us, crying out, "Here, get up off the floor!" —yanking Ignacio by the hand, lifting him like a bundle of sticks to his feet. "Good heavens!" he expostulated, brushing marble dust from the count's knee, "it's all nonsense, that head of the clan business, the order of hidalgos and all. Foolish nonsense! Ought to be buried forever. *I'm* sorry, want *your* forgiveness, even nine thousand what-odd pesetas don't excuse my terrible temper, just pass me the hospital bills, hear? We'll make up accounts, settle the whole business, and forget it ever happened. Isn't that right, Marisol?"

He appealed to her over his shoulder.

"Whatever you decide, my love."

Surprisingly undisconcerted by his performance, Ignacio turned to Grau.

"I request that this man and his wife be freed, and all charges dropped. On my account, I renounce them. I request of my acquaintances in this room—out of love and respect for my mother—that they renounce whatever ancillary charges they may have against this couple and their friends."

"An excellent idea!" came wheezing from the redoubtable Carlos Lapique, Duke of Centollos. "All a mistake. Regrettable, the whole business. Good for you, Nacho! Let's end with it and get on with . . ."

He alluded, presumably, to the funeral pomps of Odette, but checked himself. An approving babble had broken out in the assembly. "Yes, just so!" "Rather enjoyed the donnybrook this morning, for my part!" "Would you believe it of Nacho? Damnedest sight . . ."

They began milling. They drifted toward the doors.

"Wait!" shouted the Deputy Inspector.

"It's too bloody hot in here!" shouted back a guest.

"Hold the doors!" cried out the Deputy Inspector, hopping on the dais as though swept by a tantrum. His voice cracked. "Anyone who attempts forcing the doors will be booked for obstructing Justice!"

"What's that!" cried a general.

"How dare the man!" exclaimed a young monsignor, flushing.

"What impertinence!" steamed Centollos, moisture dashing in a drop off the tip of his nose to splat Dos Tripas in an eye.

It was now a rebellious assembly that turned faces to the Deputy Inspector. The air was stifling, I must say. Condensation in little clouds seemed to form over the encrusted Milky Way of the dome. Stepanópoulis clearly stood in danger of losing his audience when Juan Luis, whom I had quite lost sight of, finally pressed his way through, stopping just under the choir's ballustrade.

"I'm Sigismundo del Val," he stated, addressing the Deputy Inspector. "Duke of Sacedón," he added with a blush. "I want to report . . ."

"You, sir," yelled Grau, "are under arrest: for running or permitting to be run a house of prostitution on your premises, and for the murder of Doña Herminia Lima Olivares, your wetnurse and as it happens a traitor to her country."

Well, let me tell you, *that* put any thought of leaving out of people's minds. At once, Isias stepped forward, clamping handcuffs on a gaping Juan Luis. Two uniformed policemen flanked him. The television cameras whirred like flocking locusts. The assembly sibilated with shock.

All attention was again on Stepanópoulis Grau—the eyes of the mighty of Madrid; the eyes of the world!

He drew in a deep breath, at last resuming his discourse.

"Servants of Holy Mother Church," he stated in ringing tones, "loyal officers of the invincible Army, ministers of New Spain, Her Majesty of Bulgaria, His Majesty of Albania, Señor, Señor," (to the royal Spanish cousins) "nobles of the realm, noblemen of the press, and you other distinguished ladies and gentlemen: you are gathered here at the first disclosures in a case dealing with corruption, scandal, and treason. The Marchioness of the Pilgrim, God grant her soul rest, was murdered in a plot that compromises the whole of Society from high to low. As further investigations will bear out, the Duke of Sacedón and his late nurse, the said Herminia Lima Olivares, colluded with others—shortly to be named—to bring Society and the ever glorious Regime down. With full knowledge of the incumbent Duke, this perfidious handmaiden of Satan plotted with the Santo Dominican gangster by name Diego Muñoz González to most foully do in the incumbent Duke's late and noble father, Luis del Val Sacedón, Baron of the Revenge of Jerez, Governor General of Vizcaya, the unforgettable Duke of Steel, permitting the unworthy second son—liquidator of the true heir!—to inherit rank and fortune, which he would use to corruptest purposes. Between the three, they established a house of such degradation as would have strained the morbidity of a Marquis of Sade, using the Duke's premises on the sixth floor of Calle Almagro—, an Orbaneja building, ladies and gentlemen, mark you well that, an Orbaneja building, I will be speaking more of Señor Don Jaime Orbaneja, Count of the Caribs . . . Sergeant!" he barked now, addressing Isias, "pass these photographs to the press. Sergeant!" he barked at another plainclothesman, "cause to be detained the following persons as I name them." And Grau began the naming, with each denunciation handing a warrant to another aide while law officers fished into the crowd, snapped handcuffs on the accused, and brought them forward to join Juan Luis below the choir. "Señor Don Julio Caro y Borbón, putative Marqués de la Romana: accused of licentiousness, depravity, perversions of the sexual act, and cannibalism."

This last word acted like a bellows on us all, rib cages forcing the breath out of our lungs. *Cannibalism!* There were horrified expressions among members of the press, even, as they pored over the unspeakable glossies. Women snatching peeks at them fainted. The cardinal embraced the heads of all three nuns, pressing their faces to his girth as his shocked eyes sought the ceiling in prayer. *Cannibalism? Julio? Could that be Inmaculada and Asunción doing . . . doing . . . doing . . . !*

But Grau granted us little time for single shocks to be fully experienced. A veritable Daniel, he rolled on above the uproar. "Lady Mary Hume de Montesquieu: accused of licentiousness, depravity, perversions of the sexual act specifically including fellatio, sodomy, and cunnilingus, and also cannibalism." She showed fight. "Why you bigoted little Spic," she screamed at Grau, fighting off the handcuffs, "I'm a consenting adult, I never bit off more than I wanted to chew, I . . ." A hand was clapped over her mouth. One by one was the roll called, and Asunción Mendoza, the Duke of Amontefardo, Count Magascal, Inmaculada Urquijo, Countess of Cáceres, and Beltrán, Marquis of the Marinada, arrested and escorted (or dragged) to the front of the dais.

How adorn the turmoil in the ballroom? What add other than say commotion ruled, bringing an almost unbearable intensification of emotional heat? Grau ignored it all, pitching his voice the higher. "These accused were encouraged in every vice known to humankind by Muñoz González, Sacedón, and his late nurse with the object of depraving and disgracing Society, against which they one week ago resumed their assassin's campaign by plotting the death of the late Señor Don Eugenio Pidal de Estrada, Conde de San Martín, who did not, I announce tonight, tumble accidentally into the elevator shaft: who was *pushed* into that shaft, probably by his servants, wretches who have since fled Madrid. How do I deduce foul play? Because: the late Count's building is also an Obras Orbaneja building, *and there never was an elevator in that shaft,* Señor Orbaneja's calculations were off, of course, the shaft is too narrow for the fit of any commercially produced lift!" Jaime turned at this point to run, but he was tackled by Isias. Grau continued: "Herminia Lima Olivares was in turn murdered by Sacedón, the weapon being—as the photographs show—a screwdriver driven into her brain through the socket of her right eye, fingerprints on its hilt manifesting the Duke's guilt." "Oh my God!" we heard Juan Luis groan at these words, covering his eyes with his hands. "Well may you implore His mercy now!" shouted the Deputy Inspector. Sweat slicked like oil down his cheeks, a wetness spreading down a leg of his natty, pepper-and-salt suit. He did not notice. His pupils were dilated, as though engorged with the raptness of our attention, the rhythm of his reasoning quite mesmerizing our senses and the tics twitching across various areas of his thin face in accelerating concatenation fascinating our eyes. "Murder breeds murder!—as the incomparable Cervantes said. It commends the poisoned chalice to our own lips!—as Lope has told us. Herminia Lima Olivares drank the evil of her own paps, the motive for her liquidation being disagreement over the sharing of spoils from prostitution, which will be borne out when we more fully investigate the significance of a basket discovered in that infamous apartment, stuffed with one million, one hundred and twenty thousand pesetas! Corruption spread from this nucleus to none other than the posturing master of this house, the Count of Obregón—detain him, Sergeant!—who most atrociously murdered his mother the Marchioness of the Pilgrim, the motive there being his fear of the Marchioness declaring that he is not her son, and the proximate instrument of this murder being the demented maid, Nati, who has since hanged herself or who has been hanged, truth there remaining to be determined, is her confession false?—designed to turn suspicion from her natural son, the Count, her 'note' implying that he is the true son of his mother, the Marchioness, which if so makes him a matricide or accomplice to matricide, whereas this may very well not be so, he is actually the true son of his true mother, the maid called Nati, the treason against her mistress being an effort on her part to secure for her bastard title and palace. For this same reason did Señor Baltazar Blás—detain the man, Sergeant, go on, do what I say, don't be frightened, slap the cuffs on his wrists!—associate himself with the plot, anxious as he is to have the title descend to his grandson. Meanwhile has he been scheming with the said gangster Muñoz González to bring about revolution—yes, revolution!—the proof of which, gentlemen of the press, you will observe with your own eyes when you follow me in a few moments to the munitions storage dumps owned by Señor Blás and let to Señor Don Guillermo Smith-Burton, consort-Count of a Thousand Tears—he's right here, Sergeant, inches from your nose!—who has constructed an infernal war machine intended for the destruction of city and State. Incredible? You will see! The plot, ladies and gentlemen, ripples in ever widening circles across the social spectrum of our city, involving in its mesh the previously mentioned and notorious architect, Señor Don Jaime Orbaneja—don't let him try to run again, Sergeant, pinch him right back, hold him, manacle him!—who has several times attempted through his buildings to bring the roof down on people, and to such as the mantequero, Jacobo Rivas, and these other felons with him, said Rivas a former Red of Basque terrorist background, the electrician an atheist who this morning with the help of an Orbaneja mason bricked his wife into the grave alive, the dress designer an invert and shameless consort of such as the accused Count of Magascal, O, madre Mía! and the manicurist, well, a Murcian, no other explanation is needed, all of them deep, deep, deep in complicity. But I!" he croaked now in peroration, waving his arms and dancing on the dais as though the marble had turned into a red-hot skillet, "I, Stepanópoulis Grau, Deputy Inspector for the Barrio de la Latina, have foreseen their evil designs, sniffed out their murderous treachery, and caught them in the stew of their treason; and if you gentlemen of the press will follow me, I will at this time escort you to the very incubation center of the planned rebellion, to the Blás munitions proving grounds near the Casa de Campo, where we will surely discover such as Muñoz González in the act of loading . . ."

"Fire!" shrieked a lady to my right, wheeling about with the alarm.

It was so. We had all been suffering from the heat, but the cause of it was not the sultry night, nor our numbers, nor our emotions, but an inferno that with a crackle and a roar now suddenly burst through the solid old oak and iron of the chapel's door—which, unnoticed by us, had until this instant withstood what must have been the heat of a steel mill's furnaces.

With that searing explosion of flame, and with the virtual disintegration of the door, fire seemed to break out everywhere, melting the blue enamel of the Milky Way off the dome, consuming tapestries on the walls, cracking apart marble under our feet and erupting in trenches of flame from the ancient timbers supporting it. From the furnace of the chapel, fire had raced through the entire palace, feeding on those timbers and draughted into rushing voluminous balls of flame by the suck of oxygen in walled-up corridors. I had one vivid surreal glimpse of the interior of the chapel, glowing like a liquified ruby, like a rage of blood in the brain. The chapel had been turned into a burial pyre for Odette. Just the retained shadow of her casket remained, before dissolving under the crash of the retablo in white-hot hunks of burning wood.

Terror seized us. Panic consumed us. "Bully for you, Don Emilio!" came horribly from Billy Smith-Burton, followed by an awful rumbling. Just about where Odette surrendered her life to Nati, a whole section of floor gave way, half a dozen bankers tumbling into the pit, their wives reaching for them and screaming. We were all dancing on the frying pan of the marble now, and I know that inarticulate yells—call them screams—were being torn repeatedly from my throat, which with every fresh inhalation of the blistering atmosphere was scalded. People rushed the exits. Policemen struggled to open doors, but they were fused into their frames, iron and brass fissioning with the wood. The fire was worse anyhow in the overstuffed salons. The sliding double doors of the rose parlor ignited suddenly in a livid sheet of flame, shooting a tongue of incandescence into the ballroom that hurled people back with shrieks. "Here! Here!" rose up the cry of Juan Luis Sacedón. Who heard him! *Pop!* exploded light bulbs in their tinkling sconces. *Thump*-pity *thump!*-*thump!* sounded amplifiers from the next-door discothèque. *Crash!* came down the dripping crystal parachute of a huge chandelier, splintering on the marble, and *thud!* fell planets from the dissolving celestial system of the dome. "*My wig!*" ululated the widow-Duchess of Sacedón, clutching at it and reeling about like a bullrush in a phosphorous gale before yanking it right off to show a bald pate. "*Socorro!*" cried frantic financiers from their fiery pit as shrieking fat womenfolk tugged at their hands. "*POR CRISTO Y EL REY!*" spiraled forth the desperate ducal voice, turning us to it at last.

Juan Luis had hopped up on the dais, pushing an as though paralyzed Grau aside. He was waving his manacled fists. A chunk of wall had disintegrated behind the choir stall. Smoke billowed from the gaping black hole of a passageway.

"Women and children first!" shouted the Duke of Centollos, looking about him for a child, and finding none, grasping Consuelo and shoving her onto the dais, where Juan Luis grabbed her and propelled her on hands and knees toward the hole.

As instantly as it had possessed the assembly, panic now vanished. Spaniards truly are God's Chosen. The three good sisters, kneeling at the skirted feet of the cardinal, began variously chanting a *De Profundis* and a *Te Deum*, concerting finally on the latter. Others took up the chant, and shortly three hundred voices were lifted in thanks to Almighty God, and the roar of faith overwhelmed the roar of Don Emilio's apocalypse. In a mix of rank and function, the Dukes of Sacedón and Centollos, the Marquis-*manqué* de la Romana, the Counts of Dos Tripas, of the Caribs, and of Obregón, Baltazar Blás the financier, Jacobo Rivas, the electrician, the manicurist, and even the elegant young man from the dress shop—the manacled and the unmanacled, the noble and the commoner, the tradesman and the aristocrat, the poor man and the magnate—linked arms to form an inverted *V*, a wedge, a funnel into the passageway, through which first the women were hurried, and then, by *lowest* rank to begin with, the men. It was an old escape route they tramped, initiating under the altar of the chapel, skirting the ballroom, and winding through the stable quarters to emerge under a grating on Calle Los Mancebos. They proceeded in haste but with dignity. Many awaiting their turn were hit by disintegrating stone or burned by falling shards of plaster. Others in the passageway were overcome by the black smoke. They were picked up by their fellows, brushed off if still able to stand on their feet, carried otherwise. The heat in the ballroom was terrific by this time. The heat and the rumbling of structural collapse were a vertigo by the time the last of the guests was hurried into the passageway, the cardinal, the Governor General, and a senior Prince of the Blood disputing at the entrance as to who should have the honor of escaping last, an argument of historical antiquity that the wedge rudely aborted by closing in behind them.

It was then that I fainted. Luckily, Juan Luis saw me, turning back for me; and with Julio Caro and Ignacio Prades assisting, dragged me into the hole just as the supports gave and with a horrendous grinding of stone the mouth of salvation shut down.

TWENTY-THREE
Showdown

I cannot tell how long it was before we debouched into Calle Los Mancebos. Hands and arms stretched to pull me up from the grating; someone helped push me by the buttocks. The street resembled a Hell as imagined by some twentieth-century descendant of Hieronymus Bosch. It could have been a World War II bombing under that garish sky, or a revolution. There was a mob of the aghast, the terrified, and the wounded, some moaning, some cursing, some calling on the Almighty. Here and there through the police cordon burst men and women to charge loved ones among the refugees from the palace and embrace them. Among us were the stark naked, all rosy buttocks or rosy breasts, the scrawny and the luscious, the full and the withered, but these poor souls were of course instantly collared by the ever-vigilant vice squad, which upholds Spanish morals with handy denim sacks. Children raced gleefully up and down gutters, ducking under the arms of puffing Civil Guards in their green uniforms and black, patent leather Napoleonic kepis, flattened at the back. Civil Guard Land-Rovers, police vehicles, and firemen's wagons were parked everywhere. Sirens were squealing or whooping from, it seemed, everywhere in the city. The sky was volcanic, black and filled with soot and insane with mushrooming clouds of orange, yellow, and red. Beams as though from antiaircraft emplacements played blindingly across our faces and the façades of houses, half a dozen more television batteries having arrived to film the conflagration. "Everybody back!" someone yelled. "Everyone up the street and into the plaza!" Jets of water had been trained on Número Catorce, but they were a piddle in a pond of flame. A call had gone out for Army demolition crews. Adjacent buildings, including the palace of Marisa Magascal, were beginning to ignite. Total destruction threatened all the old palaces trailing down from the plaza between Calles Don Pedro and Los Mancebos. We were herded to safety. Neighbors were being evacuated from proximate buildings, hundreds of them, including long-haired youths of nearly indistinguishable sex from Muñoz González's nightclub. Ambulance after ambulance wailed into the plaza, stretcher-bearers leaping from rear doors. Six or seven first-aid stations were in operation, treating the more serious cases, including those unfortunates of the financial community who had fallen through the ballroom floor, and of which Marisa Magascal and I were not the least affected, rubber masks being clamped to our mouths and oxygen pumped into our lungs. I heard detonations, but at a seeming distance, as though my inner ears were clogged from sudden descent in an unpressurized airliner. Número Catorce was coming down.

"Sabotage!" cried Grau in a frenzy. One whole side of his face was popping with blisters, eyebrows charred and hair gone as frizzled and gray as the lint in a vacuum cleaner. He tore free from a Red Cross nurse. "It's begun—earlier than planned! Isias! Isias! Get us a squad car. They know I know! They've stepped up the schedule. These demolition teams, the firemen, the police—they're all counterfeits, traitors, imposters, saboteurs: they're going to blow up Madrid! To the proving grounds, Isias, to the proving grounds! All loyal officers and men to the AESA proving grounds! Radio the Guardia Civil, Isias. *They*'re loyal!"

He was, it appeared to me, quite mad, hopping up and down in a frenzy, like a troll on a Pogo stick. Two caterwauling squad cars rolled up at that moment. But they were not for Stepanópoulis's disposal. No, the poor lunatic suddenly found himself face to face with his cousin, the Inspector. Grau, apparently, wasn't particularly adept at knots. He wasn't very good at tapping people over the head. The police driver had recovered before very long, and after another half hour or so, had managed to loose himself and his chief.

"Stepanópoulis," said Grau's groggier-than-ever-before cousin, "you are under arrest."

But the Deputy Inspector was not to be thwarted now. He wheeled away in a run, dashing for a third squad car that had been abandoned below the head of Calle Don Pedro. "Stop him!" came from the Inspector, who hobbled in pursuit. Police from everywhere sprinted after Stepanópoulis, who was racing in the direction of Número Catorce, from which monster columns of black-and-red smoke kept geysering into the night, rooftops buckling with the rumble of tons-weight, and walls being blown out by repeated quakes of dynamite. "Stop or we'll shoot!" cried out Grau's cousin, but Stepanópoulis had by this time reached the sedan. He scrambled into the front seat, starting it and heading the hood around toward us.

Meanwhile I glimpsed Marisol Rivas, standing nearby and gazing with blasted eyes at Jacobo, who was being treated with others of the prisoners. "Did you hear what the Deputy Inspector said?" she asked her husband. "A house of perversion, our Soledad!"

Jacobo, streaked with soot, face also pusing from burns, nodded dumbly. "She . . . went there just this afternoon. The game was up— thank God. Thank God!"

"The young assistant, the beanpole, slipped me this note."

Marisol handed it to Jacobo, who raised paper to lurid sky. *Rivas! I have your flower, and I will drag her through Babylon!*

A wounded dog's howl, a bull's enraged bellow, issued from Jacobo's mighty lungs. He was guarded by two officers, but his manacles had not been replaced. He seemed to rise up between them—that's the way I saw it, I can describe it in no other manner. They fell from his sides, toppling away from what blows my singed and smarting eyes were not quick enough to catch. But he turned to me, grasping me by the shoulders and shaking me so that my bones ached. "Can you drive!" he roared into one of my ears. "Yes!"

We heard shots, then. The police were firing on the sedan Stepanópoulis had commandeered. Before I knew it, I found myself flung into one of the squad cars near us, Jacobo beside me. I started the engine. "Where to!" "The proving grounds the Inspector talked about, where the gangster has my Soledad!"

He set the siren going while I bucked the car into motion and through the throng (I haven't driven myself in fifteen years), the night a pit of embers above us, repeated thunderations from Número Catorce behind us, the crack of pistol and then rifle fire to one side of us. We must have been confused for other police giving chase to Stepanópoulis. Whatever the reason, no attention was paid us. Soon I had cleared the plaza, swinging left in a direction opposite to the chase and heading down through a maze of crooked alleyways that empty on the boulevard running across the front of the Royal Palace, wheeling left another time at the Plaza de España and again downhill toward the Extremadura highway. Just as we were approaching the narrow bridge at the Manzanares River, we heard behind us the hysteria of a siren and then saw, some quarter of a kilometer back of us, the scarlet flashing of the police beam.

"Faster!" yelled Jacobo Rivas. "As fast as you can make the machine go!"

We were over the bridge well ahead of the pursuing car. *Our* beam was flashing, *our* siren whooping. Traffic was stopped or cleared in front of us. I held the accelerator to the floor. Our lead had stretched to several kilometers by the time I skidded into the Boadilla turn-off.

A guard at the proving grounds came forward to stop us as we went hurtling for the gate. "Pay no attention—run him down if you have to!" came rasping from the mantequero, who had been breathing in a hard and rasping manner the whole way, like a woman in labor. Horn blaring, I crashed right through the gate, braking in a series of mechanical shudders at the hut.

Jacobo was out of the sedan and running before I had fully stopped. He bludgeoned down the hut's door, running inside. And there saw his daughter, his rose, engaging with evident gusto in perhaps the most anathematized of the reproductive sacrileges, Muñoz González as helpless under her as the male spider in the clutches of the female.

The mantequero halted, bringing the backs of both hands up to his eyes, blotting the sight out. "Papá!" shrilled Soledad, leaping off her victim, he springing up all naked from the cot after her, a bronzed panther facing a wine-red bull. *"Ybarra!"* now exploded from the Rivas chest. *"Rival!"* exploded from the Ybarra chest. *"The Seven are One!"* exploded from both their chests—and they flung themselves on each other, Muñoz González driving for the pit of Jacobo's great stomach, Jacobo falling back with the ram's blow but gathering Muñoz González to him and lifting him in a spine-cracking hug. Bear (or bull) and panther, they wrestled in the center of the hut, knocking over a table, crashing against a wall, ricocheting back toward the center, and then crashing against the opposite wall. I was by that time at the doorway. "Papá!" shrieked Soledad again, wrapping herself in a blanket, "Diego!" But bull (or bear) and panther were locked in death-struggle, Muñoz González clutching at Jacobo's throat and reaching with the stiff fingers of the other hand for his eyes, Jacobo constricting ever more tightly with the panting of his enemy's lungs and crushing Muñoz González's backbone.

A small, thin, blood-soaked figure rushed by me and into the hut, waving a revolver. It was Stepanópoulis Grau. In a sequence of flashed glances, I took in his squad car, took in the shattered windscreen, took in the jagged wounds on his burned face and forehead, and took in the blood pumping from his back and breast. "Surrender!" he cried, waving his pistol at the two men. No one can say whether he intended to shoot. He was mortally wounded, delirious. But, "Oh, Mother of Heaven, no!" came from Soledad, and in the instant that she lunged forward, the policeman's pistol went off, its bullet puncturing her between the eyes.

What more is there to add, except that Jacobo and Diego Muñoz González trampled poor Stepanópoulis to quick death, tearing him apart from limb to limb and then stamping on the parts until little more was left than a sparrow's mash of bone and blood and gristle.

A Respite

Servants and Their Masters is dedicated to Margaret Cousins of New York and Inés Sainz Vicuña of Madrid, two extraordinary women: with my deepest love.

On the whole, I have respected fact, history, and geography throughout. Whenever convenient, I have played fact, history, and geography false. I have invented where the spirit willed. *He dicho barbaridades, y quién sabe si he sacado verdad?* No character in this novel bears the foggiest resemblance to anyone I personally know, excepting such public figures as dukes and counts and other notables in Spanish society, or a Getty, or John Cage, or a General Franco. The characters are *inventions.* I have yanked names and titles out of thin air; should by chance any living person share a name or title, this is wholly coincidental and on my part unintentional. Should anyone recognize himself in a character, I apologize, and that person has my condolences; but I disclaim responsibility for chance.

I want to thank Walter Bradbury of Doubleday for sensitive criticism, and, very much indeed, my sister, Jane Buckley Smith de Sharon y Sacedón, for helping edit this chronicle.

I am deeply grateful to the Spanish nation for what fourteen years as a guest have taught me. The erudite Marqués de Gauna bears my special gratitude for bringing his expertise to the sorting out of genealogies and opening my astonished eyes to the intricacies of noble succession. The Spaniard possesses my complete admiration. To individual friends and acquaintances in Spain, too numerous to list, I am formidably indebted for insights into the national character, which they every one admirably represent in its most idiosyncratic contrariness, their very madness in this mad world being a blessed sanity. My thanks.

But this book hasn't ended, has it?

EPILOGUE

It took me all week and exhausted heaps of the good will I have collected during my off-and-on quarter century living in Madrid to penetrate the official fastness within which, as much as by Carabanchel's cold stone walls, the prisoners were kept.

Those were a harrowing six days for the Government. The fire had raged thirty-two hours. Número Catorce, Marisa Magascal's palace, and several adjoining buildings were gutted. Heat had been so intense that iron bars on grills across the way softened into intoxicated shapes. There was no paving over what had gone on. There were too many witnesses to the events in the ballroom. Too much had been recorded by television. Foreign correspondents risked their carnets filing with their home offices what they had heard and seen. The ever-quick Protestant animus against Catholic, formerly imperial Spain leaped next morning to front pages of newspapers everywhere. Especially in France and Italy, where Spain's success in attracting tourist hordes is so resented, the incredible scandal chased even Middle East fears off top headings. Spanish afternoon tabloids were perforce permitted renditions, although as much as possible these were toned down by haggardly overworked censors.

Rumor cannot be controlled. All Spain buzzed. Angry young priests ranted from village pulpits. The PRM (*Partido Revolucionario Marxista*) whipped students into a sequence of mindless window-smashings. *Resign! Resign!* greeted the Minister of Public Works when he stepped up to address a convocation of labor syndicates. Two full days nevertheless went by before a communique from Seguridad released the names of arrested principals—leaving off titles. That was a weak gesture of no efficacy. Lady Hume. The Countess of Cáceres. The Dukes of Amontefardo and Sacedón. Blás, the mogul. Such were too prominent. *Sinvergüenzas!* hissed a crowd at society folk gathering for a cinema premiere. At Toledo's venerable bullring, José Torres "Bombita," among the best of the novilleros, stalked toward the shadowed area below the Presidential Box when it came time for him to dedicate his second bull;

and turned his back to the dignitaries; and peeled down his tight breeches of lights; and shat on the sand.

People thought the worst; and there was no way in the world of toning down the officially processed arraignments listing sexual orgies, murder, and cannibalism. Stepanópoulis Grau had seen to that with his prepared "denuncias." The Government did their best to emphasize that all charges were unproved, straining to minimize the wilder fantasies about insurrection; but poor Stepanópoulis's every allegation had its kernel of fact, and his hysterical hypotheses respecting an unholy collusion its germ of truth; and that he should have been quite literally torn apart by Jacobo Rivas and Muñoz González made pooh-poohing the more difficult. Authorities reluctantly decided that Grau had to be painted the hero police inspector and martyr that, actually, in a sense indeed he had been. He was posthumously decorated with the Order of Civil Merit. His burial was attended by platoons of police officers and the Director General de Seguridad himself; although he and other high functionaries would have liked nothing better than to tear the cadaver from limb to limb all over again, or, *faute de mieux,* churn up Grau's somewhat sloshy remains in the screws of a giant Mixmaster and feed them to the pigs.

Matters worsened for the Regime on that Tuesday morning, the second of June, when police supported by a platoon of Civil Guards arrived at San Andrés to arrest Don Emilio. Their purpose instantly spread among the populace. By the time officers reappeared on the steps of the church, the holy man manacled between them, a mob had gathered. The mob attacked, overturning the paddywagon and assaulting the Civil Guards. Shots rang out. Several people were wounded—respectable burghers of both sexes, a miniskirted nun, curates, and the inevitable university students again, who, as they crumpled, screamed impartially *Arriba Cristo!* and *Arriba Mao!* Martial law had to be imposed that afternoon in Madrid, and that night a curfew on the major cities of all Spain. Because: Don Emilio, demented arsonist that he may be, had proved his sainthood to his countrymen. On the afternoon of the first of June, firemen in gas masks and asbestos suits finally penetrated the still smoking rubble, to discover him prostrate in the well under the thick marble altar of the chapel, comatose but otherwise unscathed in the very matrix of what had been an inferno that liquified metal and split huge blocks of stone into fragments. It is—how can one doubt it?—a miracle. As much to the pious soul as to the political radical, Don Emilio has become the living symbol of God's wrath, his several public protestations to the contrary notwithstanding. "I was possessed by the Devil," he has since stated at his trial; but who believes that? (And who bothers to remember that he added, "But it is Satan Who possesses the world.")

What came to the rescue of the Regime was mounting world-wide concern over—as daily it seemed—the hourly more imminent hostilities between Israel and Egypt. Who did not fear involvement of Russia and the United States? Not since the Cuban missiles confrontation had sober people more reason to dread the outbreak of atomic war. By Wednesday, the Spanish scandal was taking a back seat internationally to the crisis. Thursday and Friday it was scarcely mentioned, in part thanks to the blackout on fresh news decreed by Madrid. Saturday morning, 5 June, when I walked into Carabanchel, not even the scurrilous French and English tabloids carried a line on it.

I had finally got permission to see Rivas, Muñoz González, Baltazar, Juan Luis, Ignacio, Jaime and Julio Caro. (I had not asked to see Billy Smith-Burton. He remains to this day in coma, at the prison hospital—a pathological degeneration of the shock he went into upon being summoned to identify Sofía's scorched skull.) As they assembled in the courtyard, each flanked by a pair of muscular guards, my pity for them grew. All seemed wasted from their six days in solitary detention, and sad enough in their convict garb. Baltazar dragged his left leg. Juan Luis looked bewildered, Jacobo Rivas resigned from the quick, and Ignacio mortally, irredeemably . . . blessé (I resort to the French, because somehow nor "wounded" nor "herido" suffice). I felt sorry for them every one —until I noticed the irrespressible Jaime craning his head about and blinking into the sun.

Only a fellow Orbaneja, perhaps, is able to imagine what Jaime was imagining. How he would like to get his hands on Carabanchel, and brighten its grim masonry! What reforms in design he would initiate, using architecture for the moral redemption of inmates. Why, he would convert this huge sterile courtyard into a complex of ingenious labyrinths! Yes! Each maze individually would be conceived for purgative therapy. Vivid dioramas executed by Spain's finest sculptors and painters would portray the Christian virtues—and also, most hideously, mankind's sins, inducing revulsion. The mazes would be time-spaced for two hours of hard exercise. (One would have to labor over the high, runged, collapsible trompe l'oeil of Deceitfulness to get at the iced water fountain of Truth, or struggle through the steamy rubberized coils of Sensuality in order to reach the crystal bathing pool of Purity.) As convicts progressed, they would be promoted to mazes offering more of sweetness than of difficulty, with fewer false turns and increasing rewards, the final labyrinth providing as an ultimate test the opportunity of illicit escape through a gap in the main walls.

All this and much more bubbled in the architect's brain while everyone gathered as we were marched to a cramped visitor's reception room. Closely escorted by suspicious officials, I was permitted to assume a stance facing the prisoners. The conditions of our meeting were these. No prisoner was to speak, nor attempt in any manner to exchange information with me or fellow prisoners. I was to mention nothing evidential.

"You all know me," I began, somewhat uncomfortably (Muñoz González alone had retained his composure, and with it his chulo's twist of poisonous lips), "some of you by reputation primarily, some of you as acquaintances and guests at my house, and you, Baltazar," I said, nodding at him, "as a friendly adversary. Well, so I am—C. O. Jones, something of an American Challenge, I suppose. Ha-hah. Eh, you've read the book, surely." No one smiled. Their morale was very low. "But," I persisted, "I am American by attribution only. By birth I am English, of which several of you may be unaware. I am in fact French by origin; and back further in time, antedating the long Gallic sojourn of my line, why," and I paused here for effect, "Spanish, Basque and native to Sacedón!"

There was no reaction.

"You see," I announced next, "I am myself descended from Diego de Bustamante, first Duke of Sacedón." Juan Luis blinked. "Truly. 'S why you have all intrigued me. I am the direct issue of Diego el Bobo, the duff who relinquished his rights to the ducal title, taking to himself the Marquisate of the Pilgrim, of which he became the tenth Spanish holder, removing then with his Orbaneja bride to France. C. O. Jones. Charles Orr Jones. Ha-hah! Do you see? I am a direct and legitimate descendant of Roget de Bustamante, XIVth Marquis of the Pilgrim, and his wife Marthe de Levis Mire-Poix, both whom unfortunate souls, as some of you know, lost their heads in the Terror. What is not generally known is that two months earlier, in prison, Marthe was delivered of a healthy infant boy, little Carlos Orbaneja Bustamante, who was spirited away by his faithful Catholic Scottish nurse and brought by her after many perilous trials to Britain. Or-baneja. Separate the Or, add an *r*. Drop the *b* and fiddle with the vowels: Charles Orr Jones. My true, un-Anglicized name is Carlos Orbaneja—de Bustamante! The facts are all registered in our family Bible."

This information did arch the brows of Ignacio. Baltazar's mouth popped. Juan Luis, I thought, struggled with an impulse to giggle, but suppressed it. I have represented to so many Spaniards the vulgar and often risible American magnate.

"Now," I continued, "I never intended to make a point of my claim to the Marquisate of the Pilgrim, but matters have come to such a pass that I feel I had might as well do so, and buck it down to my grandson—as you, Baltazar, intended for your grandson. I'm sorry, but this should simplify things for all of you. Person by person . . ."

I turned to the architect. "You, Jaime, my closest kinsman in the lot, there is nothing serious hanging over your head except debts—that is, nothing as serious as what hangs over the heads of tenants in your buildings. I am salvaging your company. You will draw plans for it. You won't touch construction. I think you will be extremely happy and produce wonders of the romantic imagination.

"You, Julio Caro," I said next, addressing that pitiable leftover from another era, "I am going to finance to your father's title; but in return, you are going to assign to me the voting rights of your stock in Financiera Sacedón. I imagine it is permitted to announce that the charge of cannibalism will be dropped, now that your stomach contents have been analyzed and Muñoz González has admitted to the trumped-up nature of the scene; but you stand to serve time on the other counts. Still, it is all at the State's expense, your dividends from Financiera will meanwhile accumulate, and under new management will grow. You had might as well compose a book while you're in jail, or pop at the pigeons from your cell, they're a universal pest, authorities are sure to condone it once they see what a crack shot you are. You'll be all right."

I turned then toward the fellow I felt sorriest for. "You, Ignacio, will be found guilty of nothing, and I am confident you won't grieve for your mother's title now that you know me to be the true heir. I'll want you heading up my Comptroller's Division. By and by you'll get used to Dorada taking vows, I doubt her determination will last, but if so, I'm sure she will rise to Mother Superior one of these days . . .

"Juan Luis." I pondered him a moment. "You certainly *do* face problems in court. A plea of unintentional homicide. The difficulty of convincing judges or anyone else for that matter that you were truly ignorant of everything going on under your roof . . .

"I fear you may be in for a goodly stretch behind walls. Actually, however, where else would you prefer to be? You had might as well think about Holy Orders too. The enforced discipline of prison life is in all likelihood just the ticket for you. What I suggest you do is renounce your dukedom in favor of Cousin Ignacio, and that way, Baltazar, your grandson will be all the grander, no? I mean" —and I beamed at them all— "it's rather a happy solution, don't you agree?"

Juan Luis, I think, did agree: I can't be sure of the others. I now regarded my grand old colleague in finance. "Baltazar—old friend: I'm sure you won't begrudge my taking over Financiera and Utilidades. Given your age, mercy is sure to prevail for the man whose fleet came to the rescue of The Crusade, and you'll shortly find yourself among your beloved geraniums."

He nodded at my words, resigned to his fate. It was then that I turned to the thorniest of the cases, Jacobo Rivas, over whom the sword hung.

"Jacobo," I told him bluntly, "you *are* in a *pickle*. As are you, Muñoz González, although I can't feel as sorry for you as perhaps I should. Whatever got into you both, tearing that poor fellow to pieces? Well, I'm more than certain he was mortally wounded before you touched him, if not dead on his feet, and I have so deposed; and for you, Jacobo, since I feel you have experienced tragedy sufficient, I intend to put my resources to work in constructing a defense, the police inspector did shoot your unfortunate daughter, whether intentionally or not—a Spanish Court is bound to take into account the emotions of a loving father. There is something else I have to say to you. You may or may not be aware of it—perhaps it makes no difference to you—but you are the true Duke of Sacedón, lineal descendant of the lawful son of Beatitud, the hunchback, who was raped by your something-to-the-something grandfather, afterward her husband at pike-point."

There was general astonishment at this revelation. "Yes," I went on sorrowfully, "people tend to forget the Beatituds of this world, but the Duchy *was* confirmed to her in Madrid before she conceived, which makes you the indisputable heir. Still, what would you do with it? Is a title able to ennoble you more than your great heart?

"Tell you what!" I was inspired by the occasion. "If Don Emilio proves mistaken on this particular prophecy—that is, if you do escape the garrote, as I earnestly hope—how about taking up Señor Blás's old offer, work for him, garden for him in Lanzarote when you both get out? You'll enjoy little Borja Prades y Blás's visits, just as you once did Fedi Sacedón's, and when little Borja becomes Duke, he'll kiss your scarred old hand reverentially, because you—yes, this is so—you are the true Sacedón, the truest Spain: the perfect gentle knight."

I had reached this optimistic point when a prison warden burst in, shouting, "War! It's war! Israel has attacked!"

This momentous news, picked up from a French broadcast, terminated the meeting. My kinsmen were bustled away to their cells. I hurried with the police to an office, where an ancient wireless had been turned on as loudly as its speaker permitted. It was not yet noon. Israel had flung her columns across the Sinai Peninsula during the early dawn hours. That was about all anybody knew. Had Russia taken a stand? Had the United States? Was nuclear annihilation already speeding to targets across the rim of outer space?

We huddled fearfully around. The speaker croaked and crackled. It beeped. It sang the highest of ear-splitting shortwave decibels; but no amount of fussing connected us with a comprehensible foreign newscast.

The national band was hopeless. Nothing—not a bulletin. Programs of popular music. Home education series. Messages promoting the virtues of *Omo,* a detergent, and endlessly advertising rock recordings.

Two and a half hours dragged by. We exchanged desultory talk. We consumed coffee. Finally, finally—at two-thirty—the midday round-up news broadcast began.

As I am sure did hundreds of thousands other souls in Spain on that day, we listened fearfully. "This morning," we heard, "His Excellency the Most General Francisco Franco continued his triumphal tour through the northern provinces, where he was acclaimed at every stop with outbursts of applause and acclamations of the most fervent loyalty and affection. His Excellency the Mayor of San Vicente de la Barquera, Don Ricardo Ruiz Montalbán, presented the Caudillo with a perpetual honorary Mayorship, to the tumultuous applause of the assembled distinguished guests, including . . ."

It was half an hour more describing the Chief-of-State's peregrination that morning through the province of Santander before we were permitted to learn that the world was not about to be incinerated, that it had not stopped, that in fact for ill or good it had not changed. Apocalypse, you see, exists only in the soul.

FINIS

February 1967—March 19[?2]
Madrid—Comillas—Madrid

ROSENDALE LIBRARY
ROSENDALE, N.Y.

DISCARDED

DIEGO DE BUSTAMANTE, I DUQUE DE SACEL

THE MARQUESA

SOFÍA   IGNACIO   CONSUEL